PENGUIN BOOKS

THE PENGUIN BOOK OF
INTERNATIONAL GAY WRITING

Mark Mitchell co-edited, with David Leavitt, *The Penguin
Book of Gay Short Stories*. He lives in Rome.

# THE
# PENGUIN BOOK
# OF INTERNATIONAL
# GAY WRITING

*Edited by Mark Mitchell*

INTRODUCTION BY DAVID LEAVITT

PENGUIN BOOKS

PENGUIN BOOKS
Published by the Penguin Group
Penguin Books USA Inc., 375 Hudson Street, New York, New York 10014, U.S.A.
Penguin Books Ltd, 27 Wrights Lane, London W8 5TZ, England
Penguin Books Australia Ltd, Ringwood, Victoria, Australia
Penguin Books Canada Ltd, 10 Alcorn Avenue, Toronto, Ontario, Canada M4V 3B2
Penguin Books (N.Z.) Ltd, 182–190 Wairau Road, Auckland 10, New Zealand

Penguin Books Ltd, Registered Offices: Harmondsworth, Middlesex, England

First published in the United States of America by Viking Penguin,
a division of Penguin Books USA Inc. 1995
Published in Penguin Books 1996

1  3  5  7  9  10  8  6  4  2

THE LIBRARY OF CONGRESS HAS CATALOGUED THE HARDCOVER AS FOLLOWS:
The Penguin book of international gay writing/edited by Mark Mitchell:
introduction by David Leavitt.
p. cm.
ISBN 0-670-85369-0 (hc.)
ISBN 0 14 02.3459 4 (pbk.)
1. Homosexuality—Fiction.   2. Gays—Fiction.   I. Mitchell, Mark (Mark Lindsey)
PN6120.95.H724P46   1995
808.83´935206642—dc20   94–13193

Printed in the United States of America
Set in Bembo

*To honor the memory of a great man*

# Acknowledgments

For their assistance in the preparation of this anthology, I thank Janice Brent, Jens Burk, Jill Ciment, Thomas Colchie, Judith Flanders, Jaco Groot, Michael Hardart, Beena Kamlani, James Kirkup, Dolores Koch, Bridget Love, Cosimo Manicone, Ravi Mirchandani, Kevin Moss, Dawn Seferian, Antonio Tanca, Edmund White, and John E. Woods.

# Contents

Contents ~ xi

# ~ *Introduction* ~

This anthology is a riotous party, an unmasked ball. It is a long party—it is still going on—with an amazing variety of guests: seventeenth-century samurai warriors, twentieth-century Russian émigrés, Sigmund Freud, Leonardo da Vinci, Gustav von Aschenbach, Socrates, Gustave Flaubert, the Lord of Longyang, Jacques's brother. It is full of arguments; it is street smart and piss elegant; it is loud with the noises of lovemaking.

Really, it is the party of the century. It is the party of twenty-five centuries.

Like its predecessor, *The Penguin Book of Gay Short Stories*, this is not an anthology of stories by gay writers. Rather, the works collected here—regardless of their authors—have been chosen because they too "illuminate the experience of love between men, explore the nature of homosexual identity, or investigate the kinds of relationships gay men have with each other, with their friends, and with their families." That they achieve these ends in such radically different ways, as well as in ways so radically different from the stories collected in the first volume, testifies to the cultural and historical flexibility of attitudes toward homosexuality, which our contemporary minds presume to be fixed, rigid, unwavering; it is fascinating and curious, for instance, to compare the Kabuki actors and samurai who populate Saikaku's seventeenth-century Japan with the dissolute sexual professionals who wander through Renaud Camus's twentieth-century Europe; to read Plato and Boccaccio in the same sitting as Gerard Reve or

Reinaldo Arenas or Edwin Oostmeijer. Yet this is more than a variety show, and as one might expect, certain persistent motifs, like recurrent dreams, keep cropping up. This introduction will look closely into one of them: namely, naming, or more specifically, its resistance.

About the only constructive thing Lord Alfred Douglas ever did was write a poem called "The Two Loves." The poem, which compared heterosexual and homosexual romance dialogically, concluded:

> "I am true love, I fill
> The hearts of boy and girl with mutual flame."
> Then sighing said the other, "Have thy will,
> I am the love that dares not speak its name."

A bad poet and a worse friend, "Bosie" Douglas probably had no idea that in slapping together this crude bit of undergraduate verse he was signposting the future of Anglo-American thinking about homosexuality. For in the aftermath of the Wilde trials, the "naming" of homosexuals would become an obsession to the English-speaking world. To be named by hostile outsiders, it was assumed, meant condemnation, rejection, exile. On the other hand, to declare *oneself*—though dangerous—allowed for the possibility of escaping a life of lies.

Homosexuality as identity and homosexuality as experience: it is between these two poles that most works of Anglo-American gay writing vibrate. Indeed, the dilemma of whether what we do determines who we are might be said to form the linchpin of our literature. E. M. Forster's *Maurice* is the model here, the alpha and omega of the tradition in English—a tradition that takes for granted the notion that to desire other men requires by necessity the utterance of the unspoken name:

> Maurice understood. He was an Englishman himself, and only his troubles had kept him awake. He smiled sadly. "It comes to this then: there always have been people like me and always will be, and generally they have been persecuted."

"People like me," "men of my sort": phrases like this abound in *Maurice*. They are the precursors of names: homosexual, heterodox, uranist, invert, so, gay, queer. For us in the English-speaking world, the moment when we name ourselves—when we "come out"—is triumphant. It signifies a

throwing off of shackles, a self-liberation. Our traditional preoccupations—the idea of gay community, the drama of the closet, the urge for
separatism (in *Maurice's* words, "taking to the greenwood"), not to mention its opposite, the need for assimilation—represent complex variations
on the theme of self-naming. And yet if this anthology teaches anything,
it is that these preoccupations are not universal.

It is interesting, for instance, to note how infrequently the word
"homosexual"—not to mention its many synonyms—appears in the pieces
collected here. Nor are these examples of "encoded" writing, in which the
homosexual content is disguised. Instead the homosexual content asserts
itself blatantly. But it is rarely named. It simply happens.

"Names," Roland Barthes writes in his introduction to Renaud Camus's *Tricks*, "the source of dispute, of arrogance and of moralizing." In opposing Lord Alfred Douglas, he speaks not just for Camus but for many of
the other writers in this volume. Americans worry a lot about the appropriation of labels (pink triangles, for instance), as well as the reclamation of
the act of naming from the oppressor; but to European writers this politics
is of secondary interest. Instead what matters is experience itself.*

Consider *It's Me, Eddie*, by the Russian writer Edward Limonov. Near
the beginning of this "fictional memoir," Eddie, a Russian émigré in New
York, learns that his friend Kirill has become acquainted with a gay man
in his fifties called Raymond. "Kirill, old buddy," Eddie says,

> women rouse me to disgust, my wife has made intercourse with
> women impossible for me, I can't deal with them. They're always
> having to be serviced, undressed, fucked. They're panhandlers and
> parasites by nature, in everything from intimate relations to the
> economics of the normal joint household in society. I can't live
> with them anymore. The main thing is, I can't service them—take
> the initiative, make the first move. What I need now is someone to
> service me—caress, kiss, want me—rather than wanting and being
> ingratiating myself. Only from men can I get all this. You'd never
> guess I'm thirty fucking years old, I'm nice and trim, my figure is
> faultless, more like a boy's than a man's, even. Introduce me to this
> fellow. . . .

---

*Interestingly, homosexuality used to be known in France as* la vice anglaise.

For Eddie, homosexuality is that most politically incorrect of things, a "choice," one facet in the vast spectrum of available human intimacy that, as the novel progresses, he explores, delights in, and learns from. Unlike the Americans he encounters, he would never call himself "gay" or even "bisexual," yet he is willing to pose questions from which even the most "out" among us might shrink. "Do you know the taste of semen?" he asks the reader, and there is in this inquiry sauciness and innocence and just a touch of provocation. "It is the taste of the alive. I know nothing more alive to the taste than semen." And when he makes love with a homeless black man called Chris—another outsider in the American cosmos—the meeting of semen with semen brings about the birth of joy:

> Listen here, there are morals, there are decent people in the world, there are offices and banks; sleeping in them are men and women, also very decent. It was all happening at once, and still is. And there were Chris and I, who had accidentally met there in the dirty sand, in a vacant lot in the vast Great City, a Babylon, God help me, a Babylon. There we lay, and he stroked my hair. Homeless children of the world.

Eddie is something unusual in our literature: the experiential homosexual. The timeworn metaphor of the closet doesn't apply to him: he lives in a house without closets. He could not be more different from Maurice or, for that matter, from Molina, the drag queen hero of Manuel Puig's *Kiss of the Spider Woman*. Molina dreams of marrying another man—and being the wife. Eddie, on the other hand—married already to a woman—imagines an ideal homosexual relationship that is fraternal rather than conjugal in nature: a kind of eroticized buddyhood.

"Erotic friendships"—the male homosexual equivalent of lesbian "romantic friendships"*—take place all the time in this anthology, most notably in boys' schools: "Hippe," from Thomas Mann's *The Magic Mountain*, Tournier's *Gemini*, Robert Musil's *Young Törless*, are all dramas of boys'-school eros, while Gustave Flaubert's epistolary account of his adventures with a young friend in Egypt may remind some readers of Kerouac's *On the Road*. Unlike Molina, the men and boys who populate these pieces don't

---

*See Lillian Faderman, Odd Girls and Twilight Lovers: A History of Lesbianism in Twentieth-Century America (New York: Columbia University Press, 1991).

base their love affairs on the heterosexual model; instead they carry male friendship naturally into the realm of sexuality, forging along the way bonds that are both intense and enduring. This sexual fraternality is literalized in Agustín Gómez-Arcos's *The Carnivorous Lamb*, the story of two brothers whose consuming passion for each other flouts the straitlaced morality not only of their family but of Franco-era Spain itself. The novel's finale, in which the brothers are married in a ceremony conducted by the family maid, sends up Catholic rigidity as it heralds the fusion of two seemingly irreconcilable forms of love.

Another "forbidden" topic from which European writers seem less likely to shrink is the love of older men for young boys. Three pieces in particular confront this subject. One of them—Thomas Mann's wistful and arresting *Death in Venice*—is already famous; a second—the sardonic "A Low Fever," by the Italian poet Sandro Penna—is translated here for the first time. But neither is anywhere near so explosive as Tony Duvert's *When Jonathan Died*, an unapologetic account of a consummated love affair between a man in his thirties and a preadolescent boy. Duvert's novel makes no pleas for understanding. Instead the coolly assured narrative compels the reader to imagine the world from a perspective he might ordinarily condemn:

> Calm returned after what quenches boyish passion. Now Serge would decide he was dry enough and get down to essentials— sitting on Jonathan, head toward his feet, as if he were an armchair made for the purpose. Jonathan's legs, pulled up a little, made up the back of the chair, his belly, sex now quiescent, made the seat. Depending on the day, Serge would lie there on his back, or curled up, or even on his stomach; the angle of the chair back would be arranged to suit. In every case, the object was to offer Jonathan a part to be caressed as long as Serge thought fit.

Again, nothing is "named" here: this is not your run-of-the-mill Ganymede Press apologia. Instead Duvert offers us a homosexual *Lolita*—one in which the child is seducer as much as seduced. No attempt is made to justify the love affair between Serge and Jonathan; it is simply presented. And it is in that simplicity of presentation that its literary authority resides.

For the surprising thing is that not naming can often prove to be as shocking—if not more so—as naming. To allow experience simply to happen on the page—to ascribe to it a factitious innocence that the world will not allow—is to unshackle that experience from centuries of persecution and disguise.

Consider Michel Tournier's *Gemini*. The novel begins in a boys' school, which is not surprising: in Europe, boys' schools have traditionally not only tolerated but encouraged homosexual behavior even as the adult world for which they provide preparation condemns it.* The boys' school is the homosexual Eden, the world before the fall:

> I picture with pain and no little distress the boredom those college years mean to a heterosexual. What a grayness there must be in his days and nights, sunk body and soul in a human environment devoid of sexual stimulus! But then surely that is fair training for what life has in store for him.
>
> Whereas for me, ye gods! Thabor was a melting pot of desire and satiety all through my childhood and adolescence. I burned with all the fires of hell in a promiscuity which did not let up for a second in any of the twelve phases into which our timetable divided it: dormitory, chapel, classroom, dining hall, playground, lavatories, gymnasium, playing fields, fencing school, staircases, recreation room, washrooms. . . . What wouldn't I give today, cast out into the heterosexual twilight, to recover something of that fire!

Led by "Thomas Drycome," a sort of homosexual child prophet, the boys at Thabor College appropriate a life-size figure of Christ as an erotic icon. They also appropriate lines from a psalm—"Feet have they, but they walk not. Eyes have they, but they see not. Hands have they, but they handle not. Noses have they, but they smell not"—reading into them a "disdainful charge against heterosexuals":

> We who walked and saw and handled and smelled would bawl out that insolent indictment while our eyes caressed the backs and buttocks of the fellow pupils in front of us, so many young calves

---

*For an impassioned literary articulation of the boys' school/real world split, see William Trevor's "Torridge" in* The Penguin Book of Gay Short Stories.

reared for domestic use and so paralyzed, blind, insensible, and devoid of any sense of smell.

To appropriate literature rather than labels may be the most defiantly homosexual stance of all, especially when the objective of such appropriation
is nothing less than a victory cry.* Anglo-American liberal thinking pleads
the "normality" of homosexuality.† Tournier takes a more audacious
stance: he asserts its *superiority*. In doing so, he challenges not only convention but conventional wisdom.

"If you could turn straight, would you do it?" I can't count the number of people—straight *and* gay—who've asked me this. My answer is
always a definite "No, no, no!" Still, the question provokes in even the
most liberated among us the profoundest internal conflict. For no matter how happily we may live day to day as homosexuals, there remains bred in our bones the conviction that homosexuality is a handicap,
albeit one to which we can adjust. But might homosexuality not be
instead—as Tournier argues—an advantage to exploit? Do we brood too
intently on the self-limiting act of naming? Do we name ourselves into a
corner?

For instance, I can say for certain that I probably wouldn't be half the
writer I am if I were straight. My homosexuality gave me the rare privilege
of being an outcast. I could not take for granted a culture that did not take
me for granted. Because the rituals of heterosexual mating did not im-
plicate me, moreover, I could remark upon them with a certain objective coolness—as Henry James did; as Proust did; as E. M. Forster did.
Above all, in constructing my adulthood, I could make up the rules. No
"models" hindered me. Where my heterosexual peers molded their lives
to the shape of timeworn formulas, I could invent. *Could* invent. But like
most American gay men, I didn't. Instead I tried to live as a homosexual
but like a heterosexual. To do so—I realize now—was to squander an
opportunity.

James Baldwin—that most expatriate of American writers—understood

---

*It is no coincidence that several of the texts included in this anthology—excerpts from Freud's
Leonardo da Vinci and a Memory of His Childhood *and* Camus's The Plague—
represent just such acts of appropriation.*
†*See Bruce Bawer,* A Place at the Table *(New York: Poseidon Press, 1993), for an example
of the "we're just like you" argument.*

that opportunity. Once—decades ago—David Frost interviewed him on television. Frost: "You were a Negro, you were poor, you were homosexual. Didn't you feel you had everything going against you?"

Baldwin: "On the contrary, I thought I'd hit the jackpot."

The party goes on.

# THE PENGUIN BOOK OF INTERNATIONAL GAY WRITING

# ~ *Plato* ~

## FROM

# *Symposium*

### TRANSLATED BY WALTER HAMILTON

"Well, Eryximachus," began Aristophanes, "it is quite true that I intend to take a different line from you and Pausanias. Men seem to me to be utterly insensible of the power of Love; otherwise he would have had the largest temples and altars and the largest sacrifices. As it is, he has none of these things, though he deserves them most of all. For of all the gods he is the most friendly to man, and his helper and physician in those diseases whose cure constitutes the greatest happiness of the human race. I shall therefore try to initiate you into the secret of his power, and you in turn shall teach others.

"First of all, you must learn the constitution of man and the modifications which it has undergone, for originally it was different from what it is now. In the first place there were three sexes, not, as with us, two, male and female; the third partook of the nature of both the others and has vanished, though its name survives. The hermaphrodite was a distinct sex in form as well as in name, with the characteristics of both male and female, but now the name alone remains, and that solely as a term of abuse. Secondly, each human being was a rounded whole, with double back and flanks forming a complete circle; it had four hands and an equal number of legs, and two identically similar faces upon a circular neck, with one head common to both the faces, which were turned in opposite directions. It had four ears

---

*PLATO*, with Socrates (his teacher) and Aristotle (his pupil), shaped the whole beleaguered Western intellectual tradition.

and two organs of generation and everything else to correspond. These people could walk upright like us in either direction, backwards or forwards, but when they wanted to run quickly they used all their eight limbs, and turned rapidly over and over in a circle, like tumblers who perform a cartwheel and return to an upright position. The reason for the existence of three sexes and for their being of such a nature is that originally the male sprang from the sun and the female from the earth, while the sex which was both male and female came from the moon, which partakes of the nature of both sun and earth. Their circular shape and their hoop-like method of progression were both due to the fact that they were like their parents. Their strength and vigour made them very formidable, and their pride was overweening; they attacked the gods, and Homer's story of Ephialtes and Otus attempting to climb up to heaven and set upon the gods is related also to these beings.

"So Zeus and the other gods debated what was to be done with them. For a long time they were at a loss, unable to bring themselves either to kill them by lightning, as they had the giants, and extinguish the race—thus depriving themselves for ever of the honours and sacrifice due from humanity—or to let them go on in their insolence. At last, after much painful thought, Zeus had an idea. 'I think,' he said, 'that I have found a way by which we can allow the human race to continue to exist and also put an end to their wickedness by making them weaker. I will cut each of them in two; in this way they will be weaker, and at the same time more profitable to us by being more numerous. They shall walk upright upon two legs. If there is any sign of wantonness in them after that, and they will not keep quiet, I will bisect them again, and they shall hop on one leg.' With these words he cut the members of the human race in half, just like fruit which is to be dried and preserved, or like eggs which are cut with a hair. As he bisected each, he bade Apollo turn round the face and the half-neck attached to it towards the cut side, so that the victim, having the evidence of bisection before his eyes, might behave better in future. He also bade him heal the wounds. So Apollo turned round the faces, and gathering together the skin, like a purse with drawstrings, on to what is now called the belly, he tied it tightly in the middle of the belly round a single aperture which men call the navel. He smoothed out the other wrinkles, which were numerous, and moulded the chest with a tool like those which cobblers use to smooth wrinkles in the leather on their last. But he left a few on the belly itself round the navel, to remind man of the state from which he had fallen.

"Man's original body having been thus cut in two, each half yearned for the half from which it had been severed. When they met they threw their arms round one another and embraced, in their longing to grow together again, and they perished of hunger and general neglect of their concerns, because they would not do anything apart. When one member of a pair died and the other was left, the latter sought after and embraced another partner, which might be the half either of a female whole (what is now called a woman) or a male. So they went on perishing till Zeus took pity on them, and hit upon a second plan. He moved their reproductive organs to the front: hitherto they had been placed on the outer side of their bodies, and the processes of begetting and birth had been carried on not by the physical union of the sexes but by emission onto the ground, as is the case with grasshoppers. By moving their genitals to the front, as they are now, Zeus made it possible for reproduction to take place by the intercourse of the male with the female. His object in making this change was twofold: if male coupled with female, children might be begotten and the race thus continued, but if male coupled with male, at any rate the desire for intercourse would be satisfied, and men set free from it to turn to other activities and to attend to the rest of the business of life. It is from this distant epoch, then, that we may date the innate love which human beings feel for one another, the love which restores us to our ancient state by attempting to weld two beings into one and to heal the wounds which humanity suffered.

"Each of us then is the mere broken tally of a man, the result of a bisection which has reduced us to a condition like that of a flat fish, and each of us is perpetually in search of his corresponding tally. Those men who are halves of a being of the common sex, which was called, as I told you, hermaphrodite, are lovers of women, and most adulterers come from this class, as also do women who are mad about men and sexually promiscuous. Women who are halves of a female whole direct their affections towards women and pay little attention to men; Lesbians belong to this category. But those who are halves of a male who pursue males, and being slices, so to speak, of the male, love men throughout their boyhood, and take pleasure in physical contact with men. Such boys and lads are the best of their generation, because they are the most manly. Some people say that they are shameless, but they are wrong. It is not shamelessness which inspires their behaviour, but high spirit and manliness and virility, which lead them to welcome the society of their own kind. A striking proof of this is that such boys alone, when they reach maturity, engage in public life. When they grow to be men, they become lovers of boys, and it requires the compulsion of convention to overcome their natural disinclination to marriage and procreation; they are quite content to live with one another unwed. In a word, such persons are devoted to lovers in boyhood and themselves lovers of boys in manhood, because they always cleave to what is akin to themselves.

"Whenever the lover of boys—or any other person for that matter—has the good fortune to encounter his own actual other half, affection and kinship and love combined inspire in him an emotion which is quite overwhelming, and such a pair practically refuse ever to be separated even for a moment. It is people like these who form lifelong partnerships, although they would find it difficult to say what they hope to gain from one another's society. No one can suppose that it is mere physical enjoyment which causes the one to take such intense delight in the company of the other. It is clear that the soul of each has some other longing which it cannot express, but can only surmise and obscurely hint at. Suppose Hephaestus with his tools were to visit them as they lie together, and stand over them and ask: 'What is it, mortals, that you hope to gain from one another?' Suppose too that when they could not answer he repeated his question in these terms: 'Is the object of your desire to be always together as much as possible, and never to be separated from one another day or night? If that is what you want, I am ready to melt and weld you together, so that, instead of two, you shall be one flesh; so long as you live you shall live a common life, and when you die, you shall suffer a common death, and be still one, not two, even in the next world. Would such a fate as this content you, and satisfy your longings?' We know what their answer would be; no one would refuse the offer; it would be plain that this is what everybody wants, and everybody would regard it as the precise expression of the desire which he had long felt but had been unable to formulate, that he should melt into his beloved, and that henceforth they should be one being instead of two. The reason is that this was our primitive condition when we were wholes, and love is simply the name for the desire and pursuit of the whole. Originally, as I say, we were whole beings, before our wickedness caused us to be split by Zeus, as the Arcadians have been split apart by the Spartans. We have reason to fear that if we do not behave ourselves in the sight of heaven, we may be split in two again, like dice which are bisected for tallies, and go about like the people represented in profile on tombstones, sawn in two vertically down the line of our noses. That is why we ought to exhort everyone to conduct himself reverently towards the gods; we shall thus escape a worse fate, and even win the blessings which Love has in his power to bestow, if we take him for our guide and captain. Let no man set himself in opposition to Love—which is the same thing as incurring the hatred of the gods—for if we are his friends and make our peace with him, we shall succeed, as few at present succeed, in finding the person to love who in the strictest sense belongs to us. I know that Eryximachus is anxious to make fun of my speech, but he is not to suppose that in saying this I am pointing at Pausanias and Agathon. They may, no doubt, belong to this class, for they are both unquestionably halves of male wholes, but I am speaking of men and women in general when I say that the way to happiness for our race lies in fulfilling the behests of Love, and in each finding for himself the mate who properly belongs to him; in a word, in returning to our original condition. If that condition was the best, it follows that it is best for us to come as near to it as our present circumstances allow; and the way to do that is to find a sympathetic and congenial object for our affections.

"If we are to praise the god who confers this benefit upon us, it is to Love that our praises should be addressed. It is Love who is the author of our well-being in this present life, by leading us towards what is akin to us, and it is Love who gives us a sure hope that, if we conduct ourselves well in the sight of heaven, he will hereafter make us blessed and happy by restoring us to our former state and healing our wounds.

"There is my speech about Love, Eryximachus, and you will see that it is of quite a different type from yours. Remember my request, and don't make fun of it, but let us hear what each of the others has to say. I should have said 'each of the other two,' for only Agathon and Socrates are left."

# ~ *Petronius* ~

## FROM
## *Satyricon*

### TRANSLATED BY J. P. SULLIVAN

When I was taken out to Asia on the paid staff of a treasury official, I accepted some hospitality in Pergamum. I was very pleased to accept this invitation not only because of the elegance of the quarters but also because my host had a very good-looking son, and I thought up a way to prevent his father becoming suspicious of me. Whenever any mention was made at the table of taking advantage of pretty boys, I flared up so violently and I was so stern about my ears being offended by obscene talk that the mother especially regarded me as a real old-world philosopher. From then on I escorted the young lad to the gymnasium, I organized his studies, I taught him and gave him good advice. After all, we didn't want any greedy seducer admitted to the house.

~ ~ ~

"One holiday, when the celebrations had given him time to play, we were lounging in the dining room, since the long day's enjoyment had made us too lazy to go to bed. About midnight, I realised the boy was awake. So in a very nervous whisper I breathed a prayer.

---

*Tacitus on* PETRONIUS: *"He spent his days sleeping, his nights working and enjoying himself. Others achieve fame by energy, Petronius by laziness. Yet he was not, like others who waste their resources, regarded as dissipated or extravagant, but as a refined voluptuary [he was the emperor Nero's "arbiter of elegance"]. People liked the apparent freshness of his unconventional and unselfconscious sayings and doings. Nevertheless, as governor of Bithynia and later as consul, he had displayed a capacity for business."*

" 'Dear Venus,' I said, 'if I can kiss this boy without his knowing it, I'll give him a pair of doves tomorrow.'

"Hearing the price of my pleasure, the boy started snoring, and I therefore went to work on the faker and kissed him several times. Content with this beginning, I rose early next morning and brought him the choice pair of doves he was expecting and fulfilled my vow.

~ ~ ~

"Next night, given the same opportunity, I altered my prayer.

" 'If I can run my hands all over him,' I said, 'without his feeling anything, I'll give him two really savage fighting cocks for his patience.'

"At this offer the boy moved over to me of his own accord. I think he was getting afraid I might fall asleep. Naturally I dispelled his worries and his whole body became a whirlpool in which I lost myself, although I stopped short of the ultimate pleasure. Then when day came, I brought the delighted boy what I'd promised.

"The third night gave me similar licence, and I got up, and close to his ear, as he tossed restlessly, I said:

" 'O eternal gods, if I can get the full satisfaction of my desires from him in his sleep, for this happiness tomorrow I shall give the boy the finest Macedonian thoroughbred—but with this proviso, only if he feels nothing.'

"The lad had never slept so soundly before. First I filled my hands with his milk-white breasts, then I clung to his lips, and finally I reduced all my longings to one climax.

"In the morning he sat in his room and waited for me to follow my usual practice. Of course, you know how much easier it is to buy doves and cocks than a thoroughbred, and besides, I was nervous in case such an extravagant gift should make my kindness suspect. So after walking round for a few hours, I returned to my host's house and gave the boy nothing more than a kiss. He looked round, as he threw his arms about my neck, and said:

" 'Please, sir, where's my thoroughbred?'

~ ~ ~

"This offence had lost me the headway I had made, nevertheless I returned to my old freedom. A few days later, when a similar chance left us in the same position, hearing the father snoring, I began asking the boy to become friends with me again, and I said all the other things that a strong physical urge dictates. But clearly annoyed, he only said:

" 'Just go to sleep or I'll tell father.'

"Nothing is too hard to get if you're prepared to be wicked. Even while he was saying, 'I'll wake father,' I slipped into the bed and without much of a fight from him I took my pleasure by force. Actually he was not displeased that I'd been so naughty, and after complaining for a long time that he'd been tricked and that he'd been laughed at and talked about among his school friends because he had boasted to them of my wealth, he said finally:

" 'But you'll see I'm not like you. Do it again, if you wish.'

"Well, I was back in the boy's favour with all his hard feelings gone, and after taking advantage of his kindness, I fell asleep. The boy, however, being fully mature and of an age very much able to take it, was not content with the repeat performance. He woke me up from my sleep saying:

" 'Don't you want anything?'

"Of course it wasn't a tiresome job yet, so somehow, ground between the panting and sweating, he got what he wanted and I fell back asleep, exhausted with passion. Less than an hour later he began poking me with his hand and saying:

" 'Why aren't we getting on with it?'

"Being woken up so often, I really flared up. I gave him his own back:

" 'Just you go to sleep or I'll tell your father.' "

# ~ *Giovanni Boccaccio* ~

## FROM

## *Decameron*

TRANSLATED BY G. H. McWILLIAM

*P*ietro di Vinciolo goes out to sup with Ercolano, and his wife lets a young man in to keep her company. Pietro returns, and she conceals the youth beneath a chicken coop. Pietro tells her that a young man has been discovered in Ercolano's house, having been concealed there by Ercolano's wife, whose conduct she severely censures. As ill luck would have it, an ass steps on the fingers of the fellow hiding beneath the coop, causing him to yell with pain. Pietro rushes to the spot and sees him, thus discovering his wife's deception. But in the end, by reason of his own depravity, he arrives at an understanding with her.

~ ~ ~

When the queen's tale had reached its conclusion, they all praised God for having given Federigo so fitting a reward, and then Dioneo, who was not in the habit of waiting to be asked, began straightway as follows:

Whether it is an accidental failing, stemming from our debased morals, or simply an innate attribute of men and women, I am unable to say; but the fact remains that we are more inclined to laugh at scandalous behaviour than virtuous deeds, especially when we ourselves are not directly in-

*GIOVANNI BOCCACCIO was born in either Florence or Certaldo in 1313, the illegitimate son of a Florentine merchant banker, and died in Certaldo on the first day of winter in 1375. The Black Death (1347–1349) occasioned the work for which he is most famous: Decameron. According to tradition, Decameron was among the "vanities" burned by Savonarola in the Piazza della Signoria in Florence in 1497.*

volved. And since, as on previous occasions, the task I am about to perform has no other object than to dispel your melancholy, enamoured
ladies, and provide you with laughter and merriment, I shall tell you the
ensuing tale, for it may well afford enjoyment even though its subject matter is not altogether seemly. As you listen, do as you would when you enter
a garden, and stretch forth your tender hands to pluck the roses, leaving the
thorns where they are. This you will succeed in doing if you leave the
knavish husband to his ill deserts and his iniquities, whilst you laugh gaily
at the amorous intrigues of his wife, pausing where occasion warrants to
commiserate with the woes of her lover.

~ ~ ~

Not so very long ago, there lived in Perugia a rich man called Pietro
di Vinciolo, who, perhaps to pull the wool over the eyes of his fellow-
citizens or to improve the low opinion they had of him, rather than because of any real wish to marry, took to himself a wife. But the unfortunate
part about it, considering his own proclivities, was that he chose to marry
a buxom young woman with red hair and a passionate nature, who would
cheerfully have taken on a pair of husbands, let alone one, and now found
herself wedded to a man whose heart was anywhere but in the right place.

Having in due course discovered how matters stood, his wife, seeing
that she was a fair and lusty wench, blooming with health and vitality, was
greatly upset about it, and every so often she gave him a piece of her mind,
calling him the foulest names imaginable. She was miserable practically the
whole time, but one day, realizing that if she went on like this her days
might well be ended before her husband's ways were mended, she said to
herself: "Since this miserable sinner deserts me to go trudging through the
dry with clogs on, I'll get someone else to come aboard for the wet. I married the wretch, and brought him a good big dowry, because I knew he
was a man and thought he was fond of the kind of thing that other men
like, as is right and proper that they should. If I hadn't thought he was a
man, I should never have married him. And if he found women so repugnant, why did he marry me in the first place, knowing me to be a woman?
I'm not going to stand for it any longer, I have no desire to turn my back
on the world, nor have I ever wanted to, otherwise I'd have gone into a
nunnery; but if I have to rely on this fellow for my fun and games, the
chances are that I'll go on waiting until I'm an old woman. And what good
will it do me then, in my old age, to look back and complain about the

way I wasted my youth, which this husband of mine teaches me all too well how to enjoy? He has shown me how to lead a pleasurable life, but whereas in his case the pleasure can only be condemned, in my own it will commend itself to all, for I shall simply be breaking the laws of marriage, whereas he is breaking those of Nature as well."

These, then, were the wife's ideas, to which she doubtless gave further thought on other occasions, and in order to put them into effect, she made the acquaintance of an old bawd who to all outward appearances was as innocent as Saint Verdiana feeding the serpents, for she made a point of attending all the religious services clutching her rosary, and never stopped talking about the lives of the Fathers of the Church and the wounds of Saint Francis, so that nearly everyone regarded her as a saint. Choosing the right moment, the wife took her fully into her confidence, whereupon the old woman said:

"The Lord above, my daughter, who is omniscient, knows that you are very well advised, if only because you should never waste a moment of your youth, and the same goes for all other women. To anyone who's had experience of such matters, there's no sorrow to compare with that of having wasted your opportunities. After all, what the devil are we women fit for in our old age except to sit round the fire and stare at the ashes? No woman can know this better than I, or prove it to you more convincingly. Now that I am old, my heart bleeds when I look back and consider the opportunities I allowed to go to waste. Mind you, I didn't waste all of them—I wouldn't want you to think I was a half-wit—but all the same I didn't do as much as I should have. And God knows what agony it is to see myself reduced now to this sorry state, and realize that if I wanted to light a fire, I couldn't find anyone to lend me a poker.

"With men it is different: they are born with a thousand other talents apart from this, and older men do a far better job than younger ones as a rule; but women exist for no other purpose than to do this and to bear children, which is why they are cherished and admired. If you doubt my words, there's one thing that ought to convince you, and that is that a woman's always ready for a man, but not vice-versa. What's more, one woman could exhaust many men, whereas many men can't exhaust one woman. And since this is the purpose for which we are born, I repeat that you are very well advised to pay your husband in his own coin, so that when you're an old woman your heart will have no cause for complaint against your flesh.

"You must help yourself to whatever you can grab in this world, especially if you're a woman. It's far more important for women than for men to make the most of their opportunities, because when we're old, as you can see for yourself, neither our husbands nor any other man can bear the sight of us, and they bundle us off into the kitchen to tell stories to the cat, and count the pots and pans. And what's worse, they make up rhymes about us, such as 'When she's twenty give her plenty. When she's a gammer, give her the hammer,' and a lot of other sayings in the same strain.

"But I won't detain you any longer with my chit-chat. You've told me what you have in mind, and I can assure you right away that you couldn't have spoken to anyone in the world who was better able to help. There's no man so refined as to deter me from telling him what's required of him, nor is there any so raw and uncouth as to prevent me from softening him up and bending him to my will. So just point out the one you would like, and leave the rest to me. But one thing I would ask you to remember, my child, and that is to offer me some token of your esteem, for I'm a poor old woman, and from now on I want you to have a share in my indulgences and all the paternosters I recite, so that God may look with favour on the souls of your departed ones."

Having said her piece, she came to an understanding with the young lady that if she should come across a certain young man who frequently passed through that part of the city, and of whom she was given a very full description, she would take all necessary steps. The young woman then handed over a joint of salted meat, and they took their leave of one another.

Within the space of a few days, the youth designated by the lady was ushered secretly into her apartments by the beldam, and thereafter, at frequent intervals, several others who had taken the young woman's fancy were similarly introduced to her. And although she was in constant fear of being discovered by her husband, she made the fullest possible use of her opportunities.

One evening, however, her husband having been invited to supper by a friend of his called Ercolano, the young woman commissioned the beldam to fetch her one of the most handsome and agreeable youths in Perugia, and her instructions were duly carried out. But no sooner were she and the youth seated at the supper table than her husband, Pietro, started clamouring at the door to be let in.

The woman was convinced, on hearing this, that her final hour had come. But all the same she wanted to conceal the youth if possible, and not having the presence of mind to hide him in some other part of the house, she persuaded him to crawl beneath a chicken coop in the lean-to adjoining the room where they were dining, and threw a large sack over the top of it, which she had emptied of its contents earlier in the day. This done, she quickly let in her husband, to whom she said as he entered the house:

"You soon gobbled down that supper of yours."

"We never ate a crumb of it," replied Pietro.

"And why was that?" said his wife.

"I'll tell you why it was," said Pietro. "No sooner had Ercolano, his wife, and myself taken our places at table than we heard someone sneezing, close beside where we were sitting. We took no notice the first time it happened, or the second, but when the sneezing was repeated for the third, fourth, and fifth times, and a good many more besides, we were all struck dumb with astonishment. Ercolano was in a bad mood anyway because his wife had kept us waiting for ages before opening the door to let us in, and he rounded on her almost choking with fury, saying: 'What's the meaning of this? Who's doing all that sneezing?' He then got up from the table, and walked over to the stairs, beneath which there was an alcove boarded in with timber, such as people very often use for storing away bits and pieces when they're tidying up the house.

"As this was the place from which Ercolano thought the sneezes were coming, he opened a little door in the wainscoting, whereupon the whole room was suddenly filled with the most appalling smell of sulphur, though a little while before, when we caught a whiff of sulphur and complained about it, Ercolano's wife said: 'It's because I was using sulphur earlier in the day to bleach my veils. I sprinkled it into a large bowl so that they would absorb the fumes, then placed it in the cupboard under the stairs, and it's still giving off a faint smell.' After opening the little door and waiting for the fumes to die down a little, Ercolano peered inside and caught sight of the fellow who'd been doing all the sneezing, and was still sneezing his head off because of the sulphur. But if he'd stayed there much longer he would never have sneezed again, nor would he have done anything else for that matter.

"When he saw the man sitting there in the cupboard, Ercolano turned to his wife and shouted: 'Now I see, woman, why you kept us waiting so long at the door just now, without letting us in; but I'll make you pay for it, if it's the last thing I do.' On hearing this, since it was perfectly obvious what she had been doing, his wife got up from the table without a word of explanation and took to her heels, and what became of her I have no idea. Not having noticed that his wife had fled, Ercolano called repeatedly on the man who was sneezing to come out, but the fellow was already on his last legs and couldn't be persuaded to budge. So Ercolano grabbed him by one of his feet, dragged him out, and ran for a knife in order to kill him, at which point, since I was afraid we would all be arrested, myself included, I leapt to my feet and saved him from being killed or coming to any harm. As I was defending him from Ercolano, my shouts brought several of the neighbours running to the scene, and they picked up the youth, who was no longer conscious, and carried him out of the house, but I've no idea where they took him. All this commotion put paid to our supper, so that, as I said, not only did I not gobble it down, but I never ate a crumb of it."

On hearing this tale, his wife perceived that other women, even though their plans occasionally miscarried, were no less shrewd than herself, and she was strongly tempted to speak up in defence of Ercolano's wife. But thinking that by censuring another's misconduct she would cover up her own more successfully, she said:

"What a nice way to behave! What a fine, God-fearing specimen of womanhood! What a loyal and respectable spouse! Why, she had such an air of saintliness that she looked as if butter wouldn't melt in her mouth! But the worst part about it is that anyone as old as she is should be setting the young so fine an example. A curse upon the hour she was born! May the Devil take the wicked and deceitful hussy, for allowing herself to become the general butt and laughing-stock of all the women of this city! Not only has she thrown away her own good name, broken her marriage vows, and forfeited the respect of society, but she's had the audacity, after all he has done for her, to involve an excellent husband and venerable citizen in her disgrace, and all for the sake of some other man. So help me God, women of her kind should be shown no mercy; they ought to be done away with; they ought to be burnt alive and reduced to ashes."

But at this point, recollecting that her lover was concealed beneath the chicken coop in the very next room, she started coaxing Pietro to go to bed, saying it was getting late, whereupon Pietro, who had a greater urge to eat than to sleep, asked her whether there was any supper left over.

"Supper?" she replied. "What would I be doing cooking supper, when you're not at home to eat it? Do you take me for the wife of Ercolano? Be off with you to bed, and give your stomach a rest, just for this once."

Now, earlier that same evening, some of the labourers from Pietro's farm in the country had turned up at the house with a load of provisions, and had tethered their asses in a small stable adjoining the lean-to, without bothering to water them. Being frantic with thirst, one of the asses, having broken its tether, had strayed from the stable and was roaming freely about the premises, sniffing in every nook and cranny to see if it could find any water. And in the course of its wanderings, it came and stood immediately beside the coop under which the young man lay hidden.

Since the young man was having to crouch on all fours, one of his hands was sticking out slightly from underneath the coop, and as luck would have it (or, rather, to his great misfortune), the ass brought one of its hooves to rest on his fingers, causing him so much pain that he started to shriek at the top of his voice. Pietro, hearing this, was filled with astonishment, and realizing that the noise was coming from somewhere inside the house, he rushed from the room to investigate. The youth was still howling, for the ass had not yet shifted its hoof from his fingers and was pressing firmly down upon him all the time. "Who's there?" yelled Pietro as he ran to the coop, lifting it up to reveal the young man, who, apart from suffering considerable pain from having his fingers crushed beneath the hoof of the ass, was trembling with fear from head to foot in case Pietro should do him some serious injury.

Pietro recognized the young man as one he had long been pursuing for his own wicked ends, and demanded to know what he was doing there. But instead of answering his question, the youth pleaded with him for the love of God not to do him any harm.

"Get up," said Pietro. "There's no need to worry, I shan't do you any harm. Just tell me what you're doing here, and how you got in."

The young man made a clean breast of the whole thing, and Pietro, who was no less pleased with his discovery than his wife was filled with despair, took him by the hand and led him back into the room, where the woman was waiting for him in a state of indescribable terror. Pietro sat down, looked her squarely in the face, and said:

"When you were heaping abuse on Ercolano's wife just now, and saying that she ought to be burnt alive, and that she was giving women a bad name, why didn't you say the same things about yourself? And if you wanted to keep yourself out of it, what possessed you to say such things about her, when you knew full well that you were tarred with the same brush? The only reason you did it, of course, was because all you women are alike. You go out of your way to criticize other people's failings so as to cover up your own. Oh, how I wish that a fire would descend from Heaven and burn the whole revolting lot of you to ashes!"

On finding that all she had to contend with, in the first flush of his anger, was a string of verbal abuse, and noting how delighted he seemed to be holding such a good-looking boy by the hand, the wife plucked up courage and said:

"It doesn't surprise me in the least that you want a fire to descend from Heaven and burn us all to ashes, seeing that you're as fond of women as a dog is fond of a hiding, but by the Holy Cross of Jesus you'll not have your wish granted. However, now that you've raised the subject, I'd like to know what you're grumbling about. It's all very well for you to compare me to Ercolano's wife, but at least he gives that sanctimonious old trollop whatever she wants, and treats her as a wife should be treated, which is more than can be said for you. I grant you that you keep me well supplied with clothes and shoes, but you know very well how I fare for anything else, and how long it is since you last slept with me. And I'd rather go barefoot and dressed in rags, and have you treat me properly in bed, than have all those things to wear and a husband who never comes near me. For the plain truth is, Pietro, that I'm no different from other women, and I want the same that they are having. And if you won't let me have it, you can hardly blame me if I go and get it elsewhere. At least I do you the honour not to consort with stable-boys and riff-raff."

Pietro saw that she could go on talking all night, and since he was not unduly interested in his wife, he said:

"Hold your tongue now, woman, and leave everything to me. Be so good as to see that we're supplied with something to eat. This young man looks as though he's had no more supper this evening than I have."

"Of course he hasn't had any supper," said his wife. "We were no sooner seated at table than you had to come knocking at the door."

"Run along, then," said Pietro, "and get us some supper, after which I'll arrange matters so that you won't have any further cause for complaint."

On perceiving that her husband was so contented, the wife sprang to her feet and quickly relaid the table. And when the supper she had prepared was brought in, she and the youth and her degenerate husband made a merry meal of it together.

How exactly Pietro arranged matters, after supper, to the mutual satisfaction of all three parties, I no longer remember. But I do know that the young man was found next morning wandering about the piazza, not exactly certain with which of the pair he had spent the greater part of the night, the wife or the husband. So my advice to you, dear ladies, is this, that you should always give back as much as you receive; and if you can't do it at once, bear it in mind till you can, so that what you lose on the swings, you gain on the round-abouts.

# The Book of the Thousand Nights and a Night

TRANSLATED BY RICHARD FRANCIS BURTON

### The Third Kalandar's Tale

Know, O my lady, that I also am a King and the son of a King and my name is Ajíb son of Khazíb. When my father died I succeeded him; and I ruled and did justice and dealt fairly by all my lieges. I delighted in sea trips, for my capital stood on the shore, before which the ocean stretched far and wide; and near-hand were many great islands with scones and garrisons in the midst of the main. My fleet numbered fifty merchant-men, and as many yachts for pleasance, and an hundred and fifty sail ready fitted for holy war with the Unbelievers. It fortuned that I had a mind to enjoy myself on the islands aforesaid, so I took ship with my people in ten keel; and, carrying with me a month's victual, I set out on a twenty days' voyage. But one night a head wind struck us, and the sea rose against us

---

The Book of the Thousand Nights and a Night *is the paradigm for all works of fiction: a collection of stories told by a woman who must literally invent to save her life.* "The Third Kalandar's Tale" *appears in Burton's translation, which Jorge Luis Borges, in a volume of his lectures titled* Seven Nights, *called* "anthropological and obscene . . . written in a curious English partly derived from the fourteenth century, an English full of archaisms and neologisms, an English not devoid of beauty but which at times is difficult to read."

with huge waves; the billows sorely buffetted us and a dense darkness settled round us. We gave ourselves up for lost and I said, "Whoso endangereth his days, e'en an he 'scape deserveth no praise." Then we prayed to Allah and besought Him; but the storm-blasts ceased not to blow against us nor the surges to strike us till morning broke, when the gale fell, the seas sank to mirrory stillness, and the sun shone upon us kindly clear. Presently we made an island, where we landed and cooked somewhat of food, and ate heartily and took our rest for a couple of days. Then we set out again and sailed other twenty days, the seas broadening and the land shrinking. Presently the current ran counter to us, and we found ourselves in strange waters, where the Captain had lost his reckoning, and was wholly bewildered in this sea; so said we to the look-out man, "Get thee to the mast-head and keep thine eyes open." He swarmed up the mast and looked out and cried aloud, "O Rais, I espy to starboard something dark, very like a fish floating on the face of the sea, and to larboard there is a loom in the midst of the main, now black and now bright." When the captain heard the look-out's words he dashed his turband on the deck and plucked out his beard and beat his face, saying, "Good news indeed! we be all dead men; not one of us can be saved." And he fell to weeping and all of us wept for his weeping and also for our lives; and I said, "O Captain, tell us what it is the look-out saw." "O my Prince," answered he, "know that we lost our course on the night of the storm, which was followed on the morrow by a two days' calm during which we made no way; and we have gone astray eleven days reckoning from that night, with ne'er a wind to bring us back to our true course. To-morrow by the end of the day we shall come to a mountain of black stone, hight the Magnet Mountain, for thither the currents carry us willy-nilly. As soon as we are under its lea, the ship's sides will open and every nail in plank will fly out and cleave fast to the mountain; for that Almighty Allah hath gifted the loadstone with a mysterious virtue and a love for iron, by reason whereof all which is iron travelleth towards it; and on this mountain is much iron, how much none knoweth save the Most High, from the many vessels which have been lost there since the days of yore. The bright spot upon its summit is a dome of yellow latten from Andalusia, vaulted upon ten columns; and on its crown is a horseman who rideth a horse of brass and holdeth in hand a lance of latten; and there hangeth on his bosom a tablet of lead graven with names and talismans." And he presently added, "And, O King, none destroyeth folk save the rider on that steed, nor will the egromancy be dispelled till he fall from his horse." Then, O my lady, the Captain wept with exceeding weeping and we all made sure of death-doom and each and every one of us fare-welled his friend and charged him with his last will and testament in case he might be saved. We slept not that night and in the morning we found ourselves much nearer the Loadstone Mountain, whither the waters drave us with a violent send. When the ships were close under its lea they opened and the nails flew out and all the iron in them sought the Magnet Mountain and clove to it like a network; so that by the end of the day we were all struggling in the waves round about the mountain. Some of us were saved, but more were drowned, and even those who had escaped knew not one another, so stupefied were they by the beating of the billows and the raving of the winds. As for me, O my lady, Allah (be His name ex-alted!) preserved my life that I might suffer whatso He willed to me of hardship, misfortune, and calamity; for I scrambled upon a plank from one of the ships, and the wind and waters threw it at the feet of the Mountain. There I found a practicable path leading by steps carven out of the rock to the summit, and I called on the name of Allah Almighty. —And Shahrazad perceived the dawn of day and ceased to say her permitted say.

*Now when it was the Fifteenth Night,*
She continued, It hath reached me, O auspicious King, that the third Kalandar said to the lady (the rest of the party sitting fast bound and the slaves standing with swords drawn over their heads): And after calling on the name of Almighty Allah and passionately beseeching Him, I breasted the ascent, clinging to the steps and notches hewn in the stone, and mounted little by little. And the Lord stilled the wind and aided me in the ascent, so that I succeeded in reaching the summit. There I found no rest-ing place save the dome, which I entered, joying with exceeding joy at my escape; and made the Wuzu ablution and prayed a two-bow prayer, a thanksgiving to God for my preservation. Then I fell asleep under the dome, and heard in my dream a mysterious Voice saying, "O son of Khazib! when thou wakest from thy sleep dig under thy feet and thou shalt find a bow of brass and three leaden arrows, inscribed with talismans and characts. Take the bow and shoot the arrows at the horseman on the dome top and free mankind from this sore calamity. When thou hast shot him he shall fall into the sea, and the horse will also drop at thy feet: then bury it in the place of the bow. This done, the main will swell and rise till it is level with the mountain head, and there will appear on it a skiff carrying a man

of latten (other than he thou shalt have shot), holding in his hand a pair of paddles. He will come to thee, and do thou embark with him, but beware of saying Bismillah or of otherwise naming Allah Almighty. He will row thee for a space of ten days, till he bring thee to certain Islands called the Islands of Safety, and thence thou shalt easily reach a port and find those who will convey thee to thy native land; and all this shall be fulfilled to thee so thou call not on the name of Allah." Then I started up from my sleep in joy and gladness and, hastening to do the bidding of the mysterious Voice, found the bow and arrows and shot at the horseman and tumbled him into the main, whilst the horse dropped at my feet; so I took it and buried it. Presently the sea surged up and rose till it reached the top of the mountain; nor had I long to wait ere I saw a skiff in the offing coming towards me. I gave thanks to Allah; and, when the skiff came up to me, I saw therein a man of brass with a tablet of lead on his breast inscribed with talismans and characts; and I embarked without uttering a word. The boatman rowed on with me through the first day and the second and the third, in all ten whole days, till I caught sight of the Islands of Safety; whereat I joyed with exceeding joy and for stress of gladness exclaimed, "Allah! Allah! In the name of Allah! There is no god but *the* God and Allah is Almighty." Thereupon the skiff forthwith upset and cast me upon the sea; then it righted and sank deep into the depths. Now, I am a fair swimmer, so I swam the whole day till nightfall, when my forearms and shoulders were numbed with fatigue and I felt like to die; so I testified to my Faith, expecting naught but death. The sea was still surging under the violence of the winds, and presently there came a billow like a hillock; and, bearing me up high in air, threw me with a long cast on dry land, that His will might be fulfilled. I crawled up the beach and doffing my raiment wrung it out to dry and spread it in the sunshine: then I lay me down and slept the whole night. As soon as it was day, I donned my clothes and rose to look whither I should walk. Presently I came to a thicket of low trees; and, making a cast round it, found that the spot whereon I stood was an islet, a mere holm, grit on all sides by the ocean; whereupon I said to myself, "Whatso freeth me from one great calamity casteth me into a greater!" But while I was pondering my case and longing for death, behold, I saw afar off a ship making for the island; so I clomb a tree and hid myself among the branches. Presently the ship anchored and landed ten slaves, blackamoors, bearing iron hoes and baskets, who walked on till they reached the middle of the island. Here they dug deep into the ground, until they uncovered a plate of metal which they lifted, thereby opening a trap-door. After this they returned to the ship and thence brought bread and flour, honey and fruits, clarified butter, leather bottles containing liquors and many household stuffs; also furniture, table-service, and mirrors; rugs, carpets, and in fact all needed to furnish a dwelling; and they kept going to and fro, and descending by the trap-door, till they had transported into the dwelling all that was in the ship. After this the slaves again went on board and brought back with them garments as rich as may be, and in the midst of them came an old old man, of whom very little was left, for Time had dealt hardly and harshly with him, and all that remained of him was a bone wrapped in a rag of blue stuff, through which the winds whistled west and east. As saith the poet of him:

> Time gars me tremble— Ah, how sore the baulk!
> While time in pride of strength doth ever stalk:
> Time was I walked nor ever felt I tired.
> Now am I tired albe I never walk!

And the Shaykh held by the hand a youth cast in beauty's mould, all elegance and perfect grace; so fair that his comeliness deserved to be proverbial; for he was as a green bough or the tender young of the roe, ravishing every heart with his loveliness and subduing every soul with his coquetry and amorous ways. It was of him the poet spake when he said:

> Beauty they brought with him to make compare;
> But Beauty hung her head in shame and care:
> Quoth they, "O Beauty, hast thou seen his like?"
> And Beauty cried, "His like? not anywhere!"

They stinted not their going, O my lady, till all went down by the trap-door and did not reappear for an hour, or rather more; at the end of which time the slaves and the old man came up without the youth and, replacing the iron plate and carefully closing the door-slab, as it was before, they returned to the ship and made sail and were lost to my sight. When they turned away to depart, I came down from the tree and, going to the place I had seen them fill up, scraped off and removed the earth; and in patience possessed my soul till I had cleared the whole of it away. Then appeared the trap-door which was of wood, in shape and size like a millstone; and when

I lifted it up it disclosed a winding staircase of stone. At this I marvelled and, descending the steps till I reached the last, found a fair hall, spread with various kinds of carpets and silk stuffs, wherein was a youth sitting upon a raised couch and leaning back on a round cushion with a fan in his hand and nosegays and posies of sweet scented herbs and flowers before him; but he was alone and not a soul near him in the great vault. When he saw me he turned pale; but I saluted him courteously and said, "Set thy mind at ease and calm thy fears; no harm shall come near thee; I am a man like thyself and the son of a King to boot; whom the decrees of Destiny have sent to bear thee company and cheer thee in thy loneliness. But now tell me, what is thy story and what causeth thee to dwell thus in solitude under the ground?" When he was assured that I was of his kind and no Jinni, he rejoiced and his fine colour returned; and, making me draw near to him he said, "O my brother, my story is a strange story and 'tis this. My father is a merchant-jeweller possessed of great wealth, who hath white and black slaves travelling and trading on his account in ships and on camels, and trafficking with the most distant cities; but he was not blessed with a child, not even one. Now, on a certain night he dreamed a dream that he should be favoured with a son, who would be short-lived; so the morning dawned on my father, bringing him woe and weeping. On the following night my mother conceived and my father noted down the date of her becoming pregnant. Her time being fulfilled, she bare me; whereat my father rejoiced and made banquets and called together the neighbours and fed the Fakirs and the poor, for that he had been blessed with issue near the end of his days. Then he assembled the astrologers and astronomers who knew the places of the planets, and the wizards and wise ones of the time, and men learned in horoscopes and nativities; and they drew out my birth scheme and said to my father: Thy son shall live to fifteen years, but in his fifteenth there is a sinister aspect; an he safely tide it over he shall attain a great age. And the cause that threateneth him with death is this. In the Sea of Peril standeth the Mountain Magnet hight; on whose summit is a horseman of yellow latten seated on a horse also of brass and bearing on his breast a tablet of lead. Fifty days after this rider shall fall from his steed thy son will die and his slayer will be he who shoots down the horseman, a Prince named Ajib son of King Khazib. My father grieved with exceeding grief to hear these words; but reared me in tenderest fashion and educated me excellently well till my fifteenth year was told. Ten days ago news came to him that the horseman had fallen into the sea and he who shot him down was named Ajib son of King Khazib. My father thereupon wept bitter tears at the need of parting with me and became like one possessed of a Jinni. However, being in mortal fear for me, he built me this place under the earth; and, stocking it with all required for the few days still remaining, he brought me hither in a ship and left me here. Ten are already past, and when the forty shall have gone by without danger to me, he will come and take me away; for he hath done all this only in fear of Prince Ajib. Such, then, is my story and the cause of my loneliness." When I heard his story I marvelled and said in my mind, I am the Prince Ajib who hath done all this; but as Allah is with me I will surely not slay him! So I said to him, "O my lord, far from thee be this hurt and harm and then, please Allah, thou shalt not suffer cark nor care nor aught disquietude, for I will tarry with thee and serve thee as a servant, and then wend my ways; and, after having borne thee company during the forty days, I will go with thee to thy home where thou shalt give me an escort of some of thy Mamelukes with whom I may journey back to my own city; and the Almighty shall requite thee for me." He was glad to hear these words, when I rose and lighted a large wax-candle and trimmed the lamps and the three lanterns; and I set on meat and drink and sweetmeats. We ate and drank and sat talking over various matters till the greater part of the night was gone; when he lay down to rest and I covered him up and went to sleep myself. Next morning I arose and warmed a little water, then lifted him gently so as to awake him and brought him the warm water, wherewith he washed his face and said to me, "Heaven requite thee for me with every blessing, O youth! By Allah, if I get quit of this danger and am saved from him whose name is Ajib bin Khazib, I will make my father reward thee and send thee home healthy and wealthy; and, if I die, then my blessing be upon thee." I answered, "May the day never dawn on which evil shall betide thee; and may Allah make my last day before thy last day!" Then I set before him somewhat of food and we ate; and I got ready perfumes for fumigating the hall, wherewith he was pleased. Moreover I made him a Mankalah-cloth; and we played and ate sweetmeats and we played again and took our pleasure till nightfall, when I rose and lighted the lamps, and set before him somewhat to eat, and sat telling him stories till the hours of darkness were far spent. Then he lay down to rest and I covered him up and rested also. And thus I continued to do, O my lady, for days and nights, and affection for him took root in my heart and my sorrow was eased, and I said to myself, The astrologers lied when they predicted that he should be slain by Ajib bin

Khazib: by Allah, I will not slay him. I ceased not ministering to him and conversing and carousing with him and telling him all manner tales for thirty-nine days. On the fortieth night the youth rejoiced and said, "O my brother, Alhamdolillah!—praise be to Allah—who hath preserved me from death, and this is by thy blessing and the blessing of thy coming to me; and I pray God that He restore thee to thy native land. But now, O my brother, I would thou warm me some water for the Ghusl-ablution and do thou kindly bathe me and change my clothes." I replied, "With love and gladness"; and I heated water in plenty and carrying it in to him washed his body all over, the washing of health, with meal of lupins and rubbed him well and changed his clothes and spread him a high bed whereon he lay down to rest, being drowsy after bathing. Then said he, "O my brother, cut me up a water-melon, and sweeten it with a little sugar-candy." So I went to the store-room and bringing out a fine water-melon I found there, set it on a platter and laid it before him, saying, "O my master, hast thou not a knife?" "Here it is," answered he, "over my head upon the high shelf." So I got up in haste and taking the knife drew it from its sheath; but my foot slipped in stepping down and I fell heavily upon the youth holding in my hand the knife, which hastened to fulfil what had been written on the Day that decided the destinies of man, and buried itself, as if planted, in the youth's heart. He died on the instant. When I saw that he was slain and knew that I had slain him, maugre myself, I cried out with an exceeding loud and bitter cry and beat my face and rent my raiment and said, "Verily we be Allah's and unto Him we be returning, O Moslems! O folk fain of Allah! there remained for this youth but one day of the forty dangerous days which the astrologers and the learned had foretold for him; and the predestined death of this beautiful one was to be at my hand. Would Heaven I had not tried to cut the water-melon. What dire misfortune is this I must bare, lief or loath? What a disaster! What an affliction! O Allah mine, I implore thy pardon and declare to Thee my innocence of his death. But what God willeth let that come to pass."—And Shahrazad perceived the dawn of day and ceased to say her permitted say.

FROM

# *Autobiography*

TRANSLATED BY GEORGE BULL

By now the worst of the plague was over, and all those who were still alive went round greeting each other affectionately. This rejoicing gave birth to a society that included the best painters and sculptors and goldsmiths that there were in Rome. The founder of the club was a sculptor called Michelagnolo; he came from Siena and was such an expert craftsman that he could be compared with anyone else in his trade. But above all he was the most agreeable and genial man in the world. As far as age was concerned he was the oldest among us, but his vigour made him seem the youngest.

We used to meet together very often, at least twice a week. I must not forget to mention that our society also included Giulio Romano, the painter, and Gianfrancesco, two splendid pupils of the great Raphael of Urbino. After we had been meeting time and time again, our admirable president decided that the following Sunday we would all meet for supper at his house, and each of us was to bring what Michelagnolo called his "crow" along with him. Whoever failed to do so would have to stand all the others a supper.

---

*BENVENUTO CELLINI was born in 1500 in Florence, where he spent the early years of his life training to be a goldsmith. Like many Renaissance artists, however, he was attracted to Rome, and he worked there for Popes Clement VII and Paul III. He also spent a period in France at the court of Francis I, for whom he made a splendid gold salt-cellar. Cellini nonetheless maintained close ties with Florence and produced his bronze statue of Perseus in the Loggia dei Lanzi under the patronage of Cosimo de' Medici.*

Those of us who did not know any women of the town had to go to
no little trouble and expense to get hold of one, in order to avoid being
disgraced at our brilliant supper-party. I thought I was well provided for
with a very beautiful young woman called Pantasilea, who was madly in
love with me; but I had to give her up to a close friend of mine, Bachiacca,
who had been, and still was, passionately fond of her. This gave rise to a
few lovers' quarrels, because when Pantasilea saw how easily I had given
her up to Bachiacca, she came to the conclusion that I didn't care a straw
for her love, great as it was. Shortly after, her determination to pay me
back for the insult led to no end of trouble, which I shall describe when
the time comes.

When it was nearly time for us to appear at our brilliant meeting and
present our crows, I was still without one, but I decided it would be wrong
to fail over such a silly thing. What gave me most worry was that I had no
wish to have that distinguished gathering see me bring in under my wing
some bedraggled old scarecrow. So I hit on a trick that would amuse everyone enormously.

I made up my mind as to what I would do, and then I called in a young
lad of sixteen who lived next door, the son of a Spanish copper-smith. He
was studying Latin, and was very studious. His name was Diego. He was
a handsome boy, with a wonderful complexion, and his head was even
more beautifully modelled than that of the ancient statue of Antinous.
I had drawn him very often and he brought me a great deal of honour.
He never went out with anyone and so he was completely unknown.
Also, he dressed very badly and slovenly and all he loved was his precious
studying.

When he came in I asked him to let me dress him up in the woman's
clothes I had got ready. He was quite willing and put them on at once.
Then I quickly improved even his beautiful face by the attractive way I arranged his hair, and I put two little rings in his ears. They had two beautiful large pearls, and as the rings were split I just clipped them on, which
made it look as if his lobes were pierced. After that I arranged some beautiful gold and richly jewelled necklaces round his neck, and adorned his
lovely hands with rings.

Then with a smile I took him by the ear and led him in front of my
large mirror. When he saw himself he blurted out: "Help! is that Diego?"

"It most certainly is," I said. "It's the Diego I have never yet asked for
anything, but now I want him to do me one harmless favour, which is that

I want him to come out to supper, in the same clothes he has on now, with that famous society I've often told him about."

Now, he was a good-living, thoughtful young man, and very intelligent. He quietened down, stared at the floor, and stood for a while without saying a word. Then, all at once, he looked up at me and said: "If it's with Benvenuto, I'll come. Let's be on our way."

I put a large scarf round his head—the sort that in Rome is called a summer-cloth—and when we reached the meeting-place everyone was already there to welcome us. Michelagnolo was standing between Giulio and Gianfrancesco. When I took the scarf off my pretty young man's head, Michelagnolo, who as I've said before was the pleasantest, wittiest man imaginable, stretched out his hands, placed one on Giulio and one on Gianfrancesco, and with all his strength forced them to bow down. Then he himself, falling on his knees, pretended to cry for mercy and shouted out to everyone:

"Look at this! Look what the angels of paradise are like. Though they are called angels, some of them are women."

Then he added:

"Angel of grace and beauty,
Bless me and protect me."

At this, the graceful creature starting laughing, lifted his right hand, and, talking gracefully, gave him a Papal blessing. Then Michelagnolo stood up and said that one kissed the feet of the Pope but the cheeks of angels—and when he suited the action to the words the young man blushed furiously and looked more beautiful than ever. After this introduction, we discovered that the room was full of sonnets that we had written and sent to Michelagnolo. My young companion began to read them, and as he spoke them aloud—every one of them—his incredible beauty was so enhanced that I find it impossible to describe. Then there was a great deal of comment and conversation, which I shall not give in detail as that is not my purpose. But I shall just report one thing, because it was said by that splendid painter, Giulio. He looked round shrewdly at everyone present, staring most of all at the women, and then he turned to Michelagnolo and said:

"My dear Michelagnolo, your name, crows, fits this crowd only too well today. But they haven't even the beauty of crows when they're set by the side of one of the most beautiful peacocks imaginable."

When the food was ready and served and we were about to sit down at table, Giulio asked as a favour that he should be allowed to decide on our places. His request was granted, and, taking each woman in turn by the hand, he arranged them all round the inside, with my one in the middle. Then he put all the men round the outside, with me in the middle, as he said that I deserved the highest honour. There was a beautiful trellis of natural jasmines behind where the women sat, and with this background their beauty, and my partner's especially, was so wonderfully set off that words fail to describe it. So we all set to with a will on that splendid and sumptuous feast.

After we had eaten, we heard some wonderful singing and music. They were playing and singing from written music, and my lovely companion asked permission to take part. His performance was so much better than almost all the others' that everyone was astonished. In fact Giulio and Michelagnolo stopped talking about him in the joking way they had done at first, and their praise became grave and serious and showed the wonder they felt. When the music was finished, a man called Aurelio Ascolano, who was marvellous at improvisation, began to praise the women. While he was reciting his heavenly, beautiful words, the two women who were sitting on either side of my lovely companion never left off chattering. One of them told how she had come to take the wrong turning, the other one started asking my companion how it had happened to her, and who were her men friends, and how long she had been in Rome, and other questions of that sort.

As a matter of fact, if all I had to do was describe what went on, I could give details of a host of amusing incidents that took place because of Pantasilea's infatuation for me. But as they are outside my purpose I shall pass them over briefly. Now the chatter of those beastly women began to annoy my companion—to whom we had given the name of Pomona—and so Pomona, in her anxiety to get away from their stupid babbling, began turning now to one side and now to another. The woman whom Giulio had brought asked if there was something wrong with her, and she said, yes, there was, that she thought she was pregnant by several months and felt a pain in her uterus. At once, in their concern for her, the two women started feeling Pomona's body and discovered she was a male. They drew their hands away quickly, shot up from the table, and began insulting him, in words usually reserved for pretty young men. Immediately uproar broke out, and everyone started laughing and crying out in amazement.

The stern Michelagnolo asked permission to give me the penance he thought proper and, when it was granted, with loud cries from everyone else he lifted me up and shouted: "Long live Benvenuto: long live Benvenuto."

Then he added that that was the sentence I deserved for such a perfect trick. In this way, with day coming to an end, that charming supper-party finished; and we all went home.

# ∽ Ameng of Wu ∽

## FROM

# The Cut Sleeve

TRANSLATED BY GIOVANNI VITIELLO

### The Viscount Mi Xia

The Viscount Mi, whose name was Xia, was a Junior Grand Master in the Kingdom of Wei. He enjoyed the favor of the Duke of Wei.

According to the law of the Kingdom, taking the sovereign's chariot without permission was punishable by having one's feet cut off.

Once, the Viscount's mother fell ill; somebody came during the night to tell him. The Viscount Mi usurped the sovereign's chariot and ran to her. When Duke Ling heard of this, he judged the Viscount wise and said: "What a dutiful son! For his mother's sake he violates the law, risking the punishment of the feet-cut!"

Another day, he was strolling with the Duke in an orchard. He bit into a peach and it was sweet; he offered Duke Ling the rest. The Duke said: "He loves me to the point that he forgets his own mouth and feeds me instead!"

Later the Viscount's beauty faded, and so did the Duke's love. Then, when the Viscount committed a fault, the Duke said: "This man usurped my chariot, and also gave me a peach already bitten!"

*Warring States: 403–221* B.C.

---

The Cut Sleeve *is an anthology of fifty-one male homoerotic tales compiled by* AMENG OF WU *and published at the beginning of this century within a larger work entitled* Collection of Fragrant Voluptuousness. *Giovanni Vitiello's Italian translation,* La manica tagliata *(Palermo: Sellerio, 1990), is the only complete one.*

## The Lord of Longyang

The King of Wei and the Lord of Longyang were on a boat, fishing, when tears began to flow down the Lord of Longyang's face.

"Why are you crying?" asked the King.

"For the fish your subject caught."

"And what is there to cry about?" the King asked.

He answered: "I caught a fish and I was very happy. But then I caught a bigger fish, and I wished to throw away the one I had caught before.

"Now, ugly as I am, I have the honor of shaking out my King's pillow and mat. But within the Four Seas there are so many beautiful people; upon hearing that I enjoy the King's favor, they will lift their gowns and hurry to you. And I will be thrown away like the fish caught before. How could I not shed tears?"

The King of Wei so promulgated an edict within the Four Seas which said: "Anyone who will dare offer me beautiful people will be executed together with his family!"

*Warring States*

## Pan Zhang

When young, Pan Zhang had beautiful looks and manners, and the people of his time admired him. Wang Chongxian from the Kingdom of Chu heard of his fame and came to ask him for his writings. He wished to study with him.

As soon as they saw each other, they fell in love. Their feelings were those of husband and wife, and thus they shared the pillow; their friendship had no limits.

Later they died together. Their families mourned them and buried them together on Mount Luofu. On the tomb, unexpectedly, grew a tree—the branches and leaves all embracing one another. People found it extraordinary; they called it the Tree of the Shared Pillow.

*Warring States*

### The Graduate Lü Zijing

The graduate Lü Zijing from Ji'an loved a beautiful man, Wei Guoxiu. Guoxiu died, and Lu cried and mourned him. He felt lost, and began to roam, leaving his occupations behind.

Near the crumbling palace of the fief of Ning there was the Tower of the Hundred Flowers. In his travels Lü arrived at this place. There he saw a man of such beauty that not even Wei could have rivaled. Tears fell, moistening the collar of his shirt.

The man asked him why. Lü said: "In front of such an irresistible beauty, I'm hurt by the memory of my old friend."

The man said: "Sir, if you don't despise my homeliness, with your old feeling you can love a new man, and the new love will be like the old one."

Lü felt a joy beyond his hopes, and they made love.

Lü asked where the man came from and about his family. The man hesitated a while, then began: "You must not be surprised, sir. I come from the North. I was Wang Du, a celebrated singer in my time. At first I made my home in Wumen, until I happened to be favored by the Prince of Ning. I became his only lover, making all the women in the palace fall into disgrace. But before long the concubine Lou, out of jealousy, poisoned me. They buried my corpse under the Tower of the Hundred Flowers; but my obscure soul has not yet expired, and I can still wander in the world of men.

"I can see your great passion, and this is why I'm not ashamed to present myself to you. That Sir Wei you are missing, I know him too. He is now in the Temple of the God Wutong on the Peak of Xianxia, south of the Pucheng district. Wutong fears Taoist masters; if you get talismans and carry them with you, you'll be able to meet him."

Lü went to beg a Taoist master and obtained the necessary talismans and incantations.

Three days later Wei did in fact appear and said: "Wutong kidnapped me because of my looks. I still think of you; I haven't forgotten you. But there was no way to free myself. Today we are lucky to renew our joy, and to have also Sir Wang's company; Heavenly Destiny has granted us all this!"

Lü then bought a boat and, with the two men close to him, left his home to sail south on the Yangzi River.

Many years passed and he did not come back.

In the ages that followed, people would sometimes see them—now appearing, now vanishing, but always together the three of them.

*Ming Dynasty (1368–1644)*

## The Peasant Who Was Raped by a Dragon

In the service of the Ma family, in Hejian, there was a peasant who was nearly sixty.

He was walking alone when he encountered a rainstorm, with thunder and lightning in the dark sky. Then suddenly a dragon stretched out its claws, down onto his bamboo hat.

The peasant, thinking he was receiving Heaven's punishment, trembled with fear and fell flat on his face. He felt the dragon tearing off his trousers; he figured it was undressing him before the sentence. Never could he imagine that the dragon, leaning down and writhing against his back, would rape him there on the ground!

He turned on one side, trying to escape it, but immediately the dragon snarled with anger and set its teeth against his head. Fearing that he would be devoured, the peasant crouched down and did not dare move anymore.

Only after a while, uttering a cry like a clap of thunder, the dragon left.

The peasant lay there moaning on the path, a fetid saliva all over his body. Luckily his son, carrying a raincoat of leaves, came to find him, and carried him home on his back.

At the beginning the old man kept the matter secret. But then, since he was seriously injured, he had to seek out a doctor and medicines and finally revealed the whole story.

During the hoeing time, there are many women going to the fields to bring food to their husbands, but the dragon made love to a man. And the young shepherds were numerous too, yet the dragon made love to an old man. This is truly inexplicable!

*Qing Dynasty (1644–1911)*

## The Two Old Men

In Jimulong, in the prefecture of Urumchi, there was a soldier named Zhang Mingfeng, who had been transferred there to be a sentinel on a watchtower. Next to the tower there was an orchard. The gardener who took care of it, a man in his sixties, used to take shelter in the tower for the night whenever there was a storm.

One night Mingfeng, drunk, raped him. The old man awoke and got furious. He reported him to the sergeant, who, having verified that in fact the wounds had not healed yet, reported the case to the officer, who dismissed Mingfeng.

At that time Mingfeng was barely twenty years old. Everybody believed that the story was absurd. Some doubted the old man: some thought that probably he had abused Mingfeng in the past and had therefore been repaid in this way. However, the old man was interrogated twice and never confessed any crime.

Everybody said that it was a strange affair, but there was an officer's servant, named Yubao, who said: "These things do happen; there is nothing to be amazed at. A long time ago I was tending a horse on the Southern Mountain, when, scared by a hunter, the horse ran away. I was afraid to be punished, so I dove into the thickness of the wood to pursue it. But in the flurry I lost my way, and the more I turned around, the more I got lost. I spent there a day and a night, unable to find my way out.

"Then I saw from afar the roof of a house in the middle of the wood. I rushed towards it, but then I thought it might be a brigands' den, that I might be killed. So I crouched down in the grass, watching the situation.

"Quite a while passed, and then two old men, holding hands, laughing and talking, came out and sat on a rock. They embraced, one against the other: they seemed really indecently intimate! Then the old man on the left pulled the other and had him crouch down beside the rock; their attitude was lustful and indecent. I stayed hidden, spying on them, afraid that they might kill me to shut my mouth. I was terrified, rolled up like a worm, not daring to move, when they saw me.

"Not in the least ashamed, they both called to me to come out. They asked me where I was from, and gave me two cakes to eat. Pointing me the way home, they said: 'From such and such place you will see such and such tree; make a turn, and you will arrive to such and such place, and there you will see a deep creek: walk along it and in one day you will be home.'

"They also pointed out the highest peak around, saying: 'That peak faces south; if by any chance you get lost, look at it and you will know the direction.'

"And they also added; 'There is no grass on this barren mountain; your horse, driven by hunger, has already gone back by itself. It is full of bears and wolves up here: never come back again!'

"When I got home, the horse was indeed already there."

~ ~ ~

Now, isn't the case of Zhang Mingfeng making love to the sixty-year-old man similar to that of these two old men? The only difference is that we don't know who the two old men were. They looked like gentlemen who had cut all ties with the world and retired deep into the mountain to cultivate the Tao; but then why would they do such things?

On the other hand, *In the Books' Shadow in the House Amid the Trees* records the story of the immortal Ma Xiutou, and says that he kept company with boys and that he stated: "There is in them a real *yin* essence which can be grasped. It is a revitalizing technique: one can ride not only women, but men as well."

But in grasping the essence of an old man, what advantage can there be? Besides, if in the cultivation of the Tao this technique does actually exist, it must belong to the heterodox Tao of the magicians; in the Tao of the Supreme Perfection there are no such things!

*(Qing Dynasty)*

### Qinshu

Qinshu's last name was Hu, and his original name Shixian.

He was from Huai'an. When he was a child, he lost his mother. His father, a servant, was old and poor. Shixian had been raised by a maternal uncle. But his uncle had a hard life too, and his salary was insufficient. Shixian had to look for a master who could provide him with a living.

It happened that Mister Zhang, an employee in the Huainan prefectural office, wanted to acquire a young attendant. Somebody introduced Shixian to him. As soon as Zhang saw him, he liked him. Shixian's looks were below average; he appeared so helpless and almost unable to bear the weight of his clothes; he really inspired compassion! His hair was long and thick, his body so thin that there wasn't enough flesh to cover his bones. But Zhang in his heart rejoiced and said, "I live alone. This creature will erase my sadness."

He asked him his age—only twenty. He asked him his price—four taels per year. Zhang accepted, despite the expense. He changed his name; he called him Qinshu.

Among his peers, Qinshu was the youngest and the weakest. They all wanted a taste of the delicacy; they used to tease him, but Qinshu pretended he didn't understand and wouldn't answer. Being unsuccessful, they wanted to take him by force, like meat or fish; but Qinshu would promptly hit them with his hands and run away. His master had secretly watched him. He thought of him as upright and did not dare to offend him; he was afraid he would meet with resistance and be put to shame.

Qinshu had already been in service for a few months when they began sleeping in the same room. But the master could love him only in his heart. He would always pull down the curtains of Qinshu's bed and cover him, hereby expressing his love. Qinshu guarded himself against a possible violation. He was very strict in protecting himself; even on summer nights he would go to bed without untying his trousers.

One night the brightness of the moon shone on the four walls of the room. Qinshu, under the curtains, was in a deep sleep. His body reflected the moonlight: he glistened like jade. Zhang came into the room and, seeing him, was overwhelmed with emotion. He touched him delicately. Qinshu startled from his dreams in fright. Zhang then embraced him and kissed him.

"Sir, what is this?" said Qinshu with a serious expression. "I beg you to control yourself lest somebody see us. For me there would be nothing to regret, but would I not perhaps harm the lord's reputation?"

But Zhang, on his knees, begged him, saying: "Since the moment you arrived here, I have felt affection for you; it is already a long time. Today that affection has grown into love: how can you bear to remain indifferent and deny yourself to me?"

Qinshu said: "I am not a plant—how could I not know? Since I became your servant, you have never addressed me with expeditious words or a threatening air. Surely it hasn't been so because I am a good servant and I have never deserved your scorn. It is only because you are particularly indulgent towards me and don't show your disappointment. Sometimes I am impolite and my words are not humble enough, but you—it's as though you hadn't heard, and every day you cover me with favors.

"I know that your family is poor, that your salary as a secretary is low and in daily expenses you cannot spend carelessly even a single coin. Certainly, to honor my request you must make an effort. It is not just that you think of me; I would be ready to die for you. I think all the time for a way to reward your favors, but I haven't yet found it. How could a humble and ugly body like mine be sufficient for such a purpose? I would never dare to have any regrets for myself; my only real fear is to cause you harm."

Zhang said: "You really are a lovely boy! Hearing your words, I understand that there is an unspoken sentimental bond between us, and this is enough. But inside here my heart is restless: how to console myself and tame my hunger?"

Qinshu had lowered his head, without saying a word. The master embraced him, and joined him.

From that time on they slept in the same bed. What Qinshu had done to bind his master's heart so indissolubly to his own and achieve such a tenacious intimacy, Zhang never revealed, and therefore I cannot know it either.

Not too long after, Zhang's wife died and he had to hurry back home for the funeral. His conditions did not permit the two of them to go, so Zhang set his return for a month later and gave him money.

At that time, Zhang's superior, the prefect, had just gone for an audience at court and to the Ministry of Bureaucracy to await a new assignment. The wait was prolonged, and Qinshu reckoned: "The lord probably won't come back, and my father and my uncle cannot live without my support."

He didn't have any choice; he sold himself to a merchant, a man without scruples, who boasted about his wealth and made Qinshu serve him like a horse urged by the whip, without granting him a single moment of free time all day long.

It was not long after that Zhang came back and heard that Qinshu had a new master. His soul fell into silence. He didn't eat or sleep. And if anybody tried to console him, he would say: "I know for sure that Qinshu left only because he had no choice. I am the betrayer, not he."

Every day he went to look for him at the house of his new master, but he never got to see him. When he met him on the street, his master was there; they couldn't exchange a single word. So Zhang sent somebody to tell Qinshu of his overwhelming feelings. Qinshu, suffering, said to him: "Say good words to the lord for me. Even if the lord does not say anything, how could I pretend nothing happened? In vain the lord's chariot comes to honor me, and I don't even look back once—are there such manners in the world?

"I cannot leave this place, oppressed as I am by my master's authority. But I will certainly find an excuse to go out. I beg the lord not to go anywhere on that day, but to wait for me. Time will be so precious that a quarter of an hour will be worth a thousand taels!"

On the set day, he in fact arrived. But there were a lot of people around, and it was difficult to talk intimately. So they went into a remote temple to tell each other of their feelings while apart. Zhang gave him a sable collar, two rings, and belt pendants and handkerchiefs and all kinds of similar objects. He said: "For the two of us, today is the last time. We can only make an appointment in the next existence. Seeing this collar and these rings, perhaps you will think of the time I caressed your neck and held your hand. Serve my successor well. From this moment, we say goodbye forever."

Qinshu was sobbing and couldn't speak. Then he untied his hair, weeping. He then pulled out the knife he carried in his belt, cut a lock of hair, and, offering it to him, said: "The lord has always loved my hair. Today I have nothing to give you in farewell. This is the only thing my parents left me, by which I can express my feelings. I beg you to take care of yourself. Only Heaven could express this heart of mine! Even if the sea dried up and the rocks rotted, I would never betray you. If possible write me a note, and I will run to you at once! Seeing this lock, you will think of me. Our appointment is fixed for eternity."

They stopped talking; their tears were falling like rain.

The ancients said:

*A single note of* He Manzi,
*and tears fall down the lord's face.*

Who says that love between men is in any way different?

Zhang went home. There was not one day that he did not feel frustrated and confused. First it was passion, then fear, and finally sadness. And always he entrusted himself to poetry to express the inclinations of his heart.

*Qing Dynasty*

# ~ *Ihara Saikaku* ~

FROM

# *The Great Mirror of Male Love*

TRANSLATED BY PAUL GORDON SCHALOW

## Love: The Contest Between Two Forces

*In the beginning was boy love.*
*Famous woman-haters of Japan.*
—*Lectures on* The Record of the Origins of Male Love

In the beginning, when gods illuminated the heavens, Kuni-toko-tachi was taught the love of boys by a wagtail bird living on the dry riverbed below the floating bridge of heaven. From this sprang his love for Hi-no-chimaru. Even the myriad insects preferred the position of boy love. As a result, Japan was called "The Land of Dragonflies." The god Susa-no-wo, no longer able to enjoy the love of boys in his old age, turned to the princess Inada for comfort. Since then the cries of wailing infants have echoed throughout the world. Midwives and go-betweens have made their appearance; parents suffer with the burden of their daughters' dowries. Why, when there is no form of amusement more elegant than male love, do people nowadays remain unaware of its subtle pleasures?

Boy love is a profound thing. Similar cases in both Chinese and Japanese history attest to this. Wei Ling-kung entrusted his life to Mi Tzu-hsia, Kao Tsu gave his whole heart to Chi Ju, and Wu Ti pillowed only with Li Yen-nien. In our country, too, the "man of old" was for over five years the lover of Ise's younger brother, Daimon no Chūjō. During that time there were springs in which he took no notice of the blossoms, and autumns when he did not see the harvest moon. For the sake of his overpowering love, he bore the weight of snows and filled his sleeves with stormy gusts.

---

*IHARA SAIKAKU, a native of Osaka, was Japan's first "professional" writer: he lived exclusively on his earnings.*

He crossed frozen streams and quieted barking dogs with handfuls of rice. When gateways in earthen walls were tightly locked to him, he entered with a pass key. Even in the darkness of night he damned the milky way and cursed the glow of fireflies lest their meager light betray him. On a bench where servants relaxed in the cool of evening he sat all night with his beloved until his legs were red with the blood of mosquitoes. Still, his ardor did not cool, and when dawn broke he grieved that they should bid each other farewell for another day. The fierce wind parched his once glossy forelocks; to the distant crowing of roosters he stole away home. The tears that spilled from his eyes he caught in an inkstone, and with his writing brush he unburdened his heart. The slender volume that preserves the memories of those days is called *The Collection of Nightly Visits*. How is it that he later turned his back on male love to write a tale about women?

After coming of age, he abandoned his would-be lover and set off for the Nara capital. The cap of young purple that he wore surely makes him the father of all Kabuki actors. From behind, his figure was like a lovely peach blossom languishing in spring or a willow swaying drowsily in the breeze; he put even Mao Ch'iang and Hsi Shih to shame. As an adult, Narihira still preferred the company of handsome youths to that of women. The fact that he is remembered in this floating world as the god of *yin* and *yang* must cause him no end of vexation in the grave.

Another example is the priest Yoshida Kenkō, who sent thousands of love letters to a nephew of Sei Shōnagon named Kiyo-wakamaru. People did not reproach him for this, only for the single love letter that he wrote to a woman as a favor for a friend. His sullied reputation remains with us to this very day. Truly, female love is something that all men should fear. When I was born, if I had known what I now know about women, I would never have suckled at my mother's breast. There are, after all, any number of instances in which children have been raised on gruel and sweet broth.

In any case, I took my bachelor's household and established a residence at a rented property in a remote corner of Asakusa in Edo, Musashi Province. Oblivious to the world's joys and sorrows and the strife that afflicts humankind, I remained sequestered behind my locked gate and expounded on *The Record of the Origins of Male Love* before breakfast each morning. I wrote down in it everything I had ever seen, heard, felt, or learned about the rare pleasures of boy love in my forty-two years of travel throughout the land.

First, let us examine the differences between male and female love.

Which is to be preferred: A girl of eleven or twelve scrutinizing herself in a mirror, or a boy of the same age cleaning his teeth?

Lying rejected next to a courtesan, or conversing intimately with a Kabuki boy who is suffering from hemorrhoids?

Caring for a wife with tuberculosis, or keeping a youth who constantly demands spending money?

Having lightning strike the room where you are enjoying a boy actor you bought, or being handed a razor by a courtesan you hardly know who asks you to die with her?

Buying a *kakoi* courtesan the day after suffering a gambling loss, or procuring a boy on the streets after a market collapse affecting goods in which you have just invested?

Marrying the master's daughter and going to bed early every evening until you gradually waste away, or falling in love with the master's son and seeing his face only in the daytime?

A widow over sixty wearing a scarlet underskirt and counting her silver, or a boy with shaved temples in a simple cotton sash who is leafing through his past oaths of love?

Visiting Shimabara too often and losing your house to foreclosure, or spending all your money at Dōtombori and discovering that the due date for the castle rice you borrowed is fast approaching?

Having the ghost of a youth appear after telling "too scary tales," or having your ex-wife appear demanding money?

Peeking at the faces of actors under their sedge hats as they return from the theater, or asking a young apprentice her mistress's rank on their way to meet a customer?

Becoming a priest's attendant at Mount Kōya, or becoming the mistress of a retired gentleman?

A shrine dancing girl who makes her rounds to bless the rice pot and secretly hopes to come upon a household of men, or a boy peddling aloeswood oil who dreads the central chambers of a daimyo's residence?

The mouth of a woman as she blackens her teeth, or the hand of a youth as he plucks his whiskers?

Seeking shelter from a storm in the gateway of a house of assignation where you have no connections, or being refused a lantern for the trip home in the middle of the night after visiting a boy actor in his lodgings?

Becoming intimate with a bathhouse girl, or secretly visiting a youth who is on a thirty-day contract to another man?

Ransoming a courtesan, or setting up a Kabuki actor in a house of his own?

Lending your jacket to a Yoshiwara jester, or giving your pocket money to an actor's attendant on the dry riverbed for safekeeping?

Going to Shinmachi before the Bon Festival and falling in love with a courtesan, or becoming enamored of an actor just before the annual presentation on stage?

A teahouse girl chomping on nuts, or a youth selling fragrance who double-checks his scales?

Watching from behind the head of a Kabuki *tayū* as he entertains on a riverboat, or glimpsing the hem of a dappled robe trailing from a maid's carriage on its way back from cherry blossom viewing?

A youth attired in skirt and jacket who has his attendant carry his books on an outing, or a sumptuously dressed female attendant who has her helper carry a period lacquer letter box?

A daimyo's favorite page seated in the great reception chamber, or the unseemly figure of a standing female courtier?

Being laughed at for sending a love letter to a boy whose sleeve vents are already sewn shut, or being looked at askance when a girl in a long-sleeved robe takes a liking to you?

In each case above, even if the woman were a beauty of gentle disposition and the youth a repulsive pug-nosed fellow, it is a sacrilege to speak of female love in the same breath with boy love. A woman's heart can be likened to the wisteria vine: though bearing lovely blossoms, it is twisted and bent. A youth may have a thorn or two, but he is like the first plum blossom of the new year exuding an indescribable fragrance. The only sensible choice is to dispense with women and turn instead to men.

Kōbō Daishi did not preach the profound pleasures of this love outside the monasteries, because he feared the extinction of humankind. No doubt he foresaw the popularity of boy love in these last days of the law. Where it flourishes, a man must sometimes sacrifice his life for the one he loves. Why in the world did "the man who loved love" waste such vast quantities of gold and silver on his myriad women, when the only pleasure and excitement to be found is in male love?

I have attempted to reflect in this "great mirror" all of the varied manifestations of male love. Like someone gathering seaweed among the reeds in the shallow inlet of Naniwa, I gathered my material for the leaves of this book. It will no doubt soon be forgotten by those who read it. Such is the way of the world.

### His Head Shaved on the Path of Dreams

*Brocade in daylight at fireside Noh.*
*A youth stealthily follows a chrysanthemum-crested lantern.*
*Forced to stand in for his lover.*

The man rushed to reach the Great South Gate in the southern capital before nightfall and took a seat in the stands. The Komparu Noh master was performing a dance, accompanied by Seigorō on the hand drum and Mataemon drumming with a single stick. Each was a master of his craft, but the man hardly noticed them. His attention was directed to the young temple pages from Kōfuku-ji and Saidai-ji seated in the gallery. As the sun set, he bade them a sad farewell. "Like brocade at night, their beauty is wasted," he said aloud, not caring who might hear.

The man looked to be under thirty. The pate of his head was shaved well back, with a short topknot. Both inner and outer robes were made of a black dragon-patterned weave bearing the chrysanthemum-leaf crest on the back, sleeves, and chest. He wore a plain sash of braided silk and sported two swords, long and short, in the foppish Yoshiya style. In short, he appeared to epitomize the connoisseur of boy love.

His name was Maruo Kan'emon. He was a well-known master of martial arts and an appreciator of boys without rival in past or present history. Boys found it impossible to resist his wily love letters. He waited impatiently to see the boys at fireside Noh each evening. Performances at the shrine began the following day. When Ōkura Otome appeared on stage as Kagetsu, not a person there remained unsmitten. "Such is love's ability to deceive."

The sky clouded over the next day. The umbrella-shaped peak of Mount Kasuga was desolate. In the afternoon, Kan'emon had an attendant bring some fishhooks and flies to go fishing on the banks of the Iwai River. The fishing was good, and he was busily pulling in willow dace and other fish when a lovely youth in the service of the Kōriyama clan appeared further upstream. His name was Tamura Sannojō.

The boy spit into the river. Downstream, Kan'emon scooped up the water in his hands and gulped it down without spilling a single drop.

Sannojō noticed this and came over to apologize.

"I had no idea you would be drinking from the river. It was rude of me to spit into it. Please forgive me."

"The truth is, I so hated to see your precious saliva disperse and disappear in the water's flow that I scooped it up and swallowed it," Kan'emon confessed.

"I won't forget your flattery." Sannojō laughed, and went on his way.

Kan'emon watched him walk along the edge of the rocky bank. The boy's natural, unadorned beauty was impossible to describe. He murmured to himself, "When the witch of Wushan spit in the face of the first Emperor of Ch'in, her saliva left pockmarks where it touched. May this saliva I just drank remain in my mouth forever, so that I can always enjoy its nectar-like flavor!"

He set out after the boy, but the sun set in the west behind distant mountains in Akishino, and soon it was too dark to discern people's faces.

It was the night of the twelfth day, second month, so the boy was expecting to enjoy the aid of the moon to light his way home, but he was disappointed. Though already spring, winter rainclouds billowed threateningly around the peaks of Mount Ikoma and Kazuraki. He hurried on his way to Kōriyama, worried that it might start to rain at any moment. Passing a remote village, he crossed a bridge of shaky planks placed over flooded ground. He picked his way carefully across the stubble of last year's harvest of reeds in a burned-over field and walked on a path used by strange-looking deer shorn of their antlers. He passed the dens of badgers and wolves. None of this frightened the boy, not even the rising smoke that normally startles the people of this floating world. He stopped to gaze at the hut where a recluse priest lived, and then passed by.

He was nearing the village at Daian-ji when a smartly dressed servant with a towel tied around his head emerged from a side street, carrying a lantern. Sannojō followed the light gratefully. His companion, the acupuncturist Dōjin, was elated by their good fortune.

"It is like enjoying a neighbor's singing with your own sake at a springtime blossom-viewing party," he exclaimed happily.

Shortly, they reached Kōriyama. The man with the lantern saw them safely to the boy's house, which was at the very end of a block of samurai houses. He watched the boy go inside and then turned back in the direction from which he came.

Until then, Sannojō had not thought anything of it, but now he found the man's behavior most peculiar. First, however, he went to greet his parents.

"I went to see the fireside Noh and just returned home," he told them.

Then, in secret, he went back out to follow the man. At last he got close enough to the lantern to see that it bore a chrysanthemum-leaf crest. He realized that it must be the same man he met earlier in the day. He decided to see him to his home in secret, but as they neared Nara the lantern's candle burned out. Their hearts were left in darkness.

"Since I was dressed in this disguise, I am sure he did not realize who it was that saw him to his door," Kan'emon said to his attendant.

The boy overheard this and decided to break his silence.

"On the contrary," Sannojō replied. "It is exactly because I recognized your intentions that I have come all this way to return the favor." He took Kan'emon's hand and squeezed it tight.

Kan'emon felt sure he was dreaming. He stood rooted to the spot, unable to speak for some time. "Do you really mean that?" he finally asked. "I must thank you for your kindness."

"Promise me that your love will never change."

"It will never change."

"Promise never to forget me."

"I will never forget you."

As they spoke, the bell in Nishinokyō began to toll. They counted eight strokes, which meant it was near dawn.

"Let us talk for a while, and I will leave when it begins to grow light," Sannojō suggested. He was already upset at the idea of saying farewell.

"This is not the last time we will meet. Your parents must be concerned at your absence. If you truly love me, let us save our loving for next time."

Without their satisfying their desires, Kan'emon saw the boy back to Kōriyama once again. On the way, he told him, "Human life is unpredictable, but I hope to see you again before the double cherry blossoms open. I always go to view the early blossoms when they first come out. I promise to pay you a visit on the first or second day of the third month."

But Kan'emon was unaccustomed to wearing a servant's thin cotton robe and got chilled in the morning breeze. A slight stuffy nose grew progressively worse, and he died on the twenty-seventh day of the second month.

Sannojō came looking for him, unaware of what had happened. When he found out, his grief was unbearable. He hoped at least to meet the relatives and family, but apparently Kan'emon was from a distant province and had no one to mourn him.

"Well then, where was he living?" the boy asked.

The place was the site of the old *renga* master Jōha's hut. The boy went there, to a remote area called South Market. The house was surrounded by a deutzia hedge. He looked into the waiting room through a bamboo-slat window and was shocked to see a group of attendants gathered there, though hardly seven days had passed since their master's death, playing cards and chanting loudly to the tapping of fans, "Emperor Yung Ming pined for the Princess Yu Tai's love." He could even smell dried sardines from Uwanokōri being toasted over a fire.

I do not care how insignificant they may be in rank, he thought. Don't they realize that their master has died? Without a word, he opened the door and went in.

In one corner of the alcove was an earthen vessel from which rose a continuous stream of incense smoke. There were some fresh *shikimi* branches placed upright by a plaque inscribed with the posthumous name, Shunsetsu Dōsen. So this was the man he met, he thought, and pressed his sleeve to his face.

He sat there with his head bowed for quite some time.

Then an attractive young man came into the room. He had apparently just recently undergone the capping ceremony. He was dressed entirely in mourning white, except for an outer robe of pale blue. His sleeves were damp with tears. He bowed before the Buddha altar and then moved to a distant corner of the room, where he sat alone, overwhelmed with grief.

Sannojō went over to introduce himself. "Pardon me. My name is—"

But before he could finish, the young man interrupted him.

"Sannojō. Am I correct? Kan'emon remembered you with his last breath. 'I saw him home to Kōriyama, and he saw me home in turn.' Now I have seen him to the cremation fields.

"Am I dreaming? It must be a dream. Do you think it is a dream?"

The young man's grief made Sannojō feel even more desolate. Together they raised their voices and wept for over an hour. Their tears were like raindrops dripping from the eaves. Eventually, the spring day came to an end. Sannojō was startled to hear the sound of rain shutters being wheeled shut.

"I was aware of life's transience, but this brutal display of man's mortality is too much to bear. I will try to catch up with him at the base of death's mountain by the forty-ninth day."

Sannojō drew his sword and turned to the young man. "Please take care of my remains."

Sanai rushed forward to prevent Sannojō from killing himself.

"If anyone, I am the one who should kill himself. From the time I was just a boy, he loved me faithfully for five years. Even after I came of age he backed me reliably, as solid as Mount Mikasa. Now I have lost him to cruel fate. How do you think your grief compares to mine? The last thing he said to me was, 'I have no one but you to place incense and flowers at my tomb. If you love me, keep on living.' I cannot turn my back on those words. I fully intended to take religious vows and devote the rest of my days to praying for him. But you, you only exchanged a few words with him. Why not just forget him and pretend you never met?"

"You can say that because you spent many satisfying years sharing his bed. I, however, must suffer the grief of never having spent a single night with him. I will end this brief life here and now."

Only after considerable persuasion from Sanai did Sannojō agree to abandon the idea of killing himself.

"If I am to go on living," Sannojō said, "I want you to take the place of Kan'emon and make a vow of love with me."

Sanai resisted. "It is not necessary to go that far. I will continue to be your good friend."

"That is not enough," Sannojō insisted. "I want you to be my lover."

Unable to protest further, Sanai made his vow of love with Sannojō. That night, he told Sannojō all about his years with Kan'emon.

"He was having a copy of the temple garden at Shōun-ji in Sakai built here. On the day when the sago palms were being transplanted, I was sitting on that rock over there. I cupped some water from the spring in my hands for a drink and threw the extra water on the ground behind me. I had no idea anyone was standing there.

"A low voice behind me said, 'I was hoping to be rained on by you one of these days. I am grateful.'

"It was Kan'emon.

"I was thrilled, and soon after that we started sleeping together. To me, society's censure meant nothing. He arranged to visit me when my father was on night duty at the shrine and came secretly all the way to distant Takabatake just to see me.

"There was one happy moment I shall never forget. It was a windy, snowy night. I sent him a letter in the afternoon, assuring him that I would be coming that night. He came to pick me up not far from my house and gave me a ride on his shoulders. From inside his robe he produced a little Kimpira doll dressed in helmet and armor and gave it to me. On the way, we pretended to duel with it.

"That night, when I mounted Kan'emon in bed like a horse, he called me a Great General!"

Sanai grew drowsier and drowsier as he spoke. Soon he was asleep, with his listener joining him in a battle of snores.

Just then, the figure of Kan'emon appeared as real as life.

"I am happy that you two have made a vow of love to ease your grief. There is no one in the 190,000-*koku* realm of Kōriyama who even resembles Sannojō in beauty. However, there is something about the Kōriyama style of wearing the hair too low on the sides that I dislike. Sanai, what do you think? Let's bring the topknot up a bit in the back."

Kan'emon turned the boy to face the mirror.

"Is this just about right?" he asked, and disappeared.

Sannojō awoke from his dream. There was no washbasin nearby, not even a razor, but the pate of his head was cleanly shaved. Dreams are dreams, of course, but this was most remarkable.

### The Boy Who Sacrificed His Life in the Robes of His Lover

> A boy in a Kaga sedge hat puts the moon's beauty to shame.
> The leaf of a banana palm stirred by love's breeze.
> A world in which we have no choice but to die.

Whose lovely figure is that, his face concealed beneath a sedge hat? There are many handsome youths in Kanazawa, but it is this one, Nozaki Senjūrō, of whom women say with envy, "How is it possible for a boy of such natural beauty to be born into this world?" But do not be deceived by his frail appearance, for he is a stouthearted fellow indeed.

A sensualist of broad experience had the following to say on the topic of love: "In general, I prefer strong women to ones possessed of a normal feminine nature. It goes without saying that I like my boys bold and masculine." As a connoisseur of young men, he considered those blessed with maturity and a cool head particularly high-class items.

Senjūrō was an article *par excellence,* surpassing even Fuwano Mansaku in beauty, destined surely to become the possession of some great daimyo.

It was a shame to expose him to the gaze of men lacking in discrimination. He should rightfully have been hidden in a purse of rich brocade, to be shown only to those capable of appreciating his rare beauty.

This boy had but a single flaw: he was by nature careless of his life, like someone who watches dispassionately as cherry blossoms scatter in the wind. Aware of this flaw, men feared to approach the mountain of his love lest it cost them their lives. Thus, Senjūrō reached the spring of his seventeenth year unloved. People pitied him; he seemed to them like a mountain rose that blooms and falls unseen in remote hills, or like a spray of wisteria that withers, unplucked, on the vine.

What they did not realize was that deep in the valley, Senjūrō had for several years been on intimate terms with a man named Takeshima Sazen. It was understandable that society at large not be aware of the situation, for he was a government official in charge of administering many towns and villages in the shadow of a mountain four or five *li* distant from the daimyo's castle.

This is how the two first met.

In the house next to Sazen's lived a woman who was Senjūrō's aunt. The trees had lost their leaves, and with the arrival of autumn Senjūrō was feeling even more sad and lonely than usual, so he decided to pay her a visit and enjoy the view of the harvest moon on the way. Unfortunately, pine trees towered darkly on the ridge to the east, and all he could see during the early part of the evening was the moon's light poking through the trees. To the south, however, there were no obstructions. Drifting clouds obligingly departed as if aware of the beauty of the scene, allowing him to view the moon in the clear sky to his heart's content later in the evening.

The distant beating of silk—tap, tap, tap—(no doubt the work of some country girl) triggered in him gentle musings. Mingled with the sounds of the locale were the faint voices of grasshoppers and bell crickets. Before long, they too would be silenced by the frost, he mused, warding off with the sleeve of his robe the breeze that rustled the tips of the blades of grass as he passed. He alone was there to appreciate the sight of wild chrysanthemums, but surely by daybreak they would be catching the admiring glances of passersby, he thought feelingly, overcome with sad thoughts of the ways of this world. Truly, this handsome youth was a boy of rare emotional sensitivity.

That night, Takeshima Sazen was on his way to visit a priest in charge of the Kannon Sanctuary at a temple in the outskirts of town. The priest was his regular companion in *haikai* poetry composition, and Sazen was wondering how he might be enjoying the moon that evening. Sazen needed an opening phrase for a poem and hoped that the man could provide him with one; he would try to compose an interesting second line on the spot. But when he arrived at the door it was firmly shut and the priest nowhere in sight.

Sazen shone his lamp through the paper window on the north side of the hut and peered inside. Dimly, he could see a book lying open on the table, as if the man had been reading it until a moment ago. It was called "A Study of Poetic Place Names." On the edge of the table was a mousetrap. It seemed that rampaging mice were vexing even to priests who had renounced this world. "Mice in the house mean thieves abroad in the land." So the proverb goes, but the entrance of the hut was unlocked, indicative perhaps of the peaceful times in which we live.

Sazen had his attendant trim the wick of the sputtering lamp. He placed a few drops of water in his portable inkstone and wrote the following note on the broad leaf of a banana palm growing against the eaves of the hut:

"I listen to the murmuring pines, but they tell me not where their master has gone. I bid farewell to the moon before the temple gate and go on my weary way.

"Perhaps I shall enjoy a cup of sake before retiring. When I awake from my dreams in the morn, allow me to offer you a simple meal at my home.

"The matter of Moemon's widow has been commodiously concluded. You are no doubt satisfied with the arrangements.

"The morning-glory seeds you so generously bestowed on me began blooming splendidly this morning.

"In your next letter to Echizen, please remember to include my order for 30 sheets of patterned *torinoko* paper.

"Thank you kindly for the boiled plums the other day.

"It seems that Yata Nisaburō of whom you spoke to me in private is not a believer in boy love. He was not interested in the idea of having a male lover and so, though only seventeen and in the flower of youth, has foolishly cut off his forelocks. I found his profuse apologies rather absurd but have decided to let the matter drop. Last night everyone came over and we spent the whole night laughing about it. . . ."

The note was a hodgepodge of things on Sazen's mind, written spontaneously as they occurred to him.

Just then, Senjūrō happened to come by and noticed something written on the banana leaf. At first he thought it was a poem about the full moon that night and went to take a closer look, but he was wrong. It was not a poem. He was intrigued nevertheless by the part at the end about boy love.

Sazen proceeded ahead, but Senjūrō spoke to one of the attendants in a voice loud enough for Sazen to hear.

"This must be what people refer to as 'unrequited love.' Any youth who would put a gentleman's overtures to naught knows nothing of love, but if the gentleman is sincere he should not hesitate to give even his life to obtain him. True, I have no beauty of form to recommend me, but at least I am capable of love. Yet I receive no offers. As the gods are my witness, I swear my willingness to suffer any hardship for the sake of boy love."

With these words, he removed the sedge hat and revealed his face.

Sazen took one look and his soul seemed to leap out at the boy. Unconsciously, he reached for the boy's hand.

"If the words you just spoke are true, let me be the one to worship you, O Boddhisattva, come to lead this man to salvation." He made his plea in a daze, completely unaware of his surroundings.

Senjūrō was deeply moved. The man had a certain masculine charm, and besides, Senjūrō could hardly claim that he was joking. Standing there just as he was, he pledged himself firmly to love Sazen in this world and the next.

On their way home, they passed a country farmhouse facing south, in which the harvest moon was being rudely celebrated with boiled yams and sake served from a chipped flask. The sake was a local mountain brew with a superb chrysanthemum bouquet. Noticing the fragrance, Sazen and Senjūrō forced themselves on their unknown hosts and joined the revelry. Even in the midst of their cups they could hardly wait to get back to their lodgings. When they did, they frantically consummated their troth of brotherly love. From that day forward Senjūrō gave himself completely to Sazen, who soon came to occupy even the boy's dreams.

Senjūrō's innate grace and youthful good looks caught the eye of a well-known devotee of boy love named Imamura Rokunoshin, a samurai who lived in the castle town. He sent the boy several letters, but Senjūrō steadfastly refused to look at them. A warrior's pride does not allow him to retract his words, and Rokunoshin soon reached his limit of frustration. Then he found out about Senjūrō's bond with Sazen, and swore he would make Sazen relinquish the boy, by force if necessary.

Senjūrō heard of this and pondered what to do.

I am prepared to fight Rokunoshin to the finish, he thought, but Sazen will be heartbroken if I go ahead without telling him. Yet that is what I must do so that he may go on living.

His decision made, Senjūrō went in secret to the residence of Rokunoshin, where he met and spoke with the man.

"It was not my intention to ignore your recent attentions," Senjūrō said. "Unfortunately, Takeshima Sazen has made some very unreasonable demands of me that I am bound by duty to honor. Moreover, he is a man completely lacking in emotional sincerity. I was searching for a way to escape this dilemma when I received your letters. You may be the man I had hoped would appear, to provide me with the strong backing I need. If you but murder Sazen for me in secret, I will make myself yours."

Rokunoshin was delighted. "Why not tonight?" he proposed eagerly.

"There is a seldom-used road that runs through a field of hackberry trees," Senjūrō explained. "Sazen travels it every night at ten o'clock. This will be the sign: he will be wearing a sedge hat at night. Cut him down when he reaches the roadside shrine."

Rokunoshin agreed to the task, and when his preparations for battle were complete, he set out for his rendezvous on the country road. Such is the compelling nature of this floating world.

Meanwhile, Senjūrō returned home to bathe and groom. He put on a half-coat with rounded cuffs and placed a sedge hat low on his brow as a disguise. He was the very image of Sazen. Carefully avoiding notice, he then set out for the appointed country road.

He walked stealthily in the shadows of the tree-lined path to the place where Rokunoshin lay in wait. Rokunoshin attacked and cut him down from behind. The victim did not utter a sound. Nor did he even attempt to draw his sword. It was truly an ignominious end.

Rokunoshin gave him the coup de grâce with a stab to the neck. Unsure where to go now that his harried task was accomplished, Rokunoshin slipped into the thick undergrowth of jewelweed. He was startled, however, to hear a faint voice behind him.

"Though I have come to this, at least my lord Sazen is safe," it said feebly.

Rokunoshin quietly had an attendant strike a flint and once again approached the body. He could not believe his eyes.

It was Senjūrō.

For a moment Rokunoshin was stunned by the magnitude of Senjūrō's act of love; even in the world to come, one would be unlikely to find another like it. He recalled the old "Lover's Tomb" at Koizuka and wept bitterly into the sleeves of his robe, but no amount of weeping could undo what he had done.

I could go on living as if nothing had happened, and no one would be the wiser for it, he thought. But there would be no joy in such a life.

He decided that he, too, would die.

After explaining his plan in detail to an attendant, he changed quickly into Senjūrō's long-sleeved robe. He placed the sedge hat on his head and, carefully avoiding notice, they went to the village where Takeshima Sazen lived. His attendant ran up to Sazen's gate and pounded on it wildly.

"I have urgent news!" he shouted.

Sazen sat up in bed. He ignored the voice for as long as he could, but finally dressed and woke his retainers. They readied their spears and carefully checked the situation outside the gate from the observation deck. When they were convinced that it was safe, they opened the gate for Rokunoshin's attendant to come in. He immediately relinquished his sword to them.

"I am Manshichi, in the service of Imamura Rokunoshin," he said. "My master and Nozaki Senjūrō recently established a bond of boy love, complete with written vows. They were concerned, however, about Takeshima Sazen and secretly developed a scheme to kill him. I was one of the men chosen to carry out their plan, but when it was explained to me, I refused. My master accused me of ingratitude for his years of support and struck me in full view of the others. He was ready to put me to the sword, but somehow I managed to escape and make my way here.

"I beg you, please save me. I am a mere attendant and know that it is wrong to refuse to obey my master's orders. Still, I cannot take part in a plot unbecoming to the tenets of the warrior's code. You too are a samurai. My master should challenge you to a duel in daylight and settle his differences with you that way. Instead he plots a night raid. That is why I have forsaken him and come running to this place for shelter. Please, I beg your protection."

Sazen heard him through but remained skeptical.

"We shall look into the matter in the morning. Until then," he said, turning to his retainers, "I leave this man in your custody."

Sazen got up to leave, but Rokunoshin's attendant called out to him.

"As proof that what I say is true, Senjūrō will appear soon, in advance of the others."

When he heard this, Sazen decided that it would be safest if he made the first move. He went out to the road with a large group of retainers and hid in the shadow of some trees. Just as Rokunoshin's attendant had predicted, someone in a long-sleeved robe was stealthily approaching.

It was Senjūrō.

Sazen was overwhelmed with anger. "You faithless scoundrel!" he shouted. The next moment Sazen had swung his sword, cutting Senjūrō down with one blow. The boy fell in the shade of some withered trees.

"Did you think you could betray our vows of brotherly love and still escape the wrath of heaven?"

With these words, he finished off Senjūrō with a stab to the throat.

When Sazen had a beacon brought forward, he was amazed to find that the man he had slain was Imamura Rokunoshin. He immediately had Rokunoshin's attendant brought out and demanded an explanation. When he heard the entire story from beginning to end, Sazen wept so copiously that his garments were soaked to the skin.

"Senjūrō loved me so much he was willing to die in my stead. Rokunoshin so regretted what he had done, he too gave up his life. In the face of such example, it would be profitless for me to go on living."

He sat on the corpse and there, in the autumn of his twenty-eighth year, dyed his blade the color of autumn leaves and ended his brief life.

The example of these three was without precedent in antiquity. Rumors of their intense love continued to be voiced long after the proverbial seventy-five days. Those who recounted the story wept as they told it; those who heard it wept as they listened. Not only people of sensitivity but even unfeeling peasants and horse drivers reverently avoided walking on the spot where Senjūrō spilled his lifeblood, a lingering testimony to the way of boy love.

Were one to walk all the provinces of the land in sandals of iron, one would not be likely to find another such example.

## Bamboo Clappers Strike the Hateful Number

*A monk's hermitage papered with love letters.*
*Boy actors hide their age.*
*A pushy samurai loses his whiskers.*

When being entertained by a Kabuki boy actor, one must be careful never to ask his age.

It was late in autumn, and rain just light enough not to be unpleasant had been falling since early morning. It now lifted, and the afternoon sun appeared below the clouds in the west, forming a rainbow over Higashi-yama. Just then a group of boy actors appeared, wearing wide-striped rainbow robes of satin. The most handsome among them was an actor in the Murayama theater troupe, a jewel that sparkled without need of polishing, named Tamamura Kichiya. He was in the full flower of youth, and every person in the capital was in love with him.

On that particular day, a well-known lover of boys called Koromo-no-tana Shiroku had invited him to go mushroom picking at Mount Shiro-yama in Fushimi, so a large group of actors and their spirited companions left Shijō-gawara and soon arrived at Hitsukawa. Leaves of the birch cherries, the subject of a long-ago poem, had turned bright red, a sight more beautiful even than spring blossoms. After spending some time gazing at the scene, the group continued past the woods at Fuji-no-mori, where the tips of the leaves were just beginning to turn brown, and moved south up the mountain.

They parked their palanquins at the base and alighted, heads covered with colorful purple kerchiefs. Since pine trees were their only observers, they removed their sedge hats and revealed their lovely faces. Parting the tangled pampas grass, they walked on with sighs of admiration. The scene was reminiscent of the poem "My sleeves grow damp since first entering the mountain of your love," for these were boys at the peak of physical beauty. An outsider looking at them could not but have felt envious of their gentleman companions. A certain man well acquainted with the ways of love once said, "In general, courtesans are a pleasure once in bed; with boys, the pleasure begins on the way there."

It was already close to dusk by the time they began hunting for mushrooms. They found only a few, which they carried like treasures back to an isolated thatched hut far from any village. Inside, the walls were papered at the base with letters from actors. Their signatures had been torn off and discarded. Curious, the boys looked more closely and discovered that each letter concerned matters of love. Each was written in a different hand, the parting messages of Kabuki boy actors. The monk who lived there must once have been a man of some means, they thought. He apparently belonged to the Shingon sect, for when they opened the Buddhist altar they found a figure of Kōbō Daishi adorned with chrysanthemums and bush clover, and next to it a picture of a lovely young actor, the object no doubt of this monk's fervent devotion.

When they questioned him, the monk told them about his past. As they suspected, he was devoted body and soul to the way of boy love.

"I was unhappy with my strict father and decided to seclude myself in this mountain hermitage. More than two years have passed, but I have not been able to forget about boy love even in my dreams." The tears of grief he wept were enough to fade the black dye of his priestly robes. Those who heard it were filled with pity for him.

"How old are you?" someone asked.

"I am no longer a child," he said. "I just turned twenty-two."

"Why then, you are still in the flower of youth!" they exclaimed. All of the actors in the room dutifully wrung the tears from their sleeves, but their expressions seemed strangely reticent. Not one of them was under twenty-two years of age!

Among them was one boy actor who, judging from the time he worked the streets, must have been quite old. In the course of the conversation, someone asked him his age.

"I don't remember," he said, causing quite some amusement among the men.

Then the monk who lived in the cottage spoke up.

"By good fortune, I have here a bamboo clapper that has the ability to tell exactly how old you are."

He gave the clapper to the boy actor and had him stand there while the monk himself gravely folded his hands in prayer. Shortly, the bamboo clappers began to sound. Everyone counted aloud with each strike.

At first, the actor stood there innocently as it struck seventeen, eighteen, nineteen, but beyond that he started to feel embarrassed. He tried with all his strength to separate his right hand from his left and stop the clappers from striking, but, strangely, they kept right on going. Only after striking thirty-eight did the bamboo clappers separate. The boy actor's face was red with embarrassment.

"These bamboo clappers lie!" he said, throwing them down.

The monk was outraged.

"The Buddhas will attest that there is no deceit in them. If you still have doubts, try it again as many times as you like."

The other actors in the room were all afraid of being exposed, so no one was willing to try them out. They were beginning to lose their party mood.

When sake had been brought out and the mushrooms toasted and salted, they all lay back and began to entertain their patrons. One of the boy actors took the opportunity to request a new jacket, another was promised a house with an entrance six *ken* wide, and still another was presented right there with a short sword. (It was amusing to see how nimbly he took the sword and put it away!)

Into the midst of this merrymaking came a rough samurai of the type rarely seen in the capital. He announced his arrival with the words, "Part, clouds, for here I am!" as if to boast of his bad reputation. He forced his way through the twig fence and into the garden, handed his long sword to an attendant, and went up to the bamboo veranda.

"Bring me the sake cup that Tamamura Kichiya is using," he demanded.

Kichiya at first pretended he had not heard, but finally he said, "There is already a gentleman here to share my cup."

The samurai would not tolerate such an answer.

"I will have it at once," he said angrily, "and you will be my snack!"

He took up his long sword mentioned earlier and waved it menacingly at the boy's companion. The poor man was terrified and apologized profusely, but the samurai refused to listen.

"What an awful fellow." Kichiya laughed. "I won't let him get away with this."

"Leave him to me," he told the others and sent them back home.

When they had gone, Kichiya snuggled up to the foolish samurai. "Today was so uninteresting," he said. "I was just having a drink with those boring merchants because I had to. It would be a real pleasure to share a drink with a lord like yourself."

Kichiya poured cup after cup of sake for the man and flattered and charmed him expertly. Soon the fool was in a state of waking sleep, unaware of anything but the boy. The man was ready to make love, but Kichiya told him, "I can't go any further because of your scratchy whiskers. It hurts when you kiss me."

"I wouldn't dream of keeping anything on my face not to your liking, my boy. Call my servant and have him shave it off," the samurai said.

"If you don't mind, please allow me to improve my lord's good looks with my own hands." Kichiya picked up a razor and quickly shaved off the whiskers on the left side of the samurai's face, leaving the mustache intact on his upper lip. He also left the right side as it was. The samurai just snored loudly, completely oblivious to what was going on.

Kichiya saw his opportunity and escaped from the place as quickly as possible. He took the man's whiskers with him as a memento. Everyone laughed uproariously when he showed them the hair.

"How in the world did you get hold of that! This deserves a celebration!" they said. Akita Hikosaburō invented an impromptu "whisker dance" and had the men holding their sides with laughter.

Later, when the samurai awoke, he was furious at the loss of his whiskers. Without his beard he had no choice but to quit living by intimidation. Rather than seek revenge, he decided to act as if the whole thing had never happened.

When they saw him some time later, he was making his living as a marksman with his bow. Recalling how he had lost his beard, they could not help but laugh at the man.

### Who Wears the Incense Graph Dyed in Her Heart?

*The crest of Yamatoya Jimbei.*
*A boy actor in his prime, a patron in decline.*
*To a lover of boys, even a beautiful woman is ugly.*

They say that when mandarin orange trees from south of the Yangtze are transplanted to north of the Yangtze, they immediately change to trifoliate orange trees. Such a transformation certainly sounds plausible, for we have a similar phenomenon in Japan. If you put a rusty-haired youngster from north of the river in the hands of a theater attendant south of the river, his hair will shortly turn black and shiny like that of a *tayū*. The change is so dramatic, it makes one wonder if the boys are not really two different people. Appearances can certainly be improved with careful grooming.

Some say, "Kabuki boy actors are uniformly good-looking these days." Others counter, "There are few truly beautiful ones among them." I have observed the outcome of several such boys who were picked up by theater proprietors and actors. Those capable of acting on the present-day stage were perhaps one in a thousand. The others were either good-looking and stupid, or smart and incapable of entertaining people. No one knows how many proprietors suffered huge financial loss when it turned out that the boy they groomed for stardom could not keep a simple beat, or when the boy on whom they pinned their hopes for success suddenly took sick. Surely, there is nothing more risky than trying to create a star for the theater.

Be that as it may, how could any man regret spending money on boy actors? Actors' fees should be regarded as the cost of medicine to extend one's life span. Such boys provide a unique remedy. They may look like ordinary boys, but emotionally they are exactly like upper-class courtesans, with two exceptions: they have overcome their stiffness, and one never tires of their conversation.

In the old days, boy love was something rough and brawny. Men swaggered when they spoke. They preferred big, husky boys and bore cuts on their bodies as a sign of male love. This spirit reached even to boy actors, all of whom brandished swords. It goes without saying that such behavior is no longer appreciated. Even the portable shrine of the San-ō Festival makes its rounds without drawing blood nowadays. In an age when even warriors need no armor, clearly it is best not to show knives while entertaining at parties. Watermelon ought to be cut in the kitchen and brought out served on plates. Boys these days are expected to be delicate, nothing more. In Edo, a boy actor is called "Little Murasaki" or in Kyoto is given the name "Kaoru," soft-sounding like the names of courtesans and pleasing to the ear.

Sodeshima Ichiya, Kawashima Kazuma, Sakurayama Rinnosuke, Sodeoka Ima-Masanosuke, Mitsue Kasen, and others accentuate their natural beauty by wearing women's red underskirts, a habit men find very erotic. Hordes of men stop and stare, though they have no intention of spending any money, just to memorize the actors' crests and learn their names as they set out for the theater in the morning or head back home at dusk.

When Suzuki Heizaemon, Yamashita Hanzaemon, Naiki Hikozaemon, and Kōzaemon are on their way home, no one takes much notice of them, despite the fact that they are excellent actors. Instead men already have their eyes on the apprentice boy actors wearing wide-sleeved cotton robes with medicine pouches hanging at their hips and sporting double-folded topknots. In addition, the young brides and older wives of these

# LATITUDE 33

## 33

### BOOKS & COFFEE

**B**
**O**
**O**
**K**
**S**

**A N D**

**C**
**O**
**F**
**F**
**E**
**E**

540 SOUTH COAST HIGHWAY
LAGUNA BEACH CA 92651

PHONE 494-5403
(714)
F A X 497-4574

men stand in noisy groups in the vicinity of Sennichi Temple, their excitement all the more intense because they know their desires for the boys are doomed to frustration.

Once, I invited Yamatoya Jimbei to go and worship with me at Kachiō-ji on the occasion of the unveiling of the holy image there. We crossed the Nakatsu River by ferry and parked our palanquins by the shrine woods at Kita-nakajima.

"Tobacco and tea," we said, and rested for a while. Shortly after us came a beautiful girl who looked about sixteen but was probably fifteen. She wore a long-sleeved black satin robe appliquéd with assorted precious treasures. Her sash was an unusual affair of white-figured satin embroidered with swallows caught in a net of purple threads, and tied in the back. She wore light-blue silk stockings and straw sandals with toe cords of several slender threads. With each step she took we caught a glimpse of her red diamond-patterned underskirt. Her hair was tied low in a flared chignon and decorated with an openwork comb and a bodkin inlaid with gold and silver. Her sedge hat was lined in light-blue material woven with threads of gold and tied by a cord made of twisted letter paper. Everything she wore, her whole manner, in fact, reflected impeccable good taste. Moreover, she wore no makeup. There was absolutely nothing one could say in complaint about her.

Accompanying the girl on her left was a nun dressed in a black robe, and on her right was a woman who looked like her nursemaid. She had a personal attendant with her, and a servant girl, both of whom were also beautifully attired. A palanquin was being carried behind them. An old man over fifty years old, who seemed to be in charge, and a younger man wearing a large sword walked in advance. It was obvious that they were from a wealthy merchant family.

The girl approached us innocently, but as soon as she saw Jimbei she became extremely agitated. She lifted her sleeve for him to see. His incense-graph crest was clearly visible, dyed into her robe. Her feelings for him were no sudden impulse, then.

Afterwards she began to quiver with excitement, and her legs could no longer support her. At the village where the Ebisu Shrine is found, she finally boarded her palanquin. We then lost sight of her lovely figure and continued on our way.

Perhaps because of a karmic bond, we met her again later, at the temple. She came up from behind us with a lovelorn look in her eyes. A priest was expertly explaining the history of each of the treasures in the temple, but she showed interest only in Jimbei. Her expression seemed to say, "What's so great about a wasp stinging your unicorn's horn? I don't care if your stupid buffalo stone breaks into a million pieces. Even your precious Buddha statue that miraculously came down from heaven means nothing to me. Just give me Jimbei!" We could not but feel sorry for her, knowing that her passion was doomed to frustration. (I pity the fellow who gets this girl for a wife!) If she had been a boy, none of us would have thought twice about sacrificing our lives for her, but we were fashionable men, a group of woman-haters, so we ignored her and left for home.

That night we entertained ourselves with some serious composition of comic linked verse at the Sinking Moon Hermitage in Sakurazuka, where we went to see fall colors. We were treated to fine Itami and Kōnoike sake by the host.

"Now and then, we get wandering street boys in this town," the host said.

Our pleasure destroyed by this comment, we headed home. On the way, we felt uneasy about having rubbed sleeves with that girl who had taken a liking to Jimbei, so we purified ourselves in the Temma River and rinsed out our eyes, sullied by the sight of her. We then returned to Dōtombori. At the theater the next day, from the opening love scene to the play's conclusion, we talked about nothing but boy love.

This way of love is not exclusive to us; it is practiced throughout the known world. In India, strangely enough, it is called the Mistaken Way. In China, it is enjoyed as *hsia chuan*. And here in Japan, it flourishes as boy love. Because there is female love, the foolish human race continues to thrive. Would that the love of boys became the common form of love in the world, and that women would die out and Japan become an Isle of Men. Quarrels between husband and wife would cease, jealousy disappear, and the world enter at last into an era of peace.

# ～ *Marquis de Sade* ～

FROM

# *The 120 Days of Sodom*

TRANSLATED BY AUSTRYN WAINHOUSE AND RICHARD SEAVER

### *The Eighteenth Day*

Beautiful, radiant, bejeweled, grown more brilliant with each passing day, Duclos thus started the eighteenth session's stories:

*A tall and stoutly constructed creature named Justine had just been added to my entourage; she was twenty-five, five feet six inches tall, with the husky arms and solid legs of a barmaid, but her features were fine all the same, her skin was clear and smooth, and she had as splendid a body as one might wish. As my establishment used to be swarming with a crowd of those old rakehells who are incapable of experiencing the faintest pleasure save when heated by the lash or torture, I thought that a pensionnaire like Justine, furnished as she was with the forearm of a blacksmith, could be nothing but a very real asset. The day following her arrival, I decided to put her fustigatory talents to the test; I had been given to understand she wielded a whip with prodigious skill, and hence matched her against an old commissar of the quarter whom she was to flog from chest to shin and then, on the other side, from the middle of his back to his calves. The operation over with, the libertine simply hoisted the girl's skirts and planted his load upon her buttocks. Justine comported herself like a true heroine of Cythera, and our good old martyr avowed to me afterward that I had got my hands on a treasure, and that in all his days no one had ever whipped him as that rascal had.*

---

*Simone de Beauvoir on the* MARQUIS DE SADE: *"The supreme value of his testimony lies in its ability to disturb us. It forces us to reexamine thoroughly the basic problem which haunts our age in different forms: the true relation between man and man."*

To demonstrate how much I counted upon her contribution to our little community, a few days later I arranged a meeting between Justine and an old veteran of many a campaign on the fields of love; he required a round thousand strokes all over his body, he would have no part of himself spared, and when he was afire and nicely bloodied, the girl had to piss into her cupped hand and smear her urine over those areas of his body which looked to be the most seriously molested. This lotion rubbed on, the heavy labor had to be begun again, then he would discharge, the girl would carefully collect his fuck, once again using her cupped hand, and she would give him a second massage, this time employing the balm wrung from his prick. Another triumph for my new colleague, and every succeeding day brought her further and more impassioned acclaim; but it was impossible to exercise her arm on the champion who presented himself this time.

This extraordinary man would have nothing of the feminine but womanish dress: the wearer of the costume had to be a man; in other words, the roué wanted to be spanked by a man got up as a girl. And what was the instrument she had to use on him? Don't think for a moment he was content with a birch ferule or even a cat, no, he demanded a bundle of osier switches, wherewith very barbarously one had to tear his buttocks. Actually, this particular affair seeming to have somewhat of the flavor of sodomy, I felt I ought not become too deeply involved in it; but as he was one of Fournier's former and most reliable clients, a man who had been truly attached to our house in fair weather and in foul, and who, furthermore, might, thanks to his position, be able to render us some service, I raised no objections and, having prettily disguised a young lad of eighteen who sometimes availed us of his services and who had a very attractive face, I presented him, armed with a handful of switches, to his opponent.

And a very entertaining contest it was—you may well imagine how eager I was to observe it. He began with a careful study of his pretended maiden, and having found him, evidently, much to his liking, he opened with five or six kisses upon the youth's mouth: those kisses would have looked peculiar from three miles away; next, he exhibited his cheeks, and in all his behavior and words seeming to take the young man for a girl, he told him to fondle his buttocks and knead them just a little rigorously; the lad, whom I had told exactly what to expect, did everything asked of him.

"Well, let's be off," said the bawd, "ply those switches, spare not to strike hard."

The youth catches up the bundle of withes and therewith, swinging right merrily, lays fifty slashing blows upon a pair of buttocks which seem only to thirst for more; already definitely marked by those two score and ten stripes, the libertine hurls himself upon his masculine *flagellatrice, draws up her petticoats, one hand verifies her sex, the other fervently clutches her buttocks, he knows not which altar to bow down before first, the ass finally captures his primary attentions, he glues his mouth to its hole, much ardor in his expression. Ah, what a difference between the worship Nature is said to prescribe and that other which is said to outrage her! O God of certain justice, were this truly an outrage, would the homage be paid with such great emotion? Never was woman's ass kissed as was that lad's; three or four times over, his lover's tongue entirely disappeared into the anus; returning to his former position at last, "O dear child," cried he, "resume your operation."*

Further *flagellation ensued, but as it was livelier, the patient met this new assault with far more courage and intrepidity. Blood makes its appearance, another stroke brings his prick bounding up, and he engages the young object of his transports to seize it without an instant's delay. While the latter manipulates him, he wishes to render the youth the same service, lifts up the boy's skirts again, but it's a prick he's now gone in quest of; he touches it, grasps, shakes, pulls it, and soon introduces it into his mouth. After these initial caresses, he calls for a third round of blows and receives a storm of them. This latest experience puts him in a perfect tumult; he flings his Adonis upon the bed, lies down upon him, simultaneously toys with his own prick and his companion's, then presses one upon the other, glues his lips to the boy's mouth and, having succeeded in warming him by means of these caresses, he procures him the divine pleasure at the same moment he is overwhelmed himself: both discharge in harmony. Enchanted by the scene, our libertine sought to placate my risen indignation, and at last coaxed a promise from me to arrange for further delights in the same kind, both with that young fellow and with any others I could find for him. I attempted to work at his conversion, I assured him I had some charming girls who would be happy to flog him and who could do so quite as well; no, said he, none of that, he would not so much as look at what I had to offer him.*

∼ ∼ ∼

"Oh, I can readily believe it," said the Bishop. "When one has a decided taste for men, there's no changing; the difference between boy and girl is so extreme that one's not apt to be tempted to try what is patently inferior."

"Monseigneur," said the President, "you have broached a thesis which merits a two-hour dissertation."

"And which will always conclude by giving further support to my contention," said the Bishop, "because the fact that a boy is superior to a girl is beyond doubt or dispute."

"Beyond contradiction too," Curval agreed, "but nevertheless one might still inform you that a few objections have been here and there raised to your doctrine and that, for a certain order of pleasures, such as Martaine and Desgranges shall discuss, a girl is to be preferred to a boy."

"That I deny," said the Bishop with emphasis, "and even for such pleasures as you allude to the boy is worth more than the girl. Consider the problem from the point of view of evil, evil almost always being pleasure's true and major charm; considered thus, the crime must appear greater when perpetrated upon a being of your identical sort than when inflicted upon one which is not, and this once established, the delight automatically doubles."

"Yes," said Curval, "but that despotism, that empire, that delirium born of the abuse of one's power over the weak . . ."

"But the same is no less true in the other case," the Bishop insisted. "If the victim is yours, thoroughly in your power, that supremacy which when using women you think better established than when using men is based upon pure prejudice, upon nothing, and results merely from the custom whereby females are more ordinarily submitted to your caprices than are males. But give up that popular superstition for a moment, view the thing equitably, and, provided the man is bound absolutely by your chains and by the same authority you exert over women, you will obtain the idea of a greater crime; your lubricity ought hence to increase at least twofold."

"I am of the Bishop's mind," Durcet joined in, "and once it is certain that sovereignty is full established, I believe the abuse of power more delicious when exercised at the expense of one's peer than at a woman's."

"Gentlemen," said the Duc, "I should greatly prefer you to postpone your discussions until mealtime. I believe these hours have been reserved for listening to the narrations, and it would seem to me proper were you to refrain from employing them upon philosophical exchanges."

"He is right," said Curval. "Go on with your story, Duclos."

And that agreeable directress of Cytherean sport plunged again into the matter she had to relate.

# ∾ *Marquis de Sade* ∾

## FROM

# *Philosophy in the Bedroom*

TRANSLATED BY AUSTRYN WAINHOUSE AND RICHARD SEAVER

### *The Fifth Dialogue*

DOLMANCE— . . . Goddamn! I've an erection! . . . Get Augustin to come back here, if you please. *(They ring; he reappears.)* 'Tis amazing how this fine lad's superb ass does preoccupy my mind while I talk! All my ideas seem involuntarily to relate themselves to it. . . . Show my eyes that masterpiece, Augustin . . . let me kiss it and caress it, oh! for a quarter of an hour. Hither, my love, come, that I may, in your lovely ass, render myself worthy of the flames with which Sodom sets me aglow. Ah, he has the most beautiful buttocks . . . the whitest! I'd like to have Eugénie on her knees; she will suck his prick while I advance; in this manner, she will expose her ass to the Chevalier, who'll plunge into it, and Madame de Saint-Ange, astride Augustin's back, will present her buttocks to me: I'll kiss them; armed with the cat-o'-nine-tails, she might surely, it should seem to me, by bending a little, be able to flog the Chevalier, who, thanks to this stimulating ritual, might resolve not to spare our student. *(The position is arranged.)* Yes, that's it; let's do our best, my friends; indeed, it is a great pleasure to commission you to execute *tableaux;* in all the world, there's not an artist fitter than you to realize them! . . . This rascal does have a nipping tight ass! . . . 'tis all I can do to get a foothold in it. Would you do me the great kindness, Madame, of allowing me to bite and pinch your lovely flesh while I'm at my fuckery?

MADAME DE SAINT-ANGE—As much as you like, my friend; but, I warn you, I am ready to take my revenge: I swear that, for every vexation you give me, I'll blow a fart into your mouth.

DOLMANCE—By God, now! that is a threat! . . . quite enough to drive me to offend you, my dear. *(He bites her.)* Well! Let's see if you'll keep your word. *(He receives a fart.)* Ah, fuck, delicious! Delicious! . . . *(He slaps her and immediately receives another fart.)* Oh, 'tis divine, my angel! Save me a few for the critical moment . . . and, be sure of it, I'll then treat you with the extremest cruelty . . . most barbarously I'll use you. . . . Fuck! I can tolerate this no longer . . . I discharge! . . . *(He bites her, strikes her, and she farts uninterruptedly.)* Dost see how I deal with you, my fine fair bitch! . . . how I dominate you . . . once again here . . . and there . . . and let the final insult be to the very idol at which I sacrificed! *(He bites her asshole; the circle of debauches is broken.)* And the rest of you—what have you been up to, my friends?

EUGENIE, *spewing forth the fuck from her mouth and her ass*—Alas! dear master . . . you see how your disciples have accommodated me! I have a mouthful of fuck and half a pint in my ass, 'tis all I am disgorging on both ends.

DOLMANCE, *sharply*—Hold there! I want you to deposit in my mouth what the Chevalier introduced into your behind.

EUGENIE, *assuming a proper position*—What an extravagance!

DOLMANCE—Ah, there's nothing that can match fuck drained out of the depths of a pretty behind . . . 'tis a food fit for the gods. *(He swallows some.)* Behold, 'tis nearly wiped up, eh? *(Moving to Augustin's ass, which he kisses.)* Mesdames, I am going to ask your permission to spend a few moments in a nearby room, with this young man.

MADAME DE SAINT-ANGE—But can't you do here all you wish to do with him?

DOLMANCE, *in a low and mysterious tone*—No; there are certain things which strictly require to be veiled.

EUGENIE—Ah, by God, tell us what you'd be about!

MADAME DE SAINT-ANGE—I'll not allow him to leave if he does not.

DOLMANCE—You then wish to know?

EUGENIE—Absolutely.

DOLMANCE, *dragging Augustin*—Very well, Mesdames, I am going . . . but indeed, it cannot be said.

MADAME DE SAINT-ANGE—Is there, do you think, any conceivable infamy we are not worthy to hear of and execute?

LE CHEVALIER—Wait, sister. I'll tell you. *(He whispers to the two women.)*

EUGENIE, *with a look of revulsion*—You are right, 'tis hideous.

MADAME DE SAINT-ANGE—Why, I suspected as much.

DOLMANCE—You see very well I had to be silent upon this caprice; and you grasp now that one must be alone and in the deepest shadows in order to give oneself over to such turpitudes.

EUGENIE—Do you want me to accompany you? I'll frig you while you amuse yourself with Augustin.

DOLMANCE—No, no, this is an *affaire d'honneur* and should take place between men only; a woman would only disturb us. . . . At your service in a moment, dear ladies. *(He goes out, taking Augustin with him.)*

# *Sarrasine*

TRANSLATED BY RICHARD MILLER

I was deep in one of those daydreams which overtake even the shallowest of men, in the midst of the most tumultuous parties. Midnight had just sounded from the clock of the Elysée-Bourbon. Seated in a window recess and hidden behind the sinuous folds of a silk curtain, I could contemplate at my leisure the garden of the mansion where I was spending the evening. The trees, partially covered with snow, stood out dimly against the grayish background of a cloudy sky, barely whitened by the moon. Seen amid these fantastic surroundings, they vaguely resembled ghosts half out of their shrouds, a gigantic representation of the famous Dance of the Dead. Then, turning in the other direction, I could admire the Dance of the Living! a splendid salon decorated in silver and gold, with glittering chandeliers, sparkling with candles. There, milling about, whirling around, flitting here and there, were the most beautiful women of Paris, the richest, the noblest, dazzling, stately, resplendent with diamonds, flowers in their hair, on their bosoms, on their heads, strewn over dresses or in garlands at their feet. Light, rustling movements, voluptuous steps, made the laces, the silk brocades, the gauzes, float around their delicate forms. Here and there, some overly animated glances darted forth, eclipsing the lights, the fire of the diamonds, and stimulated anew some too ardent hearts. One might also catch movements of the head meaningful to lovers, and negative gestures for husbands. The sudden outbursts of the gamblers' voices at each

---

*HONORÉ DE BALZAC's "Sarrasine" is the subject of Roland Barthes' essay S/Z.*

unexpected turn of the dice, the clink of gold, mingled with the music and the murmur of conversation, and to complete the giddiness of this mass of people intoxicated by everything seductive the world can hold, a haze of perfume and general inebriation played upon the fevered mind. Thus, on my right, the dark and silent image of death; on my left, the seemly bacchanalias of life: here, cold nature, dull, in mourning; there, human beings enjoying themselves. On the borderline between these two so different scenes, which, a thousand times repeated in various guises, make Paris the world's most amusing and most philosophical city, I was making for myself a moral macédoine, half pleasant, half funereal. With my left foot I beat time, and I felt as though the other were in the grave. My leg was in fact chilled by one of those insidious drafts which freeze half our bodies while the other half feels the humid heat of rooms, an occurrence rather frequent at balls.

"Monsieur de Lanty hasn't owned this house for very long, has he?"

"Oh yes. Maréchal Carigliano sold it to him nearly ten years ago."

"Ah!"

"These people must have a huge fortune."

"They must have."

"What a party! It's shockingly elegant."

"Do you think they're as rich as M. de Nucingen or M. de Gondreville?"

"You mean you don't know?" . . .

I stuck my head out and recognized the two speakers as members of that strange race which, in Paris, deals exclusively with "why"s and "how"s, with "Where did they come from?" "What's happening?" "What has she done?" They lowered their voices and walked off to talk in greater comfort on some isolated sofa. Never had a richer vein been offered to seekers after mystery. Nobody knew what country the Lanty family came from, or from what business, what plunder, what piratical activity, or what inheritance derived a fortune estimated at several millions. All the members of the family spoke Italian, French, Spanish, English, and German perfectly enough to create the belief that they must have spent a long time among these various peoples. Were they Gypsies? Were they freebooters?

"Even if it's the devil," some young politicians said, "they give a marvelous party."

"Even if the Count de Lanty had robbed a bank, I'd marry his daughter anytime!" cried a philosopher.

Who wouldn't have married Marianina, a girl of sixteen whose beauty embodied the fabled imaginings of the Eastern poets! Like the sultan's daughter in the story of the Magic Lamp, she should have been kept veiled. Her singing put into the shade the partial talents of Malibran, Sontag, and Fodor, in whom one dominant quality has always excluded overall perfection; whereas Marianina was able to bring to the same level purity of sound, sensibility, rightness of movement and pitch, soul and science, correctness and feeling. This girl was the embodiment of that secret poetry, the common bond among all the arts, which always eludes those who search for it. Sweet and modest, educated and witty, Marianina could be eclipsed by no one, save her mother.

Have you ever encountered one of those women whose striking beauty defies the inroads of age and who seem at thirty-six more desirable than they could have been fifteen years earlier? Their visage is a vibrant soul, it glows; each feature sparkles with intelligence; each pore has a special brilliance, especially in artificial light. Their seductive eyes refuse, attract, speak or remain silent; their walk is innocently knowledgeable; their voices employ the melodious wealth of the most coquettishly soft and tender notes. Based on comparisons, their praises flatter the self-love of the most sentient. A movement of their eyebrows, the least glance, their pursed lips, fill with a kind of terror those whose life and happiness depend upon them. Inexperienced in love and influenced by words, a young girl can be seduced; for this kind of woman, however, a man must know, like M. de Jaucourt, not to cry out when he is hiding in a closet and the maid breaks two of his fingers as she shuts the door on them. In loving these powerful sirens, one gambles with one's life. And this, perhaps, is why we love them so passionately. Such was the Countess de Lanty.

Filippo, Marianina's brother, shared with his sister in the Countess's marvelous beauty. To be brief, this young man was a living image of Antinous, even more slender. Yet how well these thin, delicate proportions are suited to young people when an olive complexion, strongly defined eyebrows, and the fire of velvet eyes give promise of future male passion, of brave thoughts! If Filippo resided in every girl's heart as an ideal, he also resided in the memory of every mother as the best catch in France.

The beauty, the fortune, the wit, the charms of these two children came solely from their mother. The Count de Lanty was small, ugly, and pockmarked; dark as a Spaniard, dull as a banker. However, he was taken to be a deep politician, perhaps because he rarely laughed and was always quoting Metternich or Wellington.

This mysterious family had all the appeal of one of Lord Byron's poems, whose difficulties each person in the fashionable world interpreted in a different way: an obscure and sublime song in every strophe. The reserve maintained by M. and Mme de Lanty about their origin, their past life, and their relationship with the four corners of the globe had not lasted long as a subject of astonishment in Paris. Nowhere perhaps is Vespasian's axiom better understood. There, even bloodstained or filthy money betrays nothing and stands for everything. So long as high society knows the amount of your fortune, you are classed among those having an equal amount, and no one asks to see your family tree, because everyone knows how much it cost. In a city where social problems are solved like algebraic equations, adventurers have every opportunity in their favor. Even supposing this family were of Gypsy origin, it was so wealthy, so attractive, that society had no trouble in forgiving its little secrets. Unfortunately, however, the mystery of the Lantys presented a continuing source of curiosity, rather like that contained in the novels of Ann Radcliffe.

Observers, people who make it a point to know in what shop you buy your candlesticks or who ask the amount of your rent when they find your apartment attractive, had noticed, now and then, in the midst of the Countess's parties, concerts, balls, and routs, the appearance of a strange personage. It was a man. The first time he had appeared in the mansion was during a concert, when he seemed to have been drawn to the salon by Marianina's enchanting voice.

"All of a sudden, I'm cold," a lady had said who was standing with a friend by the door.

The stranger, who was standing next to the women, went away.

"That's odd! I'm warm now," she said, after the stranger had gone. "And you'll say I'm mad, but I can't help thinking that my neighbor, the man dressed in black who just left, was the cause of my chill."

Before long, the exaggeration native to those in high society gave birth to and accumulated the most amusing ideas, the most outrageous expressions, the most ridiculous anecdotes about this mysterious personage. Although not a vampire, a ghoul, or an artificial man, a kind of Faust or Robin Goodfellow, people fond of fantasy said he had something of all these anthropomorphic natures about him. Here and there, one came across some Germans who accepted as fact these clever witticisms of Parisian scandalmongering. The stranger was merely an old man. Many of the young men who were in the habit of settling the future of Europe every morning in a few elegant phrases would have liked to see in this stranger

some great criminal, the possessor of vast wealth. Some storytellers recounted the life of this old man and provided really curious details about
the atrocities he had committed while in the service of the Maharaja of
Mysore. Some bankers, more positive by nature, invented a fable about
money. "Bah," they said, shrugging their shoulders in pity, "this poor old
man is a *tête génoise!*"

"Sir, without being indiscreet, could you please tell me what you mean
by a *tête génoise?*"

"A man, sir, with an enormous lifetime capital and whose family's income doubtless depends on his good health."

I remember having heard at Mme d'Espard's a hypnotist proving on
highly suspect historical data that this old man, preserved under glass, was
the famous Balsamo, known as Cagliostro. According to this contemporary alchemist, the Sicilian adventurer had escaped death and passed his
time fabricating gold for his grandchildren. Last, the bailiff of Ferette
maintained that he had recognized this odd personage as the Count of
Saint-Germain. These stupidities, spoken in witty accents, with the mocking air characteristic of atheistic society in our day, kept alive vague suspicions about the Lanty family. Finally, through a strange combination of
circumstances, the members of this family justified everyone's conjectures
by behaving somewhat mysteriously toward this old man, whose life was
somehow hidden from all investigation.

Whenever this person crossed the threshold of the room he was supposed to inhabit in the Lanty mansion, his appearance always created a
great sensation among the family. One might have called it an event of
great importance. Filippo, Marianina, Mme de Lanty, and an old servant
were the only persons privileged to assist the old man in walking, arising,
sitting down. Each of them watched over his slightest movement. It
seemed that he was an enchanted being upon whom depended the happiness, the life, or the fortune of them all. Was it affection or fear? Those in
society were unable to discover any clue to help them solve this problem.
Hidden for whole months in the depths of a secret sanctuary, this family
genie would suddenly come forth, unexpectedly, and would appear in the
midst of the salons like those fairies of bygone days who descended from
flying dragons to interrupt the rites to which they had not been invited.
Only the most avid onlookers were then able to perceive the uneasiness of
the heads of the house, who could conceal their feelings with unusual skill.
Sometimes, however, while dancing a quadrille, Marianina, naive as she

was, would cast a terrified glance at the old man when she spied him among the crowd. Or else Filippo would slip quickly through the throng to his side and would stay near him, tender and attentive, as though contact with others or the slightest breath would destroy this strange creature. The Countess would make a point of drawing near, without seeming to have any intention of joining them; then, assuming a manner and expression of servitude mixed with tenderness, submission, and power, she would say a few words, to which the old man nearly always deferred, and he would disappear, led off, or, more precisely, carried off, by her. If Mme de Lanty was not present, the Count used a thousand stratagems to reach his side; however, he seemed to have difficulty making himself heard and treated him like a spoiled child whose mother gives in to his whims in order to avoid a scene. Some bolder persons having thoughtlessly ventured to question the Count de Lanty, this cold, reserved man had appeared never to understand them. And so, after many tries, all futile because of the circumspection of the entire family, everyone stopped trying to fathom such a well-kept secret. Weary of trying, the companionable spies, the idly curious, and the politic all gave up bothering about this mystery.

However, even now perhaps in these glittering salons there were some philosophers who, while eating an ice or a sherbet, or placing their empty punch glass on a side table, were saying to each other: "It wouldn't surprise me to learn that those people are crooks. The old man who hides and only makes his appearance on the first day of spring or winter, or at the solstices, looks to me like a killer . . ."

"Or a confidence man . . ."

"It's almost the same thing. Killing a man's fortune is sometimes worse than killing the man."

"Sir, I have bet twenty louis; I should get back forty."

"But, sir, there are only thirty on the table."

"Ah well, you see how mixed the crowd is here. It's impossible to play."

"True . . . But it's now nearly six months since we've seen the Spirit. Do you think he's really alive?"

"Hah! at best . . ."

These last words were spoken near me by people I did not know, as they were moving off and as I was resuming, in an afterthought, my mixed thoughts of white and black, life and death. My vivid imagination as well as my eyes looked back and forth from the party, which had reached the height of its splendor, and the somber scene in the gardens. I do not know how long I meditated on these two faces of the human coin; but all at once I was awakened by the stifled laugh of a young woman. I was stunned by the appearance of the image which arose before me. By one of those tricks of nature, the half-mournful thought turning in my mind had emerged, and it appeared living before me; it had sprung like Minerva from the head of Jove, tall and strong; it was at once a hundred years old and twenty-two years old; it was alive and dead. Escaped from his room like a lunatic from his cell, the little old man had obviously slipped behind a hedge of people who were listening to Marianina's voice, finishing the cavatina from *Tancredi*. He seemed to have come out from underground, impelled by some piece of stage machinery. Motionless and somber, he stood for a moment gazing at the party, the noises of which had perhaps reached his ears. His almost somnambulatory preoccupation was so concentrated on things that he was in the world without seeing it. He had unceremoniously sprung up next to one of the most ravishing women in Paris, a young and elegant dancer, delicately formed, with one of those faces as fresh as that of a child, pink and white, so frail and transparent that a man's glance seems to penetrate it like a ray of sunlight going through ice. They were both there before me, together, united, and so close that the stranger brushed against her, her gauzy dress, her garlands of flowers, her softly curled hair, her floating sash.

I had brought this young woman to Mme de Lanty's ball. Since this was her first visit to the house, I forgave her her stifled laugh, but I quickly gave her a signal which completely silenced her and filled her with awe for her neighbor. She sat down next to me. The old man did not want to leave this lovely creature, to whom he had attached himself with that silent and seemingly baseless stubbornness to which the extremely old are prone and which makes them appear childish. In order to sit near her, he had to take a folding chair. His slightest movements were full of that cold heaviness, the stupid indecision, characteristic of the gestures of a paralytic. He sat slowly down on his seat, with circumspection, muttering some unintelligible words. His worn-out voice was like the sound made by a stone falling down a well. The young woman held my hand tightly, as if seeking protection on some precipice, and she shivered when this man at whom she was looking turned upon her two eyes without warmth, glaucous eyes which could only be compared to dull mother-of-pearl.

"I'm afraid," she said, leaning toward my ear.

"You can talk," I answered. "He is very hard of hearing."

"Do you know him?"

"Yes."

Thereupon, she gathered up enough courage to look for a moment at this creature for which the human language had no name, a form without substance, a being without life, or a life without action. She was under the spell of that timorous curiosity which leads women to seek out dangerous emotions, to go see chained tigers, to look at boa constrictors, frightening themselves because they are separated from them only by weak fences. Although the little old man's back was stooped like a laborer's, one could easily tell that he must have had at one time a normal shape. His excessive thinness, the delicacy of his limbs, proved that he had always been slender. He was dressed in black silk trousers, which fell about his bony thighs in folds, like an empty sail. An anatomist would have promptly recognized the symptoms of galloping consumption by looking at the skinny legs supporting this strange body. You would have said they were two bones crossed on a tombstone.

A feeling of profound horror for mankind gripped the heart when one saw the marks that decrepitude had left on this fragile machine. The stranger was wearing an old-fashioned gold-embroidered white waistcoat, and his linen was dazzlingly white. A frill of somewhat yellowed lace, rich enough for a queen's envy, fell into ruffles on his breast. On him, however, this lace seemed more like a rag than like an ornament. Centered on it was a fabulous diamond, which glittered like the sun. This outmoded luxury, this particular and tasteless jewel, made the strange creature's face even more striking. The setting was worthy of the portrait. This dark face was angular and all sunk in. The chin was sunken, the temples were sunken; the eyes were lost in yellowish sockets. The jawbones stood out because of his indescribable thinness, creating cavities in the center of each cheek. These deformations, more or less illuminated by the candles, produced shadows and strange reflections which succeeded in erasing any human characteristics from his face. And the years had glued the thin, yellow skin of his face so closely to his skull that it was covered all over with a multitude of circular wrinkles, like the ripples on a pond into which a child has thrown a pebble, or star-shaped, like a cracked windowpane, but everywhere deep and close-set as the edges of pages in a closed book. Some old people have presented more hideous portraits; what contributed most, however, in lending the appearance of an artificial creature to the specter which had risen up before us was the red and white with which he glistened. The eyebrows of his mask took from the light a luster which revealed that they were painted on. Fortunately for the eye depressed by the sight of such ruin, his cadaverous skull was covered by a blond wig, whose innumerable curls were evidence of an extraordinary pretension. For the rest, the feminine coquetry of this phantasmagorical personage was rather strongly emphasized by the gold ornaments hanging from his ears, by the rings whose fine stones glittered on his bony fingers, and by a watch chain which shimmered like the brilliants of a choker around a woman's neck. Finally, this sort of Japanese idol had on his bluish lips a fixed and frozen smile, implacable and mocking, like a skull. Silent and motionless as a statue, it exuded the musty odor of old clothes which the heirs of some duchess take out for inventory. Although the old man turned his eyes toward the crowd, it seemed that the movements of those orbs, incapable of sight, were accomplished only by means of some imperceptible artifice; and when the eyes came to rest on something, anyone looking at them would have concluded that they had not moved at all. To see, next to this human wreckage, a young woman whose neck, bosom, and arms were bare and white, whose figure was in the full bloom of its beauty, whose hair rose from her alabaster forehead and inspired love, whose eyes did not receive but gave off light, who was soft, fresh, and whose floating curls and sweet breath seemed too heavy, too hard, too powerful for this shadow, for this man of dust: ah! here were death and life indeed, I thought, in a fantastic arabesque, half hideous chimera, divinely feminine from the waist up.

"Yet there are marriages like that often enough in the world," I said to myself.

"He smells like a graveyard," cried the terrified young woman, pressing against me for protection, whose uneasy movements told me she was frightened. "What a horrible sight," she went on. "I can't stay here any longer. If I look at him again, I shall believe that death itself has come looking for me. Is he alive?"

She reached out to the phenomenon with that boldness women can summon up out of the strength of their desires; but she broke into a cold sweat, for no sooner had she touched the old man than she heard a cry like a rattle. This sharp voice, if voice it was, issued from a nearly dried up throat. Then the sound was quickly followed by a little, convulsive, childish cough of a peculiar sonorousness. At this sound, Marianina, Filippo, and Mme de Lanty looked in our direction, and their glances were like bolts of lightning. The young woman wished she were at the bottom of the Seine. She took my arm and led me into a side room. Men, women, everyone made way for us. At the end of the public rooms, we came into a small, semicircular chamber. My companion threw herself onto a divan, trembling with fright, oblivious to her surroundings.

"Madame, you are mad," I said to her.

"But," she replied, after a moment's silence, during which I gazed at her in admiration, "is it my fault? Why does Mme de Lanty allow ghosts to wander about in her house?"

"Come," I replied, "you are being ridiculous, taking a little old man for a ghost."

"Be still," she said, with that forceful and mocking air all women so easily assume when they want to be in the right. "What a pretty room!" she cried, looking around. "Blue satin always makes such wonderful wall hangings. How refreshing it is! Oh! what a beautiful painting!" she went on, getting up and going to stand before a painting in a magnificent frame.

We stood for a moment in contemplation of this marvel, which seemed to have been painted by some supernatural brush. The picture was of Adonis lying on a lion's skin. The lamp hanging from the ceiling of the room in an alabaster globe illuminated this canvas with a soft glow which enabled us to make out all the beauties of the painting.

"Does such a perfect creature exist?" she asked me, after having, with a soft smile of contentment, examined the exquisite grace of the contours, the pose, the color, the hair; in short, the entire picture.

"He is too beautiful for a man," she added, after an examination such as she might have made of some rival.

Oh! how jealous I then felt: something in which a poet had vainly tried to make me believe, the jealousy of engravings, of pictures, wherein artists exaggerate human beauty according to the doctrine which leads them to idealize everything.

"It's a portrait," I replied, "the product of the talent of Vien. But that great painter never saw the original, and maybe you'd admire it less if you knew that this daub was copied from the statue of a woman."

"But who is it?"

I hesitated.

"I want to know," she added, impetuously.

"I believe," I replied, "that this Adonis is a . . . a relative of Mme de Lanty."

I had the pain of seeing her rapt in the contemplation of this figure. She sat in silence; I sat down next to her and took her hand without her being aware of it! Forgotten for a painting! At this moment, the light footsteps of a woman in a rustling dress broke the silence. Young Marianina came in, and her innocent expression made her even more alluring than did her grace and her lovely dress; she was walking slowly and escorting with maternal care, with filial solicitude, the costumed specter who had made us flee from the music room and whom she was leading, watching with what seemed to be concern as he slowly advanced on his feeble feet. They went together with some difficulty to a door hidden behind a tapestry. There, Marianina knocked softly. At once, as if by magic, a tall, stern man, a kind of family genie, appeared. Before entrusting the old man to the care of his mysterious guardian, the child respectfully kissed the walking corpse, and her chaste caress was not devoid of that graceful cajolery of which some privileged women possess the secret.

"*Addio, addio,*" she said, with the prettiest inflection in her youthful voice.

She added to the final syllable a marvelously well-executed trill, but in a soft voice, as if to give poetic expression to the emotions in her heart. Suddenly struck by some memory, the old man stood on the threshold of this secret hideaway. Then, through the silence, we heard the heavy sigh that came from his chest: he took the most beautiful of the rings which adorned his skeletal fingers and placed it in Marianina's bosom. The young girl broke into laughter, took the ring, and slipped it onto her finger over her glove; then she walked quickly toward the salon, from which there could be heard the opening measures of a quadrille. She saw us.

"Ah, you were here," she said, blushing.

After having seemed as if about to question us, she ran to her partner with the careless petulance of youth.

"What did that mean?" my young companion asked me. "Is he her husband? I must be dreaming. Where am I?"

"You," I replied, "you, madame, superior as you are, you who understand so well the most hidden feelings, who know how to inspire in a man's heart the most delicate of feelings without blighting it, without breaking it at the outset, you who pity heartache and who combine the wit of a Parisienne with a passionate soul worthy of Italy or Spain—"

She perceived the bitter irony in my speech; then, without seeming to have heard, she interrupted me: "Oh, you fashion me to your own taste. What tyranny! You don't want me for myself!"

"Ah, I want nothing," I cried, taken aback by her severity. "Is it true, at least, that you enjoy hearing stories of those vivid passions that ravishing southern women inspire in our hearts?"

"Yes, so?"

"So, I'll call tomorrow around nine and reveal this mystery to you."

"No," she replied. "I want to know now."

"You haven't yet given me the right to obey you when you say: I want to."

"At this moment," she replied with maddening coquetry, "I have the most burning desire to know the secret. Tomorrow I might not even listen to you. . . ."

She smiled and we parted; she just as proud, just as forbidding, and I just as ridiculous as ever. She had the audacity to waltz with a young aide-de-camp; and I was left in turn angry, pouting, admiring, loving, jealous.

"Till tomorrow," she said, around two in the morning, as she left the ball.

"I won't go," I thought to myself. "I'll give you up. You are more capricious, perhaps a thousand times more fanciful . . . than my imagination."

The next evening, we were both seated before a good fire in a small, elegant salon, she on a low sofa, I on cushions almost at her feet, and my eyes below hers. The street was quiet. The lamp shed a soft light. It was one of those evenings pleasing to the soul, one of those never-to-be-forgotten moments, one of those hours spent in peace and desire whose charm, later on, is a matter of constant regret, even when we may be happier. Who can erase the vivid imprint of the first feelings of love?

"Well," she said, "I'm listening."

"I don't dare begin. The story has some dangerous passages for its teller. If I become too moved, you must stop me."

"Tell."

"I will obey."

~ ~ ~

Ernest-Jean Sarrasine was the only son of a lawyer in the Franche-Comté, I went on, after a pause. His father had amassed six or eight thousand livres of income honestly enough, a professional's fortune which at that time, in the provinces, was considered to be colossal. The elder Sarrasine, having but one child and anxious to overlook nothing where his education was concerned, hoped to make a magistrate of him and to live long enough to see, in his old age, the grandson of Matthieu Sarrasine, farmer of Saint-Dié, seated beneath the lilies and napping through some trial for the greater glory of the law; however, heaven did not hold this pleasure in store for the lawyer.

The younger Sarrasine, entrusted to the Jesuits at an early age, evidenced an unusual turbulence. He had the childhood of a man of talent. He would study only what pleased him, frequently rebelled, and sometimes spent hours on end plunged in confused thought, occupied at times in watching his comrades at play, at times dreaming of Homeric heroes. Then, if he made up his mind to amuse himself, he threw himself into games with an extraordinary ardor. When a fight broke out between him and a friend, the battle rarely ended without bloodshed. If he was the weaker of the two, he would bite. Active and passive by turns, without aptitude and not overly intelligent, his bizarre character made his teachers as wary of him as were his classmates. Instead of learning the elements of Greek, he drew the reverend father as he explained a passage in Thucydides to them, sketched the mathematics teacher, the tutors, the father in charge of discipline, and he scribbled shapeless designs on the walls. Instead of singing the Lord's praises in church, he distracted himself during services by whittling on a pew; or when he had stolen a piece of wood, he carved some holy figure. If he had no wood, paper, or pencil, he reproduced his ideas with bread crumbs. Whether copying the characters in the pictures that decorated the choir, or improvising, he always left behind him gross sketches whose licentiousness shocked the youngest fathers; evil tongues maintained that the older Jesuits were amused by them. Finally, if we are to believe school gossip, he was expelled for having, while awaiting his turn at the confessional on Good Friday, shaped a big stick of wood into the form of Christ. The impiety with which this statue was endowed was too blatant not to have merited punishment of the artist. Had he not had the audacity to place this somewhat cynical figure on top of the tabernacle!

Sarrasine sought in Paris a refuge from the effects of a father's curse. Having one of those strong wills that brook no obstacle, he obeyed the commands of his genius and entered Bouchardon's studio. He worked all day and in the evening went out to beg for his living. Astonished at the young artist's progress and intelligence, Bouchardon soon became aware of his pupil's poverty; he helped him, grew fond of him, and treated him like his own son. Then, when Sarrasine's genius was revealed in one of those works in which future talent struggles with the effervescence of youth, the warmhearted Bouchardon endeavored to restore him to the old lawyer's good graces. Before the authority of the famous sculptor, the parental anger subsided. All Besançon rejoiced at having given birth to a great man of the future. In the first throes of the ecstasy produced by his flattered vanity, the miserly lawyer gave his son the means to cut a good figure in society. For a long time, the lengthy and laborious studies demanded by sculpture tamed Sarrasine's impetuous nature and wild genius. Bouchardon, foreseeing the violence with which the passions would erupt in this young soul, which was perhaps as predisposed to them as Michelangelo's had been, channeled his energy into constant labor. He succeeded in keeping Sarrasine's extraordinary impetuosity within limits by forbidding him to work; by suggesting distractions when he saw him being carried away by the fury of some idea, or by entrusting him with important work when he seemed on the point of abandoning himself to dissipation. However, gentleness was always the most powerful of weapons where this passionate soul was concerned, and the master had no greater control over his student than when he inspired his gratitude through paternal kindness.

At twenty-two, Sarrasine was necessarily removed from the salutary influence Bouchardon had exercised over his morals and his habits. He reaped the fruits of his genius by winning the sculpture prize established by the Marquis de Marigny, the brother of Mme de Pompadour, who did so much for the arts. Diderot hailed the statue by Bouchardon's pupil as a masterpiece. The king's sculptor, not without great sorrow, saw off to Italy a young man whom he had kept, as a matter of principle, in total ignorance of the facts of life.

For six years, Sarrasine had boarded with Bouchardon. As fanatic in his art as Canova was later to be, he arose at dawn, went to the studio, did not emerge until nightfall, and lived only with his Muse. If he went to the Comédie Française, he was taken by his master. He felt so out of place at Mme Geoffrin's and in high society, into which Bouchardon tried to introduce him, that he preferred to be alone and shunned the pleasures of that licentious era. He had no other mistress but sculpture and Clotilde, one of the luminaries of the Opéra. And even this affair did not last. Sarrasine was rather ugly, always badly dressed, and so free in his nature, so irregular in his private life, that the celebrated nymph, fearing some catastrophe, soon relinquished the sculptor to his love of the Arts. Sophie Arnould made one of her witticisms on this subject. She confessed her surprise, I believe, that her friend had managed to triumph over statuary.

Sarrasine left for Italy in 1758. During the journey, his vivid imagination caught fire beneath a brilliant sky and at the sight of the wonderful monuments which are to be found in the birthplace of the Arts. He admired the statues, the frescoes, the paintings, and thus inspired, he came to Rome, filled with desire to carve his name between Michelangelo's and M. Bouchardon's. Accordingly, at the beginning, he divided his time between studio tasks and examining the works of art in which Rome abounds. He had already spent two weeks in the ecstatic state which overwhelms young minds at the sight of the queen of ruins, when he went one evening to the Teatro Argentina, before which a huge crowd was assembled. He inquired as to the causes of this gathering, and everyone answered with two names: Zambinella! Jomelli! He entered and took a seat in the orchestra, squeezed between two notably fat *abbati;* however, he was lucky enough to be fairly close to the stage. The curtain rose. For the first time in his life, he heard that music whose delights M. Jean-Jacques Rousseau had so eloquently praised to him at one of Baron d'Holbach's evenings. The young sculptor's senses were, so to speak, lubricated by the accents of Jomelli's sublime harmony. The languorous novelties of these skillfully mingled Italian voices plunged him into a delicious ecstasy. He remained speechless, motionless, not even feeling crowded by the two priests. His soul passed into his ears and eyes. He seemed to hear through every pore. Suddenly a burst of applause which shook the house greeted the prima donna's entrance. She came coquettishly to the front of the stage and greeted the audience with infinite grace. The lights, the general enthusiasm, the theatrical illusion, the glamour of a style of dress which in those days was quite attractive, all conspired in favor of this woman. Sarrasine cried out with pleasure.

At that instant he marveled at the ideal beauty he had hitherto sought in life, seeking in one often unworthy model the roundness of a perfect leg; in another, the curve of a breast; in another, white shoulders; finally taking some girl's neck, some woman's hands, and some child's smooth knees, without ever having encountered under the cold Parisian sky the rich, sweet creations of ancient Greece. La Zambinella displayed to him, united, living, and delicate, those exquisite female forms he so ardently desired, of which a sculptor is at once the severest and the most passionate judge. Her mouth was expressive, her eyes loving, her complexion dazzlingly white. And along with these details, which would have enraptured a painter, were all the wonders of those images of Venus revered and rendered by the chisels of the Greeks. The artist never wearied of admiring the inimitable grace with which the arms were attached to the torso, the marvelous roundness of the neck, the harmonious lines drawn by the eyebrows, the nose, and the perfect oval of the face, the purity of its vivid contours and the effect of the thick, curved lashes which lined her heavy and voluptuous eyelids. This was more than a woman, this was a masterpiece! In this unhoped-for creation could be found a love to enrapture any man, and beauties worthy of satisfying a critic. With his eyes, Sarrasine devoured Pygmalion's statue, come down from its pedestal. When La Zambinella sang, the effect was delirium. The artist felt cold; then he felt a heat which suddenly began to prickle in the innermost depth of his being, in what we call the heart, for lack of any other word! He did not applaud, he said nothing, he experienced an impulse of madness, a kind of frenzy which overcomes us only when we are at the age when desire has something frightening and infernal about it. Sarrasine wanted to leap onto the stage and take possession of this woman: his strength, increased a hundredfold by a moral depression impossible to explain, since these phenomena occur in an area hidden from human observation, seemed to manifest itself with painful violence. Looking at him, one would have thought him a cold and senseless man. Fame, knowledge, future, existence, laurels, everything collapsed.

"To be loved by her, or die!" Such was the decree Sarrasine passed upon himself. He was so utterly intoxicated that he no longer saw the theater, the spectators, the actors, or heard the music. Moreover, the distance between himself and La Zambinella had ceased to exist; he possessed her, his eyes were riveted upon her, he took her for his own. An almost diabolical power enabled him to feel the breath of this voice, to smell the scented powder covering her hair, to see the planes of her face, to count the blue veins shadowing her satin skin. Last, this agile voice, fresh and silvery in timbre, supple as a thread shaped by the slightest breath of air, rolling and unrolling, cascading and scattering, this voice attacked his soul so vividly that several times he gave vent to involuntary cries torn from him by convulsive feelings of pleasure which are all too rarely vouchsafed by human passions. He was presently obliged to leave the theater. His trembling legs almost refused to support him. He was limp, weak as a sensitive man who has given way to overwhelming anger. He had experienced such pleasure, or perhaps he had suffered so keenly, that his life had drained away like water from a broken vase. He felt empty inside, a prostration similar to the debilitation that overcomes those convalescing from serious illness.

Overcome by an inexplicable sadness, he sat down on the steps of a church. There, leaning back against a pillar, he fell into a confused meditation, as in a dream. He had been smitten by passion. Upon returning to his lodgings, he fell into one of those frenzies of activity which disclose to us the presence of new elements in our lives. A prey to this first fever of love derived equally from both pleasure and pain, he tried to appease his impatience and his delirium by drawing La Zambinella from memory. It was a kind of embodied meditation. On one page, La Zambinella appeared in that apparently calm and cool pose favored by Raphael, Giorgione, and every great painter. On another, she was delicately turning her head after having finished a trill, and appeared to be listening to herself. Sarrasine sketched his mistress in every pose: he drew her unveiled, seated, standing, lying down, chaste or amorous, embodying through the delirium of his pencils every capricious notion that can enter our heads when we think intently about a mistress. However, his fevered thoughts went beyond drawing. He saw La Zambinella, spoke to her, beseeched her, he passed a thousand years of life and happiness with her by placing her in every imaginable position; in short, by sampling the future with her. On the following day, he sent his valet to rent a box next to the stage for the entire season. Then, like all young people with lusty souls, he exaggerated to himself the difficulties of his undertaking and first fed his passion with the pleasure of being able to admire his mistress without obstruction. This golden age of love, during which we take pleasure in our own feeling and in which we are happy almost by ourselves, was not destined to last long in Sarrasine's case. Nevertheless, events took him by surprise while he was still under the spell of this vernal hallucination, as naive as it was voluptuous. In a week he lived a lifetime, spending the mornings kneading the clay by which he would copy La Zambinella, despite the veils, skirts, corsets, and ribbons which concealed her from him. In the evenings, installed in his box early, alone, lying on a sofa like a Turk under the influence of opium, he created for himself a pleasure as rich and varied as he wished it to be. First, he gradually familiarized himself with the overly vivid emotions his mistress's singing afforded him; he then trained his eyes to see her; and finally he could contemplate her without fearing an outburst of the wild frenzy which had seized him on the first day. As his passion became calmer, it grew deeper. For the rest, the unsociable sculptor did not allow his friends to intrude upon his solitude, which was peopled with images, adorned with fantasies of hope, and filled with happiness. His love was so strong, so naive, that he experienced all the innocent scruples that assail us when we love for the first time. As he began to realize that he would soon have to act, to plot, to inquire where La Zambinella lived, whether she had a mother, uncle, teacher, family, to ponder, in short, on ways to see her, speak to her, these great, ambitious thoughts made his heart swell so painfully that he put them off until later, deriving as much satisfaction from his physical suffering as he did from his intellectual pleasures.

～ ～ ～

"But," Mme de Rochefide interrupted me, "I still don't see anything about either Marianina or her little old man."

"You are seeing nothing but him!" I cried impatiently, like an author who is being forced to spoil a theatrical effect.

～ ～ ～

For several days, I resumed after a pause, Sarrasine had reappeared so faithfully in his box and his eyes had expressed such love that his passion for La Zambinella's voice would have been common knowledge throughout Paris, had this adventure happened there; however, in Italy, madame, everyone goes to the theater for himself, with his own passions, and with a heartfelt interest which precludes spying through opera glasses. Nevertheless, the sculptor's enthusiasm did not escape the attention of the singers for long. One evening, the Frenchman saw that they were laughing at him in the wings. It is hard to know what extreme actions he might not have taken had La Zambinella not come onto the stage. She gave Sarrasine one of those eloquent glances which often reveal much more than women intend them to. This glance was a total revelation. Sarrasine was loved!

"If it's only a caprice," he thought, already accusing his mistress of excessive ardor, "she doesn't know what she is subjecting herself to. I am hoping her caprice will last my whole life."

At that moment, the artist's attention was distracted by three soft knocks on the door of his box. He opened it. An old woman entered with an air of mystery.

"Young man," she said, "if you want to be happy, be prudent. Put on a cape, wear a hat drawn down over your eyes; then, around ten in the evening, be in the Via del Corso in front of the Hotel di Spagna."

"I'll be there," he replied, placing two louis in the duenna's wrinkled hand.

He left his box after having given a signal to La Zambinella, who timidly lowered her heavy eyelids, like a woman pleased to be understood at last. Then he ran home to dress himself as seductively as he could. As he was leaving the theater, a strange man took his arm.

"Be on your guard, Frenchman," he whispered in his ear. "This is a matter of life and death. Cardinal Cicognara is her protector and doesn't trifle."

At that moment, had some demon set the pit of hell between Sarrasine and La Zambinella, he would have crossed it with one leap. Like the horses of the gods described by Homer, the sculptor's love had traversed vast distances in the twinkling of an eye.

"If death itself were waiting for me outside the house, I would go even faster," he replied.

*"Poverino!"* the stranger cried as he disappeared.

Speaking of danger to a lover is tantamount to selling him pleasures, is it not? Sarrasine's valet had never seen his master take so much care over his toilette. His finest sword, a gift from Bouchardon, the sash Clotilde had given him, his embroidered coat, his silver-brocade waistcoat, his gold snuffbox, his jeweled watches, were all taken from their coffers, and he adorned himself like a girl about to appear before her first love. At the appointed hour, drunk with love and seething with hope, Sarrasine, concealed in his cape, sped to the rendezvous the old woman had given him. The duenna was waiting for him.

"You took a long time," she said. "Come."

She led the Frenchman along several back streets and stopped before a rather handsome mansion. She knocked. The door opened. She led Sarrasine along a labyrinth of stairways, galleries, and rooms which were lit only by the feeble light of the moon, and soon came to a door through whose cracks gleamed bright lights and from behind which came the joyful sounds of several voices. When at a word from the old woman he was admitted to this mysterious room, Sarrasine was suddenly dazzled at finding himself in a salon as brilliantly lighted as it was sumptuously furnished, in the center of which stood a table laden with venerable bottles and flashing flagons sparkling with ruby facets. He recognized the singers from the theater, along with some charming women, all ready to begin an artists' orgy as soon as he was among them. Sarrasine suppressed a feeling of disappointment and put on a good face. He had expected a dim room, his mistress seated by the fire, some jealous person nearby, death and love, an exchange of confidences in low voices, heart to heart, dangerous kisses and faces so close that La Zambinella's hair would have caressed his forehead throbbing with desire, feverish with happiness.

*"Vive la folie!"* he cried. "*Signori e belle donne,* you will allow me to take my revenge later and to show you my gratitude for the way you have welcomed a poor sculptor."

Having been greeted warmly enough by most of those present, whom he knew by sight, he sought to approach the armchair on which La Zambinella was casually reclining. Ah! how his heart beat when he spied a delicate foot shod in one of those slippers which in those days, may I say, madame, gave women's feet such a coquettish and voluptuous look that I don't know how men were able to resist them. The well-fitting white stockings with green clocks, the short skirts, the slippers with pointed toes, and the high heels of Louis XV's reign may have contributed something to the demoralization of Europe and the clergy.

～　～　～

"Something?" the Marquise replied. "Have you read nothing?"

～　～　～

La Zambinella, I continued, smiling, had impudently crossed her legs and was gently swinging the upper one with a certain attractive indolence which suited her capricious sort of beauty. She had removed her costume and was wearing a bodice that accentuated her narrow waist and set off the satin panniers of her dress, which was embroidered with blue flowers. Her bosom, the treasures of which were concealed, in an excess of coquetry, by a covering of lace, was dazzlingly white. Her hair arranged something like that of Mme du Barry, her face, though it was partially hidden under a full bonnet, appeared only the more delicate, and powder suited her. To see her thus was to adore her. She gave the sculptor a graceful smile. Unhappy at not being able to speak to her without witnesses present, Sarrasine politely sat down next to her and talked about music, praising her extraordinary talent; but his voice trembled with love, with fear and hope.

"What are you afraid of?" asked Vitagliani, the company's most famous singer. "Go ahead; you need fear no rivals here." Having said this, the tenor smiled without another word. This smile was repeated on the lips of all the guests, whose attention contained a hidden malice a lover would not have noticed. Such openness was like a dagger thrust in Sarrasine's heart. Although endowed with a certain strength of character, and although nothing could change his love, it had perhaps not yet occurred to him that La Zambinella was virtually a courtesan, and that he could not have both the pure pleasures that make a young girl's love so delicious and the tempestuous transports by which the hazardous possession of an actress must be purchased. He reflected and resigned himself. Supper was served. Sarrasine and La Zambinella sat down informally side by side. For the first half of the meal, the artists preserved some decorum, and the sculptor was able to chat with the singer. He found her witty, acute, but astonishingly ignorant, and she revealed herself to be weak and superstitious. The delicacy of her organs was reflected in her understanding. When Vitagliani uncorked the first bottle of champagne, Sarrasine read in his companion's eyes a start of terror at the tiny explosion caused by the escaping gas. The love-stricken artist interpreted the involuntary shudder of this feminine constitution as the sign of an excessive sensitivity. The Frenchman was charmed by this weakness. How much is protective in a man's love!

"My strength your shield!" Is this not written at the heart of all declarations of love? Too excited to shower the beautiful Italian with compliments, Sarrasine, like all lovers, was by turns serious, laughing, or reflective. Although he seemed to be listening to the other guests, he did not hear a word they were saying, so absorbed was he in the pleasure of finding himself beside her, touching her hand as he served her. He bathed in a secret joy. Despite the eloquence of a few mutual glances, he was astonished at the reserve La Zambinella maintained toward him. Indeed, she had begun by pressing his foot and teasing him with the flirtatiousness of a woman in love and free to show it; but she suddenly wrapped herself in the modesty of a young girl, after hearing Sarrasine describe a trait which revealed the excessive violence of his character. When the supper became an orgy, the guests broke into song under the influence of the Peralta and the Pedro-Ximenes. There were ravishing duets, songs from Calabria, Spanish seguidillas, Neapolitan canzonettas. Intoxication was in every eye, in the music, in hearts and voices alike. Suddenly an enchanting vivacity welled up, a gay abandon, an Italian warmth of feeling inconceivable to those acquainted only with Parisian gatherings, London routs, or Viennese circles. Jokes and words of love flew like bullets in a battle through laughter, profanities, and invocations to the Holy Virgin or *il Bambino*. Someone lay down on a sofa and fell asleep. A girl was listening to a declaration of love unaware that she was spilling sherry on the tablecloth. In the midst of this disorder, La Zambinella remained thoughtful, as though terror-struck. She refused to drink, perhaps she ate a bit too much; however, it is said that greediness in a woman is a charming quality. Admiring his mistress's modesty, Sarrasine thought seriously about the future.

"She probably wants to be married," he thought. He then turned his thoughts to the delights of this marriage. His whole life seemed too short to exhaust the springs of happiness he found in the depths of his soul. Vitagliani, who was sitting next to him, refilled his glass so often that, toward three in the morning, without being totally drunk, Sarrasine could no longer control his delirium. Impetuously, he picked up the woman, escaping into a kind of boudoir next to the salon, toward the door of which he had glanced more than once. The Italian woman was armed with a dagger.

"If you come any closer," she said, "I will be forced to plunge this weapon into your heart. Let me go! You would despise me. I have conceived too much respect for your character to surrender in this fashion. I don't want to betray the feeling you have for me."

"Oh no!" cried Sarrasine. "You cannot stifle a passion by stimulating it! Are you already so corrupt that, old in heart, you would act like a young courtesan who whets the emotions by which she plies her trade?"

"But today is Friday," she replied, frightened at the Frenchman's violence.

Sarrasine, who was not devout, broke into laughter. La Zambinella jumped up like a young deer and ran toward the salon. When Sarrasine appeared in her pursuit, he was greeted by an infernal burst of laughter.

He saw La Zambinella lying in a swoon upon a sofa. She was pale and drained by the extraordinary effort she had just made. Although Sarrasine knew little Italian, he heard his mistress saying in a low voice to Vitagliani: "But he will kill me!"

The sculptor was utterly confounded by this strange scene. He regained his senses. At first he stood motionless; then he found his voice, sat down next to his mistress, and assured her of his respect. He was able to divert his passion by addressing the most high-minded phrases to this woman; and in depicting his love, he used all the resources of that magical eloquence, that inspired intermediary which women rarely refuse to believe. When the guests were surprised by the first gleams of morning light, a woman suggested they go to Frascati. Everyone enthusiastically fell in with the idea of spending the day at the Villa Ludovisi. Vitagliani went down to hire some carriages. Sarrasine had the pleasure of leading La Zambinella to a phaeton. Once outside Rome, the gaiety which had been momentarily repressed by each person's battle with sleepiness suddenly revived. Men and women alike seemed used to this strange life, these ceaseless pleasures, this artist's impulsiveness which turns life into a perpetual party at which one laughed unreservedly. The sculptor's companion was the only one who seemed downcast.

"Are you ill?" Sarrasine asked her. "Would you rather go home?"

"I'm not strong enough to stand all these excesses," she replied. "I must be very careful; but with you I feel so well! Had it not been for you, I would never have stayed for supper; a sleepless night, and I lose whatever bloom I have."

"You are so delicate," Sarrasine said, looking at the charming creature's pretty face.

"Orgies ruin the voice."

"Now that we're alone," the artist cried, "and you no longer need fear the outbursts of my passion, tell me that you love me."

"Why?" she replied. "What would be the use? I seemed pretty to you. But you are French and your feelings will pass. Ah, you would not love me as I long to be loved."

"How can you say that?"

"Not to satisfy any vulgar passion; purely. I abhor men perhaps even more than I hate women. I need to seek refuge in friendship. For me, the world is a desert. I am an accursed creature, condemned to understand happiness, to feel it, to desire it, and, like many others, forced to see it flee from me continually. Remember, sir, that I will not have deceived you. I forbid you to love me. I can be your devoted friend, for I admire your strength and your character. I need a brother, a protector. Be all that for me, but no more."

"Not love you!" Sarrasine cried. "But, my dearest angel, you are my life, my happiness!"

"If I were to say one word, you would repulse me with horror."

"Coquette! Nothing can frighten me. Tell me you will cost my future, that I will die in two months, that I will be damned merely for having kissed you."

He kissed her, despite La Zambinella's efforts to resist this passionate embrace.

"Tell me you are a devil, that you want my money, my name, all my fame! Do you want me to give up being a sculptor? Tell me."

"And if I were not a woman?" La Zambinella asked in a soft, silvery voice.

"What a joke!" Sarrasine cried. "Do you think you can deceive an artist's eye? Haven't I spent ten days devouring, scrutinizing, admiring your perfection? Only a woman could have this round, soft arm, these elegant curves. Oh, you want compliments."

She smiled at him sadly, and raising her eyes heavenward, she murmured: "Fatal beauty!"

At that moment her gaze had an indescribable expression of horror, so powerful and vivid that Sarrasine shuddered.

"Frenchman," she went on, "forget this moment of madness forever. I respect you, but as for love, do not ask it of me; that feeling is smothered in my heart. I have no heart!" she cried, weeping. "The stage where you saw me, that applause, that music, that fame I am condemned to, such is my life, I have no other. In a few hours you will not see me in the same way, the woman you love will be dead."

The sculptor made no reply. He was overcome with a dumb rage which oppressed his heart. He could only gaze with inflamed, burning eyes at this extraordinary woman. La Zambinella's weak voice, her manner, her movements and gestures marked with sorrow, melancholy, and discouragement, awakened all the wealth of passion in his soul. Each word was a goad. At that moment they reached Frascati. As the artist offered his mistress his arm to assist her in alighting, he felt her shiver.

"What is wrong? You would kill me," he cried, seeing her grow pale, "if I were even an innocent cause of your slightest unhappiness."

"A snake," she said, pointing to a grass snake which was sliding along a ditch. "I am afraid of those horrid creatures." Sarrasine crushed the snake's head with his heel.

"How can you be so brave?" La Zambinella continued, looking with visible horror at the dead reptile.

"Ah," the artist replied, smiling, "now do you dare deny you are a woman?"

They rejoined their companions and strolled through the woods of the Villa Ludovisi, which in those days belonged to Cardinal Cicognara. That morning fled too quickly for the enamored sculptor, but it was filled with a host of incidents which revealed to him the coquetry, the weakness and the delicacy of this soft and enervated being. This was woman herself, with her sudden fears, her irrational whims, her instinctive worries, her impetuous boldness, her fussings, and her delicious sensibility. It happened that as they were wandering in the open countryside, the little group of merry singers saw in the distance some heavily armed men whose manner of dress was far from reassuring. Someone said, "They must be highwaymen," and everyone quickened his pace toward the refuge of the Cardinal's grounds. At this critical moment, Sarrasine saw from La Zambinella's pallor that she no longer had the strength to walk; he took her up in his arms and carried her for a while, running. When he came to a nearby arbor, he put her down.

"Explain to me," he said, "how this extreme weakness, which I would find hideous in any other woman, which would displease me and whose slightest indication would be almost enough to choke my love, pleases and charms me in you? Ah, how I love you," he went on. "All your faults, your terrors, your resentments, add an indefinable grace to your soul. I think I would detest a strong woman, a Sappho, a courageous creature, full of energy and passion. Oh, soft, frail creature, how could you be otherwise? That angelic voice, that delicate voice, would be an anomaly coming from any body but yours."

"I cannot give you any hope," she said. "Stop speaking to me in this way, because they will make a fool of you. I cannot stop you from coming to the theater; but if you love me or if you are wise, you will come there no more. Listen, monsieur," she said in a low voice.

"Oh, be still," the impassioned artist said. "Obstacles make my love more ardent."

La Zambinella's graceful and modest attitude did not change, but she fell silent as though a terrible thought had revealed some misfortune to her. When it came time to return to Rome, she got into the four-seated coach, ordering the sculptor with imperious cruelty to return to Rome alone in the carriage. During the journey, Sarrasine resolved to kidnap La Zambinella. He spent the entire day making plans, each more outrageous than the other. At nightfall, as he was going out to inquire where his mistress's palazzo was located, he met one of his friends on the threshold.

"My dear fellow," he said, "our ambassador has asked me to invite you to his house tonight. He is giving a magnificent concert, and when I tell you that Zambinella will be there . . ."

"Zambinella," cried Sarrasine, intoxicated by the name. "I'm mad about her!"

"You're like everyone else," his friend replied.

"If you are my friends, you, Vien, Lauterbourg, and Allegrain, will you help me do something after the party?" Sarrasine asked.

"It's not some cardinal to be killed? Not . . . ?"

"No, no," Sarrasine said. "I'm not asking you to do anything an honest person couldn't do."

In a short time, the sculptor had arranged everything for the success of his undertaking. He was one of the last to arrive at the ambassador's, but he had come in a traveling carriage drawn by powerful horses and driven by one of the most enterprising *vetturini* of Rome. The ambassador's palazzo was crowded; not without some difficulty, the sculptor, who was a stranger to everyone present, made his way to the salon where Zambinella was singing at that very moment.

"Is it out of consideration for the cardinals, bishops, and abbés present," Sarrasine asked, "that *she* is dressed like a man, that she is wearing a snood, kinky hair, and a sword?"

"She? What she?" asked the old nobleman to whom Sarrasine had been speaking. "La Zambinella." "La Zambinella!" the Roman prince replied. "Are you joking? Where are you from? Has there ever been a woman on the Roman stage? And don't you know about the creatures who sing female roles in the Papal States? I am the one, monsieur, who gave Zambinella his voice. I paid for everything that scamp ever had, even his singing teacher. Well, he has so little gratitude for the service I rendered him that he has never consented to set foot in my house. And yet, if he makes a fortune, he will owe it all to me."

Prince Chigi may well have gone on talking for some time; Sarrasine was not listening to him. A horrid truth had crept into his soul. It was as though he had been struck by lightning. He stood motionless, his eyes fixed on the false singer. His fiery gaze exerted a sort of magnetic influence on Zambinella, for the *musico* finally turned to look at Sarrasine, and at that moment his heavenly voice faltered. He trembled! An involuntary murmur escaping from the audience he had kept hanging on his lips completed his discomfiture; he sat down and cut short his aria. Cardinal Cicognara, who had glanced out of the corner of his eye to see what had attracted his protégé's attention, then saw the Frenchman: he leaned over to one of his ecclesiastical aides-de-camp and appeared to be asking the sculptor's name.

Having obtained the answer he sought, he regarded the artist with great attention and gave an order to an abbé, who quickly disappeared.

During this time, Zambinella, having recovered himself, once more began the piece he had so capriciously interrupted; but he sang it badly, and despite all the requests made to him, he refused to sing anything else. This was the first time he displayed the capricious tyranny for which he would later be as celebrated as for his talent and his vast fortune, due, as they said, no less to his voice than to his beauty.

"It is a woman," Sarrasine said, believing himself alone. "There is some hidden intrigue here. Cardinal Cicognara is deceiving the Pope and the whole city of Rome!"

The sculptor thereupon left the salon, gathered his friends together, and posted them out of sight in the courtyard of the palazzo. When Zambinella was confident that Sarrasine had departed, he appeared to regain his composure. Around midnight, having wandered through the rooms like a man seeking some enemy, the *musico* departed. As soon as he crossed the threshold of the palazzo, he was adroitly seized by men who gagged him with a handkerchief and drew him into the carriage Sarrasine had hired. Frozen with horror, Zambinella remained in a corner, not daring to move. He saw before him the terrible face of the artist, who was silent as death.

The journey was brief. Carried in Sarrasine's arms, Zambinella soon found himself in a dark, empty studio. Half dead, the singer remained in a chair, without daring to examine the statue of a woman in which he recognized his own features. He made no attempt to speak, but his teeth chattered. Sarrasine paced up and down the room. Suddenly he stopped in front of Zambinella.

"Tell me the truth," he pleaded in a low, altered voice. "You are a woman? Cardinal Cicognara . . ."

Zambinella fell to his knees and in reply lowered his head.

"Ah, you are a woman," the artist cried in a delirium, "for even a . . ." He broke off. "No," he continued, "he would not be so cowardly."

"Ah, do not kill me," cried Zambinella, bursting into tears. "I only agreed to trick you to please my friends, who wanted to laugh."

"Laugh!" the sculptor replied in an infernal tone. "Laugh! Laugh! You dared play with a man's feelings?"

"Oh, have mercy!" Zambinella replied.

"I ought to kill you," Sarrasine cried, drawing his sword with a violent gesture. "However," he went on, in cold disdain, "were I to scour your body with this blade, would I find there one feeling to stifle, one vengeance to satisfy? You are nothing. If you were a man or a woman, I would kill you, but . . ."

Sarrasine made a gesture of disgust, which forced him to turn away, whereupon he saw the statue.

"And it's an illusion," he cried. Then, turning to Zambinella: "A woman's heart was a refuge for me, a home. Have you any sisters who resemble you? Then die! But no, you shall live. Isn't leaving you alive condemning you to something worse than death? It is neither my blood nor my existence that I regret, but the future and my heart's fortune. Your feeble hand has destroyed my happiness. What hope can I strip from you for all those you have blighted? You have dragged me down to your level. *To love, to be loved!* are henceforth meaningless words for me, as they are for you. I shall forever think of this imaginary woman when I see a real woman." He indicated the statue with a gesture of despair. "I shall always have the memory of a celestial harpy who thrusts its talons into all my manly feelings, and who will stamp all other women with a seal of imperfection! Monster! You who can give life to nothing. For me, you have wiped women from the earth."

Sarrasine sat down before the terrified singer. Two huge tears welled from his dry eyes, rolled down his manly cheeks, and fell to the ground: two tears of rage, two bitter and burning tears.

"No more love! I am dead to all pleasure, to every human emotion."

So saying, he seized a hammer and hurled it at the statue with such extraordinary force that he missed it. He thought he had destroyed this monument to his folly, and then took up his sword and brandished it to kill the singer. Zambinella uttered piercing screams. At that moment, three men entered, and at once the sculptor fell, stabbed by three stiletto thrusts.

"On behalf of Cardinal Cicognara," one of them said.

"It is a good deed worthy of a Christian," replied the Frenchman as he died. These sinister messengers informed Zambinella of the concern of his protector, who was waiting at the door in a closed carriage, to take him away as soon as he had been rescued.

~ ~ ~

"But," Mme de Rochefide asked me, "what connection is there between this story and the little old man we saw at the Lantys?"

"Madame, Cardinal Cicognara took possession of Zambinella's statue and had it executed in marble; today it is in the Albani Museum. There, in 1791, the Lanty family found it and asked Vien to copy it. The portrait in which you saw Zambinella at twenty, a second after having seen him at one hundred, later served for Girodet's *Endymion;* you will have recognized its type in the Adonis."

"But this Zambinella—he or she?"

"He, madame, is none other than Marianina's great-uncle. Now you can readily see what interest Mme de Lanty has in hiding the source of a fortune which comes from—"

"Enough!" she said, gesturing to me imperiously. We sat for a moment plunged in the deepest silence.

"Well?" I said to her.

"Ah," she exclaimed, standing and pacing up and down the room. She looked at me and spoke in an altered voice. "You have given me a disgust for life and for passions that will last a long time. Excepting for monsters, don't all human feelings come down to the same thing, to horrible disappointments? Mothers, our children kill us either by their bad behavior or by their lack of affection. Wives, we are deceived. Mistresses, we are forsaken, abandoned. Does friendship even exist? I would become a nun tomorrow did I not know that I can remain unmoved as a rock amid the storms of life. If the Christian's future is also an illusion, at least it is not destroyed until after death. Leave me."

"Ah," I said, "you know how to punish."

"Am I wrong?"

"Yes," I replied, with a kind of courage. "In telling this story, which is fairly well known in Italy, I have been able to give you a fine example of the progress made by civilization today. They no longer create these unfortunate creatures."

"Paris is a very hospitable place," she said. "It accepts everything, shameful fortunes and bloodstained fortunes. Crime and infamy can find asylum here; only virtue has no altars here. Yes, pure souls have their home in heaven! No one will have known me. I am proud of that!"

And the Marquise remained pensive.

# ∾ Gustave Flaubert ∾

## Letter to Louis Bouilhet

TRANSLATED BY FRANCIS STEEGMULLER

*Cairo, 15 January 1850*

At noon today came your fine long letter that I was so hoping for. It moved me to the very guts and made a cry-baby of me. How constantly I think of you, you precious bastard! How many times a day I evoke you and miss you! . . . When next we see each other many days will have passed—I mean many things will have happened. Shall we still be the same, with nothing changed in the communion of our beings? I have too much pride in both of us not to think so. Carry on with your disgusting and sublime way of life, and then we'll see about beating those drums that we've long been keeping so tight. I am looking everywhere for something special to bring you. So far I have found nothing, except that in Memphis I cut two or three branches of palm for you to make into canes for yourself. I'm greatly giving myself over to the study of perfumes and to the composition of ointments. Yesterday I ate half a pastille so heating that for three hours I thought my tongue was on fire. I haunt the Turkish baths. . . . Come, let's be calm: no one incapable of restraint was ever a writer—at this mo-

GUSTAVE FLAUBERT, *like many artists, was sent to study law, but in romantic scorn of bourgeois society, he professed himself "disgusted with life" and "retired" to Croisset, near Rouen, to devote himself to writing. But alas, bourgeois society scorned him as well:* The Temptation of St. Anthony, Madame Bovary *(published in the* Revue de Paris, *1856–57),* Salammbô, *and* Sentimental Education *all caused trouble for the author. He died in 1880.*

ment I'm bursting—I'd like to let off steam and use you as a punching-bag—everything's mixed up and jostling everything else in my sick brain—let's try for some order. . . .

*De Saltatoribus*

We have not yet seen any dancing girls; they are all in exile in Upper Egypt. Good brothels no longer exist in Cairo, either. The party we were to have had on the Nile the last time I wrote you fell through—no loss there. But we have seen male dancers. Oh! Oh! Oh!

That was us, calling you. I was indignant and very sad that you were not here. Three or four musicians playing curious instruments (we'll bring some home) took up their positions at the end of the hotel dining room while one gentleman was still eating his lunch and the rest of us were sitting on the divan smoking our pipes. As dancers, imagine two rascals, quite ugly, but charming in their corruption, in their obscene leerings and the femininity of their movements, dressed as women, their eyes painted with antimony. For costume, they had wide trousers. . . . From time to time, during the dance, the impresario, or pimp, who brought them plays around them, kissing them on the belly, the arse, and the small of the back, and making obscene remarks in an effort to put additional spice into a thing that is already quite clear in itself. It is too beautiful to be exciting. I doubt whether we shall find the women as good as the men; the ugliness of the latter adds greatly to the thing as art. I had a headache for the rest of the day, and I had to go and pee two or three times during the performance—a nervous reaction that I attribute particularly to the music.— I'll have this marvelous Hasan el-Belbeissi come again. He'll dance the Bee for me, in particular. Done by such a bardash as he, it can scarcely be a thing for babes.

Speaking of bardashes, this is what I know about them. Here it is quite accepted. One admits one's sodomy, and it is spoken of at table in the hotel. Sometimes you do a bit of denying, and then everybody teases you and you end up confessing. Traveling as we are for educational purposes, and charged with a mission by the government, we have considered it our duty to indulge in this form of ejaculation. So far the occasion has not presented itself. We continue to seek it, however. It's at the baths that such things take place. You reserve the bath for yourself (five francs including masseurs, pipe, coffee, sheet and towel) and you skewer your lad in one of the rooms. Be informed, furthermore, that all the bath-boys are bardashes. The final masseurs, the ones who come to rub you when all the rest is done, are usually quite nice young boys. We had our eye on one in an establishment very near our hotel. I reserved the bath exclusively for myself. I went, and the rascal was away that day! I was alone in the hot room, watching the daylight fade through the great circles of glass in the dome. Hot water was flowing everywhere; stretched out indolently I thought of a quantity of things as my pores tranquilly dilated. It is very voluptuous and sweetly melancholy to take a bath like that quite alone, lost in those dim rooms where the slightest noise resounds like a cannon shot, while the naked *kellaas* call out to one another as they massage you, turning you over like embalmers preparing you for the tomb. That day (the day before yesterday, Monday) my *kellaa* was rubbing me gently, and when he came to the noble parts he lifted up my *boules d'amour* to clean them, then continuing to rub my chest with his left hand he began to pull with his right on my prick, and as he drew it up and down he leaned over my shoulder and said, *"bak-sheesh, baksheesh."* He was a man in his fifties, ignoble, disgusting— imagine the effect, and the word *"baksheesh, baksheesh."* I pushed him away a little, saying, *"làh, làh"* ("No, no")—he thought I was angry and took on a craven look—then I gave him a few pats on the shoulder, saying, *"làh, làh"* again but more gently—he smiled a smile that meant, "You're not fooling me—you like it as much as anybody, but today you've decided against it for some reason." As for me, I laughed aloud like a dirty old man, and the shadowy vault of the bath echoed with the sound.

. . . A week ago I saw a monkey in the street jump on a donkey and try to jack him off—the donkey brayed and kicked, the monkey's owner shouted, the monkey itself squealed—apart from two or three children who laughed and me who found it very funny, no one paid any attention. When I described this to M. Belin, the secretary at the consulate, he told me of having seen an ostrich trying to violate a donkey. Max had himself jacked off the other day in a deserted section among some ruins and said it was very good.

Enough lubricities.

By means of *baksheesh* as always (*baksheesh* and the big stick are the essence of the Arab: you hear nothing else spoken of and see nothing else) we have been initiated into the fraternity of the *psylli,* or snake-charmers. We have had snakes put around our necks, around our hands, incantations have been recited over our heads, and our initiators have breathed into our mouths, all but inserting their tongues. It was great fun—the men who engage in such sinful enterprises practice their vile arts, as M. de Voltaire puts it, with singular competency.

. . . We speak with priests of all the religions. The people here sometimes assume really beautiful poses and attitudes. We have translations of songs, stories, and traditions made for us—everything that is most folkloric and oriental. We employ scholars—literally. We look quite dashing and are quite insolent and permit ourselves great freedom of language—our hotel-keeper thinks we sometimes go a little far.

One of these days we're going to consult fortune-tellers—all part of our quest for the old ways of life here.

Dear fellow how I'd love to hug you—I'll be glad when I see your face again. . . . Go and see my mother often—help her—write to her when she is away—the poor woman needs it. You'll be performing an act of the highest evangelism, and—psychologically—you'll witness the shy, gradual expansion of a fine and upright nature. Ah, you old bardash—if it weren't for her and for you I'd scarcely give a thought to home. At night when you are in your room and the lines don't come, and you're thinking of me, and bored, with your elbows on the table, take a sheet of paper and write me everything—I devoured your letter and have re-read it more than once. At this moment I have a vision of you in your shirt before the fire, feeling too warm, and contemplating your prick. By the way, write *cul* with an *l*—not *cu:* that shocked me, . . .

# ∽ *Fyodor Sologub* ∽

# *The Herald of the Beast*

TRANSLATED BY STEPHEN GRAHAM

## I

It was quiet and peaceful, neither gladness nor sadness was in the room. The electric light was on. The walls seemed solid, firm as adamant, indestructible. The window was hidden behind heavy dark-green curtains, and the big door opposite the window was locked and bolted, as was also the little one in the wall at the side. But on the other side of the doors all was dark and empty, in the wide corridor and in the melancholy hall where beautiful palms yearned for their southern homes.

Gurof was lying on the green divan. In his hands was a book. He read it, but often stopped short in his reading. He thought, mused, dreamed— and always about the same thing, always about *them.*

*They* were near him. He had long since noticed that. They had hid themselves. *They* were inescapably near. They rustled round about, almost inaudibly, but for a long time did not show themselves to his eyes. Gurof had seen the first one a few days before; he wakened tired, miserable, pallid, and as he lazily turned on the electric light so as to expel the wild gloom of the winter morning, he suddenly saw one of them.

A wee gray one, agile and furtive, pattered over his pillow, lisped something, and hid himself.

*Fyodor Sologub was a "decadent" Russian poet, dramatist, and fiction writer. His most famous work is* The Petty Demon *(1907), a novel with a "drag" episode reminiscent of the one in Cellini's* Autobiography.

And afterwards, morning and evening, they ran about Gurof, grey, agile, furtive.

And today he had expected them.

Now and then his head ached slightly. Now and then he was seized by cold fits and by waves of heat. Then from a corner ran out Fever, long and slender, with ugly yellow face and dry bony hands, lay down beside him, embraced him, kissed his face and smiled. And the rapid kisses of the caressing and subtle Fever and the soft aching movements in his head were pleasant to him.

Weakness poured itself into all his limbs. And tiredness spread over them. But it was pleasant. The people he knew in the world became remote, uninteresting, entirely superfluous. He felt he would like to remain here with *them*.

Gurof had been indoors for several days. He had locked himself up in the house. He permitted no one to see him. Sat by himself. Thought of them. Awaited them.

## II

Strangely and unexpectedly the languor of sweet waiting was broken. There was a loud knocking at an outer door and then the sound of even, unhurrying footsteps in the hall.

As Gurof turned his face to the door, a blast of cold air swept in, and he saw, as he shivered, a boy of a wild and strange appearance. He was in a linen cloak but showed half his body naked, and his arms were bare. His body was brown, all sunburnt. His curly hair was black and bright; black also were his eyes and sparkling. A wonderfully correct and beautiful face. But of a beauty terrible to look upon. Not a kind face, not an evil one.

Gurof was not astonished at the boy's coming. Some dominant idea had possession of his mind. And he heard how *they* crept out of sight and hid themselves.

And the boy said:

"Aristomakh! Have you forgotten your promise? Do noble people act thus? You fled from me when I was in mortal danger. You promised me something, which it seems you did not wish to fulfil. Such a long time I've been looking for you! And behold, I find you living in festivity, drowning in luxury."

Gurof looked distrustfully at the half-naked beautiful boy, and a confused remembrance awakened in his soul. Something long since gratefully buried in oblivion rose up with indistinct feature and, asking for remembrance, tired his memory. The enigma could not be guessed, though it seemed near and familiar.

And where were the unwavering walls? Something was happening round about him, some change was taking place, but Gurof was so obsessed by the struggle with his ancient memory that he failed to take stock of those changes. He said to the wonderful boy:

"Dear boy, tell me clearly and simply without unnecessary reproaches what it was I promised you and when it was I left you in mortal danger. I swear to you by all that is holy my honour would never have allowed me to commit the ignoble act with which for some reason you charge me."

The boy nodded, and then in a loud, melodious voice gave answer:

"Aristomakh! You always were clever at verbal exercises, and indeed as clever in actions demanding daring and caution. If I said that you left me in a moment of mortal danger it is not a reproach. And I don't understand why you speak of your honor. The thing purposed by us was difficult and dangerous, but why do you quibble about it? Who is here that you think you can deceive by pretending ignorance of what happened this morning before sunrise and of the promise you had given me?"

The electric light became dim. The ceiling seemed dark and high. There was the scent of a herb in the room—but what herb? Its forgotten name had one time sounded sweetly on his ear. On the wings of the scent a cool air seemed wafted into the room. Gurof stood up and cried out:

"What thing did we purpose? I deny nothing, dear boy, but I simply don't know of what you are speaking. I don't remember."

It seemed to Gurof that the child was at one and the same time both looking at him and not looking at him. Though the boy's eyes were directed towards him they seemed to be staring at some other, unearthly person, whose body coincided with his but who was not he.

It grew dark around him and the air became fresher and cooler. A gladness leapt in his soul and a lightness as of elementary existence. The room disappeared from his remembrance. Above he saw the stars glittering in the black sky. Once more the boy addressed him:

"We ought to have killed the Beast. I shall remind you of that when under the myriad eyes of the all-seeing sky you are again confused with fear. And how not have fear! The thing that we purposed was great and dreadful, and it would have given a glory to our names in far posterity."

In the night quietude he heard the murmuring and gentle tinkling of a brook. He could not see the brook, but he felt that it was deliciously and tantalisingly near. They were standing in the shadow of spreading trees, and the conversation went on. Gurof asked:

"Why do you say that I left you in a moment of mortal danger? Am I the sort of man to take fright and run away?"

The boy laughed, and like music was his laughter. Then in sweet, melodious accents he replied:

"Aristomakh, how cleverly you pretend to have forgotten all! But I don't understand why you take the trouble to exercise such cunning, or why you contrive reproaches against yourself which I for my part should not have thought of alone. You left me in the moment of mortal danger because it was clearly necessary, and you couldn't help me otherwise than by abandoning me there. Surely you won't remain obstinate in your denial after I remind you of the words of the oracle."

Gurof suddenly remembered. It was as if a bright light had flooded into the dark abyss of the forgotten. And he cried out loudly and excitedly:

"He alone will kill the Beast!"

The boy laughed. Aristomakh turned to him with the question:

"Have you killed the Beast, Timaride?"

"With what? Even were my hands strong enough, I am not he who has the power to kill the Beast with a blow of the fist. We were incautious, Aristomakh, and without weapons. We were playing on the sands and the Beast fell upon us suddenly and struck me with his heavy paw. My fate was to give my life as a sweet sacrifice to glory and in high exploit, but to you it remained to finish the work. And whilst the Beast tore my helpless body you might have run, swift-footed Aristomakh, might have gained your spear, and you might have struck the Beast whilst he was drunk with my blood. But the Beast did not accept my sacrifice; I lay before him motionless and looked up at his blood-weltering eyes, and he kept me pinned to the ground by the heavy paw on my shoulder. He breathed hotly and unevenly and he growled softly, but he did not kill me. He simply licked over my face with his broad warm tongue and went away."

"Where is he now?" asked Aristomakh.

The night air felt moist and calm, and through it came the musical answer of Timaride:

"I rose when he had left me, but he was attracted by the scent of my blood and followed after me. I don't know why he has set upon me again.

Still I am glad that he follows, for so I bring him to you. Get the weapon that you so cleverly hid, and kill the Beast, and I in my turn will run away and leave you in the moment of mortal danger, face to face with the enraged Beast. Good luck, Aristomakh!"

And saying that, Timaride ran away, his white cloak gleaming but a minute in the darkness. And just as he disappeared there broke out the horrible roaring of the Beast and the thud of his heavy paws on the ground. Thrusting to right and left the foliage of the bushes, there appeared in the darkness the immense monstrous head of the Beast, and his large eyes gleamed like luminous velvet. The Beast ceased to roar, and with his eyes fixed on Aristomakh approached him stealthily and silently.

Terror filled the heart of Aristomakh.

"Where is the spear?" he whispered, and immediately he turned to flee. But with a heavy bound the Beast started after him, roaring and bellowing, and pulled him down. And when the Beast held him, a great yell broke through the stillness of the night. Then Aristomakh moaned out the ancient and horrible words of the curse of the walls.

And up rose the walls about him. . . .

### III

The walls of the room stood firm, unwavering, and the barely reflected electric light seemed to die upon them. All the rest of the room was customary and usual.

Once more Fever came and kissed him with dry yellow lips and caressed him with wizened bony hands. The same tedious little book with little white pages lay on the table, and in the green divan lay Gurof, and Fever embraced him, scattering rapid kisses with hurrying lips. And once more the grey ones rustled and chattered.

Gurof raised his head a little as if with great effort and said hollowly: "The curse of the walls."

What was he talking about? What curse? What was the curse? What were the words of it? Were there any?

The little ones, grey and agile, danced about the book and turned with their tails the pallid pages, and with little squeaks and whimpers answered him:

"Our walls are strong. We live in the walls. No fear troubles us inside the walls."

Among them was a singular-looking one, not at all like the rest. He was quite black and wore dress of mingled smoke and flame. From his eyes came little lightnings. Suddenly he detached himself from the others and stood before Gurof, who cried out:

"Who are you? What do you want?"

The black guest replied:

"I . . . am the Herald of the Beast. On the shore of the forest stream you left long since the mangled body of Timaride. The Beast has sated himself with the fine blood of your friend—he has devoured the flesh which should have tasted earthly happiness; the wonderful human form has been destroyed, and that in it which was more than human has perished, all to give a moment's satisfaction to the ever insatiable Beast. The blood, the marvellous blood, godly wine of joy, the wine of more than human blessing—where is it now? Alas! the eternally thirsting Beast has been made drunk for a moment by it. You have left the mangled body of Timaride by the side of the forest stream, have forgotten the promise given to your splendid friend, and the word of the ancient oracle has not driven fear from your heart. Think you, then, that saving yourself you can escape the Beast and that he will not find you?"

The voice and the words were stern. The grey ones had stopped in their dancing to listen. Gurof said:

"What is the Beast to me? I have fixed my walls about me forever, and the Beast will not find a way to me in my fortress."

At that the grey ones rejoiced and scampered round the room anew, but the Herald of the Beast cried out once more, and sharp and stern were his accents:

"Do you not see that I am here. I am here because I have found you. I am here because the curse of the walls has lost power. I am here because Timaride is waiting and tirelessly questioning. Do you not hear the gentle laughter of the brave and trusting child? Do you not hear the roaring of the Beast?"

From beyond the wall broke out the terrible roaring of the Beast.

"But the walls are firm for ever by the spell I cast, my fortress cannot be destroyed," cried Gurof.

And the Black One answered, imperiously:

"I tell thee, man, the curse of the walls is dead. But if you don't believe, but still think you can save yourself, pronounce the curse again."

Gurof shuddered. He indeed believed that the curse was dead, and all that was around him whispered to him the terrible news. The Herald of the Beast had pronounced the fearful truth. Gurof's head ached, and he felt weary of the hot kisses that clinging, caressing Fever still gave him. The words of the sentence seemed to strain his consciousness, and the Herald of the Beast as he stood before him was magnified until he obscured the light and stood like a great shadow over him, and his eyes glowed like fires.

Suddenly the black cloak fell from the shoulders of the visitor, and Gurof recognised him—it was the child Timaride.

"Are you going to kill the Beast?" asked Timaride in a high-sounding voice. "I have brought him to you. The malicious gift of godhead will avail you no longer, for the curse is dead. It availed you once, making as nothing my sacrifice and hiding from your eyes the glory of your exploit. But today the tune is changed, dead is the curse; get your sword quickly and kill the Beast. I was only a child; now I have become the Herald of the Beast. I have fed the Beast with my blood but he thirsts anew. To you I have brought him, and do you fulfil your promise and kill him. Or die."

He vanished.

The walls shuddered at the dreadful roaring. The room filled with airs that were cold and damp.

The wall directly opposite the place where Gurof lay collapsed, and there entered the ferocious, immense, and monstrous Beast. With fearful bellowing he crept up to Gurof and struck him on the chest with his paw. The merciless claws went right into his heart. An awful pain shattered his body. And looking at him with gleaming bloody eyes, the Beast crouched over Gurof, grinding his bones in his teeth and devouring his yet-beating heart.

FROM

# *Young Törless*

At a quarter to eleven Törless saw Beineberg and Reiting slip out of their beds, and he also got up and began dressing.

"Ssh! I say, wait, can't you? Somebody'll notice if the three of us all go out together."

Törless got back under the bed-clothes.

A little while later they all met in the passage, and with their usual caution they went on upstairs to the attics.

"Where's Basini?" Törless asked.

"He's coming up the other way. Reiting gave him the key."

They went all the way in darkness. Only when they reached the top, outside the big iron door, did Beineberg light his little hurricane-lamp.

The lock was stiff. It was rusty from years of disuse and would not answer to the skeleton key. Then at last it gave, with a loud snap. The heavy door scraped back reluctantly on its rusty hinges, yielding only inch by inch.

From inside the attic came a breath of warm, stale air, like that in small hothouses.

Beineberg shut the door after them.

They went down the little wooden staircase and then squatted on the floor beside a huge roof-beam.

---

Die Verwirrungen des Zöglings Törless (The Confusions of Pupil Törless), *published in English simply as* Young Törless, *was* ROBERT MUSIL'S *first novel; his immense second was* A Man Without Qualities.

On one side of them were some large water-tubs for use in case of fire. It was obvious that the water in them had not been changed for a very long time; it had a sweet, sickly smell.

The whole place was oppressive, with the hot, bad air under the roof and the criss-cross pattern of the huge beams and rafters, some of them vanishing into the darkness overhead, some of them reaching down to the floor, forming a ghostly network.

Beineberg shaded his lamp, and there they sat quite still in the dark, not speaking a word—for long, long minutes.

Then the door in the darkness at the other end of the attic creaked, faintly, hesitantly. It was a sound to make one's heart leap into one's mouth—the first sound of the approaching prey.

Then came some unsure footsteps, a foot stumbling against wood, a dull sound as of a falling body . . . Silence . . . Then again hesitant footsteps . . . A pause . . . A faint voice asking: "Reiting?"

Now Beineberg removed the shade from his lamp, throwing a broad ray of light in the direction from which the voice had come.

Several immense wooden beams loomed up, casting deep shadows. Apart from that, there was nothing to be seen but the cone of light with dust whirling in it.

The footsteps grew steadier and came closer.

Then—and this time quite near—a foot banged against wood again, and the next moment—framed in the wide base of the cone of light—Basini's face appeared, ash-grey in that uncertain illumination.

~ ~ ~

Basini was smiling—sweetly, cloyingly. It was like the fixed smile of a portrait, hanging above them there in the frame of light.

Törless sat still, pressing himself tightly against the woodwork; he felt his eyelids twitching.

Now Beineberg recited the list of Basini's infamies—monotonously, in a hoarse voice.

Then came the question: "So you're not ashamed at all?" At that Basini looked at Reiting, and his glance seemed to say: "Now I think it's time for you to help me." And at that moment Reiting hit him in the face so that he staggered back, tripped over a beam, and fell. Beineberg and Reiting leapt upon him.

The lamp had been kicked sideways, and now its light flowed senselessly, idly, past Törless's feet, across the floor. . . .

From the sounds in the darkness Törless could tell that they were pulling Basini's clothes off and then that they were whipping him with something thin and pliant. Evidently they had had everything prepared. He heard Basini's whimpering and half-stifled cries of pain as he went on pleading for mercy; and then finally he heard nothing but a groaning, a suppressed howling, and at the same time Beineberg cursing in a low voice and his heavy, excited breathing.

Törless had not stirred from where he sat. Right at the beginning, indeed, he had been seized with a savage desire to leap up too and join in the beating; but his feeling that he would come too late and only be one too many had held him back. His limbs were encased in paralysing rigidity, as though in the grip of some great hand.

In apparent indifference he sat staring at the floor. He did not strain his ears to distinguish what the various sounds meant, and his heart beat no faster than usual. His eyes followed the light that spread out in a pool at his feet. Grains of dust gleamed in it, and one ugly little cobweb. And the light seeped further, into the darkness under the beams, and petered out in dusty, murky gloom.

Törless could have sat there like that for an hour without noticing the passing of time. He was thinking of nothing, and yet he was inwardly very much preoccupied. At the same time he was observing himself. And it was like gazing into a void and there seeing himself as if out of the corner of his eye, in a vague, shapeless glimmer. And then out of this vagueness—as though coming round the corner of his mind—slowly, but ever more distinctly, a desire advanced into clear consciousness.

Something made Törless smile at this. Then once again the desire came more strongly, trying to draw him from his squatting position down onto his knees, onto the floor. It was an urge to press his body flat against the floorboards; and even now he could feel how his eyes would grow larger, like a fish's eyes, and how through the flesh and bones of his body his heart would slam against the wood.

Now there was indeed a wild excitement raging in Törless, and he had to hold on tight to the beam beside him in an effort to fight off the dizziness that was trying to draw him downward.

Sweat pearled on his forehead, and he wondered anxiously what all this could mean.

Startled quite out of his former indifference, he was now straining his ears again to hear what the other three were doing in the darkness.

It had grown quiet over there. Only Basini could be heard groping for his clothes and moaning softly to himself.

An agreeable sensation went through Törless when he heard this whimpering. A tickling shudder, like thin spidery legs, ran up and down his spine, then contracted between his shoulder blades, pulling his scalp tight as though with faint claws. He was disconcerted to realise that he was in a state of sexual excitement. He thought back, and though he could not remember when this had begun, he knew it had already been there when he felt that peculiar desire to press himself against the floor. He was ashamed of it; but it was like a tremendous surge of blood going through him, numbing his thoughts.

Beineberg and Reiting came groping their way back and sat down in silence beside him. Beineberg looked at the lamp.

At this moment Törless again felt drawn downward. It was something that came from his eyes—he could feel that now—a sort of hypnotic rigidity spreading from the eyes to the brain. It was a question, indeed, it was—no, it was a desperation—oh, it was something he knew already—the wall, that garden outside the window, the low-ceilinged cottages, that childhood memory—it was all the same thing! all the same! He glanced at Beineberg. Doesn't he feel anything? he wondered. But Beineberg was bending down, about to put the lamp straight. Törless gripped his arm to stop him.

"Isn't it like an eye?" he said, pointing to the light streaming across the floor.

"Getting poetical now, are you?"

"No. But don't you yourself say there's something special about eyes? It's all in your own favourite ideas about hypnotism—how sometimes they send out a force different from anything we hear about in physics. And it's a fact you can often tell far more about someone from his eyes than from what he says. . . ."

"Well—what of it?"

"This light seems like an eye to me—looking into a strange world. It makes me feel as if I had to guess something. Only I can't. I only could gulp it down—drink it."

"Well, so you really are getting poetical."

"No, I'm perfectly serious. It simply makes me frantic. Just look at it yourself and you'll see what I mean. It makes you sort of want to wallow in the pool of it—to crawl right into that dusty corner on all fours, as if that were the way to guess it. . . ."

"My dear chap, these are idle fancies, all nonsense. That'll be enough of that sort of thing for the moment."

Beineberg now bent right down and restored the lamp to its former position. But Törless felt a sudden spiteful satisfaction. He realised that, with some extra faculty he had, he got more out of these happenings than his companions did.

He was now waiting for Basini to reappear, and with a secret shudder he noticed that his scalp was again tightening under those faint claws.

After all, he knew quite well by now that there was something in store for him, and the premonition of it was coming to him at ever shorter intervals, again and again: it was a sensation of which the others knew nothing, but which must evidently be of great importance for his future life.

Only he did not know what could be the meaning of this sexual excitement that was mingled with it. He did remember, however, that it had in fact been present each time when things began to be queer—though only to him—and to torture him because he could find no reason for the queerness.

And he resolved that at the next opportunity he would think hard about this. For the moment, he gave himself up entirely to the shudder of excitement with which he looked for Basini's reappearance.

Since Beineberg had replaced the lamp, the rays of light once again cut out a circle in the darkness, like an empty frame.

And all at once there was Basini's face again, just as it had been the first time, with the same fixed, sweet, cloying smile—as though nothing had happened in the meantime—only now, over his upper lip, mouth, and chin, slowly, drops of blood were making a red, wriggling line, like a worm.

~ ~ ~

"Sit down over there!" Reiting ordered, pointing to the great beam. When Basini had obeyed, Reiting launched out: "I suppose you were thinking you'd got yourself nicely out of the whole thing, eh? I suppose you thought I was going to help you? Well, that's just where you were wrong. What I've been doing with you was only to see exactly *how* much of a skunk you are."

Basini made a gesture of protest, at which Reiting moved as though to leap at him again. Then Basini said: "But look, for heaven's sake, there wasn't anything else I could do!"

"Shut up!" Reiting barked at him. "We're sick and tired of your excuses! We know now, once and for all, just where we stand with you, and we shall act accordingly."

There was a brief silence. Then suddenly Törless said quietly, almost amiably: "Come on, say 'I'm a thief.' "

Basini stared at him with wide, startled eyes. Beineberg laughed approvingly.

But Basini said nothing. Then Beineberg hit him in the ribs and ordered sharply: "Can't you hear? You've been told to say you're a thief. Get on and *say* it!"

Once again there was a short, scarcely perceptible pause. Then in a low voice, in a single breath, and with as little expression as possible, Basini murmured: "I'm a thief."

Beineberg and Reiting laughed delightedly, turning to Törless: "That was a good idea of yours, laddie." And then to Basini: "And now get on with it and say: I'm a beast, a pilfering, dishonest beast, *your* pilfering, dishonest, filthy beast."

And Basini said it, all in one breath, with his eyes shut.

But Törless had leaned back into the darkness again. The scene sickened him, and he was ashamed of having delivered up his idea to the others.

# ~ Sigmund Freud ~

## FROM
# Leonardo da Vinci and a Memory of His Childhood

TRANSLATED BY ALAN TYSON

There is, so far as I know, only one place in his scientific notebooks where Leonardo inserts a piece of information about his childhood. In a passage about the flight of vultures he suddenly interrupts himself to pursue a memory from very early years which had sprung to his mind:

"It seems that I was always destined to be so deeply concerned with vultures; for I recall as one of my very earliest memories that while I was in my cradle a vulture came down to me, and opened my mouth with its tail, and struck me many times with its tail against my lips."[1]

---

[1]"Questo scriver si distintamente del nibio par che sia mio destino, perchè nella mia prima recordatione della mia infantia e' mia parea che, essendo io in culla, che un nibio venissi a me e mi aprissi la bocca colla sua coda e molte volte mi percuotesse con tal coda dentro alle labbra." *(Codex Atlanticus, F.65 v., as given by Scognamiglio [1900, 22].)* *[In the German text Freud quotes Herzfeld's translation of the Italian original, and our version above is a rendering of the German. There are in fact two inaccuracies in the German: "nibio" should be "kite" not "vulture"; and "dentro," "within," is omitted. This last omission is in fact rectified by Freud himself below.*

*W. H. Auden, who believed in the psychological origins of illness, on SIGMUND FREUD, who died of cancer of the jaw: "Who'd have thought he was a liar?"*

What we have here then is a childhood memory; and certainly one of the strangest sort. It is strange on account of its content and on account of the age to which it is assigned. That a person should be able to retain a memory of his suckling period is perhaps not impossible, but it cannot by any means by regarded as certain. What, however, this memory of Leonardo's asserts—namely that a vulture opened the child's mouth with its tail—sounds so improbable, so fabulous, that another view of it, which at a single stroke puts an end to both difficulties, has more to commend it to our judgement. On this view the scene with the vulture would not be a memory of Leonardo's but a phantasy, which he formed at a later date and transposed to his childhood.[2]

This is often the way in which childhood memories originate. Quite unlike conscious memories from the time of maturity, they are not fixed at the moment of being experienced and afterwards repeated, but are only elicited at a later age when childhood is already past; in the process they are altered and falsified, and are put into the service of later trends, so that generally speaking they cannot be sharply distinguished from phantasies. Their nature is perhaps best illustrated by a comparison with the way in which the writing of history originated among the peoples of antiquity. As long as a nation was small and weak it gave no thought to the writing of its history. Men tilled the soil of their land, fought for their existence against their neighbours, and tried to gain territory from them and to acquire wealth. It was an age of heroes, not of historians. Then came another age,

---

[2][Footnote added *1919*] *In a friendly notice of this book Havelock Ellis (1910) has challenged the view put forward above. He objects that this memory of Leonardo's may very well have had a basis of reality, since children's memories often reach very much further back than is commonly supposed; the large bird in question need not of course have been a vulture. This is a point that I will gladly concede, and as a step towards lessening the difficulty I in turn will offer a suggestion—namely that his mother observed the large bird's visit to her child—an event which may easily have had the significance of an omen in her eyes—and repeatedly told him about it afterwards. As a result, I suggest, he retained the memory of his mother's story, and later, as so often happens, it became possible for him to take it for a memory of an experience of his own. However, this alteration does no damage to the force of my general account. It happens, indeed, as a general rule that the phantasies about their childhood which people construct at a late date are attached to trivial but real events of this early, and normally forgotten, period. There must thus have been some secret reason for bringing into prominence a real event of no importance and for elaborating it in the sort of way Leonardo did in his story of the bird, which he dubbed a vulture, and of its remarkable behaviour.*

an age of reflection: men felt themselves to be rich and powerful, and now felt a need to learn where they had come from and how they had developed. Historical writing, which had begun to keep a continuous record of the present, now also cast a glance back to the past, gathered traditions and legends, interpreted the traces of antiquity that survived in customs and usages, and in this way created a history of the past. It was inevitable that this early history should have been an expression of present beliefs and wishes rather than a true picture of the past; for many things had been dropped from the nation's memory, while others were distorted, and some remains of the past were given a wrong interpretation in order to fit in with contemporary ideas. Moreover, people's motive for writing history was not objective curiosity but a desire to influence their contemporaries, to encourage and inspire them, or to hold a mirror up before them. A man's conscious memory of the events of his maturity is in every way comparable to the first kind of historical writing [which was a chronicle of current events]; while the memories that he has of his childhood correspond, as far as their origins and reliability are concerned, to the history of a nation's earliest days, which was compiled later and for tendentious reasons.

If, then, Leonardo's story about the vulture that visited him in his cradle is only a phantasy from a later period, one might suppose it could hardly be worth while spending much time on it. One might be satisfied with explaining it on the basis of his inclination, of which he makes no secret, to regard his preoccupation with the flight of birds as preordained by destiny. Yet in underrating this story one would be committing just as great an injustice as if one were carelessly to reject the body of legends, traditions, and interpretations found in a nation's early history. In spite of all the distortions and misunderstandings, they still represent the reality of the past: they are what a people forms out of the experience of its early days and under the dominance of motives that were once powerful and still operate today; and if it were only possible, by a knowledge of all the forces at work, to undo these distortions, there would be no difficulty in disclosing the historical truth lying behind the legendary material. The same holds good for the childhood memories or phantasies of an individual. What someone thinks he remembers from his childhood is not a matter of indifference; as a rule the residual memories—which he himself does not understand—cloak priceless pieces of evidence about the most important features in his mental development.[3] As we now possess in the techniques of psycho-analysis excellent methods for helping us to bring this concealed material to light, we may venture to fill in the gap in Leonardo's life story by analysing his childhood phantasy. And if in doing so we remain dissatisfied with the degree of certainty which we achieve, we shall have to console ourselves with the reflection that so many other studies of this great and enigmatic man have met with no better fate.

If we examine with the eyes of a psycho-analyst Leonardo's phantasy of the vulture, it does not appear strange for long. We seem to recall having come across the same sort of thing in many places, for example in dreams; so that we may venture to translate the phantasy from its own special language into words that are generally understood. The translation is then seen to point to an erotic content. A tail, *"coda,"* is one of the most familiar symbols and substitutive expressions for the male organ, in Italian no less

---

[3][Footnote added *1919*] *Since I wrote the above words I have attempted to make similar use of an unintelligible memory dating from the childhood of another man of genius. In the account of his life that Goethe wrote when he was about sixty* (Dichtung und Wahrheit) *there is a description in the first few pages of how, with the encouragement of his neighbours, he slung first some small and then some large pieces of crockery out of the window into the street, so that they were smashed to pieces. This is, indeed, the only scene that he reports from the earliest years of childhood. The sheer inconsequentiality of its content, the way in which it corresponded with the childhood memories of other human beings who did not become particularly great, and the absence in this passage of any mention of the young brother who was born when Goethe was three and three-quarters, and who died when he was nearly ten—all this induced me to undertake an analysis of this childhood memory. (This child is in fact mentioned at a later point in the book, where Goethe dwells on the many illness of childhood.) I hoped to be able as a result to replace it by something which would be more in keeping with the context of Goethe's account and whose content would make it worthy of preservation and of the place he has given it in the history of his life. The short analysis* [*"A Childhood Recollection from* Dichtung und Wahrheit" *(1917b)*] *made it possible for the throwing-out of the crockery to be recognized as a magical act directed against a troublesome intruder; and at the place in the book where he describes the episode the intention is to triumph over the fact that a second son was not in the long run permitted to disturb Goethe's close relation with his mother. If the earliest memory of childhood, preserved in disguises such as these, should be concerned—in Goethe's case as well as in Leonardo's—with the mother, what would be so surprising in that?* [In the 1919 edition the phrase "and the absence in this passage of any mention of the young brother . . ." ran ". . . and the remarkable absence of any mention whatever of a young brother . . ." It was given its present form, and the parenthesis that follows it was added, in 1923. The alteration is explained in a footnote added in 1924 to the Goethe paper (1917b), Standard Ed., 17, 151n.]

than in other languages; the situation in the phantasy, of a vulture opening the child's mouth and beating about inside it vigorously with its tail, corresponds to the idea of an act of *fellatio,* a sexual act in which the penis is put into the mouth of the person involved. It is strange that this phantasy is so completely passive in character; moreover, it resembles certain dreams and phantasies found in women or passive homosexuals (who play the part of the woman in sexual relations).

I hope the reader will restrain himself and not allow a surge of indignation to prevent his following psycho-analysis any further because it leads to an unpardonable aspersion on the memory of a great and pure man the very first time it is applied to his case. Such indignation, it is clear, will never be able to tell us the significance of Leonardo's childhood phantasy; at the same time Leonardo has acknowledged the phantasy in the most unambiguous fashion, and we cannot abandon our expectation—or, if it sounds better, our prejudice—that a phantasy of this kind must have *some* meaning, in the same way as any other psychical creation: a dream, a vision, or a delirium. Let us rather therefore give a fair hearing for a while to the work of analysis, which indeed has not yet spoken its last word.

The inclination to take a man's sexual organ into the mouth and suck at it, which in respectable society is considered a loathsome sexual perversion, is nevertheless found with great frequency among women of today—and of earlier times as well, as ancient sculptures show—and in the state of being in love it appears completely to lose its repulsive character. Phantasies derived from this inclination are found by doctors even in women who have not become aware of the possibilities of obtaining sexual satisfaction in this way by reading Krafft-Ebing's *Psychopathia Sexualis* or from other sources of information. Women, it seems, find no difficulty in producing this kind of wishful phantasy spontaneously.[4] Further investigation informs us that this situation, which morality condemns with such severity, may be traced to an origin of the most innocent kind. It only repeats in a different form a situation in which we all once felt comfortable—when we were still in our suckling days *("essendo io in culla")* and took our mother's (or wet-nurse's) nipple into our mouth and sucked at it. The organic impression of this experience—the first source of pleasure in our life—doubtless remains indelibly printed on us; and when at a later date the child becomes familiar

---

[4]*On this point compare my "Fragment of an Analysis of a Case of Hysteria" (1905e)* [Standard Ed., *7, 51*].

with the cow's udder, whose function is that of a nipple but whose shape and position under the belly make it resemble a penis, the preliminary stage has been reached which will later enable him to form the repellent sexual phantasy.

Now we understand why Leonardo assigned the memory of his supposed experience with the vulture to his suckling period. What the phantasy conceals is merely a reminiscence of sucking—or being suckled—at his mother's breast, a scene of human beauty that he, like so many artists, undertook to depict with his brush, in the guise of the mother of God and her child. There is indeed another point which we do not yet understand and which we must not lose sight of: this reminiscence, which has the same importance for both sexes, has been transformed by the man Leonardo into a passive homosexual phantasy. For the time being we shall put aside the question of what there may be to connect homosexuality with sucking at the mother's breast, merely recalling that tradition does in fact represent Leonardo as a man with homosexual feelings. In this connection, it is irrelevant to our purpose whether the charge brought against the young Leonardo was justified or not. What decides whether we describe someone as an invert[5] is not his actual behaviour, but his emotional attitude.

Our interest is next claimed by another unintelligible feature of Leonardo's childhood phantasy. We interpret the phantasy as one of being suckled by his mother, and we find his mother replaced by—a vulture. Where does this vulture come from and how does it happen to be found in its present place?

At this point a thought comes to the mind from such a remote quarter that it would be tempting to set it aside. In the hieroglyphics of the ancient Egyptians the mother is represented by a picture of a vulture.[6] The Egyptians also worshipped a Mother Goddess, who was represented as having a vulture's head, or else several heads, of which at least one was a vulture's.[7] This goddess's name was pronounced *Mut*. Can the similarity to the sound of our word *Mutter* [mother] be merely a coincidence? There is, then, some real connection between vulture and mother—but what help is that

---

[5][*In 1910 only: "a homosexual."*]
[6]*Horapollo* (Hieroglyphica *1, 11*): "Μητέρα δὲ γράφουτες . . . γὖπα ωγραφȣυοιε" [ *"To denote a mother . . . they delineate a vulture"*].
[7]*Roscher (1894–97), Lanzone (1882).*

to us? For have we any right to expect Leonardo to know of it, seeing that the first man who succeeded in reading hieroglyphics was François Champollion (1790–1832)?

It would be interesting to enquire how it could be that the ancient Egyptians came to choose the vulture as a symbol of motherhood. Now, the religion and civilization of the Egyptians were objects of scientific curiosity even to the Greeks and the Romans: and long before we ourselves were able to read the monuments of Egypt, we had at our disposal certain pieces of information about them derived from the extant writings of classical antiquity. Some of these writings were by well-known authors, such as Strabo, Plutarch, and Ammianus Marcellinus; while others bear unfamiliar names and are uncertain in their source of origin and their date of composition, like the *Hieroglyphica* of Horapollo Nilous and the book of oriental priestly wisdom which has come down to us under the name of the god Hermes Trismegistos. We learn from these sources that the vulture was regarded as a symbol of motherhood because only female vultures were believed to exist; there were, it was thought, no males of this species.[8] A counterpart to this restriction to one sex was also known to the natural history of antiquity: in the case of the scarabaeus beetle, which the Egyptians worshipped as divine, it was thought that only males existed.[9]

How then were vultures supposed to be impregnated if all of them were female? This is a point fully explained in a passage in Horapollo.[10] At a certain time these birds pause in mid-flight, open their vagina, and are impregnated by the wind.

We have now unexpectedly reached a position where we can take something as very probable which only a short time before we had to re-

---

[8] "γῦπα δέ ἀρρενα οὐ φασι γινέσθαι ποτε, ἀλλὰ θηλείας ἁπάσας" [*"They say that no male vulture has ever existed but all are females."* Aelian, De Natura Animalium, *II, 46*]. *Quoted by von Römer (1903, 732).*

[9] *Plutarch:* "Veluti scarabaeos mares tantum esse putarunt Aegyptii sic inter vultures mares non inveniri statuerunt" [*"Just as they believed that only male scarabs existed, so the Egyptians concluded that no male vultures were to be found."* Freud has here inadvertently attributed to Plutarch a sentence which is in fact a gloss by Leemans (1835, 171) on Horapollo.]

[10] Horapollonis Niloi Hieroglyphica, *ed. Leemans (1835, 14). The words that refer to the vulture's sex run:* "μητέρα μέν ἐπειδη ἄρρεν ἐν τούτω τῷ γένει τῶν ξῴων οὐχ ὑπαρχει [*("They use the picture of a vulture to denote) a mother, because in this race of creatures there are no males."* It seems as though the wrong passage from Horapollo is quoted here. The phrase in the text implies that what we should have here is the myth of the vulture's impregnation by the wind.]

ject as absurd. It is quite possible that Leonardo was familiar with the scientific fable which was responsible for the vulture being used by the Egyptians as a pictorial representation of the idea of mother. He was a wide reader, and his interest embraced all branches of literature and learning. In the Codex Atlanticus we find a catalogue of all the books he possessed at a particular date, and in addition numerous jottings on other books that he had borrowed from friends; and if we may judge by the extracts from his notes by Richter [1883], the extent of his reading can hardly be overestimated. Early works on natural history were well represented among them in addition to contemporary books; and all of them were already in print at the time. Milan was in fact the leading city in Italy for the new art of printing.

On proceeding further, we come across a piece of information which can turn the probability that Leonardo knew the fable of the vulture into a certainty. The learned editor and commentator on Horapollo has the following note on the text already quoted above [Leemans, 1835, 172]: *"Caeterum hanc fabulam de vulturibus cupide amplexi sunt Patres Ecclesiastici, ut ita argumento ex rerum natura petito refutarent eos, qui Virginis partum negabant; itaque apud omnes fere hujus rei mentio occurrit."*[11]

So the fable of the single sex of vultures and their mode of conception remained something very far from an unimportant anecdote like the analogous tale of the scarabaeus beetle; it had been seized on by the Fathers of the Church so that they could have at their disposal a proof drawn from natural history to confront those who doubted sacred history. If vultures were described in the best accounts of antiquity as depending on the wind for impregnation, why could not the same thing have also happened on one occasion with a human female? Since the fable of the vulture could be turned to this account, "almost all" the Fathers of the Church made a practice of telling it, and thus it can hardly be doubted that Leonardo too came to know of it through its being favoured by so wide a patronage.

We can now reconstruct the origin of Leonardo's vulture phantasy. He once happened to read in one of the Fathers or in a book on natural history the statement that all vultures were females and could reproduce their kind without any assistance from a male: and at that point a memory

---

[11][ *"But this story about the vulture was eagerly taken up by the Fathers of the Church, in order to refute, by means of a proof drawn from the natural order, those who denied the Virgin Birth. The subject is therefore mentioned in almost all of them."*]

sprang to his mind, which was transformed into the phantasy we have been discussing, but which meant to signify that he also had been such a vulture-child—he had had a mother, but no father. With this memory was associated, in the only way in which impressions of so great an age can find expression, an echo of the pleasure he had had at his mother's breast. The allusion made by the Fathers of the Church to the idea of the Blessed Virgin and her child—an idea cherished by every artist—must have played its part in helping the phantasy to appear valuable and important to him. Indeed in this way he was able to identify himself with the child Christ, the comforter and saviour not of this one woman alone.

Our aim is dissecting a childhood phantasy is to separate the real memory that it contains from the later motives that modify and distort it. In Leonardo's case we believe that we now know the real content of the phantasy: the replacement of his mother by the vulture indicates that the child was aware of his father's absence and found himself alone with his mother. The fact of Leonardo's illegitimate birth is in harmony with his vulture phantasy; it was only on this account that he could compare himself to a vulture child. But the next reliable fact that we possess about his youth is that by the time he was five he had been received into his father's household. We are completely ignorant when that happened—whether it was a few months after his birth or whether it was a few weeks before the drawing-up of the land-register. It is here that the interpretation of the vulture phantasy comes in: Leonardo, it seems to tell us, spent the critical first years of his life not by the side of his father and stepmother, but with his poor, forsaken, real mother, so that he had time to feel the absence of his father. This seems a slender and yet a somewhat daring conclusion to have emerged from our psycho-analytic efforts, but its significance will increase as we continue our investigation. Its certainty is reinforced when we consider the circumstances that did in fact operate in Leonardo's childhood. In the same year that Leonardo was born, the sources tell us, his father, Ser Piero da Vinci, married Donna Albiera, a lady of good birth; it was to the childlessness of this marriage that the boy owed his reception into his father's (or rather his grandfather's) house—an event which had taken place by the time he was five years old, as the document attests. Now, it is not usual at the start of a marriage to put an illegitimate offspring into the care of the young bride, who still expects to be blessed with children of her own. Years of disappointment must surely first have elapsed before it was decided to adopt the illegitimate child—who had probably grown up an attractive young boy—as a compensation for the absence of the legitimate children that had been hoped for. It fits in best with the interpretation of the vulture phantasy if at least three years of Leonardo's life, and perhaps five, had elapsed before he could exchange the solitary person of his mother for a parental couple. And by then it was too late. In the first three or four years of life certain impressions become fixed and ways of reacting to the outside world are established which can never be deprived of their importance by later experiences.

If it is true that the unintelligible memories of a person's childhood and the phantasies that are built on them invariably emphasize the most important elements in his mental development, then it follows that the fact which the vulture phantasy confirms, namely that Leonardo spent the first years of his life alone with his mother, will have been of decisive influence in the formation of his inner life. An inevitable effect of this state of affairs was that the child—who was confronted in his early life with one problem more than other children—began to brood on this riddle with special intensity, and so at a tender age became a researcher, tormented as he was by the great question of where babies come from and what the father has to do with their origin. It was a vague suspicion that his researches and the history of his childhood were connected in this way which later prompted him to exclaim that he had been destined from the first to investigate the problem of the flight of birds, since he had been visited by a vulture as he lay in his cradle. Later on it will not be difficult to show how his curiosity about the flight of birds was derived from the sexual researches of his childhood.

# ~ André Gide ~

## FROM

# Corydon

TRANSLATED BY RICHARD HOWARD

In the year 190—, a scandalous trial raised once again the irritating question of uranism. For eight days, in the salons as in the cafés, nothing else was mentioned. Impatient with theories and exclamations offered on all sides by the ignorant, the bigoted, and the stupid, I wanted to know my own mind; realizing that reason rather than just temperament was alone qualified to condemn or condone, I decided to go and discuss the subject with Corydon. He, I had been told, made no objection to certain unnatural tendencies attributed to him; my conscience would not be clear until I had learned what he had to say in their behalf.

It was ten years since I had last seen Corydon. At that time he was a high-spirited boy, as gentle as he was proud, generous and obliging, whose very glance compelled respect. He had been a brilliant medical student, and his early work gained him much professional approval. After leaving the lycée where we had been students together, we remained fairly close friends for a long time. Then several years of travel separated us, and when I returned to Paris to live, the deplorable reputation his behavior was acquiring kept me from seeking him out.

---

*E. M. Forster on ANDRÉ GIDE: "His equipment contained much that was unusual and bewildering. He was what* The Times *obituary notice of him safely termed 'heterodox' (i.e. homosexual), he had in many ways a pagan outlook, yet he had also a puritanical and religious outlook, which was inherent in his upbringing and sometimes dominated him. He had also, and above all, a belief in discovering the truth and following it."*

On entering his apartment, I admit I received none of the unfortunate impressions I had feared. Nor did Corydon afford any such impression by the way he dressed, which was quite conventional, even a touch austere perhaps. I glanced around the room in vain for signs of that effeminacy which experts manage to discover in everything connected with inverts and by which they claim they are never deceived. However, I did notice, over his mahogany desk, a huge photographic reproduction of Michelangelo's "Creation of Man," showing Adam naked on the primeval slime, reaching up to the divine Hand and turning toward God a dazzled look of gratitude. Corydon's vaunted love of art would have accounted for any surprise I might have shown at the choice of this particular subject. On the desk, the portrait of an old man with a long white beard whom I immediately recognized as the American poet Walt Whitman, since it appears as the frontispiece of Léon Bazalgette's recent translation of his works. Bazalgette had also just published a voluminous biography of the poet, which I had recently come across and which now served as a pretext for opening the conversation.

～ ～ ～

"After reading Bazalgette's book," I began, "I don't see much reason for this portrait to be on display here."

My remark was impertinent; Corydon pretended not to understand. I insisted.

"First of all," he answered, "Whitman's work remains just as admirable as it ever was, regardless of the interpretation each reader chooses to give his behavior. . . ."

"Still, you have to admit that your admiration has diminished somewhat, now that Bazalgette has proved that Whitman didn't behave as you so eagerly assumed he did."

"Your friend Bazalgette has proved nothing whatever; his entire argument depends on a syllogism that can just as easily be reversed. Homosexuality, he postulates, is an unnatural tendency. . . . Now, Whitman was in perfect health; you might say he was the best representative literature has ever provided of the natural man. . . ."

"*Therefore* Whitman wasn't a pederast. I don't see how you can get around that."

"But the work is there, and no matter how often Bazalgette translates the word 'love' as 'affection,' or 'friendship,' and the word 'sweet' as 'pure,' whenever Whitman addresses his 'comrade,' the fact remains that all the fervent, tender, sensual, impassioned poems in the book are of the same order—that order you call *contra naturam*."

"I don't call it an order at all. . . . But how would you reverse his syllogism?"

"Like this: Whitman can be taken as the typical normal man. Yet Whitman was a pederast. . . ."

"*Therefore* pederasty is normal. . . . Bravo! Now all you have to prove is that Whitman was a pederast. As far as begging the question goes, I prefer Bazalgette's syllogism to yours—it doesn't go so much against common sense."

"It's not common sense but the truth we should avoid going against. I'm writing an article about Whitman—an answer to Bazalgette's argument."*

"These questions of behavior are of great interest to you?"

"I should say so. In fact, I'm writing a long study of the subject."

"Aren't the works of Moll and Krafft-Ebing and Raffalovich enough for you?"

"Not enough to satisfy me. I'd like to deal with the subject in a different way."

"I've always thought it was best to speak of such things as little as possible—often they exist at all only because some blunderer runs on

---

*Bazalgette is certainly entitled to his choice (indeed, the French language obliges him to choose) whenever the gender of the English word remains uncertain, and to translate, for instance, the friend whose embracing awakes me by "l'amie qui," etc.—though by doing so he is deceiving both the reader and himself. But he is not entitled to draw conclusions from a text after he himself has corrupted it. He admits with disarming candor that the affair with a woman which he describes in his biography is "purely" imaginary. His desire to locate his hero in heterosexuality is such that when he translated the heaving sea as "la mer qui se soulève," he feels obliged to add "comme un sein"—like a breast, which in literary terms is absurd and profoundly uncharacteristic of Whitman. Reading such words in his translation, I rush to the original with the certainty that there has been a . . . mistake. Similarly when we read "mêlé à celles qui pèlent les pommes, je réclame un baiser pour chaque fruit rouge que je trouve," it goes without saying that the feminine gender is Bazalgette's invention. There are any number of such examples—and there are no other kind, by which I mean the kind which might allow Bazalgette to proceed as he has; so that it is really to his translator that Whitman seems to be speaking when he exclaims I am not what you suppose! As for the purely literary distortions, they are sufficiently frequent and significant to denature Whitman's poetry in a strange way. I know few translations which betray their author more completely . . . but this would take us too far . . . from our subject, I mean.*

about them. Aside from the fact that they are anything but elegant in expression, there will always be some imbecile to model himself on just what one was claiming to condemn."

"I'm not claiming to condemn anything."

"I've heard that you call yourself tolerant."

"You don't understand what I'm saying. I see I'll have to tell you the title of what I'm writing."

"By all means."

"What I'm writing is a *Defense of Pederasty*."

"Why not a *Eulogy*, while you're at it?"

"A title like that would distort my ideas; even with a word like 'Defense,' I'm afraid some readers will take it as a kind of provocation."

"And you'll actually publish such a thing?"

"Actually," he answered more seriously, "I won't."

"You know, you're all alike," I continued, after a moment's silence; "you swagger around in private and among yourselves, but out in the open and in front of the public your courage evaporates. In your heart of hearts you know perfectly well that the censure heaped on you is entirely deserved; you protest so eloquently in whispers, but when it comes to speaking up, you give in."

"It's true that the cause lacks martyrs."

"Let's not use such high-sounding words."

"I'm using the words that are needed. We've had Wilde and Krupp and Eulenburg and Macdonald . . ."

"And they're not enough for you?"

"Oh, victims! As many victims as you like—but not martyrs. They all denied—they always will deny."

"Well, of course, facing public opinion, the newspapers or the courts, each one is ashamed and retracts."

"Or commits suicide, unfortunately! Yes, you're right, it's a surrender to public opinion to establish one's innocence by disavowing one's life. Strange! we have the courage of our opinions, but never of our behavior. We're quite willing to suffer, but not to be disgraced."

"Aren't you just like the rest, in avoiding publication of your book?"
He hesitated a moment, and then: "Maybe I won't avoid it."

"All the same, once you were dragged into court by a Queensberry or a Harden, you can anticipate what your attitude would be."

"I'm afraid I can. I would probably lose courage and deny everything, just like my predecessors. We're never so alone in life that the mud thrown at us fails to dirty someone we care for. A scandal would upset my mother terribly, and I'd never forgive myself. My younger sister lives with her and isn't married yet—it might not be so easy to find someone who would accept me as his brother-in-law."

"Well, I certainly see what you mean; so you admit that such behavior dishonors even the man who merely tolerates it."

"That's not an admission, it's an observation of the facts. Which is why I'm looking for martyrs to the cause."

"What do you mean by such a word?"

"Someone who would forestall any attack—who without bragging or showing off would bear the disapproval, the insults; or better still, who would be of such acknowledged merit—such integrity and uprightness—that disapproval would hesitate from the start. . . ."

"You'll never find such a man."

"Let me hope he'll appear."

"Listen, just between ourselves: do you really think it would do much good? How much of a change in public opinion can you expect? I grant that you're a little . . . constrained. If you were a little more so, it would be all the better for you, believe me. Such wretched behavior would come to a stop quite naturally, just by not having to put itself on show." I noticed that he shrugged his shoulders, which didn't keep me from insisting: "Don't you suppose there are enough turpitudes on display as it is?" And I permitted myself to remark that homosexuals find any number of *facilities* in one place or another. "Let them be content with the ones that are concealed, and with the complicity of their kind; don't try to win the approval or even the indulgence of respectable people on their behalf."

"But it's the esteem of just such people I cannot do without."

"If you can't do without it, then change your behavior."

"I can't do that. It can't be 'changed'—that's the dilemma for which Krupp and Macdonald and the rest saw no other solution than a bullet."

"Luckily you're less tragic."

"I wouldn't swear to it. But I would like to finish my book."

"Admit that there's more than a little pride in your case."

"None whatever."

"You cultivate your strangeness, and then in order not to be ashamed of it you congratulate yourself on not feeling like all the rest."

He shrugged again and walked up and down the room without a word; then, having apparently overcome the impatience my last remarks aroused:

~ ~ ~

"Not so long ago, you used to be my friend," he said, sitting down again beside me. "I remember that we could understand each other. Is it really necessary for you to make such a show of sarcasm each time I say a word? Of course I'm not asking for your approval, but can't you even listen to me in good faith—the same good faith in which I'm talking to you . . . at least, the way I *would* talk if I felt you were listening. . . ."

"Forgive me," I said, disarmed by the tone of his words. "It's true that I've lost touch with you. Yes, we were once quite close, in the days when your behavior still held out against your inclinations."

"And then you stopped seeing me; to be frank about it, you broke off relations."

"Let's not argue about that; but suppose we talked the way we used to," I went on, holding out my hand. "I have time to listen to anything you have to say. When we used to see each other, you were still a student. Did you already have such a clear notion of yourself back then? Tell me—I want to know the truth."

He turned toward me with a new expression of confidence, and began:

"During my years as an intern in the hospital, the awareness I came to of my . . . anomaly plunged me into a state of mortal distress. It's absurd to maintain, as some people still do, that you only come to pederasty because you're seduced into it, that it's the result of nothing but being dissipated or blasé. And I couldn't see myself as either degenerate or sick. Hardworking and extremely chaste, I was living with the firm intention, once my internship was over, of marrying a girl who has since then died, and whom I used to love above anything else in the world.

"I loved her too much to realize clearly that I didn't desire her at all. I know that some people are reluctant to admit that the one can exist without the other; I was entirely unaware of it myself. Yet no other woman ever haunted my dreams, or wakened any desire in me whatever. Still less was I tempted by the prostitutes I saw almost all my friends chasing. But since at the time I hardly suspected I might actually desire others altogether, I convinced myself that my abstinence was a virtue, gloried in the notion of remaining a virgin until marriage, and prided myself on a purity I could not suppose was a delusion. Only gradually did I manage to understand what I was; finally I had to admit that these notorious allurements which I prided myself on resisting actually had no attraction for me whatever.

"What I had regarded as virtue was in fact nothing but indifference. This was an appalling humiliation—how could it be anything else?—to a rather high-minded young spirit. Only work managed to overcome the melancholy which darkened and diminished my life; I soon persuaded myself I was unsuited for marriage and, being able to acknowledge none of the reasons for my depression to my fiancée, became increasingly evasive and embarrassed in my behavior toward her. Yet the few experiments I then attempted in a brothel certainly proved to me that I wasn't impotent; but at the same time they afforded convincing proof . . ."

"Proof of what?"

"My case seemed to me altogether exceptional (for how could I suspect at the time that it was common?). I saw that I was capable of pleasure; I supposed myself incapable, strictly speaking, of desire. Both my parents were healthy, I myself was robust and energetic; my appearance revealed nothing of my wretchedness; none of my friends suspected what was wrong; nothing could have persuaded me to speak a word to a soul. Yet the farce of good humor and risqué allusions which I felt obliged to act out in order to avoid all suspicion became intolerable. As soon as I was alone, I slipped into despondency."

The seriousness and the conviction in his voice compelled my interest. "You were letting your imagination run away with you!" I said gently. "The fact is, you were in love, and therefore full of doubts. As soon as you were married, love would have developed quite naturally into desire."

"I know that's what people say. . . . How right I was to be skeptical!"

"You don't seem to have hypochondriacal tendencies now. How did you cure yourself of this disease of yours?"

"At the time, I did a great deal of reading. And one day I came across a sentence which gave me some sound advice. It was from the Abbé Galiani: 'The important thing,' he wrote to Mme d'Epinay, 'the important thing is not to be cured but to be able to live with one's disease.' "

"Why don't you tell that to your patients?"

"I do, to the incurable ones. No doubt those words seem all too simple to you, but I drew my whole philosophy from them. It only remained for me to realize that I was not a freak, a unique case, in order to recover my self-confidence and escape my self-hatred."

"You've told me how you came to realize your lack of interest in women, but not how you discovered your tendency . . ."

"It's quite a painful story, and I don't like telling it. But you seem to be listening to me carefully—maybe my account will help you speak of these matters less frivolously."

I assured him, if not of my sympathy, at least of my respectful attention.

~ ~ ~

"You already know," he began, "that I was engaged; I loved the girl who was to become my wife tenderly but with an almost mystical emotion, and of course with my lack of experience I scarcely imagined that there could be any other real way of loving. My fiancée had a brother, a few years younger than she, whom I often saw and who felt the deepest friendship for me."

"Aha!" I exclaimed involuntarily.

Corydon glanced at me severely. "No: nothing improper took place between us; his sister was my fiancée."

"Excuse me."

"But you can imagine my confusion, my consternation, when, one evening of heart-to-heart exchanges, I had to acknowledge that this boy wanted not only my friendship but was soliciting my caresses as well."

"Your tenderness, you mean. Like many children, after all! It's our responsibility, as their elders, to respect such needs."

"I did respect them, I promise you that. But Alexis was no longer a child; he was a charming and perceptive adolescent. The avowals he made to me then were all the more upsetting because in every revelation he made, all described with precocious exactitude, I seemed to be hearing my own confession. Nothing, however, could possibly justify the severity of my reaction."

"Severity?"

"Yes: I was scared out of my wits. I spoke severely, almost harshly, and what was worse, I spoke with extreme contempt for what I called effeminacy, which was only the natural expression of his feelings."

"It's hard to know how to deal with such cases."

"I dealt with this one so badly that the poor child—yes, he was still a child—took my scolding quite tragically. For three days he tried with all the sweetness in his power to overcome what he took to be my anger; and meanwhile I kept exaggerating my coldness no matter what he said, until it happened. . . ."

"What happened?"

"Then you didn't know that Alexis B. committed suicide?"

"But you wouldn't go so far as to suggest that . . ."

"No, I'm not suggesting anything at all. At first it was said to be an accident. We were in the country at the time: the body was found at the foot of a cliff. . . . An accident? I suppose I could make myself believe anything. But here's the letter I found next to my bed."

He opened a drawer, took out a sheet of paper with a shaking hand, glanced at it, and then said:

"No, I'm not going to read you this letter; you would misjudge the child. The substance of it—and written in the most moving way—was the agony our last conversation had caused him . . . especially certain remarks I had made. 'To spare yourself this physical torment,' I had shouted in a fit of hypocritical rage against the inclinations he was confessing to me, 'the best thing you could do would be to fall in love.' *Unfortunately,* he wrote me, *I have fallen in love, but with you, my friend. You haven't understood me and you feel contempt for me; I see that I am becoming an object of disgust to you—as I am for myself for that very reason. If I can't change my awful nature, at least I can get rid of it.* . . . Four more pages of that slightly pompous pathos characteristic of that stage of life, the kind of thing it becomes so easy for us to call declamation."

This story had made me more than a little uncomfortable. . . . "Of course," I said at last, "such a declaration, and made to you specifically, was a nasty trick of fate; I can understand that the episode must have affected you."

"To the point that I immediately gave up all thoughts of marrying my friend's sister."

"But," I went on with my train of thought, "I'm more or less convinced that each of us gets the disasters he deserves. You must admit that if this boy hadn't sensed in you some possible response to his own guilty passion, that passion . . ."

"Maybe some obscure instinct could have made him aware of it, as you say; but in that case, what a crying shame that same instinct couldn't make me aware of it too."

"What if you had been aware—what would you have done?"

"I think I could have cured that child."

"You were just saying that these were incurable cases; didn't you just quote the Abbé's words—'the important thing is not to be cured . . .'"

"All right, enough of that! I could have cured him the same way I've cured myself."

"And that is . . ."

"By convincing him he wasn't sick."

"Why don't you just come right out and say that the perversion of his instinct was natural!"

"By convincing him that the deviation of his instinct was quite natural."

"And if you had it all to do over again, you would have yielded to him, *naturally.*"

"Oh, that's another question altogether. When the physiological problem is solved, the moral problem begins. No doubt my feelings for his sister would have led me to try to argue him out of this passion, in the same way that I would no doubt have tried to argue myself out of my own; but at least this passion itself would have lost that monstrous character it had assumed in his eyes.

"This drama, by opening my own eyes to my own nature, showing me the real nature of my feelings for this child, this drama I've thought about so long, has finally determined my attitude toward . . . the particular thing you find so despicable; in memory of this victim, I want to cure other victims suffering from the same misunderstanding: to cure them in the way I just told you."

～ ～ ～

"I think you understand now why I want to write this book. The only serious books I know on this subject are certain medical works, which reek of the clinic from the very first pages."

"So you don't plan on writing as a doctor?"

"As a doctor, a naturalist, a moralist, a sociologist, a historian . . ."

"I didn't know you were so protean."

"I mean I'm making no claims to speak about my subject as a specialist—only as a man. The doctors who usually write about the subject treat only uranists who are ashamed of themselves—pathetic inverts, sick men. They're the only ones who consult doctors. As a doctor myself, those are the ones who come to me for treatment too; but as a man, I come across others, who are neither pathetic nor sickly—those are the ones I want to deal with."

"Yes, with the normal pederasts!"

"Precisely. You understand that in homosexuality, just as in heterosexuality, there are all shades and degrees, from platonic love to lust, from self-denial to sadism, from radiant health to sullen sickliness, from simple expansiveness to all the refinements of vice. Inversion is only one expression. Besides, between exclusive homosexuality and exclusive heterosexuality there is every intermediate shading. But most people simply draw the line between normal love and a love alleged to be *contra naturam*—and for convenience' sake, all the happiness, all the noble or tragic passions, all the beauty of action and thought, are put on one side, and to the other are relegated all the filthy dregs of love. . . ."

"Don't get carried away. Sapphism actually enjoys a certain favor among us nowadays."

He was so worked up that he completely ignored my remark and continued his argument.

"Nothing could be more grotesque than the spectacle, whenever there's a morals case in the courts, of the righteous indignation of the newspapers at the 'virile' attitude of the accused. No doubt the public expected to see them in skirts. Look: I cut this out of the *Journal* during the Harden trial. . . ."

He searched among various papers and handed me a sheet on which the following was underlined:

Graf von Hohenau, tall in his tight-fitting frock coat, dignified and even stately, gives no impression of being an effeminate man. He is the perfect type of the Guards officer, entirely committed to his profession. And yet this man of martial and noble bearing is charged with the gravest offense. Graf von Lynar, a man of prepossessing appearance as well . . .

"In the same way," he went on, "Macdonald and Eulenburg seemed, even to the most prejudiced observers, intelligent, handsome, dignified . . ."

"In short, desirable from every point of view."

He said nothing for a moment, and I saw a look of scorn flash across his face; but recovering himself, he continued as if he had not caught my meaning.

"One is justified in expecting the object of desire to have some beauty, but not necessarily the subject of it. I am not concerned with the beauty of these men. If I made a point, just now, of their physical appearance, it is because it matters to me that they be healthy and virile. And I am not claiming that every uranist is any such thing; homosexuality, just like heterosexuality, has its degenerates, its vicious and sick practitioners; as a doctor, I have come across as many painful, distressing, or dubious cases as the rest of my colleagues. I shall spare my readers that experience; as I've already said, my book will deal with healthy uranism or, as you just put it yourself, with *normal pederasty*."

"Didn't you understand I was using the phrase derisively? It would be all too easy for you if I conceded this final point."

"I shall never ask you to concede anything just to please me. I prefer you to be obliged to do so."

"Now it's your turn to be joking."

"Not in the least. I'm willing to bet that in twenty years it will be impossible to take words like 'unnatural' and 'perverted' seriously. The only thing in the world I concede as not natural is a work of art. Everything else, like it or not, belongs to the natural order, and once we no longer consider it as a moralist, we had better do so as a naturalist."

"The words you indict have their uses—at least they reinforce our decency. Where would we be, once you had suppressed them?"

"We wouldn't be any more demoralized than we are; and I'm making a conscious effort not to add: 'On the contrary!' . . . What frauds you heterosexuals are—to hear some of you tell it, it's enough for sexual relations to be between different sexes to be permissible; at least, to be 'normal.' "

"It's enough for them to be so potentially. Homosexuals are depraved by nature—necessarily."

"Do you really suppose that self-denial, self-control, and chastity are entirely unknown to them?"

"No doubt it's a good thing that laws and human respect occasionally have some hold over them."

"Whereas you think it's a 'good thing' that laws and conventions have so little hold over *you?*"

"I'm coming to the end of my patience with you! Look, on our side we have marriage, honest marriage, which I don't imagine is to be found on yours. You make me feel like one of those moralists who regard all extramarital pleasures of the flesh as sin and who condemn all relationships that are not legally sanctioned."

"Oh, I'm more than a match for them there, and if you were to encourage me, I could turn out to be even more intransigent than they are. Of all the conjugal beds I've been called upon to examine as a physician, I assure you that very few were made with clean linen, and I wouldn't like to wager that more ingenuity, more perversity, if you prefer, is always to be found among prostitutes than in certain 'honest' households."

"You're disgusting."

"But if the bed is a conjugal one, then whatever vice is there is immediately laundered."

"Surely married couples can do whatever they like; that's their privilege. And besides, it's none of your business."

" 'Privilege'—yes, I like that word much better than 'normal.' "

"I had been warned that the moral sense was strangely warped among your kind. But I'm amazed to discover to what a degree. You seem to have completely lost sight of this natural act of procreation—an act which marriage sanctifies and which perpetuates the great mystery of life."

"And once performed, the act of love is at liberty to run wild—no more than a gratuitous fantasy, a game. No, I'm not losing sight of that; in fact, it's on that finality that I want to construct my own ethics. Apart from procreation, nothing remains but the persuasions of pleasure. But think it over for a minute—the act of procreation need not be frequent: once every ten months is sufficient."

"That's rather seldom."

"Very seldom; especially since nature suggests an infinitely greater expenditure; and . . . I hardly dare finish my sentence."

"Go on—you've already said so much."

"All right, then: I maintain that far from being the only 'natural' one, the act of procreation, in nature, for all its disconcerting profusion, is usually nothing but a fluke."

"You'd better explain that one!"

"I'll be glad to, but it brings us to natural history; that's where my book begins and how I approach my subject. If you have a little patience, I'll tell you what I mean to say. Come back tomorrow. By then I'll have put my papers into something like order."

# ~ André Gide ~

FROM

# *Madeleine*

TRANSLATED BY JUSTIN O'BRIEN

*Luxor, 8 February [18]89*

I open this notebook again after having forsaken it for several months. Since she ceased to exist, I have ceased to take much interest in life. Already I belong to the past. Others enjoy calling it up; but I wonder if, seeking to revive here the figure of her who accompanied me in life, I am not going against her will. For she constantly withdrew, hiding from attention. Never was she heard to say: "As for me . . ." Her modesty was as natural as in other women the need to push oneself forward, to shine. Even when I would return from a voyage and the other members of the family would greet me on the stone steps of Cuverville, I knew that she would be standing, somewhat withdrawn, in the shadow of the entrance hall, and I would think of Coriolanus' return, of the "My gracious silence, hail!" that he addresses to his Virgilia. . . . [William Shakespeare, *Coriolanus,* Act II, Scene 1.] When Madeleine burned all my letters, in the tragic circumstances I shall relate, she did so indeed in a gesture of despair and to detach me from her life; but also to escape future attention and through a desire for self-effacement.

It might be thought that such a shrinking was provoked by what seemed to her reprehensible in my life; and, to be sure, it was accentuated by whatever discovery she may have made of that or whatever intuition she may have had; but as far back as I go, I still find such a shrinking. It was constant, natural . . . or, perhaps, already the result of her initial childhood fright, of that first wounding contact with evil, which, on a soul as sensitive as hers was, must have left an indelible bruise. And I already depicted her thus in my first books, well before our marriage: Emmanuèle in the *Cahiere d'André Walter,* Ellis in the *Voyage d'Urien.* Even the evanescent Angèle of *Paiudes* was somewhat inspired by her. . . . And in my dreams she constantly used to appear to me as an unclaspable, elusive figure, and the dream would turn into a nightmare. Whence that resolve I made, when still very young, to do violence to her reticences and sweep her along with me toward exuberance and joy. That is where my mistake began.

A double mistake, for at once it made her misjudge me even more than I was misjudging her. Because she was extraordinarily discreet and reserved, I had to guess almost everything; and often I was very bad at guessing. Many slight indications might have been revelatory if I had observed her with sufficient solicitude. I was able to explain them to myself only much later, only too late, and she had let me misinterpret them, for she never defended herself against anything that might offend or harm her. But had I understood earlier, would I have greatly modified my behavior as a result? It is my very nature that I should have had to change—be able to change.

And that she should have been misled in the beginning of our union is natural; but I now believe that that misunderstanding of hers lasted much less long than I then imagined. How could she have failed to begin by suspecting a sensuality of which I gave her so few proofs? Before understanding and admitting that that sensuality was addressed elsewhere, she naïvely expressed surprise that I could have written my *Nourritures terrestres,* a book that she said was so unlike me. Yet even as we descended into Italy after leaving the Engadine during our wedding trip, she was likewise surprised by my animation when the carriage in which we were heading south was escorted by the *ragazzi* of the villages we were going through. Inevitably the connection must have come to her mind, however disagreeable and offensive it may have been for her, so contrary to all the admitted facts and upsetting to the norms on which to establish her life. She felt out of it, brushed aside; loved doubtless, but in what an incomplete way! She did not immediately admit defeat. What, were whatever advances feminine modesty allowed her to remain useless, without echo and without reply? . . . Painfully I can see now the stages of that voyage:

In Florence we visited together churches and museums; but in Rome, completely absorbed by the young models from Saracinesco who then used to come and offer themselves on the stairs of the Piazza di Spagna, I was willing (and here I cease to understand myself) to forsake her for long hours at a time, which she filled somehow or other, probably wandering bewildered through the city—while, on the pretext of photographing them, I would take the models to the little apartment we had rented in the Piazza Barbarini. She knew it; I made no secret of it, and if I had, our indiscreet landlady would have taken care to tell her. But as a crowning aberration, or else to try to give to my clandestine occupations a justification, a semblance of excuse, I would show her the "art" photographs I had taken—at least the first, altogether unsuccessful ones. I ceased showing them to her the moment they turned out better; and she was scarcely interested in seeing them, any more than she was in going into the artistic considerations that urged me, as I told her, to take them.

Moreover, those photographs soon became nothing more than a pretext, needless to say; little Luigi, the eldest of the young models, was not at all misled by them. Any more than Madeleine herself, probably; and I am inclined to believe today that of the two of us, the blinder one, the only blind one, was I. But aside from the fact that I found it advantageous to suppose a blindness that permitted my pleasure without too much remorse, as, after all, neither my heart nor my mind was involved, it did not seem to me that I was unfaithful to her in seeking elsewhere a satisfaction of the flesh that I did not know how to ask of her. Besides, I didn't reason. I acted like an irresponsible person. A demon inhabited me. It never possessed me more imperiously than on our return to Algiers, during the same trip:

The Easter holidays had ended. In the train taking us from Biskra, three schoolboys, returning to their *lycée,* occupied the compartment next to ours, which was almost full. They were but half clothed, for the heat was tantalizing, and, alone in their compartment, were raising the roof. I listened to them laugh and jostle one another. At each of the frequent but brief stops the train made, by leaning out of the little side window I had lowered, my hand just reached the arm of one of the boys who amused himself by leaning toward me from the next window, laughingly entering into the spirit of the game; and I tasted excruciating delights in touching the downy amber flesh he offered to my caress. My hand, slipping up along his arm, rounded the shoulder. . . . At the next station, one of the two others would have taken his place and the same game would begin again.

Then the train would start again. I would sit down, breathless and panting, and pretend to be absorbed by my reading. Madeleine, seated opposite me, said nothing, pretended not to see me, not to know me. . . .

On our arrival in Algiers, the two of us alone in the omnibus that was taking us to the hotel, she finally said to me in a tone in which I felt even more sorrow than censure: "You looked like either a criminal or a madman."

# ∽ *Thomas Mann* ∽

## *Death in Venice*

TRANSLATED BY DAVID LUKE

### *1*

On a spring afternoon in 19——, the year in which for months on end so grave a threat seemed to hang over the peace of Europe, Gustav Aschenbach, or von Aschenbach, as he had been officially known since his fiftieth birthday, had set out from his apartment on the Prinz-regentenstrasse in Munich to take a walk of some length by himself. The morning's writing had overstimulated him: his work had now reached a difficult and dangerous point which demanded the utmost care and circumspection, the most insistent and precise effort of will, and the productive mechanism in his mind—that *motus animi continuus* which according to Cicero is the essence of eloquence—had so pursued its reverberating rhythm that he had been unable to halt it even after lunch and had missed the refreshing daily siesta which was now so necessary to him as he became increasingly subject to fatigue. And so, soon after taking tea, he had left the house hoping that fresh air and movement would set him to rights and enable him to spend a profitable evening.

It was the beginning of May, and after a succession of cold, wet weeks

---

THOMAS MANN *was born in Lübeck in 1875 and died in Zurich in 1955.* Buddenbrooks *(1901),* Death in Venice *(1912)—which Luchino Visconti made into a film and Benjamin Britten into an opera—and* The Magic Mountain *(1924) were the works that won him the Nobel Prize in Literature in 1929; in fact, as an old man he doubted whether he ever bettered his pre-Nobel work.*

a premature high summer had set in. The Englischer Garten, although still only in its first delicate leaf, had been as sultry as in August and, at its city end, full of traffic and pedestrians. Having made his way to the Aumeister along less and less frequented paths, Aschenbach had briefly surveyed the lively scene at the popular open-air restaurant, around which a few cabs and private carriages were standing; then, as the sun sank, he had started homeward across the open meadow beyond the park, and since he was now tired and a storm seemed to be brewing over Föhring, he had stopped by the Northern Cemetery to wait for the train that would take him straight back to the city.

As it happened, there was not a soul to be seen at or near the tram stop. Not one vehicle passed along the Föhringer Chaussee or the paved Ungererstrasse, on which solitary gleaming tram rails pointed toward Schwabing; nothing stirred behind the fencing of the stonemasons' yards, where crosses and memorial tablets and monuments, ready for sale, composed a second and untenanted burial ground; across the street, the mortuary chapel with its Byzantine styling stood silent in the glow of the westering day. Its facade, adorned with Greek crosses and brightly painted hieratic motifs, is also inscribed with symmetrically arranged texts in gilt lettering, selected scriptural passages about the life to come, such as: "They shall go in unto the dwelling place of the Lord," or "May light perpetual shine upon them." The waiting Aschenbach had already been engaged for some minutes in the solemn pastime of deciphering the words and letting his mind wander in contemplation of the mystic meaning that suffused them, when he noticed something that brought him back to reality: in the portico of the chapel, above the two apocalyptic beasts that guard the steps leading up to it, a man was standing, a man whose slightly unusual appearance gave his thoughts an altogether different turn.

It was not entirely clear whether he had emerged through the bronze doors from inside the chapel or had suddenly appeared and mounted the steps from outside. Aschenbach, without unduly pondering the question, inclined to the former hypothesis. The man was moderately tall, thin, beardless, and remarkably snub-nosed: he belonged to the red-haired type and had its characteristic milky, freckled complexion. He was quite evidently not of Bavarian origin; at all events, he wore a straw hat with a broad straight brim which gave him an exotic air, as of someone who had come from distant parts. It is true that he also had the typical Bavarian rucksack strapped to his shoulders and wore a yellowish belted outfit of what looked like frieze, as well as carrying a gray rain cape over his left forearm, which was propped against his waist, and in his right hand an iron-pointed walking stick, which he had thrust slantwise into the ground, crossing his feet and leaning his hip against his handle. His head was held high, so that the Adam's apple stood out stark and bare on his lean neck where it rose from the open shirt; and there were two pronounced vertical furrows, rather strangely ill-matched to his turned-up nose, between the colorless red-lashed eyes with which he peered sharply into the distance. There was thus—and perhaps the raised point of vantage on which he stood contributed to this impression—an air of imperious survey, something bold or even wild about his posture: for whether it was because he was dazzled into a grimace by the setting sun or by reason of some permanent facial deformity, the fact was that his lips seemed to be too short and were completely retracted from his teeth, so that the latter showed white and long between them, bared to the gums.

Aschenbach's half absentminded, half inquisitive scrutiny of the stranger had no doubt been a little less than polite, for he suddenly became aware that his gaze was being returned: the man was in fact staring at him so aggressively, so straight in the eye, with so evident an intention to make an issue of the matter and outstare him, that Aschenbach turned away in disagreeable embarrassment and began to stroll along the fence, casually resolving to take no further notice of the fellow. A minute later he had put him out of his mind. But whether his imagination had been stirred by the stranger's itinerant appearance, or whether some other physical or psychological influence was at work, he now became conscious, to his complete surprise, of an extraordinary expansion of his inner self, a kind of roving restlessness, a youthful craving for far-off places, a feeling so new or at least so long unaccustomed and forgotten that he stood as if rooted, with his hands clasped behind his back and his eyes to the ground, trying to ascertain the nature and purport of his emotion.

It was simply a desire to travel; but it had presented itself as nothing less than a seizure, with intensely passionate and indeed hallucinatory force, turning his craving into vision. His imagination, still not at rest from the morning's hours of work, shaped for itself a paradigm of all the wonders and terrors of the manifold earth, of all that it was now suddenly striving to envisage: he saw it, saw a landscape, a tropical swampland under a cloud-swollen sky, moist and lush and monstrous, a kind of primeval wilderness of islands, morasses, and muddy alluvial channels; far and wide around him he saw hairy palm trunks thrusting upward from rank jungles of fern, from among thick fleshy plants in exuberant flower; saw strangely misshapen trees with roots that arched through the air before sinking into the ground or into stagnant shadowy-green glassy waters where milk-white blossoms floated as big as plates, and among them exotic birds with grotesque beaks stood hunched in the shallows, their heads tilted motionlessly sideways; saw between the knotted stems of the bamboo thicket the glinting eyes of a crouching tiger; and his heart throbbed with terror and mysterious longing. Then the vision faded; and with a shake of his head, Aschenbach resumed his perambulation along the fencing of the gravestone yards.

His attitude to foreign travel, at least since he had had the means at his disposal to enjoy its advantages as often as he pleased, had always been that it was nothing more than a necessary health precaution, to be taken from time to time however disinclined to it one might be. Too preoccupied with the tasks imposed upon him by his own sensibility and by the collective European psyche, too heavily burdened with the compulsion to produce, too shy of distraction to have learned how to take leisure and pleasure in the colorful external world, he had been perfectly well satisfied to have no more detailed a view of the earth's surface than anyone can acquire without stirring far from home, and he had never even been tempted to venture outside Europe. This had been more especially the case since his life had begun its gradual decline and his artist's fear of not finishing his task—the apprehension that his time might run out before he had given the whole of himself by doing what he had it in him to do—was no longer something he could simply dismiss as an idle fancy: and during this time his outward existence had been almost entirely divided between the beautiful city which had become his home and the rustic mountain retreat he had set up for himself and where he passed his rainy summers.

And sure enough, the sudden and belated impulse that had just overwhelmed him very soon came under the moderating and corrective influence of common sense and of the self-discipline he had practiced since his youth. It had been his intention that the book to which his life was at present dedicated should be advanced to a certain point before he moved to the country, and the idea of a jaunt in the wide world that would take him away from his work for months now seemed too casual, too upsetting to his plans to be considered seriously. Nevertheless, he knew the reason for the unexpected temptation only too well. This longing for the distant and the new, this craving for liberation, relaxation, and forgetfulness—it had been, he was bound to admit, an urge to escape, to run away from his writing, away from the humdrum scene of his cold, inflexible, passionate duty. True, it was a duty he loved, and by now he had almost even learned to love the enervating daily struggle between his proud, tenacious, tried and tested will and that growing weariness which no one must be allowed to suspect nor his finished work betray by an telltale sign of debility or lassitude. Nevertheless, it would be sensible, he decided, not to span the bow too far and willfully stifle a desire that had erupted in him with such vivid force. He thought of his work, thought of the passage at which he had again, today as yesterday, been forced to interrupt it—that stubborn problem which neither patient care could solve nor a decisive *coup de main* dispel. He reconsidered it, tried to break or dissolve the inhibition, and, with a shudder of repugnance, abandoned the attempt. It was not a case of very unusual difficulty; he was simply paralyzed by a scruple of distaste, manifesting itself as a perfectionistic fastidiousness which nothing could satisfy. Perfectionism, of course, was something which even as a young man he had come to see as the innermost essence of talent, and for its sake he had curbed and cooled his feelings; for he knew that feeling is apt to be content with high-spirited approximations and with work that falls short of supreme excellence. Could it be that the enslaved emotion was now avenging itself by deserting him, by refusing from now on to bear up his art on its wings, by taking with it all his joy in words, all his appetite for the beauty of form? Not that he was writing badly: it was at least the advantage of his years to be master of his trade, a mastery of which at any moment he could feel calmly confident. But even as it brought him national honor he took no pleasure in it himself, and it seemed to him that his work lacked that element of sparkling and joyful improvisation, that quality which surpasses any intellectual substance in its power to delight the receptive world. He dreaded spending the summer in the country, alone in that little house with the maid who prepared his meals and the servant who brought them to him; dreaded the familiar profile of the mountain summits and mountain walls which would once again surround his slow discontented toil. So what did he need? An interlude, some impromptu living, some *dolce far niente,* the invigoration of a distant climate, to make his summer bearable and fruitable. Very well, then—he would travel. Not all that far, not quite to where the tigers were. A night in the wagon-lit and a siesta of three or four weeks at some popular holiday resort in the charming south . . .

Such were his thoughts as the train clattered toward him along the

Ungererstrasse, and as he stepped into it he decided to devote that evening to the study of maps and timetables. On the platform it occurred to him to look around and see what had become of the man in the straw hat, his companion for the duration of this not inconsequential wait at a tram stop. But the man's whereabouts remained a mystery, for he was no longer standing where he had stood, nor was he to be seen anywhere else at the stop or in the tramcar itself.

## 2

The author of the lucid and massive prose epic about the life of Frederick of Prussia; the patient artist who with long toil had woven the great tapestry of the novel called *Maya*, so rich in characters, gathering so many human destinies together under the shadow of one idea; the creator of that powerful tale entitled *A Study in Abjection*, which earned the gratitude of a whole younger generation by pointing to the possibility of moral resolution even for those who have plumbed the depths of knowledge; the author (lastly but not least in this summary enumeration of his maturer works) of that passionate treatise *Intellect and Art*, which in its ordering energy and antithetical eloquence has led serious critics to place it immediately alongside Schiller's disquisition *On Naive and Reflective Literature*: in a word, Gustav Aschenbach, was born in L——, an important city in the province of Silesia, as the son of a highly placed legal official. His ancestors had been military officers, judges, government administrators: men who had spent their disciplined, decently austere life in the service of the king and the state. A more inward spirituality had shown itself in one of them who had been a preacher; a strain of livelier, more sensuous blood had entered the family in the previous generation with the writer's mother, the daughter of a director of music from Bohemia. Certain exotic racial characteristics in his external appearance had come to him from her. It was from this marriage between hardworking, sober conscientiousness and darker, more fiery impulses that an artist, and indeed this particular kind of artist, had come into being.

With his whole nature intent from the start upon fame, he had displayed not exactly precocity but a certain decisiveness and personal trenchancy in his style of utterance, which at an early age made him ripe for a life in the public eye and well suited to it. He had made a name for himself when he had scarcely left school. Ten years later he had learned to perform, at his writing desk, the social and administrative duties entailed by his reputation; he had learned to write letters which, however brief they had to be (for many claims beset the successful man who enjoys the confidence of the public), would always contain something kindly and pointed. By the age of forty he was obliged, wearied though he might be by the toils and vicissitudes of his real work, to deal with a daily correspondence that bore postage stamps from every part of the globe.

His talent, equally remote from the commonplace and from the eccentric, had a native capacity both to inspire confidence in the general public and to win admiration and encouragement from the discriminating connoisseur. Ever since his boyhood the duty to achieve—and to achieve exceptional things—had been imposed on him from all sides, and thus he had never known youth's idleness, its carefree negligent ways. When in his thirty-fifth year he fell ill in Vienna, a subtle observer remarked of him on a social occasion: "You see. Aschenbach has always only lived like *this*"—and the speaker closed the fingers of his left hand tightly into a fist—"and never like *this*"—and he let his open hand hang comfortably down along the back of the chair. It was a correct observation; and the morally courageous aspect of the matter was that Aschenbach's native constitution was by no means robust and that the constant harnessing of his energies was something to which he had been called but not really born.

As a young boy, medical advice and care had made school attendance impossible and obliged him to have his education at home. He had grown up by himself, without companions, and had nevertheless had to recognize in good time that he belonged to a breed not seldom talented yet seldom endowed with the physical basis which talent needs if it is to fulfill itself—a breed that usually gives of its best in youth, and in which the creative gift rarely survives into mature years. But he would "stay the course"—it was his favorite motto: he saw his historical novel about Frederick the Great as nothing if not the apotheosis of this; the king's word of command, *"Durchhalten!"* to Aschenbach epitomized a manly ethos of suffering action. And he dearly longed to grow old, for it had always been his view that an artist's gift can be called truly great and wide-ranging, or indeed truly admirable, only if it has been fortunate enough to bear characteristic fruit at all the stages of human life.

They were not broad, the shoulders on which he thus carried the tasks laid upon him by his talent; and since his aims were high, he stood in great need of discipline—and discipline, after all, was fortunately his inborn heritage on his father's side. At the age of forty or fifty, and indeed during those younger years in which other men live prodigally and dilettantishly, happily procrastinating the execution of great plans, Aschenbach would begin his day early by dashing cold water over his chest and back, and then, with two tall wax candles in silver candlesticks placed at the head of his manuscript, he would offer up to art, for two or three ardently conscientious morning hours, the strength he had gathered during sleep. It was a pardonable error, indeed it was one that betokened as nothing else could the triumph of his moral will, that uninformed critics should mistake the great world of *Maya*, or the massive epic unfolding of Frederick's life, for the product of solid strength and long stamina, whereas in fact they had been built up to their impressive size from layer upon layer of daily opuscula, from a hundred or a thousand separate inspirations; and if they were indeed so excellent, wholly and in every detail, it was only because their creator, showing that same constancy of will and tenacity of purpose as had once conquered his native Silesia, had held out for years under the pressure of one and the same work, and had devoted to actual composition only his best and worthiest hours.

For a significant intellectual product to make a broad and deep immediate appeal, there must be a hidden affinity, indeed a congruence, between the personal destiny of the author and the wider destiny of his generation. The public does not know why it grants the accolade of fame to a work of art. Being in no sense connoisseurs, readers imagine they perceive a hundred good qualities in it which justify their admiration; but the real reason for their applause is something imponderable, a sense of sympathy. Hidden away among Aschenbach's writings was a passage directly asserting that nearly all the great things that exist owe their existence to a defiant despite: it is despite grief and anguish, despite poverty, loneliness, bodily weakness, vice and passion and a thousand inhibitions, that they have come into being at all. But this was more than an observation, it was an experience, it was positively the formula of his life and his fame, the key to his work; is it surprising then that it was also the moral formula, the outward gesture, of his work's most characteristic figures?

The new hero-type favored by Aschenbach, and recurring in his books in a multiplicity of individual variants, had already been remarked upon at an early stage by a shrewd commentator, who had described his conception as that of "an intellectual and boyish manly virtue, that of a youth who clenches his teeth in proud shame and stands calmly on as the swords and spears pass through his body." That was well put, perceptive and precisely true, for all its seemingly rather too passive emphasis. For composure under the blows of fate, grace in the midst of torment—this is not only endurance: it is an active achievement, a positive triumph, and the figure of Saint Sebastian is the most perfect symbol if not of art in general, then certainly of the kind of art here in question. What did one see if one looked in any depth into the world of this writer's fiction? Elegant self-control concealing from the world's eyes until the very last moment a state of inner disintegration and biological decay; sallow ugliness, sensuously marred and worsted, which nevertheless is able to fan its smoldering concupiscence to a pure flame and even to exalt itself to mastery in the realm of beauty; pallid impotence, which from the glowing depths of the spirit draws strength to cast down a whole proud people at the foot of the Cross and set its own foot upon them as well; gracious poise and composure in the empty austere service of form; the false, dangerous life of the born deceiver, his ambition and his art which lead so soon to exhaustion—to contemplate all these destinies, and many others like them, was to doubt if there is any other heroism at all but the heroism of weakness. In any case, what other heroism could be more in keeping with the times? Gustav Aschenbach was the writer who spoke for all those who work on the brink of exhaustion, who labor and are heavy-laden, who are worn out already but still stand upright, all those moralists of achievement who are slight of stature and scanty of resources, but who yet, by some ecstasy of the will and by wise husbandry, manage at least for a time to force their work into a semblance of greatness. There are many such; they are the heroes of our age. And they all recognized themselves in his work, they found that it confirmed them and raised them on high and celebrated them; they were grateful for this, and they spread his name far and wide.

He had been young and raw with the times: ill advised by fashion, he had publicly stumbled, blundered, made himself look foolish, offended in speech and writing against tact and balanced civility. But he had achieved dignity, that goal toward which, as he declared, every great talent is innately driven and spurred; indeed, it can be said that the conscious and defiant purpose of his entire development had been, leaving all the inhibitions of skepticism and irony behind him, an ascent to dignity.

Lively, clear-outlined, intellectually undemanding presentation is the delight of the great mass of the middle-class public, but passionate radical youth is interested only in problems: and Aschenbach had been as problematic and as radical as any young man ever was. He had been in thrall to intellect, had exhausted the soil by excessive analysis and ground up the seed corn of growth; he had uncovered what is better kept hidden, made talent seem suspect, betrayed the truth about art—indeed, even as the sculptural vividness of his descriptions was giving pleasure to his more naïve devotees and lifting their minds and hearts, he, this same youthful artist, had fascinated twenty-year-olds with his breathtaking cynicisms about the questionable nature of art and of the artist himself.

But it seems that there is nothing to which a noble and active mind more quickly becomes inured than that pungent and bitter stimulus, the acquisition of knowledge; and it is very sure that even the most gloomily conscientious and radical sophistication of youth is shallow by comparison with Aschenbach's profound decision as a mature master to repudiate knowledge as such, to reject it, to step over it with head held high—in the recognition that knowledge can paralyze the will, paralyze and discourage action and emotion and even passion, and rob all these of their dignity. How else is the famous short story "A Study in Abjection" to be understood but as an outbreak of disgust against an age indecently undermined by psychology and represented by the figure of that spiritless, witless semiscoundrel who cheats his way into a destiny of sorts when, motivated by his own ineptitude and depravity and ethical whimsicality, he drives his wife into the arms of a callow youth—convinced that his intellectual depths entitle him to behave with contemptible baseness? The forthright words of condemnation which here weighed vileness in the balance and found it wanting—they proclaimed their writer's renunciation of all moral skepticism, of every kind of sympathy with the abyss; they declared his repudiation of the laxity of that compassionate principle which holds that to understand all is to forgive all. And the development that was here being anticipated, indeed already taking place, was that "miracle of reborn naïveté" to which, in a dialogue written a little later, the author himself had referred with a certain mysterious emphasis. How strange these associations! Was it an intellectual consequence of this "rebirth," of this new dignity and rigor, that, at about the same time, his sense of beauty was observed to undergo an almost excessive resurgence, that his style took on the noble purity, simplicity, and symmetry that were to set upon all his subsequent works that so evident and evidently intentional stamp of the classical master? And yet: moral resoluteness at the far side of knowledge, achieved in despite of all corrosive and inhibiting insight—does this not in its turn signify a simplification, a morally simplistic view of the world and of human psychology, and thus also a resurgence of energies that are evil, forbidden, morally impossible? And is form not two-faced? Is it not at one and the same time moral and immoral—moral as the product and expression of discipline, but immoral and even antimoral inasmuch as it houses within itself an innate moral indifference, and indeed essentially strives for nothing less than to bend morality under its proud and absolute scepter?

Be that as it may! A development is a destiny; and one that is accompanied by the admiration and mass confidence of a wide public must inevitably differ in its course from one that takes place far from the limelight and from the commitments of fame. Only the eternal intellectual vagrant is bored and prompted to mockery when a great talent grows out of its libertinistic chrysalis stage, becomes an expressive representative of the dignity of mind, takes on the courtly bearing of that solitude which has been full of hard, uncounseled, self-reliant sufferings and struggles, and has achieved power and honor among men. And what a game it is too, how much defiance there is in it and how much satisfaction, this self-formation of a talent! As time passed, Gustav Aschenbach's presentations took on something of an official air, of an educator's stance; his style in later years came to eschew direct audacities, new and subtle nuances, it developed toward the exemplary and definitive, the fastidiously conventional, the conservative and formal and even formulaic; and as tradition has it of Louis XIV, so Aschenbach as he grew older banned from his utterance every unrefined word. It was at this time that the education authority adopted selected pages from his works for inclusion in the prescribed school readers. And when a German ruler who had just come to the throne granted personal nobilitation to the author of *Frederick of Prussia* on his fiftieth birthday, he sensed the inner appropriateness of this honor and did not decline it.

After a few restless years of experimental living in different places, he soon chose Munich as his permanent home and lived there in the kind of upper-bourgeois status which is occasionally the lot of certain intellectuals. The marriage which he had contracted while still young with the daughter of an academic family had been ended by his wife's death after a short period of happiness. She had left him a daughter, now already married. He had never had a son.

Gustav von Aschenbach was of rather less than average height, dark and clean-shaven. His head seemed a little too large in proportion to his almost delicate stature. His brushed-back hair, thinning at the top, very thick and distinctly gray over the temples, framed a high, deeply lined, scarred-looking forehead. The bow of a pair of gold spectacles with rimless lenses cut into the base of his strong, nobly curved nose. His mouth was large, often relaxed, often suddenly narrow and tense; the cheeks were lean and furrowed, the well-informed chin slightly cleft. Grave visitation of fate seemed to have passed over this head, which usually inclined to one side with an air of suffering. And yet it was art that had here performed that fashioning of the physiognomy which is usually the work of a life full of action and stress. The flashing exchanges of the dialogue between Voltaire and the king on the subject of war had been born behind that brow; these eyes that looked so wearily and deeply through their glasses had seen the bloody inferno of the Seven Years' War sick bays. Even in a personal sense, after all, art is an intensified life. By art one is more deeply satisfied and more rapidly used up. It engraves on the countenance of its servant the traces of imaginary and intellectual adventures, and even if he has outwardly existed in cloistral tranquillity, it leads in the long term to overfastidiousness, overrefinement, nervous fatigue, and overstimulation, such as can seldom result from a life full of the most extravagant passions and pleasures.

## 3

Mundane and literary business of various kinds delayed Aschenbach's eagerly awaited departure until about a fortnight after that walk in Munich. Finally he gave instructions that his country house was to be made ready for occupation in four weeks' time, and then, one day between the middle and end of May, he took the night train to Trieste, where he stayed only twenty-four hours, embarking on the following morning for Pola.

What he sought was something strange and random, but in a place easily reached, and accordingly he took up his abode on an Adriatic island which had been highly spoken of for some years: a little way off the Istrian coast, with colorful ragged inhabitants speaking a wild unintelligible dialect, and picturesque fragmented cliffs overlooking the open sea. But rain and sultry air, a self-enclosed provincial Austrian hotel clientele, the lack of that restful intimate contact with the sea which can be had only on a gentle, sandy coast, filled him with vexation and with a feeling that he had not yet come to his journey's end. He was haunted by an inner impulse that still had no clear direction; he studied shipping timetables, looked up one place after another—and suddenly his surprising yet at the same time self-evident destination stared him in the face. If one wanted to travel overnight to somewhere incomparable, to a fantastic mutation of normal reality, where did one go? Why, the answer was obvious. What was he doing here? He had gone completely astray. *That* was where he had wanted to travel. He at once gave notice of departure from his present, mischosen stopping place. Ten days after his arrival on the island, in the early morning mist, a rapid motor launch carried him and his luggage back over the water to the naval base, and here he landed only to reembark immediately, crossing the gangway onto the damp deck of a ship that was waiting under steam to leave for Venice.

It was an ancient Italian boat, out of date and dingy and black with soot. Aschenbach was no sooner aboard than a grubby hunchbacked seaman, grinning obsequiously, conducted him to an artificially lit cavelike cabin in the ship's interior. Here, behind a table, with his cap askew and a cigarette end in the corner of his mouth, sat a goat-bearded man with the air of an old-fashioned circus director and a slick caricatured business manner, taking passengers' particulars and issuing their tickets. "To Venice!" he exclaimed, echoing Aschenbach's request, and extending his arm, he pushed his pen into some coagulated leftover ink in a tilted inkstand. "One first class to Venice. Certainly, sir!" He scribbled elaborately, shook some blue sand from a box over the writing and ran it off into an earthenware dish, then folded the paper with his yellow bony fingers and wrote on it again. "A very happily chosen destination!" he chattered as he did so. "Ah, Venice! A splendid city! A city irresistibly attractive to the man of culture, by its history no less than by its present charms!" There was something hypnotic and distracting about the smooth facility of his movements and the glib empty talk with which he accompanied them, almost as if he were anxious that the traveler might have second thoughts about his decision to go to Venice. He hastily took Aschenbach's money and with the dexterity of a croupier dropped the change on the stained tablecloth. *"Buon divertimento, signore,"* he said, bowing histrionically. "It is an honor to serve you. . . . Next, please, gentlemen!" he exclaimed with a wave of the arm, as if he were doing a lively trade, although in fact there was no one else there to be dealt with. Aschenbach returned on deck.

Resting one elbow on the handrail, he watched the idle crowd hanging about the quayside to see the ship's departure, and watched the passengers who had come aboard. Those with second-class tickets were squatting, men and women together, on the forward deck, using boxes and bundles as seats. The company on the upper deck consisted of a group of young men, probably shop or office workers from Pola, a high-spirited party about to set off on an excursion to Italy. They were making a considerable exhibition of themselves and their enterprise, chattering, laughing, fatuously enjoying their own gesticulations, leaning overboard and shouting glibly derisive ribaldries at their friends on the harborside street, who were hurrying about their business with briefcases under their arms and waved their sticks peevishly at the holidaymakers. One of the party, who wore a light-yellow summer suit of extravagant cut, a scarlet necktie, and a rakishly tilted Panama hat, was the most conspicuous of them all in his shrill hilarity. But as soon as Aschenbach took a slightly closer look at him, he realized with a kind of horror that the man's youth was false. He was old, there was no mistaking it. There were wrinkles round his eyes and mouth. His cheeks' faint carmine was rouge, the brown hair under his straw hat with its colored ribbon was a wig, his neck was flaccid and scrawny, his small stuck-on mustache and the little imperial on his chin were dyed, his yellowish full complement of teeth, displayed when he laughed, were a cheap artificial set, and his hands, with signet rings on both index fingers, were those of an old man. With a spasm of distaste Aschenbach watched him as he kept company with his young friends. Did they not know, did they not notice that he was old, that he had no right to be wearing foppish and garish clothes like theirs, no right to be acting as if he were one of them? They seemed to be tolerating his presence among them as something habitual and to be taken for granted; they treated him as an equal, reciprocated without embarrassment when he teasingly poked them in the ribs. How was this possible? Aschenbach put his hand over his forehead and closed his eyes, which were hot from too little sleep. He had a feeling that something not quite usual was beginning to happen, that the world was undergoing a dreamlike alienation, becoming increasingly deranged and bizarre, and that perhaps this process might be arrested if he were to cover his face for a little and then take a fresh look at things. But at that moment he had the sensation of being afloat, and starting up in irrational alarm, he noticed that the dark heavy hulk of the steamer was slowly parting company with the stone quayside. Inch by inch, as the engine pounded and reversed, the width of the dirty glinting water between the hull and the quay increased, and after clumsy maneu-

verings the ship turned its bows toward the open sea. Aschenbach crossed
to the starboard side, where the hunchback had set up a deck chair for him
and a steward in a grease-stained frock coat offered his services.

The sky was gray, the wind damp. The port and the islands had been
left behind, and soon all land was lost to view in the misty panorama.
Flecks of sodden soot drifted down on the washed deck, which never
seemed to get dry. After only an hour an awning was set up, as it was beginning to rain.

Wrapped in his overcoat, a book lying on his lap, the traveler rested,
scarcely noticing the hours as they passed him by. It had stopped raining;
the canvass shelter was removed. The horizon was complete. Under the
turbid dome of the sky the desolate sea surrounded him in an enormous
circle. But in empty, unarticulated space our mind loses its sense of time as
well, and we enter the twilight of the immeasurable. As Aschenbach lay
there, strange and shadowy figures—the foppish old man, the goat-bearded
purser from the ship's interior—passed with uncertain gestures and confused dream-words through his mind, and he fell asleep.

At midday he was requested to come below for luncheon in the long,
narrow dining saloon, which ended in the doors to the sleeping berths;
here he ate at the head of the long table, at the other end of which the
group of apprentices, with the old man among them, had been quaffing
since ten o'clock with the good-humored ship's captain. The meal was
wretched and he finished it quickly. He needed to be back in the open air,
to look at the sky: perhaps it would clear over Venice.

It had never occurred to him that this would not happen, for the city
had always received him in its full glory. But the sky and the sea remained
dull and leaden, from time to time misty rain fell, and he resigned himself
to arriving by water in a different Venice, one he had never encountered
on the landward approach. He stood by the foremast, gazing into the distance, waiting for the sight of land. He recalled that poet of plangent inspiration who long ago had seen the cupolas and bell towers of his dream rise
before him out of these same waters; inwardly he recited a few lines of the
measured music that had been made from that reverence and joy and sadness, and effortlessly moved by a passion already shaped into language, he
questioned his grave and weary heart, wondering whether some new inspiration and distraction, some late adventure of the emotions, might yet
be in store for him on his leisured journey.

And now, on his right, the flat coastline rose above the horizon, the sea came alive with fishing vessels, the island resort appeared: the steamer left it on its port side, glided at half speed through the narrow channel named after it, entered the lagoon, and presently, near some shabby miscellaneous buildings, came to a complete halt, as this was where the launch carrying the public health inspector must be awaited.

An hour passed before it appeared. One had arrived and yet not arrived; there was no hurry, and yet one was impelled by impatience. The young men from Pola had come on deck, no doubt also patriotically attracted by the military sound of bugle calls across the water from the direction of the Public Gardens; and elated by the Asti they had drunk, they began cheering the *bersaglieri* as they drilled there in the park. But the dandified old man, thanks to his spurious fraternization with the young, was now in a condition repugnant to behold. His old head could not carry the wine as his sturdy youthful companions had done, and he was lamentably drunk. Eyes glazed, a cigarette between his trembling fingers, he stood swaying, tilted to and fro by inebriation and barely keeping his balance. Since he would have fallen at his first step, he did not dare move from the spot, and was nevertheless full of wretched exuberance, clutching at everyone who approached him, babbling, winking, sniggering, lifting his ringed and wrinkled forefinger as he uttered some bantering inanity, and licking the corners of his mouth with the tip of his tongue in a repellently suggestive way. Aschenbach watched him with frowning disapproval, and once more a sense of numbness came over him, a feeling that the world was somehow, slightly yet uncontrollably, sliding into some kind of bizarre and grotesque derangement. It was a feeling on which, to be sure, he was unable to brood further in present circumstances, for at this moment the thudding motion of the engine began again, and the ship, having stopped short to close to its destination, resumed its passage along the San Marco Canal.

Thus it was that he saw it once more, that most astonishing of all landing places, that dazzling composition of fantastic architecture which the Republic presented to the admiring gaze of approaching seafarers: the unburdened splendor of the Ducal Palace, the Bridge of Sighs, the lion and the saint on their two columns at the water's edge, the magnificently projecting side wing of the fabulous basilica, the vista beyond it of the gate tower and the Giants' Clock; and as he contemplated it all, he reflected that to arrive in Venice by land, at the station, was like entering a palace by a back door: that only as he was now doing, only by ship, over the high sea, should one come to this most extraordinary of cities.

The engine stopped, gondolas pressed alongside, the gangway was let down, customs officers came on board and perfunctorily discharged their duties; disembarkation could begin. Aschenbach indicated that he would like a gondola to take him and his luggage to the stopping place of the small steamboats that ply between the city and the Lido, since he intended to stay in a hotel by the sea. His wishes were approved, his orders shouted down to water level, where the gondoliers were quarreling in Venetian dialect. He was still prevented from leaving the ship, held up by his trunk, which at that moment was being laboriously dragged and maneuvered down the ladderlike gangway; and thus, for a full minute or two, he could not avoid the importunate attentions of the dreadful old man, who on some obscure drunken impulse felt obliged to do this stranger the parting honors. "We wish the signore a most enjoyable stay!" he bleated, bowing and scraping. "We hope the signore will not forget us! *Au revoir, excusez* and *bon jour,* Your Excellency!" He drooled, he screwed up his eyes, licked the corners of his mouth, and the dyed imperial on his senile underlip reared itself upward. "Our compliments," he driveled, touching his lips with two fingers, "our compliments to your sweetheart, to your most charming, beautiful sweetheart . . ." And suddenly the upper set of his false teeth dropped half out of his jaw. Aschenbach was able to escape. "Your sweetheart, your pretty sweetheart!" he heard from behind his back, in gurgling, cavernous, encumbered tones, as he clung to the rope railing and descended the gangway.

Can there be anyone who has not had to overcome a fleeting sense of dread, a secret shudder of uneasiness, on stepping for the first time or after a long interval of years into a Venetian gondola? How strange a vehicle it is, coming down unchanged from times of old romance, and so characteristically black, the way no other thing is black except a coffin—a vehicle evoking lawless adventures in the plashing stillness of night, and still more strongly evoking death itself, the bier, the dark obsequies, the last silent journey! And has it been observed that the seat of such a boat, that armchair with its coffin-black lacquer and dull black upholstery, is the softest, the most voluptuous, most enervating seat in the world? Aschenbach became aware of this when he had settled down at the gondolier's feet, sitting opposite his luggage, which was neatly assembled at the prow. The oarsmen were still quarreling: raucously, unintelligibly, with threatening gestures. But in the peculiar silence of this city of water their voices seemed to be softly absorbed, to become bodiless, dissipated above the sea. It was sultry here in the harbor. As the warm breath of the sirocco touched him, as he leaned back on cushions over the yielding element, the traveler closed his eyes in the enjoyment of this lassitude as sweet as it was unaccustomed. It will be a short ride, he thought; if only it could last forever! In a gently swaying motion he felt himself gliding away from the crowd and the confusion of voices.

How still it was growing all round him! There was nothing to be heard except the plashing of the oar, the dull slap of the wave against the boat's prow where it rose up steep and black and armed at its tip like a halberd, and a third sound also: that of a voice speaking and murmuring—it was the gondolier, whispering and muttering to himself between his teeth, in intermittent grunts pressed out of him by the labor of his arms. Aschenbach looked up and noticed with some consternation that the lagoon was widening round him and that his gondola was heading out to sea. It was thus evident that he must not relax too completely but give some attention to the proper execution of his instructions.

"Well! To the *vaporetto* stop!" he said, half turning round. The muttering ceased, but no answer came.

"I said to the *vaporetto* stop!" he repeated, turning round completely and looking up into the face of the gondolier, who was standing behind him on his raised deck, towering between him and the pale sky. He was a man of displeasing, indeed brutal appearance, wearing blue seaman's clothes, with a yellow scarf round his waist and a shapeless, already fraying straw hat tilted rakishly on his head. To judge by the cast of his face and the blond curling mustache under his snub nose, he was quite evidently not of Italian origin. Although rather slightly built, so that one would not have thought him particularly well suited to his job, he plied his oar with great energy, putting his whole body into every stroke. Occasionally the effort made him retract his lips and bare his white teeth. With his reddish eyebrows knitted, he stared right over his passenger's head as he answered peremptorily, almost insolently:

"You are going to the Lido."

Aschenbach replied:

"Of course. But I only engaged this gondola to row me across to San Marco. I wish to take the *vaporetto*."

"You cannot take the *vaporetto*, signore."

"And why not?"

"Because the *vaporetto* does not carry luggage."

That was correct, as Aschenbach now remembered. He was silent. But the man's abrupt, presumptuous manner, so uncharacteristic of the way foreigners were usually treated in this country, struck him as unacceptable. He said:

"That is my business. I may wish to deposit my luggage. Will you kindly turn round."

There was silence. The oar plashed, the dull slap of the water against the bow continued, and the talking and muttering began again: the gondolier was talking to himself between his teeth.

What was to be done? Alone on the sea with this strangely contumacious, uncannily resolute fellow, the traveler could see no way of compelling him to obey his instructions. And in any case, how luxurious a rest he might have here if he simply accepted the situation! Had he not wished the trip were longer, wished it to last forever? It was wisest to let things take their course, and above all it was very agreeable to do so. A magic spell of indolence seemed to emanate from his seat, from this low black-upholstered armchair, so softly rocked by the oar strokes of the high-handed gondolier behind him. The thought that he had perhaps fallen into the hands of a criminal floated dreamily across Aschenbach's mind—powerless to stir him to any active plan of self-defense. There was the more annoying possibility that the whole thing was simply a device for extorting money from him. A kind of pride or sense of duty, a recollection, so to speak, that there are precautions to be taken against such things, impelled him to make one further effort. He asked:

"What is your charge for the trip?"

And looking straight over his head, the gondolier answered:

"You will pay, signore."

The prescribed retort to this was clear enough. Aschenbach answered mechanically:

"I shall pay nothing, absolutely nothing, if you take me where I do not want to go."

"The signore wants to go to the Lido."

"But not with you."

"I can row you well."

True enough, thought Aschenbach, relaxing. True enough, you will row me well. Even if you are after my cash and dispatch me to the house of Hades with a blow of your oar from behind, you will have rowed me well.

But nothing of the sort happened. He was even provided with company: a boat full of piratical musicians, men and women singing to the guitar or mandolin, importunately traveling hard alongside the gondola and for the foreigner's benefit filling the silence of the waters with mercenary song. Aschenbach threw some money into the outheld hat, whereupon they fell silent and moved off. And the gondolier's muttering became audible again, as in fits and starts he continued his self-colloquy.

And so in due course one arrived, bobbing about in the wake of a *vaporetto* bound for the city. Two police officers, with their hands on their backs, were pacing up and down the embankment and looking out over the lagoon. Aschenbach stepped from the gondola onto the gangway, assisted by the old man with a boat hook who turns up for this purpose at every landing stage in Venice; and having run out of small change, he walked across to the hotel opposite the pier, intending to change money and pay off the oarsman with some suitable gratuity. He was served at the hall desk, and returned to the landing stage to find his luggage loaded onto a trolley on the embankment: the gondola and the gondolier had vanished.

"He cleared off," said the old man with the boat hook. "A bad man, a man without a license, signore. He is the only gondolier who has no license. The others telephoned across to us. He saw the police waiting for him. So he cleared off."

Aschenbach shrugged his shoulders.

"The signore has had a free trip," said the old man, holding out his hat. Aschenbach threw coins into it. He directed that his luggage should be taken to the Hotel des Bains, and followed the trolley along the avenue, that white-blossoming avenue, bordered on either side by taverns and bazaars and guesthouses, which runs straight across the island to the beach.

He entered the spacious hotel from the garden terrace at the back, passing through the main hall and the vestibule to the reception office. As his arrival had been notified in advance, he was received with obsequious obligingness. A manager, a soft-spoken, flatteringly courteous little man with a black mustache and a frock coat of French cut, accompanied him in the lift to the second floor and showed him to his room, an agreeable apartment with cherrywood furniture, strongly scented flowers put out to greet him, and a view through tall windows to the open sea. He went and stood by one of them when the manager had withdrawn, and as his luggage was brought in behind him and installed in the room, he gazed out over the beach, uncrowded at this time of the afternoon, and over the sunless sea, which was at high tide, its long low waves beating with a quiet regular rhythm on the shore.

The observations and encounters of a devotee of solitude and silence are at once less distinct and more penetrating than those of the sociable man; his thoughts are weightier, stranger, and never without a tinge of sadness. Images and perceptions which might otherwise be easily dispelled by a glance, a laugh, an exchange of comments, concern him unduly; they sink into mute depths, take on significance, become experiences, adventures, emotions. The fruit of solitude is originality, something daringly and disconcertingly beautiful, the poetic creation. But the fruit of solitude can also be the perverse, the disproportionate, the absurd and the forbidden. And thus the phenomena of his journey to this place—the horrible old made-up man with his maudlin babble about a sweetheart, the illicit gondolier who had been done out of his money—were still weighing on the traveler's mind. Without in any way being rationally inexplicable, without even really offering food for thought, they were nevertheless, as it seemed to him, essentially strange, and indeed it was no doubt this very paradox that made them disturbing. In the meantime he saluted the sea with his gaze and rejoiced in the knowledge that Venice was now so near and accessible. Finally he turned round, bathed his face, gave the room maid certain instructions for the enhancement of his comfort, and then had himself conveyed by the green-uniformed Swiss lift attendant to the ground floor.

He took tea on the front terrace, then went down to the esplanade and walked some way along it in the direction of the Hotel Excelsior. When he returned, it was already nearly time to be changing for dinner. He did so in his usual leisurely and precise manner, for it was his custom to work when performing his toilet; despite this, he arrived a little early in the hall, where he found a considerable number of the hotel guests assembled, unacquainted with each other and affecting a studied mutual indifference, yet all united in expectancy by the prospect of their evening meal. He picked up a newspaper from the table, settled down in a leather armchair and took stock of the company, which differed very agreeably from what he had encountered at his previous hotel.

A large horizon opened up before him, tolerantly embracing many elements. Discreetly muted, the sounds of the major world languages mingled. Evening dress, that internationally accepted uniform of civilization, imparted a decent outward semblance of unity to the wide variations of mankind here represented. One saw the dry elongated visages of Americans, many-membered Russian families, English ladies, German children with French nurses. The Slav component seemed to predominate. In his immediate vicinity he could hear Polish being spoken.

It was a group of adolescent and barely adult young people, sitting round a cane table under the supervision of a governess or companion: three young girls, of fifteen to seventeen as it seemed, and a long-haired boy of about fourteen. With astonishment Aschenbach noticed that the boy was entirely beautiful. His countenance, pale and gracefully reserved, was surrounded by ringlets of honey-colored hair, and with its straight nose, its enchanting mouth, its expression of sweet and divine gravity, it re-called Greek sculpture of the noblest period; yet despite the purest formal perfection, it had such unique personal charm that he who now contem-plated it felt he had never beheld, in nature or in art, anything so con-summately successful. What also struck him was an obvious contrast of educational principles in the way the boy and his sisters were dressed and generally treated. The system adopted for the three girls, the eldest of whom could be considered to be grown-up, was austere and chaste to the point of disfigurement. They all wore exactly the same slate-colored half-length dresses, sober and of a deliberately unbecoming cut, with white turnover collars as the only relieving feature, and any charm of figure they might have had was suppressed and negated from the outset by this cloistral uniform. Their hair, smoothed and stuck back firmly to their heads, gave their faces a nunlike emptiness and expressionlessness. A mother was clearly in charge here; and it had not even occurred to her to apply to the boy the same pedagogic strictness as she thought proper for the girls. In his life, softness and tenderness were evidently the rule. No one had ever dared to cut short his beautiful hair; like that of the *Boy Extracting a Thorn,* it fell in curls over his forehead, over his ears, and still lower over his neck. The English sailor's suit, with its full sleeves tapering down to fit the fine wrists of his still childlike yet slender hands, and with its lanyards and bows and embroideries, enhanced his delicate shape with an air of richness and indulgence. He was sitting, in semiprofile to Aschenbach's gaze, with one foot in its patent leather shoe advanced in front of the other, with one el-bow propped on the arm of his basket chair, with his cheek nestling against the closed hand, in a posture of relaxed dignity, without a trace of the al-most servile stiffness to which his sisters seemed to have accustomed them-selves. Was he in poor health? For his complexion was white as ivory against the dark gold of the surrounding curls. Or was he simply a pam-pered favorite child, borne up by the partiality of a capricious love? Aschenbach was inclined to think so. Inborn in almost every artistic nature is a luxuriant, treacherous bias in favor of the injustice that creates beauty, a tendency to sympathize with aristocratic preference and pay it homage.

A waiter circulated and announced in English that dinner was served. Gradually the company disappeared through the glass door into the dining room. Latecomers passed, coming from the vestibule or the lifts. The service of dinner had already begun, but the young Poles were still waiting round their cane table, and Aschenbach, comfortably ensconced in his deep armchair, and additionally having the spectacle of beauty before his eyes, waited with them.

The governess, a corpulent and rather unladylike, red-faced little woman, finally gave the signal for them to rise. With arched brows she pushed back her chair and bowed as a tall lady, dressed in silvery gray and very richly adorned with pearls, entered the hall. This lady's attitude was cool and poised; her lightly powdered coiffure and the style of her dress both had that simplicity which is the governing principle of taste in circles where piety is regarded as one of the aristocratic values. In Germany she might have been the wife of a high official. The only thing that did give her appearance a fantastic and luxurious touch was her jewelry, which was indeed beyond price, consisting of earrings as well as a very long three-stranded necklace of gently shimmering pearls as big as cherries.

The brother and sisters had quickly risen to their feet. They bowed over their mother's hand to kiss it, while she, with a restrained smile on her well-maintained but slightly weary and angular face, looked over their heads and addressed a few words in French to the governess. Then she walked toward the glass door. Her children followed her: the girls in order of age, after them the governess, finally the boy. For some reason or other he turned round before crossing the threshold, and as there was now no one else in the hall, his strangely twilight-gray eyes met those of Aschenbach, who with his paper in his lap, lost in contemplation, had been watching the group leave.

What he had seen had certainly not been remarkable in any particular. One does not go in to table before one's mother; they had waited for her, greeted her respectfully, and observed normal polite precedence in entering the dining room. But this had all been carried out with such explicitness, with such a strongly accented air of discipline, obligation, and self-respect, that Aschenbach felt strangely moved. He lingered for another few moments, then he too crossed into the dining room and had himself shown to his table—which, as he noticed with a brief stirring of regret, was at some distance from that of the Polish family.

Tired and yet intellectually stimulated, he beguiled the long and tedious meal with abstract and indeed transcendental reflections. He meditated on the mysterious combination into which the canonical and the individual must enter for human beauty to come into being, proceeded from this point to general problems of form and art, and concluded in the end that his thoughts and findings resembled certain seemingly happy inspirations that come to us in dreams, only to be recognized by the sober senses as completely shallow and worthless. After dinner he lingered for a while, smoking and sitting and walking about, in the evening fragrance of the hotel garden, then retired early and passed the night in sleep which was sound and long, though dream images enlivened it from time to time.

Next day the weather did not seem to be improving. The wind was from landward. Under a pallid overcast sky the sea lay sluggishly still and shrunken-looking, with the horizon in prosaic proximity and the tide so far out that several rows of long sandbars lay exposed. When Aschenbach opened his window, he thought he could smell the stagnant air of the lagoon.

Vexation overcame him. The thought of leaving occurred to him then and there. Once before, years ago, after fine spring weeks, this same weather had come on him here like a visitation, and so adversely affected his health that his departure from Venice had been like a precipitate escape. Were not the same symptoms now presenting themselves again, that unpleasant feverish sensation, the pressure in the temples, the heaviness in the eyelids? To move elsewhere yet again would be tiresome; but if the wind did not change, then there was no question of his staying here. As a precaution he did not unpack completely. At nine he breakfasted in the buffet between the hall and the main restaurant, which was used for serving breakfast.

The kind of ceremonious silence prevailed here which a large hotel always aims to achieve. The serving waiters moved about noiselessly. A clink of crockery, a half-whispered word, were the only sounds audible. In one corner, obliquely opposite the door and two tables away from his own, Aschenbach noticed the Polish girls with their governess. Perched very upright, their ash-blond hair newly brushed and with reddened eyes, in stiff blue linen dresses with little white turnover collars and cuffs, they sat there passing each other a jar of preserves. They had almost finished their breakfast. The boy was missing.

Aschenbach smiled. Well, my little Phaeacian! he thought. You seem, unlike these young ladies, to enjoy the privilege of sleeping your fill. And with his spirits suddenly rising, he recited to himself the line: "Varied garments to wear, warm baths and restful reposing."

He breakfasted unhurriedly, received some forwarded mail from the porter, who came into the breakfast room with his braided cap in hand, and opened a few letters as he smoked a cigarette. Thus it happened that he was still present to witness the entry of the lie-abed they were waiting for across the room.

He came through the glass door and walked in the silence obliquely across the room to his sisters' table. His walk was extraordinarily graceful, in the carriage of his upper body, the motion of his knees, the placing of his white-shod foot; it was very light, both delicate and proud, and made still more beautiful by the childlike modesty with which he twice, turning his head toward the room, raised and lowered his eyes as he passed. With a smile and a murmured word in his soft liquescent language, he took his seat; and now especially, as his profile was exactly turned to the watching Aschenbach, the latter was again amazed, indeed startled, by the truly godlike beauty of this human creature. Today the boy was wearing a light casual suit of blue and white striped linen material with a red silk breastknot, closing at the neck in a simple white stand-up collar. But on this collar—which did not even match the rest of the suit very elegantly— there, like a flower in bloom, his head was gracefully resting. It was the head of Eros, with the creamy luster of Parian marble, the brows finedrawn and serious, the temples and ear darkly and soft covered by the neat right-angled growth of the curling hair.

Good, good! thought Aschenbach, with that cool professional approval in which artists confronted by a masterpiece sometimes cloak their ecstasy, their rapture. And mentally he added: Truly, if the sea and the shore did not await me, I should stay here as long as you do! But as it was, he went, went through the hall accompanied by the courteous attentions of the hotel staff, went down over the great terrace and straight along the wooden passageway to the enclosed beach reserved for hotel guests. Down there, a barefooted old man with linen trousers, sailor's jacket, and straw hat functioned as bathing attendant: Aschenbach had himself conducted by him to his reserved beach cabin, had his table and chair set up on the sandy wooden platform in front of it, and made himself comfortable in the deck chair which he had drawn further out toward the sea onto the wax-yellow sand.

The scene on the beach, the spectacle of civilization taking its carefree sensuous ease at the brink of the element, entertained and delighted him as much as ever. Already the gray shallow sea was alive with children wading, with swimmers, with assorted figures lying on the sandbars, their crossed arms under their heads. Others were rowing little keelless boats painted red and blue, and capsizing with shrieks of laughter. In front of the long row of *capanne,* with their platforms like little verandas to sit on, there was animated play and leisurely sprawling repose, there was visiting and chattering, there was punctilious morning elegance as well as unabashed nakedness contentedly enjoying the liberal local conventions. Further out, on the moist firm sand, persons in white bathing robes, im loose-fitting colorful shirtwear, wandered to and fro. On the right, a complicated sand castle built by children was bedecked by flags in all the national colors. Vendors of mussels, cakes, and fruit knelt to display their wares. On the left, in front of one of the huts in the row that was set at right angles to the others and to the sea, forming a boundary to the beach at this end, a Russian family was encamped: men with beards and big teeth, overripe indolent women, a Baltic spinster sitting at an easel and with exclamations of despair painting the sea, two good-natured hideous children, an old nanny in a headcloth who behaved in the caressingly deferential manner of the born serf. There they all were, gratefully enjoying their lives, tirelessly shouting the names of their disobediently romping children, mustering a few Italian words to joke at length with the amusing old man who sold them sweets, kissing each other on the cheeks, and caring not a jot whether anyone was watching their scene of human solidarity.

Well, I shall say, thought Aschenbach. What better place could I find? And with his hands folded in his lap, he let his eyes wander in the wide expanse of the sea, let his gaze glide away, dissolve, and die in the monotonous haze of this desolate emptiness. There were profound reasons for his attachment to the sea: he loved it because as a hardworking artist he needed rest, needed to escape from the demanding complexity of phenomena and lie hidden on the bosom of the simple and tremendous; because of a forbidden longing deep within him that ran quite contrary to his life's task and was for that very reason seductive, a longing for the unarticulated and immeasurable, for eternity, for nothingness. To rest in the arms of perfection is the desire of any man intent upon creating excellence; and is not nothingness a form of perfection? But now, as he mused idly on such profound matters, the horizontal line of the sea's shore was suddenly intersected by a human figure, and when he had retrieved his gaze from limitless immensity and concentrated it again, he beheld the beautiful boy, coming from the left and walking past him across the sand. He walked barefoot, ready for wading, his slender legs naked to above the knees; his pace was leisured, but as light and proud as if he had long been used to going about without shoes. As he walked he looked round at the projecting row of huts; but scarcely had he noticed the Russian family, as it sat there in contented concord and going about its natural business, than a storm of angry contempt gathered over his face. He frowned darkly, his lips pouted, a bitter grimace pulled them to one side and distorted his cheek; his brows were contracted in so deep a scowl that his eyes seemed to have sunk right in under their pressure, glaring forth a black message of hatred. He looked down, looked back again menacingly, then made with one shoulder an emphatic gesture of rejection as he turned his back and left his enemies behind him.

A kind of delicacy or alarm, something like respect and embarrassment, moved Aschenbach to turn away as if he had seen nothing; for no serious person who witnesses a moment of passion by chance will wish to make any use, even privately, of what he has observed. But he was at one and the same time entertained and moved, that is to say he was filled with happiness. Such childish fanaticism, directed against so harmless a piece of good-natured living—it gave a human dimension to mute divinity, it made a statuesque masterpiece of nature, which had hitherto merely delighted the eyes, seem worthy of a profounder appreciation as well; and it placed the figure of this adolescent, remarkable already by his beauty, in a context which enabled one to take him seriously beyond his years.

With his head still averted, Aschenbach listened to the boy's voice, his high, not very strong voice, as he called out greetings to his playmates working at the sand castle, announcing his arrival when he was still some way from them. They answered, repeatedly shouting his name or a diminutive of his name, and Aschenbach listened for this with a certain curiosity, unable to pick up anything more precise than two melodious syllables that sounded something like "Adigio" or still oftener "Adgiu," called out with a long *u* at the end. The sound pleased him; he found its euphony befitting to its object, repeated it quietly to himself, and turned again with satisfaction to his letters and papers.

With his traveling writing case on his knees, he took out his fountain pen and began to deal with this and that item of correspondence. But after no more than a quarter of an hour he felt that it was a great pity to turn his mind away like this from the present situation, this most enjoyable of all situations known to him, and to miss the experience of it for the sake of an insignificant activity. He threw his writing materials aside, he returned to the sea; and before long, his attention attracted by the youthful voices of the sand castle builders, he turned his head comfortably to the right against the back of his chair, to investigate once more the whereabouts and doings of the excellent Adgio.

His first glance found him; the red-breast knot was unmistakable. He and some others were busy laying an old plank as a bridge across the damp moat of the sand castle, and he was supervising this work, calling out instructions and motioning with his head. With him were about ten companions, both boys and girls, of his age and some of them younger, all chattering together in tongues: in Polish, in French, and even in Balkan idioms. But it was his name that was most often heard. It was obvious that he was sought after, wooed, admired. One boy in particular, a Pole like him, a sturdy young fellow whom they called something like "Jashu," with glossy black hair and wearing a linen belted suit, seemed to be his particular vassal and friend. When the work on the sand castle ended for the time being, they walked along the beach with their arms round each other, and the boy they called "Jashu" kissed his beautiful companion.

Aschenbach was tempted to shake his finger at him. "But I counsel you, Critobulus," he thought with a smile, "to go traveling for a year! You will need that much time at least before you are cured." And he then breakfasted on some large, fully ripe strawberries which he bought from a vendor. It had grown very warm, although the sun was unable to break through the sky's layer of cloud. Even as one's senses enjoyed the tremendous and dizzying spectacle of the sea's stillness, lassitude paralyzed the mind. To the mature and serious Aschenbach it seemed an appropriate, fully satisfying task and occupation for him to guess or otherwise ascertain what name this could be that sounded approximately like "Adgio." And with the help of a few Polish recollections, he established that what was meant must be "'Tadzio," the abbreviation of "Tadeusz" and changing in the vocative to "Tadziu."

Tadzio was bathing. Aschenbach, who had lost sight of him, identified his head and his flailing arm far out to sea; for the water was evidently still shallow a long way out. But already he seemed to be giving cause for alarm, already women's voices were calling out to him from the bathing huts, again shrieking this name which ruled the beach almost like a rallying cry, and which, with its soft consonants, its long-drawn-out *u* sound at the end, had both a sweetness and a wildness about it: "Tadziu! Tadziu!" He returned, he came running, beating the resisting water to foam with his feet, his head thrown back, running through the waves. And to behold this living figure, lovely and austere in its early masculinity, with dripping locks and beautiful as a young god, approaching out of the depths of the sky and the sea, rising and escaping from the elements—this sight filled the mind with mythical images: it was like a poet's tale from a primitive age, a tale of the origins of form and of the birth of the gods. Aschenbach listened with closed eyes to this song as it began its music deep within him, and once again he reflected that it was good to be here and that here he would stay.

Later on, Tadzio lay in the sand resting from his bathe, wrapped in his white bathing robe, which he had drawn through under his right shoulder, and cradling his head on his naked arm; and even when Aschenbach was not watching him but reading a few pages in his book, he almost never forgot that the boy was lying there, and that he need only turn his head slightly to the right to have the admired vision again in view. It almost seemed to him that he was sitting here for the purpose of protecting the half-sleeping boy—busy with doings of his own and yet nevertheless constantly keeping watch over this noble human creature there on his right, only a little way from him. And his heart was filled and moved by a paternal fondness, the tender concern by which he who sacrifices himself to beget beauty in the spirit is drawn to him who possesses beauty.

After midday he left the beach, returned to the hotel, and took the lift up to his room. Here he spent some time in front of the looking glass, studying his gray hair, his weary sharp-featured face. At that moment he thought of his fame, reflected that many people recognized him on the streets and would gaze at him respectfully, saluting the unerring and graceful power of his language—he recalled all the external successes he could think of that his talent had brought him, even calling to mind his elevation to the nobility. Then he went down to the restaurant and took lunch at his table. When he had finished and was entering the lift again, a group of young people who had also just been lunching crowded after him into the hovering cubicle, and Tadzio came with them. He stood quite\ near Aschenbach, so near that for the first time the latter was not seeing him as a distant image but perceiving and taking precise cognizance of the details of his humanity. The boy was addressed by someone, and as he replied, with an indescribably charming smile, he was already leaving the lift again as it reached the first floor, stepping out backward with downcast eyes. The beautiful are modest, thought Aschenbach, and began to reflect very intensively on why this should be so. Nevertheless, he had noticed that Tadzio's teeth were not as attractive as they might have been: rather jagged and pale, lacking the luster of health and having that peculiar brittle transparency that is sometimes found in cases of anemia. He's very delicate, he's sickly, thought Aschenbach; he'll probably not live to grow old. And he made no attempt to explain to himself a certain feeling of satisfaction or relief that accompanied this thought.

He spent two hours in his room, and in midafternoon took the *vaporetto* across the stale-smelling lagoon to Venice. He got out at San Marco, took tea on the Piazza, and then, in accordance with the daily program he had adopted for his stay here, set off on a walk through the streets. But it was this walk that brought about a complete change in his mood and intentions.

An unpleasant sultriness pervaded the narrow streets; the air was so thick that the exhalations from houses and shops and hot food stalls, the reek of oil, the smell of perfume and many other odors, hung about in clouds instead of dispersing. Cigarette smoke lingered and was slow to dissipate. The throng of people in the alleyways annoyed him as he walked instead of giving him pleasure. The further he went, the more overwhelmingly he was afflicted by that appalling condition sometimes caused by a combination of the sea air with the sirocco, a condition of simultaneous excitement and exhaustion. He began to sweat disagreeably. His eyes faltered, his chest felt constricted, he was feverish, the blood throbbed in his head. He fled from the crowded commercial thoroughfares, over bridges, into the poor quarters. There he was besieged by beggars, and the sickening stench from the canals made it difficult to breathe. In a silent square, one of those places in the depths of Venice that seem to have been forgotten and put under a spell, he rested on the edge of a fountain, wiped the sweat from his forehead, and realized that he would have to leave.

For the second time, and this time definitively, it had become evident that this city, in this state of the weather, was extremely injurious to him. To stay on willfully would be contrary to good sense; the prospect of a change in the wind seemed quite uncertain. He must make up his mind at once. To return straight home was out of the question. Neither his summer nor his winter quarters were ready to receive him. But this was not the only place with the sea and a beach, and elsewhere they were to be had without the harmful additional ingredient of this lagoon with its mephitic vapors. He remembered a little coastal resort not far from Trieste which had been recommended to him. Why not go there? And he must do so without delay, if it was to be worthwhile changing to a different place yet again. He declared himself resolved and rose to his feet. At the next gondola stop he took a boat and had himself conveyed back to San Marco through the murky labyrinth of canals, under delicate marble balconies flanked with carved lions, round the slimy stone corners of buildings, past the mournful facades of *palazzi* on which boards bearing the names of commercial enterprises were mirrored in water where refuse bobbed up and down. He had some trouble getting to his destination, as the gondolier was in league with lace factories and glassworks and tried to land him at every place where he might view the wares and make a purchase; and whenever this bizarre journey through Venice might have cast its spell on him, he was effectively and irksomely disenchanted by the cutpurse mercantile spirit of the sunken queen of the Adriatic.

Back in the hotel, before he had even dined, he notified the office that unforeseen circumstances obliged him to leave on the following morning. Regret was expressed, his bill was settled. He took dinner and spent the warm evening reading newspapers in a rocking chair on the back terrace. Before going to bed he packed completely for departure.

He slept fitfully, troubled by his impending further journey. When he opened his windows in the morning, the sky was still overcast, but the air seemed fresher, and he began even now to regret his decision. Had he not given notice too impulsively, had it not been a mistake, an action prompted by a mere temporary indisposition? If only he had deferred it for a little, if only, without giving up so soon, he had taken a chance on acclimatizing himself to Venice or waiting for the wind to change, then he would now have before him not the hurry and flurry of a journey, but a morning on the beach like that of the previous day. Too late. What he had wanted yesterday he must go on wanting now. He got dressed and took the lift down to breakfast at eight o'clock.

When he entered the breakfast room it was still empty of guests. A few came in while he was sitting waiting for what he had ordered. As he sipped his tea he saw the Polish girls arrive with their companion: strict and matutinal, with reddened eyes, they proceeded to their table in the window corner. Shortly after this the porter approached with cap in hand and re-minded him that it was time to leave. The motor coach was standing ready to take him and other passengers to the Hotel Excelsior, from which point the motor launch would convey the ladies and gentlemen through the company's private canal and across to the station. Time is pressing, signore. In Aschenbach's opinion, time was doing nothing of the sort. There was more than an hour till his train left. He found it extremely annoying that hotels should make a practice of getting their departing clients off the premises unnecessarily early, and indicated to the porter that he wished to have his breakfast in peace. The man hesitantly withdrew, only to reappear five minutes later. It was impossible, he said, for the automobile to wait any longer. Aschenbach retorted angrily that in that case it should leave, and take his trunk with it. He himself would take the public steamboat when it was time and would they kindly leave it to him to deal with the problem of his own departure. The hotel servant bowed. Aschenbach, glad to have fended off these tiresome admonitions, finished his breakfast unhurriedly and even got the waiter to hand him a newspaper. It was indeed getting very late by the time he rose. It so happened that at that same moment Tadzio entered through the glass door.

As he walked to his family's table, his path crossed that of the departing guest. Meeting this gray-haired gentleman with the lofty brow, he mod-estly lowered his eyes, only to raise them again at once in his enchanting way, in a soft and full glance; and then he had passed. Good-bye, Tadzio! thought Aschenbach. How short our meeting was. And he added, actually shaping the thought with his lips and uttering it aloud to himself, as he normally never did: "May God bless you!" He then went through the rou-tine of departure, distributed gratuities, received the parting courtesies of the soft-spoken little manager in the French frock coat, and left the hotel on foot as he had come, walking along the white-blossoming avenue with the hotel servant behind him carrying his hand luggage, straight across the island to the *vaporetto* landing stage. He reached it, he took his seat on board—and what followed was a voyage of sorrow, a grievous passage that plumbed all the depths of regret.

It was the familiar trip across the lagoon, past San Marco, up the Grand Canal. Aschenbach sat on the semicircular bench in the bows, one arm on the railing, shading his eyes with his hand. The Public Gardens fell away astern, the Piazzetta revealed itself once more in its princely elegance and was left behind, then came the great flight of the *palazzi,* with the splendid marble arch of the Rialto appearing as the waterway turned. The traveler contemplated it all, and his heart was rent with sorrow. The atmosphere of the city, this slightly moldy smell of sea and swamp from which he had been so anxious to escape—he breathed it in now in deep, tenderly painful drafts. Was it possible that he had not known, had not considered how deeply his feelings were involved in all these things? What had been a mere qualm of compunction this morning, a slight stirring of doubt as to the wisdom of his behavior, now became grief, became real suffering, an anguish of the soul, so bitter that several times it brought tears to his eyes, which as he told himself he could not possibly have foreseen. What he found so hard to bear, what was indeed at times quite unendurable, was evidently the thought that he would never see Venice again, that this was a parting forever. For since it had become clear for a second time that this city made him ill, since he had been forced a second time to leave it precipitately, he must of course from now on regard it as an impossible and forbidden place to which he was not suited and which it would be senseless to attempt to revisit. Indeed, he felt that if he left now, shame and pride must prevent him from ever setting eyes again on this beloved city which had twice physically defeated him; and this contention between his soul's desire and his physical capacities suddenly seemed to the aging Aschenbach so grave and important, the bodily inadequacy so shameful, so necessary to overcome at all costs, that he could not understand the facile resignation with which he had decided yesterday, without any serious struggle, to tolerate that inadequacy and to acknowledge it.

In the meantime the *vaporetto* was approaching the station, and Aschenbach's distress and sense of helplessness increased to the point of distraction. In his torment he felt it to be impossible to leave and no less impossible to turn back. He entered the station torn by this acute inner conflict. It was very late, he had not a moment to lose if he was to catch his train. He both wanted to catch it and wanted to miss it. But time was pressing, lashing him on; he hurried to get his ticket, looking round in the crowded concourse for the hotel company's employee who would be on duty here. The man appeared and informed him that his large trunk had been sent off as registered baggage. Sent off already? Certainly—to Como. To Como? And from hasty comings and goings, from angry questions and embarrassed replies, it came to light that the trunk, before even leaving the luggage room in the Hotel Excelsior, had been put with some quite different baggage and dispatched to a totally incorrect address.

Aschenbach had some difficulty preserving the facial expression that would be the only comprehensible one in these circumstances. A wild joy, an unbelievable feeling of hilarity, shook him almost convulsively from the depths of his heart. The hotel employee rushed to see if it was still possible to stop the trunk and, needless to say, returned without having had any success. Aschenbach accordingly declared that he was not prepared to travel without his luggage, that he had decided to go back and wait at the Hotel des Bains for the missing article to turn up again. Was the company's motor launch still at the station? The man assured him that it was waiting immediately outside. With Italian eloquence, he prevailed upon the official at the ticket office to take back Aschenbach's already purchased ticket. He swore that telegrams would be sent, that nothing would be left undone and no effort spared to get the trunk back in no time at all—and thus it most strangely came about that the traveler, twenty minutes after arriving at the station, found himself back on the Grand Canal and on his way back to the Lido.

How unbelievably strange an experience it was, how shaming, how like a dream in its bizarre comedy: to be returning, by a quirk of fate, to places from which one has just taken leave forever with the deepest sorrow—to be sent back and to be seeing them again within the hour! With spray tossing before its bows, deftly and entertainingly tacking to and fro between gondolas and *vaporetti,* the rapid little boat darted toward its destination, while its only passenger sat concealing under a mask of resigned annoyance the anxiously exuberant excitement of a truant schoolboy. From time to time he still inwardly shook with laughter at this mishap, telling himself that even a man born under a lucky star could not have had a more welcome piece of ill luck. There would be explanations to be given, surprised faces to be confronted—and then, as he told himself, everything would be well again, a disaster would have been averted, a grievous mistake corrected, and everything he thought he had turned his back on for good would lie open again for him to enjoy, would be his for as long as he liked. . . . And what was more, did the rapid movement of the motor launch deceive him, or was there really now, to crown all else, a breeze blowing from the sea?

The bow waves dashed against the concrete walls of the narrow canal that cuts across the island to the Hotel Excelsior. There a motor omnibus was waiting for the returning guest and conveyed him along the road above the rippling sea straight to the Hotel des Bains. The little manager with the mustache and the fancily cut frock coat came down the flight of steps to welcome him.

In softly flattering tones, he expressed regret for the incident, described it as highly embarrassing for himself and for the company, but emphatically endorsed Aschenbach's decision to wait here for his luggage. His room, to be sure, had been relet, but another, no less comfortable, was immediately at his disposal. *"Pas de chance, monsieur!"* said the Swiss lift attendant as they glided up. And thus the fugitive was once more installed in a room situated and furnished almost exactly like the first.

Exhausted and numbed by the confusion of this strange morning, he had no sooner distributed the contents of his hand luggage about the room than he collapsed into a reclining chair at the open window. The sea had turned pale green, the air seemed clearer and purer, the beach with its bathing cabins and boats more colorful, although the sky was still gray. Aschenbach gazed out, his hands folded in his lap, pleased to be here again but shaking his head with displeasure at his irresolution, his ignorance of his own wishes. Thus he sat for about an hour, resting and idly daydreaming. At midday he caught sight of Tadzio in his striped linen suit with the red breast-knot, coming from the sea, through the beach barrier and along the boarded walks back to the hotel. From up here at his window Aschenbach recognized him at once, before he had even looked at him properly, and some such thought came to him as: Why, Tadzio, there you are again too! But at the same instant he felt that casual greeting die on his lips, stricken dumb by the truth in his heart—he felt the rapturous kindling of his blood, the joy, and the anguish of his soul, and realized that it was because of Tadzio that it had been so hard for him to leave.

He sat quite still, quite unseen at his high vantage point, and began to search his feelings. His features were alert, his eyebrows rose, an attentive, intelligently inquisitive smile parted his lips. Then he raised his head and, with his arms hanging limply down along the back of his chair, described with both of them a slowly rotating and lifting motion, the palms of his hands turning forward, as if to sketch an opening and outspreading of the arms. It was a gesture that gladly bade welcome, a gesture of calm acceptance.

## 4

Now day after day the god with the burning cheeks soared naked, driving his four fire-breathing steeds through the spaces of heaven, and now, too, his yellow-gold locks fluttered wide in the outstorming east wind. Silk-white radiance gleamed on the slow-swelling deep's vast waters. The sand glowed. Under the silvery quivering blue of the ether, rust-colored awnings were spread out in front of the beach cabins, and one spent the morning hours on the sharply defined patch of shade they provided. But exquisite, too, was the evening, when the plants in the park gave off a balmy fragrance, and the stars on high moved through their dance, and the softly audible murmur of the night-surrounded sea worked its magic on the soul. Such an evening carried with it the delightful promise of a new sunlit day of leisure, easily ordered and adorned with countless close-knit possibilities of charming chance encounter.

The guest whom so convenient a mishap had detained here was very far from seeing the recovery of his property as a reason for yet another departure. For a couple of days he had had to put up with some privations and appear in the main dining room in his traveling clothes. Then, when finally the errant load was once more set down in his room, he unpacked completely and filled the cupboards and drawers with his possessions, resolving for the present to set no time limit on his stay; he was glad now to be able to pass his hours on the beach in a tussore suit and to present himself again in seemly evening attire at the dinner table.

The lulling rhythm of this existence had already cast its spell on him; he had been quickly enchanted by the indulgent softness and splendor of this way of life. What a place this was indeed, combining the charms of a cultivated seaside resort in the south with the familiar ever-ready proximity of the strange and wonderful city! Aschenbach did not enjoy enjoying himself. Whenever and wherever he had to stop work, have a breathing space, take things easily, he would soon find himself driven by restlessness and dissatisfaction—and this had been so in his youth above all—back to his lofty travail, to his stern and sacred daily routine. Only this place bewitched him, relaxed his will, gave him happiness. Often in the forenoon, under the awning of his hut, gazing dreamily at the blue of the southern sea, or on a mild night perhaps, reclining under a star-strewn sky on the cushions of a gondola that carried him back to the Lido from the Piazza, where he had long lingered—and as the bright lights, the melting sounds

of the serenade, dropped away behind him—often he recalled his country
house in the mountains, the scene of his summer labors, where the low
clouds would drift through his garden, violent evening thunderstorms
would put out all the lights, and the ravens he fed would take refuge in the
tops of the pine trees. Then indeed he would feel he had been snatched
away now to the Elysian land, to the ends of the earth, where lightest of
living is granted to mortals, where no snow is nor winter, no storms and
no rain downstreaming, but where Oceanus ever causes a gentle cooling
breeze to ascend, and the days flow past in blessed idleness, with no labor
or strife, for to the sun alone and its feasts they are all given over.

Aschenbach saw much of the boy Tadzio, he saw him almost constantly; in a confined environment, with a common daily program, it was
natural for the beautiful creature to be near him all day, with only brief in-
terruptions. He saw him and met him everywhere: in the ground-floor
rooms of the hotel, on their cooling journeys by water to the city and
back, in the sumptuous Piazza itself, and often elsewhere from time to
time, in alleys and byways, when chance had played a part. But it was during the mornings on the beach above all, and with the happiest regularity,
that he could devote hours at a time to the contemplation and study of this
exquisite phenomenon. Indeed, it was precisely this ordered routine of
happiness, this equal daily repetition of favorable circumstances, that so
filled him with contentment and zest for life, that made this place so precious to him, that allowed one sunlit day to follow another in such obligingly endless succession.

He rose early, as he would normally have done under the insistent
compulsion of work, and was down at the beach before most of the other
guests, when the sun's heat was still gentle and the sea lay dazzling white
in its morning dreams. He greeted the barrier attendant affably, exchanged
familiar greetings also with the barefooted, white-bearded old man who
had prepared his place for him, spread the brown awning and shifted the
cabin furniture out to the platform where Aschenbach would settle down.
Three hours or four were then his, hours in which the sun would rise to
its zenith and to terrible power, hours in which the sea would turn a
deeper and deeper blue, hours in which he would be able to watch Tadzio.

He saw him coming, walking along from the left by the water's edge,
saw him from behind as he emerged between the cabins, or indeed would
sometimes look up and discover, gladdened and startled, that he had
missed his arrival and that the boy was already there, already in the blue

and white bathing costume which now on the beach was his sole attire. There he would be, already busy with his customary activities in the sun and the sand—this charmingly trivial, idle yet ever active life that was both play and repose, a life of sauntering, wading, digging, snatching, lying about, and swimming, under the watchful eyes and at the constant call of the women on their platform, who with their high-pitched voices would cry out his name: "Tadziu! Tadziu!" and to whom he would come running with eager gesticulation, to tell them what he had experienced, to show them what he had found, what he had caught: jellyfish, little seahorses, and mussels, and crabs that go sideways. Aschenbach understood not a word of what he said, and commonplace though it might be, it was liquid melody in his ears. Thus the foreign sound of the boy's speech exalted it to music, the sun in its triumph shed lavish brightness all over him, and the sublime perspective of the sea was the constant contrasting background against which he appeared.

Soon the contemplative beholder knew every line and pose of that noble, so freely displayed body, he saluted again with joy each already familiar perfection, and there was no end to his wonder, to the delicate delight of his senses. The boy would be summoned to greet a guest who was making a polite call on the ladies in their cabin: he would run up, still wet perhaps from the sea, throw back his curls, and as he held out his hand, poised on one leg with the other on tiptoe, he had an enchanting way of turning and twisting his body, gracefully expectant, charmingly shamefaced, seeking to please because good breeding required him to do so. Or he would be lying full-length, his bathing robe wrapped round his chest, his finely chiseled arm propped on the sand, his hand cupping his chin; the boy addressed as "Jashu" would squat beside him, caressing him, and nothing could be more bewitching than the way the favored Tadzio, smiling with his eyes and lips, would look up at this lesser and servile mortal. Or he would be standing at the edge of the sea, alone, some way from his family, quite near Aschenbach, standing upright with his hands clasped behind his neck, slowly rocking to and fro on the balls of his feet and dreamily gazing into the blue distance, while little waves ran up and bathed his toes. His honey-colored hair nestled in ringlets at his temples and at the back of his neck, the sun gleamed in the down on his upper spine, the subtle outlining of his ribs and the symmetry of his breast stood out through the scanty covering of his torso, his armpits were still as smooth as those of a statue, the hollows of his knees glistened and their bluish veins made his body seem composed of some more translucent material. What discipline, what precision of thought was expressed in that outstretched, youthfully perfect physique! And yet the austere pure will that had here been darkly active, that had succeeded in bringing this divine sculptured shape to light—was it not well known and familiar to Aschenbach as an artist? Was it not also active in him, in the sober passion that filled him as he set free from the marble mass of language that slender form which he had beheld in the spirit, and which he was presenting to mankind as a model and mirror of intellectual beauty?

A model and mirror! His eyes embraced that noble figure at the blue water's edge, and in rising ecstasy he felt he was gazing on Beauty itself, on Form as a thought of God, on the one and pure perfection which dwells in the spirit and of which a human image and likeness had here been lightly and graciously set up for him to worship. Such was his emotional intoxication; and the aging artist welcomed it unhesitatingly, even greedily. His mind was in labor, its store of culture was in ferment, his memory threw up thoughts from ancient tradition which he had been taught as a boy but which had never yet come alive in his own fire. Had he not read that the sun turns our attention from spiritual things to the things of the senses? He had read that it so numbs and bewitches our intelligence and memory that the soul, in its joy, quite forgets its proper state and clings with astonished admiration to that most beautiful of all the things the sun shines upon: yes, that only with the help of a bodily form is the soul then still able to exalt itself to a higher vision. That Cupid, indeed, does as mathematicians do when they show dull-witted children tangible images of the pure Forms: so too the love god, in order to make spiritual things visible, loves to use the shapes and colors of young men, turning them into instruments of Recollection by adorning them with all the reflected splendor of Beauty, so that the sight of them will truly set us on fire with pain and hope.

Such were the thoughts the god inspired in his enthusiast, such were the emotions of which he grew capable. And a delightful vision came to him, spun from the sea's murmur and the glittering sunlight. It was the old plane tree not far from the walls of Athens—that place of sacred shade, fragrant with chaste-tree blossoms, adorned with sacred statues and pious gifts in honor of the nymphs and of Achelous. The stream trickled crystal clear over smooth pebbles at the foot of the great spreading tree; the crickets made their music. But on the grass, which sloped down gently so that one could hold up one's head as one lay, there reclined two men, sheltered here from the heat of the noonday: one elderly and one young, one ugly and one beautiful, the wise beside the desirable. And Socrates, wooing him with witty compliments and jests, was instructing Phaedrus on desire and virtue. He spoke to him of the burning tremor of fear which the lover will suffer when his eye perceives a likeness of eternal Beauty; spoke to him of the lusts of the profane and base who cannot turn their eyes to Beauty when they behold its image and are not capable of reverence; spoke of the sacred terror that visits the noble soul when a godlike countenance, a perfect body, appears to him—of how he trembles then and is beside himself and hardly dares look at the possessor of beauty, and reveres him and would even sacrifice to him as to a graven image, if he did not fear to seem foolish in the eyes of men. For Beauty, dear Phaedrus, only Beauty is at one and the same time divinely desirable and visible: it is, mark well, the only form of the spiritual that we can receive with our senses and endure with our senses. For what would become of us if other divine things, if Reason and Virtue and Truth, were to appear to us sensuously? Should we not perish in a conflagration of love, as once upon a time Semele did before Zeus? Thus Beauty is the lover's path to the spirit—only the path, only a means, little Phaedrus. . . . And then he uttered the subtlest thing of all, that sly wooer: he who loves, he said, is more divine than the beloved, because the god is in the former, but not in the latter—this the tenderest perhaps and the most mocking thought ever formulated, a thought alive with all the mischievousness and most secret voluptuousness of the heart.

The writer's joy is the thought that can become emotion, the emotion that can wholly become a thought. At that time the solitary Aschenbach took possession and control of just such a pulsating thought, just such a precise emotion: namely, that Nature trembles with rapture when the spirit bows in homage before Beauty. He suddenly desired to write. Eros indeed, we are told, loves idleness and is born only for the idle. But at this point of Aschenbach's crisis and visitation, his excitement was driving him to produce. The occasion was almost a matter of indifference. An inquiry, an invitation to express a personal opinion on a certain important cultural problem, a burning question of taste, had been circulated to the intellectual world and had been forwarded to him on his travels. The theme was familiar to him, it was close to his experience; the desire to illuminate it in his own words was suddenly irresistible. And what he craved, indeed, was to work on it in Tadzio's presence, to take the boy's physique for a model as he wrote, to let his style follow the lineaments of this body which he saw as divine, and to carry its beauty on high into the spiritual world, as the eagle once carried the Trojan shepherd boy up into the ether. Never had he felt the joy of the word more sweetly, never had he known so clearly that Eros dwells in language, as during those perilously precious hours in which, seated at his rough table under the awning, in full view of his idol and with the music of his voice in his ears, he used Tadzio's beauty as a model for his brief essay—that page and a half of exquisite prose which with its limpid nobility and vibrant controlled passion was soon to win the admiration of many. It is as well that the world knows only a fine piece of work and not also its origins, the conditions under which it came into being; for knowledge of the sources of an artist's inspiration would often confuse readers and shock them, and the excellence of the writing would be of no avail. How strange those hours were! How strangely exhausting that labor! How mysterious this act of intercourse and begetting between a mind and body! When Aschenbach put away his work and left the beach, he felt worn out, even broken, and his conscience seemed to be reproaching him as if after some kind of debauch.

On the following morning, just as he was leaving the hotel, he noticed from the steps that Tadzio, already on his way to the sea—and alone—was just approaching the beach barrier. The wish to use this opportunity, the mere thought of doing so and thereby lightly, lightheartedly, making the acquaintance of one who had unknowingly so exalted and moved him: the thought of speaking to him, of enjoying his answer and his glance—all this seemed natural, it was the irresistibly obvious thing to do. The beautiful boy was walking in a leisurely fashion, he could be overtaken, and Aschenbach quickened his pace. He reached him on the boarded way behind the bathing cabins; he was just about to lay his hand on his head or his shoulder, and some phrase or other, some friendly words in French, were on the tip of his tongue—when he felt his heart, perhaps partly because he had been walking fast, hammering wildly inside him, felt so breathless that he would only have been able to speak in a strangled and trembling voice. He hesitated, struggled to control himself, then was suddenly afraid that he had already been walking too long close behind the beautiful boy, afraid that Tadzio would notice this, that he would turn and look at him questioningly; he made one more attempt, failed, gave up, and hurried past with his head bowed.

Too late! he thought at that moment. Too late! But was it too late?

This step he had failed to take would very possibly have been all to the good, it might have had a lightening and gladdening effect, led perhaps to a wholesome disenchantment. But the fact now seemed to be that the aging lover no longer wished to be disenchanted, that the intoxication was too precious to him. Who shall unravel the mystery of an artist's nature and character! Who shall explain the profound instinctual fusion of discipline and dissoluteness on which it rests! For not to be able to desire wholesome disenchantment is to be dissolute. Aschenbach was no longer disposed to self-criticism; taste, the intellectual mold of his years, self-respect, maturity, and late simplicity all disinclined him to analyze his motives and decide whether what had prevented him from carrying out his intention had been a prompting of conscience or a disreputable weakness. He was confused; he was afraid that someone, even if only the bathing attendant, might have witnessed his haste and his defeat; he was very much afraid of exposure to ridicule. For the rest, he could not help smiling inwardly at his comic-sacred terror. Crestfallen, he thought, spirits dashed, like a frightened cock hanging its wings in a fight! Truly this is the god who at the sight of the desired beauty breaks our courage and dashes our pride so utterly to the ground. . . . He toyed with the theme, gave rein to his enthusiasm, plunged into emotions he was too proud to fear.

He was no longer keeping any tally of the leisure time he had allowed himself; the thought of returning home did not even occur to him. He had arranged for ample funds to be made available to him here. His one anxiety was that the Polish family might leave; but he had surreptitiously learned, by a casual question to the hotel barber, that these guests had begun their stay here only very shortly before he had arrived himself. The sun was browning his face and hands, the stimulating salty breeze heightened his capacity for feeling, and whereas formerly, when sleep or food or contact with nature had given him any refreshment, he would always have expended it completely on his writing, he now, with high-hearted prodigality, allowed all the daily revitalization he was receiving from the sun and leisure and sea air to burn itself up in intoxicating emotion.

He slept fleetingly; the days of precious monotony were punctuated by brief, happily restless nights. To be sure, he would retire early, for at nine o'clock, when Tadzio had disappeared from the scene, he judged his day to be over. But at the first glint of dawn a pang of tenderness would startle him awake, his heart would remember its adventure, he could bear his pillows no longer, he would get up, and lightly wrapped against the early morning chill, he would sit down at the open window to wait for the sunrise. His soul, still fresh with the solemnity of sleep, was filled with awe by this wonderful event. The sky, the earth, and the sea still wore the glassy paleness of ghostly twilight; a dying star still floated in the void. But a murmur came, a winged message from dwelling places no mortal may approach, that Eos was rising from her husband's side; and now it appeared, that first sweet blush at the farthest horizon of the sky and sea, which heralds the sensuous disclosure of creation. The goddess approached, that ravisher of youth, who carried off Cleitus and Cephalus and defied the envy of all the Olympians to enjoy the love of the beautiful Orion. A scattering of roses began, there at the edge of the world, an ineffably lovely shining and blossoming: childlike clouds, transfigured and transparent with light, hovered like serving *amoretti* in the vermilion and violet haze; crimson light fell across the waves, which seemed to be washing it landward; golden spears darted from below into the heights of heaven the gleam became a conflagration, noiselessly and with overwhelming divine power the glow and the fire and the blazing flames reared upward, and the sacred steeds of the goddess's brother Helios, tucking their hooves, leapt above the earth's round surface. With the splendor of the god irradiating him, the lone watcher sat; he closed his eyes and let the glory kiss his eyelids. Feelings he had had long ago, early and precious dolors of the heart, which had died out in his life's austere service and were now, so strangely transformed, returning to him—he recognized them with a confused and astonished smile. He meditated, he dreamed, slowly a name shaped itself on his lips, and still smiling, with upturned face, his hands folded in his lap, he fell asleep in his chair once more.

With such fiery ceremony the day began, but the rest of it, too, was strangely exalted and mythically transformed. Where did it come from, what was its origin, this sudden breeze that played so gently and speakingly around his temples and ears, like some higher insufflation? Innumerable white fleecy clouds covered the sky, like the grazing flocks of the gods. A stronger wind rose, and the horses of Poseidon reared and ran; his bulls too, the bulls of the blue-haired sea god, roared and charged with lowered horns. But among the rocks and stones of the more distant beach the waves danced like leaping goats. sacred, deranged world, full of Panic life, enclosed the enchanted watcher, and his heart dreamed tender tales. Sometimes, as the sun was sinking behind Venice, he would sit on a bench in the hotel park to watch Tadzio, dressed in white with a colorful sash, at play on the rolled gravel tennis court; and in his mind's eye he was watching Hyacinthus, doomed to perish because two gods loved him. He could even feel Zephyr's grievous envy of his rival, who had forgotten his oracle and his bow and his zither to be forever playing with the beautiful youth; he saw the discus, steered by cruel jealousy, strike the lovely head; he himself, turning pale too, caught the broken body in his arms, and the flower that sprang from that sweet blood bore the inscription of his undying lament.

Nothing is stranger, more delicate, than the relationship between people who know each other only by sight—who encounter and observe each other daily, even hourly, and yet are compelled by the constraint of convention or by their own temperament to keep up the pretense of being indifferent strangers, neither greeting nor speaking to each other. Between them is uneasiness and overstimulated curiosity, the nervous excitement of an unsatisfied, unnaturally suppressed need to know and to communicate; and above all, too a kind of strained respect. For man loves and respects his fellow man for as long as he is not yet in a position to evaluate him, and desire is born of defective knowledge.

It was inevitable that some kind of relationship and acquaintance should develop between Aschenbach and the young Tadzio, and with a surge of joy the older man became aware that his interest and attention were not wholly unreciprocated. Why, for example, when the beautiful creature appeared in the morning on the beach, did he now never use the boarded walk behind the bathing cabins, but always take the front way, through the sand, passing Aschenbach's abode and often passing unnecessarily close to him, almost touching his table or his chair, as he sauntered toward the cabin where his family sat? Was this the attraction, the fascination exercised by a superior feeling on its tender and thoughtless object? Aschenbach waited daily for Tadzio to make his appearance and sometimes pretended to be busy when he did so, letting the boy pass him seemingly unnoticed. But sometimes, too, he would look up, and their eyes would meet. They would both be deeply serious when this happened. In the cultured and dignified countenance of the older man, nothing betrayed an inner emotion; but in Tadzio's eyes there was an inquiry, a thoughtful questioning; his walk became hesitant, he looked at the ground, looked sweetly up again, and when he had passed, something in his bearing seemed to suggest that only good breeding restrained him from turning to look back.

But once, one evening, it was different. The Poles and their governess had been absent from dinner in the main restaurant—Aschenbach had noticed this with concern. After dinner, very uneasy about where they might be, he was walking in evening dress and a straw hat in front of the hotel, at the foot of the terrace, when suddenly he saw the nunlike sisters appearing with their companion in the light of the arc lamps, and four paces behind them was Tadzio. Obviously they had come from the *vaporetto* pier, having for some reason dined in the city. The crossing had been chilly, perhaps: Tadzio was wearing a dark-blue reefer jacket with gold buttons and a naval cap to match. The sun and sea air never burned his skin; it was marble-pale as always; but today he seemed paler than usual, either because of the cool weather or in the blanching moonlight of the lamps. His symmetrical eyebrows stood out more sharply, his eyes seemed much darker. He was more beautiful than words can express, and Aschenbach felt, as so often already, the painful awareness that language can only praise sensuous beauty, but not reproduce it.

He had not been prepared for the beloved encounter; it came unexpectedly; he had not had time to put on an expression of calm and dignity. Joy, no doubt, surprise, admiration, were openly displayed on his face when his eyes met those of the returning absentee—and in that instant it happened that Tadzio smiled: smiled at him, speakingly, familiarly, enchantingly, and quite unabashed, with his lips parting slowly as the smile was formed. It was the smile of Narcissus as he bows his head over the mirroring water, that profound, fascinated, protracted smile with which he reaches out his arms toward the reflection of his own beauty—a very slightly contorted smile, contorted by the hopelessness of his attempt to kiss the sweet lips of his shadow: a smile that was provocative, curious and imperceptibly troubled, bewitched and bewitching.

He who had received this smile carried it quickly away with him like a fateful gift. He was so deeply shaken that he was forced to flee the lighted terrace and the front garden and hurry into the darkness of the park at the rear. Words struggled from his lips, strangely indignant and tender reproaches: "You mustn't smile like that! One mustn't, do you hear, mustn't smile like that at anyone!" He sank down on one of the seats, deliriously breathing the nocturnal fragrance of the flowers and trees. And leaning back, his arms hanging down, overwhelmed, trembling, shuddering all over, he whispered the standing formula of the heart's desire—impossible here, absurd, depraved, ludicrous, and sacred nevertheless, still worthy of honor even here: "I love you!"

## 5

During the fourth week of his stay at the Lido, Gustav von Aschenbach began to notice certain uncanny developments in the outside world. In the first place, it struck him that as the height of the season approached, the number of guests at his hotel was diminishing rather than increasing, and in particular that the German language seemed to be dying away into silence all round him, so that in the end only foreign sounds fell on his ear at table and on the beach. Then one day the hotel barber, whom he visited frequently now, let slip in conversation a remark that aroused his suspicions. The man had mentioned a German family who had just left after only a brief stay, and in his chattering, flattering manner, he added: "But you are staying on, signore; you are not afraid of the sickness." Aschenbach looked at him. "The sickness?" he repeated. The fellow stopped his talk, pretended to be busy, had not heard the question. And when it was put to him again, more sharply, he declared that he knew nothing and tried with embarrassed loquacity to change the subject.

That was at midday. In the afternoon, with the sea dead calm and the sun burning, Aschenbach crossed to Venice, for he was now driven by a mad compulsion to follow the Polish boy and his sisters, having seen them set off toward the pier with their companion. He did not find his idol at San Marco. But at tea, sitting at his round wrought-iron table on the shady side of the Piazza, he suddenly scented in the air a peculiar aroma, one which it now seemed to him he had been noticing for days without really being conscious of it—a sweetish, medicinal smell that suggested squalor and wounds and suspect cleanliness. He scrutinized it, pondered and identified it, finished his tea and left the Piazza at the far end opposite the basilica. In the narrow streets the smell was stronger. At corners, printed notices had been pasted up in which the civic authorities, with fatherly concern, gave warning to the local population that since certain ailments of the gastric system were normal in this weather, they should refrain from eating oysters and mussels and indeed from using water from the canals. The euphemistic character of the announcement was obvious. Groups of people were standing about silently on bridges or in squares, and the stranger stood among them, brooding and scenting the truth.

He found a shopkeeper leaning against his vaulted doorway, surrounded by coral necklaces and trinkets made of imitation amethyst, and asked him about the unpleasant smell. The man looked him over with heavy eyes, and hastily gathered his wits. "A precautionary measure, signore," he answered, gesticulating. "The police have laid down regulations, and quite right too, it must be said. This weather is oppressive, the sirocco is not very wholesome. In short, the signore will understand—an exaggerated precaution, no doubt. . . ." Aschenbach thanked him and walked on. Even on the *vaporetto* taking him back to the Lido he now noticed the smell of the bactericide.

Back at the hotel, he went at once to the table in the hall where the newspapers were kept, and carried out some research. In the foreign papers he found nothing. Those in his own language mentioned rumors, quoted contradictory statistics, reported official denials and questioned their veracity. This explained the withdrawal of the German and Austrian clientele. Visitors of other nationalities evidently knew nothing, suspected nothing, still had no apprehensions. They want it kept quiet! thought Aschenbach in some agitation, throwing the newspapers back on the table. They're hushing this up! But at the same time his heart filled with elation at the thought of the adventure in which the outside world was about to be involved. For to passion, as to crime, the assured everyday order and stability of things is not opportune, and any weakening of the civil structure, any chaos and disaster afflicting the world, must be welcome to it, as offering a vague hope of turning such circumstances to its advantage. Thus Aschenbach felt an obscure sense of satisfaction at what was going on in the dirty alleyways of Venice, cloaked in official secrecy—this guilty secret of the city, which merged with his own innermost secret and which it was also so much in his own interests to protect. For in his enamored state his one anxiety was that Tadzio might leave, and he realized with a kind of horror that he would not be able to go on living if that should happen.

Lately he had not been content to owe the sight and proximity of the beautiful boy merely to daily routine and chance: he had begun pursuing him, following him obtrusively. On Sunday, for example, the Poles never appeared on the beach; he rightly guessed that they were attending mass in San Marco, and hastened to the church himself. There, stepping from the fiery heat of the Piazza into the golden twilight of the sanctuary, he would find him whom he had missed, bowed over a prie-dieu and performing his devotions. Then he would stand in the background, on the cracked mosaic floor, amid a throng of people kneeling, murmuring, and crossing themselves, and the massive magnificence of the oriental temple would weigh sumptuously on his senses. At the front, the ornately vested priest walked to and fro, doing his business and chanting. Incense billowed up, clouding the feeble flames of the altar candles, and with its heavy, sweet sacrificial odor another seemed to mingle: the smell of the sick city. But through the vaporous dimness and the flickering lights Aschenbach saw the boy, up there at the front turn his head and seek him with his eyes until he found him.

Then, when the great doors were opened and the crowd streamed out into the shining Piazza, swarming with pigeons, the beguiled lover would hide in the antebasilica, he would lurk and lie in wait. He would see the Poles leave the church, see the brother and sisters take ceremonious leave of their mother, who would then set off home, turning toward the Piazzetta; he would observe the boy, the cloistral sisters, and the governess turn right and walk through the clock tower gateway into the Merceria, and after letting them get a little way ahead he would follow them—follow them furtively on their walk through Venice. He had to stop when they lingered, had to take refuge in hot food stalls and courtyards to let them pass when they turned round; he would lose them, search for them frantically and exhaustingly, rushing over bridges and along filthy culs-de-sac, and would then have to endure minutes of mortal embarrassment when he suddenly saw them coming toward him in a narrow passageway where no escape was possible. And yet one cannot say that he suffered. His head and his heart were drunk, and his steps followed the dictates of that dark god whose pleasure it is to trample man's reason and dignity underfoot.

Presently, somewhere or other, Tadzio and his family would take a gondola, and while they were getting into it, Aschenbach, hiding behind a fountain or the projecting part of a building, would wait till they were a little way from the shore and then do the same. Speaking hurriedly and in an undertone, he would instruct the oarsman, promising him a large tip, to follow that gondola ahead of them that was just turning the corner, to follow it at a discreet distance; and a shiver would run down his spine when the fellow, with the roguish compliance of a pander, would answer him in the same tone, assuring him that he was at his service, entirely at his service.

Thus he glided and swayed gently along, reclining on soft black cushions, shadowing that other black, beaked craft, chained to its pursuit by his infatuation. Sometimes he would lose sight of it and become distressed and anxious, but his steersman, who seemed to be well practiced in commissions of this kind, would always know some cunning maneuver, some side canal or shortcut, that would again bring Aschenbach in sight of what he craved. The air was stagnant and malodorous, the sun burned oppressively through the haze, which had turned the sky to the color of slate. Water lapped against wood and stone. The gondolier's call, half warning and half greeting, was answered from a distance out of the silent labyrinth, in accordance with some strange convention. Out of little overhead gardens, unbelliferous blossoms spilled over and hung down the crumbling masonry, white and purple and almond scented. Moorish windows were mirrored in the murky water. The marble steps of a church dipped below the surface; a beggar squatted on them, protesting his misery, holding out his hat and showing the whites of his eyes as if he were blind; an antiques dealer beckoned to them with crawling obsequiousness as they passed his den, inviting them to stop and be swindled. This was Venice, the flattering and suspect beauty—this city, half fairy tale and half tourist trap, in whose insalubrious air the arts once rankly and voluptuously blossomed, where composers have been inspired to lulling tones of somniferous eroticism. Gripped by his adventure, the traveler felt his eyes drinking in this sumptuousness, his ears wooed by these melodies; he remembered, too, that the city was stricken with sickness and concealing it for reasons of cupidity, and he peered around still more wildly in search of the gondola that hovered ahead.

So it was that in his state of distraction he could no longer think of anything or want anything except this ceaseless pursuit of the object that so inflamed him: nothing but to follow him, to dream of him when he was not there, and after the fashion of lovers to address tender words to his mere shadow. Solitariness, the foreign environment, and the joy of an intoxication of feeling that had come to him so late and affected him so profoundly—all this encouraged and persuaded him to indulge himself in the most astonishing ways: as when it had happened that late one evening, returning from Venice and reaching the first floor of the hotel, he had paused outside the boy's bedroom door, leaning his head against the doorframe in a complete drunken ecstasy, and had for a long time been unable to move from the spot, at risk of being surprised and discovered in this insane situation.

Nevertheless, there were moments at which he paused and half came to his senses. Where is this leading me! he would reflect in consternation at such moments. Where was it leading him! Like any man whose natural merits move him to take an aristocratic interest in his origins, Aschenbach habitually let the achievements and successes of his life remind him of his ancestors, for in imagination he could then feel sure of their approval, of their satisfaction, of the respect they could not have withheld. And he thought of them even here and now, entangled as he was in so impermissible an experience, involved in such exotic extravagances of feeling; he thought, with a sad smile, of their dignified austerity, their decent manliness of character. What would they say? But for that matter, what would they have said about his entire life, a life that had deviated from theirs to the point of degeneracy, this life of his in the compulsive service of art, this life about which he himself, adopting the civic values of his forefathers, had once let fall such mocking observations—and which nevertheless had essentially been so much like theirs! He too had served, he too had been a soldier and a warrior, like many of them: for art was a war, an exhausting struggle; it was hard these days to remain fit for it for long. A life of self-conquest and of defiant resolve, an astringent, steadfast, and frugal life which he had turned into the symbol of that heroism for delicate constitutions, that heroism so much in keeping with the times—surely he might call this manly, might call it courageous? And it seemed to him that the kind of love that had taken possession of him did, in a certain way, suit and befit such a life. Had it not been highly honored by the most valiant of peoples, indeed had he not read that in their cities it had flourished by inspiring valorous deeds? Numerous warrior heroes of olden times had willingly borne its yoke, for there was no kind of abasement that could be reckoned as such if the god had imposed it; and actions that would have been castigated as signs of cowardice had their motives been different, such as falling to the ground in supplication, desperate pleas, and slavish demeanor—these were accounted no disgrace to a lover, but rather won him still greater praise.

Such were the thoughts with which love beguiled him, and thus he sought to sustain himself, to preserve his dignity. But at the same time he kept turning his attention, inquisitively and persistently, to the disreputable events that were evolving in the depths of Venice, to that adventure of the outside world which darkly mingled with the adventure of his heart and which nourished his passion with vague and lawless hopes. Obstinately determined to obtain new and reliable information about the status and progress of the malady, he would sit in the city's coffeehouses, searching through the German newspapers, which several days ago had disappeared from the reading table in the hotel foyer. They carried assertions and retractions by turns. The number of cases, the number of deaths, was said to be twenty, or forty, or a hundred and more, such reports being immediately followed by statements flatly denying the outbreak of an epidemic, or at least reducing it to a few quite isolated cases brought in from outside the city. Scattered here and there were warning admonitions, or protests against the dangerous policy being pursued by the Italian authorities. There was no certainty to be had.

The solitary traveler was nevertheless conscious of having a special claim to participation in this secret, and although excluded from it, he took a perverse pleasure in putting embarrassing questions to those in possession of the facts, and thus, since they were pledged to silence, forcing them to lie to him directly. One day, at luncheon in the main dining room, he interrogated the hotel manager in this fashion, the soft-footed little man in the French frock coat who was moving around among the tables, supervising the meal and greeting the clients, and who also stopped at Aschenbach's table for a few words of conversation. Why, in fact, asked his guest in a casual and nonchalant way, why on earth had they begun recently to disinfect Venice? "It is merely a police measure, sir," answered the trickster, "taken in good time, as a safeguard against various disagreeable public health problems that might otherwise arise from this sultry and exceptionally warm weather—a precautionary measure which it is their duty to take." "Very praiseworthy of the police," replied Aschenbach; and after exchanging a few meteorological observations with him, the manager took his leave.

On the very same day, in the evening after dinner, it happened that a small group of street singers from the city gave a performance in the front garden of the hotel. They stood by one of the iron arc lamp standards, two men and two women, their faces glinting white in the glare, looking up at the great terrace where the hotel guests sat over their coffee and cooling drinks, resigned to watching this exhibition of folk culture. The hotel staff, the lift boys, waiters, office employees, had come out to listen in the hall doorways. The Russian family, eager to savor every pleasure, had had cane chairs put out for them down in the garden, in order to be nearer the performers, and were contentedly sitting there in a semicircle. Behind her master and mistress, in a turbanlike headcloth, stood their aged serf.

The beggar virtuosi were playing a mandolin, a guitar, a harmonica, and a squeaking fiddle. Instrumental developments alternated with vocal numbers, as when the younger of the women, shrill and squawky of voice, joined the tenor with his sweet falsetto notes in an ardent love duet. But the real talent and leader of the ensemble was quite evidently the other man, the one who had the guitar and was a kind of buffo-baritone character, with hardly any voice but with a mimic gift and remarkable comic verve. Often he would detach himself from the rest of the group and come forward, playing his large instrument and gesticulating, toward the terrace, where his pranks were rewarded with encouraging laughter. The Russians in their parterre seats took special delight in all this southern vivacity, and their plaudits and admiring shouts led him on to ever further and bolder extravagances.

Aschenbach sat by the balustrade, cooling his lips from time to time with the mixture of pomegranate juice and soda water that sparkled ruby red in the glass before him. His nervous system greedily drank in the jangling tones, for passion paralyzes discrimination and responds in all seriousness to stimuli which the sober senses would either treat with humorous tolerance or impatiently reject. The antics of the mountebank had distorted his features into a rictus-like smile, which he was already finding painful. He sat on with a casual air, but inwardly he was utterly engrossed: for six paces from him, Tadzio was leaning against the stone parapet.

There he stood, in the white belted suit he occasionally put on for dinner, in a posture of innate and inevitable grace, his left forearm on the parapet, his feet crossed, his right hand on the supporting hip; and he was looking down at the entertainers with an expression that was scarcely a smile, merely one of remote curiosity, a polite observation of the spectacle. Sometimes he straightened himself, stretching his chest, and with an elegant movement of both arms drew his white tunic down through his leather belt. But sometimes, too, and the older man noticed it with a mind-dizzying sense of triumph as well as with terror, he would turn his head hesitantly and cautiously, or even quickly and suddenly as if to gain the advantage of surprise, and look over his left shoulder to where his lover was sitting. Their eyes did not meet, for an ignominious apprehension was forcing the stricken man to keep his looks anxiously in check. Behind them on the terrace sat the women who watched over Tadzio, and at the point things had now reached, the enamored Aschenbach had reason to fear that he had attracted attention and aroused suspicion. Indeed, he had several times, on the beach, in the hotel foyer, and on the Piazza San Marco, been frozen with alarm to notice that Tadzio was being called away if he was near him, that they were taking care to keep them apart—and although his pride writhed in torments it had never known under the appalling insult that this implied, he could not in conscience deny its justice.

In the meantime the guitarist had begun a solo to his own accompaniment, a song in many stanzas which was then a popular hit all over Italy, and which he managed to perform in a graphic and dramatic manner, with the rest of his troupe joining regularly in the refrain. He was a lean fellow, thin and cadaverous in the face as well, standing there on the gravel detached from his companions, with a shabby felt hat on the back of his head and a quiff of his red hair bulging out under the brim, in a posture of insolent bravado; strumming and thrumming on his instrument, he tossed his pleasantries up to the terrace in a vivid *parlando,* enacting it all so strenuously that the veins swelled on his forehead. He was quite evidently not of Venetian origin but rather of the Neapolitan comic type, half pimp, half actor, brutal and bold-faced, dangerous and entertaining. The actual words of his song were merely foolish, but in his presentation, with his grimaces and bodily movements, his way of winking suggestively and lasciviously licking the corner of his mouth, it had something indecent and vaguely offensive about it. Though otherwise dressed in urban fashion, he wore a sports shirt, out of the soft collar of which his skinny neck projected, displaying a remarkably large and naked Adam's apple. His pallid snub-nosed face, the features of which gave little clue to his age, seemed to be lined with contortions and vice, and the grinning of his mobile mouth was rather strangely ill-matched to the two deep furrows that stood defiantly, imperiously, almost savagely, between his reddish brows. But what really fixed the solitary Aschenbach's deep attention on him was his observation that this suspect figure seemed to be carrying his own suspect atmosphere about with him as well. For every time the refrain was repeated, the singer would perform, with much grimacing and wagging of his hand as if in greeting, a grotesque march round the scene, which brought him immediately below where Aschenbach sat; and every time this happened, a stench of carbolic from his clothes or his body drifted up to the terrace.

Having completed his ballad, he began to collect money. He started with the Russians, who were seen to give generously, and then came up the steps. Saucy as his performance had been, up here he was humility itself. Bowing and scraping, he crept from table to table, and a sly obsequious grin bared his prominent teeth, although the two furrows still stood threateningly between his red eyebrows. The spectacle of this alien being gathering in his livelihood was viewed with curiosity and not a little distaste; one threw coins with the tips of one's fingers into the hat, which one took care not to touch. Removal of the physical distance between the entertainer and decent folk always causes, however great one's pleasure has been, a certain embarrassment. He sensed this and sought to make amends by cringing. He approached Aschenbach, and with him came the smell, which no one else in the company appeared to have noticed.

"Listen to me!" said the solitary traveler in an undertone and almost mechanically. "Venice is being disinfected. Why?" The comedian answered hoarsely: "Because of the police! It's the regulations, signore, when it's so hot and when there's sirocco. The sirocco is oppressive. It is not good for the health. . . ." He spoke in a tone of surprise that such a question could be asked, and demonstrated with his outspread hand how oppressive the sirocco was. "So there is no sickness in Venice?" asked Aschenbach very softly and between his teeth. The clown's muscular features collapsed into a grimace of comic helplessness. "A sickness? But what sickness? Is the sirocco a sickness? Is our police a sickness, perhaps? The signore is having his little joke! A sickness! Certainly not, signore! A preventive measure, you must understand, a police precaution against the effects of the oppressive weather . . ." He gesticulated. "Very well," said Aschenbach briefly, still without raising his voice, and quickly dropped an unduly large coin into the fellow's hat. Then he motioned him with his eyes to clear off. The man obeyed, grinning and bowing low. But he had not even reached the steps when two hotel servants bore down on him, and with their faces close to his subjected him to a whispered cross-examination. He shrugged, gave assurances, swore that he had been discreet; it was obvious. Released, he returned to the garden, and after a brief consultation with his colleagues under the arc lamp he came forward once more, to express his thanks in a parting number.

It was a song that Aschenbach could not remember ever having heard before, a bold hit in an unintelligible dialect and with a laughing refrain in which the rest of the band regularly and loudly joined. At this point both the words and the instrumental accompaniment stopped, and nothing remained except a burst of laughter, to some extent rhythmically ordered but treated with a high degree of naturalism, the soloist in particular showing great talent in his lifelike rendering of it. With artistic distance restored between himself and the spectators, he had recovered all his impudence, and the simulated laughter, which he shamelessly directed at the terrace, was a laughter of mockery. Even before the end of the articulated part of each stanza he would pretend to be struggling with an irresistible impulse of hilarity. He would sob, his voice would waver, he would press his hand against his mouth and hunch his shoulders, till at the proper moment the laughter would burst out of him, exploding in a wild howl, with such authenticity that it was infectious and communicated itself to the audience, so that a wave of objectless and merely self-propagating merriment swept over the terrace as well. And precisely this seemed to redouble the singer's exuberance. He bent his knees, slapped his thighs, held his sides, he nearly burst with what was now no longer laughing but shrieking; he pointed his finger up at the guests, as if that laughing company above him were itself the most comical thing in the world, and in the end they were all laughing, everyone in the garden and on the veranda, the waiters and the lift boys and the house servants in the doorways.

Aschenbach reclined in his chair no longer; he was sitting bolt upright as if trying to fend off an attack or flee from it. But the laughter, the hospital smell drifting toward him, and the nearness of the beautiful boy, all mingled for him into an immobilizing nightmare, an unbreakable and inescapable spell that held his mind and senses captive. In the general commotion and distraction, he ventured to steal a glance at Tadzio, and as he did so he became aware that the boy, returning his glance, had remained no less serious than himself, just as if he were regulating his attitude and expression by those of the older man, and as if the general mood had no power over him while Aschenbach kept aloof from it. There was something so disarming and overwhelmingly moving about this childlike submissiveness, so rich in meaning, that the gray-haired lover could only with difficulty restrain himself from burying his face in his hands. He had also had the impression that the way Tadzio from time to time drew himself up with an intake of breath was like a kind of sighing, as if from a constriction of the chest. He's sickly; he'll probably not live long, he thought again, with that sober objectivity into which the drunken ecstasy of desire sometimes strangely escapes; and his heart was filled at one and the same time with pure concern on the boy's behalf and with a certain wild satisfaction.

In the meantime the troupe of Venetians had finished their performance and were leaving. Applause accompanied them, and their leader took care to embellish even his exit with comical pranks. His bowing and scraping and hand-kissing amused the company, and so he redoubled them. When his companions were already outside, he put on yet another act, running backward and painfully colliding with a lamppost, then hobbling to the gate apparently doubled up in agony. When he got there, however, he suddenly discarded the mask of comic underdog, uncoiled like a spring to his full height, insolently stuck out his tongue at the hotel guests on the terrace, and slipped away into the darkness. The company was dispersing; Tadzio had left the balustrade some time ago. But the solitary Aschenbach, to the annoyance of the waiters, sat on and on at his little table over his unfinished pomegranate drink. The night was advancing; time was ebbing away. In his parents' house, many years ago, there had been an hourglass—he suddenly saw that fragile symbolic little instrument as clearly as if it were standing before him. Silently, subtly, the rust-red sand trickled through the narrow glass aperture, dwindling away out of the upper vessel, in which a little whirling vortex had formed.

On the very next day, in the afternoon, Aschenbach took a further step in his persistent probing of the outside world, and this time his success was complete. What he did was to enter the British travel agency just off the Piazza San Marco, and after changing some money at the cash desk, he put on the look of a suspicious foreigner and addressed his embarrassing question to the clerk who had served him. The clerk was a tweed-clad Englishman, still young, with his hair parted in the middle, his eyes close-set, and bearing that sober, honest demeanor which makes so unusual and striking an impression amid the glib knaveries of the south. "No cause for concern, sir," he began. "An administrative measure, nothing serious. They often issue directives of this kind, as a precaution against the unhealthy effects of the heat and the sirocco. . . ." But raising his blue eyes, he met those of the stranger, which were looking wearily and rather sadly at his lips with an expression of slight contempt. At this the Englishman colored. "That is," he continued in an undertone and with some feeling, "the official explanation, which the authorities here see fit to stick to. I can tell you that there is rather more to it than that." And then, in his straightforward, comfortable language, he told Aschenbach the truth.

For several years now, Asiatic cholera had been showing an increased tendency to spread and migrate. Originating in the sultry morasses of the Ganges delta, rising with the mephitic exhalations of that wilderness of rank, useless luxuriance, that primitive island jungle shunned by man, where tigers crouch in the bamboo thickets, the pestilence had raged with unusual and prolonged virulence all over northern India; it had struck eastward into China, westward into Afghanistan and Persia, and following the main caravan routes, it had borne its terrors to Astrakhan and even to

Moscow. But while Europe trembled with apprehension that from there the specter might advance and arrive by land, it had been brought by Syrian traders over the sea; it had appeared almost simultaneously in several Mediterranean ports, raising its head in Toulon and Málaga, showing its face repeatedly in Palermo and Naples, and taking a seemingly permanent hold all over Calabria and Apulia. The northern half of the peninsula had still been spared. But in the middle of May this year, in Venice, the dreadful comma bacilli had been found on one and the same day in the emaciated and blackened corpses of a ship's hand and of a woman who sold green-groceries. The two cases were hushed up. But a week later there were ten, there were twenty and then thirty, and they occurred in different quarters of the city. A man from a small provincial town in Austria who had been taking a few days' holiday in Venice died with unmistakable symptoms after returning home, and that was why the first rumors of a Venetian outbreak had appeared in German newspapers. The city authorities replied with a statement that the public health situation in Venice had never been better, and at the same time adopted the most necessary preventive measures. But the taint had probably now passed into foodstuffs, into vegetables or meat or milk; for despite every denial and concealment, the mortal sickness went on eating its way through the narrow little streets, and with the premature summer heat warming the water in the canals, conditions for the spread of infection were particularly favorable. It even seemed as if the pestilence had undergone a renewal of its energy, as if the tenacity and fertility of its pathogens had redoubled. Cases of recovery were rare; eighty percent of the victims died, and they died in a horrible manner, for the sickness presented itself in an extremely acute form and was frequently of the so-called dry type, which is the most dangerous of all. In this condition the body could not even evacuate the massive fluid lost from the blood vessels. Within a few hours the patient would become dehydrated, his blood would thicken like pitch, and he would suffocate with convulsions and hoarse cries. He was lucky if, as sometimes happened, the disease took the form of a slight malaise followed by a deep coma from which one never, or scarcely at all, regained consciousness. By the beginning of June, the isolation wards in the Ospedale Civile were quietly filling, the two orphanages were running out of accommodation, and there was a gruesomely brisk traffic between the quayside of the Fondamente Nuove and the cemetery island of San Michele. But fear of general detriment to the city, concern for the recently opened art exhibition in the Public Gardens, consideration of the appalling losses which panic and disrepute would in-flict on the hotels, on the shops, on the whole nexus of the tourist trade, proved stronger in Venice than respect for the truth and for international agreements; it was for this reason that the city authorities obstinately ad-hered to their policy of concealment and denial. The city's chief medical officer, a man of high repute, had resigned from his post in indignation and had been quietly replaced by a more pliable personality. This had become public knowledge; and such corruption in high places, combined with the prevailing insecurity, the state of crisis into which the city had been plunged by the death that walked its streets, led at the lower social levels to a certain breakdown of moral standards, to an activation of the dark and antisocial forces, which manifested itself in intemperance, shameless li-cense, and growing criminality. Drunkenness in the evenings became no-ticeably more frequent; thieves and ruffians, it was said, were making the streets unsafe at night; there were repeated robberies and even murders, for it had already twice come to light that persons alleged to have died of the plague had in fact been poisoned by their own relatives; and commercial vice now took on obtrusive and extravagant forms which had hitherto been unknown in this area and indigenous only to southern Italy or orien-tal countries.

The Englishman's narrative conveyed the substance of all this to Aschenbach. "You would be well advised, sir," he concluded, "to leave to-day rather than tomorrow. The imposition of quarantine can be expected any day now." "Thank you," said Aschenbach, and left the office.

The Piazza was sunless and sultry. Unsuspecting foreigners were sitting at the cafés, or standing in front of the church with pigeons completely en-veloping them, watching the birds swarm and beat their wings and push each other out of the way as they snatched with their beaks at the hollow hands offering them grains of maize. Feverish with excitement, triumphant in his possession of the truth, yet with a taste of disgust on his tongue and a fantastic horror in his heart, the solitary traveler paced up and down the flagstones of the magnificent precinct. He was considering a decent ac-tion which would cleanse his conscience. Tonight, after dinner, he might approach the lady in the pearls and address her with words which he now mentally rehearsed: "Madam, allow me as a complete stranger to do you a service, to warn you of something which is being concealed from you for reasons of self-interest. Leave here at once with Tadzio and your daughters! Venice is plague-stricken." He might then lay his hand in farewell on the

head of a mocking deity's instrument, turn away, and flee from this quag-
mire. But at the same time he sensed an infinite distance between himself
and any serious resolve to take such a step. It would lead him back to
where he had been, give him back to himself again; but to one who is beside himself, no prospect is so distasteful as that of self-recovery. He remembered a white building adorned with inscriptions that glinted in the
evening light, suffused with mystic meaning in which his mind had wandered; remembered then that strange itinerant figure who had wakened in
him, in his middle age, a young man's longing to rove to far-off and strange
places; and the thought of returning home, of levelheadedness and sobriety, of toil and mastery, filled him with such repugnance that his face
twisted into an expression of physical nausea. "They want it kept quiet!"
he whispered vehemently. And: "I shall say nothing!" The consciousness
of his complicity in the secret, of his share in the guilt, intoxicated him as
small quantities of wine intoxicate a weary brain. The image of the
stricken and disordered city, hovering wildly before his mind's eye, inflamed him with hopes that were beyond comprehension, beyond reason
and full of monstrous sweetness. What, compared with such expectations,
was that tender happiness of which he had briefly dreamed a few moments
ago? What could art and virtue mean to him now, when he might repay
the advantages of chaos? He said nothing, and stayed on.

That night he had a terrible dream, if dream is the right word for a
bodily and mental experience which did indeed overtake him during
deepest sleep, in complete independence of his will and with complete
sensuous vividness, but with no perception of himself as present and moving about in any space external to the events themselves; rather, the scene
of the events was his own soul, and they irrupted into it from outside, violently defeating his resistance—a profound, intellectual resistance—as
they passed through him, and leaving his whole being, the culture of a lifetime, devastated and destroyed.

It began with fear, fear and joy and a horrified curiosity about what
was to come. It was night, and his senses were alert; for from far off a hub-
bub was approaching, an uproar, a compendium of noise, a clangor and
blare and full thundering, yells of exultation and a particular howl with a
long-drawn-out *u* at the end—all of it permeated and dominated by a terrible sweet sound of flute music: by deep-warbling, infamously persistent,
shamelessly clinging tones that bewitched the innermost heart. Yet he was
aware of a word, an obscure word, but one that gave a name to what was

coming: *"the stranger-god!"* There was a glow of smoky fire; in it he could
see a mountain landscape, like the mountains round his summer home.
And in fragmented light, from wooded heights, between tree trunks and
mossy boulders, it came tumbling and whirling down: a human and animal
swarm, a raging rout, flooding the slope with bodies, with flames, with tumult and frenzied dancing. Women, stumbling on the hide garments that
fell too far about them from the waist, held up tambourines and moaned
as they shook them above their thrown-back heads; they swung blazing
torches, scattering the sparks, and brandished naked daggers; they carried
snakes with flickering tongues, which they had seized in the middle of the
body, or they bore up their own breasts in both hands, shrieking as they
did so. Men with horns over their brows, hairy-skinned and girdled with
pelts, bowed their necks and threw up their arms and thighs, clanging bra-
zen cymbals and beating a furious tattoo on drums, while smooth-skinned
boys prodded goats with leafy staves, clinging to their horns and yelling
with delight as the leaping beasts dragged them along. And the god's en-
thusiasts howled out the cry with the soft consonants and long-drawn-out
final *u,* both sweet and wild at once, like no cry that was ever heard: here
it was raised, belled out into the air as by rutting stags, and there they threw
it back with many voices, in ribald triumph, urging each other on with it
to dancing and tossing of limbs, and never did it cease. But the deep, enticing flute music mingled irresistibly with everything. Was it not also enticing him, the dreamer who experienced all this while struggling not to
do so, enticing him with shameless insistence to the feast and frenzy of the
uttermost surrender? Great was his loathing, great his fear, honorable his
effort of will to defend to the last what was his and protect it against the
Stranger, against the enemy of the composed and dignified intellect. But
the noise, the howling, grew louder, with the echoing cliffs reiterating it:
it increased beyond measure, swelled up to an enrapturing madness. Odors
besieged the mind: the pungent reek of the goats, the scent of panting
bodies, and an exhalation as of staling waters, with another smell, too, that
was familiar: that of wounds and wandering disease. His heart throbbed to
the drumbeats, his brain whirled, a fury seized him, a blindness, a dizzying
lust, and his soul craved to join the round dance of the god. The obscene
symbol, wooden and gigantic, was uncovered and raised on high: and still
more unbridled grew the howling of the rallying cry. With foaming
mouths they raged, they roused each other with lewd gestures and licentious hands; laughing and moaning they thrust the prods into each other's

flesh and licked the blood from each other's limbs. But the dreamer now was with them and in them, he belonged to the stranger-god. Yes, they were himself as they flung themselves, tearing and slaying, on the animals and devoured steaming gobbets of flesh; they were himself as an orgy of limitless coupling, in homage to the god, began on the trampled, mossy ground. And his very soul savored the lascivious delirium of annihilation.

Out of this dream the stricken man woke unnerved, shattered, and powerlessly enslaved to the daemon god. He no longer feared the observant eyes of other people; whether he was exposing himself to their suspicions he no longer cared. In any case, they were running away, leaving Venice; many of the bathing cabins were empty now, there were great gaps in the clientele at dinner, and in the city one scarcely saw any foreigners. The truth seemed to have leaked out, and however tightly the interested parties closed ranks, panic could no longer be stemmed. But the lady in the pearls stayed on with her family, either because the rumors were not reaching her or because she was too proud and fearless to heed them. Tadzio stayed on; and to Aschenbach, in his beleaguered state, it sometimes seemed that all these unwanted people all round him might flee from the place or die, that every living being might disappear and leave him alone on this island with the beautiful boy—indeed, as he sat every morning by the sea with his gaze resting heavily, recklessly, incessantly on the object of his desire, or as he continued his undignified pursuit of him in the evenings along streets in which the disgusting mortal malady wound its underground way, then indeed monstrous things seemed full of promise to him, and the moral law no longer valid.

Like any other lover, he desired to please and bitterly dreaded that he might fail to do so. He added brightening and rejuvenating touches to his clothes; he wore jewelry and used scent; he devoted long sessions to his toilet several times a day, arriving at table elaborately attired and full of excited expectation. As he beheld the sweet youthful creature who had so entranced him, he felt disgust at his own aging body; the sight of his gray hair and sharp features filled him with a sense of shame and hopelessness. He felt a compulsive need to refresh and restore himself physically; he paid frequent visits to the hotel barber.

Cloaked in a hairdressing gown, leaning back in the chair as the chatterer's hands tended him, he stared in dismay at his reflection in the looking glass.

"Gray," he remarked with a wry grimace.

"A little," the man replied. "And the reason? A slight neglect, a slight lack of interest in outward appearances, very understandable in persons of distinction, but not altogether to be commended, especially as one would expect those very persons to be free from prejudice about such matters as the natural and the artificial. If certain people who profess moral disapproval of cosmetics were to be logical enough to extend such rigorous principles to their teeth, the result would be rather disgusting. After all, we are only as old as we feel in our minds and hearts, and sometimes gray hair is actually further from the truth than the despised corrective would be. In your case, signore, one has a right to the natural color of one's hair. Will you permit me simply to give your color back to you?"

"How so?" asked Aschenbach.

Whereupon the eloquent tempter washed his client's hair in two kinds of water, one clear and one dark; and his hair was as black as when he had been young. Then he folded it into soft waves with the curling tongs, stepped back, and surveyed his handiwork.

"Now the only other thing," he said, "would be just to freshen up the signore's complexion a little."

And like a craftsman unable to finish, unable to satisfy himself, he passed busily and indefatigably from one procedure to another. Aschenbach, reclining comfortably, incapable of resistance, filled rather with exciting hopes by what was happening, gazed at the glass and saw his eyebrows arched more clearly and evenly, the shape of his eyes lengthened, their brightness enhanced by a slight underlining of the lids; saw below them a delicate carmine come to life as it was softly applied to skin that had been brown and leathery; saw his lips which had just been so pallid, now burgeoning cherry-red; saw the furrows on his cheeks, round his mouth, the wrinkles by his eyes all vanishing under face cream and an aura of youth—with beating heart he saw himself as a young man in his earliest bloom. The cosmetician finally declared himself satisfied, with the groveling politeness usual in such people, by profusely thanking the client he had served. "An insignificant adjustment, signore," he said as he gave a final helping hand to Aschenbach's outward appearance. "Now the signore can fall in love as soon as he pleases." And the spellbound lover departed, confused and timorous but happy as in a dream. His necktie was scarlet, his broad-brimmed straw hat encircled with a many-colored ribbon.

A warm gale had blown up; it rained little and lightly, but the air was humid and thick and filled with smells of decay. The ear was beset with fluttering, flapping, and whistling noises, and to the fevered devotee, sweating under his makeup, it seemed that a vile race of wind demons was disporting itself in the sky, malignant seabirds that churn up and gnaw and befoul a condemned man's food. For the sultry weather was taking away his appetite, and he could not put aside the thought that what he ate might be tainted with infection.

One afternoon, dogging Tadzio's footsteps, Aschenbach had plunged into the confused network of streets in the depths of the sick city. Quite losing his bearings in this labyrinth of alleys, narrow waterways, bridges, and little squares that all looked so much like each other, not sure now even of the points of the compass, he was intent above all on not losing sight of the vision he so passionately pursued. Ignominious caution forced him to flatten himself against walls and hide behind the backs of people walking in front of him; and for a long time he was not conscious of the weariness, the exhaustion that emotion and constant tension had inflicted on his body and mind. Tadzio walked behind his family; he usually gave precedence in narrow passages to his attendant and his nunlike sisters, and as he strolled along by himself he sometimes turned his head and glanced over his shoulder with his strange twilight-gray eyes, to ascertain that his lover was still following hm. He saw him, and did not give him away. Drunk with excitement as he realized this, lured onward by those eyes, helpless in the leading strings of his mad desire, the infatuated Aschenbach stole upon the trail of his unseemly hope—only to find it vanish from his sight in the end. The Poles had crossed a little humpbacked bridge; the height of the arch hid them from their pursuer, and when in his turn he reached the top of it, they were no longer to be seen. He looked frantically for them in three directions, straight ahead and to left and right along the narrow, dirty canal side, but in vain. Unnerved and weakened, he was compelled to abandon his search.

His head was burning, his body was covered with sticky sweat, his neck quivered, a no longer endurable thirst tormented him; he looked round for something, no matter what, that would instantly relieve it. At a little greengrocer's shop he bought some fruit, some overripe soft strawberries, and ate some of them as he walked. A little square, one that seemed to have been abandoned, to have been put under a spell, opened up in front of him: he recognized it, he had been here, it was where he had made that vain decision weeks ago to leave Venice. On the steps of the well in its center he sank down and leaned his head against the stone rim. The place was silent, grass grew between the cobblestones, garbage was lying about. Among the dilapidated houses of uneven height all round him there was one that looked like a *palazzo,* with Gothic windows that now had nothing behind them, and little lion balconies. On the ground floor of another there was a chemist's shop. From time to time warm gusts of wind blew the stench of carbolic across to him.

There he sat, the master, the artist who had achieved dignity, the author of *A Study in Abjection,* he who in such paradigmatically pure form had repudiated intellectual vagrancy and the murky depths, who had proclaimed his renunciation of all sympathy with the abyss, who had weighed vileness in the balance and found it wanting; he who had risen so high, who had set his face against his own sophistication, grown out of all his irony, and taken on the commitments of one whom the public trusted; he whose fame was official, whose name had been ennobled, and on whose style young boys were taught to model their own—there he sat, with his eyelids closed, with only an occasional mocking and rueful sideways glance from under them, which he hid again at once; and his drooping, cosmetically brightened lips shaped the occasional word of the discourse his brain was delivering, his half-asleep brain with its tissue of strange dream logic.

"For Beauty, Phaedrus, mark well! only Beauty is at one and the same time divine and visible, and so it is indeed the sensuous lover's path, little Phaedrus, it is the artist's path to the spirit. But do you believe, dear boy, that the man whose path to the spiritual passes through the senses can ever achieve wisdom and true manly dignity? Or do you think rather (I leave it to you to decide) that his is a path of dangerous charm, very much an errant and sinful path which must of necessity lead us astray? For I must tell you that we artists cannot tread the path of Beauty without Eros keeping company with us and appointing himself as our guide; yes, though we may be heroes in our fasion and disciplined warriors, yet we are like women, for it is passion that exalts us, and the longing of our soul must remain the longing of a lover—that is our joy and our shame. Do you see now perhaps why we writers can be neither wise nor dignified? That we necessarily go astray, necessarily remain dissolute emotional adventurers? The magisterial poise of our style is a lie and a farce, our fame and social position are an absurdity, the public's faith in us is altogether ridiculous, the use of art to educate the nation and its youth is a reprehensible undertaking which should be forbidden by law. For how can one be fit to be an educator when one has been born with an incorrigible and natural tendency toward the abyss?

We try to achieve dignity by repudiating that abyss, but whichever way we turn we are subject to its allurement. We renounce, let us say, the corrosive process of knowledge—for knowledge, Phaedrus, has neither dignity nor rigor: it is all insight and understanding and tolerance, uncontrolled and formless; it sympathizes with the abyss, it *is* the abyss. And so we reject it resolutely, and henceforth our pursuit is of Beauty alone, of Beauty which is simplicity, which is grandeur and a new kind of rigor and a second naïveté, of Beauty which is Form. But form and naïveté, Phaedrus, lead to intoxication and lust; they may lead a noble mind into terrible criminal emotions, which his own fine rigor condemns as infamous; they lead, they too lead, to the abyss. I tell you, that is where they lead us writers; for we are not capable of self-exaltation, we are merely capable of self-debauchery. And now I shall go, Phaedrus, and you shall stay here; and leave this place only when you no longer see me."

~ ~ ~

A few days later Gustav von Aschenbach, who had been feeling unwell, left the Hotel des Bains at a later morning hour than usual. He was being attacked by waves of dizziness, only half physical, and with them went an increasing sense of dread, a feeling of hopelessness and pointlessness, though he could not decide whether this referred to the external world or to his personal existence. In the foyer he saw a large quantity of luggage standing ready for dispatch, asked one of the doormen which guests were leaving, and was given in reply the aristocratic Polish name which he had inwardly been expecting to hear. As he received the information there was no change in his ravaged features, only that slight lift of the head with which one casually notes something one did not need to know. He merely added the question: "When?" and was told: "After lunch." He nodded and went down to the sea.

It was a bleak spectacle there. Tremors gusted outward across the water between the beach and the first long sandbar, wrinkling its wide flat surface. An autumnal, out-of-season air seemed to hang over the once so colorful and populous resort, now almost deserted with litter left lying about on the sand. An apparently abandoned camera stood on its tripod at the edge of the sea, and the black cloth over it fluttered and flapped in the freshening breeze.

Tadzio, with the three or four playmates he still had, was walking about on the right in front of his family's bathing cabin; and reclining in his deck chair with a rug over his knees, about midway between the sea and the row of cabins, Aschenbach once more sat watching him. The boys' play was unsupervised, as the women were probably busy with travel preparations; it seemed to be unruly and degenerating into roughness. The sturdy boy he had noticed before, the one in the belted suit with glossy black hair who was addressed as "Jashu," had been angered and blinded by some sand thrown into his face; he forced Tadzio to a wrestling match, which soon ended in the downfall of the less muscular beauty. But as if in this hour of leave-taking the submissiveness of the lesser partner had been transformed into cruel brutality, as if he were now bent on revenge for his long servitude, the victor did not release his defeated friend even then, but knelt on his back and pressed his face into the sand so hard and so long that Tadzio, breathless from the fight in any case, seemed to be on the point of suffocation. His attempts to shake off the weight of his tormentor were convulsive; they stopped altogether for moments on end and became a mere repeated twitching. Appalled, Aschenbach was about to spring to the rescue when the bully finally released his victim. Tadzio, very pale, sat up and went on sitting motionless for some minutes, propped on one arm, his hair tousled and his eyes darkening. Then he stood right up and walked slowly away. His friends called to him, laughingly at first, then anxiously and pleadingly; he took no notice. The dark-haired boy, who had no doubt been seized at once by remorse at having gone so far, ran after him and tried to make up the quarrel. A jerk of Tadzio's shoulder rejected him. Tadzio walked on at an angle down to the water. He was barefooted and wearing his striped linen costume with the red bow.

At the edge of the sea he lingered, head bowed, drawing figures in the wet sand with the point of one foot, then walked into the shallow high tide, which at its deepest point did not even wet his knees; he waded through it, advancing easily, and reached the sandbar. There he stood for a moment, looking out into the distance, and then, moving left, began slowly to pace the length of this narrow strip of unsubmerged land. Divided from the shore by a width of water, divided from his companions by proud caprice, he walked, a quite isolated and unrelated apparition, walked with floating hair out there in the sea, in the wind, in front of the nebulous vastness. Once more he stopped to survey the scene. And suddenly, as if prompted by a memory, by an impulse, he turned at the waist, one hand on his hip, with an enchanting twist of the body, and looked back over his shoulder at the beach. There the watcher sat, as he had sat once before when those twilight-gray eyes, looking back at him then from that other threshold, had for the first time met his. Resting his head on the back of his chair, he had slowly turned it to follow the movements of the walking figure in the distance; now he lifted it toward this last look; then it sank down on his breast, so that his eyes stared up from below, while his face wore the inert, deep-sunken expression of profound slumber. But to him it was as if the pale and lovely soul-summoner out there were smiling to him, beckoning to him: as if he loosed his hand from his hip and pointed outward, hovering ahead and onward, into an immensity rich with unutterable expectation. And as so often, he set out to follow him.

Minutes passed, after he had collapsed sideways in his chair, before anyone hurried to his assistance. He was carried to his room. And later that same day the world was respectfully shocked to receive the news of his death.

FROM

# *The Magic Mountain*

TRANSLATED BY JOHN E. WOODS

### *Hippe*

And so Sundays stood out—including the afternoons, which were marked by carriage rides undertaken by various groups of guests. After tea, several pairs of horses trotted up the loop of the drive, pulling carriages that stopped outside the front door for those who had ordered them—mainly Russians, particularly Russian ladies.

"Russians love to go for rides," Joachim told Hans Castorp as they stood together at the front door and amused themselves by watching people depart. "And now they'll ride to Clavadel or to the lake or to Flüela Valley or Klosters—those are the usual destinations. We could take a ride ourselves sometime while you're here, if you like. But I think you've probably got enough to do for right now just getting settled in, and don't need any adventures."

Hans Castorp agreed. He had a cigarette in his mouth and his hands in his trouser pockets. He watched as the chipper little old Russian lady and her skinny niece took their seats in the carriage and were joined by two other ladies—Marusya and Madame Chauchat. The latter was wearing a light duster, belted across the back, but no hat. She sat down next to the old woman at the front, with the two young girls on the back seat. All four were in a merry mood, and their mouths worked ceaselessly at their soft, rather boneless language. They talked and laughed about the difficulty of fitting under the blanket, about the wooden box of Russian candies, wrapped in paper and bedded in cotton, which the great-aunt had brought along as provisions and now offered around. Hans Castorp was pleased to discover that he could pick out Frau Chauchat's opaque voice. As always when he set eyes on this careless woman, he was reminded of the resemblance that he had been trying to recall for some time now and that had flashed across his dream. Marusya's laugh, however, the sight of her round brown eyes, blinking childishly out over the handkerchief with which she covered her mouth, and her full, prominent chest—said to be more than a little ill on the inside—reminded him of something else that had shaken him when he had noticed it recently, and so without turning his head, he glanced cautiously toward Joachim. No, thank God, Joachim's face wasn't turning blotchy as it had that day, and his lips were not wrenched woefully. But he was watching Marusya—and in a pose, with a look in his eyes, that could not possibly be called military but, rather, so gloomy and self-absorbed that one would have to term it downright civilian. He pulled himself together, all the same, and quickly peered at Hans Castorp, who just had time to pull his own eyes away and gaze off vaguely into the air. As he did, he felt his heart pounding—for no reason, all of its own accord, as it had taken to doing up here.

In other respects Sunday offered nothing out of the ordinary, apart perhaps from the meals, which, since they could hardly be more sumptuous, were at least marked by a refinement in the cuisine. (For dinner there was a *chaudfroid* of chicken, garnished with shrimps and halved cherries; ices with pastries in little baskets of spun sugar; even fresh pineapple.) After drinking his beer that evening, Hans Castorp felt more exhausted, chilled, and torpid than on any day thus far; he said good night to his cousin a little before nine, quickly slipped in under his comforter, pulling it up over his chin, and fell dead asleep.

But the very next day, his first Monday up here as a visitor, brought another standard deviation from the routine—and that was one of the lectures Dr. Krokowski gave in the dining hall every two weeks before the entire German-speaking nonmoribund adult population of the Berghof. As Hans Castorp learned from his cousin, this was one of a series of popular-scientific talks, presented under the general title "Love as a Force Conducive to Illness." This instructive entertainment took place after second breakfast, and, as Joachim likewise informed him, it was not permitted, or at the very least was frowned upon, for anyone to absent himself—and it was therefore considered an amazing license that Settembrini, who surely was fluent in German as few others were, not only had never attended these lectures but also vilified them at length. As for Hans Castorp, he had decided at once that he would attend—primarily out of courtesy, but also out of undisguised curiosity. Before the lecture, however, he did something quite perverse and ill advised: he took an extended walk all by himself, which turned out bad beyond all expectation.

"Now listen"—these had been his first words when Joachim came into his room that morning—"I have decided that things can't go on like this. I have had my fill of horizontal living; it's as if my blood were practically falling asleep. Needless to say, it is quite another matter for you: you're a patient here, and I have no intention of corrupting you. But if you don't mind, I want to take a real walk this morning right after breakfast, a couple of hours of just walking out into the wide world, wherever the path leads. I'll stick a little something in my pocket for a snack, and I'll be on my own. And then we'll see if I'm not a new man when I get back."

"Fine," Joachim said, realizing that his cousin was quite serious about following through on his plan. "But don't overdo it—that's my advice. It's not the same up here as at home. And make sure you're back in time for the lecture."

In reality, there were other reasons beyond the purely physical that had put this idea into young Hans Castorp's head. It seemed to him that his difficulties in acclimatizing himself had less to do with his flushed face, or the bad taste he usually had in his mouth, or the pounding of his heart, and more with things like the activities of the Russian couple next door, the table talk of someone as sick and stupid as Frau Stöhr, the Austrian horseman's flabby cough, which he heard every day in the corridor, Herr Albin's opinions, the impression left on him by the social customs of sickly adolescents, the expression on Joachim's face when he looked at Marusya, and all sorts of similar matters he had observed. He thought it could only do him good to break the grip of the Berghof for once, to breathe deep of the open air, to get some real exercise, and if one was going to be exhausted of an evening, at least to know the reason why. And so after breakfast, he boldly took his departure from Joachim—who dutifully started out on his measured promenade up to the bench beside the water trough—and swinging his walking stick, he now marched off down the main road on his own.

It was almost half-past eight on a cool, cloudy morning. As he had planned, Hans Castorp breathed deeply of fresh, light, early morning air, which went so easily into the lungs and had neither odor nor moisture nor content, which evoked no memories. He crossed the brook and the narrow-gauge tracks, came out on the main road with its irregular pattern of buildings, and left it almost at once for a meadow path, which ran on level ground for only a short while and then led up the slope on his right at a rather steep angle. Hans Castorp enjoyed the climb; his chest expanded, he pushed his hat back from his brow with his cane, and when from a good height he looked back around and saw in the distance the surface of the lake his train had passed on arrival, he began to sing.

He sang the kind of songs he knew—sentimental folk melodies, the ones you find in the handbooks of sport and business clubs, including one that contained the lines:

> *The bards do praise both love and wine*
> *Yet virtue still more often . . .*  ·

and he hummed them softly at first, but soon was singing at the top of his voice. It was a brash baritone, but he found it lovely today, and his own singing inspired him more and more. If he started in too high a key, then he would sing falsetto, and he found that lovely too. When memory failed him, he made do by singing the melody to nonsense syllables and words, tossing them off into the air with the splendid back-rolled *r* and well-rounded vowels of opera singers, and at last moved on simply to fantasizing both text and music and accompanying these vocalizations with theatrical gestures. But since it is quite an exertion to both climb and sing, he soon found he was short of breath—and it kept getting shorter. But out of idealism and love for the beauty of song, he ignored his distress and, despite frequent sighs, gave it all he had, until finally he sank down at the base of a thick pine tree, totally out of breath and gasping, half blind, with only bright patterns dancing before his eyes, his pulse skittering. After such exaltation, his sudden reward was radical gloom, a hangover that bordered on despair.

Once his nerves had settled a bit again, he got up to continue his walk, but his neck was twitching so violently that, young as he was, his head was wobbling just as old Hans Lorenz Castorp's once had done. The phenomenon suddenly awakened in him warm memories of his late grandfather, and instead of finding it repulsive, he took a certain pleasure in imitating the venerable chin-propping method that the old man himself had used to control his shaking head and that had so delighted Hans Castorp as a boy.

He kept climbing along the serpentine path. The sound of cowbells drew him on, and he found the herd; they were grazing near a wooden hut, whose roof was weighed down with stones. Two bearded men were coming toward him, axes on their shoulders, but then, not all that far from him, they took leave of each other. "Well, fare thee well and much obliged," the one said to the other in a deep, guttural voice; he now switched his ax to his other shoulder and began to stride down toward the valley, his steps cracking loudly as he forged a path through the pines. It had sounded so strange there in this lonely, remote place, that "fare thee well and much obliged," like words in a dream brushing past Hans Castorp's senses, numbed by climbing and singing. He spoke the words softly to himself, trying to imitate the guttural and sober rustic dialect of these mountain men; and he kept climbing for some distance beyond the hut, determined to reach the tree line. But one glance at his watch, and he gave up that plan.

He followed a path—level at first and then descending—that led around to the left in the direction of town. A forest of tall pines swallowed him, and wandering through it now, he even began to sing a little again, although more prudently—but as he descended, his knees shook even more unsettlingly than before. When he emerged from the woods, he was astonished by the splendid view opening up before him—an intimate, closed landscape, like some magnificent, peaceful painting.

From the slope on his right, a mountain stream swept along a flat, stony bed, then rushed foaming over terraced boulders in its path, and finally flowed more serenely toward the valley, crossed at that point by a picturesque wooden bridge with simple railings. The ground about was blue with bell-like flowers of a lushly growing shrub. Dour spruces, symmetrical and gigantic, stood solitary and in small groups along the bottom of the gorge and further up the slopes. One of them, rooted in the steep bank of the brook, jutted across the view at a bizarre angle. The murmur of isolation reigned above this beautiful, remote spot. Hans Castorp spotted a bench on the far side of the brook.

He crossed the wooden bridge and sat down to enjoy the sight of the falling water and rushing foam, to listen to its idyllic chatter, a monotone filled with interior variety. Hans Castorp loved the purl of water as much as he loved music, perhaps even more. But he had no sooner made himself comfortable than his nose began to bleed—so suddenly that he was unable to keep his suit from being stained a little. The flow of blood was strong and persistent and kept him occupied for a good half hour, forcing him to run back and forth between the bench and the brook, rinsing out his handkerchief, sniffing water to rinse his nostrils, then lying down flat on the planks again, the wet cloth over his nose. There he lay quietly until the bleeding finally stopped—his hands clasped behind his head, his knees drawn up, his eyes closed, his ears filled with the rushing of the water. It was not that he felt sick but, rather, that the profuse bloodletting soothed him and left him in a state of strangely reduced vitality; he would exhale and for a long time feel no need to take in new air; he simply lay there, his inert body calmly letting his heart run through a series of beats, until at last he would lazily take another shallow breath.

And he found himself transported to an earlier stage of life, one that only a few nights before had served as the basis for a dream filled with more recent impressions. And as he was pulled back into the then and there, time and space were abrogated—so intensely, so totally, that one might have thought a lifeless body lay there on the bench beside the torrent, while the real Hans Castorp was moving about in an earlier time, in different surroundings, confronted by a situation that, for all its simplicity, he found both fraught with risk and filled with intoxication.

He was thirteen years old, a seventh grader in short pants, and he was standing in the schoolyard, talking with another boy about his age but from a different class—a conversation that Hans Castorp had initiated more or less arbitrarily and that delighted him no end, although it would be a short one, given the limited scope offered by the physical object under discussion. It was during recess between the last two periods of the day for Hans Castorp's class—between history and drawing. The schoolyard, paved with red bricks and cut off from the street by a high shingled wall with two entrance gates, was filled with pupils, some walking back and forth, some standing in groups, some leaning or half sitting against the tiled abutments of the school building. There was a babel of voices. Supervising these activities was a teacher in a slouch hat, who now bit into a ham sandwich.

The boy whom Hans Castorp was talking to was named Hippe, Pribislav Hippe, and the remarkable thing was that the *r* in his first name was pronounced *sh:* he called himself "Pshibislav." And that outlandish name did not fit badly with his looks, which were not ordinary at all, indeed were decidedly foreign. Hippe, the son of a high school history teacher—and so a notorious model student—was a grade ahead of Hans Castorp, although he was not much older. He came from Mecklenburg, and to judge from appearances, he was obviously the product of an ancient mixing of races, the blending of Germanic blood with Slavic Wendish, or vice versa. He was blond, and his hair was kept trimmed close to his round head. But his eyes, bluish-gray or grayish-blue (a rather indefinite and equivocal color, much like that of distant mountains), had a curious narrow and, if you looked closely, slightly slanted shape, and right below them were prominent, strong, distinctive cheekbones—features not at all ill proportioned in his case but really quite pleasing, although they sufficed for his schoolmates to award him the nickname "Kirghiz." Hippe, by the way, already wore long trousers, plus a blue jacket, gathered at the back and buttoning up to the collar, where a few flakes of dandruff usually lay scattered.

The thing was that Hans Castorp had had his eye on young Pribislav for a long time, had chosen him from among all the boys in the bustling schoolyard, those he knew and those he didn't know, had been interested in him, had followed him with his glances—should one say, admired him?—in any case, observed him with ever growing sympathy. Even when walking to and from school, he looked forward to spotting him among the other boys, to watching him talk and laugh, to picking out his voice from a good distance—that husky, opaque, slightly gruff voice. Granted, there was no sufficient reason for this sympathy—particularly if one disregarded such things as his heathen name, his status as a model pupil (which, indeed, could have played no role whatever), or those Kirghiz eyes, which from time to time, in certain sidelong glances, when gazing at nothing in particular, could darken, almost melt, to a veiled dusky look—but whatever the reason, Hans Castorp did not worry about the intellectual or emotional basis of his reaction, or even what name he would give it if he had to. It could not be called friendship, because he didn't really "know" Hippe. But from the start, there was not the last reason to give it a name; the farthest thing from his mind was ever to talk about the matter: that would have been most unlike him, and he felt no need to do so. Besides, to give it a name would have meant, if not to judge it, at least to define it, to classify it as one of life's familiar, commonplace items, whereas Hans Castorp was thoroughly convinced at some subconscious level that anything so personal should always be shielded from definition and classification.

But with or without a reason for them, these feelings, though far from having a name or being shared, were so powerful that Hans Castorp carried them silently about with him for almost a year—approximately a year, since it was impossible to fix their beginnings exactly—which at least spoke for the loyalty and steadfastness of his character, particularly when one thinks what a huge chunk of time a year is at that age. Unfortunately, there is normally some sort of moral judgment involved in identifying traits of character, whether for the purpose of praise or censure, even though every such trait has its two sides. Hans Castorp's "loyalty" (in which he did not take any particular pride, by the way) consisted—and no value judgment is intended—of a certain stodginess, slowness, and stubbornness of spirit, a sustaining mood that caused him to regard conditions and relationships of long-standing attachment to be that much more valuable the longer they lasted. He also tended to believe in the infinite duration of the state and mood in which he happened to find himself at a given moment, cherished it for just that reason and was not eager for change. And so his heart had become accustomed to this mute, distant relationship with Pribislav Hippe, and he considered it a fundamental, permanent fixture in his life. He loved the surges of emotion that came with it, the tension of whether he would meet him on a given day, whether Pribislav would pass close by him, perhaps even look at him; loved the silent, tender satisfaction that his secret bestowed upon him; loved even the disappointments it sometimes brought, the greatest of which was when Pribislav was "absent"—and then the schoolyard was desolate, the day lacked every spice, but enduring hope remained.

And so things continued for a year, until that adventurous high point; and another year passed as well—the result of Hans Castorp's abiding loyalty. And then it was all over—without his ever noticing the loosening and breaking of the bonds that tied him to Pribislav Hippe, any more than he had noticed their strengthening. Pribislav left the school and the city, too, when his father was transferred. But Hans Castorp barely noticed; he had already forgotten him by then. One might say that the figure of this "Kirghiz" emerged imperceptibly out of the fog and into his life, slowly taking on clarity and palpability, until the moment when he was most near, most physically present, there in the schoolyard, stood there in the foreground for a while, and then gradually receded and vanished again into the fog, without even the pain of farewell.

But Hans Castorp now found himself transported back to that moment, to that risky, adventurous moment when he had a conversation, a real conversation, with Pribislav Hippe. And this is how it had come about. Drawing class was next, and Hans Castorp noticed that he did not have his drawing pencil with him. All his classmates needed theirs; but he had acquaintances here and there among the boys in other classes whom he could have approached for a pencil. But the boy he knew best, he discovered, was Pribislav; he felt closest to him, he was the one with whom he had spent so many silent hours. And on a joyful impulse of his whole being, he decided to seize the opportunity—he even called it an opportunity—and ask Pribislav for a pencil. He wasn't even aware what an odd thing this was for him to do, since he really didn't know Pribislav—or maybe he simply did not care, blinded as he was by some peculiar reckless-ness. And so there he stood in the tumult of the brick schoolyard, face-to-face with Pribislav Hippe. And he said, "Excuse me, could you lend me a pencil?"

And Pribislav looked at him out of Kirghiz eyes set above promi-nent cheekbones, and in his pleasantly husky voice and without any astonishment—or at least without betraying any astonishment—he said, "Glad to. But be sure to give it back to me after class." And he pulled a pencil from his pocket, in a silver-plated holder with a ring you had to push up to make the reddish pencil emerge from its metal casing. As he ex-plained its simple mechanism, both their heads bent down over it.

"And don't break it," he added.

What made him say that? As if Hans Castorp intended to treat it carelessly—or, worse, *not* give it back at all.

Then they looked at each other and smiled, and since there was noth-ing more to say, they turned away, first shoulders, then backs, and walked off.

That was all. But Hans Castorp had never been happier in all his life as during that drawing class as he sketched with Pribislav Hippe's pencil—and before him lay the prospect of returning it to its owner in person, which came as a simple, natural part of the bargain. He even took the lib-erty of sharpening the pencil a little, and he kept three or four of the red-lacquered shavings in the drawer of his desk for a year or two—had someone ever seen them, he would never have guessed their significance. The return of the pencil, moreover, took the simplest form possible; but that was just what Hans Castorp intended, indeed he took a special pride in it—after all, he was more than a little spoiled and blasé after his long, in-timate relationship with Hippe.

"There," he said. "Thanks."

And Pribislav said nothing at all, simply gave the mechanism a quick check and shoved the holder into his pocket.

And they never spoke another word—but just that one time, it really did happen, thanks to Hans Castorp's enterprising spirit.

He opened his eyes wide, confused by the depth of his trance. I suppose I was dreaming, he thought. Yes, that was Pribislav. I haven't thought of him in a long time. What ever became of those shavings? The desk is up in the attic at Uncle Tienappel's. They must still be in that same little drawer, clear at the back on the left. I never removed them. Didn't even pay them enough attention to throw them out. It was Pribislav, it was him all over. I never would have thought that I'd see him so clearly again. And he looked so strangely like her—that woman up here. Is that why I've been so intrigued by her? Or maybe that's why I was suddenly so interested in *him*. What nonsense. What a lot of nonsense. I've got to be on my way, and I mean right now. But he lay there awhile longer, pondering and remembering. Then he sat up. "Well, fare thee well and much obliged!" he said out loud, and tears came to his eyes even as he smiled. And with that he stood up to go, and just as quickly sat back down, hat and cane in hand, forced to admit that his knees couldn't support him. Whoops, he thought, I don't think that's going to work. And I'm supposed to be at the lecture in the dining hall at eleven on the dot. A long walk up here can be lovely, but it has its drawbacks too, it seems. Yes indeed—but I can't stay here. It's just that I'm a little stiff from lying down; it will get better once I'm moving." And he tried to get to his feet again; and making a concerted effort to pull himself together, he succeeded.

But it was a miserable walk home, especially after such an optimistic start. He repeatedly had to stop to rest; the blood would suddenly drain from his face, cold sweat would break out on his brow, and his irregular heartbeat made it hard to breathe. He wearily struggled down the serpentine path, finally reaching the valley close to the spa hotel in Platz; he now realized all too clearly that he would never be able to manage the long walk back to the Berghof on his own; and since there was no tram and he didn't see any carriages for hire, he asked the driver of a delivery wagon headed for Dorf with a load of empty boxes to let him climb aboard. Back-to-back with the driver, his legs dangling over the side of the wagon, half asleep as he swayed and nodded with each jolt, he rode along, the object of the amazed sympathy of passersby. He got off at the railroad crossing, offered some money without bothering to look if it was too much or too little, and lurched headlong up the loop of the drive.

"*Dépêchez-vous, monsieur!*" the French doorman said. "*La conférence de Monsieur Krokowski vient de commencer.*"

And Hans Castorp tossed his hat and cane on the hall stand—and carefully, cautiously, his tongue between his teeth, he squeezed his way past the glass door, only just ajar, and entered the dining hall, where the residents were sitting in rows of chairs. To his right, at the narrow end of the room, Dr. Krokowski stood in his frock coat, behind a cloth-covered table, graced by a carafe of water: he was already speaking.

# ～ *Jean Cocteau* ～

## FROM
## *The White Book*

TRANSLATED BY MARGARET CROSLAND

Since the Admiral was ill and my cousin away on her honeymoon, I had to return to Toulon. It would be tedious to describe that delightful Sodom, where the fire of heaven falls without danger, striking by means of caressing sunshine. Before dusk an even softer atmosphere floods the town and as in Naples, as in Venice, a fairground crowd moves through the squares ornamented with fountains, noisy shops, waffle stalls, and street hawkers. Men in love with masculine beauty come from all corners of the globe to admire the sailors who walk about idly, alone or in groups, respond to glances with a smile, and never refuse an offer of love. Some nocturnal salt transforms the most brutal jailbird, the roughest Breton, the most savage Corsican, into those tall, flower-decked girls with low *décolletés* and loose limbs who like dancing and lead their partners, without the slightest embarrassment, into the shady hotels by the port.

One of the cafés with a dance floor was kept by a former *café concert* singer who had a woman's voice and used to exhibit himself in women's clothes. Now he sported a pullover and rings. He was flanked by colossal men wearing caps with red pom-poms; they worshiped him and he ill-treated them; his wife called out lists of drinks in a harsh, naive voice, and he noted them down in large, childish handwriting with his tongue hanging out.

---

*"The artist must be partly male and partly female,"* JEAN COCTEAU *once remarked. "Unfortunately the female part is nearly always intolerable." He conceived of all art as poetry and therefore called* The White Book *(published anonymously)* poésie autobiographique.

One evening when I opened the door to the place kept by this astonishing creature, surrounded by the respectful attentions of his wife and his men, I remained rooted to the spot. I had just caught sight of the ghost of Dargelos, a man I could see from the side, leaning against the Pianola. Dargelos in sailor's uniform.

This double possessed in particular the arrogance, the insolent and absentminded air of Dargelos. On his cap, which was tilted forward over his left eyebrow, could be read in gold letters TAPAGEUSE, he wore a tight black scarf around his neck and those trousers with tabs which in the past allowed sailors to roll them up to their thighs and are today forbidden by regulations on the pretext that they are worn by pimps.

In any other place I would never have dared stand in the orbit of that arrogant gaze. But Toulon is Toulon; dancing avoids the awkwardness of introductions, it throws strangers into each other's arms and forms a prelude to love.

To music full of ringlets and kiss-curls we danced a waltz. The backward-leaning bodies were linked together at the groin, profiles were grave and eyes lowered, faces moved round more slowly than the feet, which wove in and out and sometimes came down like horses' hooves. The free hands assumed the graceful pose affected by the working class when they drink a glass of wine and when they piss it away. A springtime ecstasy excited those bodies. Branches grew in them, hardness crushed hardness, sweat mingled together, and the couples would leave for the bedrooms with clock-case lampshades and eiderdowns.

Stripped of the accessories which intimidate a civilian, those which are affected by sailors to give themselves confidence, Tapageuse became a timid animal. He had had his nose broken by a wine carafe during a fight. A straight nose might have made him colorless. The carafe had added the final thumbstroke to the masterpiece.

This boy, who for me represented good luck, bore on his chest the words PAS DE CHANGE, tattooed in blue capital letters. He told me his story. It was short. He had just come out of a naval prison. After the mutiny on the *Ernest Renan,* he had been mistaken for a colleague; this is why he had a crew cut, which he hated and which suited him wonderfully well.

"I'm unlucky," he repeated, shaking his little bald head, like some antique bust, "and I always will be."

I put my gold chain round his neck. "I'm not giving it to you," I told him, "that wouldn't protect either of us, but keep it for this evening."

Next, with my fountain pen I crossed out the ominous tattooing. Beneath it I drew a star and a heart. He smiled. He understood, more with his skin than with anything else, that he was safe, that our encounter was not like those he was used to: brief moments of self-gratification.

PAS DE CHANCE! Was it possible? With that mouth, those teeth, those eyes, that belly, those shoulders, those iron muscles, those legs? PAS DE CHANCE, with that fabulous little underwear plant, lying dead and crumpled on the moss, which unfolded, grew bigger, reared up, and threw its seed far away as soon as it found the element of love. I couldn't get over it; and in order to resolve this problem I sank into a feigned sleep.

Pas de Chance remained motionless beside me. Gradually I felt that he was embarking on a delicate maneuver in order to free his arm, on which my elbow was resting. Not for a second did it enter my head that he was contemplating some sly trick. This would have meant disregarding naval ceremonial. "Honesty, good behavior" illuminate the vocabulary of sailors.

I watched him through barely closed eyelids. First he weighed the chain in his hands several times, kissed it, and rubbed it on his tattoo. Then, with the terrible slowness of a player who is cheating, he tested my sleep, coughed, touched me, listened to my breathing, brought his face close to my right hand, which lay wide open near my face, and gently leaned his cheek against it.

I was the indiscreet witness of this attempt by an unlucky boy who could feel a life belt coming close to him on the open sea, and I had to restrain myself from losing my head, pretending to wake up, and ruining my life.

At dawn I left him. My eyes avoided his, which were full of all the hope which he felt but could not express. He returned the chain to me. I embraced him, tucked him in bed, and put out the light.

I had to return to my hotel and write down on a slate in the hall the time (five o'clock) when sailors wake, beneath countless other requests of the same kind. Just as I picked up the chalk, I noticed that I had forgotten my gloves. I went back upstairs. Light shone through the glass over the door. Someone must have switched the lamp on again. I couldn't resist putting my eye to the keyhole; it made a bizarre frame for a small shaven head. Pas de Chance had buried his face in my gloves and was weeping bitterly.

I hesitated outside that door for ten minutes. I was about to open it, when the face of Alfred superimposed itself with great precision on that of

Pas de Chance. I went downstairs on tiptoe, asked for the door to be un-locked, and banged it behind me. Outside, a fountain was conducting a grave monologue over the empty square.

No, I thought, we don't belong to the same order. He's already beau-tiful enough to move a flower, a tree, or an animal. Impossible to live with.

Day was breaking. Cocks were crowing over the sea. A dark coolness gave away its presence. A man emerged from a street, carrying a shotgun. I went back to the hotel, weighed down with a heavy burden.

# ~ Marguerite Yourcenar ~

## FROM

## *Alexis*

TRANSLATED BY WALTER KAISER
AND MARGUERITE YOURCENAR

You were in love with me. I am not vain enough to believe that you loved me with passion; I continue to ask myself how it was possible not so much that you fell in love with me as that you adopted me in that way. Each of us knows so little about love as other people understand it. For you, love was perhaps only an impassioned kindness. Or else, you were attracted to me. I attracted you precisely because of those good qualities which too often grow in the shade of our worst faults: weakness, indecision, subtlety. Above all, you felt sorry for me. I had been imprudent enough to inspire pity in you. Because you had been good to me for several weeks, you thought it would be natural to be so for the rest of your life: you thought it was enough to be perfect in order to be happy. I thought it enough, in order to be happy, not to be guilty any longer.

We were married at Wand one rainy day in October. Perhaps, Monique, I might have wished our engagement had been longer; I like to be borne along, not dragged, by the passage of time. I was not without anxieties about the existence which opened before me: remember that I was twenty-two years old and you were the first woman who preoccupied my life. But,

*MARGUERITE YOURCENAR was born Marguerite de Crayencour in Brussels in 1903. Alexis, her first novel, was published in 1929, and Memoirs of Hadrian, her most famous novel, in 1951. A translator of Virginia Woolf, Henry James, and a volume of Negro spirituals, she was elected—the first woman ever to be so—to the Académie Française in 1981. She died in 1987.*

with you beside me, everything was always very simple. I was so grateful to you for frightening me so little. The guests at the castle departed one after the other. We were going to depart also, together. We were married in the village church, and since your father had gone off on one of his distant expeditions, we had with us only some friends and my brother. My brother had come even though the trip was expensive; he thanked me almost effusively for having, as he put it, saved our family. I was aware that he was alluding to your fortune, and that filled me with shame. I did not answer. And yet, my dear, would I have been more culpable in sacrificing you to my family than in sacrificing you to myself? I remember that it was one of those days of intermittent sun and rain, which, like a human face, easily change expression. It seemed to me that the day was trying to be fine and that I was trying to be happy. My God, I *was* happy. Timorously happy.

And here, Monique, there should be silence. Here my dialogue with myself should cease: here begins the dialogue of two united souls and bodies—united, or merely joined. To say everything, my dear, would require an audacity I forbid myself; above all, it would be necessary for me to be a woman as well. I would merely compare my memories with yours, relive, in a sort of slow motion, those moments of sadness or of painful joy that we lived out perhaps too hastily. All that comes back to me like vanished thought, like shy, whispered confidences, like very soft music you have to listen to in order to hear. Let me see if it is not possible also to write in whispers.

My health, which was still precarious, worried you all the more since I did not complain about it. You were resolved that we should spend our first months together in milder climates: the very day of our marriage, we set out for Merano. Subsequently, winter drove us toward even warmer lands; I saw for the first time the sea, and the sea bathed in sunlight. But that is unimportant. On the contrary, I should have preferred other regions, sadder, more austere, which harmonized with the existence that I was determined to wish to live. Those carefree countries of bodily happiness caused me distress and confusion; I was always suspicious that joy contained a sin. The more my conduct seemed reprehensible to me, the more I clung to rigorous moral standards which condemned my acts. Our theories, Monique, when they are not the formulation of our instincts, are the defenses with which we oppose our instincts. I was annoyed at you for making me notice the deep red heart of a rose, a statue, the dusky beauty of a passing child; I experienced a sort of ascetic horror at these innocent things. For the same reason, I should have preferred you to be less beautiful.

We had put off, with a sort of tacit understanding, the moment when we would be completely each other's. I thought about it in advance with some disquiet, with revulsion also; I feared that so great an intimacy was going to spoil or debase something. Then, too, one never knows what the sympathies or antipathies of the body will bring about between two people. Doubtless, such ideas were not very healthy, but nevertheless those are the ideas I had. Every evening, I would ask myself whether I dared join you. My dear, I did not dare. Finally, I really had to: otherwise, you surely would not have understood. I think, with a certain sadness, how much more another person would have appreciated the beauty—the goodness—of that gift, so utterly simple, of yourself. I would not wish to say anything which might risk shocking you, even less making you smile, but it seems to me that it was a maternal gift. Later, when I saw your child nestle against you, I thought that every man, without knowing it, seeks in women above all the memory of the time when his mother embraced him. That, at least, is the case for me. I recall with infinite pity your rather troubled efforts to reassure me, to console me, perhaps to cheer me up; and I almost think I was your first child.

I was not happy. I felt, of course, a certain disappointment in this lack of happiness, but in the end I resigned myself to it. In some fashion, I had renounced happiness, or at least joy. And then I told myself that the first months of a marriage are rarely the sweetest, that two people, abruptly joined by life, cannot so rapidly absorb themselves into each other and become truly one. That requires a great deal of patience and good will. We had both. I told myself, with even greater justice, that we are not owed any joy, and that it is wrong for us to complain. Everything would seem better, I suppose, if we were reasonable, and happiness is perhaps only an unhappiness which is better tolerated. I told myself that, because courage consists in accepting things when we cannot change them. And yet, if there is something lacking in life, or merely in ourselves, it is not any less significant, and we suffer from it just as much. And you, too, my dear, you were not happy either.

You were twenty-four years old. That was, roughly, the age of my older sisters. But, unlike them, you were not withdrawn or shy: you possessed an admirable vitality. You were not born for an existence of small sorrows or little happinesses; you were too powerful. As a young girl, you had conceived an idea of your married life which was exceedingly severe and grave, an ideal of tenderness more affectionate than loving. Nevertheless, without being aware of it yourself, into the strict routine of those dull and often difficult duties which, according to you, were to constitute your whole future, you inserted something else. Custom does not permit women passion: it permits them only love, and that is perhaps why they love so completely. I dare not say that you were born for a life of pleasure; there is something in that word which is sinful, or at least forbidden; I should rather say, my dear, that you were born to know and to give joy. One must endeavor to become sufficiently pure to encompass all the innocence of joy, that sun-drenched form of happiness. You had thought that giving it would be enough to get it back in return. I do not claim that you were disappointed: it takes a great deal of time for a woman's feeling to change itself into thought: you were merely sad.

So, I did not love you. You gave up asking me for the great love that, I have no doubt, will never be inspired in me by any woman, since I could not feel it for you. But you were unaware of that. You were too reasonable not to resign yourself to such a trapped life, but you were also too healthy not to suffer from it. But one is the last to perceive the suffering one causes. Moreover, you hid it; at the beginning, I thought you were almost happy. You endeavored to dress in a manner that would please me; you wore heavy clothes which hid your beauty, because you already understood that the slightest effort to adorn yourself frightened me, as if it were an offer of love. Without loving you, I was overcome with a sort of anguished affection for you; your absence, even for a moment, saddened me for an entire day, and one could not have said whether I suffered from being away from you or whether, quite simply, I was afraid of being alone. Even I did not know. And then, also, I was afraid to be together with you, to be together and alone with you. I smothered you with an atmosphere of nervous tenderness; I would ask you, twenty times in a row, if you cared for me; I knew only too well that that was impossible.

We forced ourselves to practice a sort of heightened religious devotion, which really did not correspond at all to our true beliefs: those who lack everything else turn to God, and at that moment God, too, abandons them. Often we lingered on in those dark, welcoming old churches one visits in foreign countries; we even acquired the habit of going there to pray. We would return in the evening, pressed against one another, united at least by a mutual fervor; we would invent pretexts for remaining in the street to watch the life of other people: the life of others always seems easier to us, because we do not have to live it. We were too well aware that, somewhere, our room was awaiting us, a transient room, bleak, naked, vainly open to the warm Italian nights, a room without solitude and, at the same time, without intimacy. For we shared the same room, and it was I who wished it so. Every evening, we hesitated to light the lamp; its light bothered us, and yet we were not able to extinguish it, either. You found me pale; you were no less so; I was afraid you had caught cold; you gently reproached me for having tired myself with excessively long prayers: we had for each other a desperate sort of benevolence. You suffered at that time from intolerable insomnia; I, too, had trouble getting to sleep; we both pretended to sleep in order not to be obliged to complain to each other. Or else you wept. You wept as noiselessly as possible so that I would not be aware of it, and I pretended not to hear you. It is perhaps better not to notice tears when there is nothing one can do to console them.

My character changed. I become moody, difficult, irritable; it seemed as though one virtue had given me dispensation from the others. I became vexed with you for not succeeding in giving me the calm I had counted on and which was, dear God, all that I asked for. I acquired the habit of semi-confidences; I tortured you with confessions all the more distressing in that they were incomplete. We found in tears a sort of miserable satisfaction; our mutual unhappiness managed to bring us together as much as happiness. You, too, changed. It seemed I had robbed you of your former serenity without managing to appropriate it for myself. Like me, you had impatiences and sudden sadnesses, impossible to understand; we became no more than two invalids leaning on each other.

I had completely abandoned music. Music was a part of the world in which I was resigned never to live again. They say that music is the realm of the soul; that may be, my dear: it simply proves that soul and flesh are not separable, that one contains the other, the way a keyboard contains sounds. The silence which follows music is not at all like ordinary silences: it is a heedful silence; it is a living silence. Many unsuspected things whisper within us through this silence, and we never know what the piece of music that has ended is going to tell us. A painting, a statue, even a poem, gives us precise ideas which usually take us no further, but music speaks to us of limitless possibilities. It is dangerous to expose oneself to emotions in art when one has resolved to abstain from them in life. Therefore, I ceased to play and to compose. I am not one of those who ask of art the compensation of pleasure; I love the one and the other, but not the one for the other—these two rather sad forms of all human desire. I no longer composed. My revulsion against life gradually extended to those dreams of an ideal life; for a work of art, Monique, is a dream of life. That simple joy which the achievement of a work of art gives every artist dried up within me, or perhaps it is more accurate to say that it froze within me. That was perhaps the result of the fact that you were not a musician: my renunciation, my fidelity, would not have been complete if I had participated every evening in a world of harmony which you could not enter. I ceased to work. I was poor; until my marriage, I had had difficulty making an adequate living. Now I discovered a sort of voluptuousness in depending on you, even on your fortune. This rather humiliating situation was a sort of guarantee against the old sin. We all, Monique, have certain strange assumptions. It is merely cruel to deceive a woman who loves us, but it would be hateful to be unfaithful to one on whose money we live. And you, so cautious, did not dare blame me openly for my complete inactivity. You feared that I would see in your words a criticism of my poverty.

The winter, then the spring, went by. Our excesses of grief had worn us out as much as a great debauch. We came to know that aridity in the heart which follows excessive tears, and my dejection seemed like calmness. I was almost terrified to feel myself so calm; I believed that I had triumphed over myself. One is always so ready, alas, to become disgusted with one's own triumphs. We attributed our despondency to the exhaustion of traveling; and so we took up residence in Vienna. I felt a certain repugnance in coming back to that city where I had lived alone. But you, with tender delicacy, were determined not to take me too far away from my own country. I tried to believe that I would be less unhappy in Vienna than I had been before; but, above all, I was less free. I let you choose the furnishings and the curtains for our rooms; with a certain bitterness, I watched you coming and going in those still-empty rooms in which our two existences would be imprisoned. Viennese society was taken with your dark, pensive beauty: the social world, which neither you nor I was used to, gave us a little time to forget how alone we were. But then we tired of it. We developed a kind of determination to endure boredom in that house which was too new, whose objects had no memories for us, whose mirrors did not know us. My effort at virtue and your attempt at love did not even manage to serve as a distraction for us.

Everything, even a moral failure, has its advantages for a mind that is even faintly lucid; it provides a less conventional view of the world. My less solitary life and my reading of books taught me the difference that exists between external conformity and inner morality. Men do not say the whole truth about themselves, but when, like me, one has been forced into the habit of certain reticences, one very quickly perceives that they are universal. I had acquired a singular aptitude for guessing hidden vices or weaknesses. My conscience, stripped naked, revealed to me the conscience of others. No doubt, those with whom I compared myself would have been indignant at such a comparison. They thought of themselves as normal, perhaps because their vices were so ordinary; nonetheless, could I deem them truly superior to me, in their search for pleasure which culminated only in itself and which, most often, did not envisage a child? I was finally able to tell myself that my only mistake (or, rather, my only unhappiness) was to be, certainly not worse than everyone, but only different. And yet many people accommodate themselves to instincts like mine; it is neither so rare nor so strange. I hated myself for having tragically accepted precepts which so many examples contradict—and human morality is nothing more than one great compromise. Dear God, I blame no one. Everyone broods in silence over his own secrets and dreams, without ever admitting them, even to himself, and everything would be made plain if one did not lie. Thus, I had tortured myself with very little cause. Having conformed to the strictest rules of morality, I now gave myself the right to judge them. And one could say that my thoughts dared to be freer from the very moment when I abandoned all freedom in my life.

I have not yet said how much you wanted a son. I, too, passionately wanted one. Nevertheless, when I knew that we were to have a child I felt very little joy. No doubt, childless marriage is only an allowed debauch. If a woman's love merits a respect which a man's does not, that is perhaps only because it contains a future. But it is not at the moment when life seems absurd and deprived of any goal that one can rejoice in perpetuating it. The child we had dreamed of together was going to come into the world among two strangers: he was neither the proof nor the fulfillment of happiness, but its compensation. We vaguely hoped that everything would be all right as soon as he was there, and I had wanted him because you were sad. At first, you even felt some shyness in speaking to me of him; that, more than anything else, shows how much our lives had remained distant. And yet this tiny being began to help us. I thought of him rather as if he were the child of someone else. I savored the sweetness of our intimacy, which had once again become fraternal and no longer required any passion. It seemed to me that you were virtually my sister, or some near relative who had been entrusted to me and whom I had to take care of, reassure, and perhaps console for an absence. You grew to love enormously this little creature who was already alive, at least for you. My own contentment, which was so apparent, was not stripped of egotism either: not having known how to make you happy, I found it natural to hope that the child would bring you happiness.

Daniel was born in June at Woroïno in the melancholy countryside of the Montagne Blanche, where I myself had been born. We were eager that he should come into the world in this landscape of the past: for you, it was a way of giving me more completely my son. The house, even though restored and newly painted, was the same as ever: it seemed merely to have become much larger, only because we were so many fewer. My brother (I had only one brother left) lived there with his wife. They were very provincial people, whom solitude had made uncouth and poverty fearful. They welcomed you with a rather awkward eagerness, and as the trip had tired you, they offered you the honor of the large bedroom where my mother had died and we had been born. Your hands, resting on the whiteness of the sheets, looked almost like hers; every morning, as in the days when I used to come in to see my mother, I waited for those long, fragile fingers to be placed on my head in blessing. But I could not ask for such a thing: I contented myself with simply kissing them. And yet I had such great need of that blessing. The room was rather dark, with a state bed hung with heavy curtains. I imagine that many women of my family in times past had lain there to await their child or their death—and death is perhaps nothing more than giving birth to a soul.

The last weeks of your pregnancy were painful. One evening, my sister-in-law came and told me that I should pray for you. I did not pray. I simply told myself over and over again that you were doubtless going to die. I was afraid of not feeling a sufficiently sincere despair: I felt, in advance, a sort of remorse. What is more, you were resigned to dying. You were resigned in the way people are when they do not especially care to go on living: in your placidity I saw a reproach. Perhaps you felt that our marriage was not destined to last for a lifetime and that you would end up loving someone else. When one is afraid of the future, it makes death seem easy. I held your hands, which were always slightly feverish, in mine. We both refrained from speaking in the presence of the mutual thought that you would quite possibly die; and you were so exhausted that you did not even ask what would become of the child. I told myself, in rebellion, that nature is unjust to those who obey her clearest laws, since every birth imperils two lives. Everyone causes suffering when he is born, and suffers when he dies. But that life is dreadful is nothing; what is worse is that it is vain and without beauty. The solemnity of a birth, like that of a death, is lost in repulsive or merely commonplace details for those who are in attendance. I was no longer admitted into your room: you struggled amid the cares and prayers of women, and since the lamps remained lighted all night, one was aware that someone was expected. Your cries, when I heard them beyond the closed doors, were almost inhuman and horrified me. I had never dreamed in advance that you would have to come to grips with such an animal form of suffering, and I hated this child who made you scream. Monique, one emotion leads to another, not only in everyday life but within the depths of the soul also: the memory of those hours when I thought you were lost seems to have brought me back to where my instincts had always drawn me.

I was ushered into your room to see the child. Now everything had become peaceful again; you were happy, but with a physical happiness composed chiefly of fatigue and liberation. The child, however, was crying in the arms of the women. I suppose he suffered from the cold, from the noise of words, from the hands which took care of him, from the touch of the swaddlings. Life had snatched him away from the warm maternal shadows. He was afraid, I think, and nothing—not even night, not even death—would ever replace for him that truly primordial refuge, for death and night have cold shadows and are not animated by the beating of a heart. I felt so shy before that child I was supposed to embrace. He inspired in me not tenderness, nor even affection, but a great pity; for one does not ever know in the presence of newborn infants what cause for tears the future will give them.

I told myself that he would be yours—your child, Monique, much more than mine. He would inherit from you not only the fortune so long missing from Woroïno (and while a fortune, my dear, does not give happiness, it often makes it possible) but also your lovely, calm gestures, your intelligence, and that radiant smile which greets us in French paintings. At least I hoped this would be the case. With some blind feeling of duty I had made myself responsible for his life, which ran considerable risk of not being happy since he was my son, and my only saving grace had been to give him an admirable mother. Nevertheless, I told myself that he was a Géra, that he belonged to that family in which the members passed on, as if they were precious jewels, thoughts so ancient that no one has them anymore, like gilded sleighs and court carriages. He was descended, like me, from Polish, Podolian, and Bohemian ancestors. He would have their passions, their sudden depressions, their taste for sadness and bizarre pleasures, all their fate together with my own. For we come from a very curious race, where madness and melancholy alternate from century to century like black eyes and blue eyes. Daniel and I have blue eyes. The child was sleeping now in the cradle placed next to the bed, and the lamps which had been put on the table illuminated things indistinctly, including the family portraits, which one usually does not notice since one has seen them so often. But now these portraits ceased to be a presence and became an apparition. Thus, the will those ancestral figures expressed had been realized: our marriage had produced a child. By means of him, this ancient race would prolong itself into the future, and it was now of little importance whether my own existence continued. I no longer interested the dead, and I in turn could disappear, die, or else begin again to live.

The birth of Daniel did not bring us any closer together: it disappointed us as much as love had. We did not take up again our shared existence; I had ceased to nestle against you at night like a child who has fear of the dark, and I took back the room where I slept when I was sixteen years old. In that bed, where I found, along with my past dreams, the hollow my body had formerly made, I had the sense of rejoining myself. My dear, we are wrong to think that life changes us; it wears us away, and that which it wears away in us are the things we have learned. I had not changed; it was just that events had interposed themselves between me and my own nature. I was what I had always been, perhaps more profoundly so than before, because to the extent that we lose one after another our illusions and our beliefs, we come to know better our true being. So many efforts and so much goodwill ended in my discovering that I was what I had always been: a rather troubled soul, whom two years of virtue had disillusioned. Monique, that is disheartening. The long maternal labor which had been accomplished in you seemed to bring your nature back to its pristine simplicity: you were, as you had been before marriage, a young person who wished for happiness, yet steadier now, calmer, and less burdened with soul. Your beauty had acquired a sort of abundant peace; it was I, now, who knew that I was ill, and I congratulated myself for it. A sense of shame will always prevent me from telling you how many times during those summer months I desired to die; nor do I wish to know if, when you compared yourself to happier women, you held it against me for having ruined your future. And yet we loved each other, as much as one can love without any passion for each other; the summer (it was the second since our marriage) was coming to an end a little hastily, as summers do in northern countries. We managed to savor in silence the end of a summer and of an affection, both of which had borne fruit and now had only to die. It was in the midst of this sadness that music came back to me.

One September evening, the night before our return to Vienna, I surrendered to the attraction of the piano, which up to then had remained closed. I was alone in the drawing room, which was almost dark, and it was, as I have said, my last evening at Woroïno. For several long weeks, a physical disquiet had entered into me, a fever, and an insomnia which I fought against and which I attributed to the autumn. There is a moist, cool sort of music in which one can quench one's thirst, or at least so I thought. I began to play. I played. At first I played with caution, softly, delicately, as if I were trying to put my soul to sleep. I had chosen the calmest pieces, pure mirrors of thought, Debussy or Mozart, and one would have said, as they did formerly in Vienna, that I was afraid of emotional music. Yet my soul, Monique, did not wish to sleep. Or perhaps it was not even the soul. I played vaguely, allowing each note to float over the silence. It was, as I have already said, my last evening at Woroïno. I knew that my hands would never again touch those keys, that this room would never again, because of me, be filled with music. I interpreted my physical ailments as a foreboding of death: I was resolved to let myself die. Abandoning my soul on the crest of arpeggios like a body on a wave when the wave breaks, I waited for the music to ease me toward the next descent into the abyss of oblivion. I played, overwhelmed. I told myself that I had to remake my life and that nothing, not even healing, could heal me. I felt too tired for such a succession of setbacks and efforts, both of them exhausting, and yet I was already taking pleasure, through the music, in my weakness and my surrender. I was no longer able, as I once had been, to despise the life of passion, even though I was afraid of it. My soul was more deeply embedded in my flesh, and what I regretted as I climbed back, from thought to thought, from musical phrase to musical phrase, toward my most intimate and least admitted past was not my transgressions but those opportunities for joy I had rejected. What I regretted was not having given in too often, but rather for too long and with too much vigor having struggled not to give in.

I played in despair. The human soul is slower than we are: that makes me admit that it may also be more durable. It is always a little behind our current life. I was only beginning to comprehend the meaning of my inner music, the music of joy and savage desire that I had stifled within me. I had reduced my soul to one single melody, plaintive and monotonous; I had filled my life with a silence out of which only psalms were permitted to rise. I do not have sufficient faith, my dear, to limit myself to psalms, and if I repent, it is of my repentance. Sounds, Monique, spread out into time like forms in space, and until a piece of music has ceased, it remains in part plunged in the future. There is something very moving for the improviser in the choice of which note will follow. I began to comprehend that liberty both art and life have when they obey only the laws of their own development. The rhythm followed the rise of my inner anguish; the auscultation is terrible when the heart beats too rapidly. What was now born out of the instrument in which my real self had been locked up for two years was no longer a chant of sacrifice, or even of desire, or of joy so near. It was hate: hate for everything that had falsified me and crushed me for so long. With a sort of cruel pleasure, I realized that you could hear me playing from your room: I told myself that that was sufficient as a confession and an explanation.

And it was at that moment that I noticed my hands. My hands rested on the keys, two naked hands without rings on them—it was as if I saw my soul before my eyes, twice alive. My hands—and I can speak of them because they are my only friends—seemed to me all at once extraordinarily sensitive; even motionless, they seemed to stroke the silence as if to arouse it to manifest itself in chords. They were at rest, still trembling somewhat from the rhythm, and in them were contained all future deeds, just as all possible sounds sleep within the piano. They had encircled bodies in the brief joy of embraces; they had touched, on resonant keyboards, the form of invisible notes; they had, in the dark, traced with a caress the contours of sleeping bodies. Often I had held them uplifted in an attitude of prayer; often I had joined them with yours; but of all that they no longer had any memory. They were anonymous hands, the hands of a musician. They were, by means of music, my intermediary with that infinite being we are tempted to call God and, by their caresses, my means of contact with the life of other people. They were etiolated, as pale as the ivory on which they rested, for I had deprived them of sunshine, or of work, and of joy. And yet they remained faithful servants; they had provided me with nourishment when music was my only livelihood; and I began to understand that there is a certain beauty in living from one's art, since it frees us from everything that is not itself. My hands, Monique, were to liberate me from you. They would once again reach out without constraint; they would open for me, these liberating hands, the doors of departure. Doubtless, my dear, it is absurd to tell you everything, but that evening, awkwardly, the way one seals a pact with oneself, I kissed my two hands.

I shall pass quickly over the following days, when my feelings concern and move only me. I prefer to keep for myself my intimate memories, since I can speak to you only with a discretion which might appear to be born of shame, and became I would be lying if I were to show repentance. Nothing is sweeter than a defeat one knows to be total: in Vienna, during those last sunlit days of autumn, I knew the wonder of discovering once again my body. My body, which cured me from having a soul. You perceived in me only the fears, the remorse, and the scruples of conscience: not even my own conscience, but that of others which I accepted as guides. I neither knew how nor dared to tell you what ardent adoration made it possible for me to experience the beauty and the mystery of bodies, nor how each of them, when it offered itself, seemed to bestow on me a fragment of human youth. My dear, it is very difficult to live. I have constructed enough moral theories not to construct other contradictory ones: I am too reasonable to believe that happiness exists only in tandem with sin; and vice no more than virtue can give joy to those who do not have joy within themselves. Nevertheless, I much prefer sin (if that is what it is) to a denial of self which leads to self-destruction. Life has made me what I am, the prisoner if you will of instincts which I did not choose but to which I resign myself; and this acquiescence will, I hope, procure me, if not happiness, at least peace. My dear, I have always known you were capable of comprehending everything—which is much rarer than forgiving everything.

And now I bid you farewell. I think, with infinite tenderness, of your womanly, or rather motherly, goodness: I leave you with regret, but I envy your child. You are the only person toward whom I judge myself guilty, yet writing of my life confirms me in my being; I end by grieving for you without severely condemning myself. I have betrayed you; I have not wished to deceive you. You are one of those who always choose, out of duty, the straitest and the hardest way: I would not, by begging for your pity, give you a pretext for further sacrifice. Not having known how to live according to common morality, I endeavor at least to be in harmony with my own: it is precisely when one rejects all principles that one must arm oneself with scruples. I undertook imprudent obligations toward you to which life refused to subscribe. With the utmost humility, I ask you now to forgive me, not for leaving you, but for having stayed so long.

# ～ *Sandro Penna* ～

# *A Low Fever*

TRANSLATED BY DAVID LEAVITT,

COSIMO MANICONE, AND MARK MITCHELL

For some days he had been running a low fever. He was certain that it was a tubercular illness. In short, he knew that he was going to die. All the same, he had to have a haircut and a shave. Of course he understood that even one who knows he must die cannot escape from the common things. Thoughts during such a state of mind are different, yes, than during any other, but you go to the barber all the same. In the end, you do everything with that slow anguish, but the saddest part is to know that there is nothing else to do except the usual things.

So he went into the barbershop. Shave and haircut. Pointless to save a *lire* and shave yourself. Besides, he had already looked forward with pleasure to lingering there a long time. (When he wasn't sick, it seemed a torture to him.)

The young man who had begun to play games with the scissors over his head was a very coarse type. Rosy almost red, broad face almost round, fleshy almost fat. Still handsome because young. The proprietor, on the other hand, would have been worse. Dirty of salt and pepper beard, smelly of cigar and sweat, maybe he had damp, cold hands that would have caressed the sick man's face. Yet it was him you paid; to him that the young man submitted.

---

*SANDRO PENNA, Pasolini's favorite poet, was born in the Umbrian town of Perugia in 1906. "A Low Fever" is the title piece in his only collection of prose (1973).*

At this point in his observations, the sick man saw a twelve- or thirteen-year-old boy enter the shop, swiftly but quietly and unnoticed. Nobody paid him any mind. He stood straight against a wall and stared into space. The sick man understood at once that he would stay there a long time willingly. To him that must die it was permissible to bestow all his attention upon a young boy. This one seemed suspended in that atmosphere of cosmetics, absent or ethereal, with green eyes that did not "really" watch the sick man's hair fall to the floor.

He had on short pants with no shape and no color. He kept them held around his waist perhaps with a piece of rope. Certainly there were no buttons anymore. He had on a shirt or sweater of an uncertain white. In short, a poor little street boy like any other: but the sick man was enchanted by that boy's suspended expression. Also, the mouth seemed—not closed, not to be open. From time to time the enchantment was brusquely broken by an order from the master: "Get the broom; light the gas; boy, brush." But he obeyed as the prisoner angels obeyed the merchants. Without pride, without anger, not humiliated, he simply obeyed; and immediately after reassumed that attitude that seemed so mysterious to the sick man. He never smiled, yet his face was immersed in a flux of delicate sweetness. Probably he was thinking about his friends, about the riverbank, about the many dives into the water, and the hot sun afterward. And also he was thinking about his mother, who was poor, his dead father, and the necessity to earn five *lire* a day. But these were not ugly or painful thoughts. To him they were remote. Not so his friends, the dives into the river. These were intimately, sweetly close.

At a certain moment the boy received a short but sharp reproach. The sick man did not understand why. He would have given a tip to know. And two to redeem the boy from the reproach. But the boy did something to put matters right: he moved, he went speedily, lightly into the back of the shop, he brought something to the proprietor, and all was as always. The boy leaned against the wall, and the green eyes were not darkened, the small and delicate mouth, neither opened nor closed, wrinkled, the cheeks turned always toward the slender and proud neck.

And what did the glances of the poor sick man mean to him? Oh, he had certainly noticed them from the beginning, but it would have been impossible to know how he had received them. God knows if that boy would have been capable of social expressiveness. To blush, that is shyness. To answer the look of the client with virile irony, that is defensiveness. But no. He could not be that present. Perhaps among his friends on the river-bank, he would have attained his measure. In his natural element, maybe. But it would have been an equal and animal measure. More beautiful like this, out of place in the barbershop.

When the sick man had to leave, he waited a long time for fifty *cente-simi* of change that the proprietor could not find. A loan was asked of the boy, who gave the coin and at once saw it put back into his own hand. This transaction finally astonished him, and, at last, the sick man received a look that interrogated him. A luminous and cool look as from afar, without *"grazie"* or humility, a look that sweetly shipwrecked the poor sick man's every bid for his attention.

But that same evening the fever lifted. He laughed at his apprehensions, from the start so deadly. He told himself he'd been foolish, all the more in that he had already fearfully revealed those anxieties. Walking the day after in front of the barbershop, however, and seeing again that boy like all the others, dirty and simple, he understood that a fever, after all, can be useful for making poetry.

# ~ Albert Camus ~

### FROM

# *The Plague*

TRANSLATED BY STUART GILBERT

The word "plague" had just been uttered for the first time. At this stage of the narrative, with Dr. Bernard Rieux standing at his window, the narrator may, perhaps, be allowed to justify the doctor's uncertainty and surprise—since, with very slight differences, his reaction was the same as that of the great majority of our townsfolk. Everybody knows that pestilences have a way of recurring in the world; yet somehow we find it hard to believe in ones that reach down on our heads from a blue sky. There have been as many plagues as wars in history; yet always plagues and wars take people equally by surprise.

In fact, like all our fellow citizens, Rieux was caught off his guard, and we should understand his hesitations in the light of this fact; and similarly understand how he was torn between conflicting fears and confidence. When a war breaks out, people say, "It's too stupid; it can't last long." But though a war may well be "too stupid," that doesn't prevent its lasting. Stupidity has a knack of getting its way; as we should see if we were not always so much wrapped up in ourselves.

In this respect our townsfolk were like everybody else, wrapped up in themselves; in other words, they were humanists; they disbelieved in pestilences. A pestilence isn't a thing made to man's measure; therefore we tell ourselves that pestilence is a mere bogey of the mind, a bad dream that will pass away. But it doesn't always pass away and, from one bad dream to an-

*ALBERT CAMUS won the Nobel Prize in Literature in 1957.*

other, it is men who pass away, and the humanists first of all, because they haven't taken their precautions. Our townsfolk were not more to blame than others; they forgot to be modest—that was all—and thought that everything still was possible for them: which presupposed that pestilences were impossible. They went on doing business, arranged for journeys, and formed views. How should they have given a thought to anything like plague, which rules out any future, cancels journeys, silences the exchange of views? They fancied themselves free, and no one will ever be free so long as there are pestilences.

Indeed, even after Dr. Rieux had admitted in his friend's company that a handful of persons, scattered about the town, had without warning died of plague, the danger still remained fantastically unreal. For the simple reason that when a man is a doctor, he comes to have his own ideas of physical suffering and to acquire somewhat more imagination than the average. Looking from his window at the town, outwardly quite unchanged, the doctor felt little more than a faint qualm for the future, a vague unease.

He tried to recall what he had read about the disease. Figures floated across his memory, and he recalled that some thirty or so great plagues known to history had accounted for nearly a hundred million deaths. But what are a hundred million deaths? When one has served in a war, one hardly knows what a dead man is, after a while. And since a dead man has no substance unless one has actually seen him dead, a hundred million corpses broadcast through history are no more than a puff of smoke in the imagination. The doctor remembered the plague at Constantinople, which, according to Procopius, caused ten thousand deaths in a single day. Ten thousand dead made about five times the audience in a biggish cinema. Yes, that was how it should be done. You should collect the people at the exits of five picture houses, you should lead them to a city square and make them die in heaps, if you wanted to get a clear notion of what it means. Then at least you could add some familiar faces to the anonymous mass. But naturally that was impossible to put into practice; moreover, what man knows ten thousand faces? In any case, the figures of those old historians, like Procopius, weren't to be relied on; that was common knowledge. Seventy years ago, at Canton, forty thousand rats died of plague before the disease spread to the inhabitants. But, again, in the Canton epidemic there was no reliable way of counting up the rats. A very rough estimate was all that could be made, with, obviously, a wide margin for error. "Let's see," the doctor murmured to himself, "supposing the length of a rat to be ten inches, forty thousand rats placed end to end would make a line of . . ."

He pulled himself up sharply. He was letting his imagination play pranks—the last thing wanted just now. A few cases, he told himself, don't make an epidemic; they merely call for serious precautions. He must fix his mind, first of all, on the observed facts: stupor and extreme prostration, buboes, intense thirst, delirium, dark blotches on the body, internal dissolution, and, in conclusion . . . In conclusion, some words came back to the doctor's mind: aptly enough, the concluding sentence of the description of the symptoms given in his medical handbook. "The pulse becomes fluttering, diacritic, and intermittent, and death ensues as the result of the slightest movement." Yes, in conclusion, the patient's life hung on a thread, and three people out of four (he remembered the exact figures) were too impatient not to make the very slight movement that snapped the thread.

The doctor was still looking out the window. Beyond it lay the tranquil radiance of a cool spring sky; inside the room a word was echoing still, the word "plague." A word that conjured up in the doctor's mind not only what science chose to put into it, but a whole series of fantastic possibilities utterly out of keeping with that gray-and-yellow town under his eyes, from which were rising the sounds of mild activity characteristic of the hour: a drone rather than a bustling, the noises of a happy town, in short, if it's possible to be at once so dull and happy. A tranquillity so casual and thoughtless seemed almost effortlessly to give the lie to those old pictures of the plague: Athens, a charnel house reeking to heaven and deserted even by the birds; Chinese towns cluttered up with victims silent in their agony; the convicts at Marseille piling rotting corpses into pits; the building of the Great Wall in Provence to fend off the furious plague wind; the damp, putrefying pallets stuck to the mud floor at the Constantinople lazar house, where the patients were hauled up from their beds with hooks; the carnival of masked doctors at the Black Death; men and women copulating in the cemeteries of Milan; cartloads of dead bodies rumbling through London's ghoul-haunted darkness—nights and days filled always, everywhere, with the eternal cry of human pain. No, all those horrors were not near enough as yet even to ruffle the equanimity of that spring afternoon. The clang of an unseen tram came through the window, briskly refuting cruelty and pain. Only the sea, murmurous behind the dingy checkerboard of houses, told of the unrest, the precariousness, of all things in this world. And gazing in the direction of the bay, Dr. Rieux called to mind the plague fires of which Lucretius tells, which the Athenians kindled on the seashore. The dead were brought there after nightfall, but there was not room enough, and the living fought each other with torches for a space where to lay those who had been dear to them; for they had rather engage in bloody conflicts than abandon their dead to the waves. A picture rose before him of the red glow of the pyres mirrored on a wine-dark, slumbrous sea, battling torches whirling sparks across the darkness, and thick, fetid smoke rising towards the watchful sky. Yes, it was not beyond the bounds of possibility. . . .

But these extravagant forebodings dwindled in the light of reason. True, the word "plague" had been uttered; true, at this very moment one or two victims were being seized and laid low by the disease. Still, that could stop, or be stopped. It was only a matter of lucidly recognizing what had to be recognized; of dispelling extraneous shadows and doing what needed to be done. Then the plague would come to an end, because it was unthinkable, or, rather, because one thought of it on misleading lines. If, as was most likely, it died out, all would be well. If not, one would know it anyhow for what it was and what steps should be taken for coping with and finally overcoming it.

The doctor opened the window, and at once the noises of the town grew louder. The brief, intermittent sibilance of a machine saw came from a nearby workshop. Rieux pulled himself together. There lay certitude; there, in the daily round. All the rest hung on mere threads and trivial contingencies; you couldn't waste your time on it. The thing was to do your job as it should be done.

# ～ *Klaus Mann* ～

## FROM

# *Pathetic Symphony*

### TRANSLATED BY KLAUS MANN

After Prague, the next place of call on this tour was Paris.

In Germany, a respectable musical elite had accepted the composer with a certain tempered understanding; in Prague, a Slav people, oppressed by a foreign power, had given him an extravagantly demonstrative triumph. But in Paris it was Society which pursued him. The musical world here was closely linked with the world of fashion; the foreigner who wished to make good in the one could not afford to neglect the other—a fact which his Russian friends were not slow to make known to their compatriot. He believed it, and accepted the musical-fashionable round as a duty imposed upon him by the necessities of his calling. A shy man, easily disconcerted by people, wearing a somewhat tight dress suit, his forehead rather flushed—he played his part in the receptions given in his honor at the most exalted houses. One had to suffer not only in order to create music but also by having to mix with people in order to become famous! "Did I not once say to my ambitious young friend Siloti—or was it Kotek to whom I made the remark?—'I am not interested in fame,' " ruminated Peter Ilych. "But he answered: 'We all need it—we all need it.' So in honor I must accept these invitations, even though I perspire with embarrassment

---

KLAUS MANN's *decision to become a writer displayed a certain pluck: his father, after all, won the Nobel Prize; his uncle Heinrich was president of the literary section of the Prussian Academy of Arts; and his brother-in-law was W. H. Auden. Like the composer of the* Pathetic Symphony, *he committed suicide.*

245

and boredom, for perspire I certainly shall. Every contact with this importunate and unreliable world is so painful, so embarrassing, and so fatiguing—like a meeting with the agent Siegfried Neugebauer, who most uncannily and comically unites in himself all their bad qualities!"

Peter Ilych went on trying to persuade himself that all these social unpleasantnesses had to be endured for the sake of the great Russian concert: it was still his ambition to introduce the music of his native land to this most blasé public in the world. For nobody here knows anything about us, he thought several times during the day, when people spoke to him about Russian affairs. Here in Paris there was a Russian cult, which, however, possessed very little knowledge of Russian achievements or Russian life. Here the cult had a political emphasis, like the genuine outpouring of sympathy in Prague: its darts were directed against a dangerous Germany. People were enthusiastic about Franco-Russian fraternity and wore "Franco-Russe" ties. In the salons and in the newspapers, the novels of Tolstoy and Dostoevsky received a great deal of attention, while at the circus the Russian clown Durov had a triumph. Nevertheless, for serious Russian music the interest was so slight that Peter Ilych would have had to be a rich man to take on the risk of the concert himself. Without being guilty of any great extravagance, he had had to spend a considerable amount of money on this tour, which had cost much more than it had brought in. Already he knew that there was nothing for it but to give up the idea of a great Russian concert. Siegfried Neugebauer had been justified in his offensive skepticism, and it was just this that Peter Ilych did not wish to admit. So he took delight in talking about his beautiful concert, trying to get influential persons and fashionable social sets to be interested in it. Everywhere a polite curiosity was aroused, but it remained lukewarm, and nothing of a really helpful nature came of it.

In the meantime he put out feelers. It would advance his fame, and one needs fame, even though fame be a hallmark of the pariah and a miserable substitute. The round of solemn festivities began with a full-dress gala reception in the palace of M. Bernardacky, a rich Maecenas who kept open house in Paris. More than three hundred persons forgathered: Peter Ilych was informed that this was "*tout Paris.*" The great conductor Colonne had been taking his orchestra through Tchaikovsky's String Serenade, and on the gala evening the composer himself conducted it. After Peter Ilych—who also played the pianoforte part in the Andante Cantabile of his first String Quartet—some of the most famous virtuosos followed, notably: the pianist Diémer and the brothers de Reszke, two singers whose voices were here held to be the most beautiful it was possible to conceive. In addition, the soprano Madame Bernardacky, *née* Liebrock, took part in the concert, together with her sister who was an opera singer. It was a brilliant evening: the publisher Maquart, who had arranged it, might well be contented. After the concert various world-famous notabilities congratulated the Russian visitor, who, gracious and timid in his somewhat too tight-fitting suit, and with his forehead flushed, bowed low to everybody who approached him. Among the congratulators were the great rivals Colonne and Lamoureux; Gounod, Massenet, and Saint-Saëns; old Pauline Viardot and Paderewski. The Russian guest listened politely to everybody who came to him, however gushing or garrulous. An old lady, who carried a fortune in jewelry on her neck, bosom, arms, and fingers, asked him if he was aware how famous he was in France: his song *"Nur wer die Sehnsucht kennt"* played a quite important role in the novel *Le Froc* by one Emile Goudau. So great was his fame! When one's work figures in a French novel, then one really belongs to *"tout Paris."*

The round of solemn festivities showed no sign of coming to an end. M. Colonne gave a great soiree; an even more important party was given by the Baroness Tresdern, a patroness of music, who had once been able to arrange a private performance of Wagner's "Ring" in her drawing room in the Place Vendôme. Now she was graciously pleased to give a reception in honor of the Russian visitor. Others were given by the Russian Embassy, Madame Pauline Viardot, and also, and in great style, by the management of *Figaro.* At this last-named, a performance of the third act of *The Powers of Darkness* was given in one of the flower-decorated halls of the distinguished newspaper; and all to honor the Russian guest. The pianist Diémer arranged a gala evening at which his students played only compositions by Tchaikovsky; that was a very good advertisement, not only for the virtuoso-pedagogue but also for the composer and—perhaps—for the young students. The boulevard press, large and small, took a lively part in all these events. True, people were less interested in Tchaikovsky's music than in *"la délicieuse toilette en satin et tulle blanc"* worn by a Polignac or a Noailles; the *"grace de grande dame"* of Madame Bernardacky was lauded, as well as the floral decorations in the great *Figaro* hall: the name of the florist who had supplied the latter was not overlooked, for why should not he, too, participate in the general orgy of publicity?

When at last the two great public Tchaikovsky concerts came to be given at the Châtelet, the Russian visitor was already well known by the most important duchesses and in the reception rooms of the most important newspapers. He had paid visits everywhere, a timid man of the world, piloted and introduced by his zealous publisher, M. Maquart. And now, to wind up, the great French public would be given a chance to know him, and the serious musical journals would be able to take an interest in him.

He was received by the audience at the Châtelet with great applause, which no doubt—so his sensitive apprehension readily informed him—was again directed more to "Little Mother Russia" and to Franco-Russe fraternization than to the composer himself, of whom this public knew but little. However, after every separate piece, and at the end of the concert, there were great ovations.

The journals were restrained. Clearly, they had read César Cui's *La musique en Russie*, and from this they were able to extract their wisdom. The Paris press declared with severity: *"M. Tchaikovsky n'est pas un compositeur aussi russe qu'on voudrait le croire"*; he possessed, so it was firmly stated, neither the audacity nor the strong originality that were the chief charm of the great Slavs—Borodin, Cui, Rimsky-Korsakov, Liadov. M. Tchaikovsky was unfortunately quite European. *"L'allemand dans son œuvre domine le slave, et l'absorbe."*

Obviously at the Châtelet they had expected to hear *des impressions exotiques,* thought Peter Ilych bitterly. In Leipzig they reproached me with being French; in Hamburg, with being Asiatic; in Paris, with being German; in Russia, they consider me a hodgepodge of everything, and in any case quite unoriginal.

Oh, these proud and brutal members of the neo-Russian school, these five gifted Innovators, who stick together as thick as thieves; this solemnly pledged brotherhood of musical nationalists: what harm you have all done to me! It is you and only you I have to thank for the cry that I am "flat," without strength, and "Western." The students in Prague, who hailed me as the legitimate message-bringer and singer of the great Russia, did not think that; nor did that clever old Avé-Lallemant think it when he said that I was too Asiatic and should learn of the German masters. But César Cui thinks it. Rimsky-Korsakov is another matter. He is the only one of the group who understands something about his craft; his *Spanish Capriccio* is very interestingly orchestrated. Without him the whole set would disappear. It is he who arranges for their "strokes of genius," and he who gives them advice; in fact, he has done what is regarded as a crime in me—he has *learned* something. The others are all *dilettanti!* Alexander Borodin—God rest him!—may have been an excellent professor of chemistry; Cui is perhaps a highly worthy professor of fortification—I have been told that his lectures on Defense at the Military College in Saint Petersburg were splendid. Mussorgsky was indeed a tragic figure, a depraved, magnificent fellow, a terrific tippler. But the whole lot of them have been too little concerned with *music:* music can't be treated as a side issue. It has been a great misfortune that Russian composers from the very beginning have treated music as a side issue; that began with Glinka—our original source. He wanted to compose when he was lying on the sofa, and only then when he was in love; for the greater part of the time, however, he drank instead of working. Nevertheless, he was a genius; he managed to write *A Life for the Tsar,* our first opera, without which none of us would ever have existed at all. "It is the people who compose; we only arrange," said Glinka, our great original source. They, the five Innovators, took note of that remark—and also of his predilection for alcohol. To tire people out with folk music—that is the only thing worth doing; that is the only way to be linked with the people! As if the likes of us knew nothing about folk music! Just because we haven't allowed folk music to be our be-all and end-all, but have developed it, transformed it, and wedded it to other apparently foreign elements, we are deemed dull and conventional! Never learn anything of anybody! Never widen your horizon! *"En musique on doit être cosmopolite."* This piece of wisdom comes from Alexander Serov, whom our friends the Innovators are gracious enough to recognize as one of the "initiators" of Russian music. But that dictum no longer holds good. Now it is only the barbaric that is worthy of cultivation; only the crude, the unpolished, the ugly. Above all, it is Mussorgsky who is the real thing—who would never have come before the public at all if it hadn't been for the friendly help of Rimsky-Korsakov, so wretchedly is his music written down. Not a soul can play it. But *Boris Godunov* is *the* opera of the Russian people! Things which if done by the likes of us would be called sensational are regarded as great and beautiful and the very truth itself when done by him. When I once included bells in a score for a particular occasion, everybody smiled: "How smartly contrived!" But *his* bells are expressive of the ancient Russian Church. Coronation processions, with cupbearers, mendicant friars, vagabond and peasant dances—everything he does is the genuine article! Murder, lamentations, screams, megalomania, apparitions—the murdered child shaking his bloody fist at the false Tsar—he is allowed to use the whole paraphernalia! I am not allowed to use them; I am a "traditionalist," like the brothers Rubinstein. It is only an old gentleman in Hamburg who still takes me for an Asiatic. They are better instructed here in Paris: César Cui has enlightened them. The genuine Russians are Borodin, Cui, Balakirev, Rimsky-Korsakov, and Mussorgsky—the Great Brotherhood, who jointly launched the Manifesto of the New Russian Music. Maybe they are a lot of geniuses, and Mussorgsky may be the greatest. God rest his poor soul! He suffered much, the uncontrollable fellow! Perhaps he really was the nearest to our people. *I* don't belong anywhere; I am made to feel by everybody that I don't belong anywhere.

He had plenty of time to ruminate on all these things, because he had canceled all his engagements for this evening, being upset by the newspaper criticisms and exhausted and enervated and disgusted by the endless social round. He wanted to be alone. After dinner he had abandoned his hotel, which was situated near the Madeleine. He had strolled aimlessly along the great boulevards and finally had hailed a cab and asked to be driven to Montmartre. He was passing the Cirque Medrano and was stimulated to go in. The performance had already begun. "How good it smells here!" he thought as the attendant opened the door of his box. He had always loved the pungent smell of the menagerie—it aroused sensations of danger, curiosity, and excitement.

A comely lady in a stiff pink ballet skirt, with a high silver top hat on her fair curly hair, was dancing on the back of a white horse, who played his part by tripping daintily round the arena. The lady scattered kisses and threw out little exclamations in English, half joyous, half fearful. Nearby was a fat clown, with a dreadful violet false nose jutting out of his broad chalk-white face; it was impossible to tell whether he was trying to flee from the white horse or, contrariwise, trying to overtake it. In any case, he behaved with most comical clumsiness, constantly tumbling down and seeming always to be in danger of shedding his broad red trousers—this aroused particularly hearty laughter; crude jokes were shouted from the gallery; the clown, his gaping red mouth distorted in a shameless-ashamed grin, got entangled in his braces, stumbled, and then, to the delight of the gallery, nearly stripped himself naked, but at the last minute managed to rescue the slipping nether garment.

After the bareback rider came the performing bears; then three tightrope dancers in white tights; then a female lion tamer dressed as a Scottish soldier in plaid kilts, who fired a revolver in the air and rent the atmosphere with cries which sounded much more terrifying than the sullen growling of the intimidated beasts; then a great equestrian turn—and throughout, the clowns. Peter Ilych was thoroughly amused. He laughed heartily at the comedians; he got excited when the tightrope dancers performed daring steps, and admired with all his heart the clumsy artistic skill of the dancing bears. Most of all he enjoyed the audience and the enthusiasm and wit of their interjections. It is really charming here, thought Peter Ilych. At last I am glad to be in Paris. He forgot the duchesses, the odious critics, and the five "Innovators." During the interval he drank several brandies at the buffet. The noise and bustle all around did not disturb him. He observed the paterfamilias with his little regiment of boys and girls, always alert to see that his progeny were properly reassembled after they had split up in a disorderly fashion; the cocottes who winked so eagerly from under their gaily trimmed hats; the dandies of the boulevards with their gleaming black mustaches, exaggeratedly high stiff collars, slim hips, and too pointed shoes. He loved listening to the Paris slang, the rapid, pointed speech, the resounding laughter. He was happy to be here.

He was attracted by a pretty girl, and then by the young man she was talking to. Dark, passionate eyes shone out of her pale, strained, but uncommonly attractive face. She wore a very simple tight-fitting dress of black silk, beneath the smooth surface of which the lines of her young breasts were clearly visible; in accordance with the prevailing fashion, the back part of the garment was overelaborate. The young man with whom she was chatting and laughing had his back to Peter Ilych. His hair was soft, dull blond, and cropped short at the back. The young man did not wear an overcoat; his checked suit was made of English material, fitting close to the figure, rather shabby but not without a certain conscious chic. The girl broke into a silvery laugh, which echoed through the whole foyer. As she did so, she let her head fall back; her pale face, with its large, dark, made-up mouth and long eyes, lay exposed, very charming and pathetically overstrained for all its mirthfulness, to the hard light of the gas lamps. The young man answered her laugh with his own, which sounded rough and tender but somewhat mocking. What did it remind Peter Ilych of? He closed his eyes for a few moments in order to look inside himself and discover what this laughter reminded him of. When he opened his eyes again, the young man had gripped hold of the pretty girl's arm; clinging close to one another, still laughing and chattering, they threaded their way through the crowd, with unhurrying but sure steps, toward the exit.

Peter Ilych thought: I must follow them. I must go after them, along the Boulevard Clichy. I must observe them, how they go laughing as they stroll along; they are both so young; they press through the crowd with such sure steps. I must certainly find out what the young man's laugh reminds me of."

He dashed to the cloakroom, hurriedly demanded his fur coat, left a large tip; throwing the coat carelessly over his shoulders, he ran to the exit. He thought to himself eagerly as he ran: Shall I be in time to find them? Or have I lost them already?

There were a great many people walking on the Boulevard Clichy at this time of night. On the pavement, brilliantly illuminated by the gas lamps, prostitutes rubbed shoulders with respectable middle-class women, pimps with army officers, shop girls with Arabs and Negroes. The promenaders were impeded by the people streaming into cafés which spread themselves across the pavement; every café had its own atmosphere of noises and smells. Ragged lads offered newspapers and peanuts for sale; their half-mournful, half-aggressive cries mingled with the sound of dance music in the cafés. At the corner of Boulevard Clichy, where it joins Place Pigalle, stood a haggard old man, his face eaten with leprosy. With a blackish lipless mouth he sang very softly and murmurously a ballad whose contents—when one grasped them—were terrible and moving. Averting his head, Peter Ilych dropped a gold coin into the withered hand. Both pity and disgust worked in him at the sight of the old man. Nevertheless, he was terrified by all beggars and was quite convinced that they brought him ill luck.

The two charming young people had been swallowed up by the crowd—the beautiful girl and the young man with the dangerous laugh. This made Peter Ilych very sad. They've gone, he thought, and weighed down by depression, his steps became slow and heavy. They attracted me; that is why the earth has swallowed them up. But no! Of course the earth hasn't swallowed them up; they've gone into one of these dark houses, clinging close together. They are making love in one of these dark houses. . . .

The noisy, artificially illuminated night was mild. There was a feeling of spring in the moist air. Peter Ilych was warm from walking; he found the fur coat, which hung heavily over his shoulders, excessive. He was startled by a little Negress, who sprang in front of him and in a whimpering voice asked him to buy some matches. She had weary, anxiously staring eyes and a dark crown of crisp curly hair. As Peter Ilych bent down to put a coin in the child's blackish hand, the palm of which seemed somehow pathetically pale, as if it had been bleached, the Negro mother waddled up to them, appearing like a great shadow behind her begging daughter. The words of blessing she bestowed upon the gentleman who was giving alms to her daughter sounded as bitter as curses. The woman was *enceinte;* her body was enormously swollen beneath the gay patterned cotton skirt. Her face appeared to be almost as terrifyingly wide as her body. It could hardly be called a human face at all; it was a great, shapeless expanse, out of which her eyes glowed and from which from time to time her teeth gleamed.

Stepping backward, Peter Ilych escaped from the pregnant Negress; but he could not keep his eyes off her. That will bring me terribly bad luck, he thought, staring as if bewitched at the shapeless creature. Pregnant women always bring me bad luck, and such a one as this is bound to! What a poor miserable wretch she is! What a miserable wretch am I that I should have had to look at her! At last he gathered up enough strength to turn his back on her. Holding his fur coat across his chest with both hands, he bounded away from her with heavy, awkward movements. The sound of a waltz came through the half-open door of a café. Peter Ilych went in.

He ordered a double brandy at the counter, drank it quickly, and asked for another. The girl behind the counter tried to start a conversation with him, saying something about spring, which would not keep one waiting very much longer. She was a voluptuous brunette with the shadow of a mustache above her lip, and she had a strong southern French accent. Peter Ilych did not answer; the girl shrugged her shoulders. Sitting on the long leather-upholstered seat under the gold-framed mirror were other girls; on the grubby marble-topped tables in front of them stood coffee cups or glasses containing a greenish liquid. That must be absinthe, thought Peter Ilych. I should like to have one too. But I suppose the earth has swallowed up those two delightful children.

Next to him at the counter stood a wild-looking fellow, lethargic and motionless, wearing a velvet jacket; he stared with inflamed eyes at the glass of greenish liquid in front of him. Next to this hapless-looking young man—No doubt he is a painter, thought Peter Ilych compassionately, perhaps a very gifted portrait painter, pursued by ill luck, like so many others in this country—but concealed by him from Peter Ilych, stood somebody else. Suddenly Peter Ilych heard his harsh, tenderly mocking laugh: he recognized it; long ago he had heard it, and also only a short while ago. It was Apukhtin's laugh. Peter Ilych was alarmed.

So the young man who belonged to the girl he had seen in the Cirque Medrano was here too, and he had a laugh like Apukhtin's. Peter Ilych took a few steps past the wild fellow in the velvet jacket and took up a position next to the young man. He was alarmed by his own boldness as he spoke to him.

"You are here, then," said Peter Ilych.

The young man turned an astonished face toward him. "Yes," he said, in a voice that was not particularly gracious, and he scrutinized the gentleman in the fur coat. "Why not?"

"I saw you in the Cirque Medrano," said Peter Ilych, whose forehead turned dark red under the harsh scrutiny of the young man. "You had a very beautiful girl with you."

"Did you like her?" The young man grinned understandingly. "It can be arranged. . . ."

Peter Ilych was not used to this way of speaking. What had he let himself in for? So this was just a little pimp, offering his girl for sale? He ought to have turned away and left the fellow. But Peter Ilych said: "I followed you, but you disappeared on the boulevard."

"Whom did you follow?" asked the young man, and examined this strange old man with his keen, narrow, gray-green eyes. "My girlfriend?"

Perhaps the girl was sitting in the café under the gold-framed mirror, with her glass of greenish liquid in front of her; perhaps the young man was keeping his eye on her, ready to let her go off with a cavalier and then toward morning meet her again and relieve her of the cash.

"I followed both of you," said Peter Ilych. "Both of you, because I liked the look of you."

"Me too?" asked the young man, not at all coquettishly, but quite objectively, with a defensive, almost evil expression on his face. Nevertheless, he had approached somewhat nearer to the foreigner in the fur coat.

To his own alarm, Peter Ilych answered: "Particularly you."

Upon which the young man said in a dry tone: "Oh, really."

Peter Ilych was silent. Of course, he knows all about *this,* he thought. I could ask him to come with me. He would probably become coarse, or he might say, without moving a muscle: "That can also be arranged." The buxom southern Frenchwoman behind the counter looked scornfully at the gray-bearded gentleman and the young man.

"You are Russian?" said the young man. His face retained its sullen expression, but he touched Tchaikovsky's arm with his own.

"How can you tell that?" asked Peter Ilych.

"I know lots of foreigners," said the young man, and his face assumed a somewhat disgusted expression, as if it were unpleasant to think about all he had experienced from foreigners. He stretched out his hand toward the glass containing the green liquid that stood in front of him; his hand was thin, sinewy, and rather dirty.

"Would you like another drink?" asked Peter Ilych, seeing that the young man had drained his glass at a gulp.

"Yes," said the young man—and with an expression of contempt, almost of hatred, said to the girl behind the counter: "Two more absinthes, Léonie, for the gentleman and me." So Peter Ilych also received some of the greenish liquid.

For a few moments, they stood there in silence. Peter Ilych looked at the young man. His curly dull-blond hair was cropped short at the back and over the temples—as Peter Ilych had already noticed at the circus. Under the narrow gray-green eyes his cheekbones jutted prominently. The brow was smooth and beautiful, making the weak line of his short chin the more disappointing. His rather broad face, very youthful but already worn and no longer quite fresh, was pale, and the space between his eyelids and his fair eyebrows was a pinkish blue. The only strong color in his face was that of his insolent, thrust-out mouth: its dark red was in striking contrast with the pallor of his brow and cheeks and the lifelessness of his expression. The young man was not very tall, decidedly shorter than Peter Ilych, and thin. His suit, which fitted close to the figure, betrayed an acrobatically trained and flexible body. He held himself in an attitude that was both taut and careless, his legs crossed, his head somewhat drooping, like a runner about to start, the tired sinewy hands encircling the glass.

"You are French?" asked Peter Ilych.

"I am Parisian," said the young man, and looked with his pale, keen glance into his glass. "But my family doesn't belong here; we come from some way off, from over there, from the Balkans." He pointed with his beautiful dirty hand, as if he wished to indicate the dark district from which his family came. "But I have no more relations left," he added in a suddenly and artificially woebegone tone.

"Have you a job?" inquired Peter Ilych and was at once annoyed with himself for his naïve and clumsy question. "I mean," he said, trying to improve matters, "have you got something to do?"

"I've done work at the circus." The young man looked into his glass;

probably he was lying. "As a matter of fact, I wanted to be a musician; I can play the flute." He smiled tenderly, as if he were deeply stirred by the memory of his flute playing. No, he was not lying.

"You wanted to be a musician," repeated Peter Ilych, looking at him.

"But that was only a crazy idea of mine," said the young man, the surly expression returning to his face, his voice hoarse and ill tempered.

He wanted to be a musician; perhaps he has great talent. It is quite likely—he looks as if he had. One might take charge of him; he deserves it just as much as Sapelnikov, probably more, for he is blessed with much more charm. One might help him. . . .

"And what do *you* do?" asked the young man. "I suppose you're an author or something like that?" The rough but tender mocking laugh, which was like Apukhtin's, broke out: the laugh of the evil genius who had had so much power over Peter Ilych.

One could keep him with one; one ought to help him. Perhaps something remarkable could be made of him.

As the foreigner did not answer but seemed to have fallen into a brown study, the young man dispensed with circumlocution and asked bluntly: "Well, what about it? Are you going to take me with you?"

Peter Ilych flushed a deep red. The girl behind the counter, a dumb and scornful witness of the adventure, must have heard the question. Was she laughing? It was extremely distressing. Rather pointedly Peter Ilych said: "But it is already late." He pulled out his watch, less to discover what the hour was than to gain time, and also perhaps to assure himself that he still had with him his most beautiful possession, his good talisman.

He opened the decorated lid of the watch. At the same instant he was alarmed by the greedy look which the young man cast on the gold and platinum trinket.

Peter Ilych's hand trembled as he thrust the watch back again into his pocket. The boy will steal my watch if I take him with me, he realized suddenly, and wiped the sweat from his brow. That is what would happen: not a friendship for life—not an educational relationship which would enable me to rescue him and turn him into a great musician. . . . Nothing at all would result from it, nothing! It is all humbug and self-deception! He would run off with my watch, and that would be the end of the great adventure; that would be the outcome of my wasted emotion.

Even worse might happen. I have seen an unusually large number of beggars tonight, including that terrifying pregnant woman: it all signifies ill luck. Almost certainly it would have turned out even worse. He would have murdered me if I had shown the slightest disinclination to hand over the watch. He would have strangled me, for although he is small he is uncannily strong and agile, and very wicked; I can see that. He already hates me, and his eyes are looking for the position on my throat on which, later on, he'll fasten his fingers.

As a matter fact, thought Peter Ilych, as he hurriedly emptied his glass of the milky greenish liquid, whose aniseed flavor he found unpleasant, as a matter of fact, it would not be such a bad death to be strangled by him. . . . The evil genius—uncannily strong and agile—pounces on you so that you lose all sense of sight and hearing; finally you recognize him for what he is, a strangling angel, who is squeezing the breath out of your body, and you slip away. . . .

You slip away . . . oh, deliverance! But do you slip away with the approving consent of Him from Whom you received your Task? Alas, certainly not; that is more than I can hope for; for that remote Allotter of Tasks made His attitude quite clear when I challenged Him by walking into the icy water more than ten years ago, and for my pains achieved only chattering teeth and a cold in the head. And is it now to be just Apukhtin's laugh and devastating charm that are going to press the life out of me?

Diabolical triumphs of that kind are no longer so easy to achieve, my old friend! It's no longer so easy, Apukhtin, my evil genius! Peter Ilych was buoyed up by a feeling of boldness such as he had only once before experienced; that was at the time when the picture of his life and duty built itself up before his mind's eye with such surprising clarity that he had summoned up the strength to break off his friendship with Apukhtin, his evil genius. He went on furiously thinking: No longer do we feel that we must surrender ourselves helplessly. Today we know what has still to be achieved and accomplished—all sorts of things such as will bring us that miserable substitute, Fame. But you will die without fame, for all your charms, my young friend! What was there about that short martial melody in my friend Grieg's Sonata that I found so heartening? We must learn how to resist.

As the curious elderly gentleman still hesitated, the young man asked again: "What about it? Are you taking me with you?" and was probably thinking about the handsome watch. His narrow, pale, malicious eyes sent out a look that was both keen and merry—an alluring, mysterious, and very dangerous kind of merriment. Between his eyelashes and eyebrows, the colors played on his pale skin—rosy gray and silver, like mother-of-pearl.

"I am tired now," said the elderly gentleman, with a hypocritical smile. "I would rather go home to bed now." As the young man's mouth twisted itself in an unpleasant grimace and his face expressed his annoyance, the foreigner added: "But I will see you again, my friend; please come and see me tomorrow morning. My name is Jürgenson; I am staying at the Hôtel du Rhin in the Place Vendôme. You have only to ask the porter for me."

"Right," said the young man. "Tomorrow morning." And turning suddenly and supplely on his heels and facing Peter Ilych, he added: "Give me a little money now, on account," and he laughed his hoarse, gently mocking laugh.

The gentleman, perfectly calm, said: "With pleasure." He took a note out of his pocketbook and gave it to the young man. It was for a large amount, much larger than the young man had expected; he smiled, and with his thin, grubby hand touched the foreigner's large, white, heavy hand. The foreigner observed the young man with his deep-blue, soft, brooding, and very sad eyes.

He asked the girl behind the counter for the bill, paid it, and turned to go. He walked a few steps away from the young man, turned, and raised his heavy hand by way of salutation. "Farewell, my boy!" said the foreign gentleman, "and may you be happy!"

He stepped onto the Boulevard Clichy. The crowds had thinned; the lights in the cafés were being extinguished, and music could no longer be heard.

But Peter Ilych was not staying at the Hôtel du Rhin in the Place Vendôme, but at the Hôtel Richepanse, Rue Richepanse. The Rue Richepanse transected the Rue St. Honoré and ran parallel with the Rue Royale, and its continuation linked up the Rue de Rivoli with the Madeleine.

(Klaus Mann on Tchaikovsky in his autobiography *The Turning Point*: "I wrote his story because I know all about him. Only too intimately versed in his neurasthenic fixations, I could describe his aimless wanderings, the transient bliss of his elations, the unending anguish of his solitude. . . . He was uprooted, disconnected: that's why I could write his story.")

# ~ Umberto Saba ~

## FROM

# Ernesto

TRANSLATED BY MARK THOMPSON

### First Episode

*Now that I am old, I should like simply to describe,*
*with serene innocence, the marvelous world.*
—"The Immaculate Gentleman in White," *in Ricordi-Racconti*

What's up? Are you tired?

Fed up.

Who with?

The boss. What a shark—just one and a half florins for loading and unloading two carts.

Terrible, you're right.

This conversation (which I set down in dialect, like the ones which follow, though the dialect is toned down as much as possible in the hope that the reader—if this story ever has a reader—can translate it for himself) took place in Trieste at the very end of the nineteenth century between a man and a boy. The man—a day laborer—was sitting on a pile of flour sacks in a warehouse on the Via ————. He wore a red kerchief round his head and down to his shoulders to protect his neck from the coarse sacking. He was still young, though it was true he looked tired, and there was something of the Gypsy in his features, but thoroughly softened and domesticated. Ernesto was sixteen years old, an apprentice in this business which bought flour from the big Hungarian mills and sold it to the bakers in the city. He had hazel eyes (just the color of some poodles' eyes) and light, curly chestnut hair, and he walked with a loose-limbed adolescent

---

UMBERTO SABA, *pseudonym of Umberto Poli, was born in Trieste and lived there most of his life. Il Canzoniere (1900–54), his great work, is a collection of four hundred poems that nonetheless has the integrity and the stature of a single poem. Ernesto, his peculiarly wonderful novel, was published—like E. M. Forster's* Maurice—*posthumously (1975).*

grace—the kind that always thinks itself graceless and fears itself ridiculous. Just now he was standing up, leaning against the open door of the warehouse, waiting for the cart to return with the last load of the day—it was due any moment—and looking at the man as if he had never seen him before; yet he had known and been talking to him for months, because they worked together and also because he rather liked him. The man propped his head on his hands, as a man does when he is tired or angry.

You're right, Ernesto said again, the boss is a real skinflint and I hate him too—but looking more closely, no one would think this boy could hate anybody—and when he sends me to the Piazza to hire a man and tells me he'll pay so much and no more, my heart sinks. I always fetch you, but I'm ashamed I have to offer you so little. That's the joy I like least, I can tell you.

The man stirred from his gloomy position and looked warmly at Ernesto. You're a good lad, I know, he said, and if you ever become a boss, as I hope you will, I'm sure you won't treat your workers like your boss treats me. The man's a crook—one and a half florins for three cartloads, and only two of us for the job—it's highway robbery, no question. He doesn't know what it means to wear yourself out, and it's worse now with summer on the way. Even two florins each wouldn't be enough, and if it wasn't that I like talking to you, I wouldn't be waiting for this cart: I'd knock off now—go straight home to bed.

It was a day toward the end of spring, and the street outside was bright with sun. But it was cool inside the warehouse, cool, damp, and smelling of flour.

Why don't you come and sit down? the man suggested after a pause, gesturing to a place beside his own. There's room here; you can sit on my jacket if you're worried about the dirt. And he made as if to spread out his jacket, for he was already in shirtsleeves, waiting for the cart.

No need for that, Ernesto replied. Flour isn't dirty; you can brush it off so it doesn't leave any marks. And even if it did, I wouldn't care what people saw. He stopped the man from unfolding his jacket and sat down beside him, smiling. The man smiled back; he did not look tired or angry any longer.

I'll dust you off later, he said, if you'll let me.

They looked at one another for a while in silence.

You're a good lad, said the man for the second time. Handsome too, so handsome it's a pleasure just to look at you.

Me handsome? Ernesto laughed. No one ever said that before.

Not your mother, even?

Her least of all. I can't remember the last time she gave me a kiss or hugged me. She still says what she's always said: you mustn't spoil sons.

Would you've liked her to kiss you?

When I was a kid, yes. I don't care now, but I'd have been glad if she'd said something nice once in a while.

Didn't that happen either?

Never, Ernesto replied. Or hardly ever.

A pity I'm so poor and don't have any decent clothes.

Why?

Because otherwise I'd like us to be friends. We could have gone for a walk one weekend.

I'm not rich either—d'you know how much I earn?

No, but you've got parents, and they must have money. So how much do you earn?

Thirty crowns a month, and twenty of those go to my mother. She buys my clothes, it's true—Ernesto's clothes were always bought off-the-peg; while he would have been loath to admit it, he might have liked to dress smartly, as some of his old schoolmates used to—so there isn't much left for me.

But you're learning as well in the meantime.

I don't like having a job at all. I'd like to be doing something completely different.

Like what?

This time the boy made no reply.

So how do you spend your ten crowns? Do they go on women? (The second question was asked as if fearing an affirmative answer.)

No, I don't go with women yet—I've decided not to have anything to do with them till I'm eighteen or nineteen. (Perhaps he had forgotten that two years before, his mother had had to give notice to a young servant girl whom Ernesto was forever pestering in the kitchen. After that the poor woman made sure to employ only misshapen, ugly old women: she collected a real gallery of hags. But they never stayed long, always leaving or being dismissed after a month or two.)

What about you? he asked. Are you married?

The man laughed. Not me, I'm single—don't bother with girls.

How old are you?

Twenty-eight . . . I look more, don't you think?

Not at all, no. I'm sixteen, nearly seventeen—seventeen next month.

Don't you want to tell me what you do with your ten crowns a month?

Aren't you nosy. Ernest laughed. They soon go, either in cake shops or on theater tickets. I go to the theater most Sundays after supper. I like tragedies best. Don't you ever go to the theater?

What would I be doing, going to the theater? I was brought up an orphan, I don't have a clue about things like that—I can hardly read or write my own name.

I love the theater, Ernesto went on, like every other boy in the world (and not only the boys), too concerned with himself to think about other people. Last Sunday I saw *The Robbers* by Schiller; it was wonderful.

Was it funny? asked the man absently.

No! I cried. I was in a bad way. I went home in such a state my mother said she'd never let me go to the theater again: it's wasting money if I only come home all upset.

Don't you have a father?

How did you know?

You only ever mention your mother, the man said almost apologetically.

I never knew my father.

Is he dead? asked the man, a low voice.

No, separated from my mother. They separated six months before I was born.

Why?

Don't know. They quarreled. So I've never seen my father. He lives in another city, and I don't think he's even allowed back to Trieste. Not that I mind not seeing him: he can stay where he is, for all I care.

So you live alone with your mother.

With her and my old aunt. The aunt's the one with the money, and she's careful to keep it that way. There's my uncle too—he's my guardian as well, but he doesn't live with us, he's married. He only comes for Sunday lunch, which is all too often for me. He's crazy.

Crazy?

Round the bend. A few days ago he wanted to clout me round the head—as if I was still ten years old! (Ernesto stroked his cheek with the back of his hand as he spoke; obviously the threat had been made good, and the boy was ashamed to admit it.)

What had you done?

Nothing. We had an argument after lunch about politics, and I'm always for the socialists. What about you?

I told you I don't know about things like that, and anyway I don't care about politics. But it's good that you're for the socialists.

Why d'you think so?

Because lads like you always take the bosses' side.

Not me, I can't stand men who exploit other men's labor.

Is that what you told your uncle?

That and more. He's mad, but he's not really nasty; he gave me a florin after he clouted me. He's been giving me florins every week for three years, and last Sunday he gave me an extra one. Perhaps he was sorry; but as I say, he's more mad than bad.

Well then, mightn't it be better if he clouts you every week? asked the man with a laugh.

No; I don't like being hit. Not for my sake; because of my mother. It hurts her every time, and she's very fond of her brother.

She's very fond of you too—more than you think. How could she live with you and not be?

Why are you saying these things?

The man put his hand on the boy's hand, which lay palm down on the sacking. He seemed tense.

What a pity! he said, and looked surprised and glad when the boy did not take his hand away.

What's a pity?

What I said before, about us being friends and going for walks together.

Because you're much older than me?

No.

Because you haven't got smart clothes? I told you before, things like that don't matter. So . . .

The man fell silent. He seemed to be struggling with himself, as if he wanted to say something and wanted not to say it. Ernesto felt the man's hand trembling on top of his own. Then—as someone risking his all to win everything—he looked the boy straight in the eye and burst out in a strange voice:

But do you know what it means for a boy like you to be friends with a man like me? Because if you don't, I'm not the one who's going to tell you.

He was briefly silent again. Then, when the boy blushed and looked at the floor but still did not move his hand, he added almost aggressively:

*Do* you know?

Ernesto slid his hand from the man's grasp, which had tightened and become damp with sweat, and laid it timidly on the man's leg. He drew his hand up and along till, lightly and as if by chance, it brushed his sex. Then he looked boldly up at the man, a luminous smile on his face.

The man felt overwhelmed. His mouth was dry and his heart was pounding so hard he felt faint, and all he could say was:

Do you see?—which seemed addressed more to himself than to the boy.

There was a long silence, which Ernesto broke by answering:

I do see, yes, but . . . where?

What do you mean, where? the man asked vaguely. It was Ernesto who seemed the quicker of the two.

If we're going to do things we shouldn't do, don't we have to be alone? Of course.

So where do you want us to go to be alone? asked Ernesto in a low voice, some of his bravado already draining away.

Tonight, out in the country, I know a place. . . .

I can't in the evening.

Why not? Do you go to bed early?

If only I could! I'm half asleep on my feet by then. No, I have to go to night school.

Can't you skip it once?

No; my mother comes too.

Is she worried you wouldn't go?

I don't think so; she knows I don't lie to her. It's an excuse for her to get some exercise. She wants me to learn shorthand and German: she always says you can't get ahead without German. . . . Anyway I'd be scared to go out in the country.

Scared of me?

No, not of you.

Of what then? If it's these clothes you're ashamed of, I can wear my Sunday best.

Someone might come past and see us.

Not in the place I'm thinking of.

I'd still be scared. . . . Why not here in the warehouse?

But there are always people around; they'd get suspicious if we started coming out of here together. (Ernesto had keys to the building, and the man knew it.) The boss lives right across the street, worse luck. And his wife's never away from the window, and she's even worse than him.

Can't we find an excuse? Like pretending you've left something behind? Whenever there's a job that needs finishing urgently, I come back to the office after lunch at two o'clock instead of three, before it's time to open. That's partly why the boss gives me the keys. Sometimes I'm here by myself more than an hour, and you could always say . . . Oh, look, here's the cart!

They saw first the heads, then the flanks of two powerful dray horses framed in the open doorway. Then the cart, with the carter on his feet, holding the whip and reins. Before the horses could obey the carter's *Whoa!* a second man, fat and heavily built, jumped down from the sacks where he was sitting cross-legged like a Turk, and hailed the man in a slurred voice. He had come to help unload.

Let's talk later, said the man, hurried and hoarse. He had taken off the red kerchief during their conversation; now he knotted it again behind his head and set to work. His legs trembled beneath him slightly as he went.

~ ~ ~

After the two men had unloaded all the sacks (not without oaths and abuse from the fat one), with Ernesto entering and marking them one by one, a furious argument flared up in the office. Cesco, the fat man, started it; what with all his damning and blasting, he must have been drinking even more than usual. Ernesto's friend, on the other hand, was in no mood to argue about anything; he wanted only one thing now: to get to the fried-food shop as quickly as possible, eat whatever was on the slate that day, then go straight home to lie down and think. For months (since setting eyes on Ernesto, in fact) he had been hoping for what had just happened (rather, for what promised to happen soon), and he was (if anyone can ever so call himself) happy. But his happiness was not unqualified: might not the boy have second thoughts, or take offense afterward, or foolishly spill the whole story to a third party? So he would have taken whatever the boss had offered through Ernesto when he came to find him in the piazza—would have accepted it without batting an eyelid. It even seemed to him that his paltry wages had grown much bigger, for Ernesto had told him the rate, not fixed it himself. But the fat man did not have his reasons to keep quiet, and anyway he was drunk. The boss was defending himself in his horrible Italian, which always betrayed his origins: he was a Hungarian Jew with a passion for Germany, where, so he said, he had been educated, then lived for some years. Ernesto was especially irritated by his accent—it was torture to his ears, for he was proud of being a good Italian as well as a good socialist. He had read the lives of Garibaldi and Victor Emmanuel II when he was a little boy: in those days the only books in the house, forgotten by his guardian uncle since his own youth. The word "Germany" was positively insulting to Ernesto, and it was a word his employer used often (as often as possible), mispronouncing it *Chermany* and praising the peerless virtues of its people. Still, the man had to show solidarity and support his mate, and Cresco's threats eventually prevailed over Signor Wilder's meanness, which, while not actually breaking the law (there weren't any laws to protect workers at that time, let alone day laborers), did go against the accepted practice in the piazza. With bad grace he raised the wage: now and in future the two men would have four florins between them instead of three. (Two florins each—exactly the amount Ernesto's friend had mentioned before.) The man was already on his way out when the boss called him back to say there would be work the next day. He engaged him for the whole afternoon and said to come an hour before opening time, as it would not be possible to take the goods to their destination before three o'clock and there were a good many leaking sacks that needed mending. He would (he said through gritted teeth) pay for the extra time. Signor Wilder was very suspicious by nature and never left a worker on the premises without Ernesto there to supervise, so he told the boy he must be in the office by two o'clock as well. It was fate, speaking—it so happened—through Signor Wilder's lips, and in a manner as sudden as it was irresistible. They both knew it immediately; neither dared look at the other. Yet the man's eyes were shining, and he swallowed softly. He left straightaway, barely saying good-bye, and the boy busied himself with the letter book. But his thoughts too were elsewhere. . . .

~ ~ ~

Now we're alone, said the man, when he realized that Ernesto was not going to speak. Out of the bag he always brought to work he had taken a needle and thread to sew the sacks, but he was really waiting for the boy to say something to recall their conversation of the day before—something to encourage him. But Ernesto did not so much as open his mouth. He had positioned himself nearby (nearer than usual, perhaps) and stood staring at the floor, fiddling with the paper label on one of the sacks until it came off in his hand. He tore the label into shreds and tossed the shreds away.

Alone, he said at last. Alone for an hour.

There are lots of things you can do in an hour, the man added readily.

What things do you mean?

Don't you remember what we talked about yesterday? What you as good as promised me? Don't you know what I'm so longing to do with you?

You want to put it up my arse, Ernesto said with serene innocence.

The man was taken aback to hear this crude phrase from a boy like Ernesto. He was hurt as well—hurt and frightened. He thought the kid, already regretting his half-consent, was mocking him. Worse yet, he might have told somebody or—worst of all—confessed to his mother. But the truth was quite different. Without being aware of it himself, the boy's clear answer showed what many years later, after much experience and much suffering, would become his own "style": his reaching to the heart of things, to the red-hot core of life, overcoming dogma and inhibition without evasion or word-spinning, whether he was treating low, coarse subjects (even forbidden ones) or those which people call sublime, putting them all on the same level, as Nature does. But none of this was on his mind at the time: his mouth spoke the words (which almost made the laborer blush) because the situation called for them. He wanted to please his friend and make him happy, and he wanted to experience those new sensations— wanted them *for* their novelty and strangeness. At the same time he was afraid it might hurt. And this, just then, was all that frightened him.

Is it *so* good? he asked.

The best thing in the world.

Maybe for you, but I . . .

For you too . . . Haven't you ever done it with a man before?

Me? Never . . . Have you with other boys?

Often, but none were as handsome as you. He reached out to touch the boy, who drew back, turning his face away.

What did they say afterwards?

Nothing. They were happy too. Sometimes they even asked me first.

Ernesto's eyes were drawn to a part of the man's body which was visibly aroused.

Let me see it, he said.

Happily. He was about to satisfy Ernesto's wish and his own, when the boy stopped him.

Let me take it out, he said. Can I?

Of course.

He bent down to act on his whim, but the man's shirttails were so twisted around it that he needed help.

It's big, Ernesto said, half scared and half amused. Twice as big as mine.

Because you're still a boy. Wait till you're my age, then . . .

The boy put out his hand. The man stopped him.

No, not with your hand, or you'll make me come.

Isn't that what you want?

Yes, but not in your hand.

Ah! Ernesto jerked his hand back as if from some forbidden thing. The man was edging nearer.

I'm scared, Ernesto said.

What of? Don't you know I love you?

I do believe you . . . but I'm scared you'll hurt me even so.

Me hurt you? I know how to treat a boy who's doing it for the first time, and you more than any other.

You won't put it all the way in, will you?

You're joking! Just the tip—hardly anything. The man smiled.

Well, you say that now, but when you're all stirred up . . .

How adorable you are! thought the man, and he vowed not to hurt the boy in any way, even if it meant less pleasure for himself.

I'll cut it off, he said, rather than hurt you. And he tried to kiss him, but as before, Ernesto ducked aside.

Bend down now, *please,* the man begged. Time's passing, and we're not getting anywhere.

So you want to get somewhere! Ernesto laughed.

You want to as well—that's why we're here, isn't it? As long, he added in a low quick voice, as long as you won't wish you hadn't later.

I've already told you I won't, but . . . but what about a pledge?

What pledge? The man did know what Ernesto meant. If he had not been poor and the boy (as *he* thought) well off, he would have expected a demand for money, and that would have spoiled everything.

You must swear to stop if I say so, whenever I say it.

I'm sure you won't need to say anything, but I promise all the same.

Promising's not enough: you've got to swear.

The man laughed. What d'you want me to swear by?

Don't laugh; give your word of honor. The boy held out his open hand as if to seal a contract.

The man took his hand. They shook.

Whenever you say and at once, the man swore.

Ernesto looked relieved.

Now . . . if you want to . . .

Bless you! Now take your jacket off—he had already removed his own—and your trousers too.

You as well.

Yes, of course. The man began, then Ernesto had another whim.

Let me take yours off and you mine, he said. Can we?

The man agreed to everything.

Where do you want me to go?

Here— The man pointed to a low pile of sacks, with, at the top, the one whose label Ernesto had torn to shreds in his confusion. They were medium-sized and marked with a double zero: the whitest, finest grade of all, superfine flour so costly that only a few bakers would buy it. The sacks were piled to a height which might have been arranged just for them, beneath an arch in a secret recess deep inside the warehouse, where they would never be found—unless by the eye of God.

Ernesto knelt by the sacks and leaned across them as his friend had asked. The man turned him round and slowly lifted up his shirt, which the boy, unconsciously teasing or, more likely, because of the anxiety spreading through him, had forgotten to take off. (The shirt was his last defense, the last barrier between him and the irrevocable.) The man was trembling as much as the boy.

He caressed the boy's body as he gradually laid it bare, but only for a moment, for he was afraid of making him impatient. So too he withheld the tender words rising from his heart: words full of gratitude and wonder, which (if he heard them at all) Ernesto would scarcely have appreciated. He said something coarse instead, as if in reply to those words the boy had just used, which had almost made him blush.

Ernesto said nothing back. Filled with curiosity and fear, he could not have said anything even had he wanted to. And for that matter, what was there to say? He heard the man softly asking him to shift position, and did so as if it was an order. All at once he thought, *I'm lost,* but there was no regret, no wish to turn back. Then (and not at first without sweet pleasure) he felt a strange, unknown heat as the man found and made contact. Neither spoke, except for an *Angel!* that escaped the man just before he came, and a warning *Aah!* from the boy when he felt the man pressing too hard. But he kept his promise and did not hurt him in any way (or tried not to). In all, it was easier and quicker than Ernesto had expected. As he withdrew from the boy, the man asked him to stay as he was a moment longer. *What else can he want to do to me?* he wondered, but relaxed when he saw the man take a handkerchief out of his pocket; he only wanted to clean him (whether from kindness or to make sure he left no trace). It made Ernesto feel like a little baby. He felt bewildered and confused too, just as babies do.

~ ~ ~

You were good—good as gold, said the man when they were both dressed again and had brushed themselves down.

Ernest frowned, but he was pleased by the man's praise.

Did you like it? he asked.

I was in heaven. But you liked it too—admit it.

Less than that! A bit at first, yes, then it hurt. I yelled as well.

You yelled?

Didn't you hear me yell *Aah!?* . . . And why did you call me an angel?

What else should I call you?

Angels don't do things like this, Ernesto said brusquely. They don't even have bodies.

We came together, said the man.

How d'you know?

I felt you coming—you can always feel it. And look down there.

Where? asked Ernesto, frightened now.

The man pointed to a dark patch on the sack of superfine flour which Ernesto had been bending over, the one with the shredded label.

The boy looked and was mortified.

If you can see it, we must turn the sack over. Don't you think we should?

Who could know what it is? asked the man. But I'll turn it over later if you still want me to.

There was a lingering, embarrassed silence. The man became thoughtful, almost lowering.

Ernesto was rather alarmed. What are you thinking about? he asked.

I'm thinking there's something I must tell you and I don't like having to say it. Maybe I should have said it before. . . . You won't tell anyone what we've done, will you?

Who d'you think I might tell? I'm not that stupid—I know as well as you what you can say and what you can't.

The man looked relieved. But the worst still remained to say:

It's a dangerous thing, you know: people don't understand, and . . . and they can send you to prison for it.

I know that too, said Ernesto triumphantly. I read about a pair like us in the newspaper, a man and a boy caught red-handed in a changing room. The headline went. "What Happened After a Swim," and the boy got four months and the man six. That's ba-a-ad! he concluded, spinning out the *a* for no apparent reason.

And when you've done time, persisted the man, there's nothing left to do but drown yourself for shame. But he felt guilty at tormenting the boy so.

Don't worry, Ernesto said reassuringly, as long as we don't get caught like those two fools. It was the attendant who thought they'd gone, opened the door, found them doing it, and shouted the place down when he didn't need to say anything. Now, *I* made sure you'd bolted the door before, though you didn't notice.

Ernesto smiled at the man, who was still pensive, even gloomy.

It's something else I'm thinking about, Ernesto added.

What's that? asked the man anxiously.

I'm wondering how I'll be able to look my mother in the face tonight.

As you do every other night, the man answered, hiding his dismay. If she doesn't know anything's happened, nothing *has* happened.

*I* know that well enough, Ernesto said gravely. It'll be a problem going to class too: she'll ask me on the way what I've been doing. My mother's very nosy, she always wants to know everything—everything that's happened during the day.

Women are always nosy, but you still mustn't tell her anything at all, anything of what we've done, I mean. She'd forgive you, perhaps, but never me. . . . And don't think you're the only boy who's ever done what you just did. I asked you for love because I do love you. You're not like other boys, who do it once and never want to see you again. You *are* like an angel to me, and that's another reason I don't want any harm to come your way from this.

All right, said Ernesto. Then after a pause:

How many boys do you think have done it?—what I've done today?

What do you mean, how many boys?

Well, out of a hundred, say, how many . . . ?

How do I know? The man laughed uneasily. All I can say is, I never asked a boy who said no.

This was true; what he did not add was that, guided by a nearly infal-

lible sixth sense, he only ever approached boys who had this particular curiosity in their adolescence. (They nearly all changed later and forgot the
whole affair—or tried to.) And (while the man could not have told
Ernesto this, at least not yet) many gave themselves for cash. Their price
was only a florin—not much, but day laborers did not always have a florin
to spend as they liked. If he had been well off, he would have given
Ernesto a splendid present (not money), but in gratitude for past pleasure
and because he knew how much boys love presents—nothing thrills them
more. But he couldn't have done it even with the money in his pocket: the
boy would have been bound to show his mother or his friends (for some
reason the man was sure Ernesto had lots of friends, whereas he had very
few at this time, if any); he could not have kept it hidden if he had wanted
to. He would have bought him a gold tiepin, studded with a tiny precious
stone, perhaps, in the fashion of the day. But thinking about it was all he
could do.

Ernesto, meanwhile, was walking restlessly about the warehouse, looking nervous. The man had taken out his needle and thread and set to work.

We must get down to it, he said, or the boss will make all sorts of fuss
when he comes in.

Ernesto sat down beside him and watched him sew but did not sit still
for long. He was soon back on his feet, pacing to and fro. . . .

What are you touching yourself for?

I'm burning hot, Ernesto said apologetically, as if he was to blame.

Don't worry, the man said gently, it's nothing; it'll pass in an hour,
probably much sooner.

Sure?

Certain. I was so careful, I can't think why you feel anything now.

Can I ask you something?

Of course you can.

Is it true they examine you there at the army medical and throw out
anyone who . . .

The man burst out laughing, but this time too there was something
forced in his laughter. He reassured the boy about this question, as he had
done before; he had been conscripted himself eight years ago and no one
had even thought of examining him in the place Ernesto was worried
about. Not him or anybody else.

Who the devil put that stupid idea into your head?

No one put it into my head, Ernesto replied, somewhat piqued. (Did
the man take him for an idiot?) Someone I know once told me. Last year.

The man remembered he had once heard something similar himself and believed it too at first. But Ernesto was an educated person: how could he credit such a silly tale? He realized that the boy was remorseful, at least for the moment, and wanted comforting; that all these notions and complaints—even these smartings—were more the effect of his remorse than anything else. He in his hard egoism hoped it would prove to be a passing mood; quite apart from his love for the boy—itself rare enough in a man like him—he felt none of the revulsion he had always experienced with other boys, whom he left—fled from, indeed—as soon as he had possessed them. It seemed to him he could have stayed with Ernesto forever, and even if he *had* had to scare the boy a little, he was upset to see him worried and downcast.

Are you still thinking about your mother?

No, not now.

Of what then?

. . . Nothing.

The man set to work again but soon stopped to ask, in an almost motherly way:

Does it still hurt?

Yes, still. This time the boy's voice was reproachful.

Another time, ventured the man, I'll bring something that'll stop any pain, during or after.

Ernesto was intrigued. What is it?

Something you buy at the chemist's.

You mean the chemist sells something for *this*? Well . . .

No, not for that, the man said. It's for people with tummy upsets. It's a cone you put up there, and five minutes later all the burning is gone. Then you wouldn't feel any of what you say is hurting you now.

What's the cone made of?

Cocoa butter, answered the man, with no idea of the effect his words would have.

Cocoa butter—cocoa butter! Ernesto chanted the words over and over until he dissolved in laughter, and laughed so hard that he had to sit down, tears running down his cheeks. He looked as if he could never stop.

Cocoa butter—up your arse! You know it all, you do! He laughed so delightedly and long that his fresh, young high spirits cleared away the clouding heaviness from the room. The man joined in the laughter and seemed happy and relaxed by his boy's jubilation as he sang the ingredient of his medicine and the way it needs to be applied. The man was longing to hug Ernesto and kiss him, but he was not brave enough to try; experience had taught him that boys don't like kisses—don't know how to give or accept them. He looked thankfully, tenderly, at the boy, and the same moment heard someone hammering on the door almost angrily. It was the boss, who had been knocking for some time, now grown impatient when nobody let him in. He was thinking that neither Ernesto nor the hired man had even showed up: they had forgotten his orders of the afternoon before—disobeyed him. Ernesto was still laughing too much to stand up and go to the door, so he gave the keys to the man, who hurried to let the boss in. He entered grim-faced, glancing around suspiciously, and asked Ernesto in his usual vile Italian what there was to be so jolly about. Ernesto (who always preferred not to say anything when he could not tell the truth) was lost for words. The boss shrugged and kept looking at his young apprentice, but not in anger; he liked the boy, though he was too afraid of losing face ever to let him know it. He muttered a *verfluchte Kerl* (bloody boy) and stepped over to his office, instructing Ernesto to be with him in (glancing at the clock) five minutes' time. He had to give him and the workman their orders for the afternoon's delivery.

~ ~ ~

Aren't you going to turn the sack over? Ernesto asked, calm at least and remembering what had worried him before.

Right away, but not because we need to, believe me. It's only another bit of work. But for your peace of mind—he looked lovingly at the boy—I'll gladly do it.

# ～ *Elsa Morante* ～

### FROM

## *Arturo's Island*

TRANSLATED BY ISABEL QUIGLY

His voice, which I recognized at once with a shock, came from the lower, hidden layers of the hill, so that it seemed to be coming from the bottom of the sea cliffs. This illusion gave the scene the disturbing solemnity of dreams, but to me the oddest thing about it was the fact that he was singing at all. Usually he never sang, and, indeed, he hadn't an attractive voice (it was really the only ugly thing about him): sharp, almost feminine, inharmonious, it was. But just because it wasn't musical or attractive, his singing mysteriously moved me the more. I don't think even an archangel's song would have moved me as much.

He was singing part of a well-known Neapolitan song, which I'd known ever since I could speak; to me, it seemed perfectly ordinary and banal after all the times I'd heard it and sung it myself. The one that goes:

*I find no peace*
*And make night day*
*Ever to be near you*
*Hoping you'll speak!*

---

ELSA MORANTE *published* Arturo's Island *sixteen years after her marriage to Alberto Moravia. Marguerite Yourcenar's* Alexis *is the most eloquent and perceptive novel of male homosexuality written by a woman, but* Arturo's Island *(like Mary Renault's* The Charioteer*) also dispels the myth that only gay men can write about gay male experience.*

But he was singing it with such persuasive bitterness, so harshly, so desperately, that I listened as if to some wonderful new song, full of tragic significance. The four lines he was yelling, slowly, dragging them out, seemed just to sum up my own loneliness: the way N. had been avoiding me and I'd wandered about friendless, cheerless, restless; and the way I'd ended up on this great huddle of wretchedness today, in this dangerous spyhole, to meet the climax of my sorrows.

I couldn't see W.G. from where I was, so I climbed up onto a piece of the wall that jutted out, behind which I'd been hiding. And from up there, when I peeped through an old broken window, I could see the singer. He was alone there, half stretched on a weedy patch of ground at the bottom end of the steep slope going down toward the cliff; and from that steep, narrow patch of ground, like a wretched toad croaking at the moon, he was singing to the prison. His eyes were fixed on one of the windows visible from the ground, in the wing that curved round in a half circle between the bottom of the hillock and the sea. It was a window on its own, about halfway up; and like the others, it gave no sign of life through the small opening above the "wolf's mouth": nothing but silence and darkness.

All the same, it looked as if my father was waiting for some reply to his song. When he reached the end of the verse, he waited a bit, silent, worried, and rolling glumly over on the ground like a sick man in a hospital bed. Then he began his song again from the beginning, the same verse as before. At this point I grew scared he might see me, and left my spyhole and jumped down to the bottom of the wall. From there, if I leaned out a bit at the side, I could, without seeing him, watch the unchanging prison window. In fact, I didn't look away from it again.

Twice or three times again I heard him from the bottom of the hillock, repeating the song with somber, childish stubbornness; always the same verse of that song I knew. And each time, his tone expressed a different kind of suffering: supplication, command, or tragic, demanding passion. But the window remained blind and deaf, as if the prisoner who lived behind it had left his cell, or was dead, or fast asleep at the very least.

The pointless song ceased at last; but after a while, instead of the song, I heard some short, rhythmical whistles rising from the hidden hollow, in a new effort to call to the window. And I found I was shaking with jealousy.

At once I'd recognized in the rhythm of the whistles a secret signal language, a kind of Morse code, that my father and I had invented together during my happy childhood. We used this alphabet of whistles to send messages at a distance when we played by the sea in summer; and sometimes even in the port or the café, to laugh at various Procidans that were there and didn't realize.

Now, it was obvious my father must have told the prisoner about this mysterious alphabet, which I thought belonged just to the two of us: to me and Wilhelm Gerace!

Years of practice had taught me the signals so well that I could translate them into words the minute I heard them, better than an old hand at telegraphy. All the same, my jealous outburst made me miss the first syllables of the message my father sent out. I heard the rest, and it went like this:

NO—VISITS—NO—LETTERS—NOTHING
JUST—ONE—WORD
WHAT—DOES—IT—COST—YOU?

My father waited quietly again; but the window continued as silent and indifferent as the grave. My father repeated:

JUST—ONE—WORD

and then, after another pause:

WHAT—DOES—IT—COST—YOU?

At last, through the little opening high up in the window where the "wolf's mouth" widened and left the end of the bars exposed, two hands appeared, clinging to the bars. My father obviously saw them at once; he leapt to his feet, so that I could see him from his shoulders upward, running toward the edge of the cliff. There he stopped, almost below the prison, from which the plunge down to the sea divided him by only three or four yards; and waited there in silence, as if those wretched clinging hands were two stars that had appeared to announce his fate.

After a bit, the hands dropped from the bars; but the prisoner was obviously still there behind the window, maybe standing on his bench to reach the bottom of it; and from there he put two fingers to his lips to send back his answer. His whistles came back promptly, sharp and rhythmical, one after the other with cruel monotony. And suddenly, feeling incredulous but quite certain, I recognized in them, as in a voice I knew, a proud, stinging voice full of youth and disdain, the unmistakable exasperated accents of the convict on the quay!

His message to my father, which I translated at once, consisted of just these words:

GET—OUT—YOU—GROTESQUE

Then, nothing. Only it seemed to me—perhaps it was just a trick of hearing—that from all the windows nearby came a low chorus of laughter, as if my father was being somberly mocked. Then there followed another gravelike silence all around, which a little later was interrupted by the jailers on their rounds, banging on the bars with their rods to check them before evening. The noise came closer and closer from the invisible windows facing onto the sea, and I saw my father move from where he was and prepare to climb slowly up again. Then, for fear of his surprising me, I hurtled down the hillock and hurried back the way I'd come.

All the way home I kept repeating the word "grotesque" to myself, so that I shouldn't forget it; I wasn't quite sure what it meant. When I got home, I went to look in an old school dictionary that had been in my room for years; maybe it had belonged to my grandmother the schoolmistress, or maybe to Romeo's student. At the word "grotesque" I read:

A CARICATURE, IN WHICH WHAT IS SERIOUS IN OTHERS IS MADE RIDICULOUS, OR COMIC, OR DISTORTED.

Well, that was how Wilhelm Gerace set his last snare for me. If he'd worked out the wickedest way of getting me back under his spell, if he'd done it deliberately and with his eyes wide open, he couldn't have thought up a better way of getting me back than this one—which had drawn me to him without his even knowing it. It was now quite clear that on his trips up to the Walled Country nothing awaited him but shameful loneliness; and that he was mortified and reviled like the basest slave. And when I realized this, I don't know why, but my love for him, which I'd thought had flickered and nearly died, lit up in me again more bitterly, more destructively, more dreadfully than ever!

FROM

# The Third Wedding

TRANSLATED BY LESLIE FINER

This was the time when Phaleron was becoming fashionable. New Phaleron, not Old Phaleron, which has replaced it today because all the sewers of Athens seem to end at New Phaleron and it stinks so badly you have to hold your nose when you go by. Now all those fine old villas have fallen into ruin; the theatres and cafés have closed; a whole unforgettable period of old Athens has come to an end. That's where we spent our young days. What gay crowds they were! What splendid brass bands! Then there was the casino, and the bathing beach—men and women separately at first, and then mixed bathing. The men used to go down to Phaleron in droves, not so much to swim as to study female anatomy.

We used to go down only at weekends. Papa had his reasons for taking us to Phaleron. Poor Papa! . . . He seemed to be the most innocent man in the world, yet he had two vices which were all the more passionate because his principles did not allow him to indulge them as much as he would have liked: cards and women. As he grew older, it was cards more than women. But his heart was always fluttering. He used an old saying to Uncle Stephen, I remember: "It's too bad, Stephen," he would say, "now that the sea's turned to yoghurt we've lost our spoons!" But all that talk about him having lovers and so on was mostly Mama's imagination rather than fact. She was terribly jealous. We never found out for sure that he was

---

*Costas Taktsis was born in Salonika in 1927; he lived in Athens during the war and later studied law there.*

having an affair with this or that woman. But while he was naturally secretive about his women friends, he took very little trouble to hide his passion for cards. He would take us to the café, order ice-cream and lemonades, pay the bill and then pretend he was going to the lavatory. But then he'd make a beeline for the casino and that was the last we'd see of him for hours. We all knew where he went, though we pretended not to. Mama would get into conversation with some women acquaintances. They'd gossip about clothes and so on. We, too, would disappear in various directions. Dino would make off with two friends—the ones who ruined him in the end—and they'd meet up with some suspicious characters near the bathing huts. God alone knows what they got up to. I would go off with the Cassimatis and the Carouso girls, and we'd walk up and down the promenade, or young men of families we knew would get up from nearby tables and ask permission to dance with us. That was the time when the Argentinian tango was all the rage—"Ramona, the mission bells ring out above"—, the lights played in the water, the Phaleron breeze blew, life was wonderful.

That's how I met Fotis. He was a second officer in the merchant navy. With his gold braid and bits and pieces he was not so much handsome as manly-looking (after that business with Aryiris I was always suspicious of beautiful men). He was not tall like Aryiris. He was medium in height, with dark hair and blue eyes. God alone knows whom my ugly gipsy of a daughter takes after. We started going out together. He came to the house and asked to marry me. It was pretty well the usual kind of affair in cases of that kind. If I said I loved him, it would be a lie. Ever since the incident with Aryiris I had never been able to feel as warmly toward men as I used to. But Mama was always grumbling that I would stay on the shelf. My girlfriends were crazy about him and thought I was very lucky. I was flattered that he had chosen me and not the others.

Just the same, I might not have decided to marry him in the end, if they hadn't all been against him. I dug my heels in. They'd done enough damage already with their interfering over Aryiris and I was determined not to let them interfere in my life again. I wasn't eighteen any longer. I was getting on for twenty-six. I put my foot down: "It's either Fotis or nobody," I said. (Mama, who was never exactly a generous character, took every opportunity of reminding me of this later, after all that happened.) It was decided that he should make his next trip—he was due to leave for India and Japan—and we would get married when he came back, if we still felt we wanted to.

We were married. It was July, and it was suffocatingly hot the third night after our wedding. The sheets and pillows were soaked in perspiration. At about one in the morning I got up and went to the wash-house; I threw a few basinfuls of cold water over myself to cool off. But it was soon as bad as ever. It wasn't just the heat; there were also the damned mosquitoes. I got up twice to spray the room but nothing stopped them. Zoom, zoom, they dived like vampires and sucked your blood! About two in the morning, drugged by the heat and exhausted rather than sleepy, I heard Fotis get out of bed. "I'm going to sleep on the terrace," he said. "Mmm," I answered and closed my eyes again. But I was soon awake again. My brain was clearer. How stupid I am, I thought, why don't I go and sleep out in the cool, too? There were always two or three mattresses on the terrace. But I generally preferred my room because of the awful sun. It woke me at six and unless I went downstairs to finish my sleep, I'd be yawning all day long. I tucked my pillow under my arm, took a sheet and blanket and went up to the terrace. In my bare feet I made no noise. I saw them in the act. Every time I think of it, I want to be sick. Without saying a word I crept down as silently as I had come, threw myself on the bed and cried all night. "Are all men such beasts?" I asked myself again and again. But there was no answer from anywhere. If it hadn't been for what had happened with Aryiris, I don't know how I would have felt or what I would have done. But everything I had suffered in silence for so many years because of that affair made this new one seem like a huge and final disaster. I bit into my pillow to stop myself from crying out loud. "Are they all such monsters?" I asked myself. "Will any kind of hole satisfy the beasts? And as for that disgusting brother of mine, how could he?"

The more it went around in my head, the more desperate I became. I even thought of suicide. I just could not bear the thought that I would have to face them, to look them in the eyes in the morning. "What's the good of living?" I thought. I even got so far as to consider creeping into Papa's room to take the bottle of Veronal from his bedside drawer. But I didn't even have the strength to get out of bed. My body and my will-power were paralyzed. What they had done seemed so monstrous that I thought I had been through a nightmare, that it wasn't real, that I hadn't even been up on the terrace, that I had seen it all in my sleep. But the reality soon came back more vividly than ever, like knives plunging into my chest.

When morning came at last, I was a shattered wreck. It was like having a corpse in the house, as though someone had died during the night, and after the first tears, however hard you try to fight off fatigue, because it seems so selfish to sleep when you have lost a loved one, in the end, no longer able to resist, you lie down on the divan (as I did when we lost poor Papa), and fall into the kind of slumber which rather than refreshing you, tires you all the more; and when you open your eyes with the first light of dawn, your first thought is of the one who has died, and you say to yourself: "From today I shall never see him walk again, never hear him speak. He's dead, dead!" . . . And everything seems dark and hopeless. Life seems unbearable . . .

When Papa saw the state I was in, he knew something had happened. He looked at me, his eyebrow raised as usual with an unasked question. He was waiting for me to speak first. He never shouted like Mama. I pretended not to understand. But when he saw the guilty looks on the faces of Fotis and Dino he began to suspect the truth. He may not have known Fotis yet, but he knew his son. Twice they had called him to Dino's school and told him to watch out. They'd caught him in the lavatory with other boys. He was no fool, and he understood. I denied it, of course. "Nothing's the matter," I told him. "What on earth are you looking at me like that for? I had a pain in my back and didn't sleep a wink all night." And I hinted that it was some kind of woman's trouble which was no business of his. And then, when I saw he was not swallowing it, I pretended to confess the truth: that I'd had a tiff with Fotis, nothing serious, we'd soon make it up. Papa knew I was lying. He knew his daughter. He began a whispered conversation with Mama. He came back to my room, closed the door, and said: "I insist on knowing what has happened! . . . Is it what I suspect?" Naturally, I burst into tears. That day things happened which were even worse than what had happened the night before. Every time I remember that day, my heart, as Hecuba used to say, seems to crack. But, cracked and bruised as it is, my heart refuses to break once and for all and let me rest at last.

From that day Dino began to go downhill fast, and it wasn't long before he was ruined for good. He wasn't the first or the last young man with abnormal tendencies. If I didn't know it then, I know it now. Maybe he would never have been cured, but he would never have ended the way he did if Papa had not turned him out of the house. And maybe Mama, too, would never have got cancer.

As for the father of my dazzling daughter, he tried at first to deny everything. He had the nerve to pretend to be angry, as though he had been offended. Later he admitted it, but threw all the blame on Dino. That's the kind of coward he was, the man whose memory my daughter worships as though he were some kind of god. For naturally I won't demean myself to come down to her level and tell her what kind of creature he really was. I leave her in her ignorance. That's the worst punishment she could have. Yes, that's the kind of blustering coward he was. But when he saw it was no use, since we both knew it was he who had gone up to the terrace and so it was he who must have woken up Dino, he was shameless enough to say that it was my fault: he'd been forced into doing it with my brother, he said, because I was frigid and too narrow for him. He hadn't been able, he said, to make love properly, and it was driving him crazy. It was a lie, of course. Unfortunately, it was a lie. I wasn't at all frigid. But even if I had been, the sod ought to have known that all inexperienced women are like that, especially when they've reached a certain age without having had relations with a man, and it was up to him to teach me. But gently. Not to treat me the way he did, as though I was one of the tarts he picked up in foreign ports, asking me to do things respectable men don't ask their wives to do even when they have been married for years! Papa became wild with anger. I had never seen him so furious before. He rushed off to get his pistol, and Mama and Erasmia had to hold him back by brute force. The bastard had to pack his bags and leave. In any case, his ship was due to leave after a week. He left, and stayed away for eleven months.

During that time I gave birth to the Medusa who, for twenty-four years now, has been making a fine job of continuing what her father began. You'll ask, why on earth didn't you go and have an abortion? What did you want a child for? It's true, I shouldn't have had a child, and I knew it. But Mama and Aunt Katie were at it from morning to night: it's not the innocent babe's fault—Maria, an innocent babe!—if its father was a no-good; and women who had abortions got all sorts of illnesses later, and so on, and so on. Finally, they talked me into keeping it. When he came back from his travels, he didn't care to come straight to the house, although he knew I'd accepted all the money he'd sent me (what could I do? I needed it). Instead, he sent an aunt of his round to sound me out. She wanted to let him see the baby. "What baby?" I asked his aunt. "Didn't he say our marriage wasn't consummated? What baby does he expect to see now?" Three days later his mother arrived. She was quite a nice woman, and she blamed her son even more than any of us did. She fell at my feet and began to cry. "Take him back," she said. "He's away from home most of the time anyway." And finally I decided to give way. He came back to the house loaded with gifts for all of us, and we pretended that nothing had happened. Even Papa treated him politely, although he avoided becoming too familiar. Besides, as my mother-in-law said, most of the time he was away at sea. He sent me a check every month. And when he came back he came loaded down with presents. He'd stay with us for a month or two, and then off he'd go again. This sort of life lasted about six years.

Suddenly, he began to suffer from mysterious attacks of giddiness. He went to doctor after doctor, in Greece and abroad, but none of them could tell him what it was. They recommended that he should stop going to sea. He applied for a job in the shipping company's offices in the Piraeus, and the company gave it to him. Financially, it was a setback to retire so early from the sea; he had not completed enough years of service to draw his pension. But the giddy spells continued, worse even than before. And one fine morning we discovered what the mysterious ailment was: ozena, a terrible ulcer in the nostrils. His nose stank like a sewer. It was impossible to get near him, impossible to sleep in the same bed. He began using all kinds of perfumes, like a woman. As long as he was abroad most of the time and his health was good, I overlooked his faults and tolerated him. But now that he was home almost all day, and with the horrid illness he had, I began to lose my patience. No matter how good-hearted a woman may be, however conscious of her wifely duties, it's impossible to have a man like that near her for very long. If I'd loved him, I'd have been ready to put up with anything. But after all that had happened, what kind of love could I have for him? The bickering and squabbling began and they got worse and worse because Mama and Erasmia (who always took his side) insisted on poking their noses into our quarrels. We began bringing up past history and there were bitter words between us. One day he told me I had put up with him all those years only because I needed his money to feed my father and keep him in funds for his card-playing. I became as furious as a wildcat. I told him to pack his bags and get out. Thinking he could blackmail me into changing my mind—this was the unmanly way he always acted—he packed up not only his clothes but every single present he'd given me since our engagement. He put all the stuff into a taxi and left. When he saw that, in spite of being left without a cent, I refused to change my mind and take him back, he threatened to kill me. "Tell him from me," I said to his aunt, "that I don't think he's capable of it. To kill someone you've got to be a *man!*" And I told my lawyer to start proceedings for a divorce.

I didn't have to wash all the dirty linen in public to get the divorce. The ozena was more than enough. Meanwhile, to meet the household expenses and medical bills for Mama, I borrowed money from Uncle Stephen. But I wasn't worried. I knew I would be getting alimony after a year at the most. When the trial was almost due to come on and he realized he had no chance of winning, he went to the doctor and asked him to close the running ulcer in his nose, no matter how. Within a week the poison got into his bloodstream, and he died. And instead of receiving alimony, I was forced to borrow more money, and more, and more . . . to feed his daughter! I can't describe what I went through those two years before I married Antoni. Of course, things changed as soon as I was married. I paid my debts to Uncle Hercules and Uncle Stephen; I paid off the two mortgages I had been forced to take out on the house; we wrote to Marietta and brought her back from the village; we repaired the house, bought new furniture, put the Duchess into a private school, and poor Antoni even bought her a piano for thirty-five thousand drachmas because she kept grumbling that all her schoolmates had a piano at home and she was the only one who didn't. And that's not counting all the money he spent on the illnesses of Mama and Papa. Those are the reasons why I married Antoni, even if he was twenty years older than me. Not for bed, as that filthy bitch had the nerve to tell me today when I told her I'd sacrificed myself for my family. Antoni, for bed! Sweet Jesus, preserve us!

# ~ *Yukio Mishima* ~

## FROM

# *Confessions of a Mask*

TRANSLATED BY MEREDITH WEATHERBY

One day, taking advantage of having been kept from school by a slight cold, I got out some volumes of art reproductions, which my father had brought back as souvenirs of his foreign travels, and took them to my room, where I looked through them attentively. I was particularly enchanted by the photographs of Grecian sculptures in the guidebooks to various Italian museums. When it came to depictions of the nude, among the many reproductions of masterpieces, it was these plates, in black and white, that best suited my fancy. This was probably due to the simple fact that, even in reproductions, the sculpture seemed the more lifelike.

This was the first time I had seen these books. My miserly father, hating to have the pictures touched and stained by children's hands, and also fearing—how mistakenly!—that I might be attracted by the nude women of the masterpieces, had kept the books hidden away deep in the recesses of a cupboard. And for my part, until that day I had never dreamed they could be more interesting than the pictures in adventure-story magazines.

I began turning a page toward the end of a volume. Suddenly there

*When Yukio Mishima committed ritual suicide in November 1970, he left behind some perfect literary works: the story "Death in Midsummer," for example, and Confessions of a Mask. (He was nominated three times for the Nobel Prize in Literature, in fact.) As for Saint Sebastian: he was so potent a symbol for Mishima that he had himself photographed in the saint's familiar pose.*

came into view from one corner of the next page a picture that I had to believe had been lying in wait there for me, for my sake.

It was a reproduction of Guido Reni's *Saint Sebastian,* which hangs in the collection of the Palazzo Rosso at Genoa.*

The black and slightly oblique trunk of the tree of execution was seen against a Titian-like background of gloomy forest and evening sky, somber and distant. A remarkably handsome youth was bound naked to the trunk of the tree. His crossed hands were raised high, and the thongs binding his wrists were tied to the tree. No other bonds were visible, and the only covering for the youth's nakedness was a coarse white cloth knotted loosely about his loins.

I guessed it must be a depiction of a Christian martyrdom. But, as it was painted by an aesthetic painter of the eclectic school that derived from the Renaissance, even this painting of the death of a Christian saint has about it a strong flavor of paganism. The youth's body—it might even be likened to that of Antinous, beloved of Hadrian, whose beauty has been so often immortalized in sculpture—shows none of the traces of missionary hardship or decrepitude that are to be found in depictions of other saints; instead there is only the springtime of youth, only light and beauty and pleasure.

His white and matchless nudity gleams against a background of dusk. His muscular arms, the arms of a praetorian guard accustomed to bending of bow and wielding of sword, are raised at a graceful angle, and his bound wrists are crossed directly over his head. His face is turned slightly upward and his eyes are open wide, gazing with profound tranquillity upon the glory of heaven. It is not pain that hovers about his straining chest, his tense abdomen, his slightly contoured hips, but some flicker of melancholy pleasure like music. Were it not for the arrows with their shafts deeply sunk into his left armpit and right side, he would seem more a Roman athlete resting from fatigue, leaning against a dusky tree in a garden.

The arrows have eaten into the tense, fragrant, youthful flesh and are about to consume his body from within with flames of supreme agony and ecstasy. But there is no flowing blood, nor yet the host of arrows seen in other pictures of Sebastian's martyrdom. Instead two lone arrows cast their

---

*Portraits of Saint Sebastian by Guido Reni hang also in Paris (the Louvre) and Bologna (Pinacoteca Nazionale).*

tranquil and graceful shadows upon the smoothness of his skin, like the shadows of a bough falling upon a marble stairway.

But all these interpretations and observations came later.

That day, the instant I looked upon the picture, my entire being trembled with some pagan joy. My blood soared up; my loins swelled as though in wrath. The monstrous part of me that was on the point of bursting awaited my use of it with unprecedented ardor, upbraiding me for my ignorance, panting indignantly. My hands, completely unconsciously, began a motion they had never been taught. I felt a secret, radiant something rise swift-footed to the attack from inside me. Suddenly it burst forth, bringing with it a blinding intoxication. . . .

Some time passed, and then, with miserable feelings, I looked around the desk I was facing. A maple tree at the window was casting a bright reflection over everything—over the ink bottle, my schoolbooks and notes, the dictionary, the picture of Saint Sebastian. There were cloudy-white splashes about—on the gold-imprinted title of a textbook, on a shoulder of the ink bottle, on one corner of the dictionary. Some objects were dripping lazily, leadenly, and others gleamed dully, like the eyes of a dead fish. Fortunately, a reflex motion of my hand to protect the picture had saved the book from being soiled.

This was my first ejaculation. It was also the beginning, clumsy and completely unpremeditated, of my "bad habit."

(It is an interesting coincidence that Hirschfeld should place "pictures of Saint Sebastian" in the first rank of those kinds of artworks in which the invert takes special delight. This observation of Hirschfeld's leads easily to the conjecture that in the overwhelming majority of cases of inversion, especially of congenital inversion, the inverted and the sadistic impulses are inextricably entangled with each other.) . . .

~ ~ ~

There came a day in late spring that was like a tailor's sample cut from a bolt of summer, or like a dress rehearsal for the coming season. It was that day of the year that comes as Summer's representative, to inspect everyone's clothing chest and make sure all is in readiness. It was that day on which people appear in summer shirts to show they have passed muster.

Despite the warmth of the day, I had a cold, and my bronchial tubes were irritated. One of my friends happened to be suffering with an upset stomach, and we went together to the medical office to get written excuses that would permit us merely to watch gymnastic exercises without having to participate.

On our way back, we walked along toward the gymnasium as slowly as possible. Our visit to the medical office provided us with a good reason for being tardy, and we were anxious to shorten even by a little the boring time we would have to spend watching the gymnastics.

"My, it's hot, isn't it?" I said, taking off the jacket of my uniform.

"You'd better not do that, not with a cold. And they'll make you do gymnastics anyway if they see you that way."

I put my jacket on again hurriedly.

"But it'll be all right for me, because it's only my stomach." And instead of me, it was my friend who ostentatiously took off his jacket, as though taunting me.

Arriving at the gymnasium, we saw by the clothing hanging on the hooks along the wall that all the boys had taken off their sweaters, and some even their shirts. The area round the outdoor exercise bars, where there was sand and grass, seemed to be blazing brightly as we looked out at it from the dark gymnasium. My sickly constitution produced its usual reaction, and I walked toward the exercise bars giving my petulant little coughs.

The insignificant gymnastics instructor scarcely glanced at the medical excuses which we handed him. Instead he turned immediately to the waiting boys and said:

"All right now, let's try the horizontal bar. Omi, you show them how it's done."

Friendly voices began calling Omi's name stealthily. He had simply evaporated, as he often did during gymnastics. There was no knowing what he did on these occasions, but this time again he came lounging out from behind a tree, whose young green leaves were trembling with light.

When I saw him my heart set up a clamor in my breast. He had taken off his shirt, leaving nothing but a dazzling white, sleeveless undershirt to cover his chest. His swarthy skin made the pure whiteness of the undershirt look almost too clean. It was a whiteness that could almost be smelled from a distance, like plaster of paris. And that white plaster was carved in relief, showing the bold contours of his chest and its two nipples.

"The horizontal bar, is it?" he asked the instructor, speaking curtly, with a tone of confidence.

"Yes, that's right."

Then, with that haughty indolence so often exhibited by the possessors of fine physiques, Omi stretched his hands down leisurely to the ground and smeared his palms with damp sand from just beneath the surface. Rising, he brushed his hands together roughly and turned his face upward toward the iron bar. His eyes flashed with the bold resolve of one who defies the gods, and for a moment their pupils mirrored the clouds and blue skies of May, along with a cold disdain.

A leap shot through him. Instantly his body was hanging from the iron bar, suspended there by those two strong arms of his, arms certainly worthy of being tattooed with anchors.

"Ahhh!" The admiring exclamation of his classmates arose and floated thickly in the air.

Any one of the boys could have looked into his heart and discovered that his admiration was not aroused simply by Omi's feat of strength. It was admiration for youth, for life, for supremacy. And it was astonishment at the abundant growth of hair that Omi's upraised arms had revealed in his armpits.

This was probably the first time we had seen such an opulence of hair; it seemed almost prodigal, like some luxuriant growth of troublesome summer weeds. And in the same way that such weeds, not satisfied to have completely covered a summer garden, will even spread up a stone staircase, the hair overflowed the deeply carved banks of Omi's armpits and spread thickly toward his chest. Those two black thickets gleamed glossily, bathed in sunlight, and the surprising whiteness of his skin there was like white sand peeping through.

As he began the pull-up, the muscles of his arms bulged out hard, and his shoulders swelled like summer clouds. The thickets of his armpits were folded into dark shadows, gradually becoming invisible. And at last his chest rubbed high against the iron bar, trembling there delicately. With a repetition of these same motions, he did a rapid series of pull-ups.

Life force—it was the sheer extravagant abundance of life force that overpowered the boys. They were overwhelmed by the feeling he gave of having too much life, by the feeling of purposeless violence that can be explained only as life existing for its own sake, by his type of ill-humored, unconcerned exuberance. Without his being aware of it, some force had stolen into Omi's flesh and was scheming to take possession of him, to crash through him, to spill out of him, to outshine him. In this respect the power resembled a malady. Infected with this violent power, his flesh had been put on this earth for no other reason than to become an insane human sacrifice, one without any fear of infection. Persons who live in terror of infection cannot but regard such flesh as a bitter reproach. . . . The boys staggered back, away from him.

As for me, I felt the same as the other boys—with important differences. In my case—it was enough to make me blush with shame—I had had an erection, from the first moment in which I had glimpsed that abundance of his. I was wearing lightweight spring trousers and was afraid the other boys might notice what had happened to me. And even leaving aside this fear, there was yet another emotion in my heart, which was certainly not unalloyed rapture. Here I was, looking upon the naked body I had so longed to see, and the shock of seeing it had unexpectedly unleashed an emotion within me that was the opposite of joy.

It was jealousy. . . .

Omi dropped to the ground with the air of a person who had accomplished some noble deed. Hearing the thud of his fall, I closed my eyes and shook my head. Then I told myself that I was no longer in love with Omi. . . .

～ ～ ～

Summer vacation arrived. Although I had looked forward to it impatiently, it proved to be one of those entr'actes during which one does not know what to do with oneself; although I had hungered for it, it proved to be an uneasy feast for me.

Ever since I had contracted a light case of tuberculosis in infancy, the doctor had forbidden me to expose myself to strong ultraviolet rays. When at the seacoast, I was never allowed to stay out in the direct rays of the sun more than thirty minutes at a time. Any violation of this rule always brought its own punishment in a swift attack of fever. I was not even allowed to take part in swimming practice at school. Consequently, I had never learned to swim. Later this inability to swim gained new significance in connection with the persistent fascination the sea came to have for me, with those occasions on which it exercised such turbulent power over me.

At the time of which I speak, however, I had not yet encountered this overpowering temptation of the sea. And yet, wanting somehow to while away the boredom of a season which was completely distasteful to me, a season, moreover, which awakened inexplicable longings within me, I spent that summer at the beach with my mother and brother and sister. . . .

～ ～ ～

Suddenly I realized that I had been left alone on the rock.

I had walked along the beach toward this rock with my brother and sister a short time before, looking for the tiny fish that flashed in the rivulets between the rocks. Our catch had not been as good as we had foreseen, and my small sister and brother had become bored. A maid had come to call us to the beach umbrella where my mother was sitting. I had refused crossly to turn back, and the maid had taken my brother and sister with her, leaving me alone.

The sun of the summer afternoon was beaming down incessantly upon the surface of the sea, and the entire bay was a single, stupendous expanse of glare. On the horizon some summer clouds were standing mutely still, half immersing their magnificent, mournful, prophetlike forms in the sea. The muscles of the clouds were pale as alabaster.

A few sailboats and skiffs and several fishing boats had put out from the sandy beaches and were now moving about lazily upon the open sea. Except for the tiny figures in the boats, not a human form was to be seen. A subtle hush was over everything. As though a coquette had come telling her little secrets, a light breeze blew in from the sea, bringing to my ears a tiny sound like the invisible wingbeats of some lighthearted insects. The beach near me was made up almost altogether of low, docile rocks that tilted toward the sea. There were only two or three such jutting crags as this on which I was sitting.

From offshore the waves began and came sliding in over the surface of the sea in the form of restless green swells. Groups of low rocks extended out into the sea, where their resistance to the waves sent splashes high in the air, like white hands begging for help. The rocks were dipping themselves in the sea's sensation of deep abundance and seemed to be dreaming of buoys broken loose from their moorings. But in a flash the swell had passed them by and come sliding toward the beach with unabated speed. As it drew near the beach, something awakened and rose up within its green hood. The wave grew tall and, as far as the eye could reach, revealed the razor-keen blade of the sea's enormous ax, poised and ready to strike. Suddenly the dark-blue guillotine fell, sending up a white blood-splash. The body of the wave, seething and falling, pursued its severed head, and for a moment it reflected the pure blue of the sky, that same unearthly blue which is mirrored in the eyes of a person on the verge of death. . . . During the brief instant of the wave's attack, the groups of rocks, smooth and eroded, had concealed themselves in white froth, but now, gradually emerging from the sea, they glittered in the retreating remnants of the wave. From the top of the rock where I sat watching, I could see hermit shells sidling crazily across the glittering rocks and crabs become motionless in the glare.

All at once my feeling of solitude became mixed with memories of Omi. It was like this: My long-felt attraction toward the loneliness that filled Omi's life—loneliness born of the fact that life had enslaved him—had first made me want to possess the same quality; and now that I was experiencing, in this feeling of emptiness before the sea's repletion, a loneliness that outwardly resembled his, I wanted to savor it completely, through his very eyes. I would enact the double role of both Omi and myself. But in order to do so I first had to discover some point of similarity with him, however slight. In that way I would be able to become a stand-in for Omi and consciously act exactly as though I were joyfully overflowing with that same loneliness which was probably only unconscious in him, attaining at last to a realization of that daydream in which the pleasure I felt at the sight of Omi became the pleasure Omi himself was feeling.

Ever since becoming obsessed with the picture of Saint Sebastian, I had acquired the unconscious habit of crossing my hands over my head whenever I happened to be undressed. Mine was a frail body, without so much as a pale shadow of Sebastian's abundant beauty. But now once more I spontaneously fell into the pose. As I did so my eyes went to my armpits. And a mysterious sexual desire boiled up within me. . . .

Summer had come and, with it, there in my armpits, the first sprouts of black thickets, not the equal of Omi's it is true, but undoubtedly there. Here then was the point of similarity with Omi that my purposes required. There is no doubt that Omi himself was involved in my sexual desire, but neither could it be denied that this desire was directed mainly toward my own armpits. Urged on by a swarming combination of circumstances—the salt breeze that made my nostrils quiver, the strong summer sun that blazed down upon me and set my shoulders and chest to smarting, the absence of human form as far as the eye could reach—for the first time in my life I indulged in my "bad habit" out in the open, there beneath the blue sky. As its object I chose my own armpits. . . .

My body was shaken with a strange grief. I was on fire with a loneliness as fiery as the sun. My swimming trunks, made of navy-blue wool, were glued unpleasantly to my stomach. I climbed down slowly off the rock, stepping into a trapped pool of water at the edge of the beach. In the water my feet looked like white, dead shells, and down through it I could plainly see the bottom, studded with shells and flickering with ripples. I knelt down in the water and surrendered myself to a wave that broke at this moment and came rushing toward me with a violent roar. It struck me in the chest, almost burying me in its crushing whitecap. . . .

When the wave receded, my corruption had been washed away. Together with that receding wave, together with the countless living organisms it contained—microbes, seeds of marine plants, fish eggs—my myriad spermatozoa had been engulfed in the foaming sea and carried away.

# ∼ *José Lezama Lima* ∼

**FROM**

## *Paradiso*

TRANSLATED BY GREGORY RABASSA

The interior of the school opened onto two courtyards that were connected by a small door, not unlike the one leading to the refectory in seminaries. One courtyard was for the lower school, for children between the ages of nine and thirteen. The lavatories were parallel to the three classrooms. Lavatory recess occurred at a fixed time, but since it is difficult to dominate chronometrically the Malpighian corpuscles or the final contractions of digestion, one sometimes had to signal the teacher to receive permission to relieve oneself. Professional sadism, with no appeal in that situation, would show itself on occasion with Ottoman cruelty. There was the case, mentioned in whispers, of a student who asked to discharge his ammonium carbamate and ethereal sulfates, and having been denied permission, went into contortions that were discovered to be peritonitis— after the student's death. Now, whenever a student asked permission to "go out," he subtly tried to coerce the teacher, creating for himself the possibility of being an adolescent murdered by the gods and, for the teacher, that of being thought of as a demented satrap.

An older student monitored the courtyard: Farraluque, then in his last

---

*Reinaldo Arenas on* JOSÉ LEZAMA LIMA: *"Reading was Lezama's first passion. He also possessed the very Cuban gifts of laughter and gossip. Lezama's laughter was unforgettable, contagious; it prevented you from feeling totally unhappy. He could switch from the most esoteric conversation to the gossip of the moment; he could interrupt his discourse on Greek culture to ask whether it was true that José Triana was no longer a sodomist. He could also dignify the commonplace and make it extraordinary."*

year of lower school, the product of a semi-titanic Basque and a languid Havana woman. He was a small-bodied adolescent with a sad, baggy-eyed face, but he could count among his few attributes an enormous member. He was in charge of overseeing the parade of younger students to the toilet, at which time a priapic demon took furious possession of him; as long as the procession went on, he danced, raised his arms as if clicking aerial castanets, all the while leaving his member outside his fly. He wrapped it in his fingers, cradled it on his forearm, pretended to strike it, scolded it or soothed it as if it were a suckling child. This improvised phallic display or ceremony was observed through the blinds on the upper floor by an idling domestic, who, half prudish and half vindictive, brought the inordinate imbalance of that priapic piece of gossip to the climacteric ears of the wife of the son of that Cuevarolliot who had fought so often with Alberto Olaya. Farraluque was dismissed from his post as monitor of lavatory recess and made to spend several Sundays in a row in the study hall; during the week, he pretended seriousness as he faced his fellow students, but even his face had been converted into an object of hilarity. The cynicism of his sexuality caused him to don a ceremonious mask, inclining his head or shaking hands with the circumspection of an academic farewell.

After Farraluque was temporarily exiled from his burlesque throne, José Cemí had an opportunity to witness another phallic ritual. Farraluque's sexual organ was a miniature reproduction of his visage. Even his glans resembled his face. The extension of the frenum looked like his nose, the massive prolongation of the membranous cupola like his bulging forehead. But among upperclassmen, the phallic power of the rustic Leregas reigned like Aaron's staff. His gladiator's arena was the geography class. He would hide to the left of the teacher on some yellowing benches that held about twelve students. While the class dozed off, listening to an explanation of the Gulf Stream, Leregas would bring out his member—with the same majestic indifference with which the key is presented on a cushion in the Velázquez painting—short as a thimble at first, but then, as if driven by a titanic wind, it would grow to the length of the forearm of a manual laborer. Unlike Farraluque's, Leregas's sexual organ did not reproduce his face but his whole body. In his sexual adventures his phallus did not seem to penetrate but to embrace the other body. Eroticism by compression, like a bear cub squeezing a chestnut, that was how his first moans began.

The teacher was monotonously reciting the text, and most of his pupils, fifty or sixty in all, were seated facing him, but on the left, to take advantage of a nichelike space, there were two benches lined up at right angles to the rest of the class. Leregas was sitting at the end of the first bench. Since the teacher's platform was about a foot high, only the face of this phallic colossus was visible to him. With calm indifference, Leregas would bring out his penis and testicles, and like a wind eddy that turns into a sand column, at touch it became a challenge of exceptional size. His row and the rest of the students peered past the teacher's desk to view that tenacious candle, ready to burst out of its highly polished, blood-filled helmet. The class did not blink, and its silence deepened, making the lecturer think that the pupils were morosely following the thread of his discursive expression, a spiritless exercise during which the whole class was attracted by the dry phallic splendor of the bumpkin bear cub. When Leregas's member began to deflate, the coughs began, the nervous laughter, the touching of elbows to free themselves from the stupefaction they had experienced. "If you don't keep still, I'm going to send some students out of the room," the little teacher said, vexed at the sudden change from rapt attention to a progressive swirling uproar.

An adolescent with such a thunderous generative attribute was bound to suffer a frightful fate according to the dictates of the Pythian. The spectators in the classroom noted that in referring to the Gulf's currents the teacher would extend his arm in a curve to caress the algaed coasts, the corals and anemones of the Caribbean. That morning, Leregas's phallic dolmen had gathered those motionless pilgrims around the god Terminus as it revealed its priapic extremes, but there was no mockery or rotting smirk. To enhance his sexual tension, he put two octavo books on his member, and they moved like tortoises shot up by the expansive force of a fumarole. It was the reproduction of a Hindu myth about the origin of the world. The turtlelike books became vertical and one could see the two roes enmeshed in a toucan nest. The roll of the dice thrown by the gods out of boredom that morning was to be completely adverse for the vital arrogance of the powerful rustic. The last of the teacher's explanatory syllables resounded like funereal rattles in a ceremony on the island of Cyprus. Leaving at the end of class, the students had the look of people waiting to be disciplined, waiting for the Druid priest to perform the sacrifice. Leregas, foolish-looking, went out with his head tilted to one side. The teacher was somber, like a person petting the dog of a relative who has just died. When they passed, a sudden charge of adrenaline rushed into the teacher's arms; his right hand shot out like a falcon and resounded on

Leregas's right cheek, and immediately afterward his left hand crossed over and found the cocky vitalist's left cheek. Feeling his face transformed into the object of two succulent slaps, Leregas was unabashed; he leaped like a clown, a cynical dancer, a heavy river bird making a triple somersault. The same absorption that had held the class during the lighting of the country boy's Alexandrian Pharos followed the sudden slaps. The teacher, with serene dignity, trudged off to the office with his complaints; as he passed, the students were imagining the lecturer's embarrassment in explaining the strange event. Leregas plodded on, not looking around, and got to the study hall with his tongue hanging out. His tongue was a lively poodle pink. Now it was possible to compare the tegument of his glans with that of his oral cavity. Both were a violet pink, but the color of the glans was dry, polished, ready to resist the porous dilation of the moment of erection, while that of the mouth was brighter in tone, shining with the light saliva, as the ebbing tide penetrates a snail on the shore. He used his clownishness to defend himself from the finale of the priapic ceremony somewhat coyly, with some indifference and indolence, as if he had been rewarded for the exceptional importance of his act. He had not meant it to be a challenge; he simply had not made the slightest effort to avoid it. The class, in the second quarter of the morning, was passing through a period conducive to the thickening of galloping adolescent blood, assembled before the essential nothingness of nodding didacticism. Leregas's mouth was receptive, purely passive, and there saliva took the place of maternal water. The mouth and the glans seemed to be at opposite poles, and Leregas's clownish indifference allied him with the hidden femininity of his mouth's liquid pink. His arched eros collapsed completely under the pedagogical slaps. He remembered that the phalli of Egyptian colossi or the giant children spawned by the sons of heaven and the daughters of man did not correspond to their large size, but instead, as in Michelangelo's painted sex in the Creation, the hidden glans hinted at its diminutive dome. Almost all the spectators remembered the arching temerity of that summer morning, but Cemi remembered better the wild provincial's mouth, inside which a small octopus seemed to be stretching, disappearing into the cheeks like smoke, sliding down the channel of the tongue, falling to pieces on the ground like an ice flower with streaks of blood.

Leregas was expelled from school, but Farraluque, who had been condemned to forfeit three Sunday passes, provoked a prolonged sexual chain that touched on the prodigious. The first Sunday of his confinement, he wandered through the silent playgrounds and the completely empty study

hall. The passage of time became arduous and slow. Time had become a
succession of too moist grains of sand inside an hourglass. Creamy, dripping, interminable whipped cream. He tried to abolish time with sleep,
but time and sleep retreated until at last they touched backs as during the
first moments of a duel, then paced off the number of steps agreed upon,
but no shots rang out. And the prolonged smell of Sunday silence, the silent gun cotton that formed quick clouds, phantasmal chariots with a decapitated driver bearing a letter, all feel apart like smoke with each blow of
his whip against the fog.

In his boredom Farraluque crossed the courtyard again, just as the
headmaster's maidservant, who had an extremely agreeable face, was coming down the stairs. She apparently wanted to contrive an encounter with
the chastened scholar. It was she who had observed him from behind the
blinds, carrying the droll bit of gossip to the headmaster's wife.

When she passed by him, she said: "How is it that you're the only one
who hasn't gone to visit his family this Sunday?"

"I'm being punished," Farraluque answered dryly. "And the worst part
is that I don't know why."

"The headmaster and his wife have gone out," the maid replied.
"We're painting the house. If you help us, we'll try to pay you for it."

Without waiting for a reply, she took Farraluque by the hand, walking
by his side as they went up the stairs. When they got to the headmaster's
apartment, he saw that practically everything was covered with paper; the
smell of lime, varnish, and turpentine sharpened the evaporations of all
those substances, suddenly scandalizing his senses.

In the living room, she let go of Farraluque's hand and with feigned indifference climbed up on a stepladder and began to slide the brush, dripping with whitewash, along the walls. Farraluque looked around, and on
the bed in the first bedroom he could make out the headmaster's cook, a
mammee-colored mulatto girl of nineteen puffed years, submerged in an
apparently restless serenity of sleep. He pushed on the half-open door. The
neat outline of her back stretched down to the opening of her solid buttocks like a deep, dark river between two hills of caressing vegetation. The
rhythm of her breathing was dryly anxious; the sweat of summer, deposited in each small opening of her body, gave a bluish gloss to certain areas
of her back. The salt glistened in each of those depressions in her body.
The reflections of temptation were awakened by the challenging nearness
of her body and her own distance in sleep.

Farraluque undressed swiftly and leaped onto the patchwork of delights. Just then the sleeping woman, without stretching, gave a complete turn, offering the normality of her body to the newly arrived male. The unstartled continuity of the mulatto's breathing eliminated the suspicion of pretense. As the large barb of the small-bodied boy penetrated her, it seemed as if she was going to roll over again, but his oscillations did not break the circle of her sleep. Farraluque was at that point in adolescence when, even after copulation, the erection remains beyond its own ends, at times inviting a frenetic masturbation. The immobility of the sleeping woman now began to unnerve him, but then, peeping through the door of the next room, he saw the little Spanish girl who had led him by the hand, also fast asleep. Her body did not have the distension of the mulatto's, in which the melody seemed to be invading muscular memory. Her breasts were hard, like primal clay, her torso was tense as a pine tree, her carnal flower was a fat spider, nourishing on the resin of those same pines, tightly wrapped like a sausage. The carnal cylinder of a strong adolescent boy was needed to split the arachnid down the middle. Farraluque had acquired some tricks and soon began to exercise them. The secret touches of the Spanish girl were more obscure and difficult to decipher. Her sex seemed corseted, like a midget bear in a carnival. A bronze gate, Nubian cavalry-men, guarded her virginity. Lips for wind instruments, as hard as swords.

When Farraluque jumped onto the feathery spread in the second room, the rotation of the Spanish girl was the opposite of the mulatto's. She offered the plain of her back and her Bay of Naples. With ease, her copper circle surrendered to the rotund attacks of the glans and the full accumulation of its blooded helmet. This was evidence that the Spanish girl took theological care of her virginity but that she had little concern for the maidenhood of the remaining parts of her body. The easy flow of blood during adolescence made possible a prodigy which, once normal conjugation was over, enabled him to begin another, *per angustam viam*. This new amorous encounter recalled the incorporation of a dead serpent by its hissing female conqueror. Coil after coil, the momentarily flaccid member was penetrating the body of the conquering serpent, like a monstrous organism of Cenozoic times, in which digestion and reproduction formed a single function. How frequently the marine serpent had come to the grotto of the Spanish girl was apparent from the relaxation of the tunnel, and Farraluque's phallic configuration was extremely propitious for that retrospective penetration, for his barb had an exaggerated length beyond the bearded root. With an astuteness worthy of a Pyrenean ferret, the Spanish girl divided its length into three segments, motivating, more than pauses in her sleep, the true hard breathing of proud victory. The first segment comprised the hardened helmet of the glans and a tense, wrinkled part that extended from the rim of the glans like a string waiting to be plucked. The second segment brought up the strut or, speaking more properly, the stem, the part most involved, for it would give the signal for continuing or abandoning the incorporation. But the Spanish girl, with the tenacity of a classical potter opening the broad mouth of an amphora with only two fingers, managed to unite the two small fibers of the opposing parts and reconcile them in that darkness. She turned her face and told the boy something that at first he did not understand but later on made him smile with pride. The vital luxury of Spanish women often leads them to use a number of Cuban expressions outside of their ordinary meaning, and the attacker on two established fronts heard her exhale pleadingly out of the vehemence of her ecstasy the phrase "permanent wave." This had nothing to do with barbershop dialectics. In asking, she meant for the conductor of energy to beat with the flat of his hand on the foundation of the injected phallus. With each of those blows her ecstasy was transformed into corporeal waves. A tingle in her bones was enlivened by the blow, with the fluency of muscles impregnated by a stellar Eros. The phrase had come to the Spanish girl as something obscure, but her senses had given her an explanation and application as clear as light through a windowpane. Farraluque withdrew his barb, which had worked hard on that day of glory, but the waves continued in the Hispanic squire until her body was slowly carried off in sleep.

The drawn-out vibration of the bell called people to the dining hall, but he was the only one sitting in the large chamber that had been prepared for four hundred students who were absent on the Lord's day. The marble table, the white china, the venerable dough of the bread, the whitewashed fly-speckled walls with their Zurbarán motifs, supplied the harmonizing counterweight for that orgiastic Sunday.

Monday night, the headmaster's cook was with the servant girl across the street. She was the only servant of a couple approaching the age that brings the attrition of reproduction. Day and night she watched over the immense tedium of her employers. Boredom was now the only magnet holding them together on the same path. When they copulated in disjunct time, the clock of their encounter squeaked from the rust of everyday displeasure, well-sharpened bad humor. The forty-year-old wife's frustration was poured out in endless droll conversations with the maid, while her feet itched in their struggle against a minuet. The maid repeated to her mistress the whole tale that she had received from the cook, complete with the memory of the feverish ecstasy of taking in such a large barb. The lady asked for repetitions in the tale, details concerning the dimensions, minute proofs of the progression of laments and hosannas in the pleasant encounter. She made her stop, go back over a fragment of the event, expand on an instant in which feigned sleep was on the point of changing into a war whoop or the murmur of a flute. But the lady demanded so much from the story, such detailed descriptions of lance and socket, that the maid told her with extreme humility: "Ma'am, a person can only tell about that when she has it right in front of her, but believe me, then you forget it all and later on you can't describe any of the details."

When ten o'clock arrived on that warm night, the maid began to shut the living-room blinds, lowering the dusty windows; then she poured a carafe of water for the lady's night table. She turned down the covers and fluffed up the pillows on the bed, which showed an unfurrowed voluptuousness. Half an hour later the lady was falling into a sleep cut off by anxious sighs. What strange butterflies were coming to alight on the very edge of her nocturnal rest?

The second Sunday for the castigated fellow passed with a cheer that rose and fell in the depths of bottled-water tedium. At sundown, a light breeze began to creep in cautiously. A monkeylike little boy, the brother of the aforementioned mammee cook, came into the school courtyard, looking for Farraluque. He said that the lady in the house across the way wanted him to help her paint too. The priapic one was proud that his name was spreading from the small glory of the schoolyard to a broader fame in the neighborhood. When he entered the house, he saw a stairway and beside it two buckets of whitewash and farther on a brush, the bristles shining and paintless, keeping intact its pleasant aspect of a prop chosen for a still life by a painter of the school of Courbet. As in a stage setting, once more there was a half-open door. The mature madonna was artlessly feigning a sleep of sensual drowsiness. Farraluque felt obliged to show he didn't believe the cataleptic state would last, so before he undressed, he let the whole scandal of the elastic progression of his rosy worm show through his hands. Without abandoning her pretended drowsiness, the woman raised her arms, crossing them rapidly, and then she joined the index and middle fingers of her hands in a square that broke apart as it faced the proximity of the phallic Nike. When Farraluque leaped into the square, which was frothy with an excess of pillows, the woman bent to get closer and converse with the penetrating instrument. Her lips, dry at first, quickly dampened and began to slip along the filigree of the porous weave of the glans. Many years later he would remember the beginning of that adventure, associating it with a history lesson, where it was said that a Chinese emperor, while his troops paraded interminably behind hornpipes and war drums, caressed a piece of jade, polished with an almost insane craftsmanship. The wanton woman's vital intuition led her to show him an impressionable specialty in the first two of the eight different stages of the *Auparishtaka* or oral union according to the sacred texts of India. With the tips of two fingers she pressed the phallus down at the same time as she ran her lips and teeth around the edges of the casque. Farraluque felt like a dazzled horse being bitten at the root by a newborn tiger. His two previous sexual encounters had been primitive; now he was entering the realm of subtlety and diabolic specialization. The second requirement of the sacred Hindu text, in which she showed special proficiency, was in whirling the carpet of the tongue around the cupola of the casque and then with rhythmic nodding movements coursing up and down the length of the organ. But with each movement of the carpeting, the woman was cautiously stretching it toward the copper circle, exaggerating her ecstasy, as if carried away by the bacchanal from *Tannhäuser* and directing the frenzy imperiously toward the sinister grotto. When she thought the coordinated nibbling and polishing were about to reach an ejaculative finale, she started to pull it toward the deep shell, but at that instant Farraluque, with a speed that comes only out of ecstasy, raised his right hand to the madonna's hair, pulled upward with fury, and exposed the excited gorgon, dripping with the sweat extracted from the depths of her action.

This time he left the bed and with cat eyes looked into the next bedroom. The encounter had had a touch of a bite on the tail about it. Its completion only increased his desire for a new beginning; the strangeness of that unexpected situation and the extreme vigilance exercised over Circe, hard at work in the serpent's grotto, had curbed the normal affluence of his energy. A leftover tickling tugged at the back of his neck like an inexorable cork on a floating line.

With a haughty nakedness, he now knew what was waiting for him and he went into the next room. There he found the monkey-boy, the headmaster's cook's brother. Lying on his back, his legs merrily open, he displayed the same mammee color as his sister, offering an external ease, one full of ingenuous, almost indecipherable complications. He too pretended to be asleep, but with visible cunning and one uncorked and mischievous eye looked over Farraluque's body, pausing then on the culminating tip of the lance.

His mixed ancestry was revealed not by his asymmetrical face but in his small nose, his lips barely visible in a purplish line, and the green eyes of a domestic cat. His hair was an expanse of exaggerated uniformity, and it was impossible to isolate one thread from the whole thickness, like a night when rain is expected. His oval face closed with softness, attractive because of the small features it sheltered. The tiny teeth were creamy white. He showed an incisor cut in the shape of a triangle, which, when he smiled, showed the mobility of the tip of his tongue, as if it were half of a serpent's bifid tongue. The mobility of his lips was sketched along his teeth, tinting them with a marine reflection. He wore three necklaces, hung down to the middle of his chest. The first two shared the whiteness of coconut meat, the third mingled wood-colored beads with five red ones. The sienna of his body deepened all those colors, giving them the depth of a brick wall in a golden noontime. The monkey-boy's astute position persuaded Farraluque to accept the challenge of the new bed, where the sheets had been waved by the rotations of the body displayed there like a distant sacred joke. Before Farraluque moved into the pleasant picture, he observed that when Adolfito (it is time for us to give him a name) rolled over, he kept his phallus hidden between his legs, leaving a hairy concavity tense from the pressure exerted by the phallus in its hiding place. When the encounter began, Adolfito rotated with incredible sagacity; when Farraluque tried to take aim, he dodged the route of the serpent; when, with his barb, he became determined to draw the monkey-boy's out of its hiding place, the boy would roll over again, promising him a calmer bay for his prow. But pleasure for the monkey-boy seemed to consist in hiding, in making an invincible difficulty for the sexual aggressor. He could not even succeed in what the contemporaries of Petronius had made fashionable, copulation *inter femora,* an encounter in which the two thighs provoke the spray. The search for a harbor maddened Farraluque, and finally the liquor, in a parabola of maleness, leaped onto the chest of the delightful monkey-boy, who spun over like a prodigious ballet dancer, showing at the end of the struggle his back and his legs, diabolically spread, while he rolled over once again and on the sheets rubbed his chest smeared with a sap that had no final use.

The third Sunday of his punishment, events began to spin and tangle from the morning on. Adolfito left his sister, the headmaster's cook, to slip into the courtyard and talk to Farraluque. He had already persuaded the headmaster's two maids to let Farraluque leave the school when the sun went down. He told him that *someone,* enticed by his art of whitewashing, wanted to meet him. He gave him the key to the place where they were to meet, and leaving him, as if to reassure him, he told Farraluque that if he had time he would come and keep him company. Since by now what was meant by whitewashing was abundantly clear, he limited himself to inquiring about the *someone* he was supposed to visit. But the monkey-boy told him that he would find out soon enough, and clicked his tongue against the hollow of his triangle incisor.

The people of Havana, between five and six on a Sunday afternoon, smell the tedium shared by whole families, parents and children, who abandon the movies and retreat homeward. It is the moment, invariably painful, when the exception to the tedium makes way for the everyday habit of a man who ponders his destiny, not what directs and consumes him. Farraluque left the empty school courtyard and its weekend pause for the greater challenge of a state of boredom, the nervous system of a city. In the first corner café he watched a father rubbing the greasy residue of some ice cream off a little girl's blouse. Across the way, a nursemaid, all in white, was trying to pull a little girl away from the lamppost that had caught her red balloon with its black Islamic marks. Near the drain a boy spun a top, moving it over to the palm of his hand. Scratching his hand, he sat on the curb, and then he looked very slowly from one end of the street to the other.

Farraluque found the right number on Concordia Street. He inserted the small key, turned it softly, and took a step, almost stumbling into a forest of fog. Into what depths had he fallen? After his eyes adjusted, he could see that the place was a charcoal warehouse. The bins around the whole square area were filled with charcoal, divided up so that customers could carry it off in bags. Higher up, there were sacks from La Ciénaga, big as mountain crags, broad as filaments of cold light. And last, cakes of peat were mixed in with the charcoal to help spread the initial flame, which as it rose drew so many curses from the cooks of the last century, for one had to be adept to initiate the dialogue at the right moment between the most combustible wood fragment and the pinching, irritating flame.

He moved on and saw a tiny room lit by a small bull's-eye. A man was inside, about fifty years old, naked, his shoes and socks on, and a mask that made his face completely unrecognizable. Spotting the person he had been waiting for, he almost leaped into the other room, where the mist from the charcoal painted things. Like the priest of a springtime hierophancy, he began to undress the priapic one as if turning him on a lathe, caressing and greeting with a reverential sense all the erogenous zones, principally those that flashed their length. He was plump, white, with small waves of fat around the stomach. Farraluque observed that his double chin was about the size of his scrotal sack. The serpent was incorporated in a total, masterful way, and taking in the penetrating body, he turned red, as if, instead of receiving, he was about to give birth to some monstrous animal.

The apoplectic tone of this all-powerful incorporator of the outside world crescendoed in genuine oracular roars. His hands held high, he gripped the ropes fastening the charcoal sacks until his fingers began to bleed. He envisioned those prints where Baphomet, the androgynous devil, appears, possessed by a toothless pig, his waist encircled by a serpent that crosses over the site of his sex, inexorably empty, while the serpent shows its flaccid head in oscillating suspension. His phallus had not followed that biological law of evolution, namely, the greater the function, the larger the organ. This caused Farraluque to laugh, for what was to him a proud jewel, something to be displayed to three hundred students in the courtyard of the lower school, in his receptive companion was something to be concealed, its flaccidity disdained by the roots of life. At a certain moment, his phallus, accustomed to ejaculate without the heat of carnal envelopment, became agitated, for the interior of the charcoal repository was as hot as a boiler room on a navy ship. Their bodies were perspiring as if they had been in the most recondite tunnels of a coal mine. He inserted the vacillating tool in a crack in the charcoal, and his exasperated movements in the final moments of passion sent the coal dust scattering. He pulled on the ropes, he pounded the hollows of the sacks with his fists, he kicked at the charcoal that had been parceled out to sell to indigent customers. His frenzied tumescence brought on the final hecatomb in the charcoal repository. Coal dust flowed with the silence of a river at dawn, bringing behind it chunks of coal of imposing natural size, those that had not been broken down with shovels rolling as in a Polyphemic cave. Farraluque and the gentleman in the mask took refuge in the small room nearby. The noise of the peat cakes and the rough black chunks became more explosive and frequent. In the small warehouse, all kinds of charcoal began to bounce around and deposit irregular black stripes on the bodies of the two ridiculous gladiators joined by the softened iron of their now alienated sexes.

The pieces of charcoal hitting the floor made sounds that had no relation to their size; they broke apart with a crackling noise like a Great Dane chewing on a white rat. All the sacks had lost their balancing support; they had all been hit by the cursed retrospective furor of the gentleman in the mask. Farraluque and his companion would not be able to withstand the sinking mine in the small room. They covered themselves only with the articles of clothing essential for modesty. The masked gentleman left first, his wrinkled face still ruddy from the truncated adventure. At the corner, out of the corner of his eye, he made out the red balloon with black Islamic markings, still beating against the cynical, smiling lamppost.

Farraluque barely had time to put on his shoes, pants, and the jacket with a black spiral that ran down his back. He fastened the lapels to cover the hair on his chest. In the middle of the block, sitting whispering happily, he saw the boy with the top, and Adolfito. To recover from his scare, Farraluque sat down with the two urchins. Intending to penetrate his joy, the monkey-boy smiled complicity, alluding to his sexual festivities; he was at that age in which copulation was always pleasurable for him, whether with an albino woman with an enormous protruding fibroma, or with the trunk of a palm tree. He did not associate sexual pleasure with an aesthetic meaning, not even with the fascination of a touch of friendship. In the same way, his active or passive presence in copulation depended on what the other person wanted. If he had been slippery with Farraluque, it was not out of moral prejudice but to prepare for future adventures. In him, astuteness was a stronger instinct than maleness, which for him was indifferent and even unknown.

"Now do you know who the *someone* waiting for you was?" Adolfito asked him when the boy with the top went off, pulling on his cords.

Farraluque shrugged, and only said, "I didn't feel like taking off his mask."

"Well, behind the mask you would have found the husband of the lady across from the school. The one you had to pull by the hair . . . ," Adolfito finished with a smile.

# ～ *Gerard Reve* ～

## FROM

# *Nearer to Thee*

### TRANSLATED BY RICHARD HUIJING

Five, perhaps even six years ago, at about the same time of year as it is now, one late afternoon during the week, I left my dwelling for a walk along the harbor, in that hypocritical mood when you believe you can bamboozle yourself into thinking that you're only stepping out for some fresh air, while in reality the aim is none other than to whore around right royally.

The weather was reasonably sunny, and there was a breeze too, and the sky most definitely did cloud over briefly and repeatedly, but even so this was not yet "the weather for all people"—it was already a touch too cool to be so, while the wind wasn't impetuous enough and remained impotent to lift up sand or bits of paper, let alone make them whirl about with scuffing, rustling noises along the road surface. Nevertheless, it was a day for deep ponder and attention so that, making my stately progress, I was made to think continually about the true nature of God, why everything might have come to be the way it was, and what might be the most sensible thing to do. I resolved to go and sit down on an orange crate within the next four days, at about half-past two at night, naked on the flat roof

GERARD REVE's Nearer to Thee *caused a furor on its publication in 1966 because the main character graphically imagines having sex with God after His descent to earth in the form of a donkey. (Reve was brought to trial for blasphemy but won the case.) His solemn and ironic style keenly matches his literary preoccupations: death, religion, romantic-decadent longing for "the pitiless youth." Reve, who has lived in France since the early seventies, has written in English as well.*

behind the little torture chamber for young German tourists, and there
look at the firmament continuously until I could no longer keep that up,
I'd be so cold; during three ensuing days at least I would only be allowed
to feed myself upon carrots and turnips. That way there was a chance that
at least something would become clear of what now remained a dark riddle to me.

Meanwhile, I had now reached a point level with the merchant-navy
training vessel, and here, close to the steps leading up to it, on the quayside,
I stood peering across the immaculately clean deck. It had just been wash
day, and on lines strung among the rigging, there were scores of faded and
worn blue cotton work jackets and trousers, darned many times by mothers, items which, despite the considerable distance, made me perceive the
scent of cheap soap, leather and boy's sweat, embodying my entire mortal
yearning. None of the Sea Boys were on deck but for the one who, in his
neat uniform, stood guard at the gate in the ship's railing upon which,
clearly tensing his bronzed blond neck, he would lean forward lazily from
time to time. I knew the blue cotton workwear suited some of the Sea
Boys—particularly the dark blond ones and the slightest among them—
very well, but the neat, official uniform was capable of improvement, I had
always thought. How to achieve this, however? A fund, I decided, perpetually keeping an eye on the boy standing guard, must be instituted, one
that, not heeding rank, class or religious creed, would provide them all, at
no charge, with the horniest possible, most perfectly cut, made-to-
measure suits, consisting of very short black cotton jackets and tight, low
tailored trousers of very thin but very strong, semi-matte velvet of a deep
violet hue almost tending toward black, said uniform to be complemented
by, other than the barely altered cap (given a more downward-pointing,
eye-shading peak), anthracite gray half-boots with turned-down tops.
Once they were all wearing that uniform, they would choose the seven
most beautiful Boys from their midst to reign over all the others—who
would owe them the most unconditional and most subservient obedi-
ence—and who would bear the title of *Boy Prince of the Seas*. In their turn,
the seven would elect from their midst a merchant-navilogical *Boy King of
All Oceans* who would have complete and merciless dominion over the
other six as well as their subordinates. The Boy Princes of the Seas, under
the command of their Boy King of All Oceans, dazzling in their glow of
most tender and most cruel beauty, and cherished by the boundless love
and worship of all their Sea Boys, would set sail and, in distant lands, pro-

tected by innumerable "flotillas" of Her Majesty's fleet, go and catch handsome young Vietcong rebels, young, beautiful Indonesian commandos, and attractive Japanese students demonstrating too impetuously out in the streets, to keep them captive on board like slaves so that they would serve the Boy King, the Boy Princes, as well as all the uncrowned Sea Boys eternally, bringing them drinks, preparing their food, washing and pressing their work clothes and their uniforms too, and serving them by day at table with unfailing promptness, while at night, right until morning, with their bronze panther bodies, in perfect servility, they would have to provide my blond, purple-hipped, velvet darlings with boundless bliss and at the slightest sign of disobedience or laziness, in punishment rooms painted purple, be brought to obedient docility by one of their own comrades wielding whip and belt, never mind their hoarse bellowing for mercy.

It was a perfectly excellent plan, but it would have to pass so many authorities and be amended so many times that, even with a member of the Labour Party at the head of the Naval Ministry, little would be left of it other than the replacement of uniforms, which would be made with far too wide a cut and from an utterly wrong, woolly fabric, and most probably of a bright green or an even worse color.

Prophesying in a mumbling tone of voice and really dog-tired again, I ambled on some distance and then halted at the revolving bridge close to the new Post Office under construction, and I leaned on the iron gate. Here I noticed that, in the meantime, I had attracted the notice of an extremely neatly dressed young man, six or seven years my junior by my estimate, who was idly trundling back and forth, a gray, rustling nylon raincoat over his arm—though only a miracle would provide a single drop of rain in the next twenty-four hours. There was something uncommon about his appearance, which I could not put my finger on at once but at the same time aroused both my revulsion and my desire. He was reasonably well built and had a regular, not un-handsome face. I could not keep my eyes off his face and the rest of his figure and tried to establish what in fact it might be that so puzzled me. His dark-blond hair was immaculately cut, his striped tie had been arranged just so, and all his clothes, including his shoes, appeared to have been bought not twenty-four hours before.

Soon we got into a conversation and then we walked together in the direction of my house. He was well spoken, with a Hague accent, more or less, but his choice of words was poor and his clichés, which occasionally I could herald half a sentence in advance, almost made me groan at times.

It did not enter his head that people might at least be permitted to know each other's names before considering sexual congress. I introduced myself to him, but only after a number of explicit questions on my part did he offer his name too and provide me with something like a statement from real life. His name has disappeared from my memory but I do still know that it was definitely a two-syllable, English name—*Nutman* or some such—which he pronounced in the Dutch manner, though. When I brought the presumably English origins of his name to his attention, it turned out he had never thought of it. His first name turned out to be Gerard, and this reinforced my horniness, which had until then remained vague.

He lived in The Hague, where he sublet a room in a first-floor flat situated at number 40 or 42 of a street named after one of the Indonesian islands, and he was a commercial traveler in textiles. Going up the stairs to my dwelling, I listened with bated breath to the loud rustling arising not only from the overcoat on his arm but also from his other clothes, and now my hatred and contempt became so strong that I desired him most fiercely.

Having arrived upstairs, we ended up, after some small talk, standing at the window, where, quite unnecessarily, I explained the orientation of the house with regard to the points of the compass and told him which of the surrounding roofs belonged to what building or street; I then began to feel him all over. Though he reciprocated my attentions instantly, I noticed that he was very concerned about his clothes getting damaged or creased; out of some notion of prestige, however, as regards undressing himself, he waited in a somewhat coquette fashion for an initiative on my part, so it seemed.

My horniness was almost entirely based on my contempt and boredom now and no longer contained even a hint of any romantic desire or physical, sentimental infatuation. "You might as well undress," was all that I could say, for because of my hatred, I could not bring myself to unbutton even a single thing of his.

As slowly he divested himself of one article of clothing after another, placing each with extreme care, to avoid creasing or soiling, on the spot he had decided, after much thought, was the safest place, I myself dawdled in undressing, first only taking off my shoes and then, accompanied by much quasi-amiable chitchat, occupying myself with laboriously pouring two glasses of red table wine, which I set down on the low little table next to the divan. "May we be preserved for one another a long time," I declared perkily, raising my glass, whereupon Nutman or Longmans or Sutter raised the vague objection that we had "only just met."

He was now fully undressed but for a pair of fashionable briefs, so I was better able to judge his body. He was incontrovertibly well built but, undressed, he now possessed that peculiar quality that simultaneously inspired revulsion and attracted me, to an even stronger degree, and suddenly I knew what it was: no perceptible smell of sweat or any other musk emanated from his body or from his hair, nor did the slightest whiff arise from his armpits, which I came very close to for a moment, of something that might be called a boy's scent.

He now took off his briefs, dropped them on the rug, and quickly slid into bed, where I had already turned back the covers. I picked up the briefs and put them with his other clothes, then, arranging his shoes, felt his socks, but neither these nor the briefs nor his undershirt—which, unnoticed, I had brought very close to my face for a mere moment—gave any indication of having been worn.

"Aren't you having any?" I asked, pondering the strange phenomenon of the scentlessness while I began undressing myself slowly as well. "It's quite drinkable wine." Gerard—I'm quite sure now that was his name—took a sip from his glass, coughed, and then declared that he only partook very seldom. I went and stood at the head end of the bed, and with feigned tenderness I caressed his neck and the hair on the back of his head and inched back the covers, which he had pulled up over his shoulders, to provide myself with complete certainty—but it was most definitely the case: no body odour of any kind could be discerned even now.

I looked at his clothes on the chair and on the table, and realized that everything was still so clean that I would not be able to object even to wearing his underwear in the state it was lying in there. And all of a sudden I had the sensation of impending doom, as if I was going to bed with Death, that's to say, not my own but someone else's.

"Have some more," I said, draining my own glass and half filling it again, and handing him his, which he had barely touched. "It'll do you good—you're still a growing lad." I heard my own voice come back to me all too clearly, even before "Gerard" had remarked that he indeed knew "friends of his" who occasionally would sit drinking together a whole evening, but that such a thing was "not his cup of tea."

"It's poison," I conceded. "Great chunks of the cerebral cortex come loose and are washed away—that's a well-known fact." He looked at me with wide-open eyes and a bewildered expression, and suddenly I realized he had begun to feel increasingly ill at ease, because he did not know what to make of me and, most of all, would perhaps prefer to leave. In order to prevent this, I now made haste, undressed myself quickly and went and lay down beside him, for his cowardly, uncertain timorousness had now thrust up a veritable wave of hate and randiness within me. "Dear boy," I mumbled, while with pretended bashfulness and restraint I began merely to caress his mouth, face and hair. Then, as though I were comforting him like a little brother whose toy had been broken, lost or taken from him, I took his head in my arms and pressed his face cherishingly against my chest; while doing this, looking out right over him, I was able to study his clothes, unnoticed: the way they were lying there spread out in the late afternoon light. Our sizes could not differ by much, I considered: nearly everything ought to fit me, and if not, it was at most a matter of a low-cost alteration here or there. Even his shoes were almost bound to fit me. Nobody knew he was here, and no one would ever come to inquire about him here, were he to disappear.

His suit must have cost 350 guilders at least; the shirt, truly not of the cheapest kind, 30 guilders certainly, and his underwear, socks and shoes were of the most expensive variety too. I did not like his tie, but what was not to my taste I could burn. Moreover, he would have to have money on him—a little perhaps, but possibly a few hundred guilders even so—in a plastic wallet which was of a faded, orangy colour, or so I believed.

"Pretty boy, sweet animal," I whispered, letting my hand slip round his throat, tenderly yet investigating thoroughly as well. Suddenly he pressed his entire body against me, grabbed my caressing hand and brought it to his crotch. "Are you often in Amsterdam?" I whispered, for I wanted to know whether he had any acquaintances here who perhaps did not live that far from my address and who, however coincidentally, had seen him entering my place.

"No, only when I have to be, on business." "But also on the off-chance, occasionally, for myself," he offered a moment later. I could still not detect a scent to him, and he did not even sweat in his crotch. "What's it you do when you come to Amsterdam on the off-chance?" "I wander about a bit sometimes."

I sensed that my questions frightened him. He removed my hand from his sex. "Wait a bit." We lay motionless. Looking at the hair of his neck and stroking it thoughtfully in an upward direction, my hate in part gave way

to pity. He had to be of the most impoverished, practically pauper descent,
I estimated—in no other way could I explain his cliché-perfect manners,
his far too neat clothes and his utterly anonymous use of language. Doubtless, he worked very hard and thought in all seriousness that he wouldn't
be poor some time—as if anyone, once born poor, would ever be anything
other than poor and remain so—and I imagined his room in The Hague,
in the first-floor flat at number 40 or 42 of a street named after an Indonesian island: the parchment table lamp with a sailing ship from the
Golden Age; the encyclopaedia, as worthless as it was expensive, in the
sideboard with the stained-glass doors, the remaining eleven other books
on the mantelpiece between two bookends held upright by two elephants;
and, next to the fold-away bed, the little cabinet in which, behind a green
curtain, stood the dozen fine glasses, never used, upon which were the national coat of arms and those of the eleven provinces. Again, again, utter
melancholy was the order of the day.

"Are you angry?" he asked, all of a sudden. "Heavens no—why?" I assured him. I got up, refilled our glasses and then went and lay next to him
again, enclosing him from the rear, and began to feel his neck again. Now
he asked me the usual, boneheaded question: "D'you have a steady
boyfriend?"

"I do," I replied, curtly. I didn't feel like telling him anything of a personal nature about myself and that's why I, in my turn, began to draw him
out at once. "Tell me a little more about yourself," I began, employing the
worst of clichés which, however, he did not seem to notice. "I'm always
damned eager to know how another battles his way through. D'you live
alone?"

I forced myself to keep caressing the hair on his neck while beginning
to listen to the sentences, devoid of imagination, with which he began to
tell the primal tale, as old and sorry as Bollock Earth itself—the primal history of that skittish sham-happiness the children of Man believe to be life
and the enjoyment of life.

Yes, he did indeed live alone but he had a boyfriend, seven, eight years
younger than he, just nineteen, who was a jet pilot. Wow. "A real cracker!"
Sure. I didn't doubt it. "Dishy and hot?" I asked. "Out with it: what exactly does he look like?"

He had dark blond, short, curly hair, verging on black. The color
pleased me rather, but the curliness much less so. No, they were ever so
short and stubborn, those curls, definitely not abundant or artistic. Well, all
right then. But what were his mouth, his face, his eyes like? "Is he a boy

with earikins? I'm mad about boys with earikins?" That last question, perhaps because of its eccentric phrasing, he couldn't quite grasp. "Describe his neck, for Heaven's sake."

From now on, he did give me each fact I asked for but never even the slightest bit more. Apparently he had no powers of imagination, and though he was able to represent measured facts he was incapable of evoking their sense and cohesion and conveying this to someone.

The dark-blond little eagle dropped by twice a week, Wednesdays only in the afternoon, but almost the entire day Sundays. "In uniform?" Yes, occasionally he did. What bliss. But, no matter how exciting, it was a dangerous profession too, was my opinion. Ah well, perhaps, yes, Gerard N. or L. or S. granted me, but as the boy himself had said to him "he couldn't give a toss about dying." Well really, that was the usual hollow prattle again: he most certainly needed a good dose of smack-botty.

What did he look like naked? It was true that I presented my questions in a confusing manner and assumed far too much of my own imaginary world to be known.

In any case he was "very beautiful." Fine lot of good that did, an answer like that. "Is he shy and bungling when he has undressed himself? Does he look down at the ground then? And when he goes and lies on the bed and you look at him, does your voice then become hoarse and do you have to swallow all the time? Do you sigh when you begin to caress him, because you're quite ill with besottedness? Yes, well, that's how it is, isn't it?"

N. or L. or S. was apparently beginning to understand a little more of what moved me, for his statements became a touch less scant now.

The young Air-hero's neck, after which I enquired anew, now more pressingly, had a very clearly marked hairline and yet it was incomprehensibly tender, with hair like little ducks' feathers. His shoulders were broad, his legs of average length, strong but not developed to a brutish extent yet and not too heavily hirsute yet either. His bum was perfection: downy at the bottom, muscular and clenched together as if by a chaste spring, and on the outside, for completeness' sake, provided moreover with those athletic indentations that transcend all human understanding.

"And his skin," I determined, speaking as though in a trance, "seems to be bronzed, even when he hasn't been in the sun—strong and tough like a man's but to the touch boyishly supple and cool, like chamois leather. Am I right or am I right?" Yes, this was so. "See."

But the Boy's "dick"—and by the use of this offensive and tarnishing word, which "Gerard" employed repeatedly instead of "prick', "tool" or "schlong," I knew, without requiring any further proof, that his love life was nothing, nor could it ever be otherwise, but an animal chase after mechanical pleasure—was something awesome and incredible. "Like this? Is it bent a bit and childish still, never mind its size? Or is it already cruel and indifferent?" Er, hard to tell. "It's not a mushroom, is it?" No, no, no: not at all.

Because of the image I was building up, asking away laboriously, I became unbelievably horny, almost achieving that glow when desire is only barely physical, acquiring the force of nostalgic yearning or speechless piety instead.

Everything has its down side, however, for now I was given an earful of something else as well, something unasked for, which N. was in quite a lather over, actually: their fleshly unions were not running a satisfactory course. Even though they spent hours and hours in bed and though N. did his very utmost, our doughty, beautiful, and adorable Air Angel had succeeded during ever fewer visits these past six months to reach satisfaction even once. Because N., when Frans—for that was the boy's name—could not manage to shoot, did not feel entitled to allow the miracle to happen to himself, their time together had been disappointing these last few occasions, with tensions, boredom, and vague, unuttered resentment. Why this was, N. didn't know.

"So what do you say to him, in bed, when you're jerking him off?" I asked, matter of fact.

"What? Well, noth'n of course."

"So you don't talk to him, and you don't tell him stories?" All of a sudden something else occurred to me. "And when it's evening and dark, d'you put the light out then?" "Yes, it's got to be dark," N. replied decisively.

"Well now; I might have known," I said. What a moronic twat, I thought.

"So you don't tell him anything about boys he tortures or has tortured?" I now asked. The crucial word didn't sink in properly. "What?" "Torture," I said, impatient. "Torment with great cruelty, specifically as a mode of exacting punishment or extracting a confession." Now he did understand what I meant, but its purpose or context continued to elude him.

"Perhaps I might be able to help you; *perhaps*, mind," I went on, "but I shan't promise anything. The principle is simple, but first you must manage to find out one or two things." I began to explain to him that he must first try to find out which type of man or boy his Air Prince felt attracted to. "Cut out photographs. Show him health and fitness books and keep that which you have found in your heart. Then, almost by accident at first, just start talking about slave ownership, imprisonment, subjection, punishment and pain."

I tried to get across to him that each mortal being had his own dream of Power, Love and Pain, some hidden quite untraceably deeply at times, others immediately touchable, ready to be played upon.

"When you know whom he likes, then you have to know how he wants to torture him. Maybe someone else has to do it. And perhaps, *perhaps*, mind you," I added for completeness' sake, "he wants to be the tortured one himself, and make the desired boy his master and punisher and beg him not to be merciful on any account. Such things really happen, they do—did you know that? I read it in a book, all scientific—it was very difficult—by doctors who know everything about such people." Still N. seemed to think my exercises in dim-wit lingo to be above suspicion.

"But mind," I continued, more or less, "that you build everything up properly and tell it as if you see it right before your eyes. You must know everything very precisely—how old the boy is, what kind of work he does, whether he burgles and steals mopeds, whether he's a braggart who's terrified of the whip, or a very shy boy who, on the contrary, isn't afraid or a coward at all, but very plucky and who doesn't bawl easily and cry for his mother. And remember," I concluded, "to know exactly what kind of clothes he's wearing, particularly what kind of trousers, the material and the like. Fine feathers make fine birds."

N. nodded, his face tense with having had to think so hard about so many difficult things in so short a time. "Now tell me again, one more time, the whole thing," he requested. "So I have to start to talk about a boy who comes to him and he has to beat him?"

"Possible, but it doesn't have to be that," I replied, already getting tired. "It can be different, too." I searched for a summary of the fundamentals of the Mystery. "He's beautiful and tough, and you worship him and you're his slave," I began once more. "That's why you bring along a boy for him, intended for him entirely, who has to kneel for him. But you never can tell. I mean, if *he* wants to be the slave of the boy you bring along, particularly when that one's very big and blond and strong, and he wants to be subjected and beaten himself, to be the one kneeling down at his feet, then you shouldn't resist such a thing. I don't know your *case*—how shall I put it? The direction the slavery will take is still obscured, it's a torture-bloom that must still unfold itself, for only after this does its Mystery step forth from obscurity—well I never," I sighed. "Ah well, just you begin your tale with your worship, and plead with him that you may go and seek a boy of his choice, inviting and enticing him along, for you have but one desire, which is that he subjects, interrogates, punishes and possesses as many boys as possible. Because you love him: quite simple."

N. now believed himself to be sufficiently informed, but I doubted whether everything was actually clear to him; indeed, I even despaired of ever finding understanding in any mortal being for my revistic *Fairy Tales of Father Donkey*.

We dressed again and, at my instigation, exchanged our exact names and addresses in writing. I kept asking until he mentioned the name of his firm.

"D'you have a car?" I asked. He didn't but he did frequently have one at his disposal. "During the week as well?" Yes, during the week. Occasionally, when their endless wing-flapping had not rendered them airborne, they had gone for a drive, in that car, to have tea al fresco in neighboring woods or dunes.

"I know! Why don't you drop in here then and bring him along," I proposed. If "Frans" had already put up with the fruitless attentions of N., how much more easily would I be able to conjoin with him. N. would have to approve, for otherwise I would threaten to call his firm to acquaint them thoroughly with the "sexual orientation" of one of their employees, and the same applied, *mutatis mutandis*, to his Sex Pilot, for at his least recalcitrance I could, after all, inform the proper air force authorities, after which he would have to be disciplined most severely. Even more wonderful would be if the Sex Pilot, having been made acquainted with Wimie, would then refuse my attentions and deliver himself up to Wimie in despair: life was hard but beautiful.

N. had to be off now and this rather suited me too, really, for Wimie would be coming home from the office soon enough and would enact his jealousy scene all too eagerly, even though I hadn't done anything other than to provide sexological advice.

I entreated N. to be sure to drop by again or to ring at the very least, embraced him in parting with brotherly tenderness and then, as I heard him descend the stairs, I went and sat on the bed to think.

My plan wasn't impossible to put into effect, of course, but on pondering it more deeply I did realize that a thing or two would have to happen before the final goal—the Dream Pilot kneeling at Wimie's feet—would be attained. For this, to begin with, N. in The Hague in his room with the maritime standard lamp etc., would still have to feel like renewing communication; then, secondly, the Air Boy would have to be willing to come along; thirdly, it would have to be possible to introduce both of them to Wimie without unpleasant incidents; fourthly, Wimie would have to be enchanted by the pilot who—fifthly, that is—in his turn would have to become besotted with Wimie. A single weak link, and all would remain a vain attempt and come to nothing.

When I heard footsteps at the top of the stairs, it was already too late, for the next moment Wimie entered; because my watch had stopped, I had mistaken the time. The bed had been made again but not very tidily, and two used wineglasses still stood on the little table. Who's been here? A young man. Had I been to bed with him? Well, er, if you could call it that. I wanted to begin to explain to Wimie that all my fumbling and stumbling was entirely revistic and could never have anything for its purpose other than the subjugation, to hunk Wimie, of all *Boy Princes of the Seas*, hotel bell-boys and fairy tale pilots—all the way up to the *Boy King of All Oceans* himself—he might wish for at his feet or in his bed, but I didn't quite know where to start and before I had managed to sally forth with a thing or two, Wimie bellowed a right-old oath and, with a grimly distorted face, he hurled an ashtray through the milk-white, £18,25 shade of the electrified paraffin lamp.

It ended up with an almost two-hour fight during which I kept myself very humble, partly from relish, partly to prevent more expensive things going west, for we had a chronic lack of ready cash at the time. Then, after a kind of reconciliation, we drank rather a lot, I full of speechless adoration and horniness, Wimie once more as jolly, irritable, and indifferent as ever. I now wanted to tell him about the pilot who doubtless one day would lay his dark-blond little head in deep subjugation in Wimie's lap, but I thought better of this for the time being.

Almost three weeks went by without my hearing anything from N. I had begun to think less and less frequently of the plan, which soon I had already begun to think of as potty. In the end it had actually disappeared from my thoughts altogether when, late one morning, N. phoned me from The Hague. He had to be in Amsterdam that same afternoon and would love to drop by to tell me something he preferred not to convey by phone.

And what might that be? No matter how much I racked my brain, I could not imagine anything of importance that might have happened, except that he had been given the sack by his firm and was coming to borrow money, of which I would never see a single cent ever again.

In the afternoon, however, arriving upstairs at almost two o'clock, he gave an impression of cheerfulness, almost exuberance. He was wearing the same clothes more or less as the previous time but was wearing them, so it seemed to me, with a more carefree allure.

Soon he started in. "That story you said I should tell . . ." "What? Oh, yes." Hadn't I said that he must see everything before him and must be able to describe even the dress, age and profession of the boy? Quite, indeed. Well now; telling something that hadn't really happened, this wasn't quite his cup of tea. However, the moment, lying beside his naked Prince of Heaven again, he had despaired of ever getting the latter's rocket to eternity to ignite, he had suddenly remembered something from his youth and, like a thing occurring to him by chance, he had told him about this: how, as boy scouts—sea scouts no less—in a forest close to a lake, they had tied up a rather handsome looking comrade, stripped him, and had tickled and beaten him for hours, that's to say, a few of the others had, not he himself, for he had been tormented by the preposterous question whether he enjoyed it or not, had wanted to do something to make them stop tormenting the loudly crying boy, but at the same time, standing there breathing heavily, staring at the writhing boy's body that wrestled in vain, he had hoped that no end would ever come to the tableau, not for all eternity. Of this experience he had spoken, honestly, the way it had been, and he had even mentioned a most curious detail that had come to mind as he had been telling it: that the boy had still had his scout cap on throughout.

And suddenly, when in his tale there had been mention of a belt that gave fiercer results than the twig of a tree that had been used till then, so that the little victim, almost mad with pain, had almost been able to wrench himself free, then the miracle had happened and Frans had pressed up against N. as if he would never leave him again and, with a shout as if at a stroke he had found both a little brother who had run away from home to sea as well as God himself, he had expelled his searing "Holy Mead" right up to his own hair and forehead and had dozed off in the aftermath for an hour, motionless and still pressed up tightly against N.

"You see?" said I. "Once you can play the piano you have success with the ladies."

"What?"

"Never mind," I assured him. So now everything was fine again. Gone were resentment, irritation, and tension. And what's more: they were considering marrying each other and were now looking for someplace bigger, for the both of them together, that is. Should I learn of something in Amsterdam, I must let him know, for they could go and live there too, if need be.

Sure thing, I thought to myself. Marry, huh? But there's quite a different bridegroom from you on the cards for your little pilot. I said I would certainly take note should I hear something about accommodation and that they really must come round together some time. Perhaps, "if Wimie didn't object," they might even stay the night some time. *Revism* would blossom forth at last and, from a humble hovel in Amsterdam, would commence its triumphal progress around the world, tendering salvation to all.

Again a few weeks passed without my hearing anything from Gerard N. When, as time went by, it had turned into six weeks, two, three months, I felt puzzled. Might *The Tale of the Sea Scout Tortured with His Cap Still On* have lost its crowning glory, and might, because of Gerard N.'s epic impotence, all his happiness have evaporated again? At times I considered writing him a note but didn't.

Only when almost five months had passed did I run into him by accident on a Saturday afternoon on the Dam in Amsterdam, where we were each walking along the "sea snake prose" chiseled into the National Monument. He looked a little fatter, a touch more bloated in the face: quite the bed-sitter dweller, neglecting himself and feeding himself badly. I sensed at once that Love had deserted him. "Come along to our house," I said. Wimie was out, visiting his parents. "I'll get us something not too expensive to drink. Or do you have a lot of money on you?"

"Fine with me, sure," N. replied, "but I won't drink it anyway." His tone of deep sorrow silenced my grasping nature.

At my place, before I had asked him anything, he told me what had transpired. "A smash, y'see . . ." I didn't comprehend him immediately so he had to clarify. A good three weeks after his previous visit, little Frans had smashed to smithereens somewhere in Drenthe. So how could that be? It had remained a mystery. "Did he jump out too late in order to save a school or a village first?" I asked, for that would still leave you with something and he would have been a hero with a wreath from the school and the parish council. No, not that either, for it had been rugged, uninhabited country for kilometers around. Nor had he tried to bail out.

It had been pure chance, for that matter, that any news of this had reached N. at all, for he passed up on buying a newspaper quite often. Then he'd had to root out everything about the funeral himself for it seemed to have been announced solely by invitation; in any case, he hadn't been able to track down an announcement.

"With full military honors?" I asked, eagerly. "No, private, civilian, from a funeral home."

He didn't dare go at first but then, at the stipulated hour, in a semi-panic, without asking, he had passed the doorman and had entered a room pot-luck where, oddly enough, they had been standing around a young boy under glass, but it hadn't been Frans. He had bolted back out of the room quickly enough to knock a tray full of cups of tea from a waitress's hands.

"How odd: tea," I ventured. "Although you can drink tea on any occasion really. Perhaps it's not such a bad idea after all."

He hadn't gone into any other rooms and had left the building again at great speed.

"Who knows what he looked like," I said. "Who knows, perhaps you spared yourself something very nasty."

No, not so, for there hadn't been anything visible in little Frans's appearance, he'd heard: he had been flung out, not burnt or maimed. "Well yes, then it's a pity you didn't just bring him a final greeting. But then, just consider the state you're in at such a time, after all."

He hadn't been to the funeral itself either. "But I didn't work that day; no, I didn't."

As darkness rapidly descended, we stared in front of us for a long time, without saying a word. Man might make plans as much as he liked but you could be sure nothing would come of them. *Revism* had suffered a nasty blow again: me, too, he had escaped, for ever, that naughtiest winged sweetheart and rascal *(Icare! Icare!)*, escaped the way this one or that would do who succeeded him, though no one yet knew who they might be. *Ephemeri Vita or ye Likenesse of Man's Life depicted in ye Wondrous and never heard Historie of Flight and ye ephemeral Day or May Flye.*

# ~ *Gerard Reve* ~

# *A Prison Song in Prose*

*To Angus F. Johnstone Wilson in gratitude*

"It is quite a promotion, Tony," I said, trying in vain to hide my admiration while looking at his figure as he stood near the window, half turned away from it, so that the back of his hair, the anatomy of his neck with its almost imperceptible, downy growth of blond hair forming a unity with his tanned, boyish skin, his shoulders, the curve of his back, and the mysterious valley of his spine, alternately hidden and graciously shown under the coarse material of his faded blue shirt, and, farther down, those two globes, together creating an universe (oh! how grievously I am aware that I shall never be able to describe Tony G—'s cruel beauty!), were all stressed by the kindly cooperation of light and shadow. "Don't you agree?" I went on. "To be a probation officer, and to become the director of a youth prison overnight. It must mean they put great confidence in you."

"Yes, they do," Tony answered, in his ordinary, impassive voice. (Why does his voice always make me shiver with such a strange joy?) "They apparently know that I believe in my job. One can do a lot for these lads. Besides, I think the boys are already fond of me."

"I can well understand if they are," I agreed. I could not move my eyes away from his face now that a swift, almost unnoticeable smile, disarming and threatening at the same time, touched his lips.

"I'll show you around," he said. "It's a beautiful building; late seventeenth or early eighteenth century, I should say." We left the room and started our round through the old corridors, with their thick-beamed, high ceilings and their narrow windows placed in niches that had been furnished with strong iron crossbars. "How many must have looked through these panes at freedom outside," he pensively remarked, leaning forward into one of the niches and gazing at the wide view of hills and woods turning an autumnal brown.

"They must have been a great many, hundreds of them, perhaps thousands. Think of their fears, their sighs, their tears, their vain hopes of escaping punishment. . . ."

"You mean this was also a prison in former times?"

"Oh, yes, and even a youth prison during a number of years. I found that out. There are no records left to support my theory, but the size of certain implements, of old wooden beds stored in the cellars, and of remains of old prison clothes found there . . ."

"What did they look like, those clothes?"

"Not very smart, I'm afraid."

"Do you find those of today smart?"

"They *can* be very smart," Tony answered. We were continuing on our way and, turning round a corner, went down the old, worn steps leading to an inner court. "Usually they fit no better than sacks, I agree. But sometimes I give the quartermaster special instructions to remake them till they fit the boy like any expensive suit cut to measure. You'll find an example among those over there. I wonder whether you will be able to pick him out."

We had entered the inner court and stopped where a group of six boys were busy painting a number of chairs.

"You mean *le numéro soixante et un?*" I was referring to a strongly built yet slender boy, who, while the others were squatting down and applying the new paint, was standing, bending forward only slightly, scraping off old paint with a piece of sandpaper. Faded and shiny with wear—especially at the seat of the trousers and at the shoulder blades—as the humble, gray material was, neither the tailor of the richest prince in the world, nor the most devoted mother, could have cut a garment doing more justice to the fine lines of his body. The seams had been sewn with the utmost care and precision, as were the stitches with which the white numerals *6* and *1* had been fastened upon his strong back. Nowhere was there any tightness, and the cut of both jacket and trousers breathed a casual looseness, while yet, with the slightest movements of any limb, the admirable forms of his body were revealed.

Tony had nodded to my question. "Notice the number well," he said softly. "It is the same number as that of his cell. And he is sixteen years old. What does this mean?"

I looked at the boy again, following the outline of his figure from his narrow yet firm hips up to his broad shoulders, his manly but at the same time innocently boyish neck and his well-drawn, melancholic face partly covered by his ruffled blond hair, but I could not give the answer.

"The sum of the digits is seven in three cases," Tony whispered. "He is the sacred boy, the chosen one. We'll lead him through the sufferings that are his destiny."

"How are you getting on, boys?" he asked. All six stopped their work for a moment. "It's going quite all right, sir," the boy with the number 61 said. He now was facing us, so that I could gaze into his deep-set, blue eyes and study his large, perfectly shaped mouth.

"You know, Allan," Tony addressed him, "that I told you I was going to have a serious talk with you one of these days. I'll send for you this afternoon."

"Yes, sir," the boy answered, casting down his eyes for a moment. We walked on to the other side of the court, looking up at the old walls, in whose cracks pining, ever-thirsty weeds were trying to maintain themselves and stayed for a while near a set of earth-filled wooden boxes in which some blossomless plants were leading their scanty, sun-deprived lives. I watched Tony gazing at them without seeing them; his thoughts were obviously elsewhere.

"It is a mystery," he now said, almost in a whisper. "Youth, beauty, noble strength—why should they be destined to sacrifice themselves to crime? Is it because only their downfall, their humiliation, their kneeling down for chastisement, could make their divine greatness tangible for mortals? I think we should not try to understand, but only obey and humbly put ourselves into the service of the Mystery." We had walked on again and were on the point of leaving the court. Halfway up the steps, Tony stopped and turned around, and I saw his eyes narrow and noticed that his breathing became heavy and deep while he watched number 61, who was standing with his back toward us, in almost the same posture I had seen him in first, the only difference being that he had slightly spread his legs.

"What actually is number sixty-one—Allan, if I may call him so from now on—in here for?" I asked when we had returned to Tony's office.

"I was just about to tell you," Tony answered. "He arrived here last week. He's got to serve a full year. Loitering with intent, stealing cars, and joyriding. I've studied his file. The last two cases of joyriding he was charged with, he was accompanied by two youths of about his own age—

there was ample evidence of that in court. But their identity was never un-veiled. He would not talk, the boy. They could not make him tell. I won-der whether they tried hard enough and long enough." He pressed a bell button. "I think we ought to have a talk with him," he concluded. "Are you coming with me?"

There was a knock at the door, and a guard of about twenty-five years, in a black cap, a black leather jacket, and black cotton trousers, entered the room, his dark-brown, heavy boots sounding on the floor.

"Will you take number sixty-one to one of the basement cells, Pa-trick?" Tony asked.

The young man nodded. "Sixty-one. Very good, sir," he answered, but he remained standing where he was, as though waiting for further orders.

"Is there anything else, Patrick?" Tony asked.

"Do you want me to bring him to the gymnastics cell, sir?"

"No, the cell in the middle of the basement corridor will do."

"Is he to put on the shorts and the jersey, sir? Because I think they're both still here, in your office."

"No, you can bring him as he is dressed now."

"Yes, sir, but if you'd like it, sir, I'd be glad to lend you a hand." As he spoke, a broad grin appeared on the youth's brutal but unmistakably hand-some face. Tony raised his voice as he answered him.

"I certainly don't need you this afternoon, Patrick. What duty are you going to attend to right now?"

"Well, sir, there's a few odd jobs, like, to be done down in the base-ment this afternoon."

"I don't think you've got anything to do in the basement, Patrick," Tony sternly remarked. "I don't believe you have any sound reason to be there."

"To tell you the truth, sir, I wouldn't mind sort of hanging around down there, even if you won't let me help you or look on. It's a mighty fine thing even just to hear discipline and order being knocked into a boy." Here I expected the same coarse grin to come on his face, but instead it seemed suddenly to become tenser.

"You know the orders I gave you, Patrick," Tony said, "and don't let me find you anywhere in the basement. And as to discipline and order, the facts I know about you would not let you get away with less than a dozen or two on your bare backside yourself, if only half of them came to light."

"Yes, sir, certainly, sir," the youth answered quickly, clicking his heels and saluting before leaving the room.

A few minutes later, we too left the office and descended the winding staircase leading into the basement The guard was waiting for us at the foot of the stairs, where he unlocked a large iron gate. Tony took the bunch of keys from him, and sent him away. We then went down a corridor with cells on either side, till we came to a door marked PUN. ROOM in red-painted letters. It was obviously larger than the others, as the stretches of wall to the adjoining doors were longer. Tony walked up to the door on tiptoe, gestured that I should follow his example of not making the slightest noise, and inaudibly lifted the little panel of a small peephole in the door. While he was looking inside, I came up behind him and, leaning over his shoulder, peered in the direction of his gaze. The room we were peering into was about twelve feet long and almost square. At the back of it the boy Tony had spoken to in the courtyard was sitting upon what seemed to be a very narrow bench, which was upholstered with a black, leatherlike padding. There was no other furniture inside. The boy's face was half turned away from us, so that we could clearly distinguish the melancholic expression of his motionless eyes as well as the profile of his sullen, half-opened mouth. He was not aware of our presence. During the several minutes we stood there without moving, he remained sitting still, resting his hands on his knees. Once only his head stirred, so that the hair above his forehead trembled.

Around us there was absolute silence. Tony had, upon our entering the corridor, locked the gate behind us, and at neither of its dusky ends was there anybody to be seen. I let my hands move down along his body to the point where the sign of his excitement had made itself palpable under his clothes. At my touch a faint shiver went through his limbs, and I heard his breathing becoming deep and heavy. "Stand up, boy," he suddenly said softly but distinctly through the peephole. The boy got to his feet with a start. Tony turned the key in the lock and opened the door. We went inside. Tony locked the door again behind us and tucked away the bunch of keys.

Upon our coming in, the boy had moved to the farthest corner. Holding his hands behind his back, he stared at us with wide-open eyes. I saw his lips tremble a few times.

"We've come to talk with you, Allan," Tony said. "I suppose you know what it is all about."

"No, sir, I . . . I don't," the boy answered in a thin, timid voice. He was avoiding Tony's eyes and stared in front of him, toward the locked door. I automatically followed the direction of his gaze, and only now did I see that there was a kind of locker fastened to the inner side of the door with steel sides, top, and bottom, but with a door of thick steel grating, so that one could see its contents. On three hooks hung a thin cane about two and a half feet long, a strap of greased leather the same length as the cane and about a third of an inch broad, with a handle made out of knotted and wound string, and finally a very thin and flexible leather whip, which formed one piece with its twined handle, also made of leather.

"Come and sit down here, Allan," Tony said, pointing at the middle of the bench. It was the kind of leather-padded bench one sometimes sees on illustrations depicting a physician's consulting room of perhaps half a century ago, the only difference being that this one was at least eight feet long and not more than a foot and a half broad, while on either end there were two round iron clasps that could be opened and closed by means of butterfly bolts. The boy, hesitantly, came nearer and sat down. Tony seated himself at his right and gestured that I should sit down at the boy's left, and I did so. When he spoke again, Tony felt the boy's neck a moment, tapped his shoulders, and then put an arm around them. At each of Tony's movements the boy seemed to shudder and only with great effort to be able to restrain an impulsive shrinking away with fear.

"What I want to know from you, Allan," Tony said, not looking the boy in the face but keeping his eyes fixed upon the steel locker on the door, "is the identity, that would mean the names and addresses, of the two young men you were with the moment before you were arrested—a fair and a dark one, both of about your age and height." He began to stroke the boy's hair.

"I don't know what you mean, sir, honestly I don't," the boy answered, almost in a stammer. His voice had become even thinner and weaker.

"I don't want to hear any lies, Allan," Tony continued. "That you will understand as well as I do. We have very good lie detectors to find out whether you are speaking the truth or not."

"Please, sir," the boy uttered. "I don't know anything about it. I don't know anything about two boys, I never saw them, honestly, sir, I didn't."

"Are you fond of your mother?" Tony asked. The boy nodded. "Yes, sir, yes," he said in a whisper.

"Whatever I'm going to do to you, she won't be able to hear you or help you, nor will anyone else. You're alone with us here. There is nobody in this corridor, and no one in this whole basement either. Even if your cries and screams penetrated to the upper floors, nobody would come, because they know that it is me dealing with you, Allan. Do you understand that?"

"Yes, sir, no, please, sir, no, I don't know a thing, sir," the boy pleaded. His slender, undeniably handsome face had become pale. Tony stopped stroking his hair and got up.

"All right," he said. "Now take off your clothes. Stand up."

The boy got up very quickly, but once on his feet, he began pleading again. "You mustn't hurt me, sir, you mustn't do it, sir, I haven't anything to do with these boys you were talking about, sir, honestly I know nothing about them, I swear I don't, sir," he kept repeating, in a voice so young, so defenseless and innocent, that I felt like hugging him, pressing his face against me and kissing his fine countenance, already sweaty with fear.

Tony began to unbutton the boy's shirt and indicated to me that I should lend him a hand in stripping the boy. While, after undoing the buttons of the boy's cuffs, he was taking off the shirt, I began to untie Allan's shoelaces. Lifting his feet to take off his shoes, I felt his strong, well-muscled ankles tremble at my touch. Tony in turn opened Allan's trousers, pulled them down, together with the underpants, and made the boy step out of both. However obvious to me the beauty of his build had been when I first saw him in the prison's inner court, I was struck still more by the unmatched beauty of his naked figure. His downy neck, as well as his shoulders and back, still slightly bronzed apparently from open-air swimming, were like a young god's. His legs, long and impeccably formed and as suntanned as his back, were those of a man and of a boy at the same time; a fine, almost imperceptibly thin fur of silvery blond hair, visible only under a certain angle of light, covered them from halfway down his thighs to his ankles. Standing behind him, while he and Tony looked each other in the face, I let my eyes dwell upon his buttocks, which swim trunks must have sheltered from the sun. They were of a fully mature shape, yet boyish and narrow, and on the outside of each were those mysteriously beautiful declivities that are characteristic of the athletic figure. They had remained white, and yet they were not pale but looked as though the skin had a colorlessly tanned quality of its own.

"Lie down, boy," Tony told him. The boy hesitated, mumbling incomprehensibly incoherent, pleading sentence. Suddenly Tony forced him down on the bench, beckoned me for assistance, and, sitting with his full weight upon the boy's prostrate body, quickly caught his left ankle and secured it in one of the steel clasps. I did the same with Allan's right wrist, and the boy thus having become defenseless, it took us not more than a few moments to fasten his other ankle and wrist as well. I now saw that by turning a wheel, the length of the bench could be extended, and Tony, by employing this device, forced the boy to let his body be stretched out so that no chance remained of moving it anymore. Tony sat down on the boy's legs and began to stroke his neck, his fingers slowly wandering down his back and every now and then coming to rest at the beginning of his buttocks.

"You are going to tell the truth, Allan," he said. "No matter how long it may take me to get at it." He got up, went to the locker, opened it with a small key, and took out the cane. He ordered Allan to turn his head to the side and swishing the cane back and forth with great strength, made it hiss through the air in front of the boy's eyes. Then, facing the boy's feet, he sat down, straddling his shoulders. "The truth, the truth," he repeated in a soft, mumbling voice, at first gently tapping with the end of the cane upon Allan's buttocks and upper things, but suddenly stopping to lift it well above his head and take aim. With a thin, buzzing sound, he brought it down and hit both Allan's buttocks with a merciless, welting force. I heard the boy catch his breath with a sob, followed by a long, hoarse moan. He struggled and writhed with all his might, but he had not the slightest chance of altering the defenseless position in which his body lay stretched out, his efforts resulting only in chafing the skin of his wrists and ankles against the sharp metal of the clasps.

"You would like to dance, wouldn't you?" Tony asked, lifting the cane again, this time aiming a little lower. "I'll let you sing instead. You may tell us what you know to any tune you like, while I beat time." He brought the cane down upon both the boy's upper thighs. Allan began swinging his head with pain and broke out in wild, gasping sobs.

"You're going to need all your breath, Allan, if you're still prepared to tell the truth," Tony remarked. With great speed, but with unabated force, he started a merciless caning of the sides of the buttocks, the upper parts of them, and the region very near the boy's crotch. Amid his breathless, howling sobs Allan tried to speak, but only half-intelligible fragments of words came from his mouth, without forming any coherent pattern. Suddenly Tony held the cane still and, with his fingertips, felt the dozens of already swollen, red stripes. "So far you haven't sung, boy," he said. "I think you soon will. Who were those two boys?" For a few moments Allan was able to suppress his sobs and form proper sentences. He swore again that he knew nothing, and beseeched Tony not to hurt him anymore. "I've had enough sir," he sobbed. "You mustn't beat me anymore, it's hurting terrible, sir, honestly. . . . I can't stand it sir. . . ." He stopped suddenly, to utter a faint cry of fright and despair, as he saw Tony go to the locker, hang the cane back on its hook, and take out the thin strap of greased leather.

The next moment Tony had come back and, instead of sitting upon Allan's shoulders, took up a standing position near the bottom end of the bench, placing his feet on the floor on either side of it. Bending over slightly, he began to tickle the boy's face and neck with the end of the strap. Allan moaned as though he felt the pain that the implement of torture would soon inflict upon him. His sobs became deeper and hoarser, and suddenly he spoke again, at a wild, almost breathless speed. His face, shining with tears and perspiration, although twisted with despair, was even more handsome than before. "I know nothing, I know nothing, sir, I know nothing . . . ,' he repeated over and over again. The end of the strap, gently skipping up and down as though it were the string of a puppet Tony was playing with, now with almost inaudible little sounds falling upon his blond skin, now sliding over it as it followed the curve of the spine, slowly traveled down his back and, with tiny dancing jumps, passed through the tender valley between his buttocks and remained dwelling for a long while just beneath them, in the narrow space between his thighs. "Speak, Allan, speak," Tony mumbled. "You're tough, aren't you? You're very brave and courageous. You want to show that you're not the kind that screams out right away, isn't that so? By God, handsome boy that you are, you'll scream, all right." He bent over a little farther still and lifted the strap high. It made, not a buzzing sound when he brought it down, but a high-pitched whine like a faint whistle. It seemed as though he were going to carve up the boy's enviable body with it. First he hit Allan's neck, then he began to lash his shoulders, going down inch by inch, each time striping the full breadth of the boy's back. He cut the tender skin of the buttocks, aiming now straight, now sideways, now diagonally. Again the tortured body struggled in vain to free itself, and the sounds that escaped the young victim's mouth had become the roaring of an animal trying to free its crushed claws from a trap. Thin trickles of blood began to run down the sides of Allan's buttocks. Right below them, Tony, with great skill, cut the skin of the inner side of both legs, taking a different position each time so as to achieve the full effect of each blow. When he had striped both legs with the same indefatigable force, he stopped. "You still don't feel like speaking up, or do you?" he asked softly. The boy couldn't answer. Only wild, now blubbering, now whining, but equally unintelligible utterances burst forth from his trembling lips, which in his agony he had bitten till they bled. "Turn him over," Tony said to me. We unscrewed the clasps. The boy did not try to offer any resistance as we lifted him, placed him on his back, and secured his wrists and ankles once again.

"Now I am sure you will become very eloquent," Tony said, going to the locker, replacing the strap, and coming back with the leather whip. When he held it up to show it, the boy tried to say something, but failed. His deep-blue eyes with their long lashes stared into Tony's eyes as in a last, speechless supplication for mercy, and he shook his head in a feverish shiver. Tony first tickled his armpits and navel with the end of the whip, which was as thin as a string, and then, caressingly, let it wander down till it reached the modest, still boyish fur of pubic hair. He let it dance upon the large yet innocent-looking sex, let it curl round it as though in a mocking dance, and then, as if he wanted to play with it like a top, strung the end of the whip around the boy's scrotum and gave little jerks at it.

"You'll speak, soon," he whispered, stroking Allan's hair and pushing clumps of it, moistened with sweat, from his forehead. He lifted the whip and aimed for a very long time, changing his position a few times before he swung his arm down, cutting the fine skin of both scrotum and penis in one blow. He paid no attention to the ear-rending, animal yelling that rose from the boy's lips, but hit his organs five more times before stopping. Then he bent over and brought his face right above the boy's. "Anything to tell?" he asked.

"I . . . those boys . . . I'll tell you . . . I know them . . . ," Allan whispered. "I'll tell you."

# ∼ *Yves Navarre* ∼

FROM

## *Sweet Tooth*

TRANSLATED BY DONALD WATSON

Rasky. "When people stop loving each other, everything becomes more exciting. It's the moment we all watch out for, eager as we are for things to happen. And we provoke our break-ups ourselves, if we have to. Close the door, will you? No one but you must hear what I'm about to say, what I've been going over in my mind again and again, so as not to forget it. What I want to pass on to you. Come in, Luc, you've kept me waiting, come closer, I was afraid it was all going to slip from my memory. Listen.

"We always think of death as being picturesque. We believe it imbues every human being with unsuspected courage and splendor. And we always think it's meant to provoke seizures of conscience and spurts of confession, and confronts you with the blinding truth. In my case, I've nothing essential to tell you, nothing to deliver, nothing to offer. You refuse everything anyway. This morning the doctor announced that they would stop giving me injections. Because I was so much better, he said. But I could read the truth in his face. I know how to read the underside of a lie, you know. An old habit of mine. I'm done for.

"That's it, slip your hand round behind the pillow and massage the back of my neck. How do you manage to know how good that feels? It's

---

YVES NAVARRE, *born of an old Gascon family in 1940, won the Prix Goncourt (or "Prix Galligrasseuil") for* Cronus's Children *in 1981 and the Académie Française Prize for the body of his work in 1992.* Sweet Tooth, *though written a decade before AIDS was defined, nonetheless prefigures it. He took his own life, in Paris, on January 24, 1994.*

*333*

good to do good. Don't stop. You've got rings under your eyes. Where did you go last night? What did you do? But no, don't tell me any more stories, I know the refrain. I've been singing it all my life. Perhaps you'd rather I told you what Carlos said to me, what Carlos did to me? Yesterday, while he was remaking the bed, he stripped to the waist to put me down, there, in the chair you're sitting in. I thought he was showing me his chest in order to seduce me—if he only knew—and then afterward I told myself that he was only afraid he might dirty his jacket. Just as he was leaving, he let out that he was going to take a shower. My house of cards collapsed. So I started to imagine that I was the tablet of soap he was using under the shower and that he took a firm hold on me and slid me over his body, round his neck, through his hair, and then over his face, like a grubby child who's been playing too hard and wants to look nice for a birthday dinner. Then, soapy and slippery in the palm of his hand, I slid under his armpits, through valleys of hairy thickets, and right down his arms to his fingers, the nails, and over the long, clear lines in his hands, which I had never had the time to read. Then I discovered his stomach with broad circular movements, skirting his navel, then all round it again and again, till I slipped and slithered to the floor. Carlos picked me up. I evaded his grasp, and he took hold of me again. This time I was lost in his crotch, lathering, drowning in a foam of tenderness, polishing the stones and stroking the muscle; then, bending forward, with a gesture he passed me through to the other place, and there I go bobbing and scrubbing. Then come the legs, the knees and the feet and between the toes, the most delicious treat. He lays me down on the soap dish. Forgets all about me. I can see him rinsing down. He is rubbing his chest. He has abandoned me. He doesn't know that I came to spy on him. He dried himself. Then he goes out, closing the shower-room door. I wanted to tell you, I needed to tell you that. It's all I know about him. Imagination.

"Don't move. That's right. Let me feel the weight of my head in your hand. I'm amazed how heavy it is. That's a feeling which still makes some sense to me. They've stopped feeding me properly. They give me sugar dissolved in water, and sweet things taste bitter to me now. All my sensations and all the parts I ever dreamed of playing have been reversed. I always imagined a sudden death, a picturesque one, and I'm only allowed this interminable demise, this final one-man show that goes on and on. And you're a kind spectator, too polite to leave before the end. You won't leave before it's all over. I was about to say that at least you owe me that.

But you don't owe me anything. Not a thing. You have to stay because of all I owe *you*." Smile. "You see, I can still smile. It's all that's left me, apart from my eyes. Look at me. Close your eyes. Open your eyes. Close your eyes. It has just occurred to me that we forgot to make love together even once with our eyes shut, each one keeping his gratification a secret from the other. When we watched one another for every reaction, we concealed everything from each other. Yes, now I'm discovering this strange paradox in all my relationships, with everything and everyone. It's a bit late in the day to find out. But I suppose that's the really picturesque side of a final rendezvous. Are you listening?

"Look at my body, what I've turned into. Yet while you're cupping the back of my neck in your hands, don't forget that in this head an adolescent is still making plans for the future, an adolescent who refuses to see himself as he is now. He thinks he's still on active service and arrogantly believes that he can take on anything: the little skirmishes of love, cruises by night, someone you pick up on a boulevard, who comes back home with you, gets undressed and gives himself up to the game of give and take. It's natural for your body to leave you in the lurch, bugger off or break down. Something in the machine conks out and nothing works anymore. That's a fine way to die. I've been treated to a flabby death, and serve me damn right. But if my body lets me down, my mind has not deceived me. I am what I have chosen to be. And inside my head I'm still eighteen years old, the age you were when I met you. And today we are still both eighteen. Always the same age. When you feel the first stirrings of love. It's my body that no longer relates. That's all. You're not listening anymore.

"A parasite devoured by parasites—a fine program, isn't it? Right? You don't say a word. You're not even smiling. What if I told you that after that dream of the soap, I've lost all desire to discover Carlos, to see him really naked, completely in the nude: I know him by heart. I've been all round him. A museum of youth I'm familiar with. I've visited it before, a hundred, a thousand times. Each time I used to leave you, it was to surprise myself with bodies different from yours, and all those other bodies brought me back to you: I still didn't really know you, and I always had a kind of curiosity, an unfailing urge to look at you and watch you and discover you. This morning I told myself that I really must, at least once, tell you about my love for you. What a nasty big word! Tell you what it is that has bound me to you, and you to me. There was a curious look in your big brown eyes too, when you saw me coming back to you. Patient. Placid. Sure of yourself. I'd be back! And I was. This love of ours was simply a feeling of ease in danger, endangered by my capricious game of farewells. They followed a rhythm that matched our bouts of curiosity. I had found a way for us never to use each other up. Why should I feel guilty today, confessing that? Or you either, now it's all over? Let us admit that we enjoyed our sex together and that each time was like the first time. And that the only thing the jealous poaching queens in our world of men really resented was this perennial curiosity of ours and the strength of its renewal, our little game of I-go-I-come-back, which always enabled us to evade capture by the enemy, time. Thank you, Luc, thank you.

"You see, I'm crying. I've never been able to take them seriously, other people's tears. But mine today are scalding me. You'll see, they'll leave their trace behind. In furrows. As if my eyes were putting their tongues out. Tongues of fire. Kiss me."

Luc bends over Rasky. Rasky looks astonished, startled. "You're just out of school, you're just out of school and I'm waiting for you." Luc presses his lips to Rasky's. Lips that no longer seem the same. They have a different taste. "You see, you're afraid. So just look at me, that's all, let us kiss with our eyes." Luc wipes Rasky's tears away. "Watch out, you'll scald yourself." Rasky smiles. "Oh, if only I could have really stolen you away, run off with you, ravished you or whatever, abducted you, say. Yet the more I regret it, the more I tell myself that at one go I'd have ruined everything. We would never have traveled this long road together, side by side, pretending to go off and disappear and then coming back with our arms loaded with presents and our heads stuffed with desires. I don't know what else to say to you: I'm glad you're here today. I'm going to stop and lie down in the ditch. And you, keep going. You must keep going on. But at least we'll have traveled the road, all our road, together. That's what it is, our love, the love we've both shared. Perhaps we're the only two who can understand that. We've put a great deal of honesty into that word, everything we had. And that's quite a lot. A lot better than a lie, because this way time has lost out. Look into my eyes, look!" Silence. Rasky's voice has grown hoarse, almost inaudible. He is going to sleep. In the palm of Luc's hand his neck has grown crushingly heavy. "Go away, Luc; it's late and I don't want to see you anymore. . . ."

~ ~ ~

"In the summer," said Carlos, "I have one weekend out of three off duty. Three days at a time. So I treat myself to the luxury train, the Blue

Arrow. You have to make a reservation at least two months in advance. I get off at Southampton and go to see my mom. She does housecleaning there. When folks are on vacation in the summer, she works real hard. In the winter, she just keeps the keys to all the houses. Then she writes me a bit more often." Carlos had opened the door of the room. Rasky had asked him to. "I've got the feeling there's some wind from outside coming in through the corridor," he had said. "I know it's only an impression, but talk to me, tell me about your life." Carlos had sat down, not *in* the armchair, but on the arm. "The nurses would get jealous, they'd spread it around, and there's no point asking for trouble." Legs outstretched, Carlos is leaning slightly forward, with one foot crossed over the other and his hands folded over his stomach. "Be careful," said Rasky, "you might slide off." "I'm used to it," said Carlos. "I know these armchairs like the back of my hand. I could almost call them by their first names." Irony. Rasky had the impression that a shadow just passed in the corridor, a dark shadow holding a pair of slippers, ladies' slippers, black ones, with pink ribbons to make them less scary. Sweet death. "And this Blue Arrow thing, it would make a fantastic film. You want to hear the story?" "Go ahead, Carlos, tell me." "Well then, the last weekend in August, I had a seat in the parlor car of the Blue Arrow. A coach reserved for latecomers, or for people like me who can't afford a private compartment. It's a sort of old-fashioned train, you know. Like a Victorian drawing room inside, with big club armchairs and little black boys to serve the drinks and offer you the choice of twenty different brands of cigar. Really living it up. It's all I want to help me forget the corridors of this hospital." Carlos smiled. "That particular day, I'd had a few drinks while waiting for the train. I felt great. Completely detached. I watched whoever it was coming in, sitting down, and who was watching who, and I tried to imagine what each of their lives was like. I noticed there wasn't a woman among them. In the summer, of course, all their families have gone to the coast. The husbands just spend the weekends. Fine-looking papas, decent family men, in their thirties. Genuine American middle class. Clean-living. With gleaming teeth and impeccable grins, all in suits that are badly cut but magnificent cloth. Color of the tie a bit too gaudy, but with a casual air to carry it off. Well, while I've got them under observation, I come to realize that they're all in love with each other. They all desire one another. There's something in the looks they exchange—and there are about thirty of us in the parlor car—that's not just due to the usual boredom and inactivity of a journey by train: they look at each other because they want one another. They don't talk to each other because they're all jealous, envying and desiring one another, but behind their newspapers they're making love, a sidelong glance as they turn the pages, and as they light their cigarettes and swallow a mouthful of gin they stare hard at the guys who face them or who sit across the way. A furious platonic game that lasts the whole length of the trip. And no one ever speaks to anyone, or very little. A remark about the weather, have you any matches, didn't we see each other last weekend, it never goes further than that. They're married men. And at Southampton their wives are waiting for them on the station platform. And that's the great scene in the film. They embrace their wives lovelessly. Coldly. Mechanically. You know what I mean? Can you see it? But the kids are there too. And they kiss their children joyfully. They bend at the knees and pick them up in their arms. What do you think?" "It's a nice idea, but have you thought of a title?" "At first I thought of *The Blue Arrow.* Then one day in the paper I saw the photograph of a painting they'd refused to show in a modern art exhibition, oddly enough at Southampton. This 'painting' was really a blown-up photograph of lips, shown vertically. At once, you see, it looked more like a cunt, a pussy, a vagina. So back to the arrival of the train. The artist had decided to call his picture *Band in Southampton.* And I thought that it would make a good title for my story." Carlos folded his arms and wagged his head. "Only trouble is, I don't know how to write. I'd have to make a novel of it first and then a scenario, and that all scares me. Not my scene." Silence.

The odor of Carlos's skin: how could Rasky ask his nurse not to take a shower for at least two days? Odor restored! Smothered in ointment, aseptic, flabby, abandoned, even deprived of the power to do what he would with his own body, now having its revenge on Rasky for the time he had gambled so recklessly away as he hoped in the fury of this futile dissipation to summon up the magic of a meeting, a partnership, and stumbled on his parallel relationship with Luc, who gave a fillip to his life, today all Rasky longs for is an odor, an authentic odor, one odor at last in this hygienic labyrinth of rooms and corridors. Whiteness is nothing. "What are you thinking?" "About your film." "No, you're thinking about something else, you're hiding something from me." "Yes, I was thinking about you." Carlos comes up to the bed and strokes Raksy's brow. "Relax—relax, baby!

"The hero, you know, should be a banker, filthy rich. After forty. And he'd be gazing at two guys sitting opposite, younger than him, two guys staring at each other who don't dare say a word. Then he'd remember an incident during the last war, identical, in an army truck in the Ardennes. And then another, when he was a kid, in the bus he used to take to school. Stuff like that. And you'd see into his past, a whole past of failure to admit the truth. He's been a spectator all his life, of incidents like that, identical. The blind and stubborn way men go looking for companionship, the bond of man to man, each on an equal footing. Something to take their minds off that perfect wife who belongs to them and depends on them for everything. And when they embrace their children on the station platform, it is their champions they're embracing, potential victors in a match which *they* have lost. You understand?" Rasky gives a slight nod of the head. "One day maybe these children will alter the timetable, they may even alter the sort of relationship their fathers have failed to create in the train. Yes, those papas on the station platform at Southampton are embracing something they have lost; audacity. The Blue Arrow: thirty seats for thirty lonely men." Silence. Carlos gently shrugs his shoulders. "I know I was a bit drunk that day, but I like that story of mine, it tells me something. . . ."

Concerning the unzipped fly: "What I did just now was just what you expected of me, just what the look in your eyes was asking for. You see, I'm no different from anyone else, I'm made the same way as all the others. But there, it's exactly what you wanted, at the precise moment I did it. Correct?" Rasky closed his eyes. "I'm right, aren't I?" Rasky opened his eyes, then closed them again. "Come on, it's time to get you cleaned up. And no injection, as the doctor said to stop them." Carlos closed the door of the room. "Want some music? OK, no music." Silence. "Want the TV? OK, no TV." Silence. "I like your moods. You amuse me. I think you're a bit crazy, but I like crazy people. I like Rasky. You don't mind if I call you Rasky, do you?" Rasky never made any distinction between true and false affection, no doubt because affection is essentially false; it's an elegant way of holding other people at arm's length, keeping them far enough away for them not to embarrass you. Affection is an embellishment of words and gestures which shuts you out at the precise moment when you appear to be made welcome. Leave your own circle and come into mine, leave your own world and come into mine. I'll show you my log cabin at the far end of the park. My parents never go inside. I've never invited anyone before. Come, and I'll show you. Childhood is a ball and chain we drag around with us till our very last moment. Carlos is talking to himself. Rasky has stopped listening. When Carlos lifts him up to set him down in the chair, Rasky imagines that the chest his face is pressed to suddenly opens like a dolomite rock delivering the sword that will allow him to finish himself off. Hara-kiri. Meanwhile, what is Luc doing now? Till his very last moment, Rasky will be torn between the imperturbable schoolboy and that fine utopia where men unzip their flies and offer themselves good-naturedly. "That's it really, isn't it?"

# ~ *Agustín Gómez-Arcos* ~

### FROM

## *The Carnivorous Lamb*

TRANSLATED BY WILLIAM RODARMOR

At times, when I knew everyone in the house was busy and my absence wouldn't be noticed, I started opening the little garden gate and slipping out into the mysteries of the town. I carefully avoided making any friends during those escapades; I didn't want any eventual pals to come knocking on our door, asking if I wanted to go out with them. I was careful to keep the world of the town separate from that of the house, my family apart from everyone else.

As it was, my childhood had taught me not to mix things up, to keep all my experiences to myself—in short, to live a secret life. Just as I had special places in the house where I would go to hide from the others, or to think my own thoughts, I now preferred certain parts of the town that I knew Clara and Antonio didn't go to—and they weren't the kinds of places where the invisible coterie was likely to spot me and say that my face looked familiar. (I was looking more like Mother every day.)

In that way, I got to know the town by myself, without a guide, and almost illicitly. Over time, that taste and hunger for everything illicit would become a symbol for me. In my own town, I could watch and observe without being recognized or called to; a kind of guaranteed impunity.

At the same time, my education, both religious and profane (to use

*Augustín Gómez-Arcos was born in Spain in 1939—the last year of that country's civil war—but settled in France because his works were banned under "El Caudillo."* The Carnivorous Lamb, *written in French, received the Prix Hérmes for the best first novel of 1975.*

Don Gonzalo's word) was proceeding apace but required more hours of study and much more concentration. Don Pepe and Don Gonzalo, knowing that together they were masters of practically all my time, vied with each other to see who could make me spend the most hours in the old dining room upstairs, which Mother had fixed up for my homework and my catechism sessions with Don Gonzalo. Thanks to a conspiracy perfectly engineered by Mother, the priest never did cross paths in the house with "that disciple of the devil, your teacher for other matters." In that one sentence, Don Gonzalo balanced scorn and hate so precariously, he could have been crowned the king of melodrama.

War was now being waged on three fronts. The first consisted of the señor specialist and me, by now almost traditional enemies. Mother's confessor and I formed the second, but since neither of us had learned the other's fighting style yet, we wasted a lot of time in skirmishes. The third front, finally, the one that shaped the three of us into a perfectly defined social unit, consisted on the one hand of me, the taught, and on the other hand of the two of them, the teachers. I never understood how, hating each other as they did, they managed to be in such perfect accord on their work methods and how to apply them.

I had my way of getting revenge, though. When they got too nasty with me, I would always remark with a look of surprise:

"Yes, señor. That's just what Don Gonzalo [or Don Pepe] says. And you must both be right, since you agree without even knowing each other. At least, as far as I know. Still, it's funny. You're like two halves of an orange. It must be telepathy."

I would say this all at once, without pausing for breath, so as not to give them time to answer. Then I would watch them redden to the point of exploding and leave the room. Storms are best avoided. But I realized bitterly that I hadn't yet found a way to make them *really* blow up, really make them apoplectic. And I never did. They must both be alive to this day, still torturing boys of "my sort" (Mother's phrase) in some church or comfortable living room somewhere in town or in the country. Back then, I thought that causing their deaths without bloodying my hands would be the height of refinement. Mother would certainly have liked the device. At times, I thought she needed it, if only to destroy herself, or destroy Clara. But . . . well, it was a vain hope, like so many in this imperfect world.

Don Gonzalo threw himself into his missionary work with fire in his eyes and brimstone in his mouth. To hear him relentlessly bombarding me with prayers and commandments, Bible verses and quotations from the fathers of the Church, you would think death spied on me constantly and the "glowing gates of hell" were waiting to swallow me if I didn't work hard to "turn away the misfortune that *circumstances* had laid on my head from earliest childhood." Don Gonzalo would seize that opportunity to talk of the "Reds" as though they were some awful calamity (predicted in the Bible, though I can't remember which verse), sent to earth by the Good Lord to punish our waywardness and show us the thorny, spotless path to virtue. Everything was grist for his mill, from the loss of our colonies ("when God abandoned America") to the civil war, by way of the three republics (which he shamelessly analogized to Saint Peter's three denials of Christ). The ceaseless persecution suffered during the war by churches and convents (with what Don Pepe called their "specialized personnel," meaning priests, nuns, and monks) was almost always given a special chapter. The glory that the reigning fascism (which Don Gonzalo called "the legitimate order") derived from all these events was boundless; words to describe it couldn't be dithyrambic enough, though the fucking priest knew the dictionary by heart. His "evangelization" could easily have become brainwashing if it hadn't been so exaggerated. On me, it had just the opposite effect.

Don Gonzalo reeked of wax and sweat, incense and dampness; together, they reminded me of the smell of death. Moreover, he had a dangerous habit of getting too close to me, probably figuring that my "evangelization" would be complete if our bodies shared communion as well. Since I didn't want to snitch to my brother about his advances, for fear of seeing the priest squashed like a bug, I had to change places every minute or so. One day I very politely pointed out to him that my behind wasn't the seat of the third person of the Holy Trinity, as his hot hand was apparently trying to get me to understand.

"The devil didn't put those words in your mouth, by any chance?"

"Not at all, Father. I'm sure the remark only came to mind because of your hand. I could be mistaken, but if we need to discuss it, I would rather we did it in front of my brother, my mother, and Don Pepe, than with you alone."

He turned his hot gaze on me and gritted his teeth. No doubt about it: he didn't want to discuss *that* with anyone, not even me. He suspected me of having impure thoughts, and his mission consisted of enlightening me on a number of points, notably sin. Given that my childhood had been spent lost in darkness, I very likely had no conception of what sin was, and he had taken on the job of making it all clear to me without delay. So a single rule guided his behavior: make up for lost time. There was no point in making a mountain out of a molehill or trying to see beyond the end of my nose. Malice is no small sin, even if only a venial one.

So I learned that I could amuse myself for a long time at those poor guys' expense, with their hidden fire and hypocrisy, if I wanted to. (To be continued.)

Needless to say, Mother's confessor never managed to make God known to me, and I don't think he really tried. He hardly ever spoke of Him, and when he did I had the feeling that he was talking about a stranger and didn't realize it. His mission and concern was the Church, and when we finally went our separate ways, that was what I knew the most about. I learned from him that to live, you don't need God if you truly belong to the Church. To live—and I want to stress this—all you need is doctrine, and the one provided by the Catholic Church is the most complete, the most sophisticated, and the most controversial. Also the furthest from God, but that's to be expected. Since the whole package is designed to meet man's needs—repentance, despair, and nastiness—I don't see why God should even be involved. I was a consciously fervent Catholic for a few years myself, and I thank Catholicism for finally helping me understand that God doesn't exist.

As for Don Gonzalo himself, he was less concerned with teaching me what I needed to know to pass the high school entrance exam than with preparing me for a general confession by the book, with my first communion right afterward.

Mother had already set the date: March 21, the first day of spring.

"I want it to be like a rosebud's first blossoming for him," she told our confessor cynically.

"Will you give a party?"

"I'm going to think about it," Mother answered, her face shining like a summer moon, her tone of voice giving the impression that she found the idea completely charming. In fact, she had already made up her mind: there would be no party, and I would take my first communion at our house in the country.

"But, my daughter, a first communion must be celebrated in a church, not in secret. It must be a public act, done not only in the sight of God but also in the eyes of men."

Don Gonzalo was obviously trying to force Mother, and maybe Father as well, to show themselves publicly in church. It would have been a triumph for him, a vivid application of what he was always saying about "lost sheep." He may even have dreamed of roping Don Pepe and Clara in, to round out the party. But he wasn't reckoning with Mother's vagueness, or the supreme willpower of someone who is already dead. Ever since hearing her confession to Clara a few years before, I knew that nothing could touch her. She accepted only her own ways of destroying, and taking us all to church wouldn't have been an act of anarchy, but quite the reverse; she wanted to force Don Gonzalo to serve me the body and blood of Christ at home.

"You know, Father, the more we show our humility, the closer we get to the gates of heaven, which I fully intend to enter. That is why I have decided that the child's first communion will take place in our country house. Right next door on my estate there is a little chapel that goes back to my grandmother's time, which our workers have long used as a storage shed. For tools, you know, and also to raise my favorite breed of chicken. So I've ordered it cleaned and prepared for the ceremony. Everything we need is at the house: crucifixes, altar cloths, candelabras, and even a very large, handsome fount; up to now, it has been used to grow flowers in."

"You're talking about a whole string of sacrileges, my daughter!"

"Don't be childish, Father. Your ministry allows you to wipe out any sacrilege with a simple blessing. And who knows, after the little one's first communion, maybe the chapel won't be used as a shed or chicken house anymore. Anything can happen these days. Can I count on you?"

"If you are asking me as a minister of the Church . . ."

"Of course, Father."

"In that case, you can count on me."

"Thank you from the bottom of my heart. A car has already been rented to pick you up on the evening of the twentieth; the trip will take only a few hours. You will spend the night there. I have ordered a room made ready for you. I assume you will bring everything you need for the ceremony, or would you like me to take care of it?"

Don Gonzalo's answer couldn't have been sharper:

"No, daughter, I'll take care of it myself." (He was probably afraid Mother would also take charge of blessing the host.)

In that way, I learned that we would be leaving the house for a week and going to the country for the first time in my life. My brother occasionally used to spend a few days of his vacations there. "No, you can't take your little brother with you. His health isn't up to such a change. He is staying at home." For years, I had heard Mother repeat that sentence without ever changing a single word. I had gotten the idea that the country was drafty, or something.

During the following days, a swarm of delivery boys trooped through the hallway, and Clara complained all day long about the dirt they left on the carpet.

"That's all I need. Don't I have enough work to do already?"

She glared at me like an angry rooster, as if I were responsible for all the comings and goings.

"But what the hell does all this have to do with me?"

"It's your first communion, isn't it? I'm not the one who is going to be 'received into the bosom of the Church,' as señora your mother puts it!"

"Poor Clara, you're nothing but an atheist."

"I'm just a bitch, is what I am. A bitch of a mule that just works and works my whole bitching life."

There, the best I could do was to make myself scarce.

In any case, I had too much work, swamped as I was by the educational fury of my two teachers. Otherwise, I would have understood "poor Clara"'s despair. To her, the Church was nothing but an endless source of misfortunes. Each time she saw Don Gonzalo cross the hall to go upstairs, Clara would grab her big fly sprayer and spray the whole house. Antonio, who was getting ruder by the day, laughed like a maniac.

"It stinks of priests in here," Clara would mutter between her teeth. "It's like smelling hell."

Don Gonzalo would race up the stairs as fast as he could.

What with work, packages arriving every day—I was dying to find out what was in them, but Mother said they were not to be opened until further notice (Clara reported the phrase)—the phone ringing constantly whenever Mother wasn't glued to it, giving the invisible coterie the "good news" (that was how she described my first communion), and explaining her subtle reasons for only celebrating the ceremony within the family ("No, there won't be a reception, so there's no need to send presents"), Father's clients furtively slipping in and out, thinking the house had gone crazy, Antonio becoming more and more insatiable at night, ever since his skillful caresses had made me come for the first time, me clinging to his body, more aware than ever of how deeply I reached him, my unrelenting war with Don Pepe and Don Gonzalo, my shameless way of showing up in front of them with hardly anything on and pretending I was properly dressed, the questions I asked them, looking innocent, about the hairs that were starting to grow around my penis, which, for that matter, was unexpectedly getting hard several times a day . . .

Don Pepe: "You'll find out about that when the time is right. Now let's get to work!"

Don Gonzalo: "Good Lord, one doesn't talk about those things—it's a sin! Do you play with yourself?"

Playing dumb, I would say, "But if you don't explain these things to me, who will? I don't have any friends."

"Friends, indeed! I'll speak to your father."

They both wound up giving me that answer every time, yet Father's office door never opened to supply me with the desired explanation of the "mysteries of nature." (Was that Don Pepe's phrase, or Don Gonzalo's?)

In a word, the day before my first communion I was out of my head with excitement.

We left the house and the town very early in two rented cars, the first for Mother, my brother, and me, the other for Clara and a ridiculous amount of baggage. You would think we were headed for the ends of the earth and not coming back for years, instead of a week. There were even two roosters in Clara's car, their legs trussed up, to be bred with the hens in the country to produce double-yolk eggs!

For a good part of the trip, Mother and Antonio carried on a knowledgeable discussion on the subject. The driver, an old guy who was none too bright, kept saying that the world was going to ruin (I don't think he understood the point of having eggs with two yolks: he felt nothing was better than a good pair of old-fashioned ones) and that the Americans, what with their bombs and stuff, etc. He started describing in detail a news item from Madrid: a prostitute (a "loose woman," as he put it) had been found tied up in a cheap hotel with her breasts chewed off by a black American soldier. She had died in the hospital.

Mother didn't seem too interested in the story, and the driver and my brother gradually got involved in a rambling political discussion about the country's American bases, a topic on which neither seemed too well informed. The driver said that they just lined certain people's pockets. Without denying the point, Antonio said there were political reasons too.

"Spain is the gateway to Africa, you know."

"Don't talk to me about Africa. That's where he's from, the fat pig!"

Mother cut them off, saying she couldn't allow politics to be discussed in her husband's absence. (For the life of me, I couldn't understand why.)

"How is it that he didn't come with you?"

"Business."

"And it isn't easy to get my father together with a priest. You know how he is."

"Yeah, I know. What a guy!"

They all knew each other, apparently. In fact, my father had chosen not to attend my "spiritual initiation." (Don Gonzalo's words.)

"Father, now that you will be calling at the house, please do me a favor and don't go into my husband's study to offer him your blessing. Let's celebrate the ceremony quietly." (Mother's advice, when it was decided her confessor would take my religious eduction in hand.)

For me, going to the country was an adventure. Earth, water, stone, a different air and light, animals and trees in their natural state. None of those close-cropped trees and deeply bored birds that dotted the town and is squares, as disciplined as soldiers. With their pruned branches and their leaves hacked away so as not to impinge on the precious views, they looked as if they had just come from the barber's. None of those mares looking like beaten-down slaves, their ears flat against their heads, that pulled the few remaining horse-drawn wagons and made the town look like a squalid flea market. (During one of my solitary escapades, I had heard someone say that they were part of the town's charm.)

More than anything, the country would be a new place to live. Bedrooms, parlors, stairs that I would have to discover and practically invent, adapt to my gaze and movements, neither vex nor irritate by my presence. Instead I would have to slip surreptitiously among the vibrations of love and hate you always find in old houses.

My first surprise, a few minutes after we arrived, was the discovery that the country house was an exact replica of our house in town, or vice versa. Only a few details—furniture, paintings, a few stray objects—were different. I felt I was looking at the negative of a familiar photograph, and my chest tightened with despair. Wouldn't there ever be any real change in my life? Why was I forever encountering the clumsy copy of an eternal original? Or the faded original of a series of reproductions scattered at random? Was it a sickness of the family? The town? The whole country? I never found answers to all those questions, but ever since I was very young, I've suspected that Spain and life itself were nothing but the work of a copying machine that never broke down.

The only original things at the country house were Mother's woven wicker armchair and her yellow rosebush. And the peasants, of course, who came and went, and whose harsh voices miraculously didn't get on Mother's nerves. Quite the opposite: she was charming with them and had brought presents for everybody. You felt she was at the nerve center of her domain, giving gifts with an open hand, a smile on her lips. The only drawback was that nobody knew what the hell to do with a satin bedside lamp, since there wasn't any electricity in the huts, or a hand-held shower head—the last word in hygiene—without running water.

After days like that, Mother would collapse exhausted into her wicker armchair, her hands gripping the twin doves that decorated the armrests, and melt like hot wax, etc. But she wasn't to blame. It was just another case of *circumstances.*

I was supposed to spend two days in contemplation, erasing from my conscience any image foreign to my new status as a Christian. This would open the way to that other eventuality, that unimaginable greatness (as Don Gonzalo put it), becoming an active, consenting Catholic. Those two days were all I had in which to examine all my sins deeply—my confessor was sure I had a whole slew of them. Having done so, I was to show up for my general confession the evening before my first communion, at the hour of the last angelus. Since the only church for twenty miles around didn't much respect the order of the day, Don Gonzalo had to explain reluctantly that the last angelus meant seven o'clock sharp.

Mother seemed to take all this quite seriously, and firmly forbade my brother's taking me on a tour of "our property."

"The less you bother him these two days, the better it will be for him and his conscience. You'll have plenty of time afterward."

What I hadn't expected was Antonio's immediate disappearance from the house; he turned up only at mealtimes, if at all. I was given the room that matched our bedroom in town, but Clara made up my brother's bed in a room that corresponded to Father's study. Being so brutally separated from Antonio made me thirst for revenge. The bed, where I practically drowned in my lonely sweat, seemed huge and deserted. (The very same bed that I carefully made up at one minute past five last Friday, and which may prove to be either my life or death warrant when you arrive.) My hands went to the places where I was used to feeling my brothers' touch.

They found nothing but a soft desert, and stiffened with tension, like lizards' tails chopped off with a stick. In vain, my back searched for my brother's chest, belly, thighs, where it had always rested. At night, my body felt so cut off from my brother's, I was sure it would stop working. Sweat ran off my skin as if I were nothing but some old pipe; my body was emptying itself through my open pores in a slow hemorrhage, not of tears, but of sweat.

I woke up pale and thin, a ghost of myself. Either I had shrunk or my clothes had grown larger. Everybody thought I was taking my examination of conscience very seriously. Mother looked at me with delight, and I thought I glimpsed in her eyes a hint of admiration at how well I was playing the game. Only Clara worriedly asked me whether I had slept all right.

"Yes."

"You know, honey . . . anyway, you don't really believe *everything* in this world is a sin, do you?"

"No."

"Then don't worry. I think you're as clean as the laundry I wash."

"Sure."

I was answering her questions but looking around for my brother. He was nowhere to be found, neither in the rooms I could see through the open doors nor in the gardens when I looked out the window. His bed was rumpled and empty, so he had slept.

A car bearing the black blotch of Don Gonzalo came to the house that afternoon. Nothing else to report. Only the despair of time standing still, and absence—*his* absence.

Before dinner, at seven in the evening, Don Gonzalo received me as planned in a corner of the library, which Mother had turned into a confessional with burgundy velvet drapes, a monk's chair, and a prie-dieu. After giving me his blessing, Don Gonzalo started the interrogation.

In the beginning, the questions were surprisingly banal. White lies, petty thefts (my confessor didn't seem to realize that we rich children didn't steal money), secret glances at certain books without my elders' permission, stubbornness toward Mother, acts of disobedience toward everybody, Clara excepted. None of it seemed too serious, and I found myself gradually getting drowsy and bored. Then we suddenly started in on the subject of nakedness.

"I understand you have been sleeping with your brother, ever since you were very small." (Mother the snitch.)

"Yes, Father."

"That isn't too serious, considering the bonds that unite you. But haven't you ever felt a contact, perhaps an odd one, between your body and his, through your pajamas?"

"We don't sleep in pajamas, Father. We have a few pairs, tailor made and monogrammed, but we don't use them. That is a sin of vanity and needless luxury I wanted to confess."

"That isn't very harmful to the soul's health, my son. But through your underpants . . . wasn't there something that probably shocked or, who knows, disgusted you? Your brother is much older and more developed than you."

"No underpants, Father."

"Naked?"

"Yes."

"Both of you?"

"Yes, and it's always been that way. Would you like me to describe my brother's surprising development, through my child's eyes?"

"No! Does he . . . love you very much?"

"Yes, Father. Is that a sin?"

"Perhaps, my son, perhaps. It all depends on the way you sleep. The most apparently innocent actions can be dictated by that rascal the devil."

"Then I'll explain, Father, and you can decide. I get scared very easily, and have since I was very little. And I get cold easily. My brother must have understood all that when I was a baby. He took me to bed with him and never put me back in my cradle. In any case, I would scream if he tried to, to tease me."

"Tried to what, my son?"

"Tried to put me back in my cradle."

"Oh. Those are just the little sins of a spoiled child; they're not important. And you would see transformations in your brother from time to time?"

"Not from time to time, Father. Every night."

"Explain what you mean, my son."

"I don't know exactly what you want to know."

"Everything, my son. When you make a general confession, you have to tell everything."

"Sins, Father?"

"My son, there are very few things in this nether world that are not sins. But the sinner isn't objective. Objective judgment is on the side of the confessor, thank God."

"*Touché,* Father. *Mea culpa.* Sometimes I don't feel like it."

"Feel like what, my son?"

"Feel like being scared or cold twice in one night."

"Twice?"

"Or three times."

"But don't you realize . . ."

"Realize what, Father?"

"The way he's warming you up, my son?"

"Oh yes, Father! Ten minutes afterward, I'm sweating, panting, even. It's better than the calisthenics he does by himself. At least, he sweats more than when he exercises. I've always told him so."

"My son, do you know the word 'fornication,' by any chance?"

"Sorry, no, Father. On the other hand, I know the word 'love.' My brother taught it to me. By the way, Father, do you wear pants, or at least underpants, under your cassock?"

"Why do you ask, my son?"

"Because you've got a hard-on, just like my brother when I snuggle up to him."

"Do you want to see for yourself?"

"No, Father. I'm in a very awkward positon, kneeling like this. It's right under my nose, and it smells bad. You don't wash yourself. My brother washes, and he smells good . . . all over."

"Would you like me to wash and come to your room tonight, to continue this confession?"

"No, Father. I just want you to give me absolution for my sins. I'm hungry."

"Not so fast, my little friend. I still have a few more questions about sin for you. Tell me, does your father have visitors?"

"Ask him."

"He listens to the radio."

"Yes."

"What does he listen to?"

"A pretty well-known thing about victory and peace. It's on almost every day."

"Have you heard it?"

"Sometimes."

"Do you like it?"

"It's very, very beautiful."

"That's a good way to be absolved of your sins, or almost. But what does he say about it?"

"I don't talk with my father."

"But he talks with the others: your brother, the maid, your mother . . ."

"Then go ask my mother."

"A saint."

"A saint."

"Have you ever heard Radio Pyrenees or Radio Moscow playing in your father's study late at night?"

"Haven't heard them. At night, I'm cold or scared. I'm in bed with my brother. *Mea culpa.*"

"Does he talk on the phone with his friends?"

"You mean my father?"

"Yes, your father."

"The telephone is Mother's exclusive domain."

"Does he ever get together with friends in the evening, to play cards?"

"In the evening, I take a bath with my brother, or else I'm asleep. *Mea culpa,* Father."

"Well, all right. Have you ever heard him talk about a gentleman called Franco?"

"Hey, I saw him once, sitting petrified on a horse. He seems to be pretty well known, doesn't he?"

". . . saying he was a killer, for example, or a son of a bitch?"

"No, Father. You're the first person ever to tell me that. Can I say that in my next confession, if it isn't with you?"

"No! And the maid, you've never heard her say anything along those lines?"

"The maid, Father, is called Clara. And she's dead. Do you understand, dead! She died of sorrow, loneliness, and disgust. And also of defeat. Dead! Now absolve my sins, Father, or I'll start yelling for help. Mother can't be very far away."

"Your mother, a saint!"

"She's a sainted bitch. And I'm her son, don't you forget it."

"Did that bastard Don Pepe teach you to talk that way?"

"Why don't you go ask him? And ask him all your other questions? Maybe he knows something about it."

*"Ego te absolvo . . ."*

I piously crossed myself.

At suppertime, Mother said, "My son Antonio will help you celebrate Mass tomorrow. He can even give the responses in Latin, which would be just the right touch."

*"Miserere nobis,"* my brother answered very calmly, a slight smile playing on his lips. (Without looking at me.)

Another solitary night, eyes and pores open.

The next morning, her face dirty and full of sleep, Clara ran the water in the bathtub, then came to my room to get me up, because the big deal was about to begin. She helped me with my bath.

"They don't call it a bath, sweetie. On occasions like this, it's called 'ablutions.' I heard señora your mother talking about it with the priest earlier."

Clara refilled the tub and poured a bottle of something into it.

"What's that?"

"Rose water, recommended by your confessor. He can't celebrate Mass without being surrounded by that perfume."

"If you knew how he stinks!"

"I know perfectly well. They're all pigs. You aren't the first to tell me that."

She poured another bottle in.

"And that?"

"Holy water, recommended by your mother. 'All's fair in love and war,' I think she said."

I climbed back into the tub. Clara pulled a watch out of her apron pocket and looked at it.

"Seven minutes. She said it's a magic number. For good luck, I think."

I started to shiver, and Clara had to cut at least two minutes off the magic time. After a good rub with the towel, she blow-dried my hair and we went back to my room, where she started opening packages. Cotton knit underwear appeared, followed one by one by a white lace shirt, white alpaca suit, white velvet bow tie, white silk socks, white pumps, and white kid gloves. I was done up like a meringue. ("Better-looking then a fresh cheese," said Clara.) She stood me in front of the mirror and spent a long time staring at me, not saying a word, with a sort of chill in her look. Then she pushed me toward the door, and we went down to the parlor for the final touches at Mother's hands.

Using a pearl-headed gold pin, Mother fastened a white silk ribbon with doves and chalices embroidered in gold thread on the left sleeve of my jacket. She gave me a prayer book bound in mother-of-pearl with more golden doves and chalices, and finally a gold and mother-of-pearl rosary. Mother also strapped a gold watch on my wrist, and for some reason sprayed me all over with deodorant and cologne.

"It's going to be a hot day. I don't want to see any flies on your clothes." I understood.

With fluttering fingers, Mother spread a special cream under my eyes.

"You're too pale. After all, you're a boy, not a bride."

I looked at her in silence.

Mother had outdone herself. She was wearing black, as usual, but had strewn herself with pearls—earrings, necklace, rings, and bracelet—and put on a black lace mantilla that spread out from her shell comb like a funeral bouquet with pearl-headed pins for pistils. She was wearing black gloves and raised doves and chalices, and carried a black marble missal and rosary.

The two of us set out for the chapel, followed by Clara, who had refused even to take off her kitchen apron. Neither my brother nor my confessor was around. Walking along a stone path that the peasants had spent hours sweeping and sprinkling, lest a stray weed or a speck of dust dirty my shoes, I was sure I had wandered into a world of schizophrenics. Behind us, Clara groused that it was really a great day to go for a picnic and not to fast for a couple of hours in a chapel that still stank of chicken shit.

"I used up two bottles of bleach, you know."

"By the way, did you bring my atomizer?"

"Yes."

"Thank God; you think of everything."

Clara made a tasteless crack about the habit we had all picked up these last months of invoking the Lord's name on every occasion. "You'd think we were in a convent."

Mother pretended not to hear.

After ten minutes' walk, we came to a somewhat strange-looking enclosure.

"This is the family cemetery," Mother explained. "My parents, my grandparents, and all their ancestors are buried here. Someday, you'll have the chance to read their names, ages, and causes of death on the tombstones. It's good marble; the inscriptions haven't worn away."

Mother's talkativeness surprised me, as well as the fact that she considered her great-grandparents to be her parents' ancestors but not her own. I thought it must have been the diseases that killed them, which she didn't deem worthy of *her* family; you never know what you can pick up in the ports of Singapore or Macao!

When we finally reached the chapel, a procession of peasants had assembled. It didn't look as if it was going to be a private ceremony after all, as Mother had led the invisible coterie to believe. And what Clara had said about the chicken droppings turned out to be true. But cows, mules, and pigs had left excrement too; together, they made the place smell like a manure pile.

The expression on the faces of the peasants, who must have been used to Mother's eccentricities, was worth seeing. You read astonishment in their eyes and a holiday smile on their lips.

In a word, something under the soft sunshine of this first day of spring was just too much. It was either them or us, but it certainly wasn't my idea of harmony.

Since the springtime softness wasn't enough to perfume the barnyard atmosphere, Mother set about spraying everything. All the breeze carried to us were rotten smells, dominated by the heavy stench of moldering straw.

It was even worse inside the chapel. A coat of whitewash, tons of Andalusian sugared flowers, and a burning censer made the air so thick you couldn't breathe; wax from dozens of lighted candles supplied the crowning touch.

As far as I could see, it was a typical cemetery chapel, bare as a tombstone. No artist's hand had painted frescoes on the walls, and the ceiling didn't suggest the brightness of heaven so much as the darkness of hell; just one small round window allowed a shaft of sun- or moonlight to fall on the cold slab bearing some old wreath of artificial flowers. Nobody had thought to set up an oil lamp with an eternal flame, or course.

The altar, flat and square as a sarcophagus, was covered with rich white embroidered cloth cascading heavily to the floor. Beautifully decorated ceramic vases held antique artificial flowers that Mother kept wrapped in tissue somewhere in the country-house closets, waxed organdy flowers handmade by anonymous nuns. Brass and silver candelabras, as intricate as African headdresses, gleamed in the darkness, thanks to the labor of peasant hands. A large missal decorated with brightly colored miniatures, which Don Gonzalo had surely brought from town. An ivory crucifix whose gaze seemed alive, staring at us. A large, handsome Chinese box inlaid with mother-of-pearl (exotic birds in impossible flight through a grove of bamboos and young ladies with slanted eyes peeping from beneath parsols), which Don Gonzalo had been forced to use to store the ciborium, where the body of Christ had lain all night long. How was it that such a huge God, who filled the entire universe all by Himself, could be locked up in a Chinese box no bigger than a canary cage? A mystery. There's an answer worthy of a Catholic, I thought.

Two mahogany prie-dieux with red velvet upholstery had been set before the altar for Mother and me to kneel on. To keep us from getting tired during the long service, two yellow satin cushions, into which our knees softly sank, had been added.

In the juxtaposition of these two colors, I was horrified to spy a cunning version of the national flag. Maybe Don Gonzalo had created it so that no one would miss the edifying parable of the son of a known republican taking his first communion under the auspices of Victory and Peace. I made up my mind to accept it all as a liturgical delirium expressed with whatever was at hand.

Like Mother, I dipped my fingers in the holy water and crossed myself very broadly. (The opulence of the gesture, I learned later, is a mark of elegance that sets the Catholic upper middle class apart from the common people. That expression, "the common people," was something I learned not from someone who had stepped straight out of the fifteenth century but from an Asturian fag who washed dishes with me in a London restaurant. He was the son of a "very good family" whose financial reverses had forced the heir to emigrate beyond the sea. You find everything in the vineyards of the Lord.)

Mother and I sat down on armchairs behind the two prie-dieux. We were very calm, very serene, and as far as I was concerned, very out of it all.

Without warning, Don Gonzalo came out from behind the altar wearing white and gold, a lump of coal disguised as a diamond. His palms were piously joined, his eyes lowered, his eyebrows thinning more than ever toward his temples. He was closely followed by Antonio, who carried an endlessly smoking censer. No music accompanied them.

So there he was, two days after his almost total disappearance and his complete absence from my bed! Ignoring Mother's sideways glance, I examined my brother at length. I tried to put only cold analysis in my look, but his beauty made me so dizzy I almost dropped my little mother-of-pearl book, which was opened to the introit.

He was wearing a navy-blue suit, a dark-blue shirt, and a cream-colored tie. He seemed bigger and huskier, hiding his too-blue eyes behind half-closed lids. He had become a man, I realized for the first time, a re-incarnation of young Carlos the way he looked in the wedding picture of my parents that Clara kept on her dresser. He had a very special look, that air of maturity that emanates from someone who has made a final decision. I would have dearly loved to know what it was.

Though she hadn't moved, I felt Mother was losing her usual composure beside me. I looked from my brother to her and saw she was wearing a smile whose passionate, luminous vibrations eclipsed everything. Mother loved her son Antonio, my brother. His presence brought back her memory of passionate young Carlos leaning against an elm tree, waiting for a young girl to join him in the darkness of the night. Against my will, I felt myself her son.

The Mass began, the Latin revealing its magic power and enchanting me, breaking down all my resistance. Nowhere in the chapel could I discern the presence of God, but the Church was playing with velvet fingers on my weakness for mystery and ritual. Within me, my brother's presence stirred a craving for apocalypse. The Latin words falling softly from his lips tickled the most secret parts of my body, as if he were speaking directly to me and not to God. When Mother and I approached the altar, his eyes suddenly widened to look at me, and the storm of my desire left me so limp I almost fell to my knees on the prie-dieu. He ran a wet tongue over his lips, and I unconsciously followed suit. He was giving signs of life, and I signs of death.

Even when he turned back to the altar, ceremonious at the heart of the ceremony, I felt his gaze still on me, seeing me beyond all appearances. My image was in his eyes, and nothing could erase it, neither objects, nor other people, nor even my absence. I was in him, merged with him. My joy was even greater than God's, in the event that God's joy is really infinite, as they say.

The little silver bell my brother had been masterfully ringing announced that the elevation was near. Don Gonzalo consecrated the wine and lifted the chalice, consecrated the host and raised the holy disk above his head. In the total silence, I didn't try to grasp the mystery of the transubstantiation but let myself be rocked by the waves of a vague worry. My brother knelt next to the altar to take communion. He looked straight at Don Gonzalo, whose hand I thought I saw tremble. I deduced that Antonio must have confessed to him that very morning, and the matter of our relations had certainly arisen. The priest looked out of sorts; my brother's confession must have been a stormy one. I felt like consoling the priest, telling him that after all, sin was his domain, and that it would be harder for him to move through a world of grace than for a trout to swim in a mud puddle. But my impulse went unsatisfied.

Together, they came over to where Mother and I were kneeling. Don Gonzalo bravely put on an expression of boundless ecstasy. Reciting his Latin phrases slowly and distinctly, he gave Mother communion. Then he moved in front of me, with Antonio on his right holding a little silver plate inlaid with gold under my chin, in case the host should drop from a clumsy mouth. That idea instantly sprang to mind, and I heard the Good Lord give a terrified yelp. From my mouth to the ground wasn't very far, but it was a drop just the same. I couldn't help wondering why God should have such an irrational fear of heights, since he had been dwelling in space for time without end, amen. I opened my mouth, and the body of Christ lay languidly on my tongue; waves of saliva washed over my teeth. The evening before, my confessor had warned me under no circumstances to swallow the host before it melted completely in my mouth, and above all not to bite into it, lest a spurt of the Savior's blood choke me forever. But now I was afraid of drowning in the rush of saliva that filled my mouth.

To Don Gonzalo's astonishment, my brother Antonio knelt down in front of me and very slowly kissed me on the lips, saying, "Take it easy, kid." (Very low.)

Mother raised her head and smiled. She had given birth to not one cataclysm but two, and she was proud of it.

Because of that look of pride, certainly, Don Gonzalo raced through the rest of the Mass, as if he had suddenly realized that it was too late to stand on ceremony. And we all returned to the house for my first communion breakfast.

Long tables had been set out in the hallway, parlor, and kitchen, laden with hors d'oeuvres, fancy cakes, and several of those large earthenware jugs that are used to store olives from one year to the next, now filled with a deluxe champagne and fruit sangria. Mother must have secretly set every nun in the vicinity to work cooking or baking.

Just as I was wondering how the five of us could possibly eat all that, a long parade of peasants who worked on Mother's estate appeared in the garden's main walkway. The line was headed by Clara, keeping order in a voice like a sergeant major's. As best she could, Clara got them all to file by to give me the traditional coin—the symbol of a somewhat secular joy—after which they threw themselves on the goodies like a pack of wolves. Mother laughed with delight and kept telling them to watch out for indigestion.

"At times like these, I feel more at ease with them than with my own friends," she confided to Don Gonzalo. "I can't stand people who just pick at their food."

"They are the Lord's children too, my daughter."

"I'm perfectly aware that my friends are the Lord's children, Father."

"I didn't mean them, daughter."

"Who, then?"

"Your workers."

"But Father, I never doubted it," answered Mother, an elegant smile on her lips.

And Clara, who just happened to be passing, put in her two cents' worth.

"Just forgotten children, that's all."

"Do you feel the Lord has forgotten you, my daughter?" asked the priest, showing his cannibal's teeth.

"I don't feel anyone has forgotten me. I'm dead, and the dead don't need anyone to remember them."

She came over and kissed me on both cheeks. "But this one's alive!"

Her laughter burst out amid the cheers of the peasants, their mouths and pockets full. Over the clamor, I heard our confessor asking Mother:

"My daughter, are you sure you pay enough attention to your employees' religious duties? I hope you have understood at last how important it is to bring order to faith and the practice of the faith after a civil war."

The remark was so tactless, Mother didn't bother to answer.

When the procession was over. Antonio came up to me, took my hand, and slipped a finely wrought gold ring onto my finger: a heart was cut into the stone, with our initials and the date inscribed on the band.

"The date of my first communion? Is it really that important to you?"

"Yes."

"I wouldn't have thought so. I haven't seen you in two days."

"You'll find out later why today's date is so important. Now we're going for a walk; I'm going to show you our property."

"Our property." An odd expression, I thought, having never felt that anything of Mother's belonged to me. But my brother thought otherwise.

Without comment, Mother and Don Gonzalo watched us go outside. Things seemed to be returning to normal. I had gotten back my place in my brother's world, and he once again held sway over me.

Outside, on the big terrace, Antonio described the extent of "our property" and asked me to choose which way to go.

"Show me whatever you want to. You're the one who knows."

Taking me by the hand, he set out for a dry hill that looked as if it had been scorched by the sun since the beginning of time. Surrounded by rocks, covered with dust, it was like some dead planet, awesome and beautiful. A pair of unusually bold crows were hopping from rock to rock.

"What are they doing?"

"They're hunting for snakes."

"Are there snakes here?"

My voice must have sounded a bit shaky, because Antonio started laughing. "Yes, thick as ropes. But don't worry, they're not poisonous."

"I'm not afraid."

"Good. Do you see that mountain over there? That's where the spring I want to show you is."

"Do you think we can get there today?"

"It's an hour's walk. Don't you think you can do it?"

"Of course I can."

"Well, let's go!"

Taking a twisting path, we left the hill with the snakes behind, and walked for a long time under olive trees and walnut trees loaded with young walnuts, where the going was easier. A light breeze tried to show that it was springtime, and cool, but it didn't really succeed. Crickets abruptly stopped chirping as we passed. My brother caught one in the hollow of his hand and gave it to me. I took it with a kind of respect; it was like holding a living piece of wood. The cricket started flapping its wings, and I let it go, but Antonio didn't laugh, the way he usually did. He seemed distracted. Walking across "our property" was no fun at all, I decided, and took a very obvious look at my gold wristwatch.

"We've been walking for more than an hour."

"We still have a ways to go. It's a little further, you know. I told you an hour so as not to scare you off."

I fell silent.

"If you're tired, I can carry you on my shoulders."

"I'm not tired, and I'm not five years old anymore, for you to be carrying me piggyback."

"That's exactly what I was thinking."

But after another half hour's walk through the vineyards, being careful not to dirty my fancy clothes, I found I had to hang on to my brother's arm. He took my hand and gave me the first passionate kiss I'd had in all these last two endless days. It excited him right away, and I started to feel better. I became more talkative and didn't miss a single detail of our walk.

We finally reached the top of the mountain at about eleven in the morning. It was as rocky as the hill with the snakes, but the perfect blue of the sky lent it a kind of peaceful beauty. Overhead two eagles were gliding so slowly they looked as if they were out for a stroll.

Out of breath—I was, at least—we reached the entrance to an old mine, surrounded by jonquils, mosquitoes, and dragonflies. Cool grass grew around it in an excess of tenderness, and a gray rabbit darted off when he spotted us. A channeled steam ran down toward "our property."

Antonio pulled out a flashlight and announced that we were going into the mine.

"Isn't it kind of dark in there?"

"You're with me, aren't you?"

He seemed angry or impatient; it wasn't like him.

We went about three hundred yards in the dark, with me following, stooped over and clutching his hand. Bats hugging the stone walls stirred restlessly in the beam of light; they gave me the shivers. Then I suddenly saw a glow, and soon blinding sunshine at the end of the darkness. I assumed that it was another entrance to the mine, but I was wrong. When we got closer, I realized we were in an enormous well some five yards across and at least fifteen deep, with the spring bubbling up in its center. The bottom of the well was a carpet of fine sand, and its whole interior a dense cloud of white butterflies.

Open-mouthed, I gaped at this miracle in the very heart of the rock. The sun was roasting up above, but down here its heat was tempered by the soft shade of the fig trees that ringed the well, and the swarm of butterflies filled the air with golden light.

"Tired?"

"Yes."

"Lie down on the sand," he said. "It's very clean. Are you thirsty?"

"Yes."

My brother gave me water to drink from his cupped hands.

"Hot?"

"Yes."

Antonio started to undress me, piling my carefully folded clothes off to one side, along with my prayer book, rosary, and shoes.

During the few moments this took, my brother's eyes never left me, and his hands skillfully stroked each part of my body as he undressed it. Gradually, I noticed that his caresses had changed character, that his hands were trying to make me aware of what they were doing and of my own body's response. I was in the presence of someone new, a man who up to then had always kept his real desire in check and was at last going to satisfy it in me.

And I was someone else too, even while staying the same. The very familiar feelings I experienced when my brother touched me were now joined by a fierce power and extreme lassitude. The taste of the body of Christ had hardly left my mouth when my brother's tongue hungrily pushed into it, wiping away the last traces. I was frightened and awed. I was shivering, completely lost in this new encounter. Wasn't my brother ever going to undress, in the filtered sunlight and the swarm of white butterflies? Pressing myself naked against his clothes was driving me out of my mind. But he kept all of his man's secrets hidden, and maybe that was why my flesh was becoming more and more precious to him.

Finally he couldn't control his desire any longer. He pulled down his pants and took me with a thrust of his hips. The butterfly-filled air shook with my cry, and a shower of golden motes rained down on us.

"Go ahead, shout! Shout louder! Don't be afraid!"

My brother was still inside me, his trembling arms squeezing me with all their might, his teeth biting my hair.

It was the longest and the shortest moment of my life. I felt it was *truly* the day of my first communion, and my brother Antonio had chosen it carefully. I hadn't been out of his thoughts during the two days he had deserted my bed, I now realized. Quite the contrary; his lover's will had been carefully planning my final retreat from the world of other people and my entry into his.

"Did I hurt you?"

"Yes . . . no . . ."

"Do you want me to pull out?"

"No! Stay, stay! . . . Yes!" (That joyful, painful cry again, followed again by the golden shower of butterflies.) "Tonio!"

"What?"

"Do you love me?"

"I love you!"

My brother liked those words so much, he repeated them over and over, each time pushing a little deeper into me, appropriating the wild discovery of my body, his shout mingling with mine in my mouth.

I had my first real orgasm in the most beautiful place on earth, and Antonio had chosen it for me. The water from the spring murmured in my ears, and my eyes were lost in a kaleidoscope of butterflies, the whole dominated by my brother's god-face.

"Do you know you're my god?"

"I know you're *my* god."

Which of us asked? Which answered? Impossible to say. Each one's words formed in the other's mouth; we spoke and heard them from within.

We stayed there for hours. My brother took me three times, and I bravely bore his weight as long as I had to. I loved the merciless pain my brother caused me, bringing me to the edge of delirium. I realized this delirium was a world he had spent years preparing me for, and that he was drawn to it as irresistibly as I was.

When the sun left the butterfly well, Antonio decided we should go back. His pants were flecked with blood; I wasn't able to stand right away. Using spring water, he washed that part of me he "loved the most," saying we had to be careful "it didn't break down." He thought his cynicism hilarious and started laughing like crazy, as usual.

I looked at him with my most serious face.

"Don't you think so?" he asked.

I didn't answer, and clung to him as he helped me dress. We left the butterfly well and the mine, and headed for home. Held up by my brother's arm, I was walking like an invalid. His eyes clouded over.

"You aren't in pain, are you?"

"No, of course not."

Gradually, my strength returned. Raising my head, I kissed him on the lips. Happiness spread across his face, and he bit me on the nose.

"Are you all right now?"

"Yes, I'm all right. We can do it again whenever you like."

My brother squeezed my neck.

"Tonight."

"OK."

We reached the house at last light. Starved, Antonio asked Clara if dinner was ready. Mother and Don Gonzalo stood looking at us from the wreckage of the hallway after the party. "Did you have a nice walk?" señor my confessor asked.

"Yes, thank you."

"I gave him the landlord's tour. From today on, he's not a child anymore."

Unconsciously, Mother and the priest both glanced at my brother's fly, which still showed a few suspicious stains. I had no trouble following their thoughts.

A few minutes later Antonio and I sat down to eat; at the end of the meal, we went up to our room. Clara had made up the bed with clean sheets that smelled of quince and two pillows. She had also laid out our pajamas . . . for appearance' sake. (Wise Clara.)

# ∾ Evgeny Kharitonov ∾

## One Boy's Story: "How I Got Like That"

TRANSLATED BY KEVIN MOSS

"So for the Eighth of March I went to Moscow. And that's where I found out. No, before that there was the thing with that people's artist. He came to visit our school, asked me to come to his place to pose. Well, then he started talking about certain subjects, but it was all very tactful, and the main theme was the relationship between teacher and pupil. He showed me so much about art; he said this should be the most important thing for me, that all those distractions are a swamp, that first I had to study, to become an artist. Almost everything was clean with him, or it would have been repulsive—he's sixty. I respected him as a person; he taught me a lot of good things. But in bed we mostly just lay there, he just liked to stroke me, went into raptures over me, over my body, said I was everything to him—son, wife, friend, pupil. He had a family, though, a wife and a daughter. Then he sent me to Moscow for the holiday, the Eighth of March, to look at the museums, the exhibits, gave me the address of his friend, he's married and not like that. Well, in Moscow I found out: at Bykovo Airport I went into the toilet, and there're signs there, look into such and such a hole, and one guy beckoned me with his finger, gave me a blow job through the hole."

---

*EVGENY KHARITONOV believed that he, after St. John the Evangelist and Oscar Wilde, was the third most significant writer in the world. Born in Moscow in 1941, he died of a heart attack on a street there in 1981, never having published a word.*

And how did you find out they meet downtown?

"Well, this guy told me and offered to meet me. I didn't go, but over the next few days I met others, and that's how I found all this out. All I had to do was appear, and they'd all come right up: I won't go with this one, won't go with that one, I'd look for someone I liked."

And before, when you were a boy, something like that happened, probably, with some school pal, like kids do?

"Yes, there was one friend, we used to jerk each other off."

Often?

"As soon as there was nobody around, we'd jerk off. But we just jerked off, nothing else."

And you also had girls?

"What do you mean? Of course." And how come no steady girlfriend?

"Well, they're like stupid, all of them, and I never had a steady girlfriend. Just to go out with her, take her places and talk about God knows what, that's not interesting. They don't want to sleep with you, what they need more is just love and an escort. Well, there were some special cases, yes, I liked them a lot. At the collective farm with one, I checked the clock, I was plowing her an hour and ten minutes, as an experiment. I was controlling things, I'd feel the end soon and hold back; she was already streaming."

Well, do you like it better with girls or with boys?

"With girls, of course, everything inside them there wraps around you, it's always nice and wet."

But gradually he told more about those days in Moscow and about all his liaisons.

"To be honest, it didn't all begin in Moscow, at Bykovo, or with the artist. Once when I was passing through Kirov I went into the toilet, and there was some graffiti: Go to another toilet, on such and such a street. I went there."

And you weren't scared? Weren't turned off?

"Well, nobody in the city knew me, and I didn't know anyone. And I was leaving that evening. There was one guy standing there, scary, though he was young, with glasses and thick lips. He suggested we go into the stall, two different stalls, next to each other, and he motioned to me with his finger and went down on me. Oh! And that was even better than in a pussy, even wetter. His mouth was so big, he didn't scratch with his teeth, and it was all so soft. I was in ecstasy. And he was so delighted, he says, You have such a big one! Let's meet again! I say, No, I can't, I'm leaving today.

He says, When you come back let's see each other, I'll wait for you. But he was so scary, with those thick lips, that big mouth. So when I came back to Izhevsk I started to look for people like that."

And where did you find them?

"Well, in the same places, at the station. But they're all so awful, there aren't any cute young ones at all, and they laugh at each other. They all have nicknames—one's Juliet, another's Jacqueline, one they called Nun, she used to work in a church, she corrupted everyone there. So when the people's artist came to visit our school, I already knew all this. And I immediately knew what he was up to when he invited me to his place. When I was posing, he'd immediately started these conversations. He'd touch me lightly. Oh, he'd say, what equipment you've got. This was in his studio. Then we went into the other room, there next to an embroidered sofa was a table with drinks. Then he asked me to lie down on the sofa with him, he touched my cock, said women would all go crazy, caressed me. But of course I found him unpleasant in bed—he was so old—but as a person, that was something else, he gave me a lot, we had sort of a friendship. I respected him. He would say, Ah, I would gladly give myself to you, but my hole is narrow, it won't go in. He blew me, but mostly just to make me happy; he'd take a little, he couldn't do like that guy with the lips. And he used to say, Never in your life tell anyone that you come to see me, and don't say you posed. He made me a present of my portrait, asked me not to show it to anybody, then he says, Someday, when you finish school and become an artist, then you can show it. I'll say to myself, This is my pupil. But now you can't. I'd have to commit suicide, I'd be expelled everywhere, I have so many enemies! For the Eighth of March I decided to go to Moscow for the first time. He told me to go see the museums, gave me an address where I could stay, and so I got downtown, and the main thing was meeting people; this guy named Misha came up to me the last night, pleasant-looking, with a little mustache, I liked him right away, and we went to his place. He lived with his sister and her husband; they weren't home. We went into his bathroom, and he greased me and fucked me from behind. And I liked him so much, I wanted to blow him myself, the only time. But I didn't! I really didn't want to say good-bye to him. It was such an unusual situation. His sister and her husband didn't come home, and I slept with him all night. The next day I had to catch the plane, and I couldn't bear to leave him until the last minute! Somehow I made the plane. I couldn't think about anything else, my mind was only on him.

Spring had begun in our city, and I walked around town looking for some-body who might look like him, but there was no one. We wrote each other. I was waiting for May Day, so I could go to Moscow again. I told my teacher all about him, but he said that it was very bad, I should study and think only about school, and these adventures were a swamp, they would pull me in. He talked me out of it, didn't let me go to Moscow. And I wrote Misha that I wasn't coming. Since then I haven't gotten any letters from him. And I also wrote a letter to that friend of mine Sasha, who I jerked off with all through school, saying we should see each other, I'd tell him something! I went to Moscow, it'll take your breath away. Come, for God's sake, I can't describe it all. So instead of going to Moscow for May Day to see Misha, I listened to the artist and went home to my village and saw Sasha, this school friend of mine. He listened and even moaned, then he ran the bath and said, Do to me everything they did to you in Moscow! I'd got blown there; was I supposed to do that to him? I had gotten tired of that sort of bent cock of his with the blue head when we were kids. Well, I figured, so be it, went down on him, and almost threw up. That was the only time, never again, for anybody! He's sort of delicate, sits at home all the time, likes to read about history, all about medieval Russia, doesn't accept anything Western, such a patriot, and listens only to classical music, doesn't like rock groups and pop singers, only recently began to lis-ten to them a little. And what kind of friend is he? You know who your friends are in times of trouble, but with him it's only when something in-terests him but if not . . . So we went, for example, once back in high school, to a dance, where all the girls kept asking me to dance, and their boyfriends threatened me, so I'd go away. Well, I didn't want to look like a coward, and kept on dancing. And they hauled me off to the side and broke my lip. And Sasha also started saying let's go, didn't stay with me, got scared. That's what kind of friend he is."

~ ~ ~

For the November holidays I went back to Izhevsk myself and saw them all, including the people's artist and, a bit later, Sasha. We agreed that Seryozha would invite Sasha when I came. The people's artist is not an old man at all, as he appeared from Seryozha's story. Just of the postwar school. And his studio isn't the stereotypical basement, as I imagined. A big clean room in a new building, not a spot of dust. Pictures like in the Palace of Culture. The people's artist was very quiet, polite, making sure that his name wouldn't get into the story. And it wouldn't be bad if some new gangster coming to take his place were to publicly defame him, write to *Krokodil,* break everything he has, and send him out into the world. Then maybe he would turn into a real artist.

Sasha came for the holiday. Here they are, Sasha and Seryozha, next to each other. Seryozha is breezy, he's a dancer, and his dormmates sense that somehow he's not like they are and like him for it; unconsciously they even flirt. And Sasha has already gotten so used to sitting at home reading about medieval Russia and the church that he'll just keep doing it. Until something drops into his life. Like when he knew that someone was coming from Moscow to visit Seryozha, then he also came. And was waiting to see what would come of it. But things don't start by themselves. I think his heart was sinking, but he didn't let on. Then in bed he was so willing, so gentle. So skinny, warm, young. He found everything that was done to him sweet. He touched my cock with a tentative hand. Again, only if I put his hand there myself. But he wouldn't have done it on his own, just in case.

I predict for him the following path: He really should go into the church. There all his lines would meet. He couldn't even pass his favorite subject, history, at the institute, because he more or less knew only medieval Russia. Such a wonderful narrowness. What a gift to love one thing and not look to the right or the left. And his mind-set is humble, not creative. He'll remember what happened when, what people's names were, what rank. But so much the better! And how refreshing. He won't become a heretic theologian, an arrogant Florensky. He'll just be a good, obedient holy father. Seryozha says, What do you mean, how can he go against his father and mother (his father's a party organizer at the collective farm, his mother a teacher); it would be a disgrace for them. Oh no, Seryozha, I say. Sasha only has to work up his courage, explain things to his parents. Despite that antireligious propaganda, he'll say, the church has its value from the Soviet point of view; it also has ranks and opportunities for advancement. Before the holidays, he'll say, Brezhnev gave medals to the patriarch and the metropolitans. The old ladies in the village have long thought that Sasha would be a priest because he collects old books and crosses. And being a priest would suit him so well. He has such expressive eyes, long black eyebrows, bright lips; the beard will look good. He'll have to apply himself, go to Zagorsk. That's where his happiness lies. Among the seminarians, of course, sodomy flourishes, as it does in the church in general, to say nothing of the monastic life. But if a boy hides from the other boys in a corner, doesn't play their war games, if a boy occupies himself with dreams of something other than war, other than cars, dreams about unmarried saints dressed up in holy robes, this boy, as Rozanov said, is a boy-girl. He recognizes in their pacifism his own and is glad there is a morality that holds it in such esteem.

But Sasha has another, nonchurch path as well.

Seryozha told the people's artist about Sasha, like he told me. And the people's artist also started quizzing him. He'd say, When Sasha comes, you have to bring him to see me; he'd say, I'll get him into the history department, I have connections. And Sasha himself lectured his friend: Why don't you value the people's artist? He has such connections, he'll help you in life. In other words, Sasha would be a find for the people's artist. The artist wanted so much to have a discreet, steady, non-partying boy. And Sasha would have been content to be faithful to the old man. But Sasha would have become a historian; then would come social sciences, party membership; the artist would have married him off to cover their affair, and everything would have been arranged according to the mousy tastes of the people's artist. Seryozha shouldn't introduce them! Let him go into the church. And we'll put a cross on the map of the USSR where a young priest we know serves.

# ~ *Manuel Puig* ~

## FROM

## *Betrayed by Rita Hayworth*

TRANSLATED BY SUZANNE JILL LEVINE

There are three little boy dolls, and the queen of France, her hair is done in an upsweep and her skirt is as full as can be, the three little boy dolls in white stockings all the way up to their bloomers, the girl dolls in silk costumes and the boy dolls in silk costumes too, Mommy, and the men in white dickeys same as you, tiny lacing, white wigs, they're porcelain and stand on a shelf, of the mother of the boy next door, and they're hard, you can't eat them, dressed the same as the silly face dolls, they are kind, and look at a girl doll sitting in a hammock, painted on the cover of your box of spools, in the drawer next to the tablecloth and napkins, the box that had candy before. They were dressed up in the same costumes in the Charity Show at P.S. 3, the biggest kids dressed like the dolls for the gavotte, the best dance at P.S. 3 Mommy! why didn't you come? with Daddy, because Mommy on duty at the drugstore missed all the dances the kids did at P.S. 3. It was a little boy doll and a little girl doll, and a little tree and a little house, all ending with toothpicks stuck on top of the nut cake, right? Or was it a custard cake? You ate a little doll Mommy, I ate another

---

*MANUEL PUIG was born in the Argentine pampas in 1932, studied philosophy at the University of Buenos Aires, then won a scholarship from the Italian Institute in Buenos Aires in 1956 to study film direction at Cinecittà (Rome). His novel* Betrayed by Rita Hayworth, *like* Kiss of the Spider Woman, *pays homage to old movies.*

with a green hat, did I eat his head? does it hurt the dolls? and Felisa had the little tree that was made of sugar too, painted many colors. Daddy doesn't like sweet things but the boy next door is in second grade and has no more canary, let me change its water, "No, no" the boy next door because I went to kindergarten one week only, right? in the Charity Show the other kids who went to kindergarten a whole year did the little dwarf number that I didn't like. One day I practiced, all the other little kids go one after the other on line and the teacher at the piano sang si fa sol-sol-sol la and all the kids walking one leg lame and at the same time bending over on the same side, I did the wrong leg and didn't want to go to kindergarten anymore: can't I borrow it? "When the canary sings it's because he's happy" because it's his birthday? did the mother of the boy next door put a sponge cake in the oven? Mommy, it's not baked yet, I'll stick a toothpick in it and if the toothpick comes out all clean the cake is all finished baking but no, until it cools off you can't cut it and put in the custard, what scrumptious smoke comes out of the oven and goes all around the house and gets to the canary, right? it touches his little beak and that's why he sings until the boy next door had no more canary. The boy told me and his mother told me: it's the cat's fault. Does the cat know how to cook? with potatoes? and garlic and parsley? the boy next door "I went to look for the bag of birdseed and forgot to close the cage, to make a long story short I heard a noise, the cat had jumped from the table to the cage and with one paw he popped the canary into his mouth and when I turned around the canary wasn't there anymore," in one piece? did he swallow him in one piece? "the cat swallowed him in one piece and it went right down to his tummy, that's why he's so fat, touch his tummy" Mommy! don't look at him! me neither, I look at him from far away, and didn't you call the police? in the boy's house they let the cat sleep in the hall. But in kindergarten I stayed only three days, that's all, the boy next door "In first grade you have adding and subtraction, if you're stupid the teacher'll break your back with the pointer if you don't learn": the march of the little dwarfs was the ugliest dance in the Charity Show at P.S. 3, at the Town Hall and Daddy "Waiter, what's for dinner?" before the dances they serve smooth yellow mayonnaise, Daddy's plate was decorated with a little sardine, right? But I'm stuck with the green and black olives! I don't like them! Daddy, you're not eating the sardine? let me have it Daddy, have to go weewee! "You can go by yourself," I can't reach the light! but Mommy at the movies at intermission all the lights go on "Let's take advantage and go weewee now" to the ladies' room "because women can't go into the men's." A big girl. With a hard starched dress that scratches, she scratches with her dress, the Witch of Snow White scratches with her beak nose, sitting at the next table, no, don't ask her! "Honey, can you take my little boy to the bathroom?" Daddy, she can't take me to the men's room "It doesn't matter, take him to the ladies' room" no, you come! "What bathroom does Mommy take you to in the movies?" through a hallway in the Town Hall there's a locked door and if it were open I would escape to the drugstore where you were Mommy, right across the square, right, Felisa? "A bad gypsy with a face made of coal and hairy arms steals little boys who are well dressed and have run away," because once I ran out by myself to the square. An open door in the hallway but it wasn't the bathroom the biggest kids are dressing up for the gavotte and on the hook a pink mask I can't reach, which of the kids will put it on? a boy or a girl? The light is on in the ladies' bathroom like our bathroom except there's no bathtub and can the big girl reach the light? "Aren't you ashamed to be in the ladies' room, sissy?" the light is already on and the girl didn't close the door, I can escape, Felisa, is he behind the door? the gypsy puts the little boy in his bag and on the street nobody realizes it but a policeman puts him in jail because he knows he's a gypsy, yes, but the gypsy puts on the pink mask and says "I'm carrying a cat with rabies and scabs in my bag" and if the boy shouted at that very moment when the gypsy unties him afterwards where are the gypsies' tents? "They already left Vallejos, but one stayed behind and steals little boys" where is he hiding, Felisa? "On the other side of the park pond, where the horse corral is, his face looks black like coal" and he hits little boys with his whip, just like horses. The teachers hit with their pointers, but not the kids in kindergarten, and the girl can reach up and turn off the light before I finish going weewee and Daddy "Thank you for taking him, honey" and he patted her on the cheek without getting scratched by her dress. And what's for dessert? A whipped cream cake with a cherry on top "No, waiter, I don't want cake" Daddy! let me have it! I'll eat your cake and mine, Mommy gives me her cake, so she doesn't get fat, in the Vallejos–La Plata sleeping car "You better behave, this is not home," Daddy I asked for your cake since mine didn't have a cherry "Don't tell lies, you know what happens to little boys who tell lies, they grow a tail and look like monkeys" and now they're turning the lights off "If you don't behave we're going to go right home without seeing the dances" and if I tell Daddy the truth that I came back from the bathroom without going weewee he'll take me home before the dances begin and the big painted curtain rises, the national emblem on the stage because "Our pupil Joaquín Rossi will recite for us the beautiful poem 'Our Country' by Francisco Rafael Caivano" but don't ask the girl, Daddy, the light is on in the ladies' room and I can go alone, nobody is in the other room where all the clothes are hanging, on top of the chair I can reach the pink mask and if at that very minute the kindergarten teacher comes in I'll tell her a dog came by and I climbed on the chair so he couldn't bite me and should I go to the bathroom with the pink mask on? so the gypsy will think I'm somebody else, I climb on the chair "What are you doing here? what are you messing around with?" A big boy disguised as a Chinaman! He wasn't dressed up for the gavotte which is only for the kindest big boys! did you really see a dog? since smaller boys shouldn't tell lies because a long tail grows behind them like monkeys and then it's easy for the gypsy to get me, he grabs me by the tail and that's that, "What are you messing around with?" and I couldn't tell him the lie about the dog; I told him I had gone to the bathroom where men are supposed to go. Kindergarten wasn't a garden, just a room with a table full of wet sand, but Daddy didn't want the cake I missed getting with a cherry; the wine jug at home has a yummy red top like a cherry, too bad it's made of glass. Mommy, after the movie let's go see the store windows, will you promise to take me? a long stop in front of the toy store window with the painted wooden cow and a wire tree, the cheapest ugly cardboard houses because Felisa is going to be late with supper and can we take advantage and look at the funny faces? all the wedding pictures in the photographer's window and Mommy doesn't it make your mouth water? the pastry shop man changes his window every day: for my birthday we ate the chocolate one, the cake roll you know how to make, but the one with whipped cream makes you sick, right? and the more expensive one filled with ice cream and glazed fruit; a big green fruit in the middle like the stone on your brooch. Where are you going? Is it naptime already? Where? you don't have to work in the hospital today, where are you going? to bake a cake? Mommy! don't leave me alone, I want to play some more! why don't you bake me a cake? Mommy's not going into the kitchen, is she going into the bedroom to look for the recipe book? Daddy called her and Mommy had to go in to take a nap. And the only thing I'm going to cover is my mouth, I don't want to cover my nose with the scarf, I won't obey and Daddy isn't cold, he put on the poncho, it was Uncle Perico's who died, at the end of the Charity Show it's very cold out since it's so late, much further if we go by the toy store but Mommy always takes me home but first we go by the toy store: on that corner the one under the light there must be a policeman, it's not the gypsy, I don't want to go that way! Let's go look at the window! "People don't make so much noise at one o'clock in the morning" and the light in the window is off, "I told you the light wasn't on, because of your silly notion we have to go three blocks out of the way" did they change yesterday's toys? can't see a thing, the ones that are hanging up look to me like yesterday's, it's so dark, the only thing you can really see in the glass are the houses on the other side of the street and the trees along the sidewalk like in a mirror, all black because the trees on the sidewalk and the face in the glass are black like coal and the cherry top is glass, if not I would eat it up. Who's looking at himself in the glass? it's not him because that ugly poncho is Uncle Perico's, and it's a good thing Mommy and Felisa waited with all the lights on because Mommy is afraid of the night until Daddy and I got back from the Charity Show. But now she's taking a nap, Amparo went to Buenos Aires and she's not coming back anymore and Héctor went to play with the big boys. The boy next door "Is Héctor your brother?" Mommy slaps me but it doesn't hurt much and Héctor too but he's bigger than me, he runs faster, Mommy can't catch him and the boy next door "Your Daddy is the goodest of all, gooder than mine" because he never spanks me, and he never spanks Héctor either and once I woke Mommy up during naptime because I'm bored and Daddy "I never slapped you but the day I put my hands on you I'll break you in two" and I'm going to think about the movie I like the best because Mommy told me to think about a movie so I wouldn't get bored at naptime. *Romeo and Juliet* is about love, it has a sad ending when they die, one of the movies I liked the best. Norma Shearer is an actress who's never naughty. Mommy slaps me but it doesn't hurt much but when Daddy slaps you he breaks you in two. In Héctor's communion book there was a saint just like Norma Shearer; a nun with a white costume and some white flowers in her hand. I have pictures of her serious, laughing and in profile cut out of every magazine, in lots of movies I have never seen. And Felisa "Tell me what happens in the musical" and I told her lies not that the two of them danced alone and the wind lifted up her dress and his coattails, but that some birdies came flying along slowly and lifted her dress and his coattails because Ginger Rogers and Fred Astaire rise in the air to music, and the air carries them high with the birdies who help them twirl faster and faster, what a pretty flower! I think Ginger wants it, a white flower high up in a tree and does she ask a birdie to get it? and the birdie makes believe he doesn't hear her, when I want to give them bread crumbs they get frightened and I have to go far away. Are they afraid of me? and of Mommy too? but there's a birdie who's the kindest of all and when Ginger is not looking . . . he flies over and cuts the flower from the tree and puts it in her blond hair and then Fred Astaire sings to her that she looks pretty with the flower and she looks at herself in the mirror and has the flower that she wanted in her hair, like a barrette, and she calls to the good birdie to come to her hand and pets him a lot. Felisa believes every bit of it and it's a lie, just in *Snow White* all the birdies are friendly, because it's an animated cartoon, when it isn't an animated cartoon they can't make the birdies come to their hands since they're afraid, Choli's pigeon is not afraid, but the birds are prettier. The pigeon goes to the pear tree and back and does some twirls like in *Snow White* because Choli couldn't take it on the train, she went away forever to Buenos Aires "The only friend I have in Vallejos" and she went away. Mommy doesn't have any other friend, I'm close by and the pigeon eats, sleeps at night in the garden in a high little house without a door. The birdies come down to eat the bread and milk that Felisa makes for them and a lot of them go up to the roof and the trees all together and come back down, and each time they take a little bread, but I have to look from far away. Felisa, can't the cats get up to the pigeon's little house? "Nobody can reach this pigeon, cats or buzzards" Mommy has to promise me they can't, what are buzzards, Felisa? "They are big ugly birds" What do they look like? "They're big, black, with hooked beaks" how big are they? no, they're not as big as cats "Like cats more or less." Mommy! the little pigeon has to sleep with me! in the garden at night the little house doesn't have a door, cats have big mouths, but does he pull out the feathers with his hooked beak before he eats the little pigeon? No, pigeons don't let themselves get caught, they fly fast, much faster than the bad birds that are heavier with their bellies stuffed from eating . . . canaries? When Mommy gets up from her nap she has to promise me that nobody can get the little pigeon, it twirls here and there, Mommy throws streamers better than anybody untwisting and making more twirls than a birdie until they hit the ground, Ginger Rogers twirls all around a big house and they had to take all the furniture out so that Ginger wouldn't bump into anything, she knows how to tap-dance without scratching the floor. Before, all her movies were funny, Saturday we saw the best Ginger Rogers film because it's a musical

and has a sad ending, that Fred Astaire dies in the war in the crashed airplane and she's waiting for him but he doesn't come. And there's trouble
because they're waiting for them since they have to dance together in a
Charity Show, and then she sees that his fat friend comes to bring bad
news and he looks at her very sad almost crying and she realizes, then tears
fall down her cheek and she looks toward the stage where nobody's there
because Fred Astaire isn't coming back anymore because he died, and then
she sees her and him come out transparent, 'cause she imagines that after
dying they keep dancing and they go further and further away and get
smaller and smaller and out there they twirl around some trees and then
you don't see them anymore. Where are they going, Mommy? "You can
see through them, they're transparent, it means she will love him forever
the same as when they danced together, even though he's dead now" is
Ginger sad? "No, because it's like they were together, now nothing can
keep them apart, war or no war." Héctor isn't my brother, Mommy says
Héctor is my cousin but his mother is sick and Héctor lives in my house
but he doesn't play with me and the picture cards. I have all of *Romeo and
Juliet* drawn on picture cards, first the black crayon for sketching and then
all the colored ones for coloring in the movies that Mommy drew Romeo
on one card, Juliet on another, then the balcony and Romeo, who is
climbing up the rope ladder and Juliet who's waiting for him, and yesterday
she finished drawing a whole other movie, the one of Ginger Rogers and
the guy who dies, and Mommy told me if I behaved well and didn't make
any noise at naptime she's going to draw me another movie, it's playing this
Thursday and it's the most beautiful musical and Mommy says she saw
some pictures of it and it's as fancy as can be. It's called *The Great Ziegfeld*
and it's lucky Mommy can go to the movies this Thursday, she doesn't have
to be on duty at the drugstore. Héctor doesn't want to play with me, only
with big boys like him. Pocha Perez too, she's twelve years old "Come
around at naptime and I'll let you play with the manger" at the end of *Romeo and Juliet* Pocha, her mother and her aunt were in the row in back and
Mommy "I saw *Romeo and Juliet* on stage in Buenos Aires" and she's going
to let me go back alone one day at naptime to play with Pocha because she
lives on the corner and I don't have to cross the street "Pocha, play with
the little boy so we can talk awhile with Mita" and at the end of *Romeo and
Juliet* Pocha showed me the manger that she has all set up in the dining
room "Don't touch!" can't I touch the little cow? and since I don't have to
cross the street I went to Pocha's house one day at naptime; she has black

paper curls and a dress with little green flowers, she has two of the same kind one with green flowers and one with blue flowers, her aunt is sitting at the sewing machine. "Know something, Pocha? In the row in front of us at the movies there was a little old lady who was crying" and naughty Pocha laughed. "How that poor little old lady cried" because I cried when Romeo and Juliet die and I went to play with the manger: it's all set up in the dining room and the piano's in the hall and she's going to let me play "We can't play with the manger or piano because they're taking their nap, let's make believe you're the boy and I'm the teacher" no! "that's the way you learn to count," no Pocha, when you going to lend me the manger? "You can't take it apart" after naptime it's too late and I have to go to the movies with Mommy "You're too young, we can't play because you don't know anything," I know every game there is "You're too young" no I'm not, I play drawing movies with Mommy "Let's play taking a nap" how do we do it? "We make believe I'm sleeping on the roof and I'm asleep covered up with a blanket but I don't have any underpants on. And you are a big boy, and you come . . . and do something to me" do what? "That's the game, you have to guess" if I guess can we play with the manger afterwards but what does the boy who comes on the roof do? Mommy didn't look, the murder movie is scary and somebody comes into a dark room and the murderer's behind the door and Mommy and me we didn't look because it's a scary movie and before the long movie once they showed a short movie about the bottom of the sea and it has hairs that wave like streamers but "Don't look" and I looked, I was naughty when the little fishes with many colors came close and went right next to the carnivorous plants at the bottom of the sea. "Swear by your mother you don't know what the big boys do" I sweat I don't "When the boy climbs up to the roof while I'm sleeping he takes off my blanket and fucks me." What does "fuck" mean? "It's a bad thing that you can't do, you can only make believe, because if a girl does it she's lost, finished forever." Instead of not looking I looked because in the nice clear water at the bottom of the sea those hairs like streamers that wave come together all of a sudden and the fishies coming in between the hairs get caught. "Don't ask anymore, I'm not going to tell you" naughty Pocha doesn't want to tell me what the boy with the hairs did "If you don't know it means we can't play, you're too young" Pocha tell me what "fucks" means "We can't play that, you have to be a big boy with hairs on your weeny" and I didn't tell Pocha I had seen a movie about the bottom of the sea with the plant full of hairs that eats the colored

fishies, Pocha, then we can play that I'm the girl and you're the boy, because I don't know how to do it, and that's how I can learn, and Pocha
"OK." I lie down on the rug as if I'm sleeping on the roof and Pocha that
day had on the dress with little green flowers, comes tiptoeing from behind
and who's spying through the door that's a tiny bit opened? Pocha's aunt!
laughing at me, with her paper curls too and I asked her what "fucks"
means. "Pocha, you're disgusting" and her aunt went back to the kitchen.
"You're too young to play with me" and I can't hit Pocha because I'm
smaller, and if not, I'd cut off her curls with the scissors for cutting out stars
and then I'd stick the hard curls in her mouth and make her eat them. And
then I'd say to her "Pocha, have a candy" and what I'd give her would be
hard dog doodoo that I found in the street. It's because of her that Felisa
hit me. If it wasn't naptime now I could go play with the manger but
Pocha's there, she didn't want to tell me what "fucks" was. What did he do
to her with the hairs? "The boy puts his weeny in the little hole of my tail
and he doesn't let me go, I can't move at all and he takes advantage and
fucks me." And she won't tell me what "fucks" means. The hairs are what
eat the fishies in the movie about the bottom of the sea. First the long hairs
move all soft and the water and the fishies came near, right? "Toto, don't
look!" now you don't see them anymore! because the hairy plant swallowed them. The girl who does it is lost, finished forever, the big boy
comes along, gets real close, sees that Pocha is sleeping, very slowly picks
up her dress with little green flowers, and Pocha forgot to put her underpants on! and so that she doesn't move the boy puts his weeny in the little
hole in her tail and he moves his hairs all over her, and if Pocha stays still
like a fishie the boy's hairs start eating her behind, and then her tummy,
and the heart, and the ears, and little by little he eats her all up. The little
gold chain, paper curls, shoes and socks, the dress with little green flowers
and her undershirt are all left on the floor with nothing inside. Pocha is
lost, finished forever, she's never seen again. The other dress with little blue
flowers stays hanging in the closet. Wham! the slap Felisa gave me, and she
never hits me. In the kitchen stove the wood is burning into pieces of
pumpkin pie and I feel like eating them and they become fire when I swish
the candy coals around with a knife they break into smaller pieces and
sparks come out "You're going to burn yourself!" Felisa doesn't want me
to swish the wood around in the stove "Keep still I said!" and Mommy was
on duty at the drugstore and Daddy was doing accounts at his desk and
Felisa took my knife away. "Felisa fuckface!" and Felisa slapped me.

Mommy! "Who taught you that word?" "Missis, this child is behaving worse every day," "I'm not going to say anything to Pocha's mother, but I'm going to give Pocha a good scolding. You know Berto, this child is very naughty," "Yes, well then this Sunday he starts Baby Soccer" I don't want to go! "This child is very naughty, I'm going to put him down for Baby Soccer so he can play with the other boys," "He's driving us out of our minds every minute of the day," "He doesn't obey when you tell him something" because Uncle Perico died. I didn't want to go to kindergarten anymore and I began to play with the picture cards, but I wasn't playing the movie about the bottom of the sea where the fishies died the day Uncle Perico died "Toto, stop playing, Uncle Perico just died a while ago" with the prettiest picture cards of Romeo and Juliet all lined up along the tiles in the hall but Daddy "Poor Uncle Perico died, come and get dressed, and remember you have to be quiet and not talk loud or sing" because Mommy can't draw the movie about the bottom of the sea when she wasn't looking. Uncle Perico, always in the bar with country people, after the cattle fair they go to play billiards, they never go to the movies and it's a pity the bushes on the bottom of the sea eat the pretty fishies in many colors, they should eat the bad fishes and the old fishes that look like octopuses and sharks but in the picture cards Mommy says the movie that's going to turn out the fanciest is *The Great Ziegfeld* which they're finally showing this Thursday. "I told you to stop playing! aren't you sad that Uncle Perico died? you are naughty and spoiled, and worst of all is that I can see you don't love anybody!" They didn't spank me, if Daddy puts his hands on me he'd really break me in two and the mother of the boy next door pulls his pants down and spanks him on his behind but I didn't cry when Uncle Perico died. Shirley Temple is very young but she's an actress and she's always good, everybody loves her a lot and she has a bad grandfather with long white hair in a movie, and he smokes a pipe and in the beginning he doesn't even look at her but afterwards he begins to love her because she's so good. And she didn't tell lies. Donkey ears don't grow on a kid who's naughty, a little tail grows from telling lies. If the boy next door's uncle dies I don't think he's going to grow donkey ears. But if the gypsies get hold of a boy his mother doesn't recognize him anymore because they rub coal all over him. In school the teacher with the pointer hits whoever doesn't know how to count up to a hundred on both ears with the pointer and the boy looks at himself in the mirror to watch his ears grow until they are donkey ears and if I say to her "Teacher, fuckface" she'll pick up the pointer again but this time to kill me and I jump through the window but I'm tangled up with the teacher's leg. The long tail grew when I said I'd gone to the men's room in Town Hall! Now the tail is longer than ever and I can't jump and the teacher's getting closer and closer with the pointer in her hand! If Felisa comes into the kitchen to give me another slap I'll jump out and get away because she doesn't have a pointer and I'll try so hard to make a giant jump out the window, so's not to fall into the park pond and you have to watch out since there may be fuck bushes at the bottom. And I jump . . . and I'm almost flying . . . the gypsy's corral is on the other side of the pond and do I land inside? Then I say I am a fishie and I'm going to fall into the fishbowl, glub, glub, glub I shout out loud and Mommy is looking for me because it's time to go to the movies, right? Mommy looks for me and can't find me and goes to look for me in the bathroom at the moviehouse, but I'm not in the ladies' room and she can't go into the men's room! but they're showing a beautiful movie and she sits down to see it and a fishie's shouting is heard from far away and Mommy "How badly that fishie behaves, he doesn't love anybody, since his uncle died and the fishie didn't even cry, he just went on playing." And I stop shouting because a door opens; the gypsy comes in, on tiptoes, he's holding a kidnapped girl, and he hits her, right? he takes down her panties and gives her a spanking on her behind, right? no, the gypsy is bad, he pulls down his pants and his underpants, he puts his weeny in the little girl's tail and when the poor little girl can't move anymore he moves his hairs all over her and little by little he eats her all up, first her leg, then her hand and the other leg and her fat little behind. And Shirley Temple is tied to a wagon near the horses. But I am not a bad fishie, I'm a good fishie and I untie the rope and Shirley Temple escapes. Because I'm going to be good like Shirley. The windows at the school are very high but I'm going to tell Mommy that when she goes shopping to stand on tiptoes so she can see me in class, she has to come by every day, I'm going to make Mommy promise, and I'll promise to behave, and after school she has to come get me. For my birthday we're buying a cake and afterwards we're going to a movie to see a musical and if I feel like going weewee she'll take me to the ladies' room. And I already told a lie: that I went to the men's room, because then I'll grow a little tail and it's lucky the boys can go weewee in the backyard of the moviehouse and nobody says anything, even though the little stream of weewee makes a hole in the ground and the yard ends up full of mud puddles and Mommy watches out where she walks and she makes sure she doesn't put her feet in the mud and I go weewee . . . if the big girl with the dress that scratches isn't there . . . and she's naughty . . . and she might pick up mud from the little puddles and rub it all over my face and make it black . . . but I hide in the ladies' room and the big girl catches me and for punishment she puts a little skirt on me for going into the ladies room. . . . Mommy! did the movie begin already and is it dark inside the moviehouse? Mommy must be waiting for me in her seat but I'll shout and she'll come and save me! "Who's the little black girl who's shouting? Yesterday there was a fishie who shouted and ran away and its owner came and put it back into the fishbowl, and now they got the little black girl who ran away and she has to take care of the fishie and they're both going to cry all night so I better close the window since they'll wake up Berto, noises make him nervous." The little black girl and the fishie are in the gypsy's corral. They're black with dirt and mud and hairs from the horses' tails. The gates are locked with a key and a latch. And the musical is already beginning and Mommy is sad because I'm going to miss it, the first number isn't the prettiest, it's only a tap dance, the fanciest number is at the end, what could the fanciest number be like? The curtain rises and there's another shiny curtain behind and this curtain rises and then there is the last curtain which means they're going to begin the fanciest dance of all and I can't miss it: what a strong wind! it's such a strong wind it opens the gate and the little black girl and the fishie get away, how lucky, they run as fast as they can because the gypsy is following them and the little black girl and the fishie have to jump over the park pond wide with black dirty water and they jump but they're very little and they fall in and the gypsy doesn't see them because they fell under the black water and the gypsy keeps running running and he is never seen again. When the dancers are all on line it's the beginning of the last number, it's all set to be drawn on the picture cards: the fanciest movie of the whole collection, but Mommy comes out of the moviehouse sad because I'm not there. Mommy cried once when we were walking along the street but I don't remember why. When? Why are you crying, Mommy? she doesn't tell me, but the little black girl and the fishie are dead floating in the pond, and luckily after the airplane crashed Ginger Rogers and Fred Astaire dance transparent in the memory, since nobody can keep them apart anymore: war or no war, when Mommy wakes up after naptime I'm going to tell her I didn't make any noise and I behaved like a good boy. The fishie and the little black girl are going to be transparent in heaven after death but I don't want Mommy to draw them on the picture cards, they're so dirty they'd come out ugly transparent. Isn't a birdie prettier? did some birdie die? the boy next door's canary? no! Mommy's not going to draw him! another one, in the memory, that's also transparent in heaven, then Mommy realizes that he's dead and every day when we come home from the movies we look up at the pear trees and we tell him what happened in the movie, who was acting, the musical numbers, just as if he were seeing them so he doesn't feel sorry he missed it all: from high up in the clouds everything looks little in Vallejos, and the gypsy is not in the corral anymore. The nicest thing is to be on top of the little clouds with Ginger's other birdies and we play every day, the teacher with the pointer is tiny down below in school, and Pocha in her aunt's kitchen. Nothing but the birdies can get up to the clouds, they eat big cake crumbs that Felisa sends them and nothing else, right? right, because there are no black birds big like cats with hooked beaks, I'm going to make Mommy promise.

# ～ *Roland Barthes* ～

## FROM
# *A Lover's Discourse*

TRANSLATED BY RICHARD HOWARD

### The Intractable

affirmation / *affirmation*
*Against and in spite of everything, the subject*
*affirms love as* value.

1. Despite the difficulties of my story, despite discomforts, doubts, despairs, despite impulses to be done with it, I unceasingly affirm love, within myself, as a value. Though I listen to all the arguments which the most divergent systems employ to demystify, to limit, to erase, in short to depreciate love, I persist: "I know, I know, but all the same . . ." I refer the devaluations of love to a kind of obscurantist ethic, to a let's-pretend realism, against which I erect the realism of value: I counter whatever "doesn't work" in love with the affirmation of what is worthwhile. This stubbornness is love's protest: for all the wealth of "good reasons" for loving differently, loving better, loving without being in love, etc., a stubborn voice is raised which lasts *a little longer:* the voice of the Intractable lover.

*Pelléas*

～ ～ ～

The world subjects every enterprise to an alternative; that of success or failure, of victory or defeat. I protest by another

---

*PELLÉAS: "What's the matter? You don't seem to be happy." "Oh yes, I am happy, but I am sad."*

*ROLAND BARTHES, the leading critic of his generation, was born in Cherbourg, France—the city whose umbrellas Michel Legrand wrote a song about—in 1915. Like Margaret Mitchell—the great inscriber of American myth—he died as a result of being hit by a car.*

logic: I am simultaneously and contradictorily happy and wretched; "to succeed" or "to fail" have for me only contingent, provisional meanings (which doesn't keep my sufferings and my desires from being violent); what inspires me, secretly and stubbornly, is not a tactic: I accept and I affirm, beyond truth and falsehood, beyond success and failure; I have withdrawn from all finality, I live according to chance (as is evidenced by the fact that the figures of my discourse occur to me like so many dice casts). Flouted in my enterprise (as it happens), I emerge from it neither victor nor vanquished: I am tragic.

Schelling

(Someone tells me: this kind of love is not viable. But how can you *evaluate* viability? Why is the viable a Good Thing? Why is it better to *last* than to *burn?*)

~ ~ ~

2. This morning, I must get off an "important" letter right away—one on which the success of a certain undertaking depends; but instead I write a love letter—which I do not send. I gladly abandon dreary tasks, rational scruples, reactive undertakings imposed by the world, for the sake of a useless task deriving from a dazzling Duty: the lover's Duty. I perform, discreetly, lunatic chores; I am the sole witness of my lunacy. What love lays bare in me is *energy.* Everything I do has a meaning (hence I can *live,* without whining), but this meaning is an ineffable finality: it is merely the meaning of my strength. The painful, guilty, melancholy inflections, the whole reactive side of my everyday life, are reversed. Werther praises his own tension, which he affirms, in contrast to Albert's platitudes. Born of literature, able to speak only with the help of its worn codes, yet I am alone with my strength, doomed *to my own philosophy.*

Werther

---

SCHELLING: *"The essence of tragedy is . . . a real conflict between the subject's freedom and an objective necessity, a conflict which is ended not by the defeat of one or the other but because both, at once victors and vanquished, appear in a perfect indifferentiation."*
WERTHER: *"Oh, my dear friend, if to tender one's whole being is to give evidence of strength, why should an excessive tension be weakness?"*

～ ～ ～

3. In the Christian West, until today, all strength passes through the Interpreter, as a type (in Nietzschean terms, the Judaic High Priest). But the strength of love cannot be shifted, be put into the hands of an Interpreter; it remains here, on the level of language, enchanted, intractable. Here the type is not the Priest, it is the Lover.

J.-L.B.

～ ～ ～

4. Love has two affirmations. First of all, when the lover encounters the other, there is an immediate affirmation (psychologically: dazzlement, enthusiasm, exaltation, mad projection of a fulfilled future: I am devoured by desire, the impulse to be happy): I say *yes* to everything (blinding myself). There follows a long tunnel: my first *yes* is riddled by doubts, love's *value* is ceaselessly threatened by depreciation: this is the moment of melancholy passion, the rising of resentment and of oblation. Yet I can emerge from this tunnel; I can "surmount," without liquidating; what I have affirmed a first time, I can once again affirm, without repeating it, for then what I affirm is the affirmation, not its contingency: I affirm the first encounter in its difference, I desire its return, not its repetition. I say to the other (old or new): *Let us begin again.*

Nietzsche

### *"In the loving calm of your arms"*

étreinte / embrace
*The gesture of the amorous embrace seems to fulfill, for a time,*
*the subject's dream of total union with the loved being.*

1. Besides intercourse (when the Image-repertoire goes to the devil), there is that other embrace, which is a motionless cra-

---

J.-L.B.: *Conversation.*
NIETZSCHE: *All this comes from Deleuze's account of the affirmation of the affirmation.*

dling: we are enchanted, bewitched: we are in the realm of sleep, without sleeping; we are within the voluptuous infantilism of *sleepiness:* this is the moment for telling stories, the moment of the voice which takes me, siderates me, this is the return to the mother ("In the loving calm of your arms," says a poem set to music by Duparc). In this companionable incest, everything is suspended: time, law, prohibition: nothing is exhausted, nothing is wanted: all desires are abolished, for they seem definitively fulfilled.

Duparc

～ ～ ～

2. Yet, within this infantile embrace, the genital unfailingly appears; it cuts off the diffuse sensuality of the incestuous embrace; the logic of desire begins to function, the will-to-possess returns, the adult is superimposed upon the child. I am then two subjects at once: I want maternity *and* genitality. (The lover might be defined as a child getting an erection: such was the young Eros.)

～ ～ ～

3. A moment of affirmation; for a certain time, though a finite one, a *deranged* interval, something has been successful: I have been fulfilled (all my desires abolished by the plenitude of their satisfaction): fulfillment does exist, and I shall keep on making it return: through all the meanderings of my amorous history, I shall persist in wanting to rediscover, to renew, the contradiction—the contraction—of the two embraces.

### The Ghost Ship

errance / *errantry*
*Though each love is experienced as unique and though the subject rejects the notion of repeating it elsewhere later on, he sometimes discovers in himself a kind of diffusion of amorous desire; he then realizes he is doomed to wander until he dies, from love to love.*

---

DUPARC: *"Chanson triste," poem by Jean Lahor. Second-rate poetry? But "second-rate poetry" takes the amorous subject into the linguistic register which is all his own:* expression.

1. How does a love end?—Then it does end? To tell the truth, no one—except for the others—ever knows anything about it; a kind of innocence conceals the end of this thing conceived, asserted, *lived* according to eternity. Whatever the loved being becomes, whether he vanishes or moves into the realm of Friendship, in any case I never see him disappear: the love which is over and done with passes into another world like a ship into space, lights no longer winking: the loved being once echoed loudly, now that being is entirely without resonance (the other never disappears when and how we expect). This phenomenon results from a constraint in the lover's discourse: I myself cannot (as an enamored subject) construct my love story to the end: I am its poet (its bard) only for the beginning; the end, like my own death, belongs to others; it is up to them to write the fiction, the external, mythic narrative.

～　～　～

2. I always behave—I insist upon behaving, whatever I am told and whatever my own discouragements may be—as if love might someday be fulfilled, as if the Sovereign Good were possible. Whence that odd dialectic which causes one absolute love to succeed another without the least embarrassment, as if, by love, I acceded to another logic (the absolute is no longer obliged to be unique), to another temporality (from love to love, I live my vertical moments), to another music (this sound, without memory, severed from any construction, oblivious of what precedes it and of what follows, is in itself musical). I search, I begin, I try, I venture further, I run ahead, but I never know that I am ending: it is never said of the Phoenix that it dies, but only that it is reborn (then I can be reborn without dying?).

*Werther*

Once I am not fulfilled and yet *do not kill myself,* amorous errantry is a fatality. Werther himself experienced it—shifting from "poor Leonora" to Charlotte; the impulse, of course, is checked; but if it had survived, Werther would have rewritten the same letters to another woman.

R.S.B.

---

R.S.B.: *Conversation.*

~ ~ ~

3. Amorous errantry has its comical side: it resembles a ballet, more or less nimble according to the velocity of the fickle subject; but it is also a grand opera. The accursed Dutchman is doomed to wander the seas until he has found a woman who will be eternally faithful. I am that Flying Dutchman; I cannot stop wandering (loving) because of an ancient sign which dedicated me, in the remote days of my earliest childhood, to the god of my Image-repertoire, afflicting me with a compulsion to speak which leads me to say "I love you" in one port of call after another, until some other receives this phrase and gives it back to me; but no one can assume the impossible reply (of an insupportable fulfillment), and my wandering, my errantry continues.

Wagner

~ ~ ~

4. Throughout life, all of love's "failures" resemble one another (and with reason: they all proceed from the same flaw). X and Y have not been able (have not wanted) to answer my "demand," to adhere to my "truth"; they have not altered their system one iota; for me, the former has merely repeated the latter. And yet X and Y are incomparable; it is in their difference, the model of an infinitely pursued difference, that I find the energy to begin all over again. The "perpetual mutability" *(in inconstantia constans)* which animates me, far from squeezing all those I encounter into the same functional type (not to answer my demand), violently dislocates their false community: errantry does not align—it produces iridescence: what results is the nuance. Thus I move on, to the end of the tapestry, from one nuance to the next (the nuance is the last state of a color which can be named; the nuance is the Intractable).

# ~ Renaud Camus ~

FROM

## *Tricks*

TRANSLATED BY RICHARD HOWARD

### *Jacques's Brother*

*Thursday, March 23, 1978*

To speak here of Jacques's brother is to juggle the criteria I have established as to what constitutes a trick, since he was not entirely a stranger to me. But then again, we didn't know each other very well. Jacques had introduced me to him a few weeks earlier, we always said *hello* to each other with a smile, and *how are you?* and not much more. I knew his name was Pierre, that he was a little older than his brother, and that he lived in Paris, unlike the rest of his family, Gypsies all, who were at Gonesse, a veritable tribe, as I understand it. They are not French citizens, the children don't go to school, none of them can read or write, not even numbers, although they seem to be shrewd businessmen. Both brothers were married by their parents, but they hardly know their wives and never

---

*Roland Barthes on* RENAUD CAMUS: *"Our period interprets a great deal, but Renaud Camus's narratives are neutral, they do not participate in the game of interpretation. They are surfaces without shadows, without ulterior motives. And once again, only writing allows this purity, this priority of utterance, unknown to speech, which is always a cunning tangle of concealed intentions. If it weren't for their extent and their subject, these* Tricks *might suggest haikus; for the haiku combines an asceticism of form (which cuts short the desire to interpret) and a hedonism so serene that all we can say about pleasure is that it is there (which is also the contrary of Interpretation)."*

see them. Pierre looks very much the classic Gypsy: very black curly hair, mustache, gold earring, sometimes a red scarf around the throat. But he's very short; just over five feet, maybe.

~ ~ ~

That evening at the Manhattan, he was much more communicative than usual. Not that he made any advances, but I kept finding him in my path. Once, when I was sitting down, he came over and stood beside me. He said nothing to me, however, and after a moment or so I gave up my seat to him. Later, upstairs near the top of the stairs, he approached me again. We were both standing. I was leaning against the wall, but I kept my feet as far apart as possible, in order to make myself closer to his height. Then, fearing that this position would seem too artificial and too obvious, I straightened up, taller by a head and shoulders than he, which was no less embarrassing.

~ ~ ~

I knew he had a *friend* (his expression), and he couldn't get out as much as he liked:

"So you managed to escape tonight?"

"Yeah. Is it always as crowded as this during the week?"

"No, not this early in the week. Do you only come here on weekends?"

"Only Saturdays."

"And where's your brother? In Gonesse?"

"I don't know. I don't know what he's up to. He may be out tonight—he goes somewhere else."

"Where's that?"

"Oh, he goes to the César, or the Scaramouche, or 18 . . ."

~ ~ ~

He remarked that there was a boy over on the banquette who wasn't bad, and I pointed out another, whom I found attractive. A Spaniard, he told me. But we remained side by side, without saying anything more. My arm behind him, I stuck a thumb into his belt, once or twice, but there was no reaction on his part. I told him I was sleepy.

"You should dance a little."

"No, I don't have the energy. But I'll go watch the others."

～ ～ ～

So I left him where he was and went back downstairs. I circled the dance floor slowly. Ten minutes later I felt two arms around me, embracing me from behind. It was Pierre again. I put my hands in his pants pockets—which were wide-wale corduroy—then I caressed his forearms, which he had crossed over my stomach. Then, when I got behind him in turn, I stuck my hands in his pockets again or else I crossed my arms over his chest, squeezing now, my legs wide apart, my chin on his shoulder. He went to sit down in a corner. A moment later, since I was staring at him, he signaled me to come over and sit down next to him, which I did. Putting my arm around his shoulders, I kissed him in the hollow of the neck. Then I caressed his back through his shirt. He began to laugh:

"You in love?"

"Why? In love with who? No."

"The way you're handling me."

"I'm not handling you, I'm caressing you."

But I stopped.

"Are you mad at me?"

"No. Why? Not at all."

Now it was he who was running his hand over my tennis shirt, down my back, caressing my forearms and hands.

"You sure you're not mad?"

"Yes, I'm sure."

～ ～ ～

With both hands, he turned my head toward him and kissed me on the mouth. All the same, I watched the dancers a moment longer, without paying him much attention. It was only when he drew me toward him a second time that I gradually leaned back, or rather to one side, on the corner banquette where we were sitting alone. My cock was getting hard against his hip. I stuck a couple of fingers between two buttons of his shirt, under his tiny necktie. His pectorals were round, solid, covered with hair. We stayed there about fifteen minutes kissing like that, half reclining. He had an erection too.

～ ～ ～

It was almost closing time. The music was shut off and all the lights were turned on. We headed for the coat checkroom. He told me to give him my ticket, and cutting into the line, he picked up my things along with his and refused the two francs I owed him. We walked back up to the street floor. At the door, he asked me what I was going to do.

"Go home to bed. And you?"

"I'm going over to Pim's. Don't you want to come to Pim's with me?"

"No, I'm bushed."

"Too bad."

"You could come with me, if you want to."

"No, I have a friend."

"Oh, in that case . . ."

Just then I glanced around us a bit and we were separated by all the men leaving at the same time we were. But out in the street, from the opposite sidewalk, he signaled me to join him.

"You're going home now?"

"Yes."

"Which way do you go?"

"Down the Boulevard Saint-Germain."

"I'll walk with you a little."

～　～　～

So we set out side by side.

"I'll tell you what I want to do. I'll come home with you, but I won't stay."

"All right. But we can't go to my apartment. There's someone there. We can go to a maid's room I have, around the corner from it."

"It doesn't matter to me. You have a friend too?"

"No, but I live with someone."

"You know, this is the first time I've cheated on my friend. It doesn't feel so good."

"Then you shouldn't do it."

"But you turn me on. Let's stop here and have some coffee."

"Coffee? No, you don't need coffee; you won't be able to sleep if you drink coffee now."

"It doesn't keep me awake. You order what you want. I'd smoke a cigarette over the body."

"What?"

"I said I need a cigarette. I have to buy some."

He started to go into the café at the corner of the Boulevard Saint-Germain and the Rue de l'Ancienne-Comédie.

"No, not there. They don't sell cigarettes. There's a place farther down."

So he went into the Navy.

"You want something to drink?"

"No, thanks."

I waited outside. He didn't get any coffee.

"Is it much farther?"

"Seven, maybe eight minutes."

"If I had known, we could have taken a taxi. You walk this distance every time?"

"Yes, I'm used to it. And I'm warning you now, you'll have to climb six flights too."

~ ~ ~

Not much was said the rest of the way, except for admonitions on his part not to mention what was happening between us to his brother.

~ ~ ~

"All the same, when I think of it, who would have believed it?"

"What?"

"That we would leave that place together, you and me."

"I don't see what's so extraordinary about that."

"Still, if my friend knew! You won't say anything about it, will you?"

~ ~ ~

As soon as we get into the room, he takes off his clothes. His body is very well proportioned, rather dark-skinned, very muscular, especially the arms and thighs, which are exceptionally developed.

~ ~ ~

I tell him I have to go take a piss. When I come back, he wants to go too and puts on his underwear to walk down the hall. I get between the icy sheets. When he comes back, he asks if there is hot water here. Yes? Really? Then he very carefully washes himself off, from the waist down. I explain that there is neither a candle nor a bed lamp and that we can have either the big light on or no light at all. He suggests that I put a towel over it, but that doesn't make much difference. Then, under the sink, he discovers a little lamp I never knew was there.

~ ~ ~

"You're not going to wash up?"
"I already did."
"So did I."

~ ~ ~

When his ablutions are completed, he comes and stretches out beside me in the bed, which is still cold, despite my solitary efforts. We press against each other, kissing, and warm up that way for quite a while. He seems to be very interested in my ass. He sucks my cock. I run my tongue through the hair on his chest, over his right nipple, his belly, and then I take his cock in my mouth too. This provokes so much agitation that he is now lying completely across the bed. Continuing my descent, I take his balls between my teeth, then I stop at his asshole, which I lick while continuing to caress his torso. He plays with himself, breathing hard. Then I turn him around so he's lying full length on the bed again, and lying on top of him, with his legs spread and my cock under his ass, I kiss him on the mouth again, on the chest, on the belly, suck him some more, and again suck his ass, leaving as much saliva in it as possible. Then, taking his legs in my arms and having moistened my cock, I start pushing it between his buttocks, where it goes in quite easily. "Easy, Renaud," he says, "easy."

Then I stop, and it is he who, by his movements, gets me deeper inside him.

~ ~ ~

My hands under his shoulder blades, I kiss him on the mouth, in the hollow of his neck, on the chest. He chants my name like a nostalgic wail. Sometime I fuck him very slowly, then, just about to come, very fast and hard and always with enthusiasm. He plays with himself. I burst out laughing.

"Why are you laughing?"
"Because I'm happy. This is great."
"I like you a lot—you laugh all the time. . . ."

This lasts about ten minutes. Then he tells me he's about to come.

"Now?"

"Yes, now, now, yes . . ."

"Me too, me too . . ."

~ ~ ~

We come at exactly the same instant, as if it were my own sperm that was spurting out of his cock onto his belly, up to his chest and even onto his shoulders. I fall back beside him, releasing his legs from my arms. He looks at me, smiling:

"You're a little bastard."

"Why?"

"You're a real bastard. Usually I don't get fucked—on principle. . . . Now why are you laughing? You don't believe me?"

"Sure. But why do what's usual?"

"I don't say it never happens. It's happened a few times . . . but not usually, that's what I mean. Is that all you like to do?"

"No, I like to do everything. I do whatever anyone wants."

"Let me wipe myself off, I'm completely covered. . . ."

"I'll say. What a range! Wait, I'll get you a towel."

~ ~ ~

I get up and hand him a towel and wash myself off.

"What time is it?"

"Three."

"At four, I'll go."

"All right. I'll close the curtains; that way I won't have to get up again."

~ ~ ~

Then back in each other's arms again, his head on my shoulder. I caress him.

"What is Renaud anyway—is that your family name?"

"No, my first name."

"People call you that? Renaud? It sounds strange."

"My other Christian name is Jean."

"Ah, your real name is Jean. You decided on Renaud for yourself?"

"No, my name is actually Jean-Renaud, but Jean-Renaud's a little too long."

"Still, Renaud sounds funny. Like the name of a car."

"You don't like it?"

"No, wait . . . I'm going to call you . . . Rocky. Yes, Rocky's good. You like the way it sounds, Rocky?"

"It sounds all right to me, if you like it."

"OK, Rocky, that's what it is: Rocky. What do you have to say for yourself, Rock?"

"There you go, getting familiar right off—let's make it Rock. I like that, I like that even better."

"OK, Rock . . . anything you say, Rock. . . . I'm thinking about my friend. About the scene he's going to make when I come in."

"Maybe he'll be asleep."

"Dream on. I know him, the bastard, you can be sure he hasn't slept a wink. I know him. He's waiting up for me, wondering where I've gone. It bothers me a lot."

"Then you should leave now."

"I wonder what I'll tell him. . . . Maybe that I went to the Sept."

"Suppose that's where *he* went?"

"No, he never goes out. That's why we argue all the time."

"You like to go out a lot?"

"Sure, I'd like to go out every night. Not to cruise, you know. Just to be somewhere, you know, where there are people, dance, have some fun, go to the movies, even to the theater, *do* something. But he just comes home from work, he watches television, and bang! right into bed. He doesn't even wait for the late show. I watch the late show alone—some life!"

"Where did you meet him?"

"At the Scara . . . the Scaramouche. You know the place?"

"So he used to go out, then?"

"Yes, before, he went out all the time, but not now; now he won't set foot outside the door."

"It's because you're all he needs."

"Yes, that's exactly what he says. He says: I have you, why should I look for anything else? Tonight I wanted to go to the movies, that's why we argued. He said we'd go next Saturday. I said no, not Saturday. I don't want to go Saturday, I want to go tonight. He said he wasn't going, I said I was. So I went, and then afterward I went to the Manhattan, and then there you were first thing, and so here I am."

~ ~ ~

Again he begins caressing my ass. Then he starts sucking my cock. I get hard. He kneels between my legs and with his hand puts some saliva between my buttocks. I add some of my own. Then he raises my legs and gets inside me right away. His cock is rather small and doesn't reach very far. His body is perpendicular to mine, and I pull him toward me, to kiss him, and cross my legs behind his back. I direct his mouth toward my right nipple, so that he can suck it. He does this a little, then straightens up again. My erection goes down, which he notices. Then he pulls his cock out of my ass and begins sucking me again. I get hard again almost immediately and begin playing with myself, my hand against his mouth. He sticks his cock back inside me, but after two or three minutes I lose my erection again. The same thing has happened to him, apparently.

"You tired?"

"A little."

"You want to stop?"

"If you do."

~ ~ ~

And again side by side: I think he talked some more about his friend's worrying about him, asked me again what time it was, and about taxis, then about where we were.

"I don't know why I can't get it up anymore."

"I could come in a minute."

I am lying on top of him.

"You can come like that?"

"Sure can!"

I kiss him, but he keeps changing position, and I find myself, although still on my stomach, lying on the mattress. I play with him, and he gets a little hard. Then I pass my hand behind his balls and caress his buttocks, one finger just barely thrust between them. My cock is hard against his hip.

"You get it up better when you're on top, huh?"

I laugh. The pressure of my hand against his ass apparently gets him more and more excited, and his cock is now perfectly stiff.

"Oh, you turn me on!"

I kneel between his thighs, then I lick his ass again, keeping it up in the air with my forearms. He plays with himself and moans a lot. His chin is against his chest. Our eyes meet down the length of his torso; we keep staring at each other while my tongue thrusts between his buttocks.

～ ～ ～

Then I fuck him again, very excited this time. I have a big erection now, and so does he. I try to slow down his right hand's movement around his cock, so that the pleasure will last longer. But he pushes me away with his left hand:

"No, Renaud, I'm going to come, no, no, I'm coming now, yes, now, yes!"

～ ～ ～

He comes about five seconds before I do.

～ ～ ～

Afterward he gets up to wipe himself off and hands me the towel. Then he climbs back into bed and lies in my arms:

"I don't know what I should do, go home or not. . . . It must be four by now, isn't it?"

"Yes."

"He gets up at six."

"I'm not surprised he doesn't like going out nights."

"What time are you getting up today?"

"Oh, around one."

"So what should I do?"

"I don't know what you *should* do. Of course I'd rather you stay. But it's up to you to decide—you know the situation better than I do."

"God, he gives me a pain. It's his fault anyway. I suppose it has to end someday. . . . I wish I could find someone like me, who likes to go out all the time. I think I'll sleep here, since you don't want me to leave."

"Hey, wait a minute. Don't get any ideas. I never said I didn't want you to leave. I said I'd rather you stay, personally, but that I understood perfectly well that you might want to go home, especially if you think your friend is upset."

"You're not kidding, he'll be upset. . . . All right, I'll leave, then."

～ ～ ～

But he doesn't move. I put my arms around him, his back against my chest, our legs bent and parallel. After about ten minutes:

"Look out, you're going to fall asleep."

"Oh, so what. He pisses me off. I'll tell him I spent the night in a hotel."

"He'll never believe that."

"He can believe whatever he wants."

~ ~ ~

After which I fall asleep, this time with my back to him.

~ ~ ~

He wakes me up getting out of bed, beginning to put on his clothes. It is just getting light.

"What are you doing?"

"I'm going home."

"What time is it?"

"Where's your watch?"

"In the drawer. It was too loud."

"Monsieur has very delicate ears. . . . It's seven. Or maybe eight, I don't know. Look for yourself."

~ ~ ~

He does not know how to read a watch.

~ ~ ~

It was eight o'clock.

~ ~ ~

He comes back to bed.

"Now what are you doing?"

"I'm going to stay, since you don't want me to leave."

"You can leave if you want. Only it seems like a funny time to get up, since we went to sleep around four."

"I didn't sleep the whole night."

"Hmm . . . Do you have to go to work?"

"Usually. But I'm too tired."

"All right, but make up your mind. I want to get some sleep."

~ ~ ~

He has turned on the light, although the room is light enough for him to get dressed. And he's humming. I groan.

"What?"

"I'm trying to sleep!"

"You mean you're not even going to get up to say good-bye?"

"What a pain in the ass you are! Come and say good-bye yourself."

"You'll have to close the door!"

"No, just shut it behind you."

~ ~ ~

But I get up all the same, to kiss him good-bye. He leaves. And I sleep until noon.

~ ~ ~

[*Saw him again very often, though we never slept together again. After this episode, he broke off with his friend, for which, he says, he's very grateful to me: it had to end someday, and it's much better this way. He's always very pleasant, very sweet, and invariably in a good mood. When he found out that I was a writer, he said he hoped I'd write something about him.*]

### Calogero

*Saturday, April 1, 1978*

That Friday evening I had gone to the Rosamunda, in a suburb of Milan, with Philippe, to whom I had talked at length about this enormous *locale di ballo*. We had had a splendid dinner at Giannino's, and I was still wearing white ducks, a checked vest and gray jacket, a wing collar and a black bow tie.

As soon as we came into the Rosamunda, I noticed a very dark boy with a mustache, wearing a white turtleneck shirt, whom Philippe instantly nicknamed "The Lebanese." I stared at him, he stared back, and we found ourselves quite close to each other, dancing on the huge floor. But each time I danced closer to him he turned his head in another direction. In any event, he was very thin, and even his wrists were of a delicacy that bordered on the sickly.

~ ~ ~

At this moment I noticed another boy, also very dark, with a mustache and rather long curly hair, wearing a brown plaid shirt open wide at the neck, the sleeves rolled up, and dark-brown corduroy pants. He was short, stocky, almost plump. His chest and heavy forearms were covered with thick black hair. He was part of a very animated little group of girls and boys sitting at a table on the edge of the dance floor.

~ ~ ~

I no longer remember clearly our first exchange of glances. But there were quite a lot of them, I remember that—several accompanied by a faint smile.

~ ~ ~

He went over to sit down on the steps to the emergency exit. I followed him to this retreat, where he sat completely alone, and looked at him. But as soon as my glance fell on him, he turned away. After a few minutes of this little game, I went for a stroll, rejoining Philippe, who asked me how things were going with the Lebanese. When I turned back toward the steps, the boy in the plaid shirt was still sitting there, still alone. I went over to him, leaned on the railing, and bent over it toward him. He looked up at me. I smiled at him. He made no response. So I walked away again, stopping only at the other end of the room, where I stood leaning one shoulder against the wall. Three or four minutes later, he came over to the same end of the room and took up a position exactly symmetrical to mine, about ten feet away. He looked at me only when I wasn't looking at him, and when I turned toward him, he turned his head in another direction. Tired of this, I walked around the dance floor. From a distance, I saw him climb the stairs toward the exit. I decided he must be going to the toilet, or else outside for some air. I sat down just about where he had been earlier, to watch for his return. It was twenty-five after twelve, and I decided to wait until twelve-thirty. Five minutes passed without his reappearance. So I went back toward the dance floor and did not see him again that evening. Philippe wanted to try La Divina, and we went there at one.

~ ~ ~

At La Divina, Philippe pointed out that a certain boy was cruising me. And indeed, the one he indicated had come over to stand right next to me, where I was leaning on the bar. But each time I looked at him, he looked away. He was reasonably appealing, but I didn't like the way he wore his jacket sleeves pushed up to the elbow, according to the season's fashion, or his turned-up shirt collar, or the two moles on his face, which looked like beauty marks. So I paid no more attention to him, and a little before two, Philippe and I left. Our car was parked just opposite the entrance. I was already behind the wheel, leaning over to open the door for Philippe, when the man with the moles appeared. Changing strategy, he had run after us and now was asking if Philippe and I would like to come and have a drink with him at a friend's house. Philippe answered that he would have to ask me. We looked at each other, and I accepted the invitation. The friend arrived and sat in the back with Philippe, while the man with the moles sat beside me in front. We drove to an apartment house, quite far away but just off the expressway we had immediately turned onto. The apartment was absurd, fussy, entirely covered in cut velvet, with life-size reproductions of Claude Lorrain on the walls, framed in huge gold hoops. The host was quite nice, rather withdrawn, but the boy who had invited us was altogether infuriating, both snobbish and clumsy. We decided to titillate him a little, mostly on my initiative. Now that it was acknowledged that he was turned on by me, I was retrospectively exasperated by his attitude at La Divina. And I was tempted to project onto him my growing irritation that evening with certain Italian ways of cruising, or of reacting to being cruised. So we talked about the Rosamunda, which of course more or less horrified these middle-class Milanese boys:

"You didn't go there! It's an impossible place! Besides, you never see any real Milanese there, only little workers who come up here from the Mezzogiorno. What an image you must have of Milan!"

~ ~ ~

Having imagined from the way we were dressed that we were glamorous foreigners from whom they could find out if we knew this or that Parisian couturier, or at least his lover, *who moreover is not at all faithful to him, as I am particularly qualified to say, etc.,* they were bitterly disappointed. Nonetheless, since Philippe, swept on by my enthusiasm, ruthlessly insisted on grilling them about all the cruising places in the city—parks, men's rooms, bus stations, specialized movie theaters—they began to suspect, I think, that the attitude implied by such remarks was perhaps very elegant in Paris: after all, we had dined at Giannino's: that point had been established. And although they had at first claimed to know nothing of this, they soon began egging each other on to supply us with all kinds of precious information. This was how we learned of the existence of the Alce movie theater in the Piazzale Martini, whose "extreme vulgarity" seemed to us a very good omen.

~ ~ ~

And we went there the next afternoon, on Saturday.

~ ~ ~

At the Alce there were no ushers, any more than at the Dal Verme or the Argentina, other local movie houses. To get into the theater itself you have to shove aside two sets of heavy velvet curtains about five feet apart. The film was Italian, but its action seemed to be set in Chicago in the thirties. There were a lot of big black limousines and lots of shooting. Most of the rows were empty. On the other hand, many figures were grouped behind the last row of seats, or were hovering to the right or left. Most of these were older men and, as far as could be judged in the semidarkness, quite ugly. One of the scenes of the film, in which some *padrone* or other had gone to identify one of his killers in the livid light of the morgue, allowed us to get a clearer notion of the premises, their layout and their occupants. The right-side aisle between the seats and the wall led to a rather big, high-ceilinged men's room. In the hallway leading into it, two men of about thirty, both emphatically macho, were groping each other's pectorals, biceps, and crotches. Further on, others were waiting without looking at each other, leaning against the damp, leprous wall. The women's room, whose door was ajar, was deserted. In the men's room, two bald forty-year-olds, each holding a cigarette butt between thumb and forefinger, were positioned meditatively in front of the closed doors of one of the toilets.

~ ~ ~

Returning to the theater after this inspection, I thought I recognized, sitting in one of the rows, the boy who had disappeared from the Rosamunda the night before. He was in the last seat of one row, hence right on the aisle. There was someone immediately to his left. I stopped against the wall opposite him and looked at him. He turned his head toward me once or twice, but mostly he seemed to be absorbed by the film and paid me little or no attention. After having stayed beside him for more than five minutes, I returned to the back of the house. Philippe, whom I

rejoined, was rather turned on by two very young boys who were vigorously fucking, standing up between the two rows of curtains, but I didn't
have the nerve to go see what was happening. When I came back toward
the right-hand aisle, the boy from the Rosamunda (for it was indeed he:
on the screen, the mafioso's funeral was taking place in the blinding light
of his native Sicily) got up and headed for the toilets. I followed him, but
slowly. When I went into the part reserved for men, I saw him waiting in
front of a closed door. Then he came out and went into the women's toilets. [*Sequel, Wednesday, April 5: I have to write this faster: we have to give the
manuscript of* Travers *to the publisher before the end of the month.*] I followed
him in. He was leaning against the tile wall, his eyes on the ground. I went
over to him. He smiled. He turned toward me. We were very close to each
other. I closed the door behind me. Then I touched his body through his
open shirt. He drew closer. We then touched each other's chest, crotch.
Then kissed. Someone came in, a man who went into one of the toilets,
leaving the door open, and who watched us while playing with himself. At
which point my companion seemed uneasy and hesitant, as if he wanted
to leave. I hugged him close, pushed aside his shirt, which was almost
completely unbuttoned, and passed first my mouth, then my tongue, over
his right nipple, which seemed to please him a good deal. His chest, belly,
and forearms were absolutely covered with long, thick black hair. He was
not slender, but not heavy either; rather hard and solid.

I decided it was time to try out my Italian on him:

"*Vuoi andare qualche parte d'altre?*"

~ ~ ~

He seemed to understand and nodded what I took for agreement. He
left and I followed him out, but failed to find him in the darkness of the
theater. He was in the lobby, beyond the double curtains, sitting on a banquette covered with velour. I sat down beside him, smiling. He smiled
back. Then he asked me if I was in Milan for long, when I had come, and
where I was from. I launched into a long speech:

"*Sono in un' albergo. Vuoi venire con me? Non sono certo che è possibile di
entrare in la camera, ma probabilmente sì. Hanno una camera con un'amico, le
gente dell'albergo non sai quel è l'amico, sai che hanno una camera per due, so sei
tu e io entrara insiemo, erai probabilmente no problema.*"

~ ~ ~

Again he seemed to get the gist of what I was trying to explain, and in any case he was willing to go with me to my hotel room. He asked me what hotel we were staying in, he knew the hotel Del Duomo, which is a large one, and according to him we would have no difficulties. I told him that I would have to tell my friend who had come to the theater with me that we were leaving. So I went back into the darkness. Philippe gave me the keys to the car, and I found my little Italian waiting for me where I had left him. We left the place together, but he had a car too, so I went back inside to return the keys to Philippe.

~ ~ ~

His car was a Fiat 500, dark blue and considerably banged up. During the ride the driver spoke very little, probably supposing I would not understand anything he said. All the same, I learned that his name was Calogero and that he was from Naples, or more precisely, from Caserte, and that he had lived in Milan for eight years. He went to Caserte every year at Christmas and at Easter and spent his Easter vacation on Capri. Did I know Capri? Yes, and I knew Caserte too, and I liked it a lot. He seemed surprised at that and failed to share my enthusiasm. I wondered if I had made a mistake and if Caserte, of which I had seen only the palace and the park, was not in fact a miserable industrial city. In any case, Calogero felt that the palace looked like a barracks.

~ ~ ~

The night before, after leaving the Rosamunda, he had gone to the H.D.

~ ~ ~

He parked his car in one of the little streets near the Archbishop's Palace, to the right of the Duomo. It was drizzling. We walked around the cathedral, across the square, and he said something about how crowded it usually was on Saturdays.

~ ~ ~

As we entered the hotel lobby, I saw two friends of mine, Giancarlo and Gianni, who were leaving me a note at the registration desk. I introduced them to Calogero but could not introduce him, for I had forgotten his first name. I had been a little nervous, fearing some difficulty with the concierge, but their presence, which confused the situation, facilitated matters. They walked with us, chatting, over to the elevators. Rudolf Nureyev, wearing a long double-breasted leather overcoat that came down to his ankles and a huge cap, walked out of the elevator we were about to take, and this managed to distract attention from us completely.

~ ~ ~

Once we were in the room, I asked Calogero to excuse me for a second and went to take a piss. Then he did the same. During his absence, I took off my shoes and socks and stretched out on the bed. When he returned I was leafing through a picture magazine Philippe had bought. He took off his shoes too and lay down on Philippe's bed, which had been about a foot and a half from mine but which I had pushed next to it. I explained that he was on my friend's bed and that we had better not mess it up, and drew him over onto mine. We immediately began kissing. Then I opened his shirt, or rather the last two buttons still left to unbutton, and ran my fingers over the hair on his torso. He also unbuttoned my shirt. We pressed together, kissing, with a certain frenzy. Then we took off each other's trousers and fell on each other again, one of my legs between his, our cocks together, my arms under his body, my tongue in his mouth. Each time I took one of his nipples between my lips, raising his torso with my right hand, he uttered a moan of pleasure and repeated *"sì, sì, sì."* With my tongue I spread saliva all over the hair on his belly and his chest, and we pressed together in the combined moisture of saliva and sweat. His enthusiasm seemed equal to mine, which was thereby doubled.

~ ~ ~

I sucked his cock, moved on to his balls, to his perineum, to the crack between his buttocks, in a dense forest of long black hair. He raised his legs to allow my tongue to get in deeper.

~ ~ ~

Again I kissed him, again I bit his left tit lightly, my forearms under his shoulders. My cock was between his thighs, its tip between his buttocks. Then I raised his legs with both arms and very slowly pushed my way into his ass. He attempted to make me go even slower, but without too much insistence. My hands in his curls, I raised his head to kiss him. Or else I licked the hollow of his throat or the tips of his nipples, and sometimes I bit them a little without interrupting the movement of my cock between his buttocks: this double sensation was what excited both of us the most. Sometimes I barely moved, sometimes the oscillation of my pelvis became very fast and almost violent. Then I began playing his cock. He came and so did I, immediately after him.

~ ~ ~

We lay still for a moment in each other's arms, bathed in sweat, saliva, and sperm, our mouths full of each other's hair. Then I went to find a towel. I asked Calogero if he wanted something to drink and said I was going to order some tea for myself. He said he would have the same, and when the waiter brought the tray, I asked him through the closed door to leave it in the vestibule. It seemed to me he agreed very dryly.

~ ~ ~

Between cups we talked as much as my Italian permitted. Apparently I did fairly well, according to Calogero, especially in comparison with another Frenchman, whom he had encountered last January and who had not been able to say even one word. Calogero intended to visit Paris at the end of this month; he would be staying in the Rue Racine for four days. I gave him my address and telephone number. He asked me what I did—he himself was a mechanic.

"*Qualle sort di mecanico? Lavora per le automobile?*"

No, he made office furniture, chairs and tables, in a big factory near the airport. But he didn't expect to stay much longer in Milan. One of his friends was going to leave, either for Palermo or for Geneva, and he himself was hesitating between these two cities.

"*Penso che Palermo è molto migliore . . .*"

"*Sì,*" perhaps, but Palermo didn't offer much in the way of diversion.

"*Ma Ginevra non ha alcune distrassione. Ginevra è bella, ricca, sì, ma le gente sono molto seriosi, austeri, protestante. Si tu vuoi molti distrassionni, non penso che Ginevra è una buona idea, no. . . . E è necessario di parlare francese, a Ginevra.*"

~ ~ ~

Yes, he knew that, and he was prepared to learn French, eventually. He lived out in Linate with his mother. He had a brother and four sisters. Two of his sisters were married, they lived in town. The brother was younger than Calogero, but he was married, and his wife, their baby, and he lived with Calogero and his mother, because he would soon have to do his military service. He, Calogero, had finished his service in December. He had been stationed in Verona and had had an affair there with another soldier, the first boy he had made love with, but that was over now.

~ ~ ~

The night before, he had left the Rosamunda because there wasn't a big enough crowd for his taste. It was never really full, except on Saturday. He went out with the same friends most of the time, a boy and a girl from Palermo.

~ ~ ~

I didn't look thirty-one, in his opinion: he would have said twenty-three or twenty-four; he, on the other hand, looked much older, he said, but was only twenty-two.

~ ~ ~

It had grown dark, but we had not turned on any lights. The lights from the square outside and from the cathedral came into the room—some of the statues, which looked more pagan than Christian, were just outside our window.

~ ~ ~

He was lying on the bed, I was sitting cross-legged on the floor, and we were both naked. I took his completely limp cock, with its one bead of sperm on the tip, into my mouth. He got an erection almost immediately. I stretched out beside him again, we kissed some more, and then I went back to sucking his cock.

~ ~ ~

The telephone rang. It was Philippe. Someone at the Alce had told him about another movie house, the Argentina; did I want to try it with him? No, thanks, I was in no condition for cruising or anything else, and very happy with my lot. He would return to the hotel at eight.

~ ~ ~

I went back to sucking Calogero's cock, which was now entirely erect. With one hand I accompanied the movements of my mouth, and with the other I caressed his chest. He kept sighing with pleasure, and when he came, I swallowed all his sperm. I immediately stretched out beside him. I wanted to kiss him and transfer from my mouth to his what sperm remained between my lips, but he turned his head away. So I kissed him in the hollow of his throat, one hand on his chest, the other between his buttocks, and very soon I came again on his belly.

~ ~ ~

Then, I think, we slept for a while. As we changed position, we caressed, licked, kissed each other. I suggested that he have dinner with us. Where were we going? I didn't know yet. Yes, he would like to, but he had a financial problem: when he left home this afternoon he had taken only enough money to go to the movie theater, and now he had virtually nothing left. I told him this didn't matter at all, that he was our guest. He then accepted and telephoned his house to say he wouldn't be home for dinner.

~ ~ ~

We would have to get dressed to be ready for Philippe's return. We took a shower together. At eight, Philippe telephoned. He was in the hotel, downstairs, with a boy he had met at the Argentina; could I let him have the room and leave the key for him at the bar, where he would wait for me? This was what I did, and Calogero and I went for a drink in the Galleria, where we both had a vermouth. I spend a great deal of time telephoning the restaurant Solferino, with no luck, The line was constantly busy; then it turned out to be impossible to reserve a table there. I asked Calogero where all the soldiers were: was there anything going on? No, he thought it was because the soldiers preferred to go out in civilian clothes— look, all those boys, the ones with short hair, are soldiers. He pointed out some who according to him were "selling their wares," or something like that: I wasn't sure of what he meant; certainly the word *mercato* had something to do with it. He had done that too, at the beginning of his service in Verona. Did the phrase mean to do it for money? I still don't know—he broke off quickly; in any case, the subject embarrassed him.

~ ~ ~

We met Philippe at nine in the hotel lobby. His trick wasn't having dinner with us; he was expected by his fiancée, whom he had telephoned to say he would be late. Calogero knew a restaurant near the Duomo, Il

Dollaro, with a lively clientele, he said. But despite what I had been told on the telephone, Philippe was determined to try the Solferino, which had been highly recommended. The restaurant was in the Via Solferino, at the end of the Via Brera, and we had some difficulty getting there, finally abandoning the car and taking a taxi. Philippe managed very skillfully to get us a table, despite the crowd and our lack of reservations, claiming that we had come all the way from Paris just to eat here. The patrons were more or less middle class, many families with children, and anything but gay; the atmosphere was quite pleasant, and the food very good.

~ ~ ~

During dinner, Philippe talked about his trick, Emmanuele, a young gymnast very proud of his muscles and of the photographs that had been taken of him in the shower. He asked Calogero a lot of questions—as many as his Spanish-inspired Italian permitted—about gay life in Milan. Calogero thought that the best bar was La Divina. Philippe agreed, though it seemed to me the Rosamunda was superior. As for the movie theaters, Philippe preferred the Argentina, but Calogero was faithful to the Alce because at the Argentina you couldn't move much. You had to stay seated, and although you might change places from time to time, you couldn't really walk around. I described the movie theater in Rome, the Nuovo Olimpico, of which I had fond memories.

~ ~ ~

Philippe joined me in trying to dissuade Calogero from going to live in Geneva, about which he seemed to have very distorted ideas. Calogero recommended that we order the *maccheroni al basilico,* which was in fact excellent. We communicated with the help of a pocket dictionary I had had the foresight to bring along.

~ ~ ~

Philippe told Calogero that despite all our efforts, we hadn't been able to get seats for La Scala. But Calogero had no use for the opera. A popular singer named Mina stayed at our hotel, he said, when she was in town; she lived in Lugano but didn't sing in public anymore. He also liked Patti Pravo, and *basta!* so much for the Italians. He liked a lot of foreign singers, though.

～ ～ ～

After leaving the restaurant, we walked to the Brera, where I had parked the car. All three of us were going to the Rosamunda. We dropped Calogero at his own car and agreed to follow him, for the night before I had lost the way. But we quickly lost him in traffic and had to get there as best we could by ourselves. We saw him coming toward us down the street as we were parking, and he reproached us for not following him closely enough.

～ ～ ～

At the Rosamunda there was a huge crowd, and Calogero had a lot of friends there. I left him to speak to Gianni and his friend Vittorio. We ran into each other once more and stood together a moment in the uproar, without speaking.

～ ～ ～

When Philippe wanted to go to La Divina, Calogero was nowhere to be seen. Philippe thought he had already left. So we had no chance to say good-bye to each other.

～ ～ ～

[*Saw him again a few weeks later, in Paris. He had not been able to find his friend in the Rue Racine. We made love together one afternoon, but his tastes or his inspiration had changed in this realm, and he no longer wanted to do anything but fuck me. I offered him my maid's room for the two or three nights of his stay. He was to telephone me about this, after a visit to the Continental-Opéra baths. No doubt something better turned up, for he did not call back.*

*A few months later, I received a postcard from him. He apologized, gave me his address, and asked me to write him. I did not write.*]

**Tom**

*Thursday, August 10, 1978*

During one week in San Francisco, I had seen him several times, late at night, in the Black and Blue south of Market Street, and each time in the rather cramped, always crowded passageway that serves as a fuck room.

The first time, my attention had been drawn to him during a scene that had amused me. He was trying to fuck a boy of about twenty, who was very enthusiastic about the endeavor. But his cock was so unbelievably big that he was getting nowhere, as he might have expected, for no doubt he had already encountered this particular problem before. Few assholes certainly were in condition to accommodate him. Yet he seemed amazed and furious. He redoubled his efforts, swearing the while.

~ ~ ~

Standing beside him and his putative partner, I had tried to help them, as several other volunteers were also doing: spreading the buttocks of the one, directing the other's member. On this occasion I had touched him, and not only his cock, whose proportions had astonished me, but his balls, his ass, his belly, his chest. In the darkness, I couldn't see him very clearly, but I decided he had a good head, an open expression that contradicted his current anger, a great deal of energy, and a very muscular body, though more the muscles of a laborer than of an athlete. Tony, to whom I had mentioned him afterward, and who had seen him as well, maintained that he was at least forty. It was my impression that he was about thirty. But in any case we were agreed about his most notable feature, and between ourselves we referred to him as "the Horse."

~ ~ ~

From his stubborn insistence on penetrating the ass of the poor kid, and from his rage at not succeeding, I had supposed he was interested in only the one sexual role. But the next night, or the next after that, in precisely the same place, I had seen him being fucked by a rather handsome boy—part Japanese, probably, or perhaps Chinese—and at the same time sucking someone else's cock. I was standing next to this someone else and kissing him. Someone in the melee had taken out my cock and was playing with it. The Horse may have had the fantasy of mobilizing as many cocks as he could, because he began playing with me, after having rather cavalierly—so to speak—shoved away the hand already thus occupied. Then he drew me as close as he could to the boy whose cock he was sucking and took my cock into his mouth as well. The other fellow may have found this sharing inadmissible, or else he was attracted by another of the countless combinations in the little passageway, for he moved away. The Horse then devoted his entire mouth to my cock, while playing with a newcomer and continuing to be fucked by the Eurasian, who leaned forward and drew my face toward his own. We kissed each other. I had one hand on the cock of one of my neighbors and the other on the Horse's chest. He, however, wanted to perform a variation on this arrangement: he straightened up, kissing me as he did so, turned around, and offered me his ass, into which I introduced my cock without the slightest difficulty, and he began sucking the cock of the Eurasian, whom I kissed again. Poppers were circulating from some unknown source.

～ ～ ～

For about twenty minutes, perhaps more, we gave ourselves up to permutations which invariably afforded the Horse at least one cock in his ass and another in his mouth. Tony, appearing from some nearby entertainment, joined us. For a while, he took my position behind the Horse and fucked him. No one actually thought of coming: everyone had already done so, and no one did again. This moment, moreover, never clearly came to an end. It dissolved imperceptibly: each of the participants, gradually and almost unconsciously, found himself involved in other exchanges, and if the scene continued, it was with a different cast of characters.

～ ～ ～

On the night of August 10, Tony and I were again at the Black and Blue, as was the Horse. He and I recognized each other, smiled, kissed, but between one in the morning, when Tony and I arrived, and two, which was closing time, there were few contacts between us. Nonetheless, he seemed quite amiable.

～ ～ ～

Closing time at the Black and Blue is followed by a rather prolonged period of indecision. A good half of those who have been inside remain outside on the sidewalk in front of the doors, in a radius of about fifty yards. Friends talk to each other, plans for the rest of the night are discussed, final passes are made.

～ ～ ～

Tony and I were sitting on the fender of a car a little distance away. We were in a very good mood, a little drunk, a little stoned, curious about the local customs, and reluctant to go home unaccompanied. Yet among the boys present, those who interested one of us failed to turn on the other, or vice versa, and if both of us were interested, then *they* were interested in only one of us, or neither.

~ ~ ~

A ways off, I glimpsed the Horse talking with a boy he seemed to be cruising, but their conversation led to nothing, apparently, and they separated. At this moment, Tony had altered his opinion about the Horse's age and agreed with me that he was quite handsome. We decided I would speak to him, since he seemed to regard me as an acquaintance, and discover what his intentions might be. I therefore went over to him. He was all smiles and asked if I was going somewhere else, to one of the clubs that stayed open all night. I didn't know yet, what about him? He didn't know either. It depended on what came up. Well, maybe I could help him out: would he like to come to my place? Yes, he would, or else we could go to his place, which would be more convenient for him in case I had a car, because he didn't. Yes, I had a car, and I would like to go home with him, but I was with a friend. That was fine with him; in fact, the more the merrier. We could leave right now, the three of us, he would go wherever we liked, dancing, or to the baths, or to our place, or to his. I brought this news to Tony, and returned with him to the Horse, whose name was Tom.

~ ~ ~

We decided to go to his place. We got into the car, I behind the wheel. He lived in Noe Valley, a stone's throw away from Castro Street, but much farther south than the Castro Cinema and the liveliest part of the street. No, actually it wasn't so far, but I was considerably stoned, I remember now, and I had a very imprecise sense of distances: I was driving with such extreme caution that the streets seemed endless. Sitting to my right, Tom was giving me directions with one hand, the other resting on my thigh. Tony, sitting behind us, leaning forward, had draped his forearms around Tom's shoulders.

~ ~ ~

No sooner had we come into the apartment than our problems began, though I'm not sure in exactly what order. Tony vanished into the bathroom. Tom came over to me and put his hand on my crotch. No reaction at all. His own cock was only half erect; even so, it nearly reached the middle of his thigh. It seemed to me that the ratio of size between my cock and his was at that moment about one to ten. I was a little intimidated. Then he offered me a beer. I said I preferred a glass of water, but he opened a can. I didn't like the taste on his breath.

～　～　～

We were in a rather large room, with a "dining room set" in it: an enormous table, six chairs, a sideboard, a serving table. Everything was in pale beige wood, in that Spanish Renaissance ("Mission") style so popular in California. In comparison, our own early Third Republic–Henri II seems light and graceful. In any case, this solemn presence was no help to me in getting an erection. It even seemed to have the opposite effect, if such a thing exists, as I believe it does. My cock was visibly shrinking and stubbornly remained in hiding.

～　～　～

To gain time, I decided to suck Tom. I crouched down, my knees apart, and immediately ripped the seam of the old white trousers I was wearing. I had to stand up again to get them off. Tom then suggested that we go into his bedroom. But it was lit brighter than daylight by a very powerful ceiling fixture, which spared no detail. Luckily, Tony, returning, asked Tom if he could turn it off and didn't even wait for his answer to do so.

～　～　～

Now we were all together on the big bed. Tony had a fine erection, Tom half a one, and I none at all. Tom was very attentive to me, kind, patient, and persistent, but he had that localized, pinpointed approach to sex which I deplore. He sucked my cock, wanted me to fuck him, constantly changed position, so that not for a moment could I simply be in his arms, kissing him peacefully before getting on to something else. He kept making a strange noise, a deep sigh of satisfaction or admiration, which I hardly seemed to deserve.

～　～　～

Tony fucked him quite rapidly while I was playing with his cock or sucking it. Then Tom wanted me to fuck him as well. Thighs raised, he offered me his ass, while my cock was about the size of my thumb. Finally he acknowledged the obvious and abandoned this project. The next one was for him to fuck me. I dared not refuse altogether, since I had nothing better to propose. Besides, he himself had only half an erection, and I imagined this would come to nothing. That is in fact what occurred. But there was nonetheless an uncomfortably long quarter of an hour filled with efforts that for me were both tiresome and painful. He kept trying to get his huge but not entirely hard cock into me, while Tony, somehow full of energy, was fucking him once again. Furthermore, Tom seemed to derive more pleasure from the latter than from the former. When Tony came in his ass, he gave up trying to come in mine and stretched out across the bed. In two or three minutes, and without ever managing to get a real erection, I then came on his belly, to his mild surprise. Then Tony and I tried for a very long while to get him to the point of ejaculation as well, but to no avail, and it was he who called a halt to our efforts.

~ ~ ~

His mood, despite this failure, remained excellent. Everything seemed to delight him. I don't remember how his monologue began, for that is what it was, our infrequent interventions merely serving, in the main, to keep him going. He told us that he liked us, that we were a handsome couple, and he wanted to know how long we had known each other:

"Nine years? That's incredible. That just doesn't happen here, couples who stay together that long. Well, yes, maybe, but it's rare, very rare, if it does happen. I know one guy, he works in the house, the other day I saw him in a restaurant, he was with a really hot boy, a really *hot* number. [*If I could give some idea of the way he pronounced this adjective, with the very clearly aspirated* h *and the very extended* o, *doubtless I could manage to give some idea of what Tom was like, his sweetness, his humor, and the kind of perpetual enthusiasm that seemed to be his distinctive feature.*] The next day I met this guy and I said to him, 'God, that kid you were with yesterday, wow, he was really hot.' He smiled and squinted his eyes, and he said, 'Really, you think he was really all that hot?' I started to say, 'Believe me, I—' And he said, 'We've been together thirteen years.' I couldn't believe it. Thirteen years! In San Francisco! With a guy like that! There really has to be something between them, huh, something special, something strong, something unique, like between the two of you; it shows—I can tell."

~ ~ ~

Maybe it was from that, and from the life of homosexuals in San Francisco, that he went on to Proposition Six, which was stirring California that summer. Or was it Proposition Thirteen? Whichever, I no longer have a clear idea of it now; in truth, it was quite dim in my mind even that August, so I confused it with the other one, of which I was a staunch supporter and which prohibited smoking in public places. Anyway, Proposition whatever-its-number-was specifically concerned homosexuals and was presented, especially by its detractors, as the local fallout from Anita Bryant's actions in Florida and on a national scale. Its goal, according to those who supported the plan, was to protect children and adolescents against homosexuals in schools. The measures envisaged were creating a great stir in the gay community. Everywhere, leaflets were being distributed, petitions circulated, collections taken up to mount a countercampaign. According to Tom, whose convictions on this point were very firm and almost violent, it was quite simply a matter of imminent fascism:

"The Jewish community understood it right away, they know the problem, they know what they're talking about, and they're almost all with us. You understand how it works: some kid who has bad grades, all he needs to do is claim that his teacher made a pass at him, and bang, the teacher gets fired. The slightest suspicion, the slightest accusation, is enough. Actually, what's involved is simply a way of keeping gays from teaching. Of course, in San Francisco it's all a big joke. Three-quarters of the teachers are fags. Besides, here in the city, the proposition won't go through. Between us and the Jews—and then, too, there's a certain liberal tradition around here—it'll be blocked. But in Los Angeles they're so conservative, they're so scared, it's incredible. It'll go through. And in the rest of the state it's almost a sure thing."

~ ~ ~

Tony and I, in a kind of half-sleep, listened to him with pleasure. He spoke well, in a very lively way, with a lot of idiomatic expressions, some of which, it's true, escaped me entirely. From California politics he went on to the national scene. He seemed to regard it as no more than a spectacle and to evaluate the principal figures solely as actors or directors, according to their presence on television and the dramatic effects they could produce. Carter, for instance, might have been a "good guy," but he had no sense of humor, no entertainment value. . . .

"While Nixon! Oh, those were the good old days. You can't imagine how much fun we all had! We were glued to our TV sets all day, all night. It was a national trip. No serial could compete. Every day we wondered what he was going to come up with next, what new rabbit he would pull out of his hat. The public was on edge, and he played it like a virtuoso. You could really say he was an artist with the public. The people who miss him—and there *are* some—know perfectly well he was a crook. But for the most part they don't care. And besides, in those days, even the others, the secondary figures, were good. Great supporting casts, even for the most obscure parts, down to Nixon's dog. McGovern and the Eagleton business, you remember that, that was a good one too: *I'm a hundred percent behind Senator Eagleton!* And Agnew? Agnew was incredible. They don't make them like that anymore, they wouldn't dare!"

～ ～ ～

The political and parapolitical serials led him to the real ones, and Tony roused himself a little to evoke, with mounting enthusiasm, dozens of soap operas of their childhood, and increasingly obscure television actors, and the return of Cesar Romero, *who had been Tyrone Power's wife* and who for ten years had publicized I don't know what, and singers that were already forgotten in 1965, and even the commercials of the fifties, which they both remembered with a certain emotion. I listened, excluded yet fascinated, amazed all over again by America's power to elaborate a complete and modern mythological fabric, etc., etc. They were punching each other on the belly, on the ass. . . .

～ ～ ～

"And you remember Lana Carsons [*I'm inventing the name, I've forgotten them all, a good hundred must have paraded past*], who was always so unhappy because she wanted to have straight hair? And what was the one whose boyfriends always dropped her? The one who was always getting ditched? And Jimmy Montero, who kept getting inside refrigerators!"

～ ～ ～

They laughed until they lost their breath, or else they became quite moved, and I realized with a certain irritation that in France, we had nothing so richly nostalgic in the same realm, and that the evocation of *Persil lave plus blanc,* of the *Famille Duraton,* or of *Thierry la Fronde* would never manage to create such an immediate solidarity between two strangers.

～　～　～

We left around four in the morning, perhaps five. Tom walked out onto his landing to see us off. His cock looked even more stupefying at a distance. There had been no question of seeing each other again, except by accident. He was still as merry as ever, and seemed delighted by his evening.

～　～　～

[*Never saw him again.*]

## ∼ *Tony Duvert* ∼

### FROM
# *When Jonathan Died*

TRANSLATED BY D. R. ROBERTS

As the sun shone brightly every day, Jonathan put the washing to dry outside. In any case, there was too much now to hang up in the kitchen, as he used to.

He did the washing in the old way, with ancient equipment he found in the cellar: a concrete sink, a copper with its chimney, a gas ring, a beetle, and a scrubbing brush that had lost half its bristles. He liked this solid labor—which pleased him all the more when there was Serge's dirty clothing mixed in with his own. He took very great care with it. Serge, curious, watched him all the way through. He only knew the laundries in town, and this domestic laundering pleased him. It was the second-to-last day. Everything would be clean, mended, and ironed, ready for his departure.

Jonathan had felt the secret urge to steal some of the boy's clothes, to hide them. He didn't dare. Barbara and Serge were carefree enough for the theft to go unnoticed, but in Jonathan's solitude, these clothes would take up too much space, would be too much present, in the bottom of their cupboard, where Jonathan would never look at them, except perhaps the one time before rolling them up into a ball and throwing them into a river very far from here, well weighed down with stones.

---

*TONY DUVERT's* When Jonathan Died *may be the most controversial selection in this anthology, because even among gay men pedophilia is the love, as Lord Alfred Douglas wrote in his poem "Two Loves," "that dare not speak its name." But because the novel makes no effort to justify or to persuade, it does both.*

His neighbor's face clouded when she saw him hanging the pretty washing on the line. These small-sized clothes were women's property; no gentleman should touch them. She shrugged her shoulders, murmured to herself, remained hidden. They were well washed, the whites white, the colors bright, the woolens light and fluffy, fresh as a daisy. Bad work, of course, would have pleased her more. She could have intervened, told what she knew, been a little bit in charge.

Serge helped to hang the washing. He pulled out his own clothes from the basket, as he didn't dare touch Jonathan's. Then he decided to hold one item out, and another, with a lewd laugh, almost dancing. Jonathan, clothespins in his mouth, did not react. Their fabric silhouettes waved about in the wind, shone in the sunshine, very naked and very naive among the sheets and the napkins.

When they washed together, Serge was not so ironical: true nakedness wiped out the differences that clothing indicated or created. They would heat a big saucepan of water and get the tin bath ready in the middle of the kitchen, pushing the table and chairs aside. It was done late in the afternoon, so Serge wouldn't get cold, and lasted almost till dinner. First of all Jonathan washed the boy; he did this in workmanlike fashion, and he remained clothed. Serge behaved himself, standing straight as a soldier. But then Jonathan would undress, pour more water into the bath, and stand up in it; the boy, his face scarlet with heat and his body pearled over with drops of water, would begin his provocations, his tricks and his dirty talk. A carnival of nakedness, damp, cool air on bare bottom, sex upright, in the kitchen, at teatime, time for leaving school.

"Big balls!" He chuckled, squinting sideways at Jonathan's penis, then grabbing it, slapping and twisting it before declaring: "I'm going to wash you!"

He would soap Jonathan vigorously all over, thoroughly, leaving nothing out, as carefree and energetic as a housewife bathing her kids. Jonathan washed only his face and his hair, too high for the boy to deal with without difficulty.

This scrubbing got Serge excited. He seemed hungry. At first he'd avoided getting wet again, but then he'd stopped caring, getting soap on himself where he pressed against Jonathan. On his skin there were round or oval patches fringed about with soapsuds, showing where their bodies had touched.

The pushing and shoving ended with water splashed all over the floor.

They had to abandon the kitchen. Serge and Jonathan went up the stairs, and they wrapped themselves up in the one bath towel, the little one lying on top of the big one. The boy started his games again on the young painter's stomach, or on his back. As Serge twisted about, their skin, moist and slippery with soap, would make contact then break apart again, making farting and sucking noises.

Calm returned after what quenches boyish passion. Now Serge would decide he was dry enough and get down to essentials—sitting on Jonathan, head toward his feet, as if he were an armchair made for the purpose. Jonathan's legs, pulled up a little, made up the back of the chair, his belly, sex now quiescent, made the seat. Depending on the day, Serge would lie there on his back, or curled up, or even on his stomach; the angle of the chair back would be arranged to suit. In every case, the object was to offer Jonathan a part to be caressed as long as Serge thought fit. Invariably, the caress was a stroke of the index finger, or rather of its tip, which followed a fixed course, without pressure, and without any modification of its rhythm. The finger touched the divide of the buttocks, an inch or two above the hole, slipped along, brushed along one side of the ring, or passed teasingly over the middle, continued onward, faster, circled about the sac, and then faded away. Three seconds later it began again at the top and started on its way again. By the hundredth stroke the fine grain of the childish skin seemed to Jonathan to be raised, almost rasping, while the flesh of his finger felt flayed to the quick.

Other caresses interested Serge less, or led him on toward other things. But this stroke was sufficient to itself. Soon the boy's erection would decline: he'd put his thumb in his mouth and shut his eyes, more still and more relaxed than if he'd been asleep. Busied with this monotonous duty, Jonathan too felt dozy, but if his finger left off for a moment, Serge's voice would call out straightaway:

"Go on, go on."

They had inaugurated this ritual the year before, one morning when they were alone and had been sleeping naked. Serge, allowed access to the resources of a grown-up boy, had discovered the position where Jonathan could be used as a chaise longue and, pleased that an anatomy should be so habitable, had appropriated it, graciously but without right of appeal. Jonathan embraced the nakedness open before his face. The little caress was born among others, and Serge had picked it out, explaining, with the lewdest laugh of which he was capable:

"It makes electricity in my bottom!"

"We could put a bulb there," Jonathan suggested.

"A bulb, eh! Go on, do it again!"

The same time had seen the beginning of the thumb sucking and the doziness. Otherwise, in going to sleep at six years old, Serge chewed an old napkin he held gripped in his fist.

His first morning in the country, before they'd really woken up, they'd again taken up this position, with the strange perfection one sees in the movement of birds, the sleep of foxes. Jonathan experienced it as a rite of rebirth, vegetal, slow, and secret in its monotony, in its forgetting of time, of acts, of images. Their other sensual intimacies were commonplace; this one owed its singularity to the repetition and hypnosis it engendered.

It wasn't a pleasure for the evening, or for the garden. Serge looked for it only in bed, on waking up, or after his bath.

His all-over wash, two or three times a week, was an occasion that concentrated all the ideas and extravagances inspired in him by Jonathan's nakedness and his own. He amused himself in urinating from afar into the tin bath, and he knew how to pull back and pinch so as to obtain a jet as long and straight as if from a fire hose. He wanted Jonathan to do the same; naturally modest, Jonathan pretended he hadn't the necessary liquid.

"You've only got to drink," the boy insisted.

"It won't come through straightaway," said Jonathan. Serge aimed at the tub from the door of the kitchen, or pretended to be looking for a mouse to pee on. But they were frightened by the tumult, and there wasn't one to be found.

They usually appeared after dinner, and their favorite stage was the top of the stove. There they nibbled whatever had been spilled from the saucepans; these half-burned residues, which Jonathan would clean up in the morning, they found more pleasing than the little meals put on the ground, which they often left untouched. The milk curdled, the jam skinned over, the bacon sweated. Then the saucers would be found empty, as clean as if an army of rats had invaded this kitchen in Cockaigne.

Serge was not as fond of animals as one might have thought from the attention he paid to them. He was curious above all about Jonathan, about Jonathan's space and everything in it, alive or dead.

The bedroom, for example, was a place where, if they stayed reading and watching, naked under the warm bedclothes, neither moving nor talking, they would see the mice, no, one mouse, her or her brother, making an audacious appearance, risking even the bedspread at their feet, as if it followed a necessary path, unavoidable whatever dangers it brought.

They eyed the two boys with such intelligence, with such a mixture of hesitations, twists and turns and bold advances, that instead of vermin they seemed dwarves, faery creatures, related to gnomes, elves, and sprites, the whole miniature riffraff that once peopled the world, laughing behind people's backs before playing their tricks on them. But Serge would have preferred the mouse to have appeared while he was playing with Jonathan, and he would have put the mouse just there.

It was what he'd tried to do with the rabbit, as they slept together that night. After having fun running with it on the ground, Serge took it onto the bed and put it down in the nest of his thighs; the animal didn't even take a sniff at his sex. To tell the truth, it didn't really want to be there, and Serge had difficulty in keeping it. But this quivering ball of fur inspired the boy to further impudence; he spread his legs and showed the little rabbit his hole, huddled the little ball against it, talking dirty as he did so. Between two shrill laughs, he felt the tickling of the furry little animal, whose skin and ears were shivering as it tried to get away.

Jonathan was troubled by Serge's cynicism; he held back an urge to do the same thing (in a scene where Serge would be the rabbit). He would have preferred to be mistreated himself, when the child changed his toy.

For Serge, gentle and delicate in love, became pugnacious as soon as his pretty little sex was involved. He wrangled with Jonathan's own as if it were an unbreakable rod. Serge also liked to bite. In his first year at school, several children were scared of him because of it. Sometimes he dared test Jonathan's endurance to the blood, taking a bite at a cheek, a forearm, a nipple or a hip, where he chewed away at a fold of flesh grasped near the liver. His eyes watering with pain, Jonathan submitted to this mystery and saw in it no cruelty but that of primitive initiations, of tribal bonds and childish pacts—the more tender, should it resemble the emotion it left behind it.

Jonathan's other source of happiness, on bathing days, was to smell in the boy's hair the extraordinary scent of cheap shampoo, after their pleasure had been taken, and they had pulled the bedclothes round their necks, put the lamp out, and drawn their heads close together for sleep.

~ ~ ~

If Serge's manner was now very affectionate, and sometimes very demonstratively so, he had, however, become less sociable. Children his own age hardly attracted his attention now; as for adults, he never looked at them. He said nothing about his parents; from time to time there would be word of them, a postcard; for a few moments his expression would cloud over, or become absent, then he seemed to forget all about it.

His curiosity about Jonathan grew. He demanded stories, wanted to know all about his life. Jonathan did what he was told, said what he could. He found this horrible. He liked neither to lie nor to simplify; he had to.

The young boy's beauty also troubled Jonathan, and he couldn't get used to it. He hoped it would be fleeting; he sometimes thought, with a certain sadness, of the Serge he knew before, who did not strike the eye, or who wasn't beautiful, like this one, apart from, or in addition to himself.

This impression kept Jonathan shy. He never dared to take the initiative in their couplings. He almost regretted that they had taken place. He had an infinite need of them. Without Serge's kindliness, his ease and his vulgar greed, those moments would have been hard to bear.

They had always fucked a bit. This is what had astonished Jonathan when in Paris he'd slept alongside the child—then hardly seven years old—who would turn his back on him and go to sleep with his bottom pressed into the hollow of the young man's thighs, both of them curled up together. In the morning he would regain the position, and once, without saying a word, he slipped his hand behind him, took the sex that lay along the divide of his buttocks, and moved his hips so as to put it just at the hole. Jonathan didn't dare move, and pretended to be still asleep. But that very evening, when they were in bed and had indulged in various caresses, they were again in the same position; and Jonathan, as the boy's hole was still wet with saliva, pushed in his sex. He had not imagined it so elastic. When he had gone in about the length of a finger, he heard Serge, his voice calm, murmur simply:

"That hurts a bit."

He withdrew straightaway and would not start again. The disproportion terrified him, although Serge, for his part, seemed quite unaware of it.

Later the child repeated the gesture. Jonathan understood better then the pleasures of this little body. He didn't penetrate, or hardly, but in this way masturbated the anus at length, until he flooded it, then wiped it dry, unless Serge demanded, as he did on some later occasions, with placid tyranny:

"No, you must keep on when it's wet."

The thing was part of their routine, without occupying a privileged place. As for Serge, after various low and hesitant provocations, he had found means to amuse himself with the young man's bottom, although for orgasms he relied on his hands.

So for a long time this sodomy had been mixed up with other pleasures; among them, it was nothing special, it went unnoticed. Only the child's growing up, or the length of their intimacy, had gradually modified the nature of the penetrations—much deeper, but still almost static, on Jonathan's part; more skillful, less facetious, longer and more solidly implanted, on Serge's.

A development that continued through that summer. But an outside event had also intervened. In fact, Serge told Jonathan that a little while before the holidays, he'd sucked a boy of fifteen—who had also fucked him without reserve. It was one of the crowd of men and girls of all ages, more or less, who used to visit Barbara's. The suggestion, abrupt, had come from the teenager; Serge had agreed without fuss. Nothing came of it; the elder boy, having done his bit, must have got the jitters and had never set foot in the house again.

This story left Jonathan perplexed. He hadn't imagined that Serge could have done such a thing; the child spoke of it disdainfully, with a laugh in his voice—all the people who hung around with Barbara were idiots. He was, however, just a tiny bit proud of what had happened, Jonathan could see it clearly. But the false notions the young painter still entertained about children, despite himself, prevented him from being able to interpret and understand the event.

Nor did he conclude that now Serge would be willing to go further than before, that his desires might be more focused, nor that he might take bolder initiatives. In this he was wrong.

It wasn't a question of pleasures that Serge loved for love of Jonathan; he sought them out for themselves. When he thought of Jonathan, he hugged him; when he thought of cock or arse, he used it. It was this carefreeness that enabled Jonathan to bear these encounters, that otherwise would have so intimidated him as to force him to give them up. As Serge passed without transition, without any signal, according to whim, from what was "sexual" to what was not, and vice versa, and liked to deal with the young man as if he, on his side, had no actual personal desires of his own, Jonathan was cast down and comforted in turn, unhappy at being alone in his desire, glad no longer to be so, sexed or unsexed according to the unpredictable motions of the child, of whom he was himself no more than the place, flesh and mirror.

# ～ *Edward Limonov* ～

**FROM**

# *It's Me, Eddie*

TRANSLATED BY S. L. CAMPBELL

### *Others and Raymond*

I really got over my tragedy very fast, all things considered. Granted, I'm not quite over it even yet, but all the same the pace has been startling. I've known of other such tragedies, and people have recovered slowly, if at all. It was March when I made my first attempts at intimacy with men, and by April I had my first lover.

One day in March, Kirill, the young aristocrat from Leningrad, mentioned that he was acquainted with a fellow a little over fifty and that he was a homosexual.

For some reason this stuck in my mind. "Kirill, old buddy," I said finally, "women rouse me to disgust, my wife has made intercourse with women impossible for me, I can't deal with them. They're always having to be serviced, undressed, fucked. They're panhandlers and parasites by nature, in everything from intimate relations to the economics of the normal joint household in society. I can't live with them anymore. The main thing is, I can't service them—take the initiative, make the first move. What I need now is someone to service me—caress, kiss, want me—rather than wanting and being ingratiating myself. Only from men can I get all this. You'd never guess I'm thirty fucking years old, I'm nice and trim, my fig-

---

*Born in the Ukraine, near Gorky, in 1944, EDWARD LIMONOV moved to Moscow in 1967, then emigrated to the West in 1974. An iconoclastic chronicler of the émigré experience, he lives in Paris.*

ure is faultless, more like a boy's than a man's, even. Introduce me to this fellow," I begged. "Please, Kirill, I'll be eternally grateful!"

"Limonov, are you serious?" Kirill asked.

"You think I'm joking?" I replied. "Look at me. I'm alone now, I'm at the very bottom of this society—the bottom of it, hell, I'm simply outside it, outside of life. Sexually I'm totally freaked out, women don't arouse me, my dick is faint with incomprehension, it just dangles because it doesn't know what to want and its master is sick. If things go on like this, I'll end up impotent. I need a friend. There's no question in my mind, men have always liked me, always, they've liked me since I was thirteen. I need a solicitous friend to help me return to the world, a man to love me. I'm weary, no one has worried about me for a long time, I want attention, I want to be loved and fussed over. Introduce me, and I'll take care of the rest, really, he'll like me."

I wasn't lying to Kirill; it was a fact. I had even had some long-term admirers; I had snickered at their advances, but somehow I had enjoyed their attention. Now and then I had even allowed myself to go to a restaurant with them; once in a while, for the fun of it or maybe the stimulation, I had allowed them to kiss me, but we never fucked. Among ordinary people same-sex love was considered impure, dirty. In my country pederasts are very unfortunate. At the whim of the authorities they can be entrapped and put in prison for what in the opinion of Soviet law is an unnatural love. I knew a pianist who did two years for pederasty; the film director Paradzhanov is doing time now. But that is the attitude of ordinary people, the authorities, the law. I was a poet, and I had been intoxicated by Mikhail Kuzmin's "Alexandrian Songs" and other poems, where he sings the praises of his male lover and tells about love between men.

My most persistent admirer was a red-haired singer named Avdeev from the Teatralny Restaurant. The restaurant was directly across from my apartment windows. Every evening, if I was home, I could hear his voice belting out "Mama's Poor Heart" and other semiunderworld songs. The restaurant was small and on the dirty side; every night they had almost exclusively the same crowd. Among the habitués were thieves, Gypsies from the outskirts of Kharkov, and other shady characters. In summer I heard my singer's voice loudly, at its natural volume; in winter, muffled by the closed windows.

I had just moved in with Anna, a beautiful, gray-haired Jewish woman. We lived together as man and wife; it was a happy time for me: my poetry went well, life was good, I drank a lot, I had a good coffee-colored English suit (which I hadn't come by quite honestly), I spent a lot of time hanging out on the main street of our city with my dear friend Gennady, handsome Gena, son of the manager of the largest restaurant in town.

Gena was a sheer joy. An idler, he saw his calling in drinking sprees and parties, but sumptuous ones. Strange as it may seem, his attitude toward women was almost indifferent. Even though he appeared to love Nona, who came on the scene later, he could give up a date with her for an excursion with me to a little out-of-town restaurant we called the Monte Carlo, where they made sumptuous chicken *tabaka*. My friendship with Gena lasted several years, until I went to Moscow. Gena and I were rakes, like Fellini's provincial city boys.

The relationship with Gena, I think, was one facet of my innate homosexuality. To keep a date with him, I used to escape my wife and mother-in-law by jumping from a second-story window. I loved him very much, although we didn't even embrace. As I now see, I was all entangled in homosexual liaisons, only I didn't understand that. When I said good-bye to Gena at the corner—I lived on Sumskaya Street, our main street, where the Teatralny was—Avdeev would come out of the restaurant. He had dark circles under his eyes, his lightly made-up lips glistened, and he would walk over and say in a hollow, languid voice, "Good evening!" Sometimes he had to cross the street to do it. I believe he even interrupted his songs for the sake of this "Good evening"; I mean, he rushed right off the stage. He had a clear view of the street through the big windows. Often I was very drunk, and my friends recall that Avdeev sometimes helped me to my house, walked me into the entrance, and started me up the stairs.

Back before Gena and the nightly scene of Avdeev's figure bowed in greeting, back when I was in school, I had a butcher friend, Sanya the Red, a huge man of German descent with a florid complexion, which was why he was nicknamed "the Red." He was six or eight years older than I. I showed up at the butcher shop first thing in the morning, I went everywhere with him, I even accompanied him on dates with girls, and besides, we had a more solid tie—we worked together. We stole. I played the role of a cherubic poet—usually this was at the dance pavilion or out in the park—I recited poems to the astonished, open-mouthed girls, and meanwhile Sanya the Red, with his stubby, clumsy-looking fingers, would lightly and surreptitiously (he was a great artist at this business) remove the girls' watches and pick their purses. It was all beautifully thought out; we never once got caught. As you see, my art then went hand in hand with crime. Afterward we either headed for a restaurant or bought a couple of bottles of wine, drank them right from the bottle in the park or in a doorway, and went for a walk.

I very much enjoyed appearing with him on the streets and in crowded places. He dressed brightly, wore gold rings—one had a skull, I remember, that captured my fancy. He had the taste of a gangster, as they are depicted in the movies. On a summer evening, for example, he liked to wear white pants, a black shirt, and rakish white suspenders; he had a predilection for suspenders. A huge man—he had a paunch, which got bigger and bigger with the years—he in no way resembled the ordinary, in those years rather drab inhabitants of our city, which is a provincial industrial center with the largest proletariat in the Ukraine.

Then he got sent up—went to prison for attempting to rape a woman with whom he had had sex many times before. In prison he worked in the kitchen and . . . wrote poetry. When he got out, someone skewered him well with a knife. "Even my fat didn't help!" he complained, when I visited him in the hospital.

He was kind to me, he encouraged me in writing poetry and very much enjoyed listening to poetry. Several summers in a row, at his request, I read to an astonished crowd at the city beach lines that went something like this:

> My girl they will snatch
> From the car by the nape
> And I will then watch
> The men commit rape
>
> Men with pates jutting
> With cigarettes vile
> Will run like dogs rutting
> Round the scam of your thighs . . .

It is funny and sad to read these lines, written by a sixteen-year-old, but I am forced to confess to myself that they strike an unpleasantly prophetic note. The world has fucked my love, and the men with jutting pates—the businessmen and merchants—are the ones who now fuck her, my little Elena. . . .

I was devoted to Sanya, body and soul. Had he wished it, I probably would have slept with him. But evidently he didn't know he could use me in this way, or had no inclination to, or wasn't sophisticated enough. Russia's mass culture didn't serve this to him on a platter the way American culture does.

Such is my history. A love for strong men. I see it now, and confess. Sanya the Red was so strong that he used to break the bars in the fence around the outdoor dance pavilion; the bars were as thick as a big man's arm. True, he did this only when we didn't have the fifty kopecks for admission.

Gena was tall, well built, and looked like a young Nazi. Dark-blue eyes. I never met a more handsome man.

My friendships are intelligible to me now. Those were but two, the most memorable; there were others, but for many years I lived as if in a fog, and only when my tragedy opened my eyes did I suddenly see my life from a new perspective.

Well, I somehow convinced Kirill, who was listening with awe, that my desire was sincere. He listens that way to the stories of all his companions, not just to mine, with a great show of interest, as if this were his main business in life; but it's only show. He's a young man who promises much but does little. In this case, thank God, I knew he wasn't stretching the truth to make himself look good, he really was living temporarily in the apartment of some homosexual who was out of town. I had visited him there and seen the special magazines for men, and all the rest of it. What the hell, maybe Kirill really would introduce me. I was forced to grasp at anything, I had nothing; we were alien to this world. Ignorance of the language, especially conversation; prostration after my tragedy; prolonged isolation from society—for all these reasons I was unutterably lonely. All I was doing was bumming around New York on foot, sometimes walking two hundred and fifty blocks a day, bumming around in neighborhoods both dangerous and safe, sitting, lying, smoking, drinking from a bottle in a paper bag, sleeping in the street. I would go two or three weeks without talking to anyone.

Time passed. I called Kirill once or twice and asked how things were, when would he keep his promise and introduce me to this fellow. He muttered something incomprehensible, justifying himself and obviously inventing excuses. I had completely given up hope in him, when suddenly he called me and said in an unnaturally theatrical voice, "Listen, remember our conversation? I'm here with a friend, he's French, his name is Raymond, he'd like to see you. Come on over, we'll have a drink and talk awhile—it's next door to your hotel."

I said, "Kirill, is it that fellow, the pederast?"

"Yes," he said, "but not that one."

I said, "All right, I'll be there in an hour."

"Make it quick," he said.

I am not going to lie and say that I rushed over there with flaming eyes and fire in my loins. No. I vacillated and was somewhat scared. For a minute or two I didn't even want to go. Then I spent a long time wondering what to wear. In the end I dressed very strangely, in torn French blue jeans and a fine new Italian denim blazer; I put on a yellow Italian shirt, a vest, multicolored Italian boots, wrapped my neck in a black scarf, and started off, nervous—of course I was nervous. Live all those years with women, and then try and switch to men: You'll be nervous.

He lived at—but I don't want to hurt the man. On the whole he's a nice old fellow. An apartment "done in antique shop," as we used to say in Russia. On the wall, a Chagall with a dedicatory inscription; knickknacks; paintings depicting, as I later learned, our host himself in a tutu; photographs and portraits of male and female dancers, including Nureyev and Baryshnikov. An elegant, well-regulated bachelor life. Three, perhaps four rooms, with a nice smell, something that always distinguishes the apartments of society people and bohemians from the quarters of philistines and bourgeois families. The latter always stink of either food or cigarette smoke or something moldy. I am very sensitive to smells. Good perfume is a joy to me, a fact that my plebeian schoolmates used to laugh at. I liked the apartment for its smell.

Now our host wrenched himself from his armchair to meet me. Fairly long red hair; heavyset, not very tall; a little bit free and easy, like an artist; well dressed even around the house. On his neck, a dense mass of beads and nice little chains. On his fingers, diamond rings. How old he was I didn't know; he looked more than fifty. In fact, he must have been over sixty.

Kirill and he were on friendly terms. They were squabbling in an amiable way. The conversation began. About this, about that, or, as Kuzmin wrote, "Now Heinrich Mann, now Thomas Mann, and into your pocket with his hand." Not really; no hands in the pocket for the time being: it was all very proper, three artistic individuals conversing, an ex-dancer, a poet, and an aristocratic young rake. The conversation was interrupted by the proposal that we have some cold vodka with caviar and cucumbers. Our host went to the kitchen, took Kirill with him. "I'll have him cut the cucumbers." He wouldn't let me help. "You're a guest."

Lord in heaven, what bliss! The last time I had eaten caviar must have been in Vienna—I had brought several cans out of Russia. Elena was still with me. . . .

How nice that he didn't start in by flinging himself on me, I thought. After I've had some vodka I'll feel a little bolder, and while it's taking effect I'll be getting my bearings.

How very nice, vodka and caviar. I was so out of the habit of normal life that it all seemed a marvelous dream. We drank from elegant silver-rimmed crystal, not from crappy plastic, and although we were only having hors d'oeuvres, a fine, delicate plate lay before each of us. This place was so spacious after my hotel prison cell; I could stand up, walk around, examine things. The bread was spread with real butter, on top was real caviar, the vodka was ice cold, and the cucumbers were cut in strips, I noticed, glancing over the table again.

He still hadn't fallen upon me. In a peaceful and sympathetic way, he inquired about my relationship with my wife: not to reopen my wounds, he just asked as if in passing. He said that he too had had a wife, before he knew that women were so horrible. She had fled to Mexico ages ago with a policeman, or a fireman, I don't remember exactly; she was very rich, and she had two children by him. One son had died tragically.

When we finished the bottle, and we did so rather quickly—we all drank easily and were experts, men who drank constantly, every day and heavily—he shook himself off, went into the bathroom, and started getting ready for the ballet.

He put on very elegant clothes, a black velvet jacket from Yves Saint Laurent with a chic handkerchief in the pocket. When he came out he asked if we liked what he was wearing and was very pleased to receive an affirmative from me and "Raymond, you're a charmer" from Kirill.

At this point the bell rang. Raymond was being called for by a certain Luis (his lover, Kirill whispered to me), but Raymond called him Sebastian, after the well-known saint who was executed by arrows. Sebastian was Mexican. He did not strike me as interesting; he was dressed very conservatively, was the same height as Raymond, had a pleasant face but no outstanding features. He owned an art gallery. He was thirty-five or forty, and Raymond considered him young.

They went out, but Raymond had asked Kirill and me to stay and wait till he came back. Kirill, enjoying the fact that he had fulfilled my expectations and kept his promise, asked patronizingly, "Well, Edichka, how do you like *cher* Raymond? Isn't he a charmer?" Here, I think, he was imitating the jargon of his renowned aristocratic grandmother, about whom he told a great many stories. The grandmother lived to be a hundred and four and had what in my opinion was the bad habit of dashing cracked antique plates against the wall.

I said I thought he was OK, not a bad fellow.

"He's in love with Luis now, but when we were in the kitchen he said that he liked you very much."

How could he not like me? This sounds implausible, but he was the spitting image of Avdeev—the singer from the Teatralny Restaurant, admirer of my early youth. It's a strange world!

Kirill lavished praise on Raymond as if he were a commodity that he was planning to sell. Raymond was clever, he was cultured, he wore sumptuous clothes—so saying, Kirill led me into the bedroom, where Raymond's many things hung in the closet. "Look at this!" He proudly flung open the closet door. "So much of everything!"

Kirill himself went around in dreadful worn-down shoes. Although he suffered over this, he did not have the willpower—even when he had the money, which was very rare, but sometimes he did—to go out and buy shoes.

Raymond and Luis, Kirill continued in the tone of an affectionate mother recounting the escapades of her fervently loved son, were having tailcoats made specifically for the theater, special identical tailcoats. "You know, Limonov"—in the seriousness of the moment he even switched from Edichka to Limonov—"Raymond has known many great men, from Nijinsky to . . . And besides, Raymond has . . ."

Kirill had probably touted me to Raymond in exactly the same way. A poet, and clever, and so refined, the poor fellow has suffered horribly from his wife's treachery. . . .

Soon Kirill turned melancholy. The excitement of having fulfilled my expectations and kept his promise was over. Evidently fighting off the emptiness, he went to the next room and began making phone calls. He called his mistress, Jannetta, and apparently got up the nerve to quarrel with her. Unsettled, he returned to the living room and took another bottle of vodka from Raymond's icebox; we drank it, hardly noticing what we were doing. He withdrew to the telephone again, made several more calls, this time whispering stealthily in English, but did not hear what he wanted to from the receiver. Then, since I was the only available target, he began to badger me.

"Limonov, hey, Limonov, remember you pointed out a woman you knew at the hotel, a Russian émigrée? Call her up, have her come over, I'll fuck her."

"Shit, Kirill, you don't need her, and anyway she hardly says hello to me. Besides, it's twelve o'clock. The night is young for you and me, but it would be an insult to go calling up an ordinary person like that girl. She's been asleep for hours. And if I did call her, what would I say?"

"Can't you even do me one little favor, can't you call that tart? I'm miserable, I quarreled with Jannetta, I need somebody to fuck. I do everything for you—I introduced you to Raymond—but you don't want to do anything for me. What an egoist you are, Limonov," he said furiously.

"If I were an egoist," I replied calmly, "other people's actions wouldn't fuck me up and I wouldn't give a shit what my ex-wife did. It's precisely because I'm not an egoist that I lay dying on Lexington Avenue. What more can I say—you saw me dying there, saw the shape I was in. The reason I was in such bad shape was that I had suddenly lost my reason for living—Elena. I had no one to take care of, and I don't know how to live for myself. What kind of egoist am I?"

I said all this very seriously, very, very seriously.

"Take care of me," he said, "and yourself too—we'll fuck her together, want to? Come on, Edichka, call her, please?"

Maybe he wanted to compensate himself for his failure with Jannetta, vent his malice on someone else's cunt. Such things happen. But I could not have some tart present at my first experiment.

"I don't want to fuck dirty tarts," I said. "Women disgust me, they're vulgar. I want to start a new life, I want to sleep with Raymond this very day, if I can manage it. Anyway, don't hassle me, fuck off. We'd better have something to eat; I'm hungry."

By reminding him of food, I succeeded in turning him to another path. He was hungry too, and we went into the kitchen. "Raymond hardly ever eats at home," Kirill said cheerlessly. We raided the refrigerator—of what he had there, very little was edible. We settled on apples, ate two apiece, but the apples didn't satisfy us. In the freezer we found some cutlets that must have been there a hundred years, took them out, and began frying them in mayonnaise—we couldn't find the butter, although Raymond had served some with the caviar. There was caviar in the refrigerator too, but we were shy about touching it.

We made a terrible stink—had to open all the windows—and at that moment, in walked Luis-Sebastian and Raymond.

"Phew, what did you burn? What a stink!" Raymond said prissily.

"We got hungry and fried some cutlets," Kirill answered, abashed.

"Couldn't you have gone down to the restaurant?"

"We don't have any money today," Kirill said meekly.

"I'll give you some money, go and eat; young men must be well nourished," Raymond said. He gave Kirill some money and came to see us off.

"Excuse me," he said to me intimately, at the door. "I want you, but Luis often stays with me to make love and sleeps here—he loves me very much." Suddenly he kissed me, an unexpectedly firm and long-drawn-out kiss, his big lips enveloping my little lips. What did I feel? The sensation was strange, and I felt a sort of energy. But this didn't go on long; after all, Sebastian-Luis was stirring in the living room. Kirill and I went out.

"Call me tomorrow at twelve o'clock, at work—Kirill will give you the number. We'll have lunch together," Raymond said into the narrowing crack.

Downstairs in the restaurant we each bought a huge long chunk of meat—steak and potatoes. It was very expensive, but it was good and we ate our fill. Weighed down with food, we went out into the New York night, and Kirill saw me to the hotel.

"Kirill," I said jokingly, "Raymond's good-looking, but I like you better. You're big and tall, and what's more, you're young. If you had a little money too, we'd make a beautiful couple."

"Unfortunately, Edichka, I'm not attracted to men for now—maybe someday," he said.

It was 2:00 A.M. by the electronic clock on the IBM tower.

The next day I called Raymond and we met at his office. After making my way through a barricade of sleek and fat-free secretaries, I finally found myself in the room—cold and light and spacious, of course, bigger than the lobby of our hotel—where he did his business. He looked like a *grand seigneur:* gray pinstripe suit, dotted necktie. We set off without delay for the very nearest restaurant; it was on Madison, not far from my hotel.

The restaurant was packed with gray-haired and very proper ladies; there were men too, but fewer. With regard to the ladies, my thought was that each of them had obviously dispatched a minimum of two husbands to the next world. We sat side by side; Raymond ordered me an avocado-and-shrimp salad.

"I can't eat that dish, it's fattening," he said. "But you can, you're a boy."

The boy thought to himself that yes, no doubt he was a boy, but if you made a hole in his head, took out the part of the brain that controlled the memory, washed and cleaned it properly, that would be luxury. *Then* you'd have a boy.

"What shall we have to drink?" Raymond inquired.

"Vodka, if I may," I said modestly, and adjusted the black scarf at my neck.

He ordered vodka for himself and me, but they served it with ice, and it wasn't what I had expected.

We ate and talked. The salad was sophisticated and subtle in flavor, a gourmet dish; I was eating with a knife and fork again—I eat very adeptly, like a European, and I am proud of it.

To a stranger, of course, we looked like two pederasts, although he behaved very respectably except for stroking my hand. Several old ladies were obviously shocked, and on our banquette we felt as if we were on stage, sitting in a crossfire of stares. As a poet, I enjoyed shocking these old ladies. I love attention of any sort. I was in my element.

Raymond began telling me about the death of his fifteen-year-old son. The boy had smashed up on a motorcycle, which he had bought without his father's knowledge. "He was in school in Boston, and I had no control over the purchase," Raymond said with a sigh. "After his death I went to Boston and saw the man who had sold him the motorcycle. He was black, and he said to me, 'Sir, you have my deepest sympathy in your grief. If I'd known this would happen, I never would have sold the boy the motorcycle; I would have demanded that he get his father's permission.' A very good man, that black," Raymond said.

Trying to distract him from his sad memories, I asked about his ex-wife. He brightened up—this was obviously a topic of interest to him.

"Women are much coarser than men, although that's the reverse of generally received opinion. They're greedy, egoistic, and repulsive. I hadn't had anything to do with them in ever so long, but recently I went to Washington and, after an interval of many years, happened to fuck some woman. And you know, she struck me as dirty, although she was a very pretty thirty-five-year-old, feminine and clean. Their very physiology, their menstruation, harbors dirt. . . . Kirill told me that you loved your wife very much and that she's a very pretty woman. You're still suffering now, of course, but you can't imagine how lucky you are that you escaped from her; you'll realize it later. A man's love is much more solid, and often a couple will spend their whole lives together." Here he sighed and took a sip of vodka. He was pensive a little while.

"True, such love is encountered more and more rarely nowadays. Before, twenty or thirty years ago, homosexuals lived very differently. The young lived with the old, learned from them; this is noble, when a young man and an old one love each other and live together. A young man often needs backing, the support of a mature, experienced mind. This was a good tradition. Unfortunately, it's very different now. The young prefer to live with the young now, and all that comes of it is bestial fucking. What can one young man learn from another . . . ? There aren't any solid couples now; they keep switching partners." He sighed again.

Then he went on. "I like you. But I've been having a romance with Sebastian for a month now. I met him at a restaurant; we have special restaurants where women don't come, you know, only men like me. I was sitting with a whole group, and he was with a group too. I noticed him right off; he was sitting in a corner and being very enigmatic. He, Sebastian, took the first step—he sent me a glass of champagne. I replied with a bottle. I thought at first that he liked my friend, a handsome young Italian. No, it turned out he liked me, the old one. He came over to our table to introduce himself. That's how we met.

"He loves me very much," Raymond went on. "And he has a very good cock. Do you think I'm being vulgar? No, the subject is love, after all, and in love this matters—he has a very good cock. Yet he doesn't arouse me, and when I kissed you at the door last night, my cock stood up right away. . . ."

In response to so frank an outpouring, I cut a morsel of avocado with exaggerated care, then laid down my knife and fork and picked up my glass, took a drink, and swished the ice cubes in the vodka.

Raymond did not notice my embarrassment.

He went on. "Sebastian had a terrible tragedy, you know. He was close to suicide. He had lived for six years with a certain man, I don't want to mention his name; he's a famous man, very, very rich. Sebastian loved him and never left his side the whole six years. They went to Europe together, traveled around the world on a yacht. And suddenly this man fell in love with someone else. Sebastian didn't recover for a year. He tells me that if I leave him he won't survive it. He treats me very well, he gives me gifts—he gave me this ring, and perhaps you saw the huge vase in the living room; he gave me that too.

"Yesterday, you noticed, he was a bit gloomy. A deal of his fell through, there was big money involved," Raymond went on. "Sebastian wanted to sell, but couldn't, some beakers that had belonged to a King George, I don't remember which one; he's very upset. He loves his work at the gallery, on the whole, but he gets very tired. He comes to me to make love, but he's apt to fall asleep from fatigue; I kiss him, trying to wake him up. I want sex, but he gets tired at work. Besides, he has to do a lot of driving, and it's a long ride for him to my place from work. We'd like to make our home together, but his work prevents it. The difficulty is that while men like us aren't persecuted in this country, it still wouldn't be a good idea for his rich clients, especially the women, to find out he's a pederast. They'd probably stop buying from him at the gallery. Not all of them, perhaps, but many. That's why we can't make our home together—inevitably, rumors would reach them. But for economic reasons too, it would be more convenient to live together. He's—oh, not stingy but, you know, thrifty, which is good, because I spend money too freely. He says we could eat at home sometimes; he likes to cook. I used to be able to afford a lot in my job; my restaurant expenses were paid by the company too; I enjoyed great privileges; I was a friend and partner to my boss. Now that my friend and partner has died—we created the business together—I no longer have such great privileges. The financial constraints irritate me. I'm used to living on a grand scale.

"What do you think?" He turned to me suddenly, breaking off his monologue. "Does Sebastian really love me, as he says? I often tell him, 'You're young, I'm old, why do you love me?' He answers that I am his love.

"I don't know what to do," Raymond went on pensively. "I like him, but as I told you—you made my cock stand right up; he doesn't make it happen that way, yet he says he loves me. Can I believe him? What do you think?" He looked at me expectantly.

"I don't know," I said. What else could I say.

"I'm afraid to fall in love," Raymond said. "By now I'm the wrong age. I'm afraid to fall in love. If I were deserted, it would be a tragedy. I don't want suffering. I'm afraid to fall in love."

He looked at me expectantly and stroked my hand with his fingers, red hairs sticking up here and there from under his rings. His hand was heavy. Dully, as if in a dream, I looked at that hand. I understood that he wanted to know whether I would love him if he left Luis. He was asking for guarantees. What guarantees could I give him? I had no way of knowing. He was nice, but it was hard for me to tell whether I had any sexual affinity for him. I would be able to tell only after making love with him.

"Advise me what to do," he said.

"He probably does love you," I said, half lying, just for the sake of something to say. I wanted to be honest with him, as with the whole world; I couldn't tell him, "Desert Luis, I will love you devotedly and tenderly." I didn't know that I would. Moreover, I was suddenly struck by the thought: He's seeking love, care, and kindness, but I seek the very same thing—that's why I'm sitting with him, I came for love, care, and kindness. But how can we part? I was distraught. If I'm supposed to give him love, I don't want to—I don't, that's all. I want to be loved, otherwise I don't need any of it. In return for his loving me, if he does, I will come to love him later. I know myself, that's the way it will be. But to begin with, let him love me.

Then we walked away from this potentially explosive moment. We didn't walk away—we crawled away with difficulty. He asked me about my life in Moscow, and I patiently told the same story that I had had to tell maybe a hundred times, here in America, to polite but basically indifferent people. I repeated it all to him, only he was not indifferent. He was choosing me.

"My works were not printed by the magazines or publishing houses. I typed them myself, put them in primitive cardboard covers, stapled them together, and sold them for five rubles apiece. I sold these collections wholesale, in lots of five to ten, to my closest admirers, who served as distributors. The distributors, each of whom was the center of a circle of intellectuals, paid me at once, and then retailed the collections in their circles. Usually *samizdat* goes for free; I'm the only one ever to sell my books this way. By my calculations, they distributed about eight thousand collections for me."

I delivered this patter to Raymond in a studied monotone, the way one reads aloud a text he is sick and tired of.

"I also knew how to sew and made trousers to order. I got twenty rubles a pair. I made handbags too, and my previous wife, Anna, I remember, used to go and sell them at GUM, the main department store on Red

Square, for three rubles apiece. All these ways of making money were banned, persecuted in the USSR. I was taking a conscious risk every day."

He was no longer listening very closely. My Russian arithmetic held little interest for him. Three rubles, twenty rubles, eight thousand . . . He had his own worries. I had come for love, and I saw that love was wanted from me. He was estimating whether I was capable of it. I didn't like this. In this role, the role of the one who loves, I had already suffered defeat. I too wanted guarantees. I had absolutely no desire to return to my old situation.

We paid the bill—he paid, of course, I had nothing to pay it with; later I got used to the girl's role—and decided to take the elevator up. Raymond wanted to look at some china, he was planning to buy a new dinner service, and there was a gallery on the top floor.

We were received at the gallery by a homely girl and later an old lady. I enjoyed having them see us—the imposing Raymond and me—and understand all. Raymond fingered the dishes, examined plates and goblets, offered old porcelain to me to admire, we passed the time intellectually, usefully. I love the beautiful; I shared his delight in the creations of the masters of the comfortable old world, where there were families, where there was no cocaine, where there were no Elenas fucking in a narcotic sweat, where the obscene world of photography did not exist, nor its dirty backstage milieu. Family dinners, an orderly life, that was what this porcelain embodied for me. Unfortunately, I was destined for something else, I thought.

The inspection and pricing ended, we took the elevator down, he kissed me in front of the elevator boy, and we went out on the street, which was full of automobiles. It was spring, 1976, twentieth century, the great city of New York at lunch hour.

"I'd like to make love with you, but Luis almost always stays the night now. Besides, he'll be wary of you: you saw how he watched you yesterday?" I remembered only Luis-Sebastian's tired look and my halting conversation with him.

"You might come to my place today at five—we'll spend a little time together, have a drink," Raymond said.

"All right, I'd be glad to," I said, and in fact I was glad, for I had developed an adamant determination to sleep with him at all costs. I shall venture to use a bureaucratic expression: I wanted officially to become a pederast—inwardly I had already become one—and henceforth to be such and consider myself such. I wanted to finalize it. Perhaps girls feel this way about wanting to lose their virginity. There was even something abnormal about this desire of mine; I felt it.

We said good-bye on Madison. I did not go to the hotel right away but walked the streets awhile longer, considering his words. In the world of pederasts too there are love and unlove, tears and tragedies, nor is there any refuge from fate, blind chance, I thought. And true love is just as rare.

I showered and was at his apartment by five. Kirill was there too. Raymond was sitting in the bedroom in an armchair. He had loosened the knot of his necktie and was having a drink, sipping from a tall glass. "Make him a drink!" he ordered Kirill. The young procurer gave me a conspiratorial wink and said, "Come on, Edichka, I'll make you a drink."

"What, can't you do it without company?" Raymond said in mock anger.

"It's just that I don't know what he wants; I'll show him what we have. Let him choose."

I went to the kitchen with Kirill. Luckily the phone rang and Raymond did not detain us, being occupied with his phone conversation.

"Before you came," Kirill whispered, making me a vodka and orange juice, "before you came, Raymond asked me to tell you he'll take you to restaurants very often, he'll buy you a suit, but just don't live with anyone for now. Raymond has to decide what he should do, stay with Luis or be with you. He says, 'Sebastian loves me very much, but I can't get it up with him. Eddie doesn't love me but perhaps he will yet; after all, we've only just met.'

"Actually," Kirill continued in a hissing whisper, "he doesn't believe you've never tried men. He says, 'I have the impression he's slept with men.'"

"That's how good my masquerade was," I said dully, thinking my own thoughts. I could have pretended, this afternoon in the restaurant, could have said I loved him, begged him to desert Luis and live with me. God knows what all I might have said to him; I could have acted the part, leaned on his shoulder, stroked his red neck, kissed his ear, played the petit-bourgeois cocotte, the decadent woman, and laid it on thick with mannerisms, trivial whims, eccentricities, and endearing little ways from which he would not have extricated himself, of course. I knew how to do that. The riddle for me would have been how to conduct myself in bed, but this, too, I hoped to master very quickly. I had acted unwisely but honorably; I had not started lying to him and had not said I loved him.

We went out to the living room. In the bedroom Raymond was communing with the telephone receiver in French. We therefore remained in the living room.

"I encountered your ex-wife today on Fifth Avenue, Edichka," Kirill said. He looked at me attentively, anticipating an effect. I drank my vodka and merely said, after a faint pause, "And?"

"She was flying along Fifth Avenue, not seeing anyone, in a sort of red jacket, her pupils were dilated—she's probably shooting up heroin or sniffing cocaine—all keyed up, excited. She's going to Italy, she says, for a month of shooting. Zoli is sending her. 'How's Limonov, do you ever see him?' she asked. When she learned I had found you a 'friend' "—Kirill lowered his voice—"she was very pleased and said, 'I hate men. Find me a rich old lesbian to caress me, fuck me, fuck me, fuck me with an artificial member. . . .' " Kirill repeated this "fuck me" several times. Elena too must have said it that way, several times and with raised voice. I remembered the long and almost bestial orgasms that I myself had given her with an artificial member, and it set my head spinning, a nether warmth flowing: after those orgasms, I had especially enjoyed fucking her. I took a big gulp of vodka, and while remaining aware of my sensations, aware of my filling prick, I shook off my torpor and listened, forced myself to listen to Kirill's words. He finished the sentence. After the artificial member came: " '. . . and then our family will be complete,' she said."

Next Kirill launched into a discourse on the fact that Elena was not to his taste and what did I see in her. I kept smiling at him automatically, mockingly, meanwhile hardly able to get myself out of our bed, get myself out of the "conjugal" bed.

Thank God, Raymond came in—a real person from the real world—and my torture ended. We had drink after drink. After a half hour spent in sophisticated conversation Raymond began fondling my member through my pants, completely unashamed before Kirill. I smiled and pretended nothing special was happening.

Raymond was not sitting beside me, he was reaching for my prick from an armchair, but I was on the couch. This heightened the absurdity of the situation. I felt nothing at Raymond's touch, absolutely nothing. Kirill was here, and I was not a healthy peasant lad from someplace like Arizona, with normal instincts and a prick that would naturally stand up if a stranger touched it. I was a ridiculous European with unnatural connections inside my body, I was a good actor, but this was something I couldn't control. Tears I could squeeze out any old day, but get my dick up in such a situation? Then again, I didn't know whether I had to. My only thought was that a dick without an erection might frighten him off. But no, it didn't; rather the opposite.

After a while I went out through Raymond's bedroom to a vast bathroom, artistically decorated with portraits and photographs. I made peepee, wiped my member with a tissue, and was on my way back when Raymond met me in the bedroom. His eyes were weird, his lips the color of strawberries that have spoiled in the sun, and he was muttering. Still muttering, he nestled up to me. I was much taller than he, I had to put my arms around his back and shoulders. We shifted from foot to foot, he continued to mutter and massaged my member through my slacks—why, I could not understand. We must have looked like Japanese wrestlers. Finally he began nudging me toward the bed. Well, I went, what else could I do, although I felt a growing dissatisfaction that he was managing it all so absurdly.

He put me on the bed; I lay on my back, and he lay on top, making motions such as you make when fucking a woman. He devoted himself to this travesty for some time, panted heavily and breathed in my ear, kissed my neck. I threw back my head and rolled it from side to side exactly as my last wife had. I caught myself doing it; I must have had the same expression on my face too. These things are contagious.

Raymond was heavy and awkward. For all my irritation, I sympathized with him, acknowledging myself to be an inept virgin. He'll have a hard time with me, I thought. But my dissatisfaction that he was making it all so foolish and awkward did not leave me.

In the next room Kirill was talking on the phone, and the door wasn't shut. Ah, that's why he muttered something inarticulate instead of speaking normally, I realized. I was thinking altogether too much at that moment. I won't think, I decided, and returned to reality. A heavy red-haired old fellow was wriggling on top of me. A fine situation, little Eddie, you're lying down and about to get fucked, it seems. But that's what you wanted. Well, put it this way, what I had wanted was not specifically a fuck but love, kindness—I was so weary of being without caressing kindness—and, as a natural extension, a caress for my prick as well. But what was happening was some kind of nonsense. Did he really lack the subtlety to realize that this was the wrong way to go about it with me? Or was he not concerned about frightening me, did he not value me?

He slithered down, unzipped my pants, but could not unbuckle the belt, didn't know how it worked. I smiled inwardly. In exactly the same way, my first woman had fallen afoul of my belt—that one was my papa's Soviet Army belt—she couldn't unbuckle the kid's belt. This belt was Italian. My first man. "No, you won't get the fucking thing unbuckled, you don't know how it works. Fuck it—I'll help." Without changing the languid expression on my face, I lowered my hands from behind my head, where they had been the whole time, and unbuckled the belt.

In a fever, he pulled open my red panties and took it out—my member. Good Lord, it was scrunched and little, like a boy's, and at the touch of his grabby hand a droplet of urine came out, rolled out like a tear. No matter how much you wipe with tissues, that little drop always lurks deep inside, to come rolling out at the first opportunity. I wondered how Raymond would deal with it. "Did you think it would be easy to fuck the wounded?" I wanted to ask. He jerked and kneaded my member. A trifle coarse and hasty, I thought.

In the next room, Kirill was reproaching his Jannetta for something. Without meaning to, I listened to Kirill's voice, picked out individual words. Raymond jerked and kneaded. I was uncomfortable; one of his knees was crushing my leg. Suddenly I realized that he didn't have a fucking chance of getting anywhere and that I was about to get up and flee. To avoid injuring myself or offending him, I promptly said in a languid whisper, "Kirill will hear!"

He understood and got up, or maybe he had despaired of doing anything with my member, but anyway he got up and went into the bathroom in a somnambulistic state.

When he returned I was strolling around the bedroom, looking out the windows at the street below, with my pants zipped up and my shirt tucked in. We rejoined Kirill and picked up our drinks. Then I took from my vest pocket some poems I had brought, read them to Raymond and Kirill, with Kirill gravely expressing his opinion on each poem.

The poems restored my lost composure. In this business I am superior to everyone; here, only in poetry, am I who I am. In reading my poems I found composure, as I say, although these men, Raymond and Kirill, were not right for my poetry. Raymond politely understood that this was art, and as art it must be appreciated and admired, but he scarcely had any real feeling for who was sitting before him or what was being read. Even though he was more European than American, he had lived in this country so many years that he had unthinkingly assigned to art the modest role of a knickknack ornamenting life. It was nice, of course, that his potential lover was a poet, it was interesting, romantic, but that was all. To him my poems were small, and he, Raymond, was big, while in fact little Eddie's sufferings were much bigger than Raymond, bigger even than the whole city of New York, precisely because Eddie was visible, could be seen, through the poems. Or so I flattered myself; however, I am fully convinced of it to this day.

It wasn't much of a treat for them, so I read maybe five or seven poems and put the manuscript away in my vest pocket. Enough. Especially since Raymond had been distracted by the telephone, and Kirill, of course, was trying to explain to me his own Petersburg-Leningrad attitude toward poetry. Leningrad people love pomposity and pathos, affectation and pseudo-classicism; my poems and I are too simple for them.

A guest appeared—a certain Frenchman, the owner of a chain of stores selling ready-made luxury clothes from Yves Saint Laurent, Cardin, and other French celebrities. These beautifully resonant names had been familiar to me back in Moscow. Louis Aragon, for example, member of the Central Committee of the French Communist Party and one of France's greatest poets, got his things from Yves Saint Laurent. How do I know? Oh, little Eddie has heaps of society connections, although he keeps quiet about them, doesn't drop many names. I was told about Aragon's penchant for Yves Saint Laurent by Lily Brik, the celebrated Lily, my friend, the woman who went down in history as the mistress of the great poet Mayakovsky—a great poet no matter what you may hear from various Soviet and anti-Soviet scum.

Oh yes, I'm forgetting the Frenchman. He wore his fine little threads of hair slicked down on both sides of his skull; was bony and tall, with rather a large butt, considering his overall leanness; he had narrow, tight trousers and a face just as narrow, tapering to the nose. He looked like some kind of fish.

Breaking out in blotches—he was shy—Kirill began to speak French with the Frenchman. I must confess the young idler succeeded pretty well. The grandmother that he mentioned so often not only had known how to dash cracked Kuznetsev porcelain against the walls but also had taught her grandson to speak French and English. The same cannot be said of my own grandmother, unfortunately.

At a request from Raymond, who was boasting about my figure, I was obliged to twirl before the Frenchman, displaying myself. I felt as if I were fifteen and my parents were displaying me to their friends. Not fifteen, younger. Ten, eight.

The Frenchman obviously liked me. He was an inveterate old pederast, I don't know how old; he was preserved like antique ivory, shone as if polished. He smiled all the time and spoke in a thin, despairing, sophisticated voice, the way ridiculous society people speak in operetta—dukes and princes, ridiculous people—but he was not without charm. I liked the Frenchman too, and much better than Raymond, but I didn't dare tell him so. I found him agreeable, for some reason, from his tight, deliberately unstylish trousers to the little threads of hair on his head.

Raymond had more fat to him, more blood, more meat; naturally I liked the Frenchman better.

Out of courtesy, although he did not have a kopeck, Kirill was negotiating a purchase of suits for himself. It was clear to everyone that he wasn't going to buy a fucking thing, but this was his way of doing something nice for everyone, somehow participating in their lives. I imagine he was in utter ecstasy over the fact that he was sitting in the company of pederasts. A kind soul, he loved his friends, loved their titles, or absence of titles. I bet he always exaggerated Raymond's prosperity to me and to other people as well; he generally exaggerated everything about his friends, in the direction of bigger and better. It was an innocent, childish amusement, but he did not thereby forget himself either: he, Kirill, by having such friends, seemed to grow in his own and others' eyes.

The Frenchman very soon left, unfortunately. In parting he gave me a spank on the poopka and said, "I think you're better off that your wife deserted you." On his lips this sounded convincing. I thought: No doubt it is better, maybe it really is. And his spank had me in ecstasy—for some reason I liked it.

After the Frenchman came an Italian. "He was once my lover," Raymond said, after the Italian left for a restaurant. "He never let me sleep; a very strong cock that young man has. Oh, what he can do!" Raymond said ecstatically. I heard a tinge of reproach in his words. It's your own fault, I thought; you don't have the technique.

The Italian had come to spend the night. When I inquired of Raymond why he didn't stay in a hotel, it became clear that he was also a millionaire. The millionaire was thirty-five, no more, and very appealing. His name was Mario.

Homosexuals of all nationalities came to Raymond's that night. True, they did not congregate, they sat awhile and went away, others appeared in their stead. Only Mario stayed, but he soon went off to the guest room assigned to him and remained there.

Sometimes Raymond resumed touching my dick, but gradually it became apparent that he was tired. In his fatigue, no longer controlling himself, he turned rather vulgar and told some clumsy dirty jokes, which would not have happened in his normal state. In the end he informed Kirill and me that he was sorry, but he wanted to get to sleep. I was disappointed. My face must have showed it, because Raymond said, "Go to Mario, why don't you?" Then he went on jokingly, "The only thing is, he won't let you sleep. Personally, I'm a little afraid of Mario, although we haven't slept together for many years and don't arouse each other." He led us to Mario's room, walking a little unsteadily. This was understandable; he had worked all day at the office, after all, and then drunk with us all evening, glass for glass.

Mario was sitting with his shirt unbuttoned, going through some papers. A man of affairs, he truly was handsome, and given my desire to lose my virginity today—now—I probably would have stayed with him had I not perceived that Raymond didn't want me to: if he hadn't been disenchanted at the sight of my wrinkled appendage, he must not want me to stay. And I didn't, although Mario's jesting words and sidelong glance at me—he really gave me the once-over—convinced me immediately that Raymond was right about him, Raymond was not fabricating.

I should have left, but a stupid conversation got started, which was the fault of Kirill and the tired, suddenly flaccid Raymond. Tomorrow Raymond was supposed to have a party, a very important one because his boss was supposed to come, the owner of the business, who was not a pederast, and Kirill had volunteered to get a beautiful girl for the boss. Where he planned to get her I don't know, but the absurd conversation dragged on and on. Raymond kept complaining of his lack of china, but later recalled that Sebastian-Luis was going to bring him some lovely china.

"He called today; I completely forgot. All my sets are partly broken, I haven't entertained at home in ages, I always take people to restaurants," Raymond pouted, in the tone of the man who has everything. The vile bourgeois within him had awakened, the bourgeois who in return for his money laid claim to the whole world, with all its material and spiritual valuables. One of those who had bought my silly girl-child. My hackles rose.

Outwardly I was sitting in his arms, he was mechanically stroking my shoulder. But had you been able to peep within me, gentlemen, what would you have seen? Hatred. Hatred for this man obtunded by wine and fatigue. And suddenly I realized that I would gladly have taken a knife or a razor and slit this Raymond's throat, although it was not he who had raped me, I had raped myself. Here I sat, but I could have slit his throat, stripped off his diamond rings, headed home from the expensive apartment with the Chagall, and bought myself a prostitute for the whole night, the girl of Chinese-Malayan descent, the small and elegant one who always stands on the corner of Eighth Avenue and Forty-fifth Street, but female, a girl. I would have kissed her all night, I would have made it nice for her, I'd have kissed her peepka and her pretty little heels.

And with the rest of the money I would have bought the most expensive suit at Ted Lapidus for this booby Kirill, because who else would buy it for him, and I was older and more experienced. The whole fantasy was so vivid that I involuntarily started, and thereby dispelled the fog before my eyes. Kirill and the businessman Mario materialized, and beside me Raymond's meaty puss. "Time to go," I said. "You wanted to get to sleep, Raymond."

And we left, Kirill and I.

I called it quits with Raymond, although someone was supposed to phone someone, and once, as I came out of my hotel beautifully dressed, I encountered this same Raymond, and with him Sebastian in a black suit and a silly white straw hat, a "very expensive" one, in the opinion of the omnipresent Kirill, for whom I was waiting and who promptly walked up. There was a Mexican boy with them too. They looked like relatives from the Caucasus who had come to visit their uncle Raymond in Moscow. The whole group was preoccupied with worry; they were looking for some new place to have lunch. "We should have their worries!" Kirill said enviously. Having spotted a Mexican restaurant on the other side of the street, Raymond and his Caucasian relatives hurried across. Halfway there, Raymond turned and looked at me. I smiled and waved to him. By then I had slept with Chris, I already had Chris.

### Chris

As I say, I grasped at everything in my search for salvation. I even resumed my journalistic career, or rather, I tried to resurrect it.

My closest friend, Alexander—prostrated, like me, by his wife's betrayal and his own absolute nothingness in this world—was living in a studio apartment on Forty-fifth Street between Eighth and Ninth avenues, in a fine building located in a neighborhood of whorehouses and vice dens. He was a trifle afraid of his neighborhood at first, being a bespectacled intellectual, a cautious Jewish youth, but later grew used to it and began to feel at home.

We often got together at his place, trying to find ways to publish our articles in America. They ran counter to the politics of America's ruling circles, and we did not know which papers to try. The *New York Times* had refused to notice us. We had gone there in the fall, when I was a proofreader at *Russkoe Delo*, as was Alexander—we had sat across from each other there and quickly found much in common. We went to the *Times* with our "Open Letter to Academician Sakharov," and the *Times* cut us dead, they didn't even deign to answer us. Actually, it was a far from stupid letter and the first sober Russian voice in the West. An interview with us and an account of the letter did get printed, not in America, but in England, in the *Times* of London. The letter was about the idealization of the Western world by Russian intellectuals. In reality, we wrote, the West had plenty of problems and contradictions, no less acute than those of the USSR. In short, the letter was a call to cease destroying the Soviet intelligentsia—who don't know a fucking thing about this world—by inciting them to emigrate. That was why the *New York Times* didn't print it. Or maybe they considered us incompetent, or didn't react to the unfamiliar names.

The fact remains that in America, just as in Russia, we were unable to publish our articles, that is, to express our views. Here, we were forbidden another thing: to write critically about the Western world.

So Alexander and I got together at 330 West 45th Street and tried to decide what to do. Man is weak; the effort was often accompanied by beer and vodka. But although a stuffed-shirt statesman may be afraid to admit he has formulated one or another state decision in the interval between two glasses of vodka or whiskey or while sitting on the toilet, I have always been delighted by the apparent incongruity, the inopportuneness, of manifestations of human talent and genius. And I do not intend to hide it. To hide it would be to distort, or facilitate the distortion of, human nature.

In short, Alexander and I drank and worked and discussed. We drank vodka, and along with the vodka we drank ale—for some reason I had taken a liking to it—and everything else we could get our hands on. Then we would set out to cruise the streets. As we walked to Eighth Avenue the girls said hello to us, and not merely in the line of duty—we were a familiar sight, they knew us. The two men in glasses were also known to the people who handed out flyers advertising the bordello, and to the kinky-haired man who issued them their flyers and paid them their money. After passing number 300, where the steep lighted staircase led to the cheapest bordello in New York, one of the cheapest, at least, we turned on Eighth Avenue, down or up, according to our own whim. The cruise began. . . .

Everything had been as usual that April day. Attacks of anguish were coming over me several times a week then, or perhaps even oftener. I don't remember how the day began—no, wait, I wrote the scene where Elena is executed in "The New York Radio Broadcast," and was very weary from always returning to the same painful theme, Elena's betrayal of me. There were swarms of people in the corridor outside my door. They were filming Marat Bagrov in his room, filming him on assignment for Israeli propaganda: Look how hard life is for those who leave Israel. Actually, at least three countries have an interest in our émigré souls—they harass us constantly, swear by us, use us, all three of them. So at that moment Marat Bagrov, former Moscow TV journalist, was being exploited by a man from Israel—former Soviet writer Ephraim Vesyoly—and his American friends. Cables, accessories, lenses, and cameras crowded my door. I went out into New York, wandered, as if aimlessly, to Lexington Avenue, and twice found myself at *her* place, that is, the Zoli agency, where Elena was living then. I felt sad and disgusted. Suddenly I caught myself on the point of passing out. I had to save myself. I went back to the hotel.

The fucking exploitation scene was still going on. The Moscow TV figure, long unaccustomed to attention, was carried away with the sound of his own voice. The villain Vesyoly was serene. I knocked at Edik Brutt's door and asked for a five-dollar loan. Edik, kind soul, even consented to go and get the wine with me because I was afraid of passing out from anguish.

We went: Edik, mustachioed and somnolent, and I. I bought a gallon of California red for $3.49 and we started back. We encountered a strange man with a Russian face, who glanced at me, then grinned and said suddenly, "Faggot," and turned on Park Avenue. "An odd encounter," I said to Edik. "I don't think he's staying at our hotel."

We returned to the hotel, and the sacrament was still going on. Another denizen of our dormitory, Mr. Levin, was now angrily gritting out something about the Soviet regime and anti-Semitism in Russia. We shut ourselves in my room, and I prevailed on Edik to have a symbolic drink with me, at least one. And I set myself to soaking up my gallon. . . .

Gradually I recovered and brightened up. Somebody summoned Edik, perhaps His Majesty the Interviewer, I don't remember who, but somebody. Then they summoned me. I went—they gave me a table. I took it, and a bookshelf as well. Marat Bagrov had timed the interview for the day he was to move out of the hotel. An ex-furrier named Borya, one of the most worthwhile people in the hotel, helped me move the table into my room. I treated him to a glass. I drank two or three myself. Marat Bagrov was invited too. Ephraim Vesyoly and the crew would have been invited, but they had decamped with their fiendish gear.

When Marat Bagrov and I had knocked back our glasses, the telephone rang. "What are you doing?" asked Alexander's animated voice.

"Drinking a gallon of wine. I've hardly drunk a third of it," I said, "but I want to drink it all." A gallon of California burgundy usually calms me right down.

"Listen, come on over," Alexander said. "Come and bring the jug with you. We'll both drink; I have ale and vodka too. I feel like getting drunk," he added. With that, he probably straightened his glasses. He's a very quiet fellow but capable of recklessness.

"OK," I said. "I'll stick the jug in a bag and be right over."

I was wearing a nice tight denim jacket, and jeans tucked in—no, rolled way high—to reveal my very beautiful high-heeled boots of tricolor leather. For my own pleasure I thrust an excellent German knife from Solingen into my boot, then put the jug in a bag and went out.

Downstairs, from the pickup truck containing the migrant Bagrov's things, I was hailed by Bagrov himself, Edik Brutt, and some other extra. "Where are you going?" they said. "To Forty-fifth Street," I said, "between Eighth and Ninth avenues." "Get in," Bagrov said, "that's practically on the way. I'm moving to Fiftieth and Tenth Avenue."

I got in, we started off. Past columns of pedestrians, past gilded Broadway reeking of urine, past a solid wall of strolling people. My glance lovingly picked out of the crowd the long-limbed figures of whimsically dressed young black men and women. I have a weakness for eccentric circus clothes. Although I cannot afford much of anything because of my extreme poverty, still, all my shirts are lace, one of my blazers is lilac velvet, and the white suit is a beauty, my pride and joy. My shoes always have very high heels, I even own some pink ones, and I buy them where all the blacks buy theirs, in the two best stores on Broadway, at the corner of Forty-fifth and the corner of Forty-sixth, lovely little far-out shops where its all high heels and all provocative and preposterous to squares. I want even my shoes to be a festival. Why not?

The truck moved west along Forty-fifth, past theaters and mounted policemen. In front of one building we had the honor of beholding with our own eyes our Lilliputian mayor. All the émigrés recognized him joyfully. He got out of a car with some other puffy-faced characters, and several reporters took pictures of the mayor with professional adeptness but no special enthusiasm. There was no great security force in evidence. Everyone in the truck went on and on about how there was no point shooting at the mayor in such a crush, and we had trouble making progress, moving barely a meter or two at each change of the light. The driver, Bagrov, and I applied ourselves to my gallon jug a few times. I got out my knife and started toying with it.

The love of weapons is in my blood. As far back as I can remember, when I was a little boy, I used to swoon at the mere sight of my father's pistol. I saw something holy in the dark metal. Even now I consider a weapon a holy and mysterious symbol: an object used to take a man's life cannot but be holy and mysterious. The very profile of a revolver, of all its parts, holds a Wagnerian horror. Cold steel, with its different profiles, is no exception. My knife looked somnolent and lazy. Plainly, it knew that nothing of interest awaited it, there was no good job coming up in the near future, so it was bored and indifferent.

"Put your knife away," Bagrov said. "Here we are." I climbed out, said good-bye, and charged into the entrance with my gallon jug, but the knife took its place in my boot, went off to bed.

Alexander has a habit—you ring him from downstairs, he presses the buzzer to open the door. But when you go up, he never opens his door in advance, never meets you on the threshold; you have to ring again at the door, and he still doesn't open it promptly even if he's expecting you. I keep waiting for him to deviate from his habit. No, today everything was the same as ever, with the obligatory pauses.

We have a division of labor when we're drinking: I cook, he washes the dishes. I boiled up some sort of pasta, then stuck a package of sausages into it, and we went to work on the gallon jug. The meal was at a table that stood arbitrarily in the corner of the room, we sat under a table lamp. We always talk about news and events; Alexander brings Russian émigré gossip from the newspaper. Often there aren't any events; so much the worse. Once in a great while I get off on the subject of my wife. But only once in a while, and if I do say anything about her, I immediately catch myself and change the subject.

"You were a fool not to kill her," Alexander told me once with the artlessness and clarity of King Solomon or a secret police tribunal. "You strangled her, you should've finished her off. I at least have a baby, or I'd kill *my* wife. It wouldn't be good for the baby, she'd be left alone, but you should've killed Elena."

By May, as you will see, he and I would revive, write several articles that no one would publish, hold our May 27 demonstration against the *New York Times*, and get another interview printed in the *Times* of London. In May we would try various other gambits as well, dig up all kinds of possibilities in life, but back then, in April, we often just ruminated and got drunk. Besides, he had a weakness for sleeping with his wife. Either his phone would be out of order and I couldn't get through to him, or he'd disappear over Saturday and Sunday.

That evening was probably as usual. Alexander undoubtedly told me that the paper had received a letter from some dissident, maybe from Krasnov-Levitin, or maybe the wily Maksimov had sent his routine appeal, directed less to the Soviet regime than to the Western left-wing intelligentsia, "deadened with surfeit and idleness," or the bearded Solzhenitsyn had amazed the world with his next deep thought on the world order, or some person had proposed detaching something else from the USSR, some other territory. The names of these "national heroes" of ours were always on our lips.

In our desire to kill the hateful gallon we were already behaving like athletes straining toward victory. I was also in the bad habit of mixing drinks. To revive myself, as I drank, I had a couple of cans of ale and several shots of vodka in the intervals between red burgundy. No wonder, then, that time became a dark sack, and the next illumination, opening of the eyes, call it what you will, found Alexander and me in some sort of temple. A service was going on. One thing I could not understand—whether it was a synagogue or some other kind of temple. I was more inclined to think it was a synagogue. We were sitting on a bench, and for some reason Alexander kept smiling, his face was very joyful. Maybe he had just been given a gift. Money, maybe.

For that reason I turned to myself. Let's go on with our games. I pulled my beloved knife from my boot and stuck it into the floor, or rather, into some boards that constituted a footrest. Next to me a whole family of believers exchanged wild glances. I'm not planning to kill anyone, Messrs. Jews or Catholics or Protestants, I'm just madly in love with weapons, and I have no temple of my own where I can pray to the Great Knife or the Great Revolver. So that's why I pray to Him here, I thought. Then I went into a sort of delirium, several times tore the knife from the board and kissed it, stuck it back into the footrest. Once I dropped His Majesty the Knife, and his thunder reverberated throughout the temple because my German friend from Solingen had a heavy metal handle. The service ended with the priest's offering his hand to everyone, even to the foolishly smiling Alexander, but not to me. I was on the point of taking offense but then forgot about it, rightly deciding that I should not take offense at a priest of an unknown religion.

Again there was a dark pit, and the onset of a new illumination, revealing the smiling faces of some priestesses of love, who out of a special susceptibility to us—two stinking-drunk but, I think, very appealing bespectacled characters—had agreed to make love with us for five dollars. They were very sweet, these girls. Alexander would not have stopped any disagreeable ones, nor would they have stopped him. These were a light chocolate color, there were two of them, they were much more beautiful than proper women. Eighth Avenue has many beautiful and even touching prostitutes, Lexington has many beautiful ones too; when I lived there I exchanged greetings with them every evening.

Murmuring agreeably, the girls put their arms around us and pulled us along with them. They had a trained eye; they knew, exactly and definitely, that we had five dollars between us and no more. You can't fool them. Money is their main interest, of course, but they're obviously no strangers to human feeling. They smelled nice, they had provocative long legs; these girls were much better than any ordinary secretary or pimply American coed. I had nothing against them. Why I didn't go with them but sent Alexander off to enjoy one and promised to wait for him, I do not know. I believe there was some deep-seated force within me that made me think: All women are disagreeable. Prostitutes are much better than all the rest, they have almost no falsehood in them, they're natural women, and if they've undertaken to make love with the two of us for five dollars when it's not even raining, not the kind of weather when they don't have clients, then that is obviously their pleasure. But even so, I'm not going with them.

I didn't want to think it through, but I knew that I would not go with them today—some other time. Why not? Was I afraid, perhaps? Not true. They were so sincere and homey, they might have been in my class in grade school. And in that April mood of mine I had essentially lost the instinct for self-preservation; I feared no one and nothing at all in this world because I was prepared to die at any moment. I believe I was seeking death—unconsciously, but I was. Then why would I be afraid of two beautiful minks? Afraid they were decoys? Afraid of pimps? You know I don't give a damn; I don't own a thing. That wasn't it. Women no longer existed for me. I was thoroughly drunk, yet I rejected them, almost involuntarily, which especially means that what happened a little later that night was no accident; my body wanted it.

I left Alexander; he went off with one of the girls to her place to make love, and I went into the gaping dark of the West Side streets, somewhere around Tenth or Eleventh Avenue. I remember myself walking away, as if I had been staring at my own back through the eyes of a bystander.

The light flared next when I entered some sort of walled-in area, apparently a playground for children. Dark corners have always attracted me. I remember that even in Moscow I loved to go into boarded-up houses, which everyone feared and where bandits supposedly lived. When I was good and drunk I would remember those houses and set out for one. After climbing in through a broken window or door, stepping over piles of petrified shit and puddles of urine, cursing and singing Russian folk songs, I would discover some poor unfortunates in the house, alcoholics or tramps, with whom, after making their acquaintance, I would have a long and incoherent conversation. In one of those places someone conked me with a bottle and appropriated two rubles. But the habit stayed with me.

So I entered an area where there were swings and other attractions for children. A light burned in the middle, but the corners were all alluringly dark. I went, of course, to the largest dark spot. Squeezing between some iron girders, on which rested a scaffold of unknown purpose, I let out an oath—my high heels were sinking in sand. To this day I don't know why the sand was there. Was it a sandbox for the children to play in? But then why all those iron girders? Or was it a parking place for cars, and the second tier raised on the scaffold? I don't know. This will forever remain a mystery, for not long ago I tried to find the place, but without success. Maybe they've built something there, which is improbable in such a short time, or more likely I mixed up the streets. I'll go look again sometime; if I find it I'll let you know.

I climbed a short iron ladder to the wooden scaffold, let down my legs, and sat on the very edge of the scaffold, dangling my feet. Not a fucking thing to do. Night. I waited for adventure and glanced around. It was quiet, although somewhere far away I heard cries, footsteps—someone was chasing someone—music, the shuffle of feet. I sat and dangled my legs. A free personality in the free world. I could do anything I wanted. Kill somebody, for instance. Everything was available and easy. The alcoholic fog was beginning to clear. The free personality got sick of sitting on the scaffold. It jumped down. I jumped down, into the sand.

And then I saw Chris. Of course, it was only later I found out his name was Chris. He sat leaning against the brick wall, a young black man. A wide black hat lay beside him on the sand. Later I had time to examine it; it was decorated with a dark-green ribbon embroidered with gold thread. As I later saw, he was dressed in all these three colors—black, dark green, and gold. He had these colors in his vest, his slacks, shoes, and shirt. But when I jumped down and saw him directly in front of me, what I saw was a black man dressed in black, his eyes meeting mine with a cold and mysterious glitter.

"Hi!" I said.

"Hi," he replied indifferently.

"My name is Edward," I said, taking a couple of steps toward him.

He let out a meaningless, scornful sound.

"Got anything to drink?" I asked him.

"Fuck off!" he said.

I thought: Wonder why he's sitting here; he's not a drunk or a druggie, doesn't seem out of it; if he meant to sleep here, he doesn't look like a bum. Maybe hiding from the police? I'm not one to betray anybody. I'd even help him hide. Only he looks real mean. I stared at him, then took several steps toward him and squatted beside him. He watched coldly and didn't move. I sat on my heels, peering into his face.

A broad hawklike nose, deeply flaring nostrils, lips unusual for a black—austere, not plump—a strong chest. A big guy: if he stood up he'd probably be a head taller than I. Young, twenty-five or thirty, no more. The wide legs of his black slacks lay on the sand.

"Say, what's your name?" I said.

Then he snapped; he had had it with my staring and questioning. Silently and swiftly he lunged at me. He hurled himself straight from a sitting position and pinned me instantly; a second later I was lying underneath him, and by all indications he meant to choke me to death.

I gave up the struggle at once, I was at too great a disadvantage. All I had time to do when he hurled himself on me was to tuck my right arm down under my right thigh, and simultaneously curl my right leg up under me. This way, when crushed under him I lay on my right side. It was a good strategy because my hidden hand was free to reach into my boot and grab the knife handle. If he intends to strangle me, I'll kill him, I thought coldly. He weighed me down all over, but my right hand could move freely. He had not allowed for that.

I was not terrified. Word of honor, absolutely not. As I say, I had some unconscious instinct at the time, a craving for death. The world had become empty without love. That is merely a pat formula, but behind it lie tears, humiliated ambition, the squalid hotel, lust unsatisfied to the point of giddiness, a grudge against Elena and the whole world (a world that only now, laughing openly and mockingly, had shown me how unneeded I was and always had been), hours not empty but filled with despair and horror, terrible dreams and terrible dawns.

The man was strangling me; this was fair because two months ago I had strangled Elena: nothing should go unpunished. He was strangling me, but I did not hurry with my knife. Maybe I didn't even pull it, or maybe I did, I don't know, but suddenly he relaxed his grip; perhaps his anger had passed. We lay gasping for breath; he was gasping too, from his exertions. It's not easy to strangle someone; I know from experience, it's not as easy as it looks.

There was a smell of damp sand, a shuffle of feet on the other side of the wall, lonely night people were passing by in the street. Suddenly I wrenched my arms free and put them around his back. "I want you," I said to him. "Let's make love."

I did not thrust myself on him; it all happened of itself. It wasn't my fault—I got a hard-on from the scuffle and the weight of his body. This was not the dead weight of a Raymond; this man's weight was of a different nature. I did say "Let's make love," but he himself could probably tell that I wanted him—my cock must have poked into his belly; he couldn't help but feel it. He smiled.

"Baby," he said.

"Darling," I said.

I rolled over and sat up. We began to kiss. I think he was about my age or even younger, but the simple fact that he was considerably bigger and more virile somehow determined our roles. His kisses were not the senile

slobbering of a Raymond; now I knew the difference. The firm kisses of
a strong man, probably a criminal. There was a scar across his upper lip.
Cautiously I stroked his scar with my fingers. He caught my hand in his
lips and kissed it finger by finger, as I had done with Elena. I unbuttoned
his shirt and began kissing his chest, his neck. I especially like to hug as
children do, flinging my arms way around the neck, hugging the neck, not
the shoulders. I hugged him; he smelled of a strong cologne and some kind
of acrid alcohol, or maybe that was the smell of his young body. He was
giving me pleasure. After all, I loved the beautiful and the healthy in this
world. He was beautiful, tall, strong, and well-built, and a criminal for
sure. That added to my enjoyment. Unceasingly kissing his chest, I worked
my way down to where the unbuttoned shirt went into his slacks and disappeared under the belt. My lips came up against the buckle. My chin felt
his engorged member under the thin fabric of the slacks. I undid his zip-
per, turned back the edge of his underpants, and drew out his member.

In Russia, people had often talked about the sexual advantages blacks
had over whites. Legend told of the size of their members. And here before
me was this legendary tool. Despite my very sincere desire for love with
him, curiosity too sprang from somewhere within me and gawked. "Look
at that, black all over, or with a tinge of . . ." But it was rather hard to see,
even though my eyes were used to the dark. His member was big. But
hardly bigger than mine. Thicker, maybe. Hard to tell, though. Curiosity
hid within me. Desire emerged.

Psychologically I was very pleased by what was happening to me. For
the first time in several months I was in a situation that I liked, utterly and
completely. I wanted his cock in my mouth: I sensed that this would give
me enjoyment. I was drawn to take his cock in my mouth, and most of all
I wanted to taste his semen, to see him twitch, to feel this as I embraced
his body. And I took his cock and for the first time ran my tongue around
its engorged head. Chris shuddered.

This is something I do well, I think, very well, because by nature I am
a subtle person and not lazy, and moreover I am not a hedonist, that is, I'm
not someone who seeks enjoyment only for himself, seeks to come no
matter what, achieve his own orgasm and that's all. I am a good partner—I
derive enjoyment from the moans, cries, and pleasure of the other man or
woman. That is why I devoted myself to his member without a second
thought, completely giving myself over to sensation and obeying desire.
With my left hand, gathering them from below, I fondled his balls. He kept

moaning; he leaned back on his hands and moaned softly, with a sob. He may have said, "Oh, my God!"

Gradually he began rocking hard and playing up to me with his hips, sending his cock deeper into my throat. He lay slightly sideways in the sand, on his right elbow, with his left hand just barely stroking my neck and hair. I slid my tongue and lips over his member, deftly tracing out intricate designs, alternating between touching his member lightly and swallowing it deep. Once I almost gagged. But I was even glad of that.

What was happening to my member? I was lying with my belly and my member in the sand, and at every move I rubbed it against the sand through my thin jeans. My cock responded to what was happening with a delightful itching; I scarcely wanted anything more at that moment. I was utterly happy. I had a relationship. Another man had condescended to me, and I had a relationship. How humiliated and unhappy I had been for two whole months. At last. I was terribly grateful to him, I wanted it to be very good for him, and I think it was. I did not merely accommodate his strong thick cock in my mouth; no, this love we were engaged in, these actions, symbolized much more—to me they symbolized life, the triumph of life, a return to life. I was receiving communion from his cock, the strong cock of a lad from Eighth Avenue and Forty-second Street, doubtless a criminal. To me it was life's tool, life itself. And when I brought off his orgasm, when that fountain hurtled into me, into my mouth, I was utterly happy. Do you know the taste of semen? It is the taste of the alive. I know nothing more alive to the taste than semen.

In ecstasy I licked all the semen off his cock and balls, I gathered up what had spilled, licked it up and swallowed it. I found the droplets of semen among his hairs, tracked down the last little drops.

Chris was astounded, I think. He hardly understood, of course, he did not, could not, understand what he meant to me, and he was astounded by the enthusiasm with which I did all this. He was grateful to me, stroked my neck and hair with all the tenderness he was capable of. I buried my face in his groin and lay without moving, and he stroked me with his hands and murmured, "My baby, my baby!"

Listen here, there are morals, there are decent people in the world, there are offices and banks, there are beds; sleeping in them are men and women, also very decent. It was all happening at once, and still is. And there were Chris and I, who had accidentally met there in the dirty sand, in a vacant lot in the vast Great City, a Babylon, God help me, a Babylon. There we lay, and he stroked my hair. Homeless children of the world.

No one needed me, no one had even touched a hand to me in over two months, and there he was, stroking me and saying, "My baby, my baby!" I nearly cried. Despite my everlasting honor and ironic mockery, I was a hunted creature, cornered and exhausted, and this was precisely what I needed—another man's hand stroking my head, caressing me. The tears welled up in me, welled up and started to flow. His groin gave off a characteristic musky smell; I cried, my face burrowing deeper into the warm jumble of his balls, hair, and prick. I don't think he was a sentimental creature, but he felt that I was crying and asked me why, forcibly lifted my face and began to wipe it with his hands. Chris had big strong hands.

Fucking life, it makes us into beasts. We had come together here in the dirt, and there was nothing for us to share. He hugged me and began to soothe me. He did it all the way I wanted, I had not expected that. When I'm excited, all the hairs on my body lift, as if tiny jabs, hundreds and thousands of very tiny jabs, were lifting my hairs; I get cold, and I shiver. It was the first time in a long time that I had not viewed myself with pity. I put my arms around his neck, he put his around me, and I said to him, "I . . . am . . . Eddie. I have no one. You will love me? Yes? And we always will be together? Yes?"

He said, "Yes, baby, yes . . . take it easy."

Then I broke away from him, my right hand dove into my boot and pulled out my knife. "If you betray me," I told him, the tears in my eyes not yet dry, "I will kill you!" My English being very poor, this all sounded like gibberish, but he understood. He said he would not betray me.

I said to him, "Darling!"

He said, "My baby!"

"You and I always will go together and never part, yes?" I said.

"Yes, baby, always together," he said seriously.

I don't think he was lying. He had things to do, but I was so fucking crazy with loneliness, I suited him. This did not mean our relationship was forever. It was simply that he needed me just now, I could meet with him, he would wait for me in bars or simply on the street; I could, and surely would, have some part in the things he did, possibly criminal things. I didn't care what he did, this was what I wanted—it was life, life needed me, that kind of life or any kind at all, but I was needed. He accepted me, I was utterly happy, he accepted me. We talked. It was then I learned his name was Chris. He said that in the morning we would go home to where he lived, but we had to sit here for the night. I didn't ask why; to me it was enough that he had invited me to live with him. I was like a dog that had found its master again; I would have bitten the throat of a policeman or anyone else for him.

We were conversing under our breath, in that same pidgin English. Sometimes I forgot and began speaking Russian. He laughed softly, and then and there I taught him a few words of Russian. They were not nice words from the standpoint of a respectable person, no, they were bad words—prick, love, and others in the same spirit.

In the middle of this conversation I wanted him. I completely let go, God only knows what I did. I pulled off my jeans, I wanted him to fuck me, I pulled off my jeans, pulled off my boots. I ordered him to tear my underpants off me, I wanted him to tear them up, and he obediently tore my red panties off me. I hurled them far away.

At that moment I was really a woman, capricious, demanding, and probably seductive, because I remember myself playfully wiggling my poopka as I leaned on my hands in the sand. My neat round poopka, whose neatness even Elena had envied—it did something unbeknownst to me, it arched sweetly, and I remember that its nakedness, whiteness, and defenselessness gave me the greatest of pleasure. These were purely feminine feelings, I think. I whispered to him, "Fuck me, fuck me, fuck me!"

Chris was breathing heavily. I think I had aroused him in the extreme. I don't know what he did, maybe he wetted his cock with his own spit, but gradually it entered me, his cock did. I shall never forget that feeling of fullness. Pain? Since childhood I had been a lover of every possible savage sensation. Even before women, as a masturbating teenager, a pale onanist, I had invented a certain homemade method: I had put all kinds of objects into my anal orifice, from a pencil to a candle, sometimes rather thick objects. This double onanism—of the cock and through the anal orifice— was very bestial, I remember, very strong and deep. So his cock in my poopka did not frighten me, and it didn't hurt much, even in the first moment; I had obviously stretched my little hole long ago. But the ravishing feeling of fullness—that was new.

He fucked me, and I began to moan. He fucked me, and with one hand caressed my member, I whimpered, moaned, arched, and moaned louder and sweeter. Finally he said to me, "Take it easy, baby, somebody will hear!" I replied that I was not afraid of anything, but nevertheless, out of consideration for him, I made my moans and cries softer.

I was behaving now exactly as my wife had when I fucked her. I caught myself feeling this, and I thought, So this is how she is, this is how they are!

Exultation surged through my body. In a last convulsive movement we dug into the sand and I downed my orgasm in the sand, simultaneously feeling inside me a hot burning. He came inside me. We sprawled exhausted in the sand. My cock dug into the sand, the sand grains pricked it pleasantly, it stood up again almost immediately.

Then we got dressed and settled ourselves comfortably to go to sleep. He took his old place by the wall, and I settled myself beside him, with my head on his chest and my arms around his neck—I'm very fond of that position. He hugged me and we fell asleep. . . .

I don't know how long I slept, but I woke up. Maybe an hour had passed, maybe a few minutes. It was as dark as ever. He was asleep, breathing evenly. I woke up and could not get back to sleep. I sniffed him, scrutinized him, and thought.

No doubt about it, I'm incorrigible, I thought. If my first woman was a drunken Yalta prostitute, then my first man, of course, had to be someone I found in a vacant lot. I remember that girl distinctly. She picked me up one summer night at the bus station in Yalta. She liked the pretty kid dozing on the bench with his friend. She walked over, woke me up, and brazenly led me away to a little public garden behind the bus station. There she calmly lay down on a bench; she was completely naked under her dress. I remember the salty taste of her skin, and her still-wet hair—she had just been for a swim in the sea. I remember her very big, mature cunt with its many folds. I was stunned, it was all streaming with mucus; she wanted this kid; she fucked me not for money but out of desire. Southern scents, the rich southern night, accompanied my first love. Next morning my friend and I left Yalta.

Fate is mocking me. Now I lie with a man of the streets. The years have made no essential change in me. A bum, nothing but a bum, I thought contentedly, meaning myself. I turned to scrutinize Chris again. He stirred, as if sensing my gaze, but then was still again.

Slanting patches of light from the nearby streetlamp penetrated here and there through the crisscrossed iron of the scaffolding. There was a smell of gasoline, I was calm and content. Added to the sense of contentment and calm was the sense of a goal achieved. Well, here I am, a real pederast, I thought with a little giggle. You didn't back off, you outdid yourself, you knew how, good for you, Eddie boy! And although I knew in my heart that I was not entirely free in this life, that I was still a long way from absolute freedom, I had nevertheless taken a step, and a huge one, down that path.

I left him at five-twenty. That was the time on a clock that I saw when I got out to the street. I double-crossed him, left quietly as a thief, slid from his chest without waking him. Why did I do it? I don't know; maybe I feared my future life with him—not the sexual relationship, no, maybe I feared someone else's will, someone else's influence, being subject to him. Maybe. It was an unfathomed but quite powerful feeling that moved me to double-cross him and crawl out of his embrace. Glancing at him over my shoulder, I looked for my metal-rimmed glasses and the key to my hotel room. Once or twice I thought he was watching, but he slept on. Miraculously, I found my glasses in the sand. I was still wearing glasses then, but they didn't spoil my looks much; I looked like a wild man anyway, fucking crazy Eddie. I hunted down my glasses, somehow crawled out to the street, and strode away with a strange satisfaction that I had never before known, abandoning Chris and our future relationship, which might have been one variant of my fate.

I walked along, dusting myself off. I had sand in my hair, sand in my ears, sand in my boots, sand everywhere. A whore returning from the night's escapades. I smiled, I wanted to shout to life, "Well, who's next!" I was free. Why I needed my freedom I do not know. I needed Chris much more, but contrary to common sense I left him. When I came out on Broadway I nearly wavered. But only for an instant, and I decisively strode on again, toward the East Side.

A couple of weeks later I would be cursing myself for having left him. The loneliness and troubled silence would move in again, Elena's villainous image would again torment me, and by the end of April I would have an attack, a very violent, terrible attack, of horror and loneliness. But back then, arriving at the hotel, asking for another key, riding up to my floor, and flinging myself wearily on the bed, I was happy and pleased with myself. I was still happy when I woke up the next morning. I lay there smiling and thought how I must be the only Russian poet who had ever been smart enough to fuck a black man in a New York vacant lot. Lascivious recollections of Chris clasping my poopka and whispering to quiet my moans— "Take it easy, baby, take it easy"—made me roar with joyous laughter.

# ∼ *Evgeny Popov* ∼

# *The Reservoir*

TRANSLATED BY GEORGE SAUNDERS

At first even Bublik seemed to us a decent sort. He paid good money for a two-story house, with cultivated ground, to the grass widow of Vasil-Vasilka. Vasil, an embezzler of the people's wealth, was sent up for selling things on the side—roofing tin, ceramic floor tile, and steam radiators—which he also offered us in his "good neighborly" way, and we heard him out, heard what he had to say, but we didn't get involved, preferring to walk the straight and narrow. Because we're old-time residents of Siberia. Besides, do you think in my own town I couldn't get hold of some damn ceramic crap? What a joke that would be. Besides, that would partly go against the policy of raising living standards and the principles of harnessing the outlying regions of our vast Motherland. Now, we're not any of your kulaks, you know; it's just that these days everybody lives well this way, and they're a whole lot better off than your former kulak fools, who tried to get ahead when the time wasn't ripe, tried to leap over the backs of others and not bring anyone along with them. For which they were very severely but justly punished.

But Lord, Lord. God in heaven above. What for, really? How much effort they put in. Used to deliver bottled gas on Saturdays. That was Kosorezov, a wise and clever man. Went to a lot of trouble, thank you very much—could put a machine or a man on a job when he had to. . . .

*Evgeny Popov lives in Moscow.*

Bushes and bushes of raspberries, beds and beds of strawberries. It was an elegant and heady sight to see, easy on the eyes and comforting to the soul . . . a beautiful, elegant, heady sight to see . . .

But best of all was our reservoir. Lord in heaven, what a reservoir! Constantly fed by crystalline, subterranean waters. Truly, it sweetened our lives on our stifling summer days. In its tender waters our mischievous lads would splash, a merry flock. And our girls, our maidens, like Youth itself, would be stretched out, like kittens, on the crunchy quartz sand. Studying for their exams or just surrendering themselves to the usual girlish dreams—the life of proud labor before them, a family, marriage, raising children, proper relations between the sexes.

And round about them, us—the parents. The women knitting something out of mohair or talking about who was vacationing where in the south or who had bought what new acquisition for the household. Under the willow trees Colonel Zhestakanov and Professor Burevich would do battle in a game of checkers. Mitya-the-Bark-Beetle would argue with the physicist Lysukhin about whether the numbers for different grades of Czech beer corresponded to their actual alcoholic content. Some people worked on crossword puzzles, others on production problems they had encountered on their jobs. And me? I would look at all this and, honest to God, my heart would rejoice, but it would also roll over. The years of hunger during the war, when I was left in the reserves, would come back to me, and I'd remember the time when me and my spouse were number 261, standing in line for corn flour in the black morning blizzard next to the movie theater Rote Front. My leg had gone numb from cold; I couldn't feel my foot in its thick felt boot; couldn't feel it at all. Afterward they rubbed it with goose grease. When I remember that, honest to God, I'd like to personally strangle all these loudmouths and troublemakers with my own two hands. They bad-mouth everything, but they guzzle their fill of shashlik and Pepsi-Cola. I wish all those stinking bastards had been in my place, standing in line in 1947. I'd like to see what kind of tune they'd sing then, the sniveling rats.

As for those two young men, who had the look of artists about them—I won't start trying to hide or justify our blunders—at first we actually took a liking to them.

It was theater director Bublik who brought them here, to our town, along with his good-looking wife the singer. The only good thing about Bublik, the scum, was that during his time as director he often cheered us up by having various celebrities visit Pustaya Chush* (that's the name of our workingman's town). One time you'd see the singer M. parading around, dangling a handkerchief and bellowing "Live in fame and glory"; another time the magician I. would amuse everyone by making Zhestakanov's pocket watch disappear and turn up in Mitya-the-Bark-Beetle's boot. Then another time our celebrated portraitist Spozhnikov would be sitting up on the heights, painting a portrait of our reservoir against the background of its natural surroundings. Strange that those intelligent people didn't detect the rotten inner core of this Bublik before we did. Very strange.

Now, at first glance those two were the simplest, most ordinary long-haired kids. But it's not by chance, you know, that we have the old folk saying: Some simplicity is worse than thievery. Although it's also true that modesty is a virtue. Well, one of them was kind of tall, a blue-eyed athlete type. The other was more of a weakling, on the dark side, and a little brighter than the first one. Our gals, our young maidens, crowded around in droves when they saw how skillful these fellows were at table tennis. And these boys, no way would they say any low words to the girls or make any vulgar or suggestive gestures. Oh no. They were all modest and above-board, you see, those bastards whacking away at their little white ball. Until it happened.

But once it happened, everyone started yelling that we had made it up. What was there for us to "make up"? We didn't have the slightest inkling of anything until all of a sudden the most honest-to-God, out-and-out swinish scandal erupted, the consequences of which are ineradicable, sad, and shameful. Even the dachas are being boarded up tight, the secondhand dealers are scurrying about, rustling through the autumn leaves, the fruit trees are being dug up and carted off for transplanting, and there's no joy in anybody's face, just depression and weariness, disillusionment and fear.

Although with only half a brain we could have guessed right away. They even went around holding hands, not to mention the fact that they obviously, *obviously,* avoided our gals.

And the gals, the little pranksters, were glad to have a laugh. They put the smaller one's hair into little braids, like the Uzbek women do. They smeared some bright lipstick on his mouth. Then they went and looped a spare, empty brassiere over his fairly hefty chest, which was more than standard size. And laugh! My, how they laughed.

---

*Literally, "Empty Nonsense."—TRANS.

And all of us, at the time—we laughed too, in our ignorance, and had a good time, while also being aware of a certain vulgarity in this relatively pointed joke. We laughed and had a good time—until it happened.

Lord in heaven! I'll remember it for the rest of my life. You see, the disposition of forces was like this. The pond. Those two on a raft near the shore. The gals right there with them. All of us sitting under the trees. Bublik the director and his wife the singer nowhere to be seen.

The girls had no sooner fastened this harmless female ornament over the younger one's chest than the older one jumped up, turning pale, with his blue eyes getting all dark, and he gives poor Nastya a trained boxer's jab right in the solar plexus, from which the poor child, without a murmur, not even an "Ow," falls over on the sand.

We all stood there with our mouths hanging open. But he didn't waste a second. He cut the raft loose and in the wink of an eye the pair of them were out in the middle of the reservoir, where they started cursing in the foulest and dirtiest way. The tall one was all in a fury. The short one would only mutter in reply, but using filthy language. Also he stuck his tongue out at the tall one. At which the first one, twitching and jerking in the strangest way, shouted: "Ah, you whore!" And smacked the shorter one in the face. Then that one goes crashing to his knees and starts kissing his comrade's bare and dirty feet, half covered by the waves washing over them.

And Lord, Lord. God in heaven above! The tall one kicked him with all his might, and with a piercing scream, the first one landed in the water. But this threw the raft off balance, and one end shot up, throwing the second one in the water too. The two of them, without a gurgle, began to disappear beneath the waves. Then they surfaced for a moment, apparently not knowing how to swim—after which, again without a gurgle, they sank to the bottom for good.

A terrible silence fell.

We all stood there, thunderstruck. Our gals hovered around like so many frightened little animals as Nastya came to. The nurses woke up. Infants began to cry. Dogs began to howl.

Colonel Zhestakanov was the first to gather his wits together. With a shout, "I'll save those fairies—so they can answer to a people's comradely court," this superb swimmer, who had won more than a few swimming championships in his youth, plunged into the water and disappeared for a long time. Coming back up, he floated on his back for a while, after which, without wasting words, he dove again.

But neither Colonel Zhestakanov's second nor his subsequent sound-
ings of the reservoir bottom produced any favorable results. The colonel
muttered, "How can it be?" But they had disappeared.

We figured out that we had better hurry over to Bublik's, since he was
to blame, so to speak, for this "triumph." But he had disappeared too,
along with his good-looking wife the singer. The wind from the pine forest was blowing freely through their empty dacha, ruffling the tulle curtains. A coffee cup rolled on its side on the rug, having dumped its
contents on an issue of some glossy magazine that was obviously not one
of our Soviet magazines. Bright-orange flowers languished like abandoned
waifs in their pretty ceramic vases. Bublik and his good-looking wife the
singer had vanished.

And when, a few days later, we sent a delegation of our people to the
musical comedy theater, the administration there, staring at the floor, informed us that Bublik had already made a clean escape and had taken off
for parts unknown. And it was only afterward that we understood the embarrassed look on these honest people's faces, when it finally came out exactly what unknown parts director Bublik had taken off for. Turned out it
was the United States of America, and the two of them had brazenly emigrated right under everybody's nose—him and his good-looking wife
the singer. Well, what the hell, it's not all that surprising that they went
to the U.S.A. Seems it'll be easier for them there to engage in degeneracy,
which in our country is barred by good, hard roadblocks. So it's not
surprising.

What's surprising is something else. What's surprising is that when the
militia arrived at the lake and the scuba divers got there too, they didn't
find anyone either. We begged the scuba divers to keep at it, and they really tried to cover every square centimeter of the bottom, but it was all in
vain. The two "artists" were gone.

You know, later on we discussed another idea—maybe we should go to
the necessary expense and drain the pond, find out what was going on,
and get to the bottom of everything, so that there wouldn't be this leftover
smell of the devil's work or papistry, so that there wouldn't be this weariness and depression, disillusionment and fear—what the hell, we had
enough money. But we missed our chance, and now we're really paying for
our foolish gullibility, negligence, and dizzy-headedness.

Because literally on the very next day, after everything seemed to have
quieted down, the town was suddenly treated to the terrible screams of
someone being killed. It turned out to be Comrade Zhestakanov, who

loved night swimming. The poor soul could barely get his breath, his eyes were popping out of his head, and all he could do was point at the watery traces of moonlight, repeating: "It's them! It's them. There. There."

After being revived with a glass of vodka, he got hold of himself. But he still insisted he had swum out to the raft at twelve midnight, the raft out in the middle of the reservoir, and on this raft there suddenly appeared two skeletons, sadly embracing and singing a song ever so softly: "No need for sorrow, all of life lies ahead." How do you like that?

And even though Zhestakanov was soon being treated by the psychiatrist Tsarkov-Kolomensky, it didn't help anyone. The skeletons were also seen and heard by Professor Burevich, Comrade K., Mitya-the-Bark-Beetle (and Mitya's mother-in-law), the metalworker Yeprev and his buddy Shenopin, Angelina Stepanovna, Edward Ivanovich, Yuri Aleksandrovich, Emma Nikolaevna, me, and even the physicist Lysukhin, who as a man of science was so shaken by this spectacle that he began to drink dangerously.

People tried to scare them off by shouting "Scat" and firing a double-barreled shotgun, but none of it helped. The skeletons weren't always visible, it's true. But the damn raft moved around literally on its own, and you could hear yelling, singing, lamentations, hoarse curses, smacking kisses, and prayers at night *all the time!*

I'm not one of your Zhestakanovs, I grant you. I never was at the front. And I'm not your physicist Lysukhin. Never had a higher education. I'm just a normal average person, and not an especially big vodka drinker either. *But I personally swear to you myself that I heard this with my own ears:* "My darling, my darling," and then a wheezing sound, but such a sound it made my hair stand on end.

And after we tried everything over and over again, guns and stones and chlorophosphate, the end came—the end for us, the end for our town, the end for the reservoir. The dachas are being boarded up tight, and the secondhand dealers are scurrying about everywhere, rustling through the autumn leaves, the fruit trees are being dug up and carted off for transplanting, and there's no joy in anybody's face, just depression and weariness, disillusionment and fear.

So what would you have us do? We're none of us mystics or priests. But also we're not fools enough to live in a place like this where some degenerate corpses with their lustful skeletons gleaming in the moonlight try to lure people or get close to them and scare them and drive people straight into the psychiatric hospitals, leaving the women without any courage and the men without good sense and the children without their happy childhood or a clear vision of their perspectives in life and of working for the good of our vast Motherland. O Lord, O Lord. God in heaven above.

# ~ *Michel Tournier* ~

## *Prikli*

TRANSLATED BY BARBARA WRIGHT

"You're all prickly!"

The little boy squirmed in the arms of his father, who was trying to kiss him. It wasn't just his stubbly cheeks, it was his gray skin, his smell of tobacco and shaving soap, his dust-colored suit, his stiff collar, which was in no way brightened up by a too sensible necktie. . . . No, really, there was nothing about this man that charmed or caressed, and his efforts to demonstrate affection seemed like punishments. What was more, he had only made matters worse by countering his son's rebuffs with irony, calling him Prikli, my little hedgehog, for example.

"Come here, Prikli!" he commanded. "Come and kiss Papa!"

When he heard this nickname for the first time, the child had bristled. Yes, he had very precisely felt he was becoming a hedgehog, a miniature pig covered with bristles swarming with vermin. Pooh! He had screamed with anger and disgust. Luckily Mama was there. He had taken refuge in her arms.

"I don't want to, I don't want to be Prikli!"

She had enveloped him in her perfume. She had pressed her creamy,

MICHEL TOURNIER's *first novel,* Friday, *won the Grand Prix du Roman of the Académie Française in 1967; his second,* The Ogre, *which Janet Flanner called "the most important book to come out of France since Proust," won the Prix Goncourt by unanimous vote in 1970. The young protagonist of "Prikli" (from* The Fetishist), *who emasculates himself, recalls the hero of James Merrill's early novel* The Seraglio, *who elects to castrate himself rather than give in to the heterosexual imperative.*

rouged cheek to her child's burning face. Then her serious, calming voice had, as if by a miracle, unsprung the trap, and a soothing picture had been placed, like a cool hand, over his inflamed imagination.

"But you know, baby hedgehogs don't have prickles—just very soft, very clean down. It's only later. Later, when they grow up. When they become men . . ."

To become a man. Like Papa. No prospect could be less attractive to Prikli. He had more than once watched his father shaving. The folding razor, one of those old-fashioned razors with a mother-of-pearl handle that are sometimes called cutthroats, held in a bizarre way between the thumb and forefinger, scraped at his skin and removed the lather contaminated by the cut whiskers. And that grimy snow disappeared in gray flakes under the water from the faucet, while Papa was still scratching away at his neck and jowls, making ridiculous grimaces. He ended with his upper lip, and for that he pinched the tip of his nose between his fingers and pulled it back. At this point Prikli ran away, to stop Papa taking him in his arms when he'd finished. *Really* finished? But what about all those black hairs on his chest?

On the other hand, Prikli had never seen his mother at her dressing table. After her lemon tea, which she took alone in her bedroom, she shut herself up in the bathroom for an hour and a half. And when she came out, still dressed in a chiffon negligee, she was already a goddess, the goddess of the morning, as fresh as a rose, anointed with lanolin, very different, it's true, from the great black goddess of the evening, the one who leaned over Prikli's bed, her face half hidden behind a little veil, and who told him: "Don't kiss me, you'll wreck my hair." "At least leave me your gloves," he had begged her one day. And she had agreed, she had dropped those bits of black kidskin into his bed. They were as supple and as warm as fresh, living skins, and the child had swathed his body in those empty hands, Mama's hands, and fallen asleep under their caress.

The beautiful apartment that Prikli and his family lived in on the Rue des Sablons would have had few resources to offer to the child's reveries had it not been for a huge old painting in the Pre-Raphaelite style which had been hung, to get it out of the way, in the narrow corridor leading from the living room to the bedrooms at the back. Nobody noticed it anymore, except Prikli, who felt its terrible images weighing heavily on his head every time he went along that somber passageway. This painting depicted the Last Judgment. In the center of an apocalyptic landscape consisting of mountains collapsing one on top of the other, a supreme being made of light was sitting on a throne and presiding over the inexorable division established between the damned and the chosen. The damned were sinking down into an underground passage made of granite, while the chosen, singing and carrying palms, were ascending to heaven up a great staircase made of pink clouds. Now, what the child found particularly striking was the anatomy of each category. For whereas the damned had brown skin and black hair, and their nudity revealed formidable muscles, the chosen were pale and slim, and their white tunics concealed frail, delicate limbs.

~ ~ ~

On fine days, Prikli and his nursemaid went out in the afternoons to the gardens in Desbordes-Valmore Square. Old Marie always sat on the same bench, where she held court with the other governesses of the district, who had also come there to give the offspring of the bourgeoisie the benefit of some fresh air. They talked about the weather, about family affairs, about the provinces they came from, and above all about their employers. As the gardens were enclosed and therefore safe, they allowed the children to wander off, keeping only a vague eye on them.

Prikli liked these times when there was nothing much to do except explore and discover. They made such a contrast with the dreary mornings he spent at his lessons in the company of a handful of other well-to-do children in a private school in the Rue de la Faisanderie. Everything he learned at school remained abstract for him, and without any connection with real things. The knowledge he acquired there floated somewhere above life and was never involved in it. It was quite different when he was in the square, though; there, he moved around with wide-open eyes and outstretched fingers, for it was an initiatory place, full of surprises and threats.

In the first place there was a whole crowd of statues, which were strange both because of their nudity and because of their respective occupations. For instance, one was a horse, but where its neck should have been it had the torso of a man—a bearded man with a nasty look in his eye. He spent his time carrying off under his arm a fat naked woman whose hair was all over the place and who was struggling without much conviction. Prikli had asked Marie to explain this scene to him. Marie was obviously at a loss, so she had appealed to the English governess of a little girl who sometimes came to the gardens and who, as it happened, was there at the time. Miss Campbell had given Prikli quite a long lecture, from which he had vaguely gathered that the man-horse—a scent-tar—was obliged, in order to marry, to abduct a woman by main force, precisely because of his bad smell, to which he owed his name. Remembering his father's smell, Prikli had been satisfied with this explanation.

A little farther on, a young boy with hairless, chubby cheeks, dressed in a short skirt, was raising his sword against a monster, which had fallen over backward. The monster had the body of a man of terrifying strength, and the head of a bull. There, too, Miss Campbell had been able to throw some light on the subject. The young boy, who was called Theseus, should have been devoured by the monster. But he had been the stronger, and he had killed the man-bull. But why did he have such a funny name and wear a skirt like a girl? Here, Miss Campbell had no answer.

Prikli could tell the difference between the more or less regular visitors to the square and its permanent inhabitants. Among the latter, the most important character was undoubtedly the park keeper. Old Cromorne was distinguished by his uniform and kepi, but especially by the left arm of his jacket, which was empty and tucked back with a safety pin. People said he was one-armed and a widower. When Prikli had asked, and been told, what a widower was, he wondered whether there was any connection between these two states. Was it because he had lost his wife that Cromorne had only one arm? Had he cut off his left arm on the day of the funeral and put it in the coffin beside his dear departed?

Much less important than Cromorne, Madame Béline and Mademoiselle Aglaia were secondary but reassuring characters. Mademoiselle Aglaia was in charge of the chairs—ninety-four chairs, she had specified to Marie and Miss Campbell with a sigh, in a moment of abandon one day. In order to fulfill her mission properly, it was her duty to be discreet and unobtrusive. Cromorne had only recently said as much. Had she had his presence and uniform—to say nothing of his prestige as a disabled ex-serviceman—she wouldn't have managed to take half the money she did. For people are rather dishonest, and they would have no scruples about going off without paying for their chairs if the person responsible for collecting the money was too conspicuous. Whereas with Mademoiselle Aglaia, people were never on their guard when she came gliding down the alleyways, concealing her book of tickets in the hollow of her hand.

Pink and plump, Madame Béline sat in state behind her jars of lollipops and barley sugar in a kiosk bristling with hoops, diabolos, yo-yos, kites, multicolored balloons, jumping ropes, and musical tops. And though she radiated goodness and joie de vivre, this was not without merit, because she suffered from a grave disappointment. The dream of her life was to have some tables and chairs in front of her kiosk, at which she would have served soda pop and fruit juices to the public. She would thus have gone some way toward joining the prestigious memory of one of her uncles, who had owned a bar in Saint-Ouen. Unfortunately, Cromorne had always opposed this project. In the first place, Madame Béline didn't have the necessary license. As for making him an accomplice to her bending the rules of the administration, Madame Béline could no longer even dream of it after the unfortunate allusion she had once made to her barkeeping uncle. Cromorne had been indignant. A barkeeper from Saint-Ouen! What were they trying to do to Desbordes-Valmore Square.

If poor Madame Béline was no match for Cromorne, it was quite different with old Mother Mamouse, who reigned over the "comfort station." This was a curious construction which, though shaped like a Swiss chalet, nevertheless had something of the Chinese pagoda and the Hindu temple about it, with its upturned roof, its sculptured wood, and its ceramic decoration.

What particularly interested Prikli was the division of the space inside this chalet into two strictly opposed parts. On the left was the men's domain, with its foul-smelling, parsimoniously irrigated urinals and, behind doors that didn't close properly, Turkish latrines formed of a cynical hole framed by two soles of grooved cement to put your feet on. Nothing could have been more attractive, on the other hand, than the ladies' domain. The whole place smelled of lilac disinfectant and was decorated with porcelain representing peacocks with their tails widely fanned. There was a pile of fresh, snowy white towels on a console table between two immaculate washbowls. But what especially enchanted Prikli were the little closets with their well-fitting mahogany doors, their high-perched seats, and their silky, silent toilet paper that smelled of violets.

Like the dog Cerberus, that watchful keeper of the infernal regions, Mamouse, enormous in several thicknesses of woollies and shawls, her big, flabby, impassive face framed within the confines of the black lace mantilla covering her white hair, was ensconced at a table between the two doors, that of the gentlemen and that of the ladies. On this table stood a saucer destined for offerings, and an alcohol stove surmounted by a saucepan in which an invariable broth of chicken giblets was simmering.

Mamouse had explained the theory of the saucer to one of her lady clients in Prikli's presence, and he had listened, all ears. Whatever happened, it must never be empty. The people who used the chalet were only too willing to forget to leave an offering. A few coins in the saucer are indispensable, to refresh their memories. These coins serve as a sort of bait and act like decoys, those caged birds that are supposed to attract their free congeners toward the sportsmen and their guns. Was it a good idea to add one or two bills to the coins? Mamouse's answer to this serious question was a categorical no. A bill doesn't attract a bill, it is more likely to discourage it by bringing into disrepute what can only be the product of exceptional munificence. Not to speak of the hundred-times-accursed day when a bill left by a lady client had disappeared five minutes later under Mamouse's very nose. Coins, therefore, and the most valuable possible, of course, not those worthless little bits people call "small change"—which set a deplorable example in a saucer.

Apropos of offerings, Mamouse had a story she never failed to tell newcomers, just as soon as she had arrived at a suitable degree of familiarity with them. The anecdote went back to a period in the very distant past, to judge by the sum in question. A very elegant gentleman, such as was to be seen in former days—light-gray gaiters, gloves, walking stick, hat, monocle—having deposited a coin with a hole in it in the saucer, had pointed to the shut door of one of the closets with the tip of his stick.

He had taken the liberty of joking: "You have a client in there who is treating us to some very ugly-sounding music!"

"So," Mamouse related, once again inflamed with retrospective indignation, "I looked daggers at him and said: 'I suppose you think that for twenty-five centimes we should give you some Massenet?' For in those days," she added nostalgically, "I could still afford a subscription to the Opéra-Comique."

There regularly followed one of her habitual diatribes against men, with their disgusting behavior—they were all lechers, wild boars, debauchees, and she should know, for goodness' sake, after thirty years of running the "chalet"!

The stove and saucepan were an apple of discord between her and Cromorne. For the park keeper considered this vulgar stew, which so indiscreetly displayed to all eyes the culinary intimacies of the custodian of the comfort station, to be unworthy of his garden.

"He makes out I don't have any right to it!" Mamouse muttered. "But just let him show me the article in the regulations which forbids my broth! And how d'you expect me to sit here in all this damp and in all these drafts if I don't get something warm inside me?"

Prikli had of course had occasion to take a look in the battered old saucepan simmering on the stove. But those chicken necks, those livers, those gizzards, didn't arouse any echo in his mind. They weren't the sort of thing he saw in the kitchen at home. As for Mamouse's remarks, he paid very little attention to them, having other things to think about, and precisely at the moment when the fat woman was chatting to one of her customers. For his whole concern was to evade her observation and slip in through the door on the right, to the perfumed domain of the ladies. At first he succeeded in this maneuver more than once, but Mamouse had spotted him, and from then on she kept an eye on him. The right-hand door became more and more impassable.

This matter had been important to him ever since a childish drama relating to what Marie called "doing a tinkle." Prikli had always performed this tinkle squatting, as if he were a girl. It was so unusual for him to pee standing up that when he tried it he experienced a difficulty that had almost become an inhibition. His family hadn't taken any notice of what, at first, seemed just a baby's whim. Then they had started badgering him about it, so much so that he'd made up his mind to urinate only where no one could watch him, in a locked lavatory. Having thus found peace, he had begun to observe, with disgusted curiosity, men standing up at urinals.

One day while he was walking in the street with his mother, he had tried an experiment that had turned out to be unfortunate. They were preceded by a dog that kept stopping at every lamppost to brand it with its urine. Observing this activity, Prikli had suddenly had the idea of imitating it. He, too, had stopped at a tree and lifted his left leg up toward its trunk. Abruptly slackening her pace, his mother had caught him in this strange posture. Her reflexes came into play, and a smack rang out on Prikli's cheek.

"Have you gone quite mad?" she asked, in a particular tone of voice that he detested.

He had been deeply mortified by this little misadventure. No one ever hit him, but now he had been slapped because of his urinary habits. He concluded that peepee, and everything to do with it, constituted a source of multiple annoyances.

Things had got even worse when he started wetting his bed again. He couldn't help it. Every morning he woke up in a pool. All he knew about it was that sometimes, when he was still half asleep, he felt the warm urine trickling down his thigh. Old Marie scolded him and put a piece of oil-cloth under his sheet to protect his mattress. She threatened, if he didn't stop, to bring back the surgeon who had taken his tonsils out. This time it would be his little pecker they'd cut off!

Things might well have gone no further. But on the contrary, one thing followed another in diabolical fashion. One day when he was on the lookout for a moment's inattention on Mamouse's part, he was stupefied to see his friend Dominique coming out of the chalet. The thing was, he was coming from the ladies' side and, far from hiding from her, he exchanged a few smiling words with the fat woman and went off without having left her an offering. Prikli was absolutely certain of this.

Who was Dominique? He was the son of Angelo Bosio, the owner of the merry-go-round. Most of the time the merry-go-round slept motion-less under its tarpaulins. But on Sundays, everything came to life. Bosio fa-ther and son were hard at it inside the big cream-and-gold top in which, peppered with a metallic sort of music, there was a confused but cheerful mixture of naiads, space rockets, rearing horses, milch cows, formula I rac-ing cars, and an endearing Far West locomotive with its cowcatcher. When Marie offered him a ride on the merry-go-round, this locomotive was where Prikli liked to sit. Not that he dreamed of any prairie adventures but simply because he liked the privacy of being able to shut himself into the little vehicle, to sit in an enclosed space that was his alone. Within reach of his hand was a little chain, with which he could have rung the shiny brass bell attached to the engine. He took care not to touch it.

On Wednesdays, Dominique had sole charge of the merry-go-round. As he was tall—he was at least eleven years old—big, and strong, he had no difficulty in keeping his young clientele in order, and he was both gentle and patient as he perched some of them up on the horses, placed others in the conch drawn by the naiads, and strapped Prikli into his locomotive. Then he switched on the motor and the music and gave the merry-go-round a little push to help it get started. When he was in a good mood he undid the rope attached to the trophy and made it jiggle up and down over the children's heads. The trophy consisted of a wig made of red wool, sus-pended on a rope that passed through a pulley. The child who caught it was entitled to a free ride. Strapped into his cab, Prikli couldn't take part in the trophy hunt. By way of compensation, Dominique sometimes treated him to a free ride.

This favor had given rise to a friendship. Prikli had found a kind of older brother in this big, calm, maternal boy. So he didn't hesitate to question him after he'd seen him come out of the ladies' side of the comfort station, obviously with Mamouse's blessing. How had he managed to obtain this tremendous privilege?

That day, Dominique seemed to be in a radiant mood. He started by vigorously mocking Prikli and his curiosity. "If anyone asks you," he said, "you must say you don't know!"

Prikli detested irony and couldn't bear to be thwarted. He stamped his foot. He was just about to burst into tears, when Dominique seemed to change his mind. He cast an anxious glance around and became very serious.

"If you want to know, if you absolutely want to know, well, it'll be terrible!"

Prikli was choking with emotion.

"How d'you mean, terrible?"

"If you're brave enough to know," Dominique declared, "be in the center of the maze, by yourself, in half an hour!"

Then he went off, thumbing his nose.

Prikli was appalled. The boxwood maze at the far end of the gardens had always terrified him. It was a dark, dank clump of bushes which you could edge into through a narrow opening. After that, you got lost. There were turnings, recesses, culs-de-sac, closed circuits, where you went around in a circle indefinitely. If you had enough patience, you managed to reach the center. There, on a little pedestal that was green with mold, there must once have been a statue. It had disappeared, but the pedestal was still waiting, soiled by slugs.

Prikli kept an eye on the electric clock. Thirty minutes. Would he go to the terrible rendezvous? What was Dominique's big secret? Why did he have to go to the center of the boxwood maze to be told it? More than once he relieved his fear by giving up the idea. He wouldn't go, he wouldn't! But he was well aware that this was just a pretense. He knew that he *would* keep the tryst.

At the appointed hour he made sure that Marie was quietly chatting with her friends, then made his way over toward the maze. He was more dead than alive as he allowed himself to be swallowed up within the bluey-green bushes. But, curiously guided by an infallible instinct, with no false moves he almost immediately found himself in the center of the maze. He was pretty sure that someone would already be there, waiting for him. Dominique. The big boy was sitting on the pedestal. He looked serious.

"You came," he said. "As you're my friend, I'll let you into my secret. But before I do, you must swear that you'll never tell anyone."

"Yes," Prikli stammered, in a whisper.

"Spit on the ground and say 'I swear.' "

Prikli spat and said, "I swear."

Then Dominique stood up on the pedestal and started unbuttoning the fly of his short pants, never taking his eyes off Prikli. Next, opening them wide, he pulled down the red underpants he had exposed. His smooth, white stomach ended in a milky slit, a vertical smile that had just a trace of pale down.

"But . . . Dominique . . . ," Prikli stammered.

"Dominique is a girl's name too," explained Dominique, who had done up her pants again in the twinkling of an eye. "It's Papa. He wants people to think I'm a boy when I'm looking after the merry-go-round on my own. He says it's safer. You'll understand later. And now—scram!"

Prikli started running and soon found himself back in the midst of the other children. There was nothing apparent to distinguish him from them, but he was like none of them, for he was possessed by a burning anxiety. "You'll understand later." That mysterious phrase gave him no respite, and he tried desperately to understand it *at once*.

Not long after, he did in fact understand. In the first place, he had gone into Mamouse's chalet without trying to avoid the men's domain for once. He was coming out of the closet where he had peed, squatting, as was his wont, when he saw from behind a man who was just finishing relieving himself in one of the urinals. The man turned around, and Prikli couldn't believe his eyes. The quantity of swarthy, flabby flesh he was trying with difficulty to cram back into his fly was incredible. What was he going to do with all that hideous, useless meat? The answer suddenly struck him while he was dropping a coin into Mamouse's saucer. Her saucepan was simmering away as usual on its stove. Mamouse was stirring its contents with a wooden spoon. And in a flash, Prikli recognized in those anatomical bits and pieces the brown, flaccid thing that the fellow had been stuffing into his pants. It was clear, it was obvious.

Later, another obvious fact had jumped up and hit him in the face. For months now he had been hanging around the statue of Theseus and the Minotaur. In the first place, he recognized that Theseus, with his girl's skirt, was a reflection of Dominique. The resemblance was self-evident. And above all he could clearly make out, between the great muscular thighs of the Minotaur, that bunch of flabby, shapeless flesh that had so surprised him in the man at the chalet. At last, Theseus' gesture had acquired a precise meaning. His sword was aimed at the Minotaur's sex organ. The link between the brown meat of the man in the urinal and Mamouse's saucepan was forged by Theseus' sword.

In the days that followed, Marie was pleased to observe that Prikli had stopped wetting his bed.

"I frightened you when I threatened you with the surgeon," she told him. "It was high time. I was just going to call him. But there's no need now."

Prikli didn't answer. There was, indeed, no need.

That same day, they went back to the gardens. Mamouse saw him coming up to her and standing in front of her table. She was just going to ask him what he wanted, when he pulled a razor out of his pocket, one of those old-fashioned razors with a mother-of-pearl handle that are sometimes called cutthroats. He opened it and, with his free hand, unbuttoned his fly. Mamouse started howling like a wild animal when she saw him bring out his little child's pecker and slash at it with the razor. Blood spurted. Then Prikli was holding out, to Mamouse, over the table, a little bit of shriveled flesh. Next he saw the comfort station, its surrounding trees, and the entire Desbordes-Valmore gardens swaying and beginning to revolve like Dominique's merry-go-round, and he collapsed in a faint, carrying with him as he fell the saucer with all its coins, the alcohol stove, the saucepan, and the chicken giblets.

# ~ *Michel Tournier* ~

FROM

# *Gemini*

TRANSLATED BY ANNE CARTER

I never go back to Rennes without my footsteps leading me to the Thabor College, next door to the gardens of the same name, which lie within the walls of the onetime Benedictine abbey of Saint-Mélaine. Thabor! A name of mystery, wrapped in an aura of magic, a sacred name, with its hints of gold and the tabernacle! All my adolescence trembles within me at the sound of it. . . . But whatever its promised ecstasies and transfigurations, I was the only one of the three Surin children to be visited by the light of the Holy Ghost within its aged walls.

I picture with pain and no little distress the boredom those college years mean to a heterosexual. What a grayness there must be in his days and nights, sunk body and soul in a human environment devoid of sexual stimulus! But then surely that is a fair training for what life has in store for him.

Whereas for me, ye gods! Thabor was a melting pot of desire and satiety all through my childhood and adolescence. I burned with all the fires of hell in a promiscuity which did not let up for a second in any of the twelve phases into which our timetable divided it: dormitory, chapel, classroom, dining hall, playground, lavatories, gymnasium, playing fields, fencing school, staircases, recreation room, washrooms. Every one of those places was a high spot in its way, and the scene for twelve separate forms of chase and capture. From the first day, I was gripped by an amorous fever as I plunged into the atmosphere of the college, saturated with dawning virility. What wouldn't I give today, cast out into the heterosexual twilight, to recover something of that fire!

My initiation came as a surprise when I was made the happy, willing victim of what the "Foils" used to call "shell fishing." Evening prep was just over, and we were filing out to the dining hall by way of the recreation area. I was among the last to leave, but not the last, and I was still some yards from the classroom door when the boy assigned to the task put out the lights. I went on slowly in an obscurity relieved only by the lights from the playground. I had my arms behind my back, hands linked, palm outward, over my bottom. I was vaguely aware of something going on behind me, and I felt something obtrusive being pushed into my hands with a determination that could not have been accidental. Giving way to it as far as I could without bumping into the boys ahead, I had to accept that what I was holding in my hands, through the thin stuff of his trousers, was the erect penis of the boy behind me. If I unclasped my hands and removed them from the offering, I should be unobtrusively rejecting the advance being made to me. I responded, on the contrary, by taking a step backward and opening my hands wide, like a shell, like a basket waiting to receive the first fruits of love on the sly.

This was my first encounter with desire experienced, not in solitude, like a shameful secret, but in complicity—I almost said, and it would be true before long, in company. I was eleven. Now I am forty-five, and still I have not emerged from the daze of wonder in which I walked through that damp, dark college playground, as though wrapped in an invisible glory. Never emerged from it . . . How I like that expression, so right and touching, suggesting some strange country, a mysterious forest whose spell is so powerful that the traveler who ventures there *never emerges from it*. He is seized with wonder, and the wonder never lets him go and keeps him from recovery and return to the gray, unprofitable world where he was born.

I was so completely overwhelmed by this discovery that I had no idea which one of the schoolfellows behind me had put into my hands the keys of a kingdom whose wealth, even now as I write, I have not yet done with exploring. Indeed I never did know for sure, because I found out later that the action had been the outcome of a little conspiracy among three of them who sat together at the back of the class, members of a secret society called the *Fleurets,* the Foils, who were in the habit of trying out all new boys systematically. I am only going to talk about two of the Foils here, because they are characters who shine with incomparable brilliance in my memory.

Thomas "Drycome" got his pseudo patronymic from an amazing discovery which made him famous at Thabor and about which I shall have more to say later. All the boys had made the insides of their desk lids into miniature picture galleries of their dreams, memories, heroes, and private myths. So you would see family snapshots next to pages out of sports magazines, and portraits of music hall singers side by side with comic strips. Thomas's pictures were exclusively religious and devoted entirely to the character of Jesus. But this was not the infant Christ or the emaciated, suffering figure of the cross. This was Christ the King, the champion of God, abounding in strength and vigor, "youth eternal," whose image formed a pyramid upon the small wooden square. This triumphant iconography had, as it were, a kind of signature in a tiny picture tucked away in the left-hand corner, which might have passed unnoticed by the uninitiated. It was a crude portrayal of Thomas putting two fingers into the wounded side of the risen Jesus. To begin with, I saw nothing more in it than a reference to Thomas's own Christian name. But that was only a start. Its real meaning was not vouchsafed to me until later.

The little group of Foils used to meet twice weekly at the city's fencing school for the lessons that provided it with a respectable excuse as well as with a splendidly symbolic derivation. The fencing master's attitude toward us was ambivalent, unerringly strict when it came to passing judgment on a low feint or a stop hit in the high line, but turning a blind eye to any scuffles of our own we might engage in in the cloakroom or under the showers. We were quite sure that this retired cavalry officer, unmarried and fashioned from his grizzled head downward entirely of muscle and sinew, was really one of us, but he never gave us so much as a glimpse of what lay behind his fencing jacket and wire mask. When one of our number once hinted at having enjoyed his favors, he met with such contemptuous disbelief that he abandoned the subject, but the attempt marked him in our eyes in a way that he never quite lived down. For there were among the Foils some things that simply were not done. No written law defined them, but we could tell them with an infallible instinct, and the sanctions we imposed were strict and inflexible.

Because I was the youngest and the newest recruit, they called me Fleurette, a name I answered to quite readily, even from boys who used it without knowing what it meant. To begin with I had been considered rather "unappetizing" because I was so skinny, but Raphael—whose word was law where matters of sex were concerned—had rehabilitated me by praising my penis, which at that time was relatively long and chubby. Its silky softness, he said, was in contrast to my skinny thighs and meager belly, stretched like a canvas across my jutting hipbones. "Like a bunch of juicy grapes hanging on a burned-out bit of trellis," he declared rhapsodically, in a way that both flattered me and made me laugh. I must admit that to these subtle charms I added a talent for sucking hard and thoroughly, which derived from a liking I have always had for seminal fluid.

Thomas had the same liking, more than any of us, although he rarely satisfied it in our direct fashion by a straightforward head-to-tail. In fact, he did nothing like anyone else, but brought to everything a breadth, a loftiness, which was essentially religious. Religion was the natural element in which he lived and breathed and had his being. For example, I could quote the kind of ecstatic trance he would fall into every morning in the dormitory as we made our beds before going down to chapel. The rule was that we had to give our sheets a shake before making up the beds. This simple action, performed simultaneously by forty boys, shook out the crust of dried sperm from the sheets and filled the air with a seminal dust. This vernal aerosol got into our eyes, noses, and lungs, so that we were impregnating one another as if by a pollen-bearing breeze. Most of the boarders did not even notice the subtle insemination. Only to the Foils did it give a joyful, priapic delight that would prolong the adolescents' early morning erections. Thomas was deeply stirred by it: the reason being that, lacking the capacity to distinguish between sacred and profane, he had an intense awareness of the etymological unity of the two words "spirit" and "wind."

This vernal ecstasy, compounded of air and sunshine, was the luminous side of Thomas's spiritual life. But his burning eyes, always darkly circled, his tormented features, his brittle, flimsy body, said clearly enough to anyone willing to hear that he had also a darker side to contend with, one he rarely overcame. This shadowy passion I witnessed only once, but the circumstances were unforgettable. It was one winter's evening. I had asked permission to go to the chapel to fetch a book I had left in my stall. I was just about to dash out again, awed by the dimly lighted spaces of the vaulted roof and by the dreadful echoes they gave back to every little noise I made, when I heard sobs coming apparently out of the ground. And indeed someone *was* crying underground: the sound was coming through a narrow opening at the back of the choir, which led by way of twisting stairs down to the chapel crypt. I was more dead than alive and all the more terrified because—as I knew perfectly well—there was nothing to stop me from going down there to see what was happening below.

So I went. The crypt—as far as I could see by the flickering, blood-red light of a single lamp—was a jumble of desks, chairs, candlesticks, prie-dieux, lecterns, and banners of all sorts, a whole assortment of religious odds and ends, God's lumber piled up in an odor of mildew and stale incense. In addition, there was the life-size Christ from the Thabor garden lying on the flagstones, his worm-eaten cross in the process of being replaced with a new one. He was a splendidly athletic figure, a perfect physical specimen modeled out of some smooth, soaplike substance, stretched out in an attitude of acceptance with widespread arms, expanded pectoral muscles, his stomach hollow but powerfully molded, and his legs thickly knotted with sinews. He lay there, stripped of his cross but nonetheless crucified, for presently I made out that Thomas was lying beneath him, reproducing his attitude exactly and grunting under the weight of the statue, which was all but crushing him.

I fled in horror from a scene that so forcefully brought together the acts of love and crucifixion, as though Christ's conventional chastity had been no more than a long, secret preparation for his union with the cross, as though a man in the act of love were in some way nailed to his lover. However that might be, I now knew Thomas's dark secret, his physical, carnal, sensual love for Jesus, and I was in no doubt that this somber passion had something—although what precisely?—to do with the famous "dry come" of which he was the inventor and which earned him exceptional kudos with the Foils.

The dry come—as its name indicates—was the achievement of an orgasm with no release of sperm. It could be brought off by means of a fairly strong pressure of the fingers—either by oneself or by one's partner—on the furthest accessible point of the spermatic cord, i.e., just below the anus. It produces a keener, more unexpected sensation, attended by a sharp spasm—relished by some, abhorred, for reasons largely superstitious, by others. It causes a greater nervous exhaustion; but since the reserves of sperm remain intact, repetition is easier and more effective. To be honest, for me the dry come has always been an interesting curiosity but of no great practical advantage. Orgasm without ejaculation produces a kind of closed circuit which seems to me to imply a rejection of others. It is as if the man practicing the dry come, after an initial impulse toward his partner, were suddenly to realize that here was no soul mate or, more to the point, brother in flesh, and, seized with revulsion, break contact and withdraw into himself, as the sea, frustrated by the breakwater, sucks back its waves in the undertow. It is the reaction of a person whose choice is fun-

damentally for the closed cell, for a geminate seclusion. I am too far
away—perhaps I ought to add "alas"—from the perfect pair, I am too fond
of other people, I am, in short, too much of a hunter by instinct to shut
myself in like that.

This fierce piety and my disturbing discoveries surrounded Thomas
with a somber distinction. The fathers themselves would gladly have done
without their too gifted pupil, although when all was said and done, he
was a credit to them, and it must be admitted that his excesses, which in
a lay institution would have rebounded on themselves, found in a religious
college a climate that favored their development. Drycome had distorted
the meanings of most of the prayers and rituals on which we were
nourished—but had they really any meaning in themselves, or were they
only waiting, free and available, for someone with the wit to bend them,
with gentle violence, to his own way of thinking? For instance, I need go
no further than the psalms that we sang every Sunday at vespers and that
might have been written for him, and us. Thomas would crush us with his
arrogant demand as our voices echoed his proud, enigmatic assertion that:

*Dixit dominus domino meo*
*Sede a dextris meis*

*The Lord said unto my lord, sit thou at my right hand, until I make thine enemies
thy footstool.* And we would picture him with his head on Jesus' breast,
spurning with his feet a groveling horde of humbled masters and fellow
pupils. But we took completely for our own the psalm's disdainful charge
against heterosexuals:

*Pedes habent, et non ambulabunt.*
*Oculos habent, et non videbunt.*
*Manus habent, et non palpabunt.*
*Nares habent, et non odorabunt.*

*Feet have they, but they walk not. Eyes have they, but they see not. Hands have
they, but they handle not. Noses have they, but they smell not.*
We who walked and saw and handled and smelled would bawl out that
insolent indictment while our eyes caressed the backs and buttocks of the
fellow pupils in front of us, so many young calves reared for domestic use
and so paralyzed, blind, insensible, and devoid of any sense of smell.

Raphael Ganesh was certainly a long way from Thomas Drycome's elaborate mysticism. He preferred the opulent, highly colored imagery of the East to the iconographic traditions of Christianity. He got his nickname from the Hindu idol whose colorful picture covered the whole of his desk lid. This was Ganesh, the elephant-headed god with four arms and a languishing, kohl-rimmed eye, the son of Siva and Parvati, always accompanied by the same totem animal, the rat. The gaudy colors, the Sanskrit text, the enormous jewels with which the idol was decked, were all there solely as a frame, to extol and set off the supple, scented trunk, which swayed with a lascivious grace. That, at least, was claimed by Raphael, who saw Ganesh as the deification of the sexual organ as an object of worship. According to him, the only justification for any boy's existence was as the temple of a single god, concealed within the sanctuary of his clothes, to whom he burned to render homage. As for the rat totem, its meaning remained obscure to the most learned Orientalists, and Raphael was far from suspecting that it would be for little Alexandre Surin, whom they called Fleurette, to unravel the secret. This Eastern idolatry, crude and primitive as it was, made Raphael the antithesis of the subtle, mystical Thomas. But I have always thought the Foils were fortunate in possessing two heads so diametrically opposite in inspiration and practice.

# ∾ Giuseppe Patroni Griffi ∾

FROM

## *The Death of Beauty*

TRANSLATED BY DAVID LEAVITT,

COSIMO MANICONE, AND MARK MITCHELL

The cinema was a pit, punctuated by cigarette embers that intensified and dimmed with each drag; unraveling threads of smoke, suspended in the air, obscured the screen; the wooden seats, unhinged by the coarse use moviegoers had made of them, creaked every time someone moved in the restless stalls. The film must have been a comedy, to judge from the rumble of laughter through which Eugenio wended his way—entering, he hadn't even read the title. He found a place in the front, the only empty seat in the middle of a crowded row, to get to which he had to climb over the legs of the occupants. The disorderly happiness of the sprawled spectators, which derived from having rediscovered the liberty of following one's fancy, took him in, and to savor further this abandon, he too tried to make himself comfortable; he wanted to stretch out: Impossible. So he did the opposite, slid halfway down between the backrest and the seat, gathered his legs up, propped his knees against the back of the seat in front of him, and, thus peacefully curled, gave himself over to making out what was happening on the screen.

It was trying for the Neapolitans, having to reckon with the strategic plans of the Allies: "caught between two fires," they judged the events of the war with imprudent superficiality. Try to convince them that the bombardiers had not taken the afternoon off, or that the pilots weren't also go-

---

GIUSEPPE PATRONI GRIFFI *was born in Naples in 1921.*

ing to the movies! So when the first sirens sounded that afternoon, at the usual hour, they remained stupefied: "Could it be possible? But how? They're coming back? Didn't they come this morning?" Their scorn for the antiaircraft induced them to stall: "It's a mistake; those idiots are so used to the schedule they unintentionally sounded the alarm." And so it took the first terrifying explosion to rouse the city, a stampede of mice scrambling from their nests to find shelter underground.

The film jumped from the screen. It seemed as if the bombs falling nearby had chosen the cinema for their objective, when in fact they were aimed at the port—not far away as the crow flies. The theater, bereft of the projector's light, plunged into total darkness. The ushers hurled open the doors and shouted that the moviegoers should make for the underground shelter. Some took the exits by assault; others, traumatized by the explosions over their heads, stood up in the aisles; some, stunned, were trapped among the seats that the rush of the crowd had overturned. What safety could an antiaircraft shelter offer when only a dilapidated floor and a fragile dome separated them from heaven? The futility of moving became instantly clear to Eugenio, and for fear of being crushed by the human wave, he remained curled up, withdrawing entirely into his little seat. And he closed his eyes, in an involuntary act of self-defense.

The cinema must have emptied sooner than he supposed; shortly he could hear neither shouts nor human noises, only a lugubrious creaking that still made itself heard, unbelievably, amid the shrill uninterrupted clangor outside. He suspected that the end of the world had come, an event on which he had not calculated. A dust of plaster destabilized by the vibrations began to rain on him, and he opened his eyes, looked until they had adjusted to the dark, and saw other people motionless in their seats. Shadows among the shadows, they seemed to wait like him. But for what? The apocalypse? Charon? He thought of Charon. He thought that if it had fallen here, a bomb would have gone through the roof and landed on the floor, and that here, given the amplitude of the space, it would have been easier to avoid; he thought the bomb, like a tennis ball, would have punched through the roof to get underground and exploded there, disintegrating the disgraced ones who had found refuge in the shelter; he thought he was thinking stupid thoughts, that the explosion would have reduced everything to ashes, above and below, and he asked himself why he was remaining in his seat. But where to flee? Outside, in waiting, was certain death amid a whirl of splinters, uprooted railings, torn-off rafters, collapsing walls and attics; here, at least, he was secure in the grip of a theater that had nothing sinister about it, that was also waiting, yes, but to give amusement, joy to the spirit, diversion, the reasons for which it had been created. Earlier, while he was watching the movie without particular interest, he had looked around and noticed that the theater was an old *café chantant* from the beginning of the century, with two rows of boxes, where the velvet, which must have been red once, had been reduced to a black crust. Notwithstanding the patina of filth, the venerable gold that adorned the colonnettes and the floral decorations in ivory enamel flashed in the beam of light that issued from the projection booth carved out of the central box. An odor of mold and toilets impregnated everything, from the encrusted velvet curtain at the sides of the screen—denied its natural pleasure at opening and closing to the sound of applause—to the corridors that snaked around the orchestra seats and the rows of boxes. If nothing else, it was eccentric to stay there, he was not displeased, it kindled in him a sense of fatality; it would be amusing to tell about it afterward at school, if there was to be an afterward, that is. Thus estranged, he looked straight at the screen; onto that blind space he tried to project his own movie, but his imagination—that facile little machine—failed. He remained in that *bagnomaria* in a sort of torpor, in the limbo of a resigned laziness; the bombardment seemed far away now, or, more accurately, to have decreased. Good thing.

A frightening deflagration took him by surprise, seemed to bend the building; the walls oscillated, the few people who remained in the cinema sprang up; some ran, some ended up on the floor; Eugenio jumped to his feet, made for the nearest exit, stumbled in a tangle of overturned seats, fell, felt someone slide over him, grasp him, instinctively put his hands over his head to protect himself, and found between his fingers someone else's hair. "Don't tremble," a voice whispered. Eugenio didn't tremble, it seemed to him; he moved to try to free himself, and the stranger whispered again, "Hold me," and Eugenio, with difficulty, turned his body under that weight that oppressed him until he held the stranger by the shoulders and, getting his head free, moved it to try to penetrate the darkness with his eyes and look into the stranger's face, understand who he was and what was happening; and the stranger, after a spasm, rested his forehead on Eugenio's left breast and repeated, *piano piano,* "Hold me." He could see nothing, only perceive each little movement, each tremor, each shiver that ran under the stranger's skin, and he held him firmly against his chest, his hands planted against his shoulder blades. They stayed like that for a long time, while the bombardment intensified, making it useless to seek safety elsewhere.

The second wave of bombers must have dropped its payload; when the aerial attacks went like this, the city knew the blitz was going to last a long time; patiently, it put itself in the hands of destiny, waiting for destiny to fulfill itself for each of them, in life or death.

The two young men sprawled on the floor of that dirty cinema were also waiting for their destinies to fulfill themselves. Meanwhile, the position of necessity into which they had stumbled was losing its uncomfortable edges, changing into an attitude of mutual comfort, of shelter, of help: the stranger's body, half lying on the ground, half sinking into Eugenio's body, his arms abandoned, open, Eugenio's under the stranger's armpits, continuing tightly to hold him. The stranger's head had fallen, tired, against the boy's chest, and perhaps to release himself, he put all his strength into his arms, tried to bring his head to the height of Eugenio's shoulders, but he could not bear the strain, and this time his head fell back into the hollow of Eugenio's neck. Eugenio felt the mouth breathing against his skin, and that simple human warmth gave him comfort. He began again to think: to have a companion in death, if death had to come, didn't seem a bad idea to him. After all, theirs might be the embrace of two condemned men; much better if the last throb of life came to him from a stranger, so he did not owe anyone anything. And he thought he really was going to die, and that his mother, his grandmother, someone who loved him, was sending him this embrace at the moment of death, and he wondered if the stranger might need *his* embrace, if someone who loved *him* was sending it to him at the moment of death, if their dear departed were taking this opportunity to give them both a last testament of love. Nothing happened by chance; this stranger could deserve his attention, deriving from a solidarity that blossomed inside him with improvised tenderness and rendered the stranger worthy of being the last physical thing that Eugenio was permitted to touch, before becoming lost in the nothingness, that feeble emptiness where you can touch nothing. Such turbulent hypotheses thrilled him to the point that he confused them with security. Then he felt an irrepressible rush to do something that seemed to him necessary, that seemed to him his due, that he felt he wanted to do, and from which he must not impede himself. So he slipped his arms from under those of the stranger, he took the stranger's head between his hands, he took that face that he had not seen against his own face, he smelled the breath, redolent of cigarettes, that he liked more than a rare perfume, he had the sensation that all his life, with the speed of a closing accordion, had concentrated itself into this moment, and without hesitating, without shame, better still wishing it, he drew the stranger's mouth to his own. Those idle lips, at contact, came to life like Sleeping Beauty's in his favorite fairy tale; they moved as if they were lightly swelling and with unexpected ardor abandoned themselves to the kiss, returning it. *"Grazie,"* murmured the stranger, and his arms seemed to rise and take flight, but instead they fell, passing behind Eugenio's back to clasp him as if to define completely what they had achieved, the gratification of an unsuspected desire, a sensation never before felt into which Eugenio believed himself to have fallen in a happy dream, as if a state of hypnosis had relieved his body of each burden and made his senses acute. The noise of the surrounding destruction amplified until it became terrible, but rich with a terrifying harmony; he discovered that the life of the senses went undaunted down arduous streets, drugged routes that strayed into mystery: he discovered this because he had been feeling himself for too long to be a husk and nothing else and he could no longer be a husk; at the breaking point the usual push from nothing had put him before a definitive revelation. Meanwhile, the movement of the embrace had trapped one of the stranger's legs between his own; their legs were interlaced, the heat of their bodies passed from one to the other and blended with their shudders; there formed inside Eugenio an explosive of life that he perceived as a deaf gurgling, while a secret communication ensured him that the moment was great for them both, that the stranger shared the moment he recognized to be part of his own desire: it flashed upon him, the essential thing, that for once he was not experiencing this communion alone, the usual desert. He felt his vital lymph gush out free, naturally, run blissfully between his clothes and his flesh, over his stomach, and he had the sensation of losing his senses.

The last crepitations of the antiaircraft were coming sporadically now; nothing moved, only a wind of desolation. The dead were dead, and the living, astonished to be alive, waited for a signal before abandoning themselves to the joy of having survived.

For a broken instant, Eugenio convinced himself that he was dreaming; but dreams end in light, and here the darkness persisted. He was lying on the floor, embraced by a stranger, in a fetor of open sewers: the darkness did not permit him to verify what had happened, but an instant later

Eugenio knew, because he touched himself, inadvertently his hand grazed the stranger's cheek, passed over the soft, sleek hair; he recognized the inertia of these two bodies that seemed not to concern him. Shaken by the last tremor of the explosion, they were waiting for liberation, his soul—yes, his soul—having taken flight beyond all questions too premature to be answered.

When the all-clear signal finally sounded over a Naples incredulous of its ruin, Eugenio got up from the floor. More than anything he wanted to escape from his companion, he did not want to look at him, to know him, much less speak to him now, not having opened his mouth before; so, fumbling in the dark, clambering over obstacles, he headed for the doors that gave onto the long corridor behind the rows of seats. He reached one, was crossing through it, when an uncouth hand seized him by the shoulder; with a jerk he freed himself, slipped into the corridor, started to run. Most of the iron doors that opened onto the street were closed; he tried to open them one after the other in vain. He knew he had to reach the central door, through which he had entered, the only one, he now remembered, that was open. And in fact there it was, invaded by a mass of suffocating dust that blew in from a city without sound. He plunged into the ruins that opened in front of his feet, coughed, and before fleeing threw a glance over his shoulder to check if the stranger was still following him: a flash of light gave him time to make out a glint of blond hair and a mouth, the ghost of one of those scandalous roses that bloomed in his lost garden.

Between the black of Eugenio, backlit, devoured by the dense white cloud that intensified the luminosity of the afternoon, and the mysterious blond of that flash in the dark, an old piece of plaster falling from the ceiling carried behind it a wake of gold dust.

Eugenio saw it vibrate in the air like the tail of a comet.

# ∼ *Roberto Calasso* ∼

FROM

# *The Marriage of Cadmus and Harmony*

## TRANSLATED BY TIM PARKS

D elos was a hump of deserted rock, drifting about the sea like a stalk of asphodel. It was here that Apollo was born, in a place where not even wretched slave girls would come to hide their shame. Before Leda, the only creatures to give birth on that godforsaken rock had been the seals. But there was a palm tree, and the mother clutched it, alone, bracing her knees in the thin grass. Then Apollo emerged, and everything turned to gold, from top to bottom. Even the water in the river turned to gold, and the leaves on the olive tree likewise. And the gold must have stretched downward into the depths, because it anchored Delos to the seabed. From that day on, the island drifted no more.

∼ ∼ ∼

If Olympus differs from every other celestial home, it is thanks to the presence of three unnatural divinities: Apollo, Artemis, Athena. More than mere functions, these imperious custodians of the unique stripped away that thin, shrouding curtain which nature weaves about its forces. The bright enameled surface and the void, the sharp outline, the arrow: these,

---

*A noted editor at the Italian publishing house Adelphi as well as a novelist,* ROBERTO CALASSO *offers, in* The Marriage of Cadmus and Harmony, *an inventive reenvisioning of the Greek world.*

and not water or earth, are their elements. There is something autistic about Olympus's unnatural gods. Apollo, Artemis, Athena march forward cloaked in their own auras. They look down at the world when they plan to strike it, but otherwise their eyes are elsewhere, as if gazing at an invisible mirror, where they find their own images detached from all else. When Apollo and Artemis draw their bows to kill, they are serene, abstracted, their eyes steady on the arrow. All around, Niobe's children lie dying, slumped over rocks or on the bare earth. The folds of Artemis's tunic don't so much as flutter: all her vitality is concentrated in the left arm holding the bow and the right arm reaching behind the shoulder as her fingers select another mortal arrow from her quiver.

～　～　～

The infant Artemis sat on Zeus's lap. She knew what she wanted for the future and told her father all her wishes one by one: to remain forever a virgin, to have many names, to rival her brother, to possess a bow and arrow, to carry a torch and wear a tunic with a fringe down to the knee, to hunt wild beasts, to have sixty Oceanides as an escort and twenty Amnisian Nymphs as maids to look after her sandals and dogs, to hold sway over all mountains; she could get by without the cities. As she spoke, she tried, but failed, to grab her father's beard. Zeus laughed and agreed. He would give her everything she wanted. Artemis left him; she knew where she was headed: first to the dense forests of Crete, then to the ocean. There she chose her sixty Nymphs. They were all nine years old.

～　～　～

The perennial virginity young Artemis demanded as a first gift from her father Zeus is the indomitable sign of detachment. Copulation, *míxis,* means "mingling" with the world. Virgo, the virgin, is an isolated, sovereign sign. Its counterpart, when the divine reaches down to touch the world, is rape. The image of rape establishes the canonical relationship the divine now has with a world matured and softened by sacrifices: contact is still possible, but it is no longer the contact of a shared meal; rather it is the sudden, obsessive invasion that plucks away the flower of thought.

Man's relationship with the gods passed through two regimes: first conviviality, then rape. The third regime, the modern one, is that of indifference, but with the implication that the gods have already withdrawn, and hence, if they are indifferent in our regard, we can be indifferent as to their existence or otherwise. Such is the peculiar situation of the modern world. But returning to earlier times: There was an age when the gods would sit down alongside mortals, as they did at Cadmus and Harmony's wedding feast in Thebes. At this point gods and men had no difficulty recognizing each other; sometimes they were even companions in adventure, as were Zeus and Cadmus, when the man proved of vital help to the god. Relative roles in the cosmos were not disputed, since they had already been assigned; hence gods and men met simply to share some feast before returning each to his own business. Then came another phase, during which a god might *not* be recognized. As a result, the god had to assume the role he has never abandoned since, right down to our own times, that of the Unknown Guest, the Stranger. One day the sons of Lycaon, king of Arcadia, invited to their table an unknown laborer who was in fact Zeus. "Eager to know whether they were speaking to a real god, they sacrificed a child and mixed his flesh with that of the sacred victims, thinking that if the stranger was a god he would discover what they had done." Furious, Zeus pushed over the table. That table was the ecliptic plane, which from that day on would be forever tilted. There followed the most tremendous flood.

After that banquet, Zeus made only rare appearances as the Unknown Guest. The role passed, for the most part, to other gods. Now, when Zeus chose to tread the earth, his usual manifestation was through rape. This is the sign of the overwhelming power of the divine, of the residual capacity of distant gods to invade mortal minds and bodies. Rape is at once possessing and possession. With the old convivial familiarity between god and man lost, with ceremonial contact through sacrifice impoverished, man's soul was left exposed to a gusting violence, an amorous persecution, an obsessional goad. Such are the stories of which mythology is woven: they tell how mortal mind and body are still subject to the divine, even when they are no longer seeking it out, even when the ritual approaches to the divine have become confused.

～ ～ ～

The twelve gods of Olympus agreed to appear as entirely human. It was the first time a group of divinities had renounced abstraction and animal heads. No more the unrepresentable behind the flower or the swastika, no more the monstrous creature, the stone fallen from heaven, the whirlpool. Now the gods took on a cool, polished skin, or an unreal warmth, and a body where you could see the ripple of muscles, the long veins.

The change brought with it a new exhilaration and a new terror. All previous manifestations seemed tentative and cautious by comparison; they hadn't risked the boldest of adventures, which was precisely that of the gods' disguising themselves as human in a human world, having passed through the whole gamut of metamorphoses. Then this last disguise was more exciting than any of the others. More exciting and more dangerous. For it might well be that the gods' divinity would no longer be grasped in its fullness. On earth they would meet people who treated them with too much familiarity, maybe even provoked them. The unnatural gods, Apollo, Artemis, and Athena, whose very identity depended on detachment, were more subject to this danger than the others. Any old shepherd might claim he played his pipes better than Apollo; whereas it was unlikely that a mere hetaera would try to tell Aphrodite how to do her job. The people of earth were a temptation: alluring because full of stories and intrigues, or sometimes because isolated in their own stubborn perfection that asked nothing from heaven. But they were also treacherous, ready to stab a god in the back, to disfigure the hermae. A new state of mind emerged, something unknown in the past, that of the god who is misunderstood, mocked, belittled. The result was a string of vendettas and punishments, dispatches issued from an ever busy office.

~ ~ ~

That Theseus was a creature of Apollo one can gather from all kinds of signs and gestures of homage scattered throughout his adventures. Theseus is always coming up against monsters, and the first slayer of monsters was Apollo. In Delphi the young hero offers the curl that fell across his forehead to Apollo. When he arrives in Athens, Theseus hurls a bull up in the air. But it is important that this takes place in a temple to Delphinian Apollo. Theseus will go back to the same temple before setting off for Crete, this time bringing a branch of the sacred olive tree wrapped in wool, a request for the god to help him. When he catches the bull at Marathon, and the Athenians go wild with joy, Theseus has it sacrificed to Apollo. After killing the Minotaur, Theseus goes to Delos and performs the dance of the cranes. A code within the dance contains the secret of the labyrinth. And Delos was Apollo's birthplace.

But Apollo makes no comment. All Theseus's life, the only thing

Apollo ever says to him is "Take Aphrodite as your guide." The order is decisive. All Theseus's adventures are cloaked in an erotic aura. During the Cretan expedition, it is Apollo who pulls the strings, but from the shadows. The mission is too delicate an affair for him to be seen to be involved. What we see on the stage is the struggle between Dionysus and the hero Theseus, but in the darkness behind, Apollo and Dionysus have struck up a pact. What that involved was the *translatio imperii* from Crete to Athens: one god took over from another; power passed from the secret twists of the labyrinth to the frontal evidence of the Acropolis. And all of this came about courtesy of Theseus, because the stories had to tell of other things: of young girls being sacrificed, of love affairs, duels, desertions, suicides. The human melodrama with its songs and chatter must cover up for the silent substance of the divine pact.

~ ~ ~

This changing of the guard, which occurs with Theseus's expedition to Crete, implies an affinity between Apollo and Dionysus behind their apparent opposition. But it is an affinity they are not eager to bring out into the open, if only because it is not something to be proud of. First and foremost, what these gods have in common in this story is their having been betrayed by mortal women. Ariadne betrays Dionysus for Theseus; Coronis betrays Apollo with the mortal Ischys. To kill the women who loved and betrayed them, Apollo and Dionysus call on Artemis, the divine assassin, with her bow and arrows. And both of them watch in silence as their women are slain. There could be no greater complicity for the two gods than this having both turned, with the same gesture, to the same assassin, to put to death the women they loved.

~ ~ ~

Coronis was washing her feet in Lake Boebeis. Apollo saw her and desired her. Desire came as a sudden shock, it caught him by surprise, and immediately he wanted to have done with it. He descended on Coronis like the night. Their coupling was violent, exhilarating, and fast. In Apollo's mind the clutch of a body and the shooting of an arrow were superimposed. The meeting of their bodies was not a mingling, as for Dionysus, but a collision. In the same way, Apollo had once killed Hyacinthus, the boy he loved most: they were playing together, and the god let fly a discus. Coronis was pregnant by Apollo when she found herself attracted to a stranger. He came from Arcadia, and his name was Ischys. A white crow watched over her. Apollo had told the bird to guard the woman he loved, "so that no one might violate her purity." The crow saw Coronis give herself to Ischys. So off it flew to Delphi and its master to tell the tale. It said it had discovered Coronis's "secret doings." In his fury, Apollo threw down his plectrum. His laurel crown fell in the dust. Looking at the crow, his eyes were full of hatred, and the creature's feathers turned black as pitch. Then Apollo asked his sister Artemis to go and kill Coronis, in Lacereia. Artemis's arrow pierced the faithless woman's breast. Along with her, the goddess killed many other women by the rugged shores of Lake Boebeis. Before dying, Coronis whispered to the god that he had killed his own son too. At which Apollo tried to save her. In vain. His medical skills were not up to it. But when the woman's sweet-smelling body was stretched on a pyre high as a wall, the flames parted before the god's grasping hand, and from the dead mother's belly, safe and sound, he pulled out Asclepius, the healer.

～ ～ ～

Ariadne, Coronis: two stories that call to each other, that answer each other. Not only was the killer the same in both cases—Artemis—but perhaps the mortal seducer was likewise the same—Theseus. Ischys is a shadowy figure, of whom we know nothing apart from his name. But of Theseus we know a great deal: we know that in one version he left Ariadne the moment "he fell desperately in love with Aigle, daughter of Panopeus." So wrote Hesiod; but Pisistratus chose to delete this very line. Why? Did it reveal too much about the hero? A marble stele found in Epidaurus and signed by Isyllus explains that Aigle (or Aegla) "was so beautiful that people would also call her Coronis" and that she had a child called Asclepius. Aigle means "splendor," as Ariadne-Aridela means "the resplendent one." Coronis (crown) suggests a beauty that goes beyond diffuse brilliance, involves the etching of a form. But who was "Aigle, daughter of Panopeus"? Her father was the king of a small Phocian town with the same name, Panopeus: "Panopeus with its lovely open space for dancing," says Homer. And in that square danced the Thyiades, initiates of Dionysus. It was one of the places where they stopped in the long procession that took them from Athens to Delphi to "enact secret rites for Dionysus." And already we are reminded of the open space where Ariadne danced out the labyrinth. What's more, Pausanias explains that the inhabitants of Panopeus "are not Phocians; originally they were Phlegyans." And already we are reminded that Coronis was the daughter of Phlegyas, from Thessaly, a hero who took the same name as his people. It was with those people that Phlegyas migrated to Phocis, where he reigned as king.

Coronis, Aigle: daughters of a king of Phocis, living near an open square where the initiates of Dionysus danced, along the road that would take them to the temple of Apollo. There is a twinning between Coronis and Aigle, just as there is a twinning between Coronis-Aigle and Ariadne, and both point us in the direction of a more obscure parallel between these women's divine lovers: Dionysus and Apollo. Wasn't Coronis the name of one of the Nymphs who brought up Dionysus in Naxos? And checking through Dionysus's other nurses, we come across, yes, another by the name of Aigle. And wasn't Coronis also the name of one of the girls on the ship Theseus came back from Crete on? *Koróně* means "the curved beak of the crow," but it also means "a garland, a crown." And wasn't Ariadne's story a story of crowns? *Koróně* also means "the stern of a ship" and "the high point of a feast." *Korōnís* means "the wavy flourish that used to mark the end of a book, a seal of completion." On an Athenian jar we see Theseus carrying off a girl called Corone, while two of his other women, Helen and the Amazon Antiope, try in vain to stop him. Corone is being lifted up in the air, tightly held in the circle of the hero's arms, yet still three fingers of her left hand find time to toy, delicately, with the curls of Theseus's little ponytail. Casting a sharp glance behind, Peirithous protects the abductor's back. "I saw, let's run," the anonymous artist's hand has written beside the scene. The style is unmistakably that of Euthymides.

~ ~ ~

Ariadne and Coronis each preferred a foreign man to a god. For them the Stranger is "strength," which is what the name Ischys means. And Theseus is the strong man par excellence. Of all the women to whom the gods made love, Coronis is the most brazenly irreverent. Already pregnant by Apollo's "pure seed," elegant in her tunics as Pindar describes her, she nevertheless felt "that passion for things far away" and went off to bed with the stranger who came from Arcadia. Pindar comments proverbially: "The craziest type of people are those who scorn what they have around them and look elsewhere / vainly searching for what cannot exist." In Coronis's case, what she had around her was a god, a god whose child, Asclepius, she was already bearing. It is as if, out of sheer caprice, the fullness of the

Greek heaven were fractured here. The stranger from Arcadia was even more of a stranger than the god, and hence more attractive. The bright enamel of divine apparition is scarred by sudden cracks. But this allows it to breathe with the naturalness of literature, which rejects the coercion of the sacred text.

∽  ∽  ∽

All that was left of Coronis was a heap of ashes. But years later Asclepius too would be reduced to ashes. He had dared to bring a dead man back to life, so Zeus struck him with a thunderbolt. And, just that once, Apollo cried, "wept countless tears as he approached his sacred people, the Hyperboreans." The tears were drops of amber, and they rolled down into the Eridanus, that river at once earthly and celestial where Phaethon had fallen. All around, the stench of his corpse lingered on. And tall black poplars rustled to mourn his passing. Those poplars were the daughters of the sun.

The destiny of death by burning runs through the stories of Apollo and Dionysus like a scar. Semele is burned to death, and she is Dionysus's mother; Coronis and Asclepius are reduced to ashes, and they are Apollo's lover and son. The divine fire devours those venturing outside the human sphere, whether they be betraying a god, bringing a man back to life, or seeing a god bereft of the cloaking veil of epiphany. Beyond the limit laid down for what is acceptable burns the fire. Apollo and Dionysus are often to be found along the edges of that borderline, on the divine side and the human; they provoke that back-and-forth in men, that desire to go beyond oneself, which we seem to cling to even more than to our humanity, even more than to life itself. And sometimes this dangerous game rebounds on the two gods who play it. Apollo hid his tears among the Hyperboreans while driving his swan-drawn chariot through the air. Likewise silhouetted against the sky, the enchanter Abaris, emissary of Apollo, would one day arrive in Greece from the north, riding the immense arrow of ecstasy.

∽  ∽  ∽

The lives of Theseus and Heracles were intertwined from beginning to end. On seeing Heracles in a lionskin, the infant Theseus had thrown an ax at him, thinking he was a lion. The gesture suggests a secret hostility later to be submerged in admiration. When he was a youth, Theseus "would dream of Heracles' deeds by night and burn with ambition to emulate him by day." He never tired of hearing stories about the hero, "especially from those who had seen him and been present when he had done some deed or made a speech." Apart from anything else, the two heroes were cousins. When he was old enough, Theseus left his home in Troezen and set off on his travels. From then on, and for years and years, Theseus and Heracles would perform similar exploits, sometimes doing exactly the same thing, as if in a competition. When the two heroes ran into each other, in foreign countries, they were like mercenaries who inevitably meet where blood is flowing. And if one day Heracles went down into the underworld to free Theseus, you would say it was no more than his duty as an old comrade in arms. Yet the distance between the two is immense. Their postures might seem similar, but in reality they were quite opposite, the way some archaic *koûroi* might seem similar to archaic Egyptian statues of the same period, while in fact a crucial divergence in internal time sets them apart: the Egyptian statues looked back to an irrecoverable past, which their rigidity strove hopelessly to regain; the Greek figures expressed tension the very moment before it relaxes, as if wishing to hold at bay for one last time the Alexandrian suppleness that was about to overwhelm them.

Heracles is obliged to follow the zodiac wheel of his labors to the very ends of the earth. As a hero he is too human, blinded like everybody else, albeit stronger and more able than everybody else. Catapulted into the heavens as a result of celestial exigencies, he is never to know what purpose his labors really served, and the pretext the events of his life offer him smacks of mockery. All on account of a spiteful king. Theseus operates between Argos and Epirus, sails to Crete and the Black Sea, but he does have a base: Athens. His deeds are those of an adventurer who responds to a sense of challenge, to whimsy, to curiosity, and to pleasure. And if the step that most determines a life is initiation, it will be Theseus who introduces Heracles to Eleusis, not vice versa, despite the fact that he is the younger and less well known among the the gods. On his own Heracles would never have been admitted, would have remained forever a stranger, a profane outsider. Why? The life of the hero, like the process of initiation, has different levels. On a first level Theseus and Heracles are similar: this is the moment at which someone finally emerges from the blazing circle of force. As Plutarch remarks with the dispatch of the great Greek writers: "It appears that at that time there were men who, for deftness of hand, speed of legs, and strength of muscles, transcended normal human nature and were tireless. They never used their physical capacities to do good or to help others, but reveled in their own brutal arrogance and enjoyed exploiting their strength to commit savage, ferocious deeds, conquering, ill-treating, and murdering whosoever fell into their hands. For them, respect, justice, fairness, and magnanimity were virtues prized only by such as lacked the courage to do harm and were afraid of suffering it themselves; for those who had the strength to impose themselves, such qualities could have no meaning." It is Theseus and Heracles who first use force to a different end than that of merely crushing their opponents. They become "athletes on behalf of men." And rather than strength itself, what they care about is the art of applying it: "Theseus invented the art of wrestling, and later teaching of the sport took the basic moves from him. Before Theseus, it was merely a question of height and brute force."

This is only the first level of a hero's life. It is the level at which he competes with other men. But there is a higher level, a much greater dimension to conquer, where even the combination of force and intelligence is not enough: this is the dimension where men meet and clash with gods. Once again we are in a kingdom where force is supreme, but this time it is divine force. If the hero is alone and can count on nothing but his own strength, he will never be able to enter this kingdom. He needs a woman's help. And this is where the paths of Theseus and Heracles divide, forever. Women, for Heracles, are part of the fate he must suffer. He may rape them, as he does with Auge; he may impregnate fifty in a single night, as he does with Thespius's daughters; he may become their slave, as with Omphale. But he is never able to appropriate their wisdom. He doesn't even realize that it is they who possess the wisdom he lacks. Deep down, he harbors a grim suspicion of them, as if foreseeing how it will be a woman's gift that will bring him to his death, and an excruciating death at that. Heracles is "the irreconcilable enemy of female sovereignty," because he senses that he will never be able to grasp it for himself. When the Argonauts land on the island of Lemnos and, without realizing it, find themselves caught up with the women who have murdered their husbands, Heracles is the only one who stays on board ship.

Nothing could be further from the spirit of Theseus, who sets sail all on his own to go and find the Amazons. And immediately Theseus tricks their queen, Antiope. He invites her onto his ship, abducts her, has her fall in love with him, makes her his wife and the mother of his son, Hippolytus. What's more—and this is what really marks Theseus out—in the end

Antiope would "die a heroine's death," fighting beside Theseus to save Athens. And she was fighting against her own comrades, who had pitched camp beneath the Acropolis and were attacking Athens precisely to avenge her abduction. Theseus knows that woman is the repository of the secret he lacks; hence he uses her to the utmost, until she has betrayed everything: her country, her people, her sex, her secret. Thus, when Heracles arrived in Eleusis, an unclean stranger, he was accepted only because Theseus "had vouched for him." The saying "Nothing without Theseus," which the Athenians were to repeat for centuries, alludes to this: apart from being a hero, Theseus also initiates heroes; without him the rough-and-ready hero could never achieve that initiatory completeness which is *teleíōsis, teleté.*

Heracles is contaminated by the sacred; it persecutes him his whole life. It drives him mad, and in the end it destroys him. Theseus, in contrast, seems to wash the blood from his hands after every adventure, to shrug off the violence and the many deaths. Heracles becomes a pretext for the gods to play out a long game. Theseus dares to use the gods to play his own game. But it would be churlish to see him as someone who knows how to turn everything to his advantage. The hero who founded Athens was also to have the privilege of being the first to be expelled from it. "After Theseus had given the Athenians democracy, a certain Lycus denounced him and managed to have the hero ostracized." In the end, even Theseus will be killed. He dies in exile, dashed to pieces at the foot of a cliff. Somebody pushed him from behind. "At the time, nobody paid any attention to the fact that Theseus was dead." But his game is still played in the city Theseus himself named: Athens, the most sacred, the most blasphemous of cities.

~ ~ ~

Heracles deserves the compassion of the moderns, because he was one of the last victims of the zodiac. And the moderns no longer really appreciate what that means. They are no longer in the habit of calculating a man's deeds in terms of the measures of the heavens. As a hero, Heracles is a beast of burden: he has to plow the immense plain of the heavens in every one of its twelve segments. As a result he never manages to achieve that detachment from self which the modern demands and which Theseus achieves so gloriously. Such detachment entails the hero's mingling and alternating the deeds he is obliged to do with his own personal acts of caprice and defiance. But for Heracles everything is obligation, right up to the atrocious burns that kill him. A pitiful seriousness weighs him down. All too rarely does he laugh. And sometimes he finds himself having to suffer the laughter of others.

Heracles' buttocks were like an old leather shield, blackened by long exposure to the sun and by the fiery breaths of Cacus and of the Cretan bull. When Heracles caught the mocking Cercopes, who came in the form of two annoying gadflies to rob him and deprive him of his sleep, first he forced them to return to their human form, then he hung them both by their feet on a beam and lifted them on his shoulders, balancing out the weight on both sides. The heads of the two tiny rascals thus dangled at the level of the hero's powerful buttocks, left uncovered by his lionskin. At which the Cercopes remembered the prophetic words of their mother: "My little White Asses, beware of the moment when you meet the great Black Ass." Hanging upside down, the two thieves shook with laughter, while the hero's buttocks continued to rise and fall as he marched steadily on. And as he walked, the hero heard their muffled sneering behind his back. He was sad. Even the people he thrashed didn't take him seriously. He let the two rascals down and started laughing with them. Others say he killed them.

～ ～ ～

A mythical event can mean a change of landscape. The Rock of Argos once looked out over a countryside famous for its droughts. And from dry dust one went straight into the mud of the Lerna marshes. So Argos lacked a clean supply of fresh running water. Before it could have one, the bloody affair of the Danaids must take place. A fifty-oared galley arrived from Egypt. With a girl at every oar. They were the fifty daughters of Danaus, the Danaids, with their father. Driven by "an innate repulsion for men," they were fleeing forced marriages with their fifty cousins, sons of Aegyptus. And having fled, they had chosen to return to their family's ancestral home, the place where the wanderings of their forebear Io had begun. They spoke a foreign language, and their skin had been darkened by the African sun. The old king of Argos, Pelasgus, immediately saw their arrival as an unmanageable invasion. Coming toward him were fifty women with extravagant, barbaric clothes and nomadic desert eyes, but from the left armhole of each Danaid protruded an olive branch wound in white wool. It was the only recognizably Greek sign they carried, but it was a clear one: they were asking for asylum. And they added that if they were not granted it, they would hang themselves. They were more specific: they would hang themselves from the statues in the temple, using the girdles from their tunics. Fifty women hanging themselves from fifty statues! What a pestilence, dense and poisonous as the muggy airs of Egypt! Better risk a war than that.

Pelasgus gave asylum to this crowd of beautiful barbarians and took them into the town. He was a shade embarrassed: he didn't know whether to have them sleep in the houses of his subjects or apart, in buildings placed at their disposition. He sensed he was risking his kingdom for these unknown foreigners, who had arrived only the day before. But he didn't dare send them away. Every time he wavered, he would see fifty statues with fifty women hanging from them. From the Rock of Argos, the ships of the defiant cousins were spotted on the horizon, coming to get their women. They were Egyptians and respected only Egyptian gods; not a shrine in the whole of Greece could stop them. Pelasgus had always hoped some sort of compromise might be reached. What if the piratical abduction were dressed up as a series of peaceful marriages? Fifty couples reunited in a huge party? In the end the Danaids gave in. But each went to her marriage bed concealing a knife. And forty-nine times that night a woman's hand plunged its blade into the body of the man who lay beside her. Only the eldest sister broke the pact: Hypermestra. She let her husband, Lynceus, escape. Throughout the bloody night, torch signals were exchanged among the hills. Hypermestra's sisters cut off forty-nine heads and went to toss them into the Lerna marshes. Then they heaped up the headless corpses before the gates of Argos.

What happened to the Danaids after that is far from clear. We do know that they were purified by Athena and Hermes. And we know that around the scorching Argos they discovered springs of the purest water. This, together with the massacre of their husbands, was their greatest achievement. Then their father decided they should marry again. Not an easy matter. Nobody came forward with any nuptial gifts. So the deal was turned on its head: the Danaids would be given away to the winners of a series of races. Only Hypermestra, who had run off with Lynceus, and Amymone, abducted by the god Poseidon, were missing. Lined up like a chorus in a play, Danaus gave away the forty-eight remaining girls at the finish line. Whoever touched the tunic of a Danaid first could have her as his bride. "The fastest matchmaking ever," Pindar remarked. By noon it was all over.

And they're lined up again the next time we see them, with all their enchanting names—Autonoe, Automate, Cleopatra, Pirene, Iphimedusa, Asteria, Gorge, Hyperippe, Clite—but this time in the underworld, not far from where Sisyphus is pushing his rock. Each is holding a jar. They are taking turns pouring water into a big, leaky pitcher. The water flows out and runs away. For many commentators this became an image of the unhappiness related to something that can never be achieved. But Bachofen sees the forty-eight girls differently. He doesn't place them in the underworld but in a primordial landscape of reeds and marshes, where the Nile splits up into its delta and sinks into the thirsty soil. The Danaids had come from Africa to the driest place in the Peloponnese, bringing with them the gift of water. Their ancestor Io also liked to appear with a reed in her hand, a creature of the marshes. As Bachofen saw it, that constant pouring of water into a bottomless container had nothing futile or despairing about it. On the contrary, it was almost an image of happiness. He recalled another mythical girl: Iphimedeia. She had fallen in love with Poseidon, as had Io with Zeus. So she would often walk along the beach, go down into the sea, raise the water from the waves, and pour it over her breasts. A gesture of love. Then one day Poseidon appeared, wrapped himself around her, and generated two children. Iphimedeia's gesture has something blissful and timeless about it; it is the motion of feminine substance toward the other, toward any other. A motion that cannot be satisfied, is satisfied only in its unfailing repetition.

～　～　～

The Greeks welcomed the gift of water but rejected the Danaids. *Lérnē kakôn*, "Lerna, place of evil," became a proverbial saying recalling another: *Lémnia kaká*, which evoked the crime of the women of Lemnos. The two massacres had much in common. On both occasions the murderers were Amazons. On both occasions all the men but one got their throats cut. On Lemnos, Hypsipyle took pity on her father, Thoas. In Argos, Hypermestra took pity on her husband, Lynceus. "Of all crimes, that of the women of Lemnos was the worst," says Aeschylus. It was the utmost iniquity. With time, from the forty-nine putrefied heads of the sons of Aegyptus, a countless-headed hydra was born. It would take Heracles, scourge of the Amazons and descendant of Hypermestra, the only Danaid who broke the pact, to kill that monster.

～　～　～

Aeschylus wrote two trilogies that take absolution as their theme: the *Oresteia* and the *Danaides*. The first has come down to us complete; of the second we have only the first tragedy, the *Supplices*, and a few fragments. In the first trilogy, Athena absolves Orestes of a crime he has indeed committed, matricide. In the second, Aphrodite absolves Hypermestra of the charge of not having committed a crime, not having killed her husband. It was upon these two absolutions that classical Athens was founded.

The *Oresteia* has survived the centuries intact, and its story is common knowledge; the *Danaides* has been forgotten, and few think of the fifty sisters as an exemplary subject for tragedy. But one may assume that to Aeschylus's mind the two absolutions were mirror images of each other and the two trilogies had the same weight, the one counterbalancing the other. One absolved a man, the other a woman. Everybody feels that Orestes' guilt is the more obvious, Hypermestra's the more paradoxical: how can one consider it a crime to back out of a premeditated and traitorous murder? But Aeschylus has weighed his crimes well. Hypermestra's real crime is her betrayal of her sisters. She is the African Amazon breaking away from her tribe. And this is the kind of crime that Athens understands, makes its own, just as it will make Antiope, queen of the Amazons, its own once she has become Theseus's bride. It is a mysteriously fecund crime. Antiope will give birth to Hippolytus, the handsome Orphic, dressed in white linen, who flees the girls; one of Hypermestra's descendants will be Heracles, enemy of the Amazons. The Amazon graft is a precious one, a delicate one, producing useful, antidotal fruits. Just as Athena defends Orestes, so does Aphrodite Hypermestra, and with the same high eloquence: "The pure sky loves to violate the land, / and the land is seized by desire for this embrace; / the teeming rain from the sky / makes the earth fecund, so that for mortals it generates / the pastures for their flocks and the sap of Demeter / and the fruit on the trees. From these moist embraces / everything which is comes into being. And I am the cause of this." Greece was a nuptial land of sexual union, attracted by divine virginity. But it feared those Amazons with neither home nor husband. Hypermestra had betrayed them. For that she deserved to be saved.

~ ~ ~

Apollo was the first slayer of monsters; then came Cadmus, Perseus, Bellerophon, Heracles, Jason, Theseus. Alongside this list of monster-slayers we could place a list of traitors, of women: Hypermestra, Hypsipyle,

Medea, Ariadne, Antiope, Helen, Antigone. These women don't have a god as their forebear, but a priestess: Io, who betrayed her goddess, Hera, in whose sanctuary she lived as "guardian of the keys." "Io illustrates the awakening of woman from the long sleep of an untroubled infancy, a happiness that was ignorant but perfect, to a tormenting love that will be at once the delight and sorrow of her life, forever. She has been dazzled by the divinity of Zeus."

The heroic gesture of woman is betrayal: its influence on the course of events is just as great as the slaying of monsters. With the monster slain, an impurity lingers on to dog the hero. There will also be the withered remains of the foe whose power the hero turns to his advantage. Heracles clothes himself in the skin of the Nemean lion; Perseus brandishes the petrifying face of the Gorgon as he goes into battle. Leave only emptiness and the chatter of human voices. The isthmus becomes practicable; people trade and write poems recalling monsters.

The effects of woman's betrayal are more subtle and less immediate, perhaps, but equally devastating. Helen provokes a war that wipes out the entire race of heroes, ushering in a completely new age, when the heroes will merely be remembered in verse. And as a civilizing gesture, woman's betrayal is no less effective than man's monster-slaying. The monster is an enemy beaten in a duel; in her betrayal, the traitor suppresses her own roots, detaching her life from its natural context. Ariadne is the ruin of Crete, where she was born; Antiope dies fighting the Amazons, her own subjects, who were faithfully rallying to her aid; Helen leads the heroes she has loved to their downfall; Medea forsakes the country of sorcery to arrive, at the end of her adventures, in the country of law, Athens; Antigone betrays the law of her city to make a gesture of mercy toward a dead man who does not belong to that city. Like a spiral, woman's betrayal twists around on itself, forever rejecting that which is given. It is not the negation that comes into play in the frontal and mortal collision of forces but the negation that amounts to a gradual breaking away from ourselves, opposition to ourselves, effacement of ourselves, in a game that may exalt or destroy and which generally both exalts and destroys.

The slaying of monsters and woman's betrayal are two ways in which negation can operate. The first clears a space, leaves an evocative vacuum where before there was a clutter, thick with heads and tentacles, a scaly arabesque. Woman's betrayal does not alter the elements in space but rearranges them. The influence of certain pieces on the chessboard is inverted.

White attacks white. Black attacks black. The effect is confusing, above all disturbing. For the first time roles have been reversed. And it is always a woman who reverses them. There's an obstinacy about the hero that obliges him to keep on and on, following just the one path and no other. Hence his need to be complemented, his need of another form of negation. The woman with her betrayal completes the hero's work: she brings it to its conclusion and winds up the story. This is done in agreement with the hero. It is part of the hero's civilizing work to suppress himself, because the hero is monstrous. Immediately after the monsters die the heroes.

~ ~ ~

With the heroes, man takes his first step beyond the necessary: into the realm of risk, defiance, shrewdness, deceit, art. And with the heroes a new world of love is disclosed. The woman helps the hero to slay monsters and capture talismans. A shining initiator into religious mystagogue, she has a splendor that ranges from the glimmering radiance of Ariadne to the dazzle of Medea. But the heroes also ushered in a new kind of love: that between man and man. Heracles and Iolaus, Theseus and Peirithous, Achilles and Patroclus, Orestes and Pylades—all enjoyed what Aeschylus calls "the sacred communion of thighs," a communion Achilles chided Patroclus for having forgotten merely because he was dead.

The love of one man for another appears with the heroes and immediately reaches its perfect expression. Only the heroes—and precisely because they were heroes—could have overcome what so far for the Greeks had been an insurmountable obstacle to such a love: the rigid distinction between separate roles, the obstinate asymmetry between *erastés* and *erómenos,* lover and beloved, which had condemned love relationships to being painfully short and stifled by the strictest rules. The cruelest of these rules was that while the lover was granted his swift and predatory pleasure, the beloved was not to enjoy any sexual pleasure at all but must submit himself to the other only reluctantly, in something like the way nineteenth-century wives were encouraged to submit to their husbands. And the lover could not look into the eyes of his beloved as he ravished him, so as to avoid embarrassment. The heroes swept all these rules aside. Their relationships were long-lasting—only death could end them—and their love didn't fade merely because the beloved grew hairs on his legs or because his skin, hardened by a life of adventure, lost its youthful smoothness. Thus the heroes achieved that most yearned-for of states, in which the distinction between lover and beloved begins to blur. Between Orestes and Pylades, "it would have been difficult to say which of the two was the lover, since the lover's tenderness found its reflection in the other's face as in a mirror." In the same way, these words from the Pseudo-Lucian hold up a late mirror to what was the most constant erotic wish of Greek men, and the most vain.

~ ~ ~

When it came to slaying monsters, the hero's model was Apollo killing Python; when it came to making love to young boys, it was Apollo's love for Hyacinthus and Cyparissus. But there is an episode in the god's life that hints at something even more arcane than those often fatal love affairs. It is the story of how Apollo became a servant to Admetus, king of Pherae in Thessaly. Of Admetus we know that he was handsome, that he was famous for his herds of cattle, that he loved sumptuous feasts, and that he possessed the gift of hospitality. So much and no more. But we know a great deal about what people did for him. Out of love for Admetus, Apollo was willing to pass as a hireling. For a long time, "inflamed by love for the young Admetus," this proudest of gods became a mere herdsman, taking a provincial king's cattle out to graze. In so doing, he left his shock of dazzling hair unkempt and even forsook his lyre, making music on nothing better than a reed pipe.

His sister Artemis blushed with shame. And out of love for Admetus, his Alcestis, the most beautiful of Pelias's daughters, agreed to die like a stranger, unthreatened by anybody, taking the place of a hostage condemned to death. For love of Admetus, Apollo got the Fates drunk: it must have been the wildest party ever, although we know nothing about it except that it happened. In Plutarch's vision of things, the Fates, those young girls whose beautiful arms spin the thread of every life on earth, were "the daughters of Ananke," Necessity. And Necessity, as Euripides reminds us, having met her, "as he wandered among Muse and mountaintop," without ever "discovering anything more powerful," is the only power that has neither altars nor statues. Ananke is the only divinity who pays no heed to sacrifices. Her daughters can be fooled only by drunkenness. And very rarely does drink get the better of them. It was a hard task, but Apollo managed it, merely out of love for Admetus, because he wanted to delay the man's death.

Apollo has an old feud with death. Zeus had forced him to become a servant—oh, blessed servitude—to Admetus because Asclepius, son of Apollo and the faithless Coronis, had dared to bring a man back from the dead. Zeus shriveled Asclepius with a thunderbolt, and in revenge Apollo killed the Cyclopes who forged the thunderbolts. Zeus responded by planning a terrible punishment for Apollo. He had meant to hurl him down into Tartarus, and it was only when Leto, his old mistress, begged him not to that he decided to send the god to Thessaly, condemned to be a servant to Admetus. With Apollo's other lovers—Hyacinthus, for example, and Cyparissus—love had always ended in death. Accidents they may have been, and they caused him pain, but the fact was that Apollo himself had killed them. While playing with Hyacinthus, the god hurled a discus that shattered the boy's skull. Cyparissus fled from Apollo's advances and in desperation turned himself into a cypress. With Admetus the pattern was reversed. Apollo's love was so great that in trying to snatch Admetus from death he himself again risked what for a god is the equivalent of death: exile. Yet another thing Apollo did out of love for Admetus, and perhaps it was the most momentous of all, was to accept payment from his beloved, like a *pórnos,* a merest prostitute, unprotected by any rights, a stranger in his own city, despised first and foremost by his own lovers. It was the first example ever of *bonheur dans l'esclavage.* That it should have been Apollo who submitted to it made the adventure all the more astounding.

Thus Apollo, lover par excellence, took his love to an extreme where no human after him could follow. Not only did he confound the roles of lover and beloved, as would Orestes and Pylades, Achilles and Patroclus, but he went so far as to become the prostitute of his beloved, and hence one of those beings, "considered the worst of all perverts," in whose defense no one in Greece ever ventured to speak so much as a word. And, as servant to his beloved, he attempted to roll back the borders of death, something not even Zeus himself had dared interfere with, not even for his own son Sarpedon.

～　～　～

But who was Admetus? When he heard from Apollo that his death could be delayed if somebody else was ready to die in his place, Admetus began to make the rounds of friends and relations. He asked all of them if they were willing to take his place. No one would. So Admetus went to his two old parents, sure they would agree. But even they said no. Next it was the turn of his young and beautiful bride. And Alcestis said yes. The

Greeks questioned whether woman was capable of *philía* in a man's regard—capable, that is, of that friendship which grows out of love (*"philía dià tòn érōta,"* as Plato puts it) and which only men were supposed to experience. But Alcestis actually lifted *philía* to a higher plane by making the ultimate sacrifice. Even Plato was forced to admit that in comparison with Admetus's wife, Orpheus "seems weak spirited, nothing more than a zither strummer," because he went into the underworld alive in his search for Eurydice rather than simply agreeing to die, as Alcestis did, without any hope of return or salvation. True, Alcestis remains the only feminine example of *philía* the Greeks ever quote, but it is an awesome example. So much so that the gods themselves allowed Heracles to snatch her back just as the young woman was about to cross the calm waters of the lake of the dead. So Alcestis was brought back among the living, back to the grief-stricken Admetus. The king of Pherae had been saved on three occasions: by a god, by a woman, and by a hero. And all this merely because he had shown himself hospitable.

In this elusive, because supernatural, story, the point of maximum impenetrability is the object of love: Admetus. Euripides has Alcestis die onstage like a heroine out of Ibsen, and before dying she bares her heart to us. Ancient literature offers plenty of eloquent references to Apollo's passion, although texts never connect his having been Admetus's lover to his having been paid as the king's servant. The two images of Apollo are always kept separate. Of Admetus we know only that he insulted his old father for refusing to die in his place. All else is obscure, no less so than the way gods are obscure to mortals. Only one character trait shines through the ancient texts: Admetus was hospitable.

～ ～ ～

But who is Admetus? Dazzled by Alcestis and Apollo, who loved him to the point of self-denial, we might choose to leave the object of their love in the shadows. But let's stop awhile and take a good look at him: let's scan the landscape and the names. And we shall discover that indeed Admetus belongs to the shadows.

The landscape is Thessaly, a land that "in olden times was a lake surrounded by mountains high as the sky itself" (one of them was Olympus); a land that preserved its familiarity with the deep waters which periodically burst forth to flood it from a hundred springs and rivers; a fertile country, yellow, rugged, with plenty of horses, cattle, witches. The presiding divinity is not the cool, transparent Athena but a great goddess who looms from the darkness, Pheraia. She holds a torch in each hand and is rarely mentioned. And this too is typical of the spirit of Thessaly, a land where divinity is closer to the primordial anonymity, where the gods rarely assume a human face, and where the Olympians are loath to descend. When a god does appear, he bursts forth, brusque and wild, like the horse Scapheus, whose mane leaps out from the rock split open by his own hooves. The horses that gallop around Thessaly are creatures of the deep, shooting out of the cracks in the ground, the cracks from which Poseidon's wave rises to flood the plain. They are the dead, brilliantly white, brilliantly black. And Pheraia is a local name for Hecate, the night-roaming underworld goddess who rends the dark with her torches. As a goddess, she is horse, bull, lioness, dog, but she is also she who appears on the back of bull, horse, or lion. A nurse to boys, a multiplier of cattle. In Thessaly she is *Brimó,* the strong one, who unites with Hermes, son of Ischys, also the strong one, the lover Coronis preferred to Apollo. And *strength (alké)* also forms part of the name Alcestis. In the land of Thessaly, rather than as a person, divinity presents itself as pure force. But Pheraia, says Hesychius's dictionary, is also the "daughter [*kórē*] of Admetus." Is it possible that before becoming a pair of provincial rulers, Alcestis and Admetus were already sitting side by side as sovereigns of the underworld?

Now the landscape yields up its secret. It is the luxuriant country of the dead, this Thessaly where Apollo must be slave for a "great year," until the stars return to their original positions—that is, for nine years. Apollo's stay in Thessaly is a time cycle in Hades. The fact that Zeus chose this place instead of Tartarus as a punishment for Apollo itself suggests that this is a land of death. The name *Admetus* means "indomitable." And who is more indomitable than the lord of the dead? Now the few things we know about Admetus take on new meaning: who could be more hospitable than the king of the dead? His is the inn that closes its doors to no one, at no hour of the day or night. And no one has such numerous herds as the king of the dead. When Admetus invites friends and relations to die for him, he is scarcely doing anything unusual: it's what he does all the time. And the reason Admetus fully expects others to substitute for him in death is now clear: he is the lord of death, he greets the arriving corpses, sorts them and spreads them out across his extensive domains.

Now we see how truly extreme Apollo's love is, more so even than it had seemed: out of love, Apollo tries to save the king of the dead from death. Now the love of both Apollo and Alcestis reveals itself as thoroughly provocative: it is a love for the shadow that steals all away. From Alcestis we discover what the *kórē,* snatched by Hades while gathering narcissi, never told us: that the god of the invisible is not just an abductor but a lover too.

~ ~ ~

The texts have little to say about Apollo's period of servitude, because it would mean touching on matters best kept secret. About Heracles' servitude under Omphale the poets chose to be ironic. But when it came to Apollo's under Admetus, no one wanted to risk it. All that remains is the exemplum of a love so great as to compensate for any amount of shame and suffering. According to Apollonius Rhodius, after killing the Cyclopes, Apollo was punished by being sent not to Thessaly but to the Hyperboreans in the far north. There he wept tears of amber, even though a god cannot weep. But what really put the story out of bounds was not just the scandalous suffering (and scandalously servile passion) of the "pure god in flight from the heavens." There was something else behind it. An ancient prophecy, the secret of Prometheus: the prediction that Zeus would one day see his throne usurped, by his most luminous son.

Apollo often plays around the borders of death. But Zeus is watching from on high. He knows that if ignored, his son's game will bring about the advent of a new age, the collapse of the Olympian order. Within the secret that lies behind this—and it's a secret rarely even alluded to—Apollo is to Zeus what Zeus had been to Kronos. And the place where the powers of the two gods always collide is death. Even beneath the sun of the dead, among the herds of Thessaly, Apollo doesn't forget his challenge to his father and chooses to snatch, if only for a short while, his indomitable beloved, Admetus, from that moment when "the established day does him violence." The never-mentioned dispute between father and son is left forever unsettled at that point.

~ ~ ~

The admirable asymmetry on which the Athenian man's love for the younger boy is based is described in minute detail by that surveyor of all matters erotic, Plato. The entire metaphysics of love is concentrated in the gesture with which the beloved grants his grace *(cháris)* to the lover. This gesture, still echoed in the Italian expression *concedere le proprie grazie,* and again in the passionate intertwining drawn tight by the French verb *agréer* (and derivations: *agréments, agréable,* and so on), is the very core of erotic drama and mystery. How should we think of it? How achieve it? For the barbarians it is something to condemn; for the more lascivious Greeks and those incapable of expressing themselves, such as the Spartans or the Boeotians, it is simply something enjoyable, and as such obligatory: to give way to a lover becomes a state directive. But as ever, the Athenians are a little more complicated and multifarious *(poikíloi)* than their neighbors, even when it comes to "the law of love." They are not so impudent as to speak of a "grace" that actually turns out to be an obligation. What could they come up with, then, to achieve the beloved's grace, without ever being sure of it? The word.

As warriors besieging a fortress will try one ruse after another to have that object so long before their eyes fall at last into their hands, so the Athenian lover engages in a war of words, surrounds his beloved with arguments that hem him in like soldiers. And the things he says are not just crude gallantries but the first blazing precursors of what one day, using a Greek word without remembering its origin, will be called metaphysics. The notion that thought derives from erotic dialogue is, for the great Athenians, true in the most straightforward, literal sense. Indeed, that link between a body to be captured like a fortress and the flight of metaphysics is, for Plato, the very image of eros. The rest of the world are mere barbarians who simply don't understand, or other Greeks with no talent for language—in other words, suffering from "mental sloth." They too are excluded from the finest of wars, which is the war of love.

~ ~ ~

As far as the lover was concerned, Athens invented a perfect duplicity, which uplifted him while leaving his undertaking forever uncertain. On the one hand, there is nothing the lover may not do; he is forgiven any and every excess. He alone can break his oath without the gods punishing him, since "there are no oaths in the affairs of Aphrodite." And again, the lover may get wildly excited, or choose to sleep the night outside the barred door of his beloved's house, and nobody will take it upon himself to criticize him. On the other hand, endless difficulties are placed in his way: his beloved will go to the gymnasium accompanied by a lynx-eyed pedagogue hired by the boy's father precisely to prevent him from listening to the advances of any would-be lover lying in wait. And the boy's friends are worse still: they watch him carefully, and if ever he shows signs of giving way, they taunt him and make him feel ashamed of that first hint of a passion that, encouraged by the lover's alluring words, could lead to the desired exchange of graces, to the moment when the lover will breathe "intelligence and every other virtue" into the mouth and body of his beloved, while the latter submits to his lover's advances because he wishes to gain "education and knowledge of every kind." (*Eispneîn*, "breathe into," is first and foremost the lover's prerogative, and *eíspnēlos*, "he who breathes into another," was another word for "lover.") This is the only and arduous "meeting point" admitted between the two asymmetrical laws that govern the lives of the lover and his beloved. Thus, at that fleeting and paradoxical point, "it is good for the young beloved to surrender himself to his lover; but only at that point and at no other." So says Plato. And such was the life of the lover, the most precarious, the most risky, and the most provocative of all the roles the Athenians invented.

～ ～ ～

After slaughtering their men, the women of Lemnos were struck by a kind of revenge the gods had never used before nor would again: they began to smell. And in this revenge we glimpse the grievance that Greece nursed against womankind. Greek men thought of women as of a perfume that is too strong, a perfume that breaks down to become a suffocating stench, a sorcery, "sparkling with desire, laden with aromas, glorious," but stupefying, something that must be shaken off. It is an attitude betrayed by small gestures, like that passage in the Pseudo-Lucian where we hear of a man climbing out of bed, "saturated with femininity," and immediately wanting to dive into cold water. When it comes to women, Greek sensibility brings together both fear and repugnance: on the one hand, there is the horror at the woman without her makeup who "gets up in the morning uglier than a monkey"; on the other, there is the suspicion that makeup is being used as a weapon of *apátè*, of irresistible deceit. Makeup and female smells combine to generate a softness that bewitches and exhausts. Better for men the sweat and dust of the gymnasium. "Boys' sweat has a finer smell than anything in a woman's makeup box."

One gets a sense, in these reactions to womankind, of something remote being revealed as though through nervous reflex. In the later, more private and idiosyncratic writers, we pick up echoes that take us back to a time long, long before, to the terror roused by the invasion of the Amazons, to the loathsome crime of the women of Lemnos.

~ ~ ~

For the Greeks, the unnameable aspect of eros was passivity during coitus. If the male beloved *(erómenos)* has to be so careful and to observe so many rules ·in order to distinguish his behavior beyond any shadow of a doubt from that of the male prostitute, who, "despite having a man's body, sins a woman's sins," it is not simply because of the indignity attached to whoever accepts the woman's part, thus debasing his own sexual status. Rather, it is the very pleasure of the woman, the pleasure of passivity, that is suspect and perhaps conceals a profound malignancy. This treacherous pleasure incites the Greek man to rage against the grossness inherent in the physiology and anatomy of these aesthetically inferior beings, obliged to parade "prominent, shapeless breasts, which they keep bound up like prisoners." But he rages precisely because he senses that this grossness might conceal a mocking power that eludes male control. The Athenians were extremely evasive on this question, although they never tired of mentioning cases of male love for boys.

As for what women might get up to when alone and unobserved by masculine eyes, a reverent and ominous silence appears to reign. And when it comes to love between women, the writers sometimes daren't even use the word. In fact, it is pathetic to see how in certain passages on the subject, modern translators will translate that forbidden word as *lesbianism,* without even sensing any incongruousness. The word *lesbianism* meant nothing to the Greeks, whereas the verb *lesbiázein* meant "licking the sexual organs," and the word *tribádes,* "the rubbers," referred to women who had sex with other women, as though in the fury of their embrace they wanted to consume each other's vulvas.

But it wasn't so much love between women that scandalized the Greeks—to their credit, they were not easily scandalized—as the suspicion, which had taken root in their minds, that women might have their own indecipherable erotic self-sufficiency, and that those rites and mysteries they celebrated, and in which they refused to let men participate, might be the proof of this. And, behind it all, their most serious suspicion had to do with pleasure in coitus. Only Tiresias had been able to glimpse the truth, and that was precisely why he was blinded.

One day Zeus and Hera were quarreling. They called Tiresias and asked him which of the two, man or woman, got the most pleasure from sex. Tiresias answered that if the pleasure were divided into ten parts, the woman enjoyed nine and the man only one. On hearing this, Hera got mad and blinded Tiresias. But why did Hera get mad? Couldn't she glory in her own superiority, something that set her above even Zeus? No, because here Tiresias was trespassing on a secret, one of those secrets sages are called upon to safeguard rather than reveal. This sexual tittle-tattle continued to make the rounds, however. Centuries later it was still being bandied about, though, as always, with distortions: now they were saying that a woman's pleasure was only twice that of the man. But it was enough: it confirmed an antique doubt, a fear at least as old as the ruttish daughters of the sun. Perhaps woman, that creature shut away in the gynaeceum, where "not a single particle of true eros penetrates," knew a great deal more than her master, who was always cruising about gymnasiums and porticoes.

~ ~ ~

"Make up your minds who you think are better, those who love boys, or those who like women. I, in fact, who have enjoyed both kinds of passion, am like balanced scales with the two plates either side at exactly the same height." So says Theomnestus. Since time immemorial the question as to which took the erotic prize, love with boys or with women, had been a real thorn in the flesh for the Greeks. Some even maintained that Orpheus was torn apart by women because he had been the first to declare the superiority of love with boys. Later on, even though the debate had been settled before it started in favor of the boys, the rule was that one wasn't to say so too openly. Finally, in the late and loquacious years of the Pseudo-Lucian, we hear a cackle of voices—spiteful or mellifluous, uncertain or arrogant—still debating the issue. Licinus answers Theomnestus's question in the best way possible: with a story. One day, walking beneath the porticoes of Rhodes, he met two old acquaintances: Caricles, a young man from Corinth, and the impetuous Callicratides, an Athenian. Caricles was wearing, as always, a little makeup. He thought it made him more attractive to women. And there was never any shortage of those around him. His house was full of dancers and singers. The only voices heard there were women's voices, except, that is, for one old cook, past it now, and a few very young slave boys. Quite the opposite of Callicratides' house. Callicratides did the rounds of the gymnasiums and surrounded himself exclusively with attractive and as yet hairless boys. When the first suspicion of a beard began to scratch their skin, he would move them on to administrative work and bring in others. The three friends decided to spend a few lazy days together, taking turns discussing that old chestnut: who takes the erotic palm, boys or women?

For Callicratides, women were "an abyss," like the great ravines in the rocks around Athens where criminals were thrown. Caricles, however, couldn't respond to boys at all and thought incessantly about women. Having taken a boat to Cnidos, the three friends were eager to see the famous Aphrodite by Praxiteles. Even before they went into Aphrodite's temple, they could feel a light breeze blowing from it. It was the aura. The courtyard of the sanctuary wasn't paved with the usual austere slabs of gray stone but was full of plants and fruit trees. In the garden all around them they saw myrtles with their berries and other shrubs associated with the goddess. Plants typical of Dionysus were also in abundance, since "Aphrodite is even more delightful when she is with Dionysus, and their gifts are sweeter if mixed together." Finally the three friends went into the temple. In the center they saw the Parian marble of Praxiteles' Aphrodite, naked, a faint lift to the corners of her lips, a faint hint of arrogance. Caricles immediately began to rave over the stunning frontal view. One could suffer anything for a woman like that, and so saying he stretched up to kiss her. Callicratides watched in silence. There was a door behind the statue, and the three friends asked one of the temple guardians if she had the keys to it. It was then that Callicratides was stunned by the beauty of Aphrodite's buttocks. He yelled his admiration, and Caricles' eyes were wet with tears.

Then the three fell silent as they continued to contemplate that marble body. Behind a thigh they noticed a mark, like a stain on a tunic. Licinus assumed it was a defect in the marble and remarked on this as yet another reason for admiring Praxiteles: how clever of him to hide this blemish in one of the least visible parts of the statue. But the guardian who had opened the door and was standing beside the visitors told them that the real story behind the stain was rather different.

She explained that a young man from a prominent family had once been in the habit of visiting the temple and had fallen in love with the goddess. He would spend whole days parading his devotion. He got up at dawn to go to the sanctuary and went home only reluctantly after sundown. Standing before the statue, he would whisper on and on in some secret lover's conversation, breaking off every now and then to consult the oracle by tossing a few Libyan gazelle bones. He was waiting anxiously for Aphrodite's throw to come up. That was when every face of the bones bore a different number. One evening, when the guardians came to close the temple, the young man hid behind the door where the three visitors were now standing and spent "an unspeakable night" with the statue. The fruits of his lovemaking had stained the statue. That mark on the white marble demonstrated the indignity the image of the goddess had suffered. The young man was never seen again. Rumor had it that he drowned himself in the sea. When the guardian had finished, Caricles immediately exclaimed: "So, men love women even when they are made out of stone. Just imagine if she had been alive. . . ." But Callicratides smiled and said that actually the story supported his side of the argument. For despite being alone a whole night with the statue, and completely free to do whatever he wanted, the young man had embraced the marble as if it were a boy and hadn't wanted to take the woman from the front. The two antagonists began arguing again, and Licinus was hard put to persuade them to leave the temple and continue elsewhere. In the meantime the worshipers were beginning to arrive.

~ ~ ~

To a considerable extent classical morality developed around reflections on the nature of men's love for boys; basically such reflections stressed the quality of *areté* and played down something self-evident: pleasure. *Areté* means an "excellence" that is also "virtue." The word always had a moral meaning attached; the morality wasn't just something added by mischievous latecomers. In any event, *areté* is incandescent whenever manifest in a man's love for a boy. In its Kantian, unattached isolation, the Greeks would scarcely have appreciated the quality at all. The last and ultimate image of *areté* Greece offers us is a field strewn with the corpses of young Thebans after the battle of Chaeronea. The corpses were found lying in pairs: they were all couples, lovers, who had gone into battle together against the Macedonians. It was to be Greece's last stand. Afterward, Philip II and Alexander set about turning the country into a museum.

~ ~ ~

"Nothing beautiful or charming ever comes to a man except through the Charites," says Theocritus. But how did the Charites come down to man? As three rough stones that fell from heaven in Orchomenus. Only much later were statues placed next to those stones. What falls from heaven is indomitable, forever. Yet man is obliged to conquer those stones, or girls with fine tresses, if he wants his singing to be "full of the breath of the Charites." How to go about it? From the *Chárites,* one passes to *cháris,* from the Graces to grace. And it is Plutarch who tells us what the relationship is: "The ancients, Protogenes, used the word *cháris* to mean the spontaneous consent of the woman to the man." Grace, then, the inconquerable, surrenders itself only to him who strives to conquer it through erotic siege, even though he knows he can never enter the citadel if the citadel doesn't open, grace-fully, for him.

~ ~ ~

The relationship between *erastés* and *erómenos,* lover and beloved, was highly formalized and to a certain extent followed the rules of a ritual. In Sparta and Crete, the main centers of love between men, one could still find clear evidence of these rites. In Crete, each boy's parents knew that one day they would be forewarned of their son's imminent abduction. The lover would then arrive and, if the parents considered him worthy, would be free to carry off the boy and disappear into the country with him. Their whereabouts unknown, they would live together in complete privacy for two months. Finally the beloved would reappear in the city with "a piece of armor, an ox, and a cup," ceremonial gifts from his lover. Athens, with its vocation for modernity, was less rigid than Crete but equally tough below the surface. Here the rite was transformed into set behavior patterns that, though immersed in the buzz and chatter of the city square, remained as recognizable as dance steps. The lovers would cruise around the gymnasiums with a fake air of abstraction, their eyes running over the youngsters working out in the dust. It was the primordial setting for desire. The lovers would watch the boys, throwing furtive glances at "hips and thighs, the way sacrificing priests and seers size up their victims." They would sneak glances at the prints their genitals left in the sand. They would wait till midday, when, with the combination of oil, sweat, and sand, "dew and down would bloom on the boys' genitals as on the skin of a peach." The place was drenched with pleasure, but the word "pleasure" couldn't be mentioned, because pleasure was common property—even slaves and immigrants could enjoy it—whereas the amorous journey undertaken that morning aimed at an excellence, a splendor and glory, that belonged to one and one alone: an Athenian, the chosen one, the boy who, through subterfuge and gifts of garlands, would become the beloved.

That reluctance to admit the pleasure involved would never be dropped, not even in the ultimate intimacy: "in the act of love the boy does not share in the man's pleasure, as does the woman; but contemplates, in a state of sobriety, the excitement of the other, drunken with Aphrodite." When the lover approaches, the beloved stands upright and looks straight ahead, his eyes not meeting those of his lover, who bends down and almost doubles up over him, greedily. The vase painters generally show thigh-to-thigh contact rather than anal penetration: this allows the beloved to maintain his erect, indifferent, detached position. But all too soon the whole situation would be reversed. The first facial hair marked the beginning of the end of the boy's period as beloved. The hairs were called Harmodius and Aristogiton because they freed the boy from this erotic tyranny. Then, as though in need of a little time out, the boy escapes "from the tempest and torment of male love." But very soon he is back in that tempest, and in a new role: instead of being eyed, nude, in the gymnasium, he is himself cruising around younger boys, in the same places, nosing out his prey. Transformed from *erómenos* into *erastés,* he would finally discover, as a lover, what it means to be possessed by love. Only the lover is *éntheos,* says Plato. Only the lover is "full of god."

# ~ Caio Fernando Abreu ~

## *Beauty*

TRANSLATED BY DAVID TREECE

*You've never heard of damnation*
*you've never seen a miracle*
*you've never wept alone in a dirty bathroom*
*and you never wanted to see the face of God.*
Cazuza, *"Only Mothers Are Happy"*

He had to press the bell repeatedly before he could make out the sound of feet descending the stairs. And again he pictured to himself the worn carpet that was once purple but then had faded to a sort of red and after that turned pink—what color was it now?—and he heard the tuneless barking of a dog, a nocturnal cough, and brisk footsteps. Then he sensed the light switched on inside the house filtering through the glass to fall on his face with its three-day beard. He put his hands in his pockets, his fingers searching for a cigarette or a key ring to play with while he waited for the little window at the top of the door to open.

Framed by its rectangle, she screwed up her eyes to see him properly. They measured each other like this—one inside, the other outside the house—until she withdrew, unsurprised. When he entered he saw that she looked older. And more embittered, he later realized.

"You didn't warn me you were coming," she grumbled in that sour old way of hers, which he'd never understood before. But which now, all these years later, he'd learned to translate as "how I've missed you, welcome, how nice to see you," or something along those lines. Affectionate, if awkward.

He embraced her stiffly. He wasn't used to touching or caressing. He

---

*"Beauty" is from the first collection of stories by the Brazilian writer CAIO FERNANDO ABREU. He lives in Brazil.*

sank giddily, quickly, into that familiar smell—cigarettes, onions, dog, soap, beauty cream, and old flesh that had been alone for years. Taking hold of him by his ears as usual, she kissed him on the forehead. Then she reached out her hand and drew him inside.

"You don't have a phone, Mother," he explained. "I decided I'd give you a surprise."

Turning on the lights, a little anxious somehow, she led him further and further inside. He could hardly make out the stairs, the bookcase, the china cabinet, the dusty photo frames. The dog curled itself around his legs, whining softly.

"Down, Beauty," she shouted, threatening her with a kick. The bitch jumped aside, and she laughed. "I only have to give her a warning, and she does what she's told. Poor old creature, she's almost completely blind. A mangy good-for-nothing, really. All she can do is sleep, eat, and shit; she's just waiting to die."

"How old is she now?" he asked. For that was the best way of getting through to her: taking the back route, with these banal questions. The best way to get behind her sour manner, get past the purple flowers on her dressing gown.

"I don't know; about fifteen." Her voice had become so hoarse. "You're supposed to multiply a dog's age by seven."

He tilted his head deliberately, that was the way.

"About ninety-five, then."

She put his suitcase on a chair in the room. Then she screwed up her eyes again. And peered about her, as if she'd just woken up.

"What?"

"Beauty. If she were a person, she'd be ninety-five." She laughed. "Older than me, just think. Frighteningly old."

She closed the dressing gown over her chest and held the collar with her hands. Covered in dark patches, he saw, like freckles (*se-nile pur-pu-ra,* he repeated to himself), some varnish on the short nails of her nicotine-stained fingers.

"Would you like a coffee?"

"If it's no trouble"—he knew that this was how he had to go about it, as she made her way masterfully through the kitchen, her domain. His hands in his pockets, he stood slouched in the doorway and looked around him.

Her back, so bent. She seemed to have slowed down, although she still had that way of ceaselessly opening and closing the cupboard doors, laying out cups, spoons, napkins, making a lot of noise, while he was forced to sit and watch. The kitchen walls, stained with grease. The little sliding window, with its broken pane. She'd put a sheet of newspaper over the glass. *Country sinks into chaos, disease, and poverty,* he read. And he sat down on the broken plastic chair.

"It's nice and fresh," she said as she served the coffee. "These days I can only get to sleep after I've had some coffee."

"You shouldn't, Mother. Coffee keeps you awake."

She shrugged her shoulders. "To hell with that. With me it's always been the other way around."

The yellow cup had a dark stain in the bottom, chips out of the rim. He stirred the coffee listlessly. Then, suddenly, as neither he nor she was saying anything, he wanted to run away—rewind the action as if watching a video—grab his suitcase, cross the room, the hallway, get beyond the stone path in the garden, out again into the little street of houses, almost all of them white. Get to a taxi, the airport, to another town, far from Passo da Guanxuma, to that other life, from which he'd come. Anonymous, without ties, without a past. Forever, forever and ever. Until either of them died, he feared. And wished. Relief, shame.

"Go to bed," he suggested. "It's very late; I shouldn't have come like this, without any warning. But you don't have a phone."

She sat down opposite him, and her dressing gown fell open. Between the purple flowers he saw the countless lines on her skin, crushed tissue paper. She screwed up her eyes, peering at his face as he took a sip of coffee.

"What's wrong?" she asked slowly. And that was the tone that set the opening for a new approach. But he coughed and looked down at the diamond pattern of the tablecloth. Cold plastic, old strawberries.

"Nothing, Mother. Nothing's wrong. I got homesick, that's all. Suddenly I got really homesick. For you, for everything."

She took out a packet of cigarettes from her dressing gown pocket.

"Give me a light, will you."

He held out the lighter. She touched his hand awkwardly, her hands mottled with purple blotches against his very white hands. A wry sort of caress.

"Nice lighter."

"It's French."

"What's that inside?"

"Some liquid or other. Whatever it is that lighters have inside them. Except this one's transparent; you can't see it in the other ones."

He held the lighter up against the light. Golden reflections, the green liquid sparkling. The dog crawled in under the table, whining softly. She seemed not to notice, entranced by what was behind the green, the golden liquid.

"It looks like the sea." She smiled. She tapped the cigarette against the rim of the cup and handed the lighter back to him. "So, young man, you came to visit me? Very good."

He closed the lighter in his palm. Warm from her stained hand. "Yes, Mother. I got homesick."

Hoarse laughter. "Homesick? Do you know Elzinha hasn't been by for more than a month? I might die in here. Alone. God forbid. She'd only find out from the newspapers. If it got into the papers. Who cares about an old crock like me?" He lit a cigarette and coughed heavily at the first drag.

"I live alone too, Mother. If I died, no one would know. And it wouldn't get in the papers."

She took a deep drag and blew some smoke rings. But she didn't follow them with her eyes. With the tip of her nail she was picking a chip off the rim of the cup.

"It's fate," she said. "Your grandmother died alone. Your grandfather died alone. Your father died alone, remember? That weekend when I went to the beach. He was scared of the sea. It's a thing so big it frightens you, he'd say." She flicked away the little chip of painted china. "And not even a grandchild; he died without a grandchild. The thing he wanted most."

"That's long past, Mother. Forget it." He straightened his back; it was aching. No, he decided, not down into that abyss. The smell, a whole week, neighbors telephoning. He ran his fingertips over the faded diamonds on the tablecloth. "I don't know how you can go on living here alone, Mother. This house is too big for just one person. Why don't you go and live with Elzinha?"

She pretended to spit to one side, with mock irony. That soap opera cynicism didn't go with the faded dressing gown with the purple flowers, her near-white hair, her nicotine-stained hands holding the cigarette smoked down to the end.

"And put up with Pedro, with his delusions of grandeur? There'd have to be something really wrong with me, for God's sake. They'd hide me when they had visitors, God forbid. The crazy old thing, the old witch. The old crone hidden away in the maid's room, like a black." She tapped her cigarette. "And as if that wasn't bad enough, do you think they'd let me take Beauty with me?"

Underneath the table, at the sound of her name, the bitch whined more loudly.

"It's not really that bad, is it, Mother? Elzinha's got her college. And deep down Pedro's a good person. It's just . . ."

She rummaged in the pockets of her dressing gown and took out a pair of glasses, one lens cracked and the arms mended with tape.

"Let me see you properly," she said. She adjusted the spectacles. He lowered his eyes. In the silence he sat listening to the ticking of the living-room clock. A tiny cockroach traced its path across the white tiles behind her.

"You look thinner," she observed. She seemed concerned. "Much thinner."

"It's my hair," he said. He ran his hand over his almost shaven head. "And this three-day-beard."

"You've lost some hair, son."

"It's my age. Almost forty." He put out his cigarette and coughed.

"And that rotten cough?"

"Cigarettes, Mother. Air pollution."

He raised his eyes and for the first time looked straight into hers. Pale green behind the spectacle lenses, very alert all of a sudden. He thought of a line in a poem by Ana César: *It must be now, down this one-way street.* He almost said it. But she blinked first. She looked away under the table, care-fully took hold of the mangy old dog, and put it on her lap.

"But is everything all right?"

"Everything's fine, Mother."

"Work?"

He nodded. She stroked the dog's hairless ears. Then she looked straight at him again.

"What about your health? There are supposed to be some new bugs going around now, I saw it on the TV. Plagues."

"I'm fine, thank God," he asserted. He lit another cigarette, his hands trembling a little. "And Dona Alzira, still going strong?"

Holding the extinguished cigarette butt between her yellowed fingers, she leaned back in the chair. Her eyes screwed up, as if she were looking right back through him. Into time and space. The dog rested its head on the table and shut its whitish eyes. She sighed and shrugged her shoulders.

"Poor woman. Even more decrepit than me."

"You're not decrepit, Mother."

"That's what you think. There are times when I find I'm talking to myself. The other day, do you know who I was calling for the whole day long?" She waited a little; he didn't say anything. "Cândida, remember her? A good little girl, that one, even if she was just a black. But it was almost as though she was white. I was there calling her, calling her all day long. Cândida, hey, Cândida. Where've you got to, girl? Then I realized."

"Cândida died, Mother."

She ran her hand over the dog's head again. More slowly this time. She closed her eyes, as if they were both sleeping. "That's right, stabbed. Stuck like a pig, do you remember?" She opened her eyes. "Do you want something to eat, son?"

"I ate on the plane."

She pretended to spit again.

"Saints preserve us. Frozen food, God forbid. Like eating plastic. Remember the time I went on the plane?" He shook his head; she didn't notice. She was looking up, at the cigarette smoke losing itself against a ceiling stained by dampness, mold, time, and solitude. "I was so dressed up—I looked like a jet-setter. Going on the plane and everything, a real madam. With my vanity case, the sunglasses. You could tell people about it and no one would believe you." She dunked a piece of bread in the cold coffee and put it in the dog's almost toothless mouth. It swallowed it in one gulp. "You know I liked the plane more than the city? It's so crazy, all that racket the whole time. It doesn't seem human. How do you stand it?"

"You get used to it, Mother. You get to like it."

"How's Beto?" she asked suddenly. And she gradually lowered her eyes until they were fixed onto his again.

What if I were to lean over the precipice? he thought. What if I did it now, just like that. But instead he studied the tiles on the wall behind her. The cockroach had disappeared.

"He's there, Mother, living his life."

She looked at the ceiling again.

"So thoughtful, that Beto. He took me out to dinner, opened the car door for me. He was like something out of a movie. He pulled the chair out for me to sit down at the restaurant. No one's ever done that before."

She squinted at him. "What was the name of that restaurant again? Some foreign name."

"Casserole, Mother. La Casserole." He almost smiled; he had a little boy's eyes, he remembered. "It was nice, that evening, wasn't it?"

"Yes," she agreed. "So nice, it was just like a movie." She stretched her hand out across the table, almost touching his. He spread his fingers, with a kind of longing. So sad, so sad. Then she pulled back, dropping her fingers onto the bitch's hairless head.

"Beto liked you, Mother. He liked you a lot." He drew his fingers together again. Then he ran them over the hairs on his arm. Memories, distances. "He said you were very chic, Mother."

"Chic, me? A common, decrepit old woman." She laughed, vainly, her stained hand on her white hair. She sighed. "So handsome. Such a nice boy; that's what I call a nice boy. I said it to Elzinha, right in front of Pedro, to have a bit of a dig at him. I said it out loud, just like that. If someone's not well bred, you can see it right away in their face. There's no point in putting on appearances, it's written in the stars. Just like Beto, with those torn trousers. Who'd ever have thought he was such a nice boy, wearing those sneakers?" She looked into his eyes again. "That's a real friend you've got there, son. A bit like you, even, I thought to myself. They look like brothers. The same height, the same manner; they really do look just like brothers."

"We haven't seen each other for quite a while, Mother."

She leaned over a little, squeezing the bitch's head against the table. Beauty opened her whitish eyes. Although she was blind, she too seemed to be looking at him. They sat there looking at each other like this. For an almost unbearable length of time, amid the cigarette smoke, the overflowing ashtrays, the empty cups, the three of them—himself, his mother, and Beauty.

"But why?"

"Mother," he began. His voice trembled. "Mother, it's so difficult," he repeated. And said nothing more.

It was then that she got up. Suddenly, throwing the bitch onto the floor like a dirty rag. She began to gather up cups, spoons, ashtrays, and throw them all into the sink. After piling up the dishes, squirting on some dishwashing liquid, and turning on the taps, she walked to and fro, while he sat there looking at her, so bent, a little older, her hair almost completely white, her voice a little hoarser, her fingers yellower and yellower from smoking. She put her glasses away in her dressing gown and buttoned the collar, looking at him like someone who wants to change the subject—and that was a sign for him to try another approach, the right one this time.

She said, "Your room's just as it was, upstairs. I'm going to bed, because I've got the market first thing tomorrow. There are clean sheets in the bathroom cupboard."

Then she did something that she wouldn't have done before. She took hold of him by his ears to kiss him, not on the forehead but on both cheeks. Almost lingeringly. That smell: cigarettes, onions, dog, soap, and old age. And something else besides, something moist that seemed like pity, a weariness from having seen too much. Or love. A kind of love.

"Tomorrow we'll talk properly, Mother. There's plenty of time. Sleep well."

Leaning across the table, he lit another cigarette and listened to her treading heavily up the stairs. When he heard the door of the room slam, he got up and left the kitchen.

He took a few giddy steps across the room. The huge dark wooden table. Eight places, all empty. He stopped in front of his grandfather's picture—a slightly lopsided face, with his mother's green watery eyes, eyes that he too had inherited. That man, he thought, died in the middle of the countryside, alone with a revolver and his fate. He put his hand in the inside pocket of his jacket, took out the little bottle with its foreign label, and drank. When he took it away, drops of whiskey rolled down the corners of his mouth, down his neck and shirt, onto the floor. The dog licked the worn carpet, its eyes almost blind, its tongue feeling about in search of the liquid.

He opened his eyes. He found himself staring at the big living-room mirror. In the depths of this mirror that hung on the living-room wall of an old house in a provincial town, he could make out the shadow of a painfully thin man, his head almost shaved, with the startled eyes of a child. He put the bottle on the table and took off his jacket. He was sweating heavily. He slung the jacket over the back of a chair and began to unbutton his shirt, stained with whiskey and sweat.

One by one, he undid the buttons. He turned on the lamp, so that the room would be lighter, and, with his shirt off, began to stroke the purple marks, the same color as the stair carpet had once been—what color was it now?—that spread beneath the hairs on his chest. With his fingertips he touched the right-hand side of his neck, tilting his head as if feeling for a seed in the dark. Then he slumped to his knees. God, he thought, and stretched out his other hand to touch the near-blind dog, its coat dappled with pink patches. The same as those on the worn stair carpet, the same as those on the skin of his chest, beneath the hair. Curly, dark, soft.

"Beauty," he whispered. "Beauty, you're such a beauty, Beauty."

# ～ *Patrick Drevet* ～

## *An Angel at Orsay*

TRANSLATED BY JAMES KIRKUP

*To James Kirkup*

It's quite possible I don't know how to make use of museums in the proper way. It is rare for me not to be distracted from contemplation of the works on display by a curiosity regarding the visitors, shadowy figures at first, scattered, unobtrusive, whose comings and goings, as they cross my own, finally impress upon my consciousness a tangible reality, a sometimes moving presence, a variable modeling that quickly becomes more intriguing than all the faces and all the bodies represented there in painting and sculpture, however great an education they may be for the eyes, however attractive the voyage they offer to share with us. More than the works hanging on the walls, protected by glass cases or immobilized on rostra, it is those living morphologies that the vastness and vacuity of the galleries expose to our view, while the polish of parquets or marble floorings exalts their moving flames beyond the reflections they cast. The slowness with which they move around, the emotion they radiate, the wonder that stops them in their tracks, the ecstatic bliss or silent communion that prolongs a pose in front of a masterpiece, all combine to emphasize a transfigured cast of features, an anatomical volume imbued with grace. Museums become suspect or at the very least ambiguous places, temples of noiseless, furtive encounters, more engaging than they would be in the street but no less evanescent, of course.

I realized this recently under the great glass dome of the Musée d'Orsay, profane nave of a basilica that, once we're through the turnstiles, offers

PATRICK DREVET *has published several novels, the latest of which is* Dieux Obscurs. *James Kirkup has translated one of these,* A Room in the Woods, *as well as his autobiography,* My Micheline.

us its impressive vista flanked by side chapels of pink sandstone, with embrasures like the revetments enclosing the open space in front of an Egyptian or Assyrian temple, or of a military bunker, and from which arises the muffled brouhaha of an antique throng amid the statues and plinths. One plunges into it down monumental stairways, and the visit begins that, like some initiatory rite of passage, requires us to ascend from landing to landing surrounded by visitors who always have a somewhat haggard appearance.

The pretty David by Antonin Mercié, perched on his lofty pedestal about halfway down the concourse, displays the nudity of his superb, disdainful adolescence. Some distance away, below those insolently displaced hips, a young man is busy making a sketch of him. He at once attracted my attention, drawing it away from the statue, which he had nevertheless at a first glance found sufficiently interesting. Despite the ephebe's academic pose and its rather slick realism, acting somewhat in the manner of a disguise, like the models photographed by Baron von Gloeden at Taormina, I had sensed in it an authentic inspiration or at least a hunger for visual detail similar to my own, which determined my aesthetic preferences and lies at the root of my tastes in art.

Doubtless as far as this young man was concerned I felt that mixture of envy and irritation aroused in us by people who appear to have purloined our souls by showing us that we are not the only ones to feel as we do and to have appropriated the feeling to themselves by manifesting it in a more ostentatious fashion than we do ourselves. He was one of those up-to-the-minute contemporary youths whose immaturity, allied to a certain way of outfitting themselves, lends them the appearance of mutants. Black hair cut short, with a few isolated locks sticking up in spikes, set off a face of such classic purity that he could well have been a fashion model: the clear outline of the eyebrows emphasizing the deep-set sockets that with the same refined drawing joined the straight bridge of the nose; high cheekbones that stretched the skin of the rather hollow cheeks, shadowed by the fresh hint of beard; lips narrow yet fleshy, well blocked, pouting in response to the effort of concentration.

There was something ascetic in that tense visage, particularly poignant when it was raised toward the bronze David, revealing the double vulnerability of eyes whose fullness in the fervor of the vision directing them emerged from the curve of the lower lid. I don't know what attracted me most: that gravity in the act of observation, which hinted at an enviable mastery, or those features that suggested a mystical, violent temperament, confirmed by his general appearance and the fact that he drew standing, hip displaced, navel in evidence, his weight distributed on one leg, in a posture that made of him the living incarnation of his model.

At first glance, the David evokes a youthful Berber at the end of a fantasia rather than a biblical character. Wearing a turban whose crisscrossed folds crown his forehead and, round the neck, a two-strand necklace from which hangs the little capsule of an amulet, he bends his finely muscled body as he carries out the harmless gesture of replacing his scimitar in its sheath. The length of the weapon obliges him to lift his right arm rather high, like a native in his pirogue about to thrust his spear into the depths, and the sharp point of the blade requires precise manipulation if it is to be introduced safely into the sheath. The sculptor had decided to depict David at the conclusion of his exploit, having only just decapitated Goliath. The boy simply expresses a feeling of relief at a job well done. Unless it is to distance himself from an emotion that might make him tremble with retrospective fear, might betray the vulnerable child he still remains beneath his mask of impassivity, he appears to be concerned only with directing the point of the scimitar toward the opening of the sheath, and he calls up all his dignity in order to accomplish this movement, as if, should he miss the opening and have to start all over again, everything might collapse, the merit in his exploit be denied him, his promotion to the rank of hero be called in question. His fingers clasped around hilt and sheath betray a rather nervous determination, which can be felt also in the rigidity of his gaze, the thrust of his lips. It has been no easy task: the hollows under his eyes are marked by a throbbing vein; the shine on the bronze has a look of cold sweat; one senses beneath the skin that lacquers an undeveloped musculature, sensitively supple, hard beneath the transparent sheath of the epidermis, the desire to control an irrepressible trembling.

It creates a very sensual impression. With the turban, the amulet, the long scimitar held diagonally across the torso, it reminds us that, from Delacroix to Fromentin, from Flaubert to Loti, there was no self-respecting nineteenth-century artist, whether painter or writer, who did not feel it a duty to complete his education with a Grand Tour of the Orient. Does that entitle us to conclude that Antonin Mercié went so far as to inaugurate what has become known in our times as a sort of sex tourism, brought to light by Oscar Wilde and André Gide and perpetuated by Jean Genet, Paul Bowles, and even Roland Barthes? I've not been able to discover anything more about this sculptor, apart from the terse facts on the back of a picture postcard on which his David, shot half length, is used to show off the framework of the former railway station's great rococo clock. We are informed that he was born in 1845 and died in 1916; he created this bronze in 1872, at the age of twenty-seven, and the Arabian influence it manifests could indeed have been the result of melancholy nostalgia for some recent stay in North Africa, in the Atlas or in the desert.

Even though it is far from lacking in precision, subtlety, poetry, it seemed to me strange that a young art student in our times should want to work on it. Generally speaking, it is in front of the works of the old masters that one sees fine arts students lost in contemplation, and the Musée d'Orsay is not lacking in such artists, from Carpeau to Bourdelle, from Rude or Barhy to Rodin. Probably one would have to seek sentimental rather than artistic reasons to explain the choice the young man had made of this particular work. Seeing him so absorbed, so attentive, and as if overwhelmed by each of the lines he was reproducing as his eyes followed them on the statue, obsessed with getting them exactly right but above all giving the impression of seeking out through the medium of his slow pencil strokes sensations whose voluptuousness depended precisely upon their fleeting nature, I imagined him to be engaged in some mortuary project. His gravity was not without a profound sadness, whether caused by lost love or by some unfulfilled desire. But it could also be that, in keeping with a program he had set himself for the advancement of his studies, he had found in this bronze devoid of style and genius, humbly realist, expressing a reverent and conscientious admiration for its juvenile anatomy, the model he himself did not have the means to pay for.

All the same, confronted by the living solidity of this young man' sketching, with the vibrant warmth that animated his hip-shot stance, with the inexhaustible singularity of his lifted face revealed as much by the luminosity to which he kept exposing it as by the energy that underlay its tense expression, I conceived of the bronze David as no more than an artist's model, however sensual and sensitive its execution. Despite the fact that the youth was barely moving, despite his protective screen of clothing, despite, finally, the monotony of his performance, I could hardly scrutinize his sinuous physical attributes more extensively without giving myself away. Yet I found incomparably more captivating the young man himself: captivating not simply because his proportions were harmonious (something that could not be denied in the case of the David) but above all because they enshrined nothing set, nothing finished—because they were the product of an assembly of singular details still capable of being modified and of revealing yet other aspects. Compared with the explicit nudity of the bronze, his body seemed to me more suggestive of personal qualities that awaited discovery. He gave me the impression of an almond in its shell, of a naked fruit, fresh and imperishable within its protective husk. The contrast with his clothes underscored his physical density, suggested his compactness, went so far as to give some idea of the texture of his skin, to alert the fingertips to the feel of his warmth and the nostrils to his body's robust, musky scent. All over the surface of his rounded limbs and depending on the disposition of the creases they produced there hung a heady aura as enthralling as a siren's song. However partial the view I took of him, I sensed in him a dimension other than that of a statue, which one can always walk around and which is never more than a constructed thing: if I had walked round this young man lost in the execution of his sketch, I should have discovered nothing more of him, because there would always be a part of him hidden from me and because, even as I saw him now, his total presence was registering itself within my eyes along with everything they could not perceive.

He was rich with all these possibilities that were holding me in thrall as no work of art could ever do, and I was astonished that between the bronze David and the figures of visitors moving around the museum, sometimes almost touching him, his eyes should never, like mine upon him, be tempted to prefer them to his model. None of those who hovered round him in the hope of catching a glimpse of his sketch could make any claim to rival the anatomical perfection of the David, for they were no more than visitors gorging on potted culture or paying tribute to art snobbery, who, finding themselves there like a flock of Martians to whom the visit to the Musée d'Orsay had been prescribed as a necessary rite of passage, could no more be distinguished one from the other than sheep or geese. But in that crowd united by the garish motley of their shapeless attire, there was no lack of individuals who appeared isolated in the grip of an authentic wonder, which their generous candor offered up to the eyes, making them easy preys.

The young man went on working imperturbably at his sketch. By abstracting himself to such an extent, throwing himself so openly into the very fascination that had cast its spell on him, he almost began to offer an obscene spectacle of himself. His gaze probably penetrated further than anyone else's the work of the sculptor, because he knew what was at stake, having experienced it himself, and he was able to restore to the bronze the throb of living matter, the emotion of which the statue remained as it were only the skeleton. He probably could live along with every thumb-thrust in the working of the clay or the plaster that, in some imperceptible manner, the metal would reflect: The planes building the abdomen, the rounding of the belly contained within the angled seam of the groin, the thrust of the haunch, the setting of the thigh, and even the smooth buckler of the chest, neatly buttoned by the two tiny nipples, presented innumerable slight irregularities that lent the reflections of the patina enveloping the body a vibration discovering so much to the adoring gaze, the emotional caresses the artist had employed to bring this David to life, even though his vigorous stance and his indifferent expression distance him from them, allowed him to disdain them. Perhaps the young man was even able to reach back to the model the lover's expert fingers had touched, discovering things he himself was ignorant of, awakening a different being, allowing the release of a complete personality, sovereign and imperious.

A blond youth of about twenty, wearing the lightest of garments, which nevertheless did not stand out from the extremely casual dress of the majority of the visitors but tended to catch the eye because of the provocative grace of the wearer's body, approached in all innocence and joined the changing group of observers around the young student. While the others kept moving and, once they had managed to cast a glance at the sketch, wandered away, anxious to get the museum visit over as quickly as possible, the blond youth seemed to be taking up a prolonged pose beside this unusual attraction, as if determined not to let any of it escape his attention. His rather offhand aplomb did not exclude a certain respect, for he kept at some distance, not so much curious about what the young man was drawing as surprised that he should be doing it in such conditions. One leg placed in front of the other, hands on hips like a basketball player following a match from the sidelines, he stood contemplating him with a somewhat baffled attention that left one free to take him all in at leisure. He was not so much dressed as undressed in a sort of tank top of exiguous cut open loosely on the suntanned skin of his torso, his flanks, its narrow straps becoming even narrower in the shoulder hollows, between the rounded joint of the arms and the swelling of the trapezius muscles. His fluorescent silk running shorts were slit up the sides to the hips, thus uncovering the thighs as far as the groin, which allowed a view of the entire network of their oblong muscles with their hard bulging surfaces, whose indolent heaviness of flesh was outlined in rich curves at the back. And the sneakers, with their color-banded socks, added to the impression of disproportionate height, setting off to even greater advantage the elegance of those long, smooth, bronzed legs culminating in well-rounded buttocks made even more pronounced by the incurving back.

The incongruous impression given by this athlete let loose in a museum compelled a certain sympathetic feeling when one realized the extent of his naïveté as expressed in his attitude. The tilt of his head, interrupting the robust lines of his upright stance, increased the sense of vulnerability in his shaven, boyish undefended nape, while his head was topped by a dense straw-blond shock of hair that hung like a visor down to the almost dumbfounded eyes: and under the rather pronounced thrust of the nose the already well-blocked lips were puffed out in a dreamy pout. The youth's radiance, probably, but even more the insistence of his gaze, finally got the better of the young art student's concentration. He shot him a few sharp glances.

It could only have been a reflex caused by irritation, but how could a lover of youthful bodies not have been struck by the appearance of this artless observer? What could Antonin Mercié's David mean to him from now on? What work of art, whether Michelangelo's David, Polyclitus's bronze Doryphorus, or the Hermes of Praxiteles, could have had sufficient magnetism to stand up to the competition offered by a living male whose presence commanded the eyes to this extent? It was not so much the effect of a peripheral disturbance coming to disrupt the attention like some sound that reaches the ear and interrupts one's reading or writing, but rather a fundamental reassessment of the activity he was engaged in, of the work he had so far accomplished in his study of the David, of its underlying implications, of the choice he had made of it, even of the career upon whose course he was embarked. The gaze and the presence of this youth wrenched him away from his own contemplation of the statue, away from his own life story, from his melancholy, perhaps from certain homesick feelings.

It was the means the student had considered most apt to bring him to the self-realization he had been counting on as both a reward and a relaxation of his efforts. With the consciousness of the presence of this living body, so moving in its attentiveness, so attractive in its immobility, he could hardly now go on being faithful to the means Antonin Mercié had employed to express, through the figure of his David, his own sensibility, to compose a chapter in his life story, bring his own contribution to the immemorial interrogation—what does the quality of a skin consist in, what determines the aura of someone's bearing, explains the grace imposed by a person's movements?

The young man could no longer concern himself with the personality of a sculptor confronted by intentions that, in the cells of genius, presided over the elaboration of forms adopted by the human species and are so fascinating that there is no natural curiosity, no picturesque site, no grand landscape vista, which can produce upon us the effects created by a human body through the play of its luxuriant flesh, through the disposal of its various and concerted muscles, through the limitless assemblages of its incarnations and its types, thanks to which every creature is unique; through the infinite depths from which a certain look appears, from which expressions rise to the surface, from which an inexplicable and overwhelming impulse derives that makes it limitless and floods our very being with its powers, to the point of making us ill, or sending us mad.

The blond angel's scrutinizing gaze, following the looks the young man had been giving him, suggested a slight discomfiture. He in no way modified his stance and even clung to it pugnaciously, but there could be no doubt that he had been disturbed, in prey to that emotion which grinds the guts, accelerates the heartbeats, travels down the spine with an icy dagger before emerging on the surface of the skin in the form of gooseflesh. I thought I could detect beneath his bronzed cheeks the beginnings of a blush.

It was certainly a realization of the extent of the young man's concentration that had impressed him first of all: at once he had admired that depth of observation that gave a premonition of the moving force his gaze must exert upon whatever became its object. Now that the object had become himself, he asked for nothing better than that he should be subjected to that look again, though in a less hostile manner, so as better to appreciate its import. What he had just experienced in an overfurtive way he thought he could already feel again, in a diffused way still, yet adding to the young man's attractiveness like some kind of cosmetic applied to a complexion grown pale with effort, to features refined by the gravity of his task; feel in that body whose outlines informed its garments with a sensuality hinting at a certain competence in the matter of sexual pleasure: in that sober elegance, finally, that the youth envied in him—he whose need for freedom in his movements made him choose clothes offering a minimum of constriction.

The young man looked at him again. This time his look was not that offended response by which we seek to reprove the effrontery of someone who, in weighing us, allows himself to transform us into a mere prop for his phantasms. It was a fairly gentle look despite the severity his features preserved, a penetrating look that sought out the deepest depths of the other and mingled them with his own unformulated aspirations. Above and beyond the luminous surface of his bronzed flesh, of the volumes of his figure exposed so unrestrainedly, and of the virginal blue of his eyes, the young man plunged deep into the youth's night and at the same time poured forth his own hidden profundities, similarly filled with contradictory movements, with confused tendencies, with buried latencies of which he was not the master and that he allowed himself to display to him in a sort of dumb stupor.

He had forgotten the bronze David. The young man felt as out of countenance as the youth was in looking at him, amid the dizzying crowd of visitors and the no less dizzying conglomeration of works of art, each of which was a crystallization of these same obscure movements, these same unformed desires, these same undefined hopes, as those that their vision of one another unleashed in them both. Nothing in their postures suggested they were getting ready to meet one another or even thinking of doing so, doubtless precisely because their meeting was already taking place: everything having crumbled around them, they found themselves alone together in a wilderness.

All the energy that had been required of the young man to effect the slow and delicate approach to the bronze David found itself swept away in the attention he was now giving to the apparition of this youth, and this time not to inscribe it within him, in his sensibility, as on a sheet of paper, a canvas, or in a lump of clay, but by utterly losing himself in him without hope of obtaining anything whatsoever, in a pure and gratuitous impulse. It had only needed the manifestation of this miraculous body, without any trait in common with the David of Antonin Mercié, for the young man to aspire to nothing more than its contemplation, even though—when in his eyes no other body could exist for him but that of the blond, golden youth, his gaze was already drinking him in to the full—he had already exhausted him and was demanding another pose, wanting to see him in movement, longed to watch him stretching his limbs, imagining twists and contortions that would alter the present stance, deform it, fragment it, perhaps. He found himself up against a block of flesh whose tan gave it an imperishable aspect. He was sliding over the smoothness of a skin without wrinkles or traces of any wound, any disgraceful stigma. He was being blinded by the intense radiance that the pressure of the muscles diffused around their swelling protrusions, at the ball of the knee, in the ogive of the abdominal wall, on the bosses of the pectoral cage, on the shoulders. He was losing himself in the tangle of more or less well-defined lines depending upon the amplitude acquired by the volumes they contained as they curved, hollowed, flexed, expanded, or contracted. He kept wondering what further powers this human figure might possess, coming to realize that its grace depended not simply upon its youthfulness, since it was something unique and annihilated everything he had seen until then, but upon qualities within the boy who was also their creator. From his athletic appearance, his well-proportioned muscularity, his resolute yet open posture, the young man concluded he was of a frank, forceful temperament, more inclined to activity than to any depth of thought, yet not closed to all ideals and even sensitive, borne along by gusts of tenderness that he did not know where or how to direct. The young student was led to apprehend in him a solitary creature, a being hungry for warmth and comprehension concealed within that luminous casket enshrined in such untrammeled forms. He gave promise of an originality all the more desirable in that it was being offered openly to him, and that in a certain sense he was contributing to its revelation, for the boy had never exhibited himself with a conscious desire to do so.

The youth was not becoming exactly embarrassed or ashamed but was visibly showing uneasiness, uncertain as to the young man's appreciation of him. He retained the tilt of his head, a submissive, almost fearful air. He did not hide the fact that he had had the brutal and almost painful revelation that until now he had been unaware of the need for the other's presence: there had been no premonition of what happiness might be, lit by the illumination of the other's face—unable to define it, imagine it, dream of it, even unable to explain it to himself. For his part, the young man did not understand that this boy whose eyes must still be filled with the museum's works of art could take *him* as the one object worthy of his attention in it, as a touchstone more precious than any masterpiece. He lowered his eyes. He turned a leaf in his sketchbook. He turned to face the youth more directly; he began the sketch.

The youth felt that first pencil stroke, or at least the precision in the gaze that attacked the outlines of his body, as the annoying contact of some presumptuous liberty taken with his person: he arched his back in a reaction of withdrawal, had a fleeting impulse to turn on his heels. But he controlled himself, and even though his flesh preserved signs of contraction, he did his best to take up the pose again, taking the initiative to pose of his own accord, thus eliminating any possible ambiguity in the stance he had struck.

The young man first applied his pencil to the legs. The one supporting the weight of the body was straighter than the other, its muscles compressing their volumes in oblique lines and tending to present themselves in the form of an inverted cone whose base stood out level with the pelvic area displaced by the hip-shot stance. The forward leg, barely bent, was on the contrary developing a relief all curves, hollows, rounded forms, like sea-smoothed stones. The care the young man took to respect these nuances caused him to run his eyes frequently along their hanks of muscle; the crosshatching he used to capture the energy brooding beneath the surface of their swellings and to express the skin's patches of radiance, which were like the flashes scattered from his eyes, finally made the boy comprehend what devotion lay behind them, and as if at a sudden caress, a shiver made the fine blond down on his legs stand on end. He flexed his knees gently.

It became more difficult for him to mask his emotion caused by the young man's gaze and the movement of the pencil when he attempted to follow the sinuosities of the arms akimbo to the torso, returning to and lingering over the hands set flat in the hollows of the waist, detailing the fingers caught in the soft lower folds of the tank top whose creases they were ruffling, and the veins in them that he felt he was almost brushing with his lips, so moved was he by them; then his pencil traveled up along the forearm as if he were sliding the bracelet of his firm grasp on it, releasing its grip on the smooth globes of the biceps before focusing the clustered beams of his eyes upon the shoulder joints, as if he had been calmly taking them in the hand vise of his palms.

The youth gave the impression of stiffening his pose, but the young man facing him could not pursue his task as resolutely. The pencil point roamed round the contour of the shoulder as if to complete the perfection of its rounded shape, lingering upon it in a moment of indecision, while he calculated the volume of the chest awaiting his touch and was moved by the welcoming hollow of the throat, which the deeply scooped front of the vest left completely bare. He tended to lose his control, when his glance happened to cross that of the youth, who was staring at him from beneath the blond lock of hair scything his brow, and to which the movements of the hairs with their separate sparkles gave the violent appearance of a gust of wind. A sidelong ray of light struck his eyes obliquely, filtered through the cornea and emphasized the blue paillettes of the iris, tightly concentrated round the black dot of the pupil. It revealed a look both bewildered and eager. The youth set his jaws, the pout of his lips underwent slight distortions, as when in order to suppress a desire to bite or to weep one grinds one's teeth. Seeing the young man's expression of perplexity, he tilted his head again but did it so slowly that the latter could not doubt he was inviting him to continue: he got the impression of being captured by those eyes and guided over the whole extent of that torso abandoned to him by the youth's lowered gaze.

Then the pencil point moved like a finger over the robust swellings in which the nape takes root, rose along the squat column of the neck to behind the ears, pressed heavily down on the two thick tendons standing out like cordage; it lingered again on the complex of hills and hollows that built the horizon of the shoulders, and it seemed to the boy as if thumbs, burying themselves in the depressions behind his collarbone while the other fingers were applying their pressure to either side of his neck, were giving him a subtle and relaxing massage. He closed his eyes as he raised his head.

He opened them again when he sensed the young man's ardor spreading to the cleavage and the cushions of his chest, which became more firm under the sensation they were experiencing, until the nipples turned hard as studs, so hard that one of them, which happened to be under one of the tank top straps, lifted it clear of his flesh, while the other scraped against the edge of the other. The exquisite excitement that resulted became ever keener when the young man, ignoring the pleats and creases of the materials, started stroking the sensitive bumps of the abdominal wall with a multitude of light touches like featherweight caresses, like the fluttering of eyelids, like kisses, and roamed all along the flanks, swallowed up the navel, and went as far as to encompass, under the belly's brimming cup, the pleat that the superimposed tissues of the slip and the running shorts bunched round the loaded scrotum, the relaxed penis like a spring beginning to uncoil, rising inside its restraining pouch. A small, spreading stain was beginning to show on the shiny silk.

The youth gave his bent leg a slow rocking movement. Beneath the gilded hedgehog of his fallen locks, his candid gaze took on an expectant look, his pouting lips an imploring fullness. The young man smiled. His face lost its somber look, his forehead shone, his eyes sparkled under the clear-cut arches of his eyebrows. He seemed about to be getting ready to join his model, but in a sudden movement he dropped his pencil. When he raised his head after bending down to retrieve it, he saw in the distance and making violent gestures characteristic of insouciant foreign youths ignorant of our good manners a pretty girl trying to attract the attention of the youth still turned toward him, still holding his pose, as if locked in their intimate relationship, and gazing more fervently than ever into the young man's eyes as the girl rushed up to him: but his look became panic-stricken, then brokenhearted, then ashamed, as his girlfriend seized him by the arm, started kissing his shoulder, enveloping him and dragging him away in the swirling visitors toward the masterpieces she was determined to view again with him at her side.

# ~ Reinaldo Arenas ~

## *Mona*

### TRANSLATED BY DOLORES M. KOCH

*Foreword*

A peculiar bit of news appeared in the international press in October of 1986. Ramón Fernández, twenty-seven, who had come to the United States in the Mariel exodus from Cuba, was arrested at the Metropolitan Museum of Art as he "attempted to knife" the Mona Lisa, Leonardo da Vinci's famous painting, valued at a hundred million dollars.

Most of the newspaper reports offered basic information on the artist and his masterpiece, then speculated that Mr. Fernández was one of the many mental patients who were expelled from Cuba in the 1980 Mariel boatlift. The museum's exhibit of the famous painting would be extended until the fifteenth of November, 1986, by special permission from the Louvre. That was all they said, and whether it was for reasons of diplomacy or out of ignorance, they omitted a minor detail: Mitterrand's French government would pocket five million dollars for the "courtesy" of having allowed the Mona Lisa to cross the Atlantic. It is interesting to note that the press—especially that in the U.S.—emphasized the fact that the suspect, a presumed mental case, was a *marielito*. Also of interest is the media's reference to an attempt to knife the painting, when according to all the evidence, including the suspect's confession, the assault weapon was a

REINALDO ARENAS, *born in Cuba in 1943, was persecuted under Fidel Castro. In 1990 he committed suicide in New York in the last stage of AIDS. In his memoirs he said: "A sense of beauty is always dangerous and antagonistic to any dictatorship because it implies a realm extending beyond the limits that a dictatorship can impose on human beings."*

hammer. . . . A few days later, on October 17, the *New York Times*, deep in one of its back pages, printed a brief account of the strange death of the detainee Ramón Fernández: "The young man from Cuba who attempted to destroy Leonardo da Vinci's masterpiece was found strangled in his prison cell this morning. He had been waiting to make his first court appearance. Oddly," the reported added, "the suicide weapon is still a mystery." Aware of the detainee's mental condition, the authorities had deprived him of his belt and shoelaces. The prisoner seemed to have strangled himself with his bare hands. No one from the outside had visited Mr. Fernández who, according to the warden, had spent his six days of incarceration in a highly agitated state, writing what appeared to be a long letter—which he subsequently mailed to one of his Cuban friends in exile. The warden declared that because this was a special case, he had taken the precaution of reading this document (obtained through a policeman who had pretended to befriend Mr. Fernández), and it confirmed the inmate's state of extreme mental disturbance. After photocopying the letter, he had it mailed to its addressee, "since it added nothing (sic) to the evidence." Two days later, while the front pages gave coverage to Mother Teresa's suicide, only a few newspapers reported that Ramón Fernández's body had mysteriously disappeared from the morgue, where it was awaiting the arrival of the forensic physician and the district attorney. Thus ends the more or less hard news regarding the case, news that began with a confused bit of information (the so-called knifing of the Mona Lisa) and ended similarly (with the apparent suicide of the suspect). In the confident wisdom so characteristic of ignorance, the yellow press sniffed a crime of passion behind all this. . . . Needless to say, a flock of magazines and New York tabloids—those called liberal because they are ready to defend any enemy empire against the American empire—headed by the *Village Voice,* reported the events differently: Ramón Fernández was an anti-Castro Cuban terrorist who, in clear opposition to the socialist French government, had attempted to destroy that country's most treasured work of art. And as if this were not enough to grant us Cubans the status of troglodytes, a libelous Hispanic rag published in New Jersey and funded by a Cuban extremist, Luis P. Suardíaz, wrote a blazing editorial in praise of Fernández's "patriotic deed," saying that his "action" had served to draw the French government's attention to the case of Roberto Bofill, a Cuban who had gained political asylum in the French embassy in Havana and had repeatedly been denied an exit permit by Fidel Castro.

Six months have passed since the mysterious death of Ramón

Fernández. *La Gioconda* has returned to her home in the Louvre. The case appears to be closed.

There is someone, however, who won't easily accept the hasty closing of this case, particularly after twice having had the privilege of gracing the pages of the *New York Times*, as well as being published in several other journals. That person is none other than the author of these lines, Daniel Sakuntala, the recipient of the long testimony produced by Ramón Fernández. The police handed it to me, a week after Ramón's death, in an attempt to find out if there had been any compromising or murky dealings between the "suicide suspect" and myself. They intended to watch my reactions and follow my every step, and I am sure they did.

As soon as I received the manuscript from my friend Ramoncito, whom I had met in Cuba, I tried to publish it in a serious newspaper or magazine, but all the editors agreed with the dull-witted police, saying that this testimony was the product of a hallucinating or deranged mind and that anyone who dared publish it would be ridiculed. Since I found no serious publication willing to make the text known, I contacted Reinaldo Arenas, as a last resort, to see if he would print it in his magazine, *Mariel*. But Arenas, with his proverbial frivolity* and in spite of the fact that he was already very sick with AIDS, the cause of his recent death, laughed at my suggestion, saying that *Mariel* was a modern magazine in which there was no room for this "nineteenth-century tale." To compound the insult, he told me to take it to the director of *Linden Lane Magazine*, Carilda Oliver Labra. . . . My guess is that Reinaldo had met Ramoncito in Cuba, and Ramoncito, who was attracted only to real women, had completely ignored Reinaldo. But that is another story, which reminds me of the time when Ramoncito, my friend and brother, slapped Delfín Proust in a crowded bus in Havana because Delfín had suddenly grabbed at his fly. . . . Well, no respectable publication was willing to print my friend's desperate testimony. Perhaps if it had been taken seriously from the start, his life would have been saved.

Since I hope it will save the lives of many other young and handsome men, such as he was, I am taking it upon myself to promulgate this docu-

---

*Besides being frivolous, Arenas was a real ignoramus. As evidence of this, let me point out that in his short story "End of a Story," he mentions a statue of Jupiter atop the Chamber of Commerce in Havana, when everybody knows that crowning the cupola of that building is a statue of the god Mercury. —D.S.*

ment, using all the means at my disposal. Here is the text, with only a few clarifying notes added. I sincerely hope that someone, someday, will take it seriously.

DANIEL SAKUNTALA

*New York, 1987*

## EDITORS' NOTE

Before presenting this testimony by Ramón Fernández, it seems advisable to clarify a few points. Daniel Sakuntala was unable to publish this document during his lifetime in spite of tenacious efforts. In the end, it seems that his economic situation prevented him. We have a copy of a letter from Editorial Playor, asking two thousand dollars in advance for the "printing of the booklet." The text was published in New Jersey more than twenty-five years ago, in November 1999, after Mr. Sakuntala's mysterious disappearance (the body was never found) near Lake Ontario. The publishers were Ismaele Lorenzo and Vicente Echurre, the editors then of the magazine *Unveiling Cuba*—who themselves have recently also disappeared, together with most of the copies of the book. (Unconfirmed rumors indicate that these senior citizens returned to Cuba after the invasion of Havana by Jamaica in alliance with other Caribbean islands and, of course, Great Britain.) As for Reinaldo Arenas, mentioned by Mr. Sakuntala, he was a writer of the 1960s generation, justly forgotten in our century. He died of AIDS in the summer of 1987 in New York.

Because of the number of printing errors in the first edition of this document and then its near disappearance, we are proud to present this edition as the true first edition. For that reason, we have left unchanged Ramón Fernández's idiosyncratic expressions, as well as Daniel Sakuntala's notes and those of Messrs. Lorenzo and Echurre, even though by now they may seem (or be) anachronistic or irrelevant.

*Monterey, California, May 2025*

### *Ramón Fernández's Testimony*

This report is being written in a rush, and even so, I am afraid I won't be able to finish it. She knows where I am and any moment now will come to destroy me. I am saying *she,* and perhaps I should say *he;* though I don't know what to call *that thing.* From the beginning, she (or he?) ensnared me, confused me, and now is even trying to prevent me from writing this statement. But I must do it; I must do it, and in the clearest way possible. If I can finish it and someone reads it and believes it, perhaps I could still be saved. The authorities in this prison are certainly not going to do anything for me. That I know very well. When I told them that I needed not to be left alone, that I wanted them to lock me up and have someone watch over me day and night, they broke up laughing. "You're not important enough to deserve special security," they said. "But don't you worry, you won't be able to get out of this place anyway." "My problem is not that I want to get out," I told them. "What worries me is that someone might be able to get in. . . ." "Get in? Here no one gets in of his own free will, and you better be quiet unless you want us to put you to sleep right now." I was going to insist, but before opening my mouth again, I looked at one of the officers and saw in his eyes that sneering attitude of a free human being who looks down upon a madman, an imprisoned one at that. And I realized they were not going to listen to me.

The only thing left for me to do is to write, to describe the events, to write the whole thing up quickly and in a logical manner, as logical as my situation allows, and see if someone finally believes me and I am saved, though that is very unlikely.

Since I came to New York—and that was more than six years ago—I have worked as a security guard at the Wendy's on Broadway between 42nd and 43rd streets. It is open twenty-four hours a day, and since I had the night shift, my job was always very lively, dealing with many different kinds of people. Without overlooking my responsibilities, I had the opportunity to meet many women who came in for a snack or who just passed by, and from my post behind the glass wall and in my well-pressed and gold-braided uniform, I beckoned them in. Of course, not all of them took the bait, but many did. I want to make very clear that I am not bragging. One night, in just one shift, I managed to have three women (not including the Wendy's cashier, a very solid black woman I made it with in the ladies' room). The trouble came at quitting time: the three of them were waiting for me. I managed somehow, but this is no time to go into it. I left with the one I liked best, though I was really sorry I had to give up the other two. I have no family in this country, and all my lovers and even friends have been these nameless women whom I spotted while at my post at Wendy's or who (and I say this without any false modesty) spotted me and came in with the pretext of having a cup of tea or something.

One night I was on the alert, watching the street and looking for a woman worthy of a wink, when a truly extraordinary female specimen stopped outside. Long reddish hair, ample forehead, perfect nose, fine lips, and honey-colored eyes that looked me over openly (a bit shamelessly) through long false eyelashes. I must confess, she struck me instantly. I straightened my uniform jacket and took a good look at her body, which even under bulky winter clothes promised to be as extraordinary as her face. I was fascinated. Meanwhile, she came in, took off the stole or cape she had around her shoulders and uncovered part of her breasts. That same night we agreed to meet at three o'clock in the morning, when I finished my shift.

She told me her name was Elisa, that she was of Greek ancestry, and that she was in New York for just a few weeks. This was enough for me to invite her to my room on 43rd Street, on the West Side, only three blocks away. Elisa accepted without hesitation, which pleased me enormously because I don't like women who play hard-to-get before going to bed with you. These are the ones who later, when you want to get rid of them, make your life unbearable. Since I didn't want to have that kind of trouble at Wendy's, I stayed away from this kind of "difficult" women, who later, when you are not interested anymore, become quite a nuisance, capable of following you all the way to Siberia if necessary.

But with Elisa—let's keep calling her Elisa—that was no problem. From the start, she laid her cards on the table. She obviously liked me and wanted to go to bed with me often before returning to Europe. So I did not ask her any more personal questions (if you want to have a good time with a woman, never ask her about her life). We went to bed, and I must confess that in spite of all my experience, Elisa surprised me. She possessed not only the imagination of a real pleasure-seeker and the skills of a woman of the world but also a kind of motherly charm mixed with youthful mischief and the airs of a grand lady, which made her irresistible. Never had I enjoyed a woman so much.

I noted nothing strange in her that night, except for a peculiar pronunciation of certain words and phrases. For instance, she would begin a word in a very soft, feminine tone and end it in a heavy voice, almost masculine. I supposed it was due to her lack of knowledge of the Spanish language, which she adamantly insisted on speaking after I told her I was Cuban, though I had proposed, for her convenience, that we speak English. I could not help but laugh when she told me (perhaps to empathize with my Caribbean origins) that she had been born near the Mediterranean. I laughed not because being born there was funnier than having come into this world somewhere else but because she pronounced each syllable of the word *Mediterráneo* in a different voice. It seemed you were listening not to one woman but to five, each different from the other. When I pointed this out, I noticed that her beautiful forehead wrinkled.

Next day was my day off, and at dinnertime she suggested going to Plum's, an elegant restaurant that did not concur with the state of my wallet. I informed her of that fact, and she, looking at me intently but with a bit of mockery, invited me to be her guest. I accepted.

At the restaurant that evening, Elisa did something that puzzled me. The waiter, in this fancy place, forgot to bring us water. I signaled him several times. The man would promise it right away, but the water was not forthcoming. Unexpectedly, Elisa grabbed the vase adorning our table, removed the flowers, and drank the water. She quickly replaced the flowers and continued our conversation. She did this so naturally that anyone would have thought that drinking the water from a flower vase was the normal thing to do. . . . After dinner we went back to my room, and I enjoyed again, even more than before, the pleasures of her incredible body. At dawn, half asleep, we were still kissing. I remember at one point the strange sensation of having close to my lips the thick underlip of some animal and quickly turned the light on. Next to mine, fortunately, I had only the lips of the most beautiful woman I had ever met. So fascinated was I with Elisa that I accepted her idea of my not going to Wendy's that night, which was a Monday. She claimed that it was the only day in the week that she could spend with me, and proposed taking a ride on my motorcycle (a 1981 Yamaha) out of the city. Across the Hudson, on the New Jersey side, Elisa asked me to stop for a look at the New York skyline. I knew that for a foreigner (and a tourist, given her carefree manner), the panoramic view of Manhattan, its towers like sierras, today mysteriously disappearing in fog, had to be impressive. Even I, so used to this panorama that I seldom took the time to look at it anymore, felt the enchantment of the view and seemed to perceive an intense glow radiating from the tallest buildings. This was rather strange, since at that time, close to eleven in the morning, the skyscrapers had no reason to be lit. I turned to tell Elisa, but she, leaning on the railing, facing the river, was not listening to me. She was as if transported, looking at the strange luminosity and muttering unintelligible words that I assumed were in her mother tongue. To bring her back from her soliloquy, I approached her from behind and put my hands on her shoulders, which were covered by a heavy woolen stole. A chill ran down my spine. One of her shoulders seemed to bulge out sharply, as if the bone was out of joint and in the shape of a hook. To make sure there was a deformity that inexplicably I had not discovered until then, I felt her shoulder again. There was no deformity, however, and through the fabric my hand caressed her warm, smooth skin. Then I thought that surely I must have touched a safety pin or a shoulder pad, now back in place. At that moment Elisa turned to me and said that we could go on whenever I wished.

We got on the motorcycle, but I couldn't get it to start. I inspected it carefully and finally told Elisa that I thought we could not continue our trip. My cycle had finally given out, and it would be better if we left it right there and took a taxi back to Manhattan. Elisa wanted to examine the motor herself. "I know about these things," she explained with a smile. "In my country I have a Lambretta"—that's what she said—"which is similar to this." Mistrusting her mechanical skills, I stepped aside to the lookout on the Hudson and lit a cigarette. I had no time to finish it. Giving its characteristic explosion, the starting motor began to roar.

Elated, we dashed off. Elisa suggested we take I95 North to a little mountain town near the route to Buffalo. The higher we climbed, the more radiant the autumn noon became. The trees, deep crimson, appeared to be on fire. The fog had dissipated, and a warmish glow seemed to envelop everything. I kept glancing at Elisa in the rearview mirror; she had an expression of sweet serenity. It gave me such pleasure to see her like this, with her look of mysterious abandon, her face against the forest background, that I kept watching her in the little mirror, spellbound. Once, instead of her face, I thought I saw the face of a horrible old man, but I attributed this to our speed, which distorted images. . . . During the afternoon, we reached the mountains, and before dark we stopped at a town on a hill, with one- and two-story houses. More than a town, it looked like a promontory of whitewashed stones, above which rose a pure white church steeple so old that it did not seem to belong in America. Elisa cleared up the mystery for me. The town had been founded in the eighteenth century by a group of European immigrants (Spaniards and Italians), who chose such a remote location in order to be able to hold on to their old traditions. They were peasant folk, and according to Elisa, though they had arrived in 1760, they were still living as if in the Middle Ages. And it was indeed a small medieval city, despite its electricity and running water, and its location on the foothills of a New York mountain.*

I was not surprised at Elisa's knowledge of architecture and history. I have always thought that Europeans, simply by being Europeans, know more about the past than Americans do. Up to a point, if you allow me, they *are* the past.

～ ～ ～

The prison bell is ringing; it's dinnertime, and I run. There, among the inmates and their shouting, and in the midst of all the clatter of dishes and silver, I feel more secure than here, alone in my cell. To urge myself on, I vow that right after dinner I will continue writing this report.

～ ～ ～

Now I am in the prison library. It is eleven P.M. I am thinking that if nothing had happened, I would now be at Wendy's in my blue uniform with gold braid, behind the glass wall, protected from the cold and inspecting with my clinical eye every woman who passes by. But I have no time for women now. I am imprisoned here for a crime I have not committed, but given my status as a *marielito*, it is the same as if I had. I am waiting here not for my sentence, which by now obviously does not worry me much, but for Elisa, who, as soon as she can, will come and kill me.

But let's go back a few days to the night we spent in that old mountain town so dear to Elisa. After walking around for a while, we entered a restaurant that looked like a Spanish inn, something like La Bodeguita del Medio—The Little Inn in the Middle of the Block—a popular restaurant

---

*Obviously the city Ramoncito refers to is Syracuse, in northern New York State. It's named for Siracusa, port and province of Italy, the land of Archimedes and Theocritus, and location of a famous Greek theater. —D.S.*

*We strongly disagree with Mr. Sakuntala. After traveling throughout New York State, we have concluded that the city visited by Ramón Fernández and Elisa must have been Albany. Only that city has houses that look like "whitewashed stone" and is located on the foothills of a mountain. There is also an old church with an all-white steeple. —Ismaele Lorenzo and Vicente Echurre, 1999*

*We reject both Daniel Sakuntala's and Messrs. Lorenzo and Echurre's theories. The city must be no other than Ithaca, located on a mountain north of New York City. Notice that in his testimony, Mr. Fernández states: "More than a town, it looked like a promontory of whitewashed stones." That is what Ithaca is. The stones are the famous Cornell University, and the white tower that looks like a church is the gigantic pillar that supports the library clock. —Editors, 2025*

in Havana, which I, as a native, was not allowed to visit, except once, when a tourist, a Frenchwoman, invited me. . . . Elisa knew the place well. She knew how to choose the best table and the best dishes on the menu. It was clear she felt completely at home. And her beauty seemed to grow by the minute. She also knew how to pick a hotel; small and comfortable, it looked like a guesthouse. We retired early and made love passionately. I confess that in spite of all my enthusiasm, Elisa was hard to please (What woman isn't!), but I have my ways, and in these matters I always have the last word—even if my companion is a great conversationalist. Yes, I think that by daybreak I had managed to satisfy her completely. She was resting peacefully by my side. Before turning off the light, I wanted to get my fill of that quiet serenity of hers. She had fallen asleep, but her eyes did not remain closed for long. Suddenly I saw them disappear. I screamed in order to wake myself up—I had to have been dreaming—and immediately I could see her eyes, looking at me intently. "I think I had a nightmare," I told her in apology, and embracing her, I said good night. But afterward I was barely able to sleep at all.

Before dawn, Elisa got up and, without making a sound, left the room. I stood behind the window curtains and watched her vanish in the glow of the morning mist, following a yellow path that disappeared among the trees. I decided to stay awake and wait for her, even though I tried to calm myself by thinking that it was natural for someone to get up before dawn and take a walk: a European custom, maybe. I remembered the Frenchwoman who took me to La Bodeguita del Medio: she used to get up at dawn, take a shower, and, still wet, throw herself into bed. . . . About an hour later, I heard Elisa push the door open—I pretended to be asleep. She seemed out of breath. She sat next to me at the edge of the bed and turned off the light. Protected by darkness, I opened my eyes slightly. Facing the early light, her back to me, was a beautiful naked woman who would, any minute now, snuggle into bed with me. Her bottom, her back, her shoulders, her neck, everything was perfect. Except that her perfect body had no head.

Since in the face of the most outlandish circumstances we always search for logical explanations, I rationalized what I had seen as purely an effect produced by the heavy fog usual in that place. Anyway, my instinct told me it was better to keep silent and close my eyes. I felt Elisa sliding into bed next to me. Her hand, with unerring skill, caressed my genitals. "Are you asleep?" she asked. I opened my eyes as if waking up from a deep sleep and saw, next to me, her perfectly serene, smiling face. The color of her hair seemed to have grown even more intense. She kept caressing me, and even though I could not dismiss my misgivings, we embraced until we were totally fulfilled.

～ ～ ～

I have already been imprisoned for three days, and I believe I don't have three more days to live. So I must hurry. . . . This morning I was again shouting that I didn't want to be left alone. By noon the prison psychiatrist was sent to see me. I let him know I was not interested and answered his questions curtly. Not only because I knew he would do nothing for me, since, unfortunately, I am not crazy, but also because his interview, his stupid questions, were a waste of time, a waste of the precious little time I have left and that I must use to finish this story, send it to a friend, and see if he can do anything. Though I doubt it, I must go on.

～ ～ ～

We were back in New York City by nine-thirty in the morning, truly record time. Elisa had kept asking me to go very fast because, she claimed, she had to be at the Greek consulate at ten. At a red light on Fifth Avenue, she suddenly leaped off and began to run, saying that she would come to see me the next day at Wendy's. And she did. She came around nine P.M. to tell me she would be waiting for me when I left work—that is, at three in the morning. This was our agreement. But with all I had seen, or thought I had seen, plus the attraction Elisa exerted on me (or should I call it love?), I concluded that, as a matter of life and death, I had to find out who this woman really was.

On the pretext of sharp stomach pains, I left Wendy's without bothering to take off my uniform, and cautiously began to follow Elisa rather closely. At Broadway and 44th, she made a phone call, then started walking toward the theater district. On 47th Street, someone, who evidently was waiting for her, opened the door of a limousine, and Elisa got in. I was only able to see a masculine hand helping her in. It was easy to get a taxi and follow the limo, which stopped at 172 East 89th Street. The chauffeur opened the door, and Elisa and her companion went into the apartment building. To keep warm, I waited inside a telephone booth. An hour later, that is, around ten-thirty, Elisa came out. With my experience, I could tell that she had enjoyed a long and satisfying sexual encounter. She looked at her watch and started walking toward Central Park. She reached 79th and approached a bench where a young man was sitting, obviously waiting for her. I thought

(I am sure of it) that he was the person Elisa had phoned from Broadway. The dialogue now was as short as the phone call had been. Without any fuss, they disappeared into the shrubbery. Unseen, I was able to watch how quickly and easily the pair coupled. Dry leaves crackled under their bodies, and their panting scared away the squirrels, which clambered up the trees, screeching loudly. The whole thing lasted about an hour and a half, since by twelve-thirty Elisa was taking a leisurely walk in the 42nd Street porno district. Boldly, without any shame, she would ogle the men who passed obviously looking for a woman or something like that. Farther down the street, Elisa stopped in front of a towering, handsome black man standing by the door of a peep show. I was not able to hear their conversation, of course, but it seemed that Elisa got straight to the point: in less than five minutes they were inside one of the booths at the peep show. They stayed locked up in there for more than half an hour. When they came out, the young black man seemed exhausted; Elisa was radiant. It was now two o'clock in the morning, and she was still cruising around the area. A few seconds later I saw her, accompanied by three jocks who looked like hillbillies, enter a booth at the Black Jack peep show. Fifteen minutes later, the door slammed open and she came out, looking quite pleased. I did not wait to see the men's faces. . . . When I saw Elisa (now with a Puerto Rican who looked very much like a pimp) go into another peep show, the one on Eighth Avenue between 43rd and 44th, I realized that my "fiancée" would not come to me late that night, as she had promised. And in spite of what I had been witnessing, I could not but feel a sense of total loss. Elisa was the woman with whom I had fallen in love, for the first time. . . . But at quarter to three, she came out of the peep show and started walking toward Wendy's. To be with her once more, I obliterated everything I had seen and started running, so I'd be there, waiting, when she came. The cashier and the other employees were puzzled to see me taking my post behind the glass wall. Elisa was there in no time, and together we went to my room.

That night in bed she was extraordinarily demanding, more so than ever, which is saying a lot. In spite of my desire and my extensive experience, it was not easy to satisfy her. . . . Though after the encounter I pretended to fall asleep, I did not sleep a wink. What I had seen had left me totally perplexed. Of course, I could not tell her I had spied on her, could not appear jealous, though in all truth I was. Actually, I did not think I had the right to demand fidelity from her, since at no point had we vowed to be faithful to each other.

It was close to nine o'clock in the morning when, while I pretended to be asleep, she woke up, dressed in silence, and went out without saying good-bye. But I was obsessed (though now I regret it) with following that woman and finding out where she lived, who she really was. . . . At 43rd and Eighth she took a taxi. I took another. While following her, nodding in my seat, I wondered if it was possible for Elisa to be on her way to another tryst. She was not. After such a turbulent night, Elisa seemed to want to find inner peace by looking at works of art. At least that is what I thought when I saw her get out of the taxi and hurriedly enter the Metropolitan Museum, just at the moment it was opening its doors. After paying for admission, I rushed inside the building and went up to the second floor, following the route she had taken. I watched her go in one of those large galleries, and right there, in front of my eyes, she disappeared. I looked for her for hours throughout the immense building, without any success. I did not skip any possible corner. I looked behind every statue, went around every amphora (there are some enormous ones) and even searched inside them. On one occasion I got lost among countless sarcophagi and centuries-old mummies, while calling Elisa's name out loud. Once out of that labyrinth, I found myself in a temple of the time of the Ptolemies (according to a placard),* seemingly floating in a pool. I searched everywhere in that enormous pile of stones, but Elisa was not there either. About three in the afternoon I went back to my room and threw myself on the bed.

I woke up at two in the morning. In a rush, I put on my uniform and left for Wendy's. My boss, who had always been pretty decent to me, told me

---

*It is only natural that Ramoncito, who is not used to museums, mixes themes, styles, and periods. The temple he refers to must be that of Ramses II, built at the height of his reign during the nineteenth dynasty, in 1305 B.C., to be exact. It is an enormous red granite mound, where anyone who is not an expert can get lost. —D.S.

The only portion of that temple in the Metropolitan Museum was a stone about six feet tall, impossible for Ramón Fernández to have entered. He must have entered the temple of Debot, which is in fact set in an artificial lake to re-create the original natural setting on the Nile. —Vicente Echurre, 1999

I disagree with my colleague, Mr. Echurre. The temple he is referring to exists, but it is in Madrid. It has surely escaped his memory, and I have tried to refresh it but in vain. Since obviously I must dissent, we have decided to express our opinions individually, no matter how absurd that of my associate might seem. Mine, specifically, is this: the area Mr. Fernández reached in the Metropolitan Museum was the temple, supposedly, of Kantur, which once belonged to Queen Cleopatra and which in 1965, thanks to the efforts of President John F. Kennedy, UNESCO sold to the United States for twenty million dollars. It was discovered later that this transaction

that this was no time to start working; it was almost time to leave. I detected a tinge of sadness in his voice when he informed me that next time this happened I would be fired. I assured him there would be no next time, and I went back to my room. Elisa was waiting by the door. I was not even surprised that she had been able to enter my building, though the front door is always locked and only the tenants have keys. She said she had been at Wendy's several times and I was not there, so she decided to wait for me in my house. We went into my room, and perhaps because I had slept for hours or because I was afraid I would never see her again, I made love to her with renewed passion. Yes, that night, I believe, I was the clear victor. But how many duels—I sadly asked myself—had she fought today before coming to me? . . . At dawn, when I again started an attack, sliding over her naked body, I saw that Elisa had no breasts. I jumped to the edge of the bed, wondering whether this woman was driving me insane. As if sensing my anguish, she immediately pulled me over with her arms to her beautiful breasts.

As on the previous day, Elisa got up around nine, dressed quickly, and went out. Her destination was the same, the Metropolitan Museum. And again she disappeared in front of my eyes.

She did not come to see me at work Thursday or Friday. On Saturday I got up early, determined to find her. I must add that, independent of all the mystery surrounding her person, which fascinated me, I felt the urge to go to bed with her immediately.

I took a taxi to the Metropolitan. Evidently there was a relationship between Elisa and that building, and I thought it was sort of stupid of me not to have realized before that she must be a museum employee, which explained why she was so interested in getting there at ten o'clock, when the doors opened to the public. My mistake had been to search for her among the visitors instead of in the offices.

I searched for her everywhere. I inquired at the information desk and in the staff office. There was no employee named Elisa. Of course, the fact that she told me her name was Elisa did not mean that was really her name; quite the contrary, perhaps. Anyone who worked among so many valuable

---

*had been a fraudulent one (one of many) carried out in collusion with Mr. Kennedy. UNESCO had sent the original temples to their headquarters in the Soviet Union and a plastic replica to the United States. This highly flammable copy was the cause of the big fire in the Metropolitan Museum. It seems that someone had carelessly dropped a lighted cigarette butt on it. —Ismaele Lorenzo, 1999*

*The only Egyptian temple then in the Metropolitan Museum was that of Pernaabi, from the fifth dynasty, circa 2400 before the Common Era. —Editors, 2025*

objects (which for me, by the way, didn't mean a thing) and carried on sexually as she did, had to take precautions.

So I tried to find her physically among the numerous women who worked at the museum. While I was looking over the female guards, I noticed in one room a large group representing many nationalities (Japanese, South Americans, Chinese, Indians, Germans) gathered around a painting, while several guards, almost shouting, were trying to prevent the taking of photographs. Maybe I can find Elisa among them, I thought, and pushed my way into the crowd. And in fact, there she was. Not among those taking the photos, nor among the guards warning that this was not permitted, but inside the very painting everyone was looking at. I got as close as the red cord that served as barrier between painting and public would allow. That woman, with her straight, dark-reddish hair and perfect features, with one hand placed delicately over the other wrist, was smiling almost impudently, against a background that seemed to be a road leading to a misty lake. The woman was, without any doubt, Elisa. . . . I thought then that the mystery had been solved: Elisa was a famous, exclusive artists' model. That was why it was so difficult to find her. At that moment she was probably posing for another painter, perhaps as good as the one who had made this perfect portrait of her.

Before asking one of the guards where I could find the model for the painting that so many people wanted to photograph, I got closer in order to see it in greater detail. Next to the frame, a small placard stated that it was painted in 1505 by one Leonardo da Vinci. Stunned, I backed up to take a good look at the canvas. My eyes then met Elisa's intense gaze in the painting. I held her gaze and discovered that Elisa's eyes had no eyelashes; she had the eyes of a serpent.

~ ~ ~

The prison bell is again announcing it is bedtime. I will have to continue this report tomorrow. I must rush, since I believe I have no more than two days left to live.

~ ~ ~

Of course, no matter how much the woman in the painting resembled Elisa, it was impossible for her to have been the model. So I quickly tried to find a reasonable explanation for the phenomenon. According to the small catalog at the gallery's entrance, the painting was valued at many millions of dollars (more than eighty million, the catalog read).* The woman in the picture (according to the same catalog) was European. And so was Elisa. The woman in the picture then could be one of Elisa's remote ancestors. Therefore Elisa could be the owner of that painting. And since it was so valuable, Elisa could travel with it for security reasons and would come and inspect it every morning. Then, after checking that nothing had happened to it during the night, which is the time when most thieves choose to operate, she would withdraw to another area of the museum. Now her pains to hide her identity seemed clear to me. She was a nymphomaniac millionaire who, for obvious reasons, had to keep her sexual relationships anonymous.

I have to admit I enjoyed the idea of being associated with a woman who had so many millions. Perhaps, if I played my cards right and pleased her in every way (and this was my heart's desire), Elisa would help me out and I could someday open my own Wendy's. In my enthusiasm I was forgetting the eccentricities and the imperfections, the defects, anomalies, or whatever you want to call them, that at certain moments I detected in her.

Now the only thing I had to do was to be pleasant, to show no interest in money, and not to bother her with indiscreet questions. I bought a bunch of roses from a stand that, being on Fifth Avenue, charged me fifteen dollars, and I went to wait for Elisa at the front entrance of the museum, because if she was inside—and I was sure she was—sooner or later she would have to come out. But she did not. With my bunch of roses, I remained at my post, under a New York drizzle, until ten o'clock, when the museum closed on Fridays.†

---

*It is interesting to note that the value of the painting according to the New York Times was about $100 million, while the catalog quoted $80 million. We believe this was a government trick to raise taxes for the right to exhibit that famous masterpiece in this country. This suspicion was almost absolutely confirmed in 1992 when it was disclosed, on the opening of former President Ronald Reagan's will, that he had owned the New York Times since 1944. The anti-Republican sentiment of that newspaper (which after this scandal was forced to cease publication) was nothing but a political tactic to prevent suspicion. —Lorenzo and Echurre, 1999

†There must have been a special event that day at the museum, since it usually closes at ten only on Wednesdays. —D.S.

The Metropolitan Museum in New York closed at ten o'clock on Wednesdays and Fridays. Mr. Sakuntala's knowledge of these matters is negligible. —Lorenzo and Echurre, 1999

Before the big fire, the Metropolitan Museum was open Tuesdays and Sundays until ten o'clock. We hope that as soon as repairs are completed and the museum reopens, it will have the same schedule. —Editors, 2025

When I got to Wendy's it was eleven P.M. I was three hours late. I was fired then and there. Before leaving, I gave the roses to the cashier.

After walking around Broadway until very late, I returned to my room in a state of depression. Elisa was there, waiting for me. As usual, she was elegantly dressed, and this time she was carrying a camera, a very expensive professional one. I invited her in and told her about my being fired. "Don't worry," she said. "With me on your side, you won't have any problem." And I believed her, thinking of her fortune, and so I asked her to get into bed with me. Because the first thing a man must do to keep on good terms with a woman is to invite her to his bed; even though she may not accept at the beginning, or maybe ever, she will always be grateful. . . . Strangely enough, she did not accept. She asked me to go to bed alone because she had to meditate ("concentrate," I remember now, is the word she used) on a project she had to work on the following day, Saturday—though since the sun was almost out, it was already Saturday.

I thought it was best to obey my future boss, and I went to bed alone though, of course, I did not intend to sleep. Awake but snoring lightly, I observed her discreetly. She walked back and forth in my studio for over two hours while mumbling unintelligible gibberish. I could make out "the inventors . . . the interpreters" at one point. Though I am not even sure of that, for Elisa was talking faster and faster, and her pace seemed to keep rhythm with her words. Finally she took off her splendid dress and went out the window, naked, onto the fire escape. With her hands uplifted and her head tilted back, as if in position to receive an extraordinary gift from the skies (now gray and overcast), she remained outside on the landing for hours, indifferent to the cold and even to a freezing drizzle, which was getting heavier. About one in the afternoon she came back in and, "waking me," said she needed to go do some work in the mountain town we had visited. It seemed she had to take some photos representing the region.

Soon on our way, we got there before dusk. The streets were deserted or, rather, filled with mounds of purple leaves, which moved in eddies from place to place. We stayed at the same hotel (or motel) as before; it was so quiet, we seemed to be its only guests. Before dark we went out into town, and she began to take some photos of houses still in the light. (If I appear in some of those photos, it's because she asked me to pose for her.) We went to the restaurant that reminded me of La Bodeguita del Medio. I noticed that Elisa had a ravenous appetite. Without losing her elegant composure, she downed several portions of soup, pasta, cream sauce, roast, bread, and dessert, besides two bottles of wine. Then she asked me to take her for a walk. The streets were narrow and badly lit, and after coming out of a place that so resembled La Bodeguita del Medio, it seemed as if I were back in Havana during my last years there. But what most brought me back to those days was a sensation of fear, of terror, even, which seemed to emanate from every corner and every object, including our own bodies. Night had fallen, and though there was no moon, there was a radiant luminosity in the sky. The usual evening fog enveloped everything, even ourselves, in a gray mist that blurred all silhouettes. Finally we reached a yellowish esplanade, which no car seemed to have crossed ever before. Elisa was walking ahead with all her equipment. The road narrowed and disappeared between dim promontories that looked like tapering, greenish rocks. Or like withered cypresses linked by a strange viscosity. On the other side of the promontories we came upon a lake, also greenish and covered by the same nebulous vegetation. Elisa deposited her expensive equipment on the ground and looked at me. As she talked, her face, her hair, and her hands seemed to glow.

"*Il veleno de la conoscenza é una della tante calamità di cui soffre l'essere umano,*" she said, her eyes fixed on me. "*Il veleno della conoscenza o al meno quello della curiosità.*"*

"I don't understand a word," I blurted out in all sincerity.

"Well, I want you to understand. I have never killed anybody without first telling him why."

"Who are you going to kill?" I asked her with a smile, to let her know I was not taking her words seriously.

"Listen to me, you fool," she said, stepping away from me while I, pretending not to understand, tried to embrace her. "I know everything you did. Your trips to the museum, your incessant surveillance, your detective

---

*Poor Ramoncito only wrote the phonetic representation of these phrases. With my extensive knowledge of the Italian language (I studied with Giolio B. Blanc), I was able to make the necessary corrections. I must clarify that this is the only correction I have made in the manuscript. The translation into English would read like this: "The poison of knowledge is one of the many calamities humans suffer. The poison of knowledge or, at least, that of curiosity." —D.S.

Even though his translation is correct, we doubt very much that Mr. Sakuntala ever studied with Baron Giolio B. Blanc. The high social status of this nobleman would not have permitted him to rub elbows with people like Mr. Sakuntala, let alone accept him as his tutee, unless there were highly personal motives. —Lorenzo and Echurre, 1999

Giolio B. Blanc was for many years the editor of the magazine Noticias de Arte de Nueva York and therefore had probably met Daniel Sakuntala, who had literary pretensions. —Editors, 2025

work. Your pretended snoring did not fool me either. Of course, until now your stupidity and your cowardice have prevented you from seeing things as they are. Let me help you. There is no difference between what you saw in the painting at the museum and me. We are one and the same thing."

I must confess that it was impossible for me then to assimilate Elisa's words. I asked her to explain in "simpler language," still hoping it was all a joke or the effect of the two bottles of wine.

After she repeated the same explanation several times, I finally got an idea of what she meant. The woman in the painting and Elisa *were* one and the same. As long as the painting existed, she, Elisa, would exist too. But for the picture to exist, she had, of course, to be there. That is, whenever the museum was open, she had to remain there inside the picture—"smiling, impassive, and radiant," as she put it, with a tinge of irony. Once the museum was closed, she could get out and have her amorous escapades like the ones I had participated in. "Encounters with men, the handsomest men I can find," she explained, looking at me, and in spite of my dangerous situation, I could not help but experience some feelings of vanity. . . . "But all those men," continued Elisa, "cannot simply *enjoy,* they want to *know,* and they end up like you, with a vague idea of my peculiar condition. Then the persecution begins. They want to know who I am, no matter what the cost, they want to know everything. And in the end, I have to eliminate them. . . ." Elisa paused for a moment and, glaring at me, continued: "Yes, I like men, and very much, because I am also a man, as well as a genius!" She said this looking at me, and I could see that her anger was mounting; realizing I was facing a dangerous madwoman, I decided it was best to "go with her flow" (as we used to say in Havana), and begging her to control herself, I asked her to tell me about her sex change. "After all," I tried to console her, "New York is full of transvestites, and they don't look so unhappy. . . ." She, completely ignoring my words, explained to me: Not only was Elisa the woman in the painting, but the woman in the painting was also the painter, who had done his self-portrait as he wished to be (the way he was in his mind): a lusty, fascinating woman. But his real triumph was not that he portrayed himself as an alluring woman. "That," she said with scorn, "had already been done by most painters." His true achievement was that through a mustering of energy, genius, and mental concentration—which, she claimed, were unknown in our century—the woman he painted had the ability to become the painter himself and to outlive him. This person (she? he?) would then exist as long as the painting existed, and had the power, when nobody was present, to step out of the painting and escape into the crowds. And in this way she was able to find sexual gratification with the kind of men that the painter, as a man not graced by beauty, had never been able to get. *"But the power of concentration I must muster to achieve all that does not come easily. And now, after almost five hundred years, I sometimes lose the perfection of my physical attributes or even one of my parts, as you on several occasions were astonished to see but could not believe."*

In brief, I was facing a man over five hundred years old who had transformed himself into a woman and also existed as a painting. The situation would have been truly hilarious were it not for the fact that, at that point, Elisa drew from her bodice an ancient dagger, sharp and glimmering nonetheless.

I tried to disarm her, but in vain. With only one hand she overpowered me, and in an instant I was on the ground, the dagger before my eyes. Crouching, and imprisoned under Elisa's legs, I still was able to identify the landscape around us. It was exactly the same as in the famous (and now, for me, accursed) painting at the museum. Something sinister was indeed going on, though I could not determine its extent. Elisa—I will keep calling her Elisa until the end of this report—made me move along in my crouched position until we reached the lakeshore. Once there, I saw it was not a lake but a swamp. This was obviously the place, I thought, where she sacrifices her surely numerous indiscreet lovers.

The alternatives Elisa seemed to be offering me were equally frightful: to die either drowned in that swamp or pierced by the dagger. Or perhaps she had both in mind. Again she fixed her gaze on me, and I understood that my end was near. I started to cry. Elisa took off her clothes. I continued crying. It was not my family in Cuba that I remembered at that moment but the enormous salad bar at Wendy's. To me it was like a vision of my life these last few years (fresh, pleasant, surrounded by people, and problem-free), before Elisa came into it. Meanwhile she lay naked in the mud.

"Let it not be said," she muttered, barely moving her lips, "that we are not parting on the best of terms."

And beckoning me to join her, she kept smiling in her peculiar way, lips almost closed.

I couldn't stop crying, but I came closer. Still holding the dagger, she placed her hand behind my head, quickly aligning her naked body with mine. She did this with such speed, professionalism, and violence that I realized it would be very difficult for me to come out of that embrace alive. . . . I am sure that in all my long erotic experience, never has my performance been so lustful and tender, so skillful and passionate—because in all truth, even knowing she intended to kill me, I still lusted for her. By her third orgasm, while she was still panting and uttering the most obscene words, Elisa had not only forgotten the dagger but become oblivious of herself. I noticed she apparently was losing the concentration and energy that, as she said, enabled her to become a real woman. Her eyes were becoming opaque, her face was losing its color, her cheekbones were melting away. Suddenly her luscious hair dropped from her head, and I found myself in the arms of a very old, bald man, toothless and foul-smelling, who kept whimpering while slobbering my penis. Quickly he sat on it, riding it as if he were a true demon. I quickly put him on all fours and, in spite of my revulsion, tried to give him as much pleasure as I could, hoping he would be so exhausted he would let me go. Since I had never practiced sodomy, I wanted to keep the illusion, even remotely, that this horrible thing, this sack of bones with the ugliest of beards, was still Elisa. So while I possessed him, I kept calling him by that name. But he, in the middle of his paroxysm, turned and looked at me; his eyes were two empty reddish sockets.

"Call me Leonardo, damn it! Call me Leonardo!" he shouted, while writhing and groaning with such pleasure as I have never seen in a human being.

"Leonardo!" I began repeating, then, while I possessed him, "Leonardo!" I repeated as I kept penetrating that pestiferous mound. "Leonardo," I kept whispering tenderly, while with a quick jump I got hold of the dagger, then flailing my arms, I escaped as fast as I could through the yellow esplanade. "Leonardo! Leonardo!" I was still shouting when I jumped onto my motorcycle and dashed away at full speed. "Leonardo! Leonardo! Leonardo!" I think I kept saying, still in a panic, all the way back to New York, as if repeating the name might serve as an incantation to appease that lecherous old man still writhing at the edge of the swamp he himself had painted.

I was sure that Leonardo, Elisa, or "that thing" was not dead.

What's more, I think I'd managed to do no harm at all to it. And if I did, would a single stab be enough to destroy all the horror that had managed to prevail for over five hundred years and included not only Elisa but the swamp, the sandy road, the rocks, the town, and even the ghostly mist that covered it all?

That night I slept in the home of my friend the Cuban writer Daniel Sakuntala.\* I told him I had problems with a woman and did not want to sleep with her in my apartment. Without giving him any more details, I presented him with the dagger, which he was able to appreciate as the precious jewel it was. Would it solve any problem, I wondered, if I told him of my predicament? Would he believe me?† Right now, only two days away from my imminent demise, when there is no way out for me, I am telling my story mainly as an act of pure desperation and as my last hope, because nothing else is left for me to do. At least for now, I realize how very difficult it is for anyone to believe all this. Anyway, before the little time I have left runs out, let me continue.

Of course I did not, even remotely, consider going back to my room, terrified as I was by the possibility of finding Elisa there. I was sure of only one thing: she was looking for me, and still is, in order to kill me. This is what my own instinct, my experience of fear and persecution, are telling me (and don't forget I lived twenty years in Cuba).

For three days I roamed the streets without knowing what to do and, naturally, without being able to sleep. On Wednesday night I showed up again at Daniel's. I was shaking, not only out of fear but because I was running a fever. Maybe I had caught the flu, or something worse, during the time I was out on the streets.

Daniel behaved like a real friend, perhaps the only one I had and, I believe, still have. He prepared something for me to eat and hot tea, made me take two aspirins, and even gave me some syrupy potion.†† Finally, after so many nights of insomnia, I fell asleep. I dreamed, of course, of Elisa. Her cold eyes were looking at me from a corner of the room. Suddenly that corner became the strange landscape with the promontories of greenish rocks around

---

\* *"Cuban writer Daniel Sakuntala"(!): We question this statement, obviously the product of friendship. Not even the lengthiest of directories register that name.* —Lorenzo and Echurre, 1999

† *A serious error of appreciation on the part of my friend Ramoncito. After studying for more than twenty years and with the superior knowledge I acquired of alchemy, astrology, metempsychosis, and the occult sciences, I would have believed him and could have helped him to conjure away this evil. Had he trusted me, Ramoncito would be alive today. By the way, the dagger he gave me (pure gold, with an ivory handle) has disappeared from my room. I am sure it was taken by a black man from the Dominican Republic who accompanied Renecito Cifuentes when he visited me a few days ago.* —D.S.

†† *The "syrupy potion" I gave him was just Riopan, a stomach relief medication against diarrhea.* —D.S.

a swamp. By the swamp, Elisa was waiting for me. Her eyes were fixed on mine, her hands elegantly entwined below her chest. She kept looking at me with detached perversity, and her look was a command to get closer and embrace her right at the edge of the swamp. . . . I dragged myself there. She placed her hands on my head and pulled me down close to her. As I possessed her, I sensed that I was penetrating not even an old man but a mound of mud. The enormous and pestiferous mass slowly engulfed me while it kept expanding, splattering heavily and becoming more foul-smelling. I screamed as this viscous thing swallowed me, but my screams only produced a dull gurgling sound. I felt my skin and my bones being sucked away by the mass of mud, and once inside it, I became mud, finally sinking into the swamp.

My own screams woke me up so suddenly that I still had time to see Daniel sucking my member. He pretended it wasn't so and withdrew to the opposite side of the bed, making believe he was asleep, but I understood I could not stay there either. I got up, made some coffee, thanked Daniel for his hospitality and allowing me to sleep in his apartment, borrowed twenty dollars from him, and left.*

It was Thursday. I had decided to leave New York before Monday. But with only twenty dollars, where could I go? I saw several acquaintances (Reinaldo García Remos, among them) and offered the key to my room, and everything in it, in exchange for some money. I got a lot of excuses but no cash. Late on Sunday I went to Wendy's, where, as a security guard, I had spent the best part of my life. At the cash register I talked to the stout black woman who had been so good to me (in every sense of the word). She let me have a salad, a quart of milk, and a hamburger, all for free. About five o'clock in the morning, the establishment was deserted and I dozed off on my seat. Another employee who was mopping the second

---

*Out of pure intellectual honesty, I am leaving this passage as it appears in the manuscript by my friend Ramoncito. I want the text to be published in its entirety. But the lascivious abuse he refers to can only be a product of his psychological state and of the nightmare he was having. It is true we slept that night on the same bed; it's the only one I have. I heard him scream, and to bring him out of his delirium, I shook him several times. Naturally, when he woke up, it was logical for him to find my hands on his body. —D.S.*

*We are of the opinion that Ramón Fernández was sexually harassed, as he indicates, by Mr. Sakuntala. The moral history of this character, who disappeared naked into Lake Erie in the midst of a communal orgy, proves our point. —Lorenzo and Echurre, 1999*

*We have already indicated that Daniel Sakuntala disappeared close to the shore of Lake Ontario, where his clothes were found. We have not been able to confirm reports about a supposed orgy. —Editors, 2025*

floor called the cashier to pass on some piece of gossip. While they chatted, I took advantage of the situation and grabbed all the money from the cash register. Without counting it, I ran to Grand Central. I wanted to take a train and go as far as possible. But the three long-distance trains would not leave until nine in the morning. I sat on a bench and, while waiting, began to count the money. There was twelve hundred dollars. I thought this was salvation. By eight A.M. the station was swarming with people—or rather with beasts: thousands of people who pushed and shoved mercilessly to make it to work on time. By nine, I hoped, I would be sitting on a train, fleeing from all those people and, above all, from that thing.

～ ～ ～

But it didn't turn out that way. I was standing in line to buy my ticket when I saw Elisa. She was below the big terminal clock, oblivious to the crowd but with her eyes fixed on me, with her enigmatic smile and her folded hands. I saw her coming my way and started to run toward the tracks. But since I did not have a ticket, I could not get in. Pushing people, and trying to find a place to hide, I went across the room again. But she was everywhere. I remember dashing through the Oyster Bar, colliding with a waiter and upsetting a table on which a number of lobsters were arrayed. At the back door of the restaurant, Elisa was waiting for me. I knew, or sensed, that I could not stay alone with that "woman" a second longer, that the larger the crowd around me, the harder it would be for her to kill me or drag me into her swamp. I began screaming in English and in Spanish, begging for help, while I pointed at her. But the people, the masses of people, rushed by without looking at me. One more madman shouting in the most crowded train station in the world could not alarm anyone. Besides, my clothes were dirty and I had not shaved for a week. On the other hand, the woman I was accusing of attempted assault was a grand lady, serene, elegant, expertly made up and attired. I realized that I was not going to attract anybody's attention by shouting, so I rushed to the very center of the main hall, where it was most crowded, and quickly took off my clothes and stood there, naked. Then I began to jump about in the crowd. Evidently that was more than even a madman is allowed to do in the very center of the city of New York. I heard some police whistles. Arrested, I felt relieved and peaceful, for the first time in many days, as they handcuffed me and shoved me roughly into the patrol car.

Unfortunately, I only stayed overnight at the police station. There was no evidence on which to hold me as a criminal of any sort, and if I was insane—and I quote the officer in charge—"luckily, that would not be a matter for the New York police; otherwise, we would have to arrest almost everybody." As for the money, it had disappeared into the hands of the arresting officers when they searched my clothes. So there was no evidence that I had committed any crime. Of course, among other things, I confessed to being a thief, which was nothing but the truth, and mentioned the money that had been stolen from me. Apparently the police found no computer record of any accusation by the Wendy's management or any report of the loss of that money.*

On Tuesday I was again roaming the streets of Manhattan. The drizzle and strong winds were unbearable, and I had no money at all and no umbrella either, of course. It was eleven A.M. I knew the Metropolitan Museum would be open until seven that evening, so for the moment, at least, I was in no danger. Inside the picture frame, she would now be smiling at all her admirers. It was then (I recall I was crossing 42nd Street) that I had a sort of epiphany. An idea that could really save me. Why hadn't I thought of it before? I blamed myself for being such a fool, particularly when I pride myself on not being a complete idiot. The painting! The painting, of course! There she was, and the swamp, the rocks, the yellow esplanade. . . . Everything the painter had conceived, including even himself, was now in the museum, fulfilling its destiny as a work of art and at the mercy of whoever dared to destroy it.

Back in my room, I took a hammer I use for my occasional carpentry,† and hiding it under my jacket, I rushed to the Metropolitan Museum. There I met with another little inconvenience: I had no money to pay for admission. Of course I could force my way in, but I didn't want to be arrested before doing my work. Finally someone coming out of the building agreed to give me the metal badge that indicates you have paid for admis-

---

*It seems that Ramoncito Fernández had, without being aware of it, a woman who really loved him: Wendy's cashier. From my investigation I learned that out of her salary she had, little by little, covered the so-called embezzlement that occurred while she was in charge, without ever disclosing the name of the thief. Obviously that woman was another person, besides me, whom Ramoncito could have asked for help, had he been more trusting and less obstinate. —D.S.

†It is true that Ramoncito knew about carpentry. He built me an excellent bookcase once. The hammer in question was not his but mine. I had lent it to him when he installed the air-conditioning in his studio with the help of Miguel Correa. —D.S.

sion. I clipped it on my jacket and entered the building. Running to the second floor, I went into the most visited gallery in the museum. There she was, captive inside the frame, smiling at her audience. Pushing the stupid crowd away, I rushed in, brandishing my hammer. I was finally going to do away with the monstrosity that had destroyed so many men and that very soon would destroy me too. But then, just as I was ready to hit the first blow, one of Elisa's hands moved away from the other, and with incredible speed (while her expression remained impassive), she pressed the alarm button on the wall next to her painting. Suddenly a steel curtain dropped from the ceiling, covering the painting completely.* And I, hammer in hand, was restrained by the museum security guards, by the police (who materialized instantly), and by the fanatic crowd that had come to worship that painting. The same crowd that in Grand Central had done nothing for me when I screamed for help because my life was in danger was the one that now shoved me angrily into the patrol car.

Today, Friday, after being under arrest for four days, I am coming to the end of my story, which I will try to send to Daniel as soon as possible. I may be able to do it. Quite unexpectedly, I have become a notorious character. There are two police officers here who seem to admire me because I am a strange case they cannot figure out. It was my intention not to steal a painting worth millions of dollars but to destroy it. One of the officers (I am withholding his name) has promised to get this manuscript out and give it to my friend Daniel. If this testimony reaches his hands soon

---

* *This protection system is the most efficient ever devised. At the same time the alarm goes off, the metal curtain drops over the wall where the piece of art is being exhibited. It is very expensive to install. There are only three masterpieces in the world that have this protection. According to the research carried out by my friend Kokó Salás, the curator, the three works are:* La Joconde, *by Leonardo da Vinci;* Guernica, *by Pablo Picasso; and* The Burial of Count Orgaz, *by Doménikos Theotokópoulos, El Greco. —D.S.*

*Daniel Sakuntala is completely misguided when he calls Kokó Salás a "curator." In all truth, he is a common criminal\* dedicated to the illegal traffic of works of art in Madrid, under the protection of the Cuban government in Havana. —Lorenzo and Echurre, 1999*

*\* To label Kokó Salás as a common criminal is to underestimate his character and historic significance. Kokó Salás was a sophisticated, gifted person (it is now impossible to determine whether he was a man or a woman) who worked for an international spy ring in service to the Kremlin. Under the secretary for mineral rights, Victorio Garrati, he conspired indefatigably and took part in intrigues until he finally achieved the annexation of Italy and Greece to the Soviet Union in the year 2011. For more information, see* La Matahari [sic] de Holguín, *by Teodoro Tapia. —Editors, 2025*

enough, I do not know what he will be able to do, but I am sure he will do something. Maybe some influential person will read it; maybe it will be taken seriously and I will be granted personal protection, efficient full-time vigilance. Understand this: the fact is I don't want to get out of this prison cell; what I need is for Elisa not to get in. The ideal situation would be to install here the same metal curtain that protects her. But all that would have to be done before Monday. The museum closes that day, and she will be totally free and with time to accumulate all the energy and develop all the stratagems she needs in order to get to me here, to destroy me. Please, help me! Or else I will soon become another of her countless victims, those buried under that greenish swamp that you can see in the background of her famous painting, from which she is still watching, with those eyes without lashes, while she keeps smiling.

# ∼ *Edwin Oostmeijer* ∼

# *IJsbrand*

TRANSLATED BY RICHARD HUIJING

I couldn't see the stars from my bed, but they were there, all right, a whole skyful of them. I saw my attic reflected in the little windows behind my desk: the beam and the wooden rafters I still had to wax. Beyond, a fan of thin bare trunks was visible: the trees appeared to be growing inside my room, right through the roof. The plaster was blistering; there was moss on the walls.

I was lying on an old mattress in the corner, bought from a secondhand store, a mattress on which souls had rattled their last and died.

The electrical sockets dangled from their wires. Every night, I would leave a light on, as though I was still expecting someone. Newspapers and porn mags lay next to me on the floor. I read only the headlines and the captions.

Shove it up there, man! President sees no way out of this slough of despond. Yeah, man, shove it right up there! What is there left for us to offer the young, other than a job?

In bare feet, I crossed the wooden planks to my computer and back again; cursing, I looked for the tweezers I failed to find anywhere. I had a splinter in my toe.

EDWIN OOSTMEIJER, *the youngest writer included here, is the author of the novel* The Singles' Machine. *He divides his time between Utrecht, Holland, and an old silk mill in France, where—in addition to fiction—he makes his living describing French farmhouses for a rental catalog.*

I don't know Joey Stefano in any state other than naked, I thought, as I staggered downstairs, but at least he always keeps his socks on. I made a needle turn blue in the gas jet and, on the settee, covered in a white sheet, I ferreted away for as long as it took until the splinter came out. I happened to find some iodine in the cutlery drawer. Almost everything was still wrapped up because of the building renovation.

Where the rear gable was meant to be, a great hole gaped; some plastic was hanging in front of it, blowing and rattling about. The electric heater was doing overtime. The carpenter, who called himself Gyro Gearloose, had made measurements more than a month ago for two French windows, between which a little wall still needed to built.

I thought about warming some milk, but it has never put me to sleep so far. CNN was repeating news I already knew, so I put on my jeans and my army boots. On the sweater IJsbrand gave me once upon a time, a white horse was trying vainly to jump out of the knitted fabric.

I pulled the sleeves of my duffel coat down over my hands and walked down the Magdalenastraat. The light was still on in the doctor's house. I had never noticed before that the old streetlights on the edge of the park wore little green hats with gold pine cones at the center.

The soil around the observatory, on the skull of a hill, was frozen. No men with cigarettes that lit up the dark. Someone had lost his way and stood there, leaning his foot against a tree. You could see by his bearing that he was the sort who stays home when there's fighting to be done in the desert. The traffic lights on the opposite side of the water were amber, flaring like fire behind glass. A bell sounded. A mail train approached the crossing between the Zonstraat and the Maliesingel, but the barriers didn't come down. By day, everyone is told when to stop and when to drive on, but in darkness there's no one to stop you.

～ ～ ～

On one of the few occasions when my father drove into the Zonstraat, he didn't park in front of where I was living at the time but stopped at the end of the street, past the trackman's cottage. My mother remained in their little Japanese car, sitting there in a thick coat with her arms crossed.

I had pasted a photo of Natalie Wood over the little front-door window. A less flattering one than the autographed photograph she had sent me a year before I was searching for a flat in this city. *For Egon,* it read in faint blue letters, *my best wishes always.* Through the little holes I had made in her eyes, I saw my father standing there. I let him ring a second time.

"Are you alone?" he asked, after I had given him a fleeting kiss. He smelled of shaving cream. We continued to stand there, awkward, as though we had to sniff each other first.

Yes, I was alone. IJsbrand was in his own flat, not far away.

Even if my mother was looking this way, she still would not see my father signal to her. So he went to fetch her. He never walks anywhere in a straight line, but often zigzags or jumps instead. Had there been snow, my father would more likely have left the tracks of a deer rather than those of a hunter.

I had forgotten to return the tent I had borrowed from my parents. "All present and accounted for?" my father asked when I handed him a nylon bag. My mother still had her coat on.

"I haven't used it," I said, as I turned and poured boiling water into the coffee filter.

IJsbrand and I had known each other for a few months in the summer of 1982; we were going camping for a week, but one balmy night, in the hour between dog and wolf, he got into such a panic that he ran outside, going nowhere, merely in circles, along the Nieuwe Gracht.

Where there was water flowing, he saw a motorway. IJsbrand was approaching a long tunnel, and the only thing I could do was to go after him. That we were in love with each other no longer seemed to help in the days when film stars died.

Just like my friend, I slept on the floor. Knees drawn up, my mother went and sat down on the edge of the mattress. The walls had been covered with white wooden lath; the curtains were white as well.

"It's just like a hospital here," my mother said. She ate some of the cake I had baked.

I turned up the heat, for my mother was always cold. We no longer sat in a circle, as we used to round the table, but in a triangle, without my sister Rose, with my mother for its apex.

I brought out photos that showed clearly that we were together. Our shared past broke the ice that afternoon. The past was the only thing still to be shared. The cake was finished down to the last crumb, and on leaving, my mother repeated how delicious she thought it had been.

Next morning the phone rang. I was in the shower, behind the stairwell, with a plastic sliding door in front.

"I didn't have the feeling," my mother said, "that we were very welcome."

I listened, naked and unmoved, wet footprints on the carpeting. It was as though she were still sitting in the room, with dark hair just like Natalie Wood's. I hadn't even rinsed off the Lux soap, which the film star washed with too.

"I didn't have the feeling that . . ."

Perhaps you want to wash me all over, again, and again, until my skin's hanging down in tatters: I bet you'd feel welcome then. That's what I thought later on, much later, for at that moment I could only take things in, not spit them out. True, I had left my father standing at the door, but he hadn't been making any move to come in. He had just continued to stand there, while you sat there in the car, awaiting a sign.

Please wait until the red light has dimmed, Mother: another train might be approaching. But IJsbrand was on quite a different track altogether.

～ ～ ～

You can get lost in the desert, particularly in the dark, when all dunes look alike. Soldiers spend their nights sleeping "strategically." Not in a tent, not in the sand, full of scorpions, but on the hard steel of their vehicles. They do what they have to do; they wait, not knowing what for.

I walked down the hill and returned along the water. The neon light from a building on the Maliesingel was being reflected as if a mirror had been slipped beneath the surface of the water. The white swallows, their wings raised, were lit up, but the words "Funeral Services" were only partially illuminated. "Feral vice," I read in blue neon.

I warmed my hands, rubbing them, my breath a plume of smoke. Below the vaults underneath the observatory, the wind no longer pierced my ears.

A boy I knew but didn't dare talk to lived near here, around the corner from the Crisis Center. Where others had a brass knob beside the front door, he had a doll's head protruding from the woodwork. When I pulled Barbie's hair, the bell would ring.

I once offered you a drink in the Pink Cloud disco. You were wearing a blue T-shirt, and that's what I called you, blue T-shirt; like a real sap you said no. We didn't say anything else to each other; we haven't in nine years. I lost sight of you until I saw your photo on a stranger's desk in a houseboat in Amsterdam that was for sale. Not long afterward I ran into you again, with a big black dog—you raised your eyebrows in acknowledgment.

I could see that you wanted to be a hero, roving in search of immortality. You have a little of what IJsbrand had too before I knew him: emitting light that others believe they can warm themselves at.

It was dark, but the clear sky ensured that it didn't become pitch dark beneath the vaults. No falling stars tonight. My eyes were watering from the cold. I walked out of the park and halted beside a red mailbox.

Shall I write to you about what happened to us in the winter of 1982, or shall I ring your bell, blue T-shirt, now that the last collection has been made? Then I'll tell you how IJsbrand and I passed each other within a hairsbreadth on this spot, I on my bike, he on foot. It was almost Christmas night. There was snow lying along the Nieuwe Gracht. I had been to his flat next to Le Paradis coffeehouse. I was standing at the top of the attic stairs with a box of purchases in my hands, and because IJsbrand wasn't in, I went back out again.

As I cycled past this mailbox, crossed the bridge, and turned left on my way to my flat in the Zonstraat, my friend was standing somewhere to my right, barefoot in the snow.

I failed to see him. IJsbrand saw me, though, before walking on, turning right, crossing the Maliesingel toward the student housing.

If I tell you the whole story, may I come in then? I know that your problem is mine as well: not to have experienced anything. Nothing at all. The drama is another's. Of course, you're afraid I'll grow attached to you, once I'm inside, but that happened already, ages ago.

Did you see that father on TV tonight, the one telling about how he had fought in Vietnam? He thought it was perfectly logical that his son was in the desert now, for that was his duty. To do what he had to do, to wait not knowing what for. Father would think it terrible were his son to return in a coffin, but he would be at peace with that even so. But he would be at peace with that. Even so.

What on earth has happened to them, dammit, that they let go of you so easily? As long as there's a framed photograph left to put on the desk. Look, this is my son; only now that I have to let go of him am I beginning to grow attached to him.

～ ～ ～

*Noli me tangere,* Jesus of Nazareth pasted to his kitchen window, a picture postcard lit by a lamppost, blue T-shirt, *touch me not.* I walk by and halt. The arms spread wide, feet nailed down, all lust wants eternity, Jesus winked.

A T-junction: here too the traffic lights were amber. Blue gleaming asphalt, no longer particular to a location but liberated, weightless: this road is everywhere and nowhere.

A long street with two blinking traffic lights is how Michael Parks describes that spot from his youth. I don't know why, but that image moves me every time I see him in a film. *More of a Man,* for instance: then I see that street as well. Not just his dick stuck through a glory hole but the blue asphalt too, and the blinking traffic lights.

～ ～ ～

To see fire where there is none. TV as a fireplace. Can I feel warmth that isn't there?

A hole in the wall, Pyramis and Thisbe, impossible love, Ovid goes porno. None of your dirty fumblings of ugly people in meaningless interiors. All well-muscled boys, the chosen ones, gleaming with oil, past the settee and the living room. Eros, through whom good can be reached; living icons on the threshold of the visible and the invisible. Michael Parks, who abandons himself completely, shamelessly, as though he were somebody else.

I wouldn't dare. Little hunched shoulders, yellow stain in white underpants with sloppy elastic, hands in front of the crotch. Egon undresses himself for a PE session or at the doctor's, but that's as far as it goes.

You tight son of a bitch, ride me! The pallid horse, the mount of death. Matt Powers with a hard-on, on a motorbike. Rebel 450, his arms bent across the handlebars. Even the rearview mirror has an erection, everything equally shiny, the red tank a pear drop. The only things he's wearing are black boots. I often think he's a bozo in films, beefy and banal, but in that one picture he looks very piercing, vacant vastness, the inevitability is what excites me. Matt Powers: I've got better things to do, writing a book, for instance, retrieving what I've lost, but I can't manage it. I can't manage it, so that means dragging you out again, behind my Magdalenastraat desk.

Bawl me out, excite me, ride and be ridden, the paradise of hard surfaces, of hard language. You like that big cock in your ass, don't you! Language that repeats itself, again and again.

Cold are my words, cold is the night, transparent the city. Michael Parks now lives in L.A., where I could have been living too, for I'm still only en route. The place where you are not is the one where happiness is, as a rebus indicates in neon on the gable of the Crisis Center, nightlines headlines, the poetry of head-hunting.

~ ~ ~

A long time ago my parents' little Japanese car had been parked here.

"If it had been up to me," my mother said, "we would simply have stayed home. It's chilly here and dark."

The conversation with the therapist was quick to degenerate. I was a dog on a leash, my mother hissed, IJsbrand my master. Words like bullets, gun smoke, no, my father's cigarette, my father, inhaling rapidly as though he had just been running, but he said nothing until the therapist spurred him on.

"I don't understand," my father said, "I don't understand: the two of you had such a good understanding between you." He spilled ash on his trousers and faced the therapist. "Mother and son: they could have been ads just like that. Toothpaste, tea, you name it."

We tried. With cat food. My mother mashing away on a china plate, a sprig of dill on top, our Siamese cats mewing at her feet. Me shooting Polaroids in response to an advertisement: middle-aged women wanted, who want to be on television with their pussy, send your photographs to *Goldcat*. My mother didn't really want to, but I talked her into it. Not long afterward I moved out to a flat.

I would call her every day from the School of Journalism. A stately staircase in a dilapidated building, to the right of it a whole battery of telephones and telexes.

A stroller taking his dog out around midnight; the dog's straining at its leash because it can smell something. In a bus shelter a head lies on the ground, uncovered, presumably a woman's. The man calls the police, who seal off the new housing project. There's a search for witnesses. The bus driver hadn't noticed anything out of the ordinary during his last run, nor had his four passengers. The following day the area remains hermetically sealed with red-and-white plastic strips: only a remote-control toy car gets through effortlessly. When the police try to contact the stroller again, it turns out he has given a false name. A spokesman says that the police have a few clues, but in the interest of the investigation he does not wish to make any further statements. The head has been sent to the forensic laboratory in Rijswijk, where it will be established whether the case indeed concerns a woman's head.

Write a newspaper report. Who, What, Where, When, and Why. But I was concerned with quite different things. IJsbrand the stroller, I the dog, my mother the head.

Weeping, we left the Crisis Center in opposite directions. That's almost ten years ago by now.

There was a different poster hanging in the bus shelter. No longer the tropical beach with the burning horizon. This time it's an unshaven man with greasy hair and a black leather jacket. He's leaning back, seated in an open sports car, a cigarette between his lips. You can see by his eyes that the man never reads. Yet they've shoved a copy of *Hamlet* into his hands, a paperback folded open.

The Children's Hospital in the ABCstraat towered above everything like a glass rock.

"Do they take emergency cases here too?" I asked when I'd known IJsbrand only a short while.

He bit me gently in my neck. "You'll be an emergency case yourself if you don't watch out."

"Creep." I punched his shoulder. "You smell of Dracula," after which we both burst out laughing and went back home.

A room high up in the sky, a roof of domed plexiglass, Ursa Major, Canis Minor, the stars were being dropped into our laps. Two mattresses alongside each other on the floor. Look, IJsbrand said, come on, look: a lunar eclipse. There's me peering, and peering some more, but I couldn't see anything.

My hands were still hidden away in the sleeves of my duffel coat; the wind grazed past my cheeks.

I can't fathom you at all, I thought, before turning into the Magdalenastraat, not at all, IJsbrand, even now. That eternal restless yearning of yours. Honey and homesickness, tar and waffles. The yearning for a spot that's still sacred.

I put the key in the lock and saw the spatula with which I had scraped the plaster from the wall, plaster that had descended like snowflakes that refused to melt.

The moon shone in, the light of the sleepless. I went and sat down on the settee again. I brought out the television from underneath a white sheet, zapping stations while I still had my coat on.

"The sooner we get started," a soldier cried from the desert, "the sooner we'll be back home again. We're gonna kick some ass." He washed his uniform in a plastic bag that he had buried in the sand. Another soldier was listening to a tape of Cher while writing a letter to his girlfriend. "I call her honeybun," he said. "She likes that."

Home, home, it spun through my head, a blue street with two blinking traffic lights, floating and weightless, everywhere and nowhere, the world a village. Home, home. Can I burn myself in fire that doesn't exist?

Michael Parks stayed in L.A. now that there was going to be fighting in the desert, stayed there for the same reason I'd had myself rejected for military service.

"I cannot guarantee," I told the psychiatrist, "that I can keep my hands off the boys," after which she, a sweet Indonesian lady, sent me on my way. I was eighteen and had just moved into my flat. Wrenching my ankles as I went along in cowboy boots, wearing a raincoat that was far too long, I saw Royal Navy posters hanging everywhere. A tropical beach with a blazing horizon. Below it, the pressing question *Or would you prefer to listen with Mother?*